The Snoopy Festival

Books by Charles M. Schulz

Peanuts
More Peanuts
Good Grief, More Peanuts!
Good Ol' Charlie Brown
Snoopy
You're Out of Your Mind, Charlie Brown!
But We Love You, Charlie Brown
Peanuts Revisited
Go Fly a Kite, Charlie Brown
Peanuts Every Sunday
It's a Dog's Life, Charlie Brown
You Can't Win, Charlie Brown
Snoopy, Come Home
You Can Do It, Charlie Brown
We're Right Behind You, Charlie Brown
As You Like It, Charlie Brown
Sunday's Fun Day, Charlie Brown
You Need Help, Charlie Brown
Snoopy and the Red Baron
The Unsinkable Charlie Brown
You'll Flip, Charlie Brown
You're Something Else, Charlie Brown
Peanuts Treasury
You're You, Charlie Brown
You've Had It, Charlie Brown
Snoopy and His Sopwith Camel
A Boy Named Charlie Brown
You're Out of Sight, Charlie Brown
Peanuts Classics
You've Come a Long Way, Charlie Brown
Snoopy and "It Was a Dark and Stormy Night"
"Ha Ha, Herman," Charlie Brown
The "Snoopy, Come Home," Movie Book
Snoopy's Grand Slam
Thompson Is in Trouble, Charlie Brown
You're the Guest of Honor, Charlie Brown
Win a Few, Lose a Few, Charlie Brown
The Snoopy Festival

The Snoopy Festival

Charles M. Schulz

with an Introduction by Charlie Brown

HOLT, RINEHART AND WINSTON
New York

An Owl Book

Published by Holt, Rinehart and Winston, 383 Madison Avenue,
New York, New York 10017.

Published simultaneously in Canada by Holt,
Rinehart and Winston of Canada, Limited.

Library of Congress Catalog Card Number: 74-4809
ISBN Hardbound: 0-03-013161-8
ISBN Paperback: 0-03-057503-6

First published in hardcover by Holt, Rinehart and Winston in 1974.
First Owl Book Edition—1980.

Printed in the United States of America
2 4 6 8 10 9 7 5 3 1

Introduction

It is a great honor for me to be asked to write this introduction to Snoopy's book. Actually, I suppose I wouldn't have to do it if I didn't want to because, after all, he is my dog and I am his master, which means that he is supposed to do what I tell him and not vice versa. Sometimes, I think he doesn't know his place.

At any rate, this seems to be a pretty good collection of some of his latest adventures, but I feel I should point out that a few of the other kids around the neighborhood are here too. In other words, without them, where would he be? And as I have told him many times, without me, he'd be no place at all.

Anyway, I hope you enjoy his book. As Lucy once said, "He isn't much of a dog, but after all, who is?"

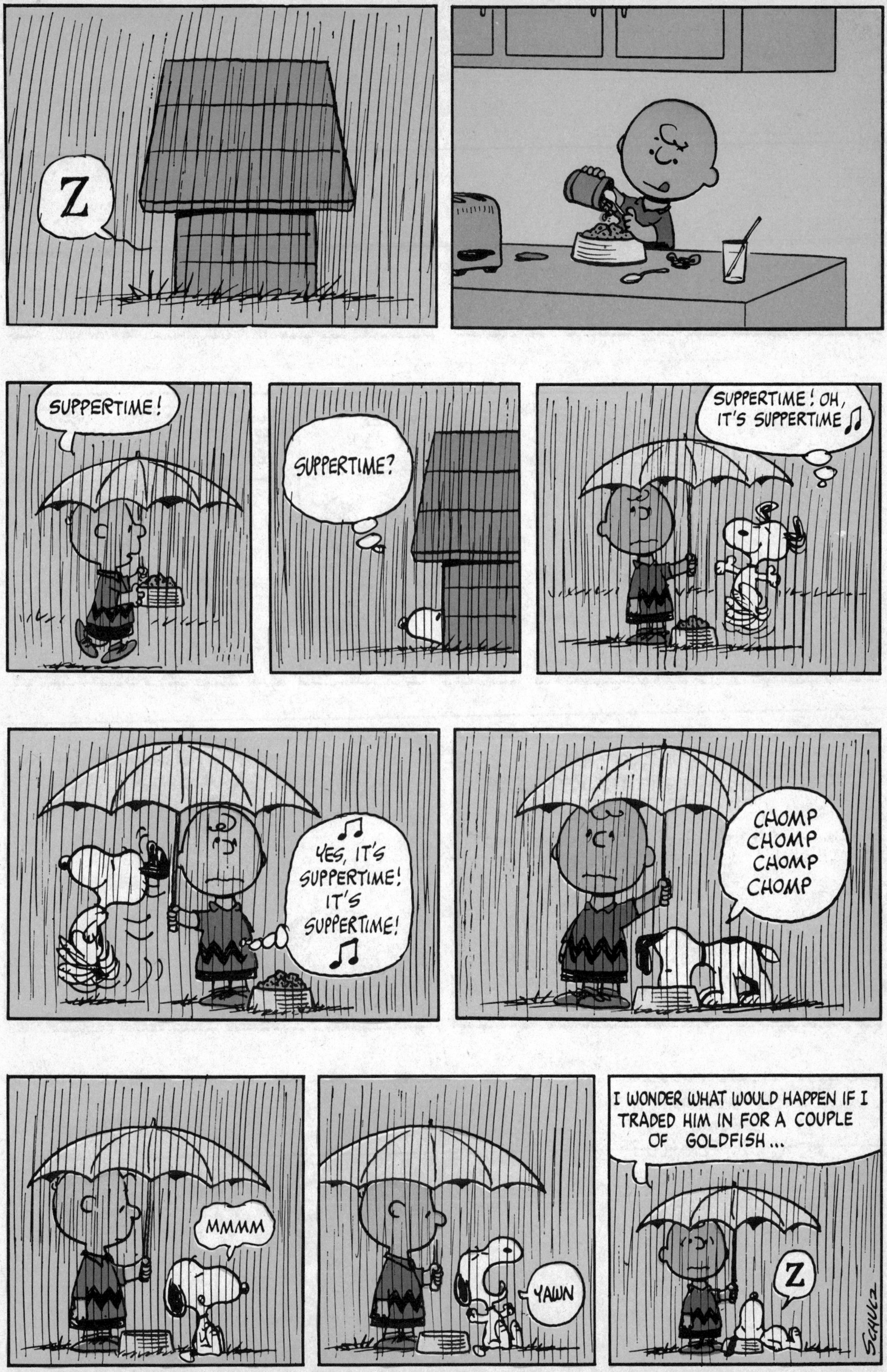
Z
SUPPERTIME!
SUPPERTIME?
SUPPERTIME! OH, IT'S SUPPERTIME ♫
♫ YES, IT'S SUPPERTIME! IT'S SUPPERTIME! ♫
CHOMP CHOMP CHOMP CHOMP
MMMM
YAWN
I WONDER WHAT WOULD HAPPEN IF I TRADED HIM IN FOR A COUPLE OF GOLDFISH...
Z
SCHULZ

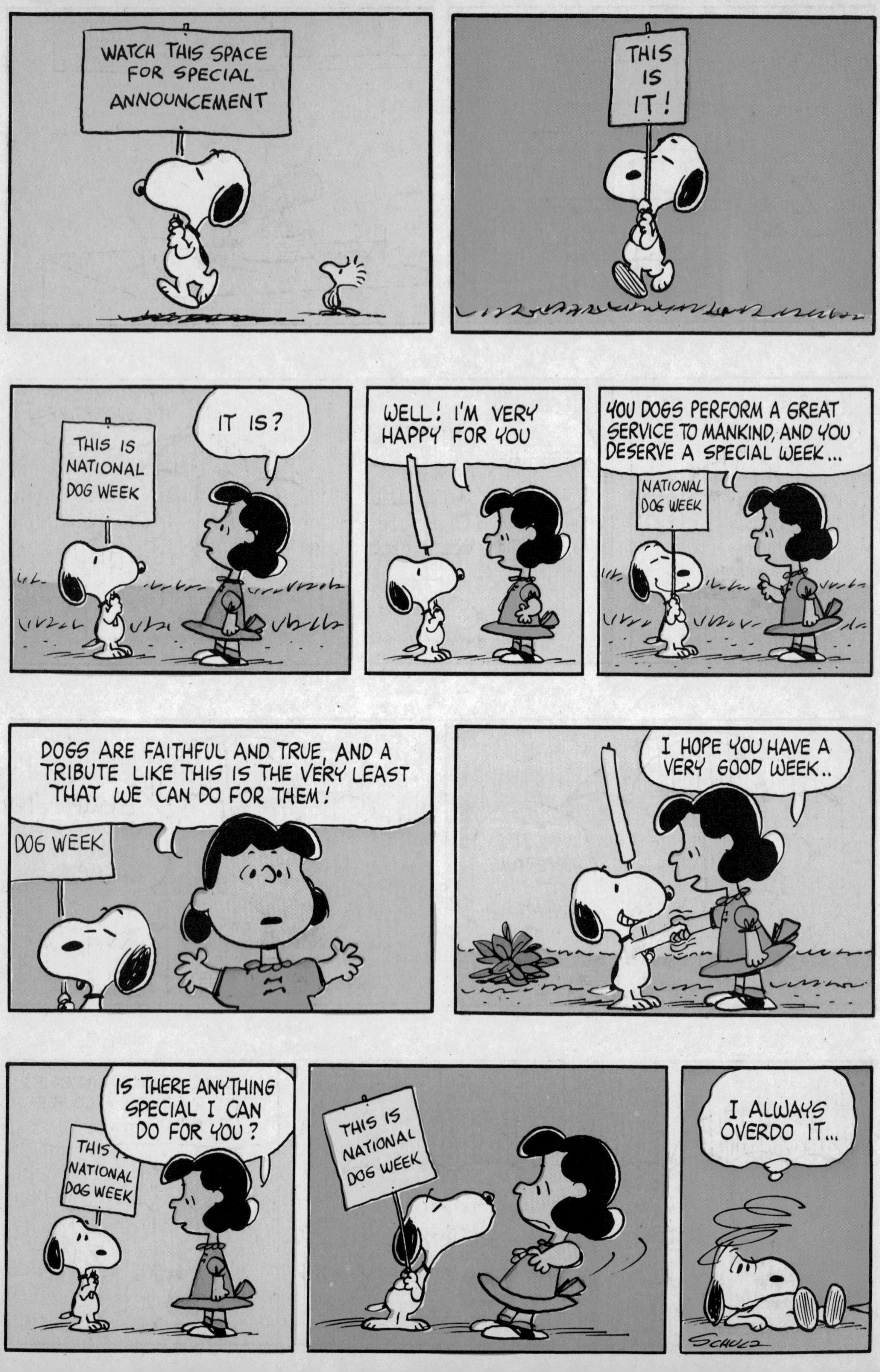

WATCH THIS SPACE FOR SPECIAL ANNOUNCEMENT
THIS IS IT!
THIS IS NATIONAL DOG WEEK
IT IS?
WELL! I'M VERY HAPPY FOR YOU
YOU DOGS PERFORM A GREAT SERVICE TO MANKIND, AND YOU DESERVE A SPECIAL WEEK...
NATIONAL DOG WEEK
DOGS ARE FAITHFUL AND TRUE, AND A TRIBUTE LIKE THIS IS THE VERY LEAST THAT WE CAN DO FOR THEM!
DOG WEEK
I HOPE YOU HAVE A VERY GOOD WEEK..
IS THERE ANYTHING SPECIAL I CAN DO FOR YOU?
NATIONAL DOG WEEK
THIS IS NATIONAL DOG WEEK
I ALWAYS OVERDO IT...
SCHULZ

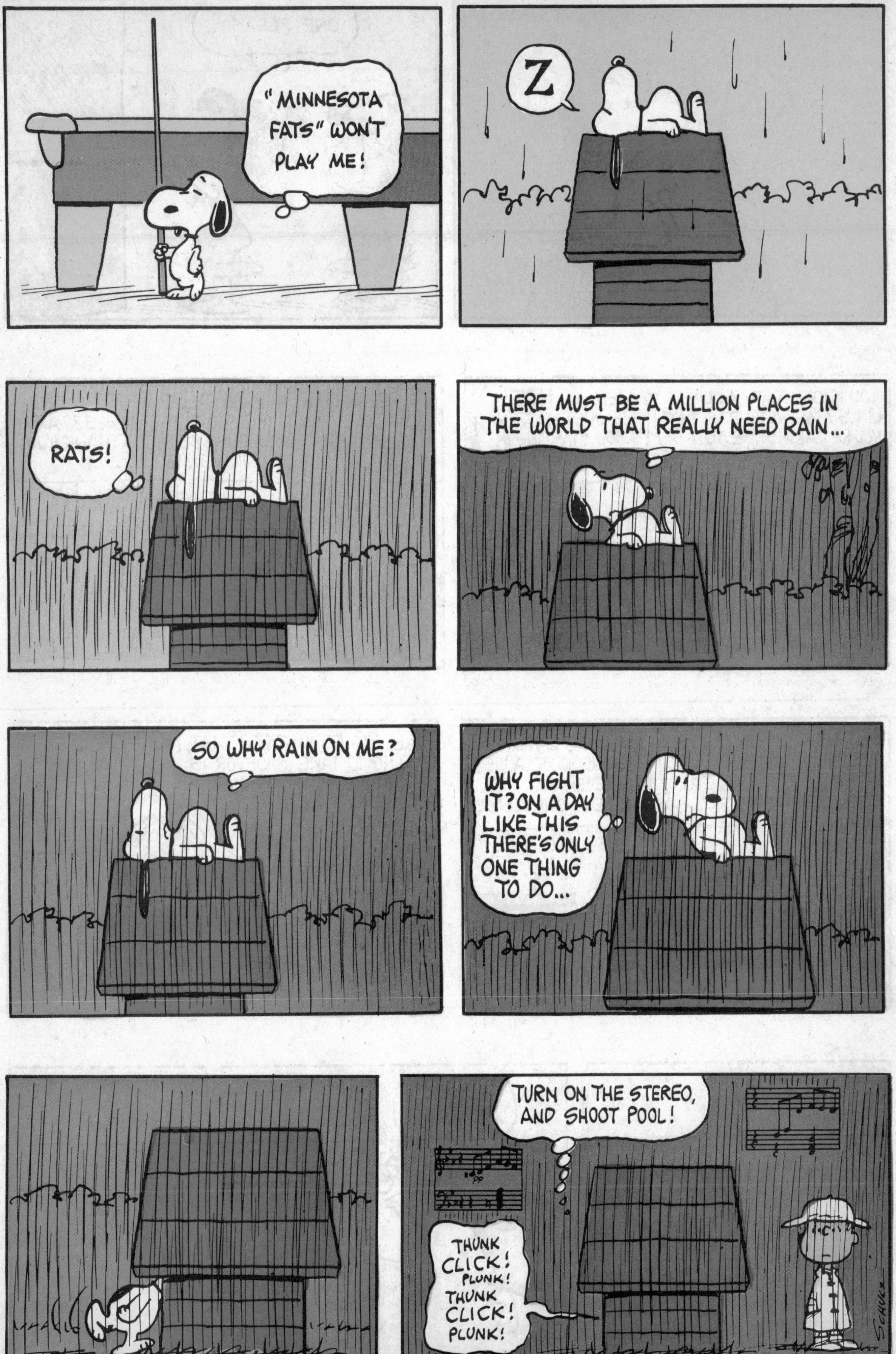
"MINNESOTA FATS" WON'T PLAY ME!
Z
RATS!
THERE MUST BE A MILLION PLACES IN THE WORLD THAT REALLY NEED RAIN...
SO WHY RAIN ON ME?
WHY FIGHT IT? ON A DAY LIKE THIS THERE'S ONLY ONE THING TO DO...
TURN ON THE STEREO, AND SHOOT POOL!
THUNK CLICK! PLUNK! THUNK CLICK! PLUNK!
SCHULZ

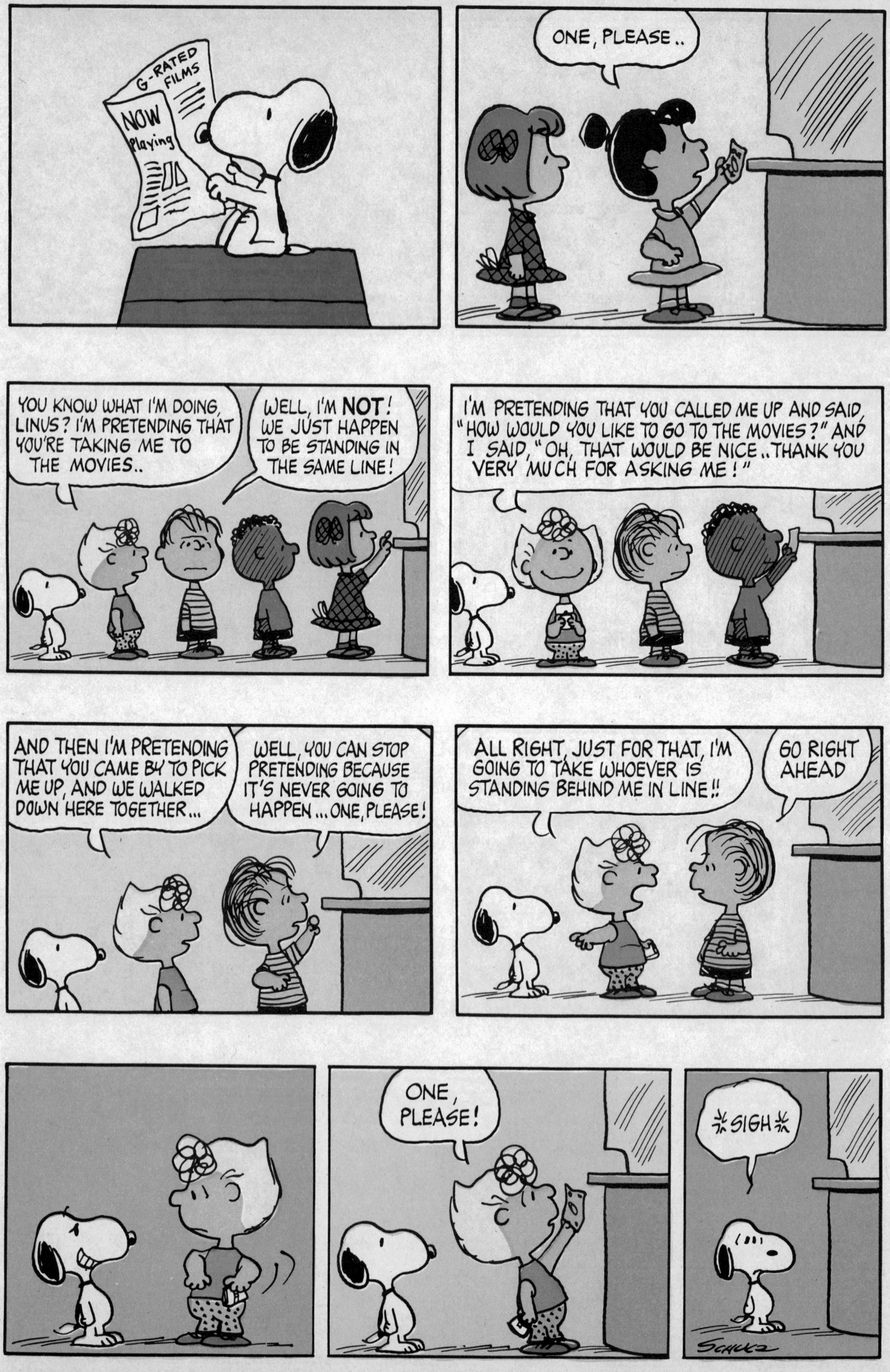
G-RATED FILMS
NOW Playing
ONE, PLEASE..
YOU KNOW WHAT I'M DOING, LINUS? I'M PRETENDING THAT YOU'RE TAKING ME TO THE MOVIES..
WELL, I'M NOT! WE JUST HAPPEN TO BE STANDING IN THE SAME LINE!
I'M PRETENDING THAT YOU CALLED ME UP AND SAID, "HOW WOULD YOU LIKE TO GO TO THE MOVIES?" AND I SAID, "OH, THAT WOULD BE NICE..THANK YOU VERY MUCH FOR ASKING ME!"
AND THEN I'M PRETENDING THAT YOU CAME BY TO PICK ME UP, AND WE WALKED DOWN HERE TOGETHER...
WELL, YOU CAN STOP PRETENDING BECAUSE IT'S NEVER GOING TO HAPPEN ... ONE, PLEASE!
ALL RIGHT, JUST FOR THAT, I'M GOING TO TAKE WHOEVER IS STANDING BEHIND ME IN LINE!!
GO RIGHT AHEAD
ONE, PLEASE!
SIGH
SCHULZ

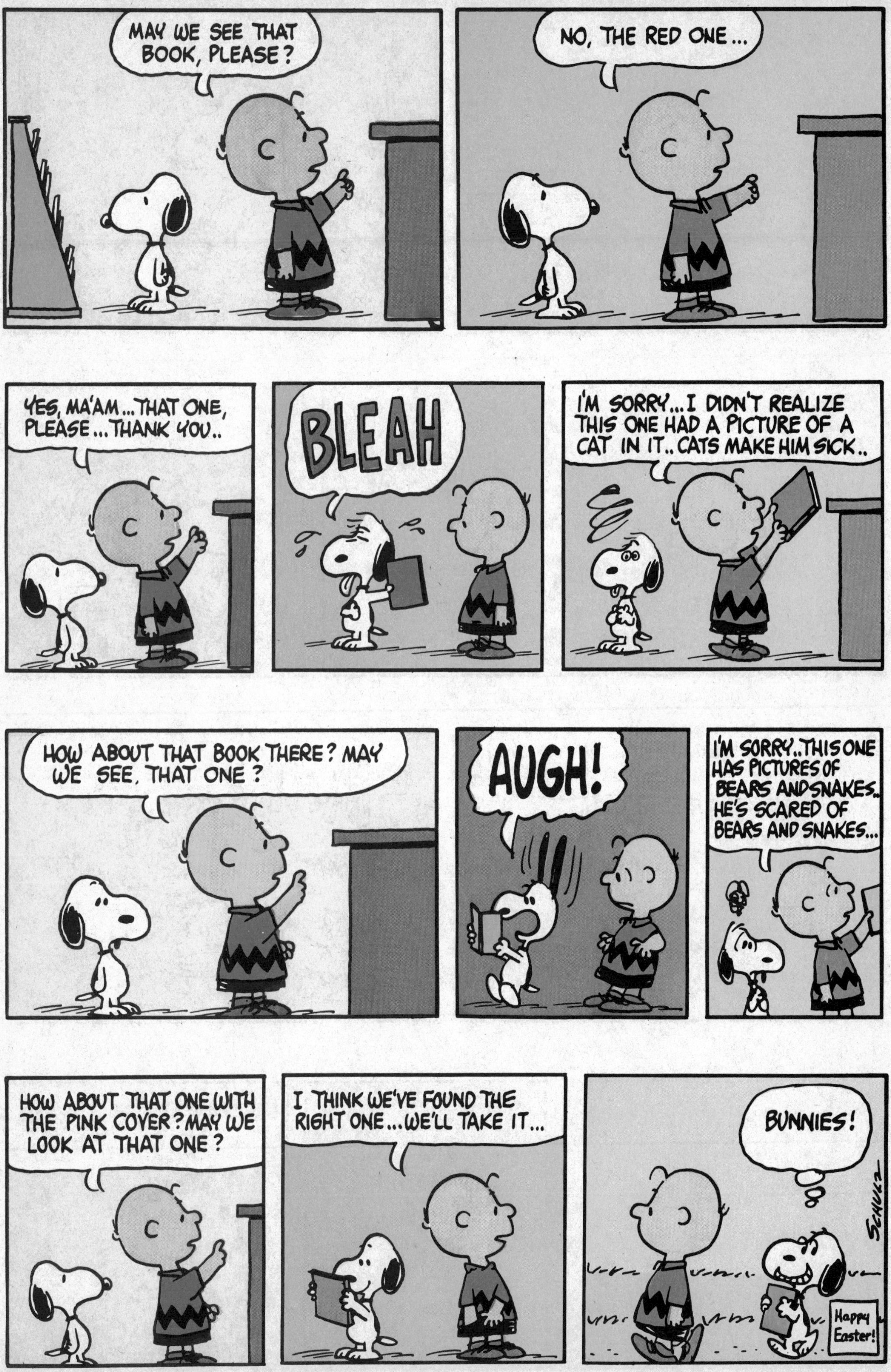
MAY WE SEE THAT BOOK, PLEASE?
NO, THE RED ONE...
YES, MA'AM...THAT ONE, PLEASE...THANK YOU..
BLEAH
I'M SORRY...I DIDN'T REALIZE THIS ONE HAD A PICTURE OF A CAT IN IT.. CATS MAKE HIM SICK..
HOW ABOUT THAT BOOK THERE? MAY WE SEE, THAT ONE?
AUGH!
I'M SORRY..THIS ONE HAS PICTURES OF BEARS AND SNAKES.. HE'S SCARED OF BEARS AND SNAKES...
HOW ABOUT THAT ONE WITH THE PINK COVER? MAY WE LOOK AT THAT ONE?
I THINK WE'VE FOUND THE RIGHT ONE...WE'LL TAKE IT...
BUNNIES!
SCHULZ
Happy Easter!

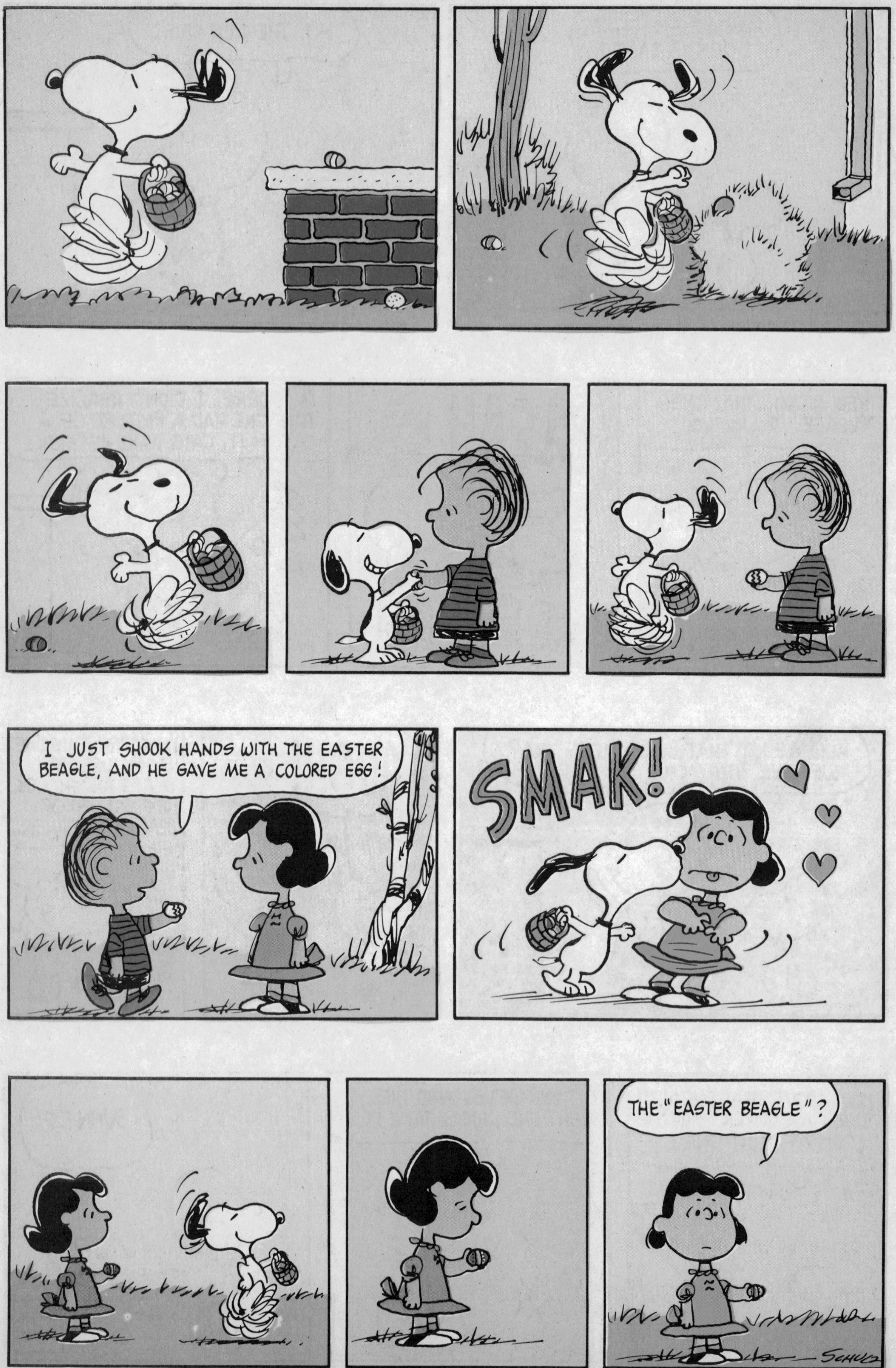
I JUST SHOOK HANDS WITH THE EASTER BEAGLE, AND HE GAVE ME A COLORED EGG!
SMAK!
THE "EASTER BEAGLE"?
SCHULZ

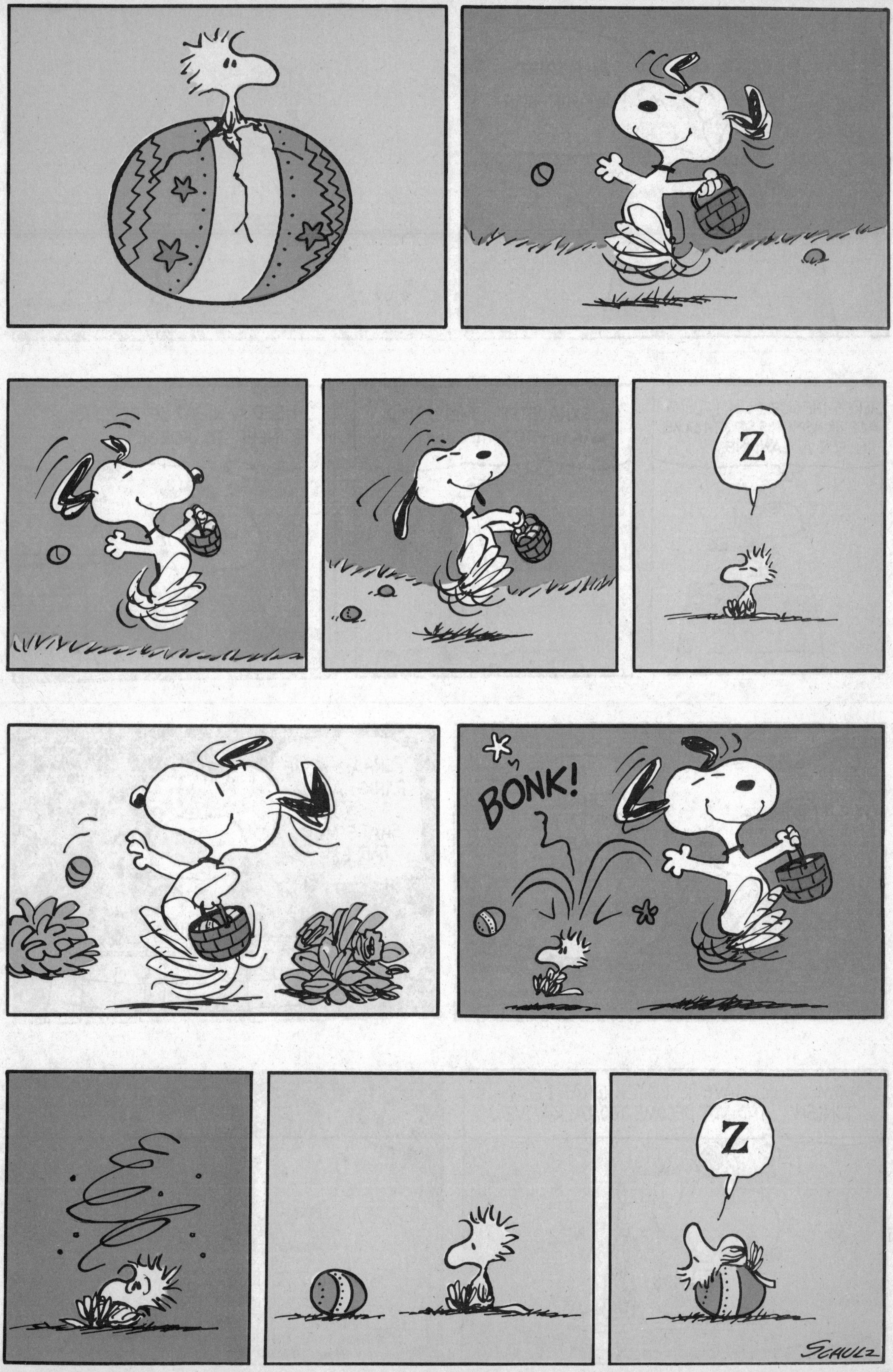
Z
BONK!
Z
SCHULZ

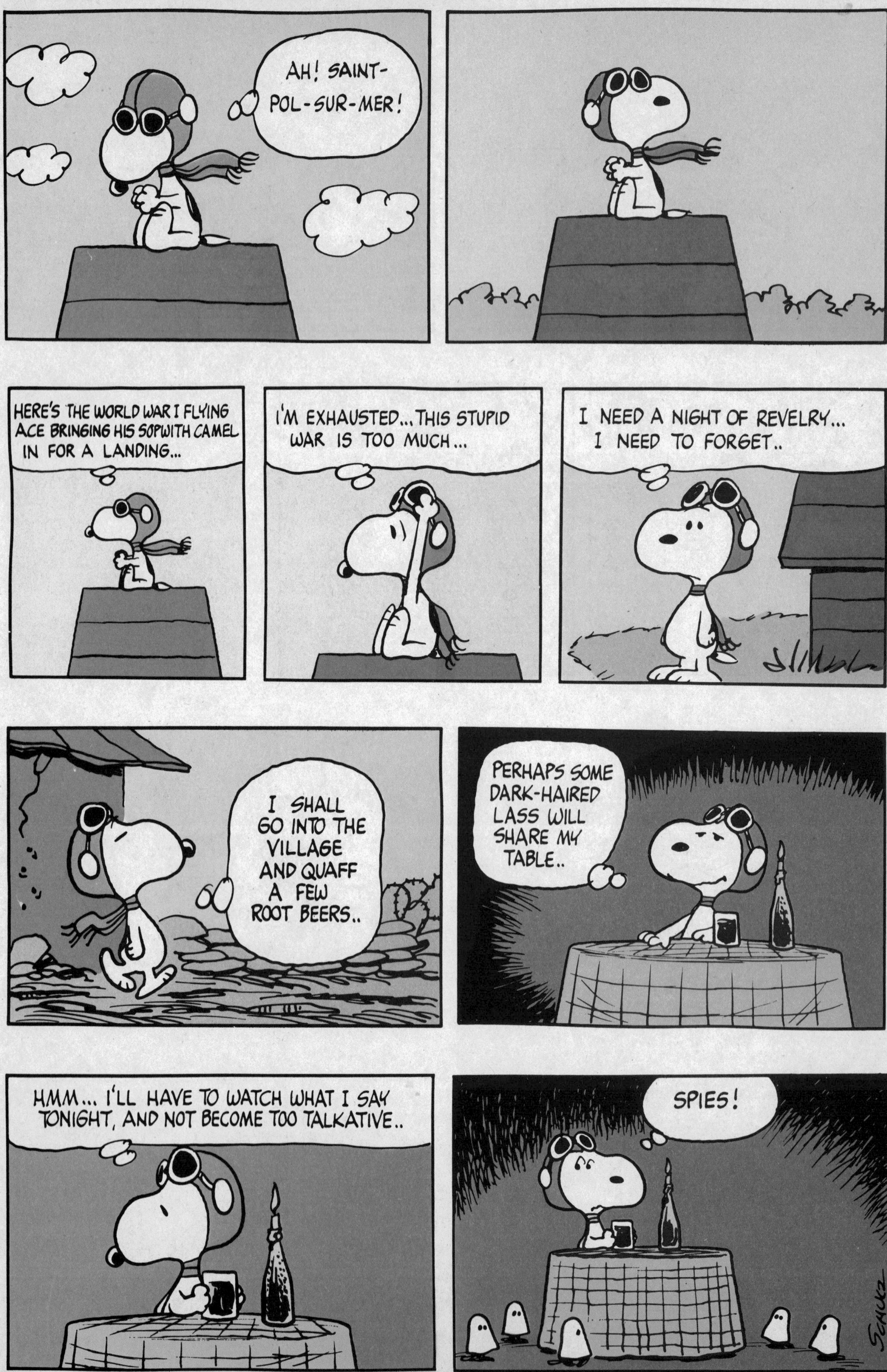
AH! SAINT-POL-SUR-MER!
HERE'S THE WORLD WAR I FLYING ACE BRINGING HIS SOPWITH CAMEL IN FOR A LANDING...
I'M EXHAUSTED... THIS STUPID WAR IS TOO MUCH...
I NEED A NIGHT OF REVELRY... I NEED TO FORGET..
I SHALL GO INTO THE VILLAGE AND QUAFF A FEW ROOT BEERS..
PERHAPS SOME DARK-HAIRED LASS WILL SHARE MY TABLE..
HMM... I'LL HAVE TO WATCH WHAT I SAY TONIGHT, AND NOT BECOME TOO TALKATIVE..
SPIES!
SCHULZ

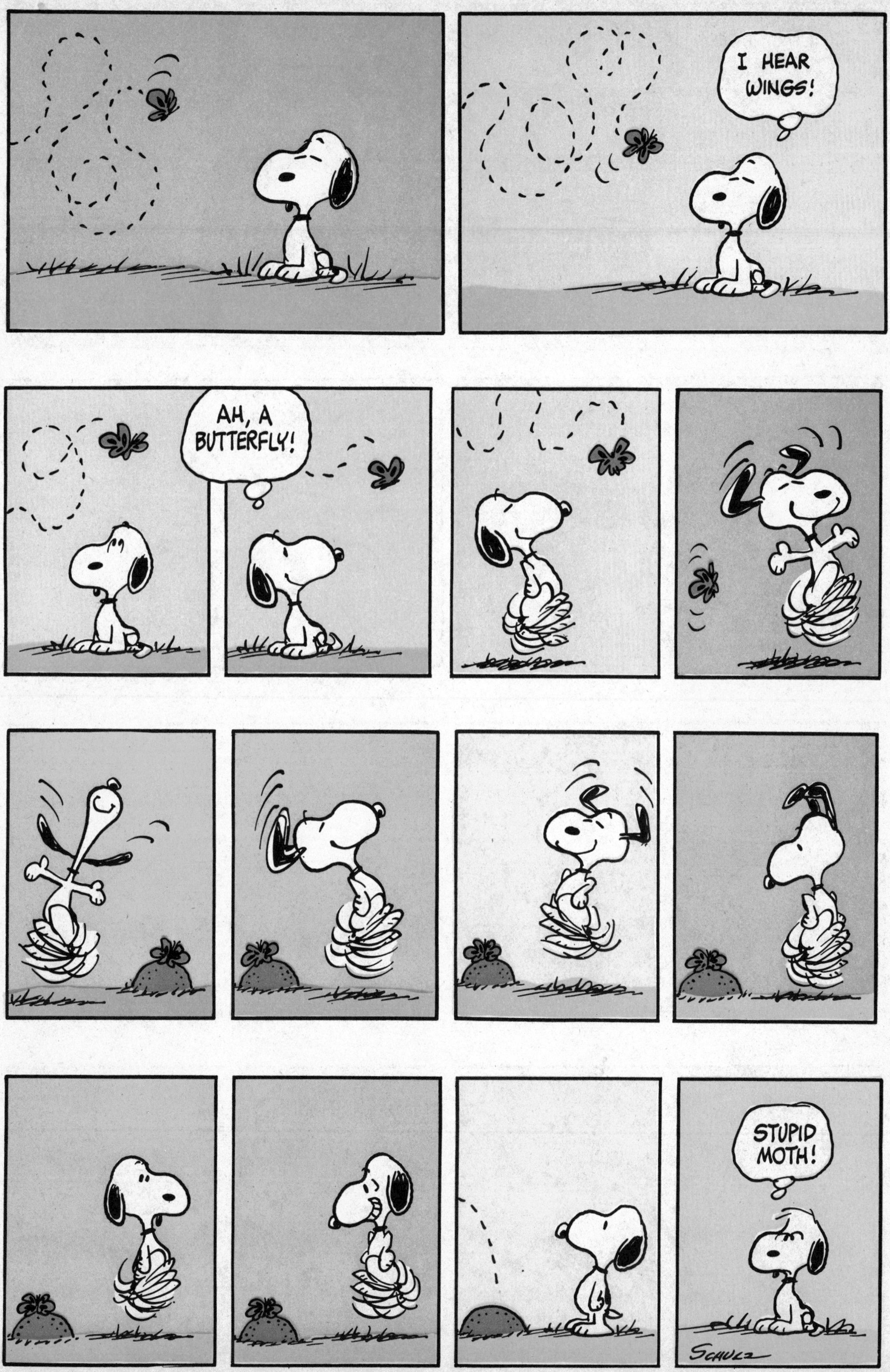

I HEAR WINGS!
AH, A BUTTERFLY!
STUPID MOTH!
SCHULZ

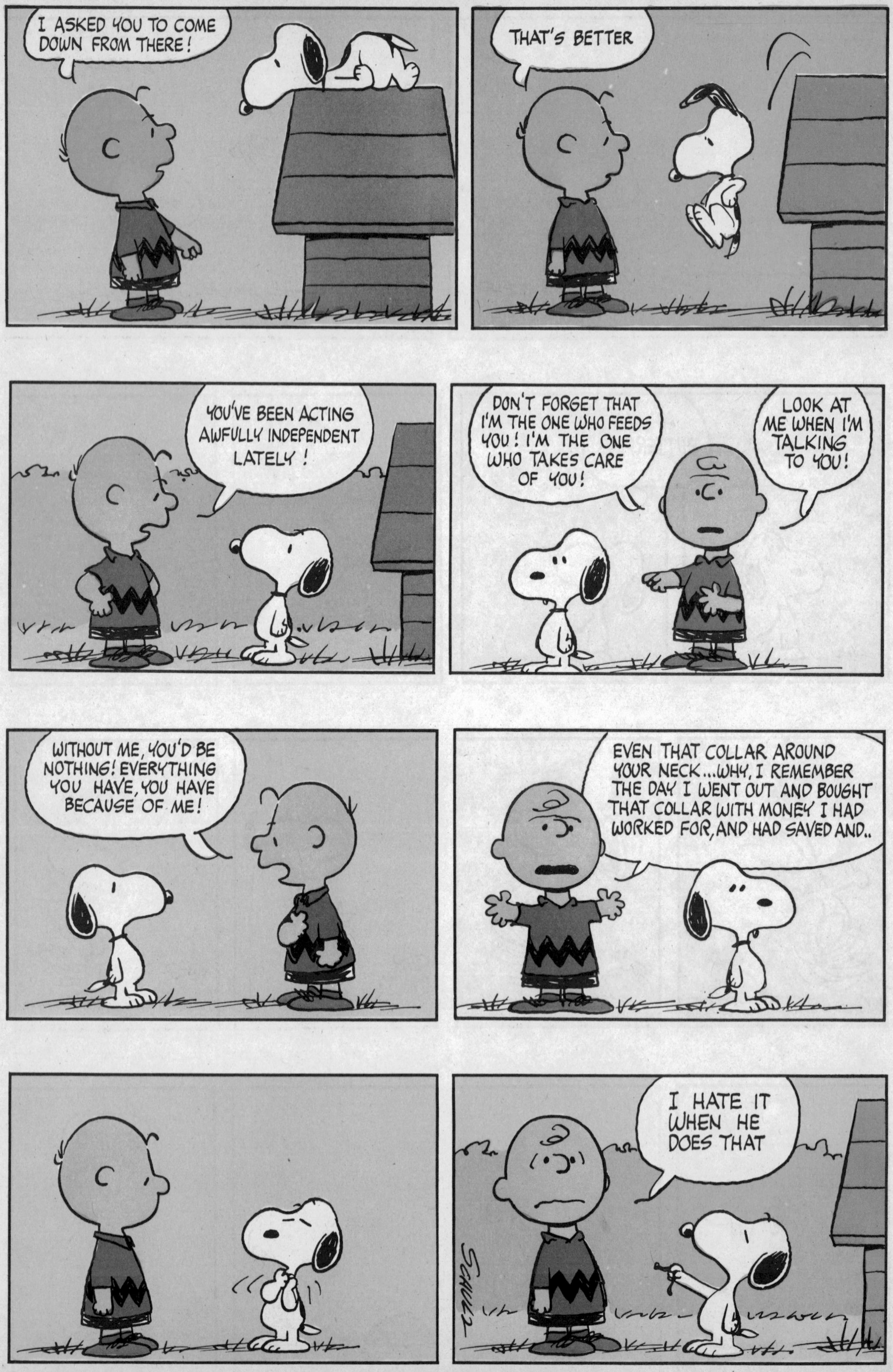
I ASKED YOU TO COME DOWN FROM THERE!
THAT'S BETTER
YOU'VE BEEN ACTING AWFULLY INDEPENDENT LATELY!
DON'T FORGET THAT I'M THE ONE WHO FEEDS YOU! I'M THE ONE WHO TAKES CARE OF YOU!
LOOK AT ME WHEN I'M TALKING TO YOU!
WITHOUT ME, YOU'D BE NOTHING! EVERYTHING YOU HAVE, YOU HAVE BECAUSE OF ME!
EVEN THAT COLLAR AROUND YOUR NECK...WHY, I REMEMBER THE DAY I WENT OUT AND BOUGHT THAT COLLAR WITH MONEY I HAD WORKED FOR, AND HAD SAVED AND..
I HATE IT WHEN HE DOES THAT
SCHULZ

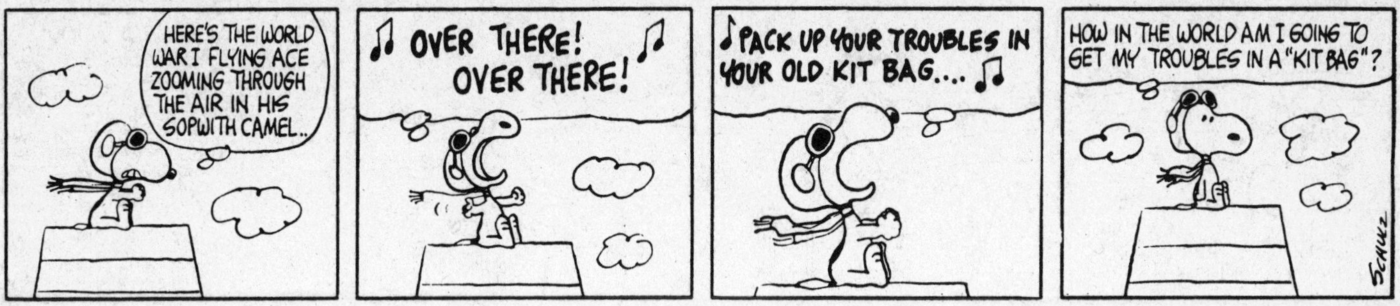
HERE'S THE WORLD WAR I FLYING ACE ZOOMING THROUGH THE AIR IN HIS SOPWITH CAMEL..
♫ OVER THERE! OVER THERE! ♫
♪ PACK UP YOUR TROUBLES IN YOUR OLD KIT BAG.... ♫
HOW IN THE WORLD AM I GOING TO GET MY TROUBLES IN A "KIT BAG"?
SCHULZ

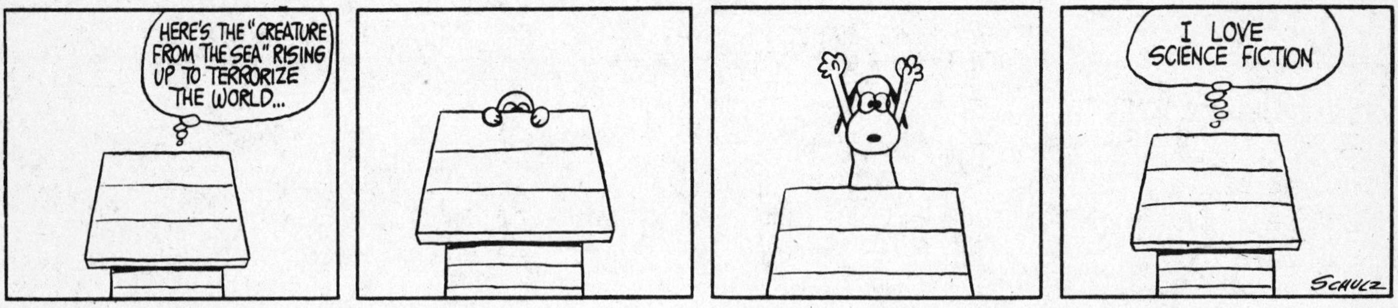
HERE'S THE "CREATURE FROM THE SEA" RISING UP TO TERRORIZE THE WORLD...
I LOVE SCIENCE FICTION
SCHULZ

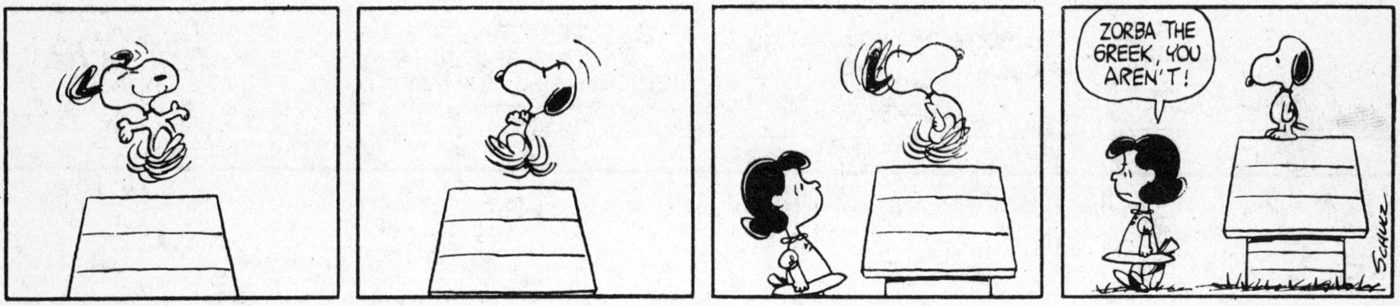
ZORBA THE GREEK, YOU AREN'T!
SCHULZ

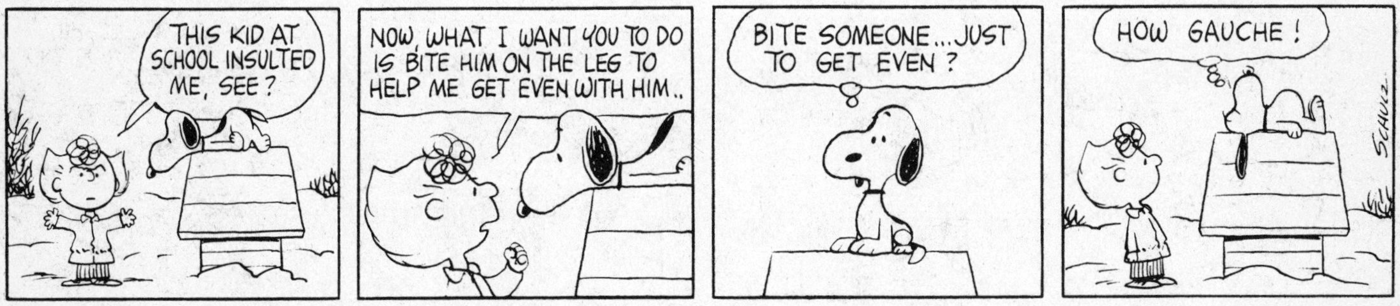
THIS KID AT SCHOOL INSULTED ME, SEE?
NOW, WHAT I WANT YOU TO DO IS BITE HIM ON THE LEG TO HELP ME GET EVEN WITH HIM..
BITE SOMEONE... JUST TO GET EVEN?
HOW GAUCHE!
SCHULZ

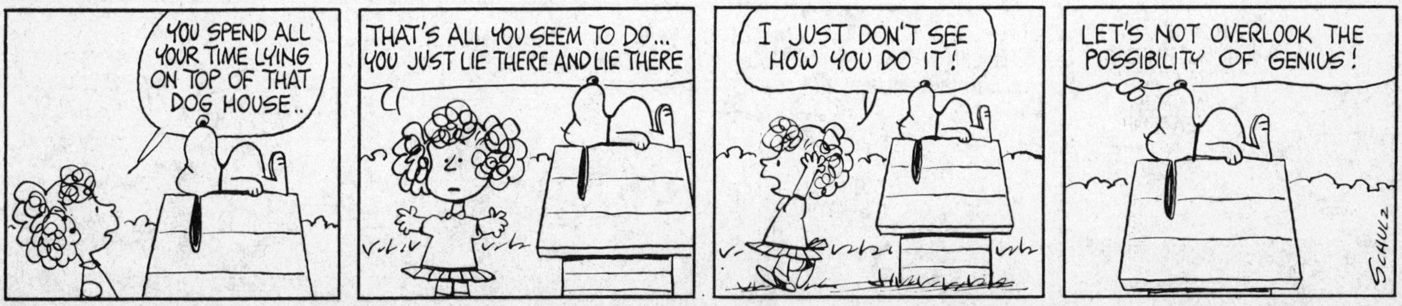
YOU SPEND ALL YOUR TIME LYING ON TOP OF THAT DOG HOUSE..
THAT'S ALL YOU SEEM TO DO... YOU JUST LIE THERE AND LIE THERE
I JUST DON'T SEE HOW YOU DO IT!
LET'S NOT OVERLOOK THE POSSIBILITY OF GENIUS!
SCHULZ

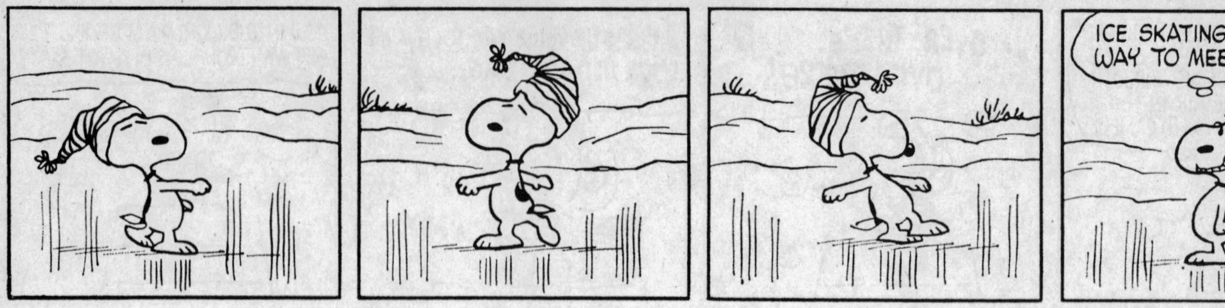
ICE SKATING IS A GOOD WAY TO MEET GIRLS!
SCHULZ

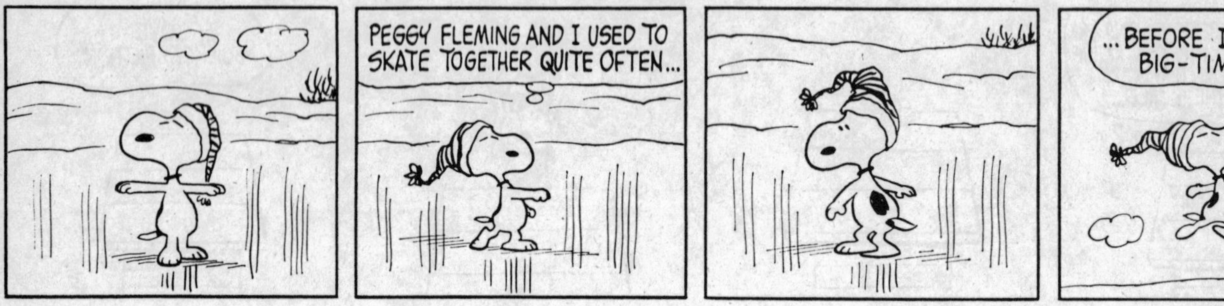
PEGGY FLEMING AND I USED TO SKATE TOGETHER QUITE OFTEN...
...BEFORE I BECAME BIG-TIME!
SCHULZ

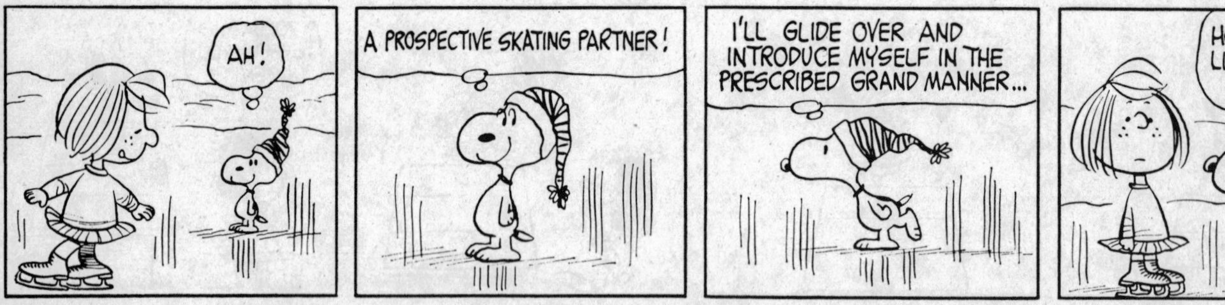
AH!
A PROSPECTIVE SKATING PARTNER!
I'LL GLIDE OVER AND INTRODUCE MYSELF IN THE PRESCRIBED GRAND MANNER...
HOW ABOUT A LITTLE SKATE, SWEETIE?
SCHULZ

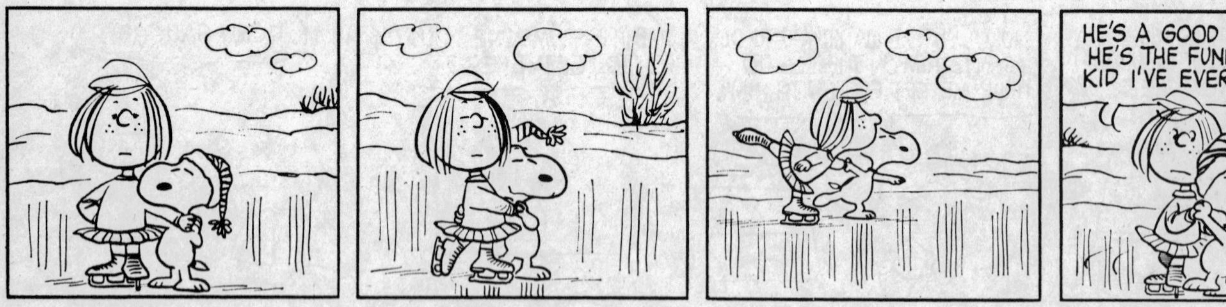
HE'S A GOOD SKATER, BUT HE'S THE FUNNIEST-LOOKING KID I'VE EVER SEEN!
SCHULZ

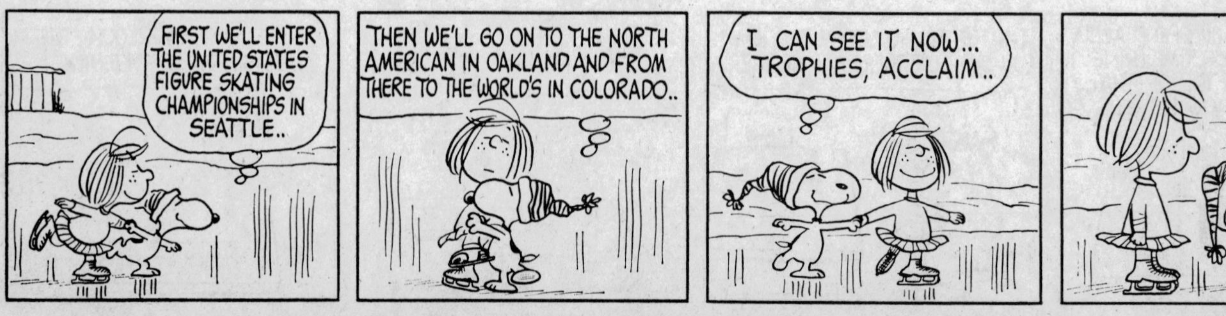
FIRST WE'LL ENTER THE UNITED STATES FIGURE SKATING CHAMPIONSHIPS IN SEATTLE..
THEN WE'LL GO ON TO THE NORTH AMERICAN IN OAKLAND AND FROM THERE TO THE WORLD'S IN COLORADO..
I CAN SEE IT NOW... TROPHIES, ACCLAIM..
..COLD FEET!
SCHULZ

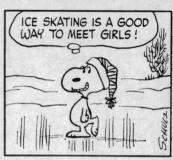

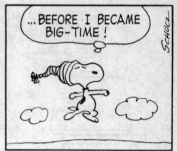

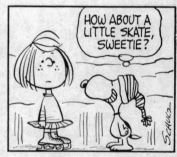

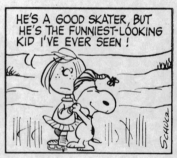

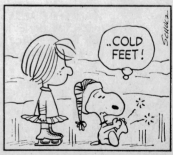

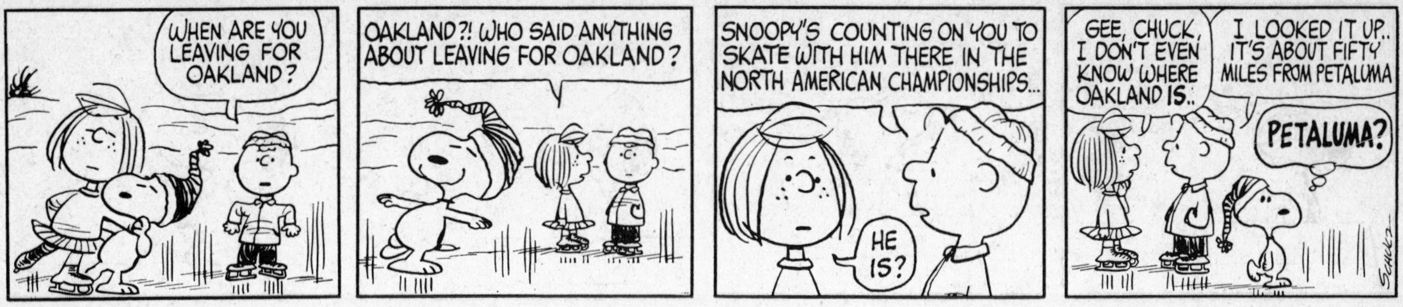
WHEN ARE YOU LEAVING FOR OAKLAND?
OAKLAND?! WHO SAID ANYTHING ABOUT LEAVING FOR OAKLAND?
SNOOPY'S COUNTING ON YOU TO SKATE WITH HIM THERE IN THE NORTH AMERICAN CHAMPIONSHIPS...
HE IS?
GEE, CHUCK, I DON'T EVEN KNOW WHERE OAKLAND IS..
I LOOKED IT UP.. IT'S ABOUT FIFTY MILES FROM PETALUMA
PETALUMA?
SCHULZ

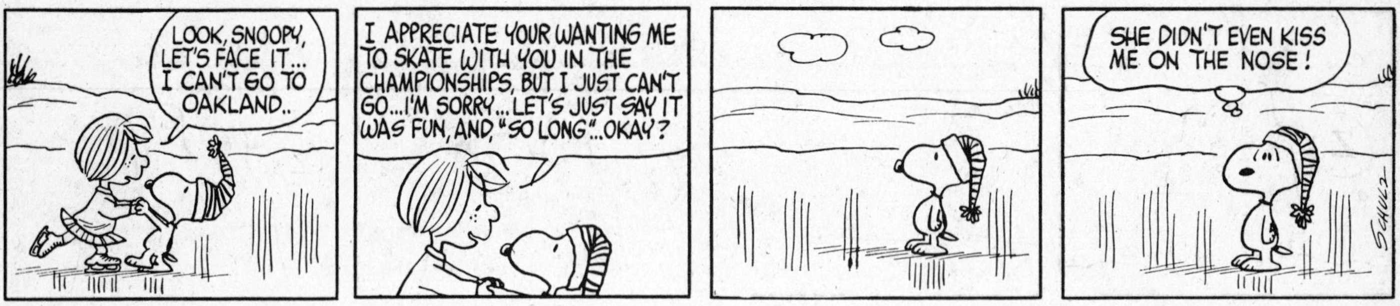
LOOK, SNOOPY, LET'S FACE IT... I CAN'T GO TO OAKLAND..
I APPRECIATE YOUR WANTING ME TO SKATE WITH YOU IN THE CHAMPIONSHIPS, BUT I JUST CAN'T GO...I'M SORRY...LET'S JUST SAY IT WAS FUN, AND, "SO LONG"...OKAY?
SHE DIDN'T EVEN KISS ME ON THE NOSE!
SCHULZ

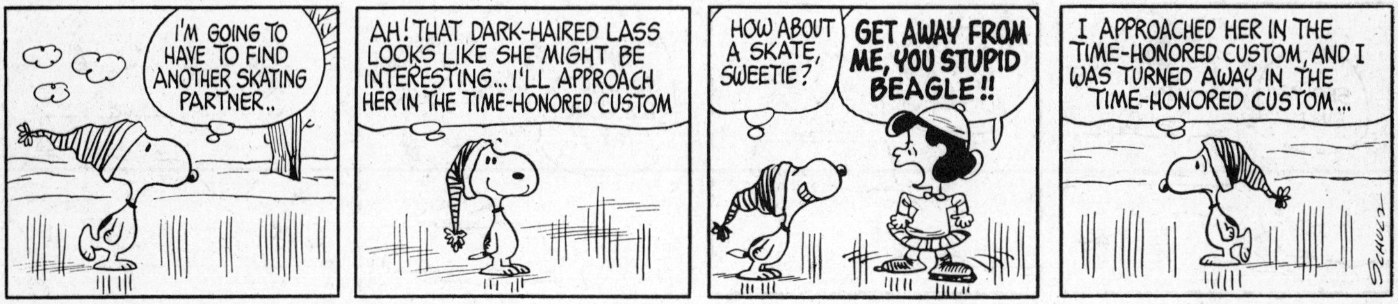
I'M GOING TO HAVE TO FIND ANOTHER SKATING PARTNER..
AH! THAT DARK-HAIRED LASS LOOKS LIKE SHE MIGHT BE INTERESTING...I'LL APPROACH HER IN THE TIME-HONORED CUSTOM
HOW ABOUT A SKATE, SWEETIE?
GET AWAY FROM ME, YOU STUPID BEAGLE!!
I APPROACHED HER IN THE TIME-HONORED CUSTOM, AND I WAS TURNED AWAY IN THE TIME-HONORED CUSTOM...
SCHULZ

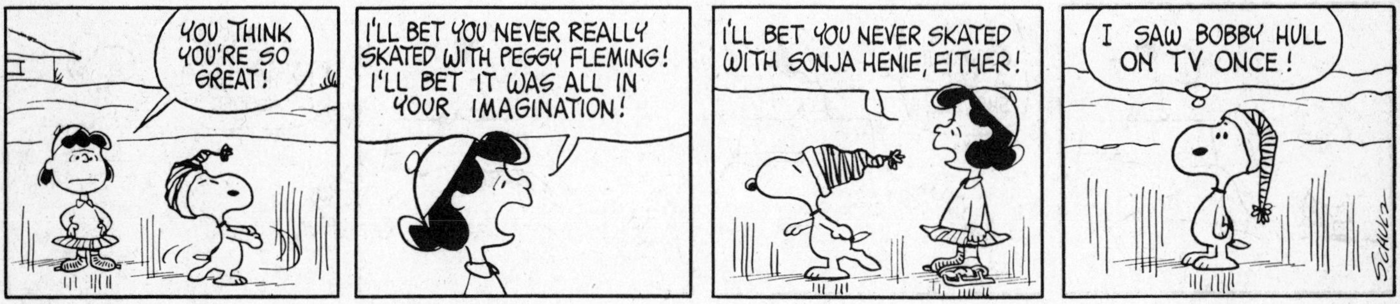
YOU THINK YOU'RE SO GREAT!
I'LL BET YOU NEVER REALLY SKATED WITH PEGGY FLEMING! I'LL BET IT WAS ALL IN YOUR IMAGINATION!
I'LL BET YOU NEVER SKATED WITH SONJA HENIE, EITHER!
I SAW BOBBY HULL ON TV ONCE!
SCHULZ

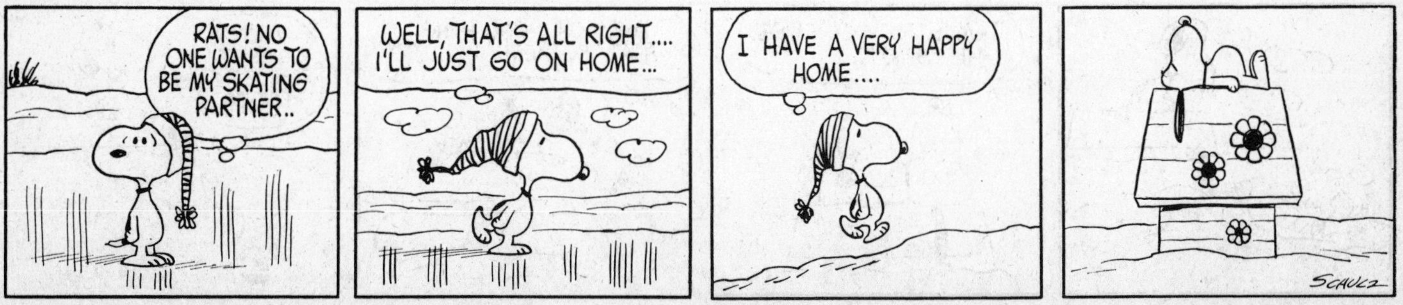
RATS! NO ONE WANTS TO BE MY SKATING PARTNER..
WELL, THAT'S ALL RIGHT.... I'LL JUST GO ON HOME...
I HAVE A VERY HAPPY HOME....
SCHULZ

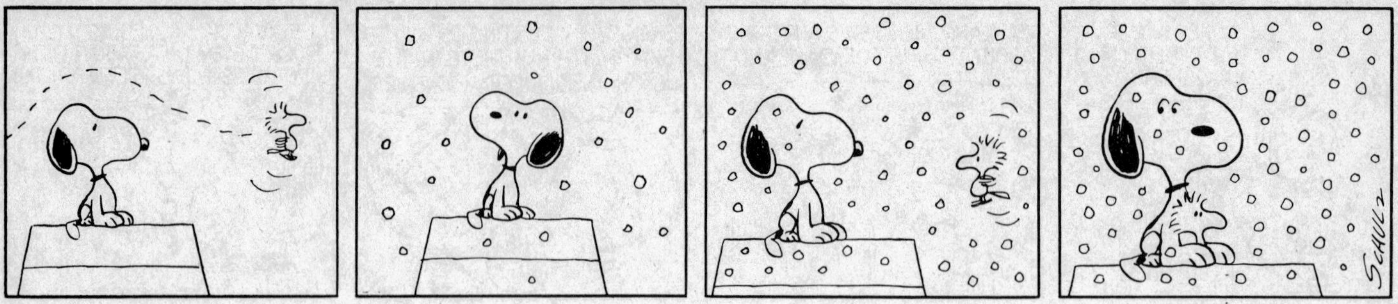
SCHULZ

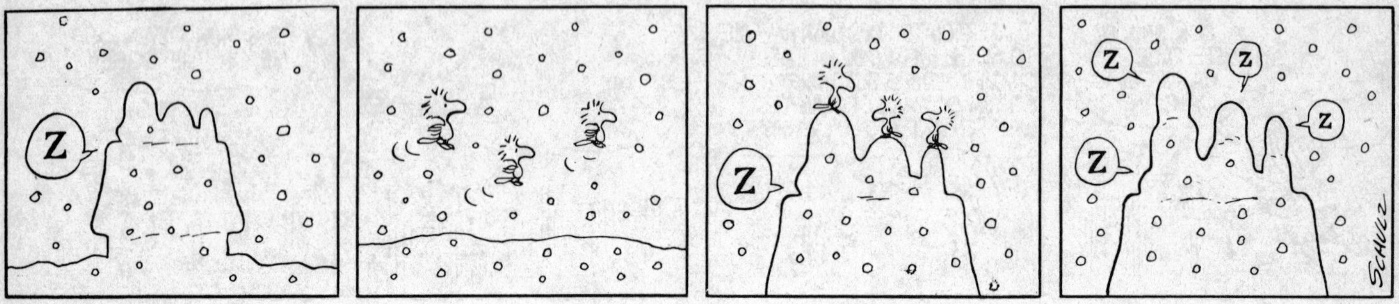
Z
Z
Z
Z
Z
SCHULZ

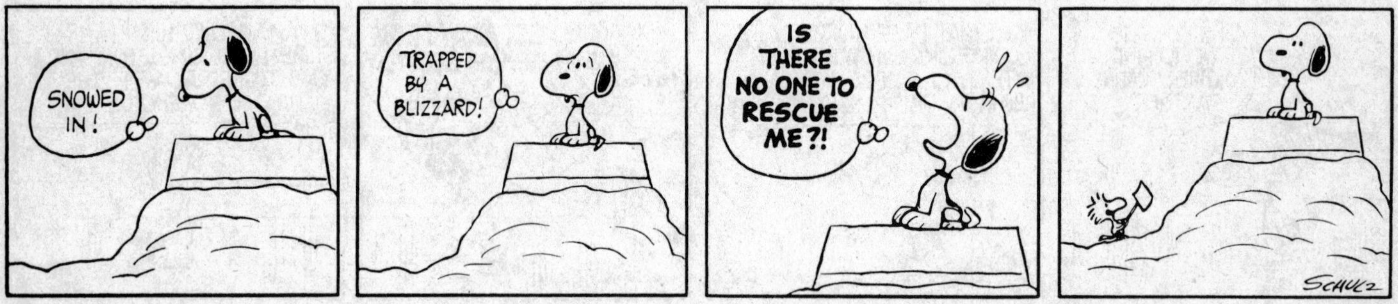
SNOWED IN!
TRAPPED BY A BLIZZARD!
IS THERE NO ONE TO RESCUE ME?!
SCHULZ

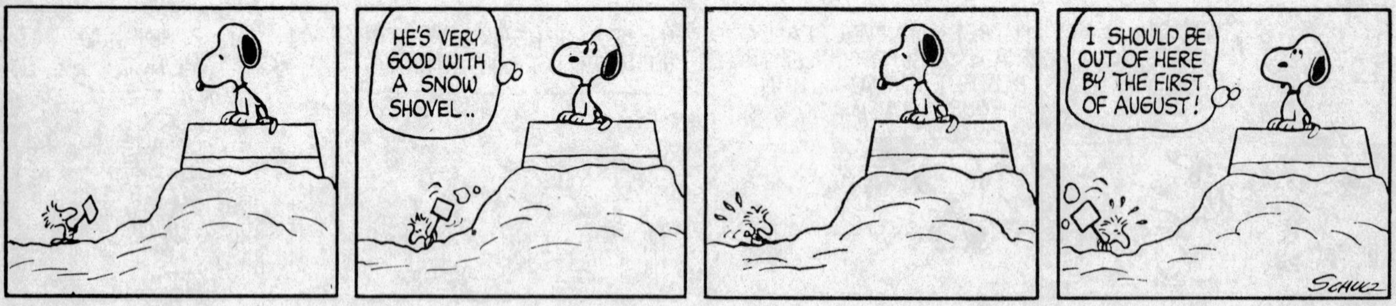
HE'S VERY GOOD WITH A SNOW SHOVEL..
I SHOULD BE OUT OF HERE BY THE FIRST OF AUGUST!
SCHULZ

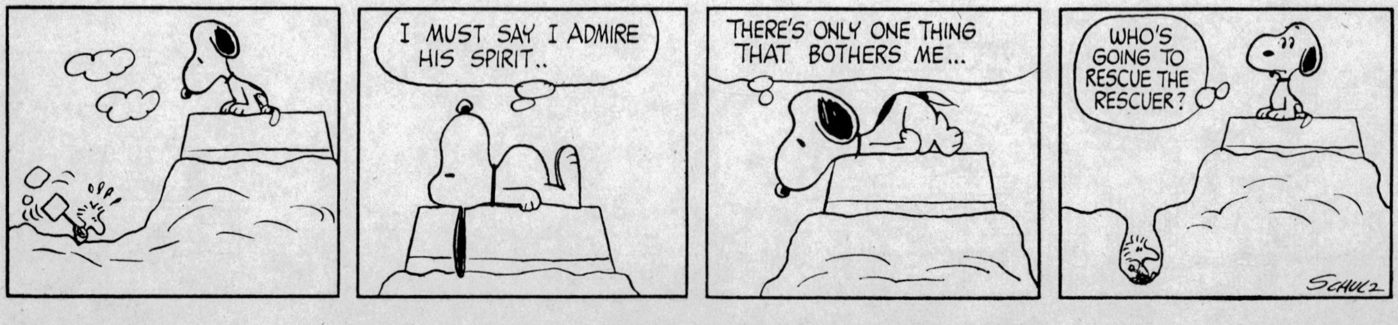
I MUST SAY I ADMIRE HIS SPIRIT..
THERE'S ONLY ONE THING THAT BOTHERS ME...
WHO'S GOING TO RESCUE THE RESCUER?
SCHULZ

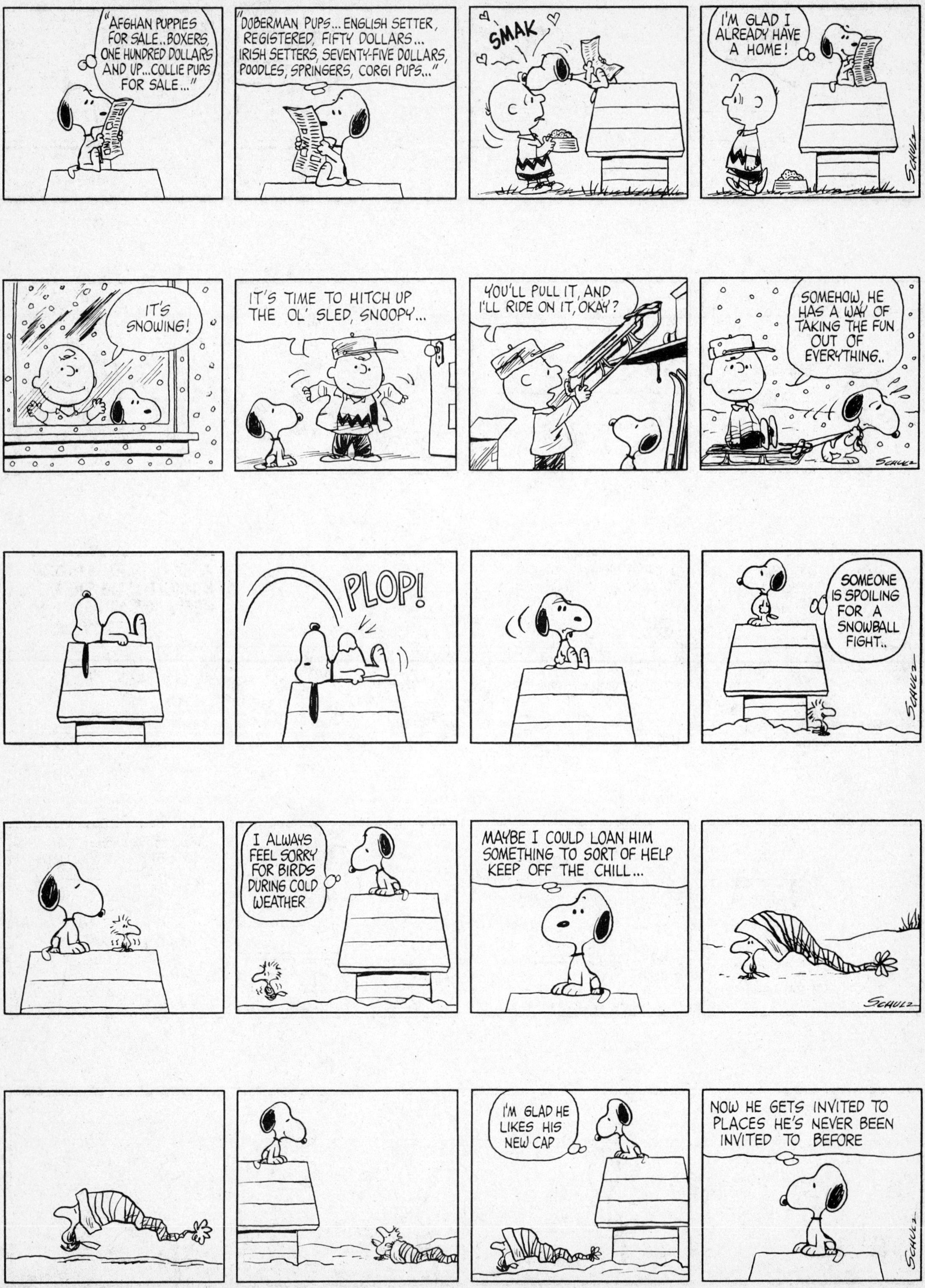
"AFGHAN PUPPIES FOR SALE..BOXERS, ONE HUNDRED DOLLARS AND UP...COLLIE PUPS FOR SALE..."
"DOBERMAN PUPS...ENGLISH SETTER, REGISTERED, FIFTY DOLLARS... IRISH SETTERS, SEVENTY-FIVE DOLLARS, POODLES, SPRINGERS, CORGI PUPS..."
SMAK
I'M GLAD I ALREADY HAVE A HOME!
SCHULZ
IT'S SNOWING!
IT'S TIME TO HITCH UP THE OL' SLED, SNOOPY...
YOU'LL PULL IT, AND I'LL RIDE ON IT, OKAY?
SOMEHOW, HE HAS A WAY OF TAKING THE FUN OUT OF EVERYTHING..
SCHULZ
PLOP!
SOMEONE IS SPOILING FOR A SNOWBALL FIGHT..
SCHULZ
I ALWAYS FEEL SORRY FOR BIRDS DURING COLD WEATHER
MAYBE I COULD LOAN HIM SOMETHING TO SORT OF HELP KEEP OFF THE CHILL...
SCHULZ
I'M GLAD HE LIKES HIS NEW CAP
NOW HE GETS INVITED TO PLACES HE'S NEVER BEEN INVITED TO BEFORE
SCHULZ

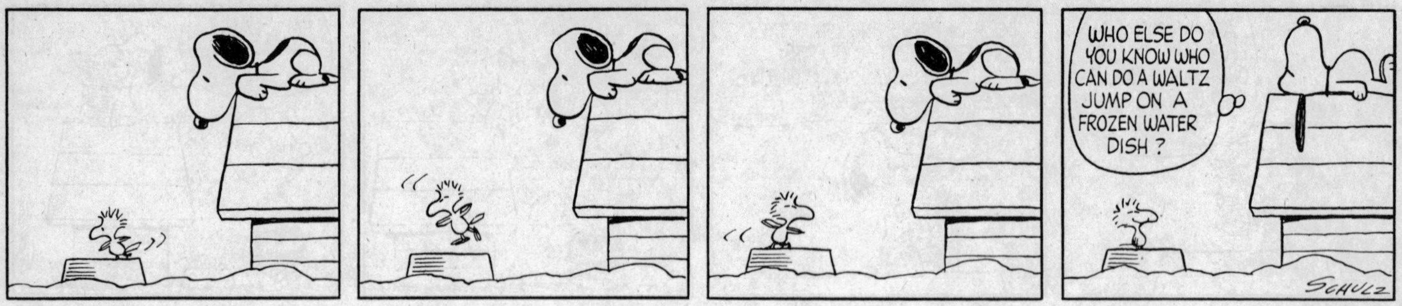
WHO ELSE DO YOU KNOW WHO CAN DO A WALTZ JUMP ON A FROZEN WATER DISH ?

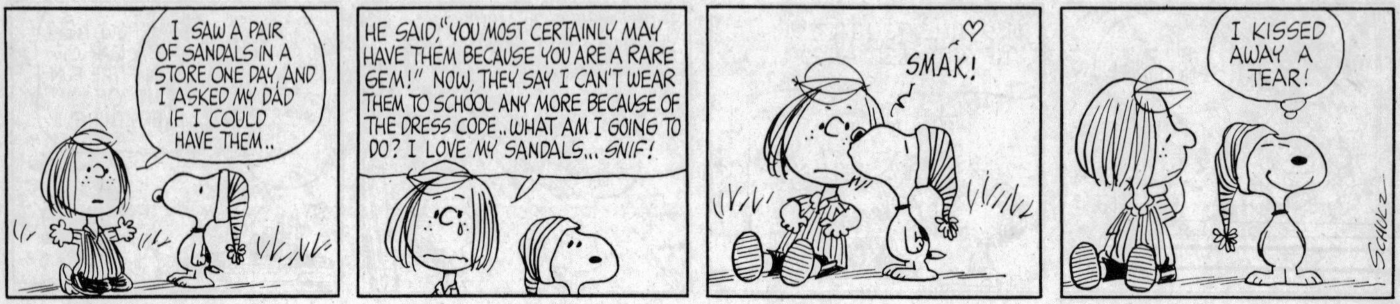
I SAW A PAIR OF SANDALS IN A STORE ONE DAY, AND I ASKED MY DAD IF I COULD HAVE THEM..
HE SAID, "YOU MOST CERTAINLY MAY HAVE THEM BECAUSE YOU ARE A RARE GEM!" NOW, THEY SAY I CAN'T WEAR THEM TO SCHOOL ANY MORE BECAUSE OF THE DRESS CODE..WHAT AM I GOING TO DO? I LOVE MY SANDALS... SNIF!
SMAK!
I KISSED AWAY A TEAR!

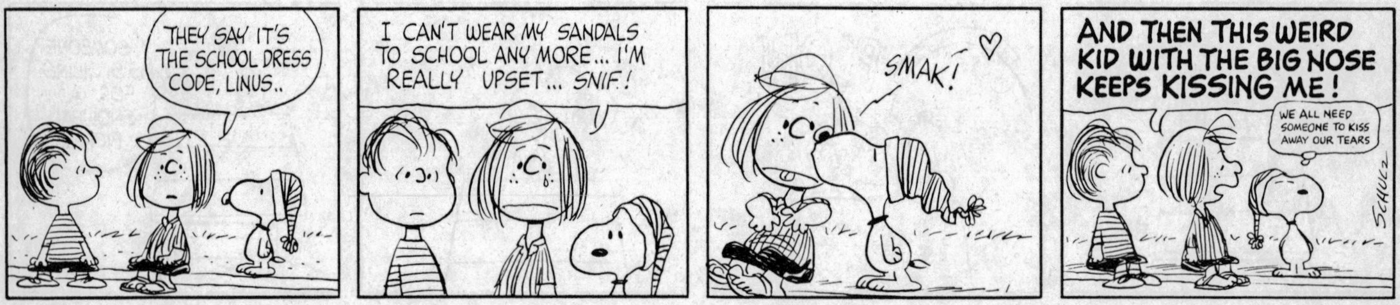
THEY SAY IT'S THE SCHOOL DRESS CODE, LINUS..
I CAN'T WEAR MY SANDALS TO SCHOOL ANY MORE... I'M REALLY UPSET... SNIF!
SMAK!
AND THEN THIS WEIRD KID WITH THE BIG NOSE KEEPS KISSING ME!
WE ALL NEED SOMEONE TO KISS AWAY OUR TEARS

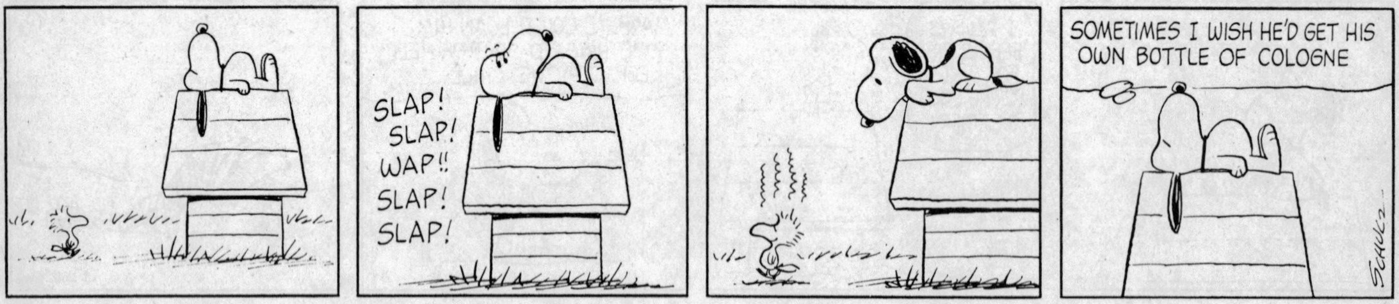
SLAP! SLAP! WAP!! SLAP! SLAP!
SOMETIMES I WISH HE'D GET HIS OWN BOTTLE OF COLOGNE

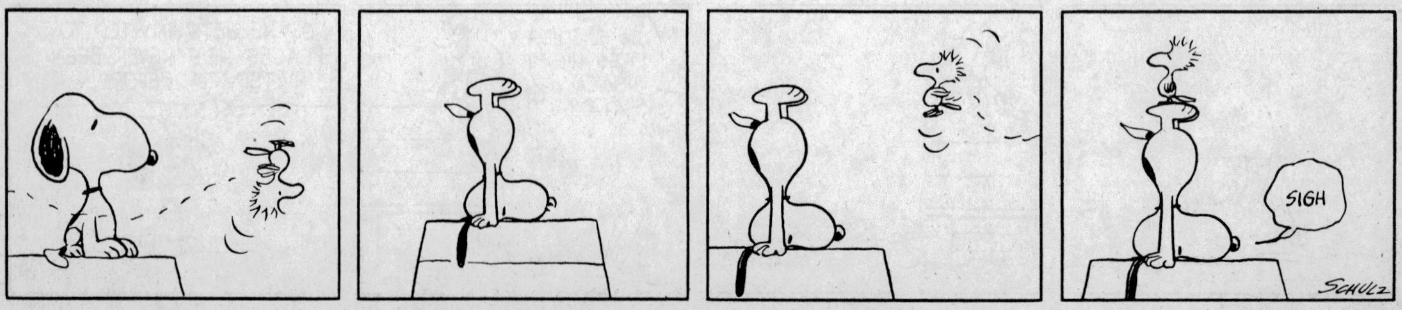
SIGH

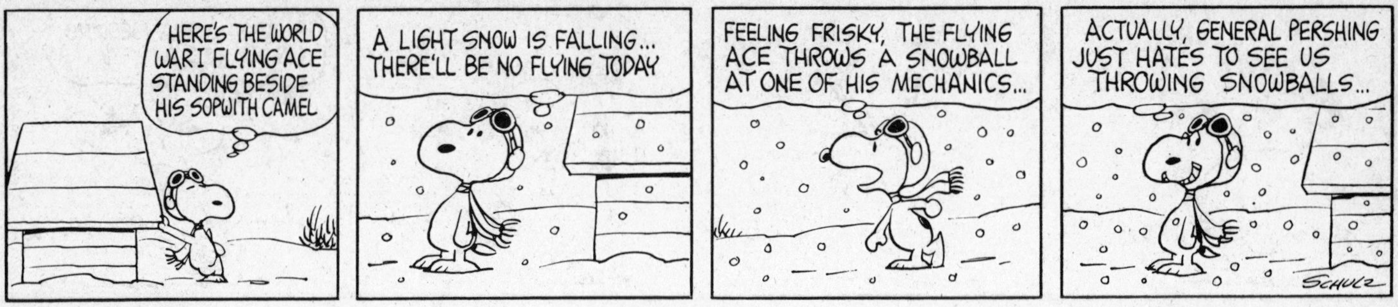
HERE'S THE WORLD WAR I FLYING ACE STANDING BESIDE HIS SOPWITH CAMEL
A LIGHT SNOW IS FALLING... THERE'LL BE NO FLYING TODAY
FEELING FRISKY, THE FLYING ACE THROWS A SNOWBALL AT ONE OF HIS MECHANICS...
ACTUALLY, GENERAL PERSHING JUST HATES TO SEE US THROWING SNOWBALLS...
SCHULZ

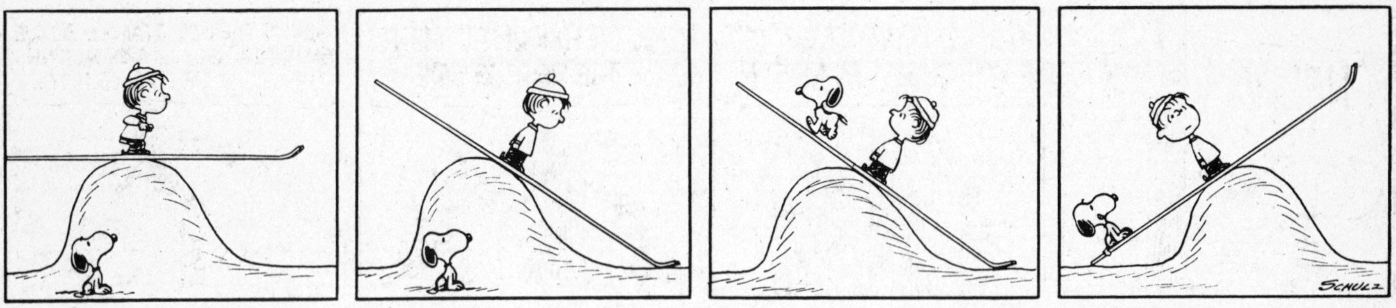
SCHULZ

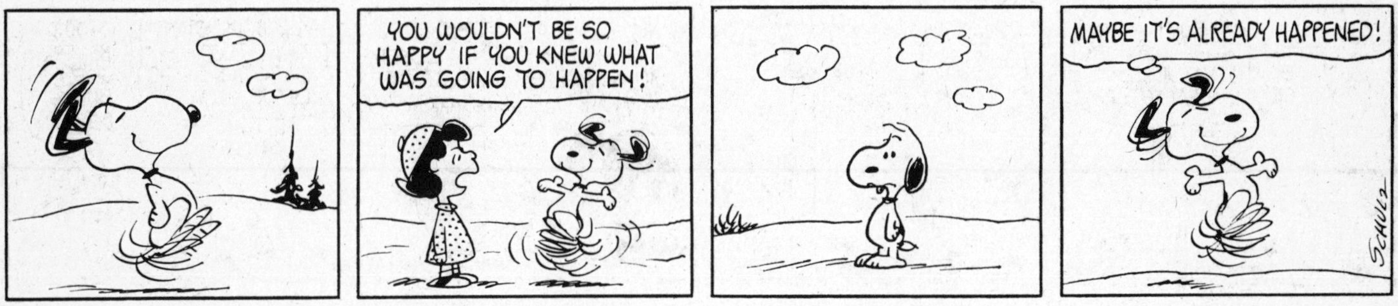
YOU WOULDN'T BE SO HAPPY IF YOU KNEW WHAT WAS GOING TO HAPPEN!
MAYBE IT'S ALREADY HAPPENED!
SCHULZ

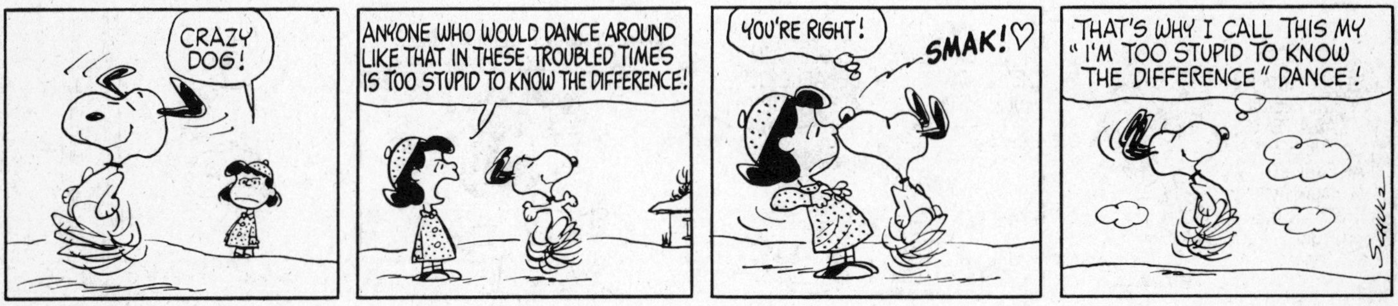
CRAZY DOG!
ANYONE WHO WOULD DANCE AROUND LIKE THAT IN THESE TROUBLED TIMES IS TOO STUPID TO KNOW THE DIFFERENCE!
YOU'RE RIGHT!
SMAK!
THAT'S WHY I CALL THIS MY "I'M TOO STUPID TO KNOW THE DIFFERENCE" DANCE!
SCHULZ

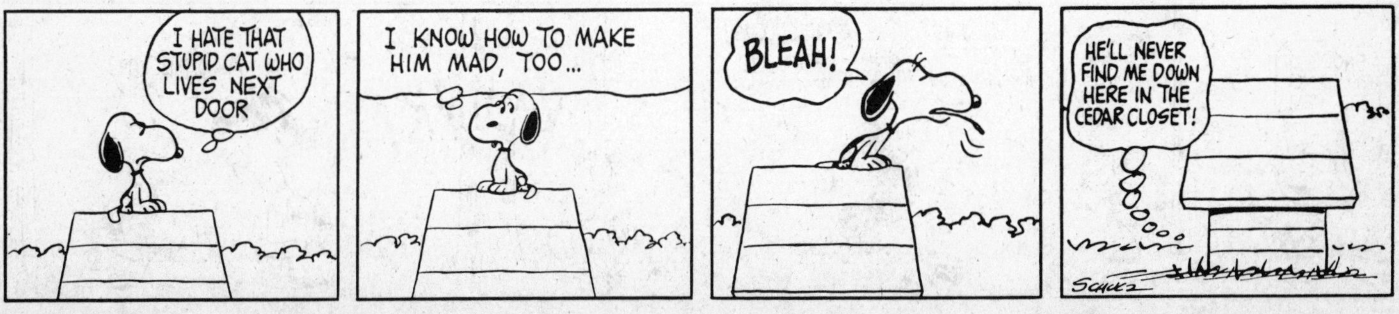
I HATE THAT STUPID CAT WHO LIVES NEXT DOOR
I KNOW HOW TO MAKE HIM MAD, TOO...
BLEAH!
HE'LL NEVER FIND ME DOWN HERE IN THE CEDAR CLOSET!
SCHULZ

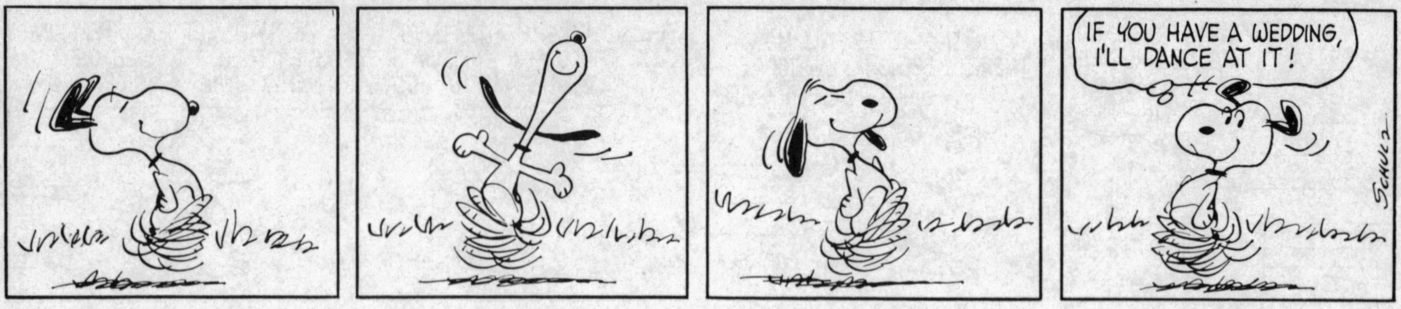
IF YOU HAVE A WEDDING, I'LL DANCE AT IT!
SCHULZ

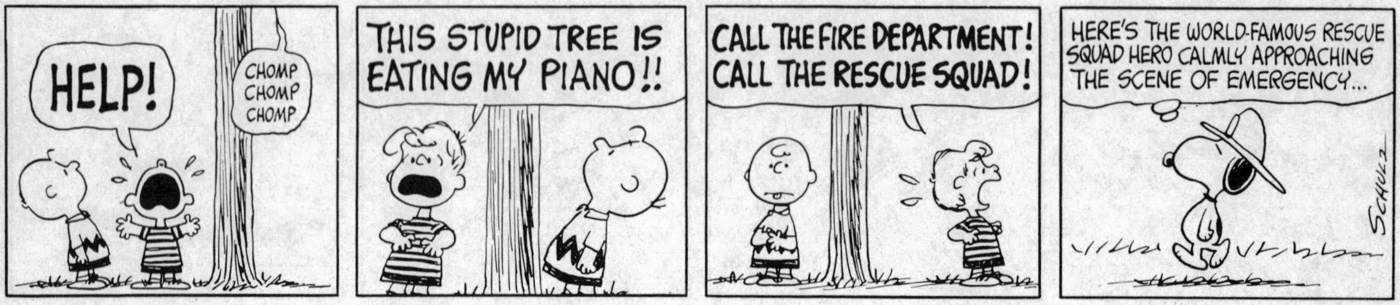
HELP!
CHOMP CHOMP CHOMP
THIS STUPID TREE IS EATING MY PIANO!!
CALL THE FIRE DEPARTMENT! CALL THE RESCUE SQUAD!
HERE'S THE WORLD-FAMOUS RESCUE SQUAD HERO CALMLY APPROACHING THE SCENE OF EMERGENCY...
SCHULZ

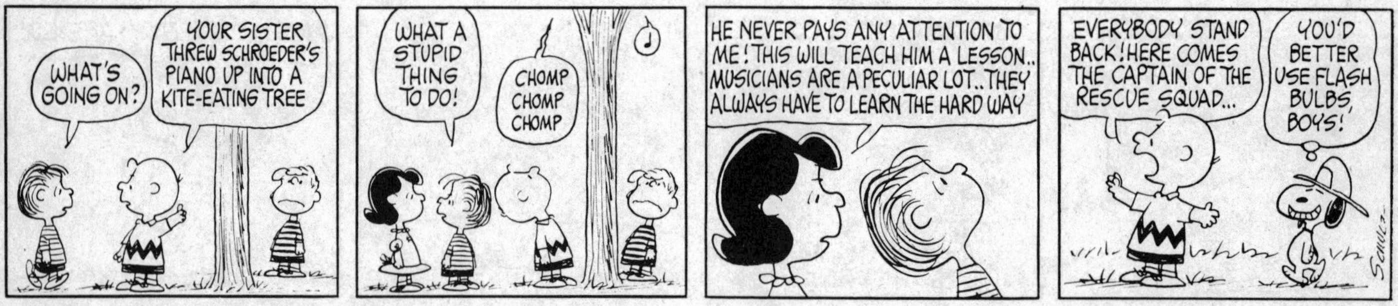
WHAT'S GOING ON?
YOUR SISTER THREW SCHROEDER'S PIANO UP INTO A KITE-EATING TREE
WHAT A STUPID THING TO DO!
CHOMP CHOMP CHOMP
HE NEVER PAYS ANY ATTENTION TO ME! THIS WILL TEACH HIM A LESSON.. MUSICIANS ARE A PECULIAR LOT..THEY ALWAYS HAVE TO LEARN THE HARD WAY
EVERYBODY STAND BACK! HERE COMES THE CAPTAIN OF THE RESCUE SQUAD...
YOU'D BETTER USE FLASH BULBS, BOYS!
SCHULZ

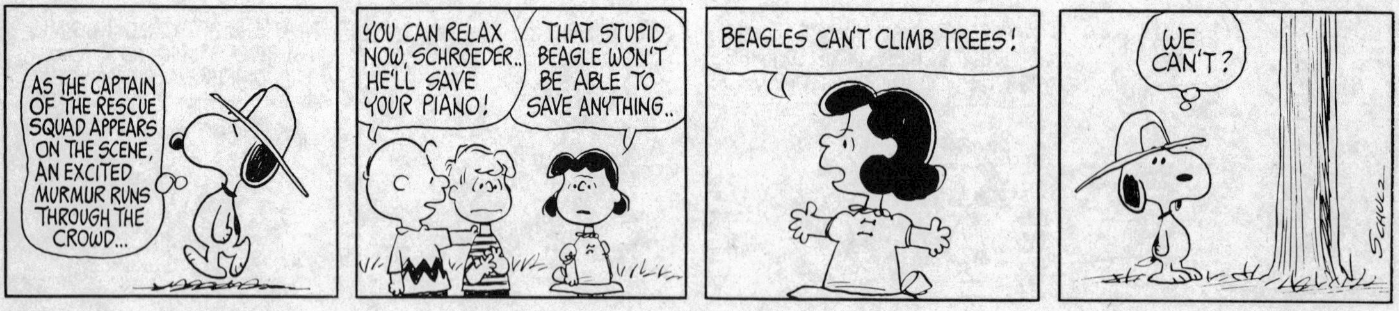
AS THE CAPTAIN OF THE RESCUE SQUAD APPEARS ON THE SCENE, AN EXCITED MURMUR RUNS THROUGH THE CROWD...
YOU CAN RELAX NOW, SCHROEDER.. HE'LL SAVE YOUR PIANO!
THAT STUPID BEAGLE WON'T BE ABLE TO SAVE ANYTHING..
BEAGLES CAN'T CLIMB TREES!
WE CAN'T?
SCHULZ

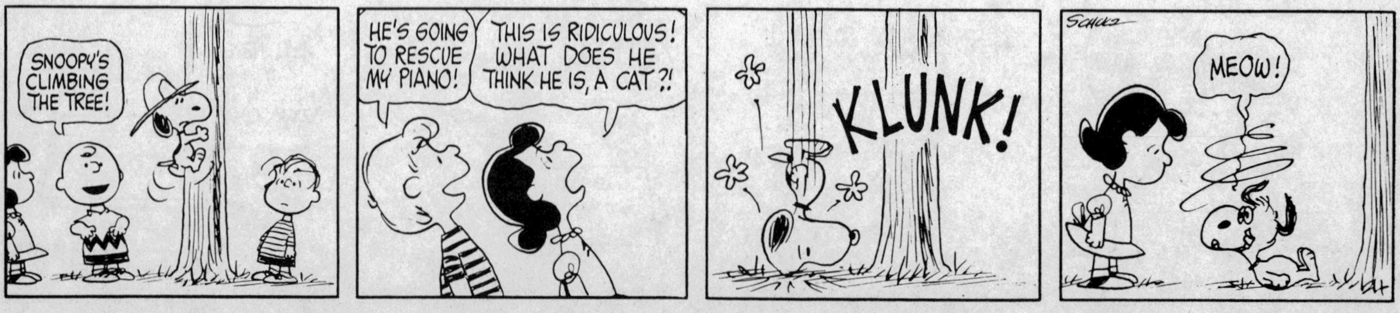
SNOOPY'S CLIMBING THE TREE!
HE'S GOING TO RESCUE MY PIANO!
THIS IS RIDICULOUS! WHAT DOES HE THINK HE IS, A CAT?!
KLUNK!
SCHULZ
MEOW!

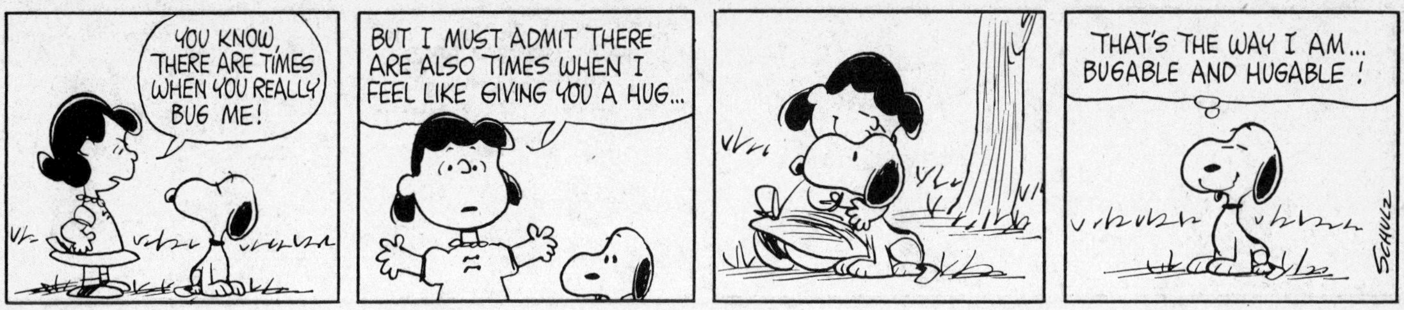
YOU KNOW, THERE ARE TIMES WHEN YOU REALLY BUG ME!
BUT I MUST ADMIT THERE ARE ALSO TIMES WHEN I FEEL LIKE GIVING YOU A HUG...
THAT'S THE WAY I AM... BUGABLE AND HUGABLE!
SCHULZ

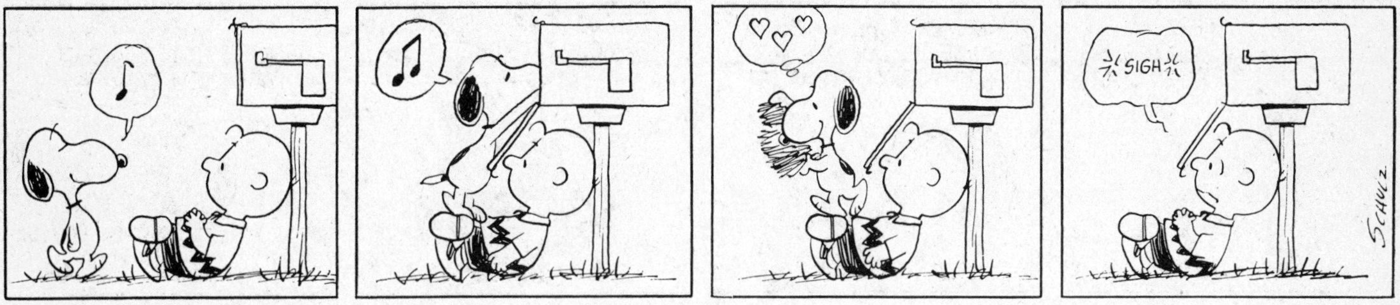
SIGH
SCHULZ

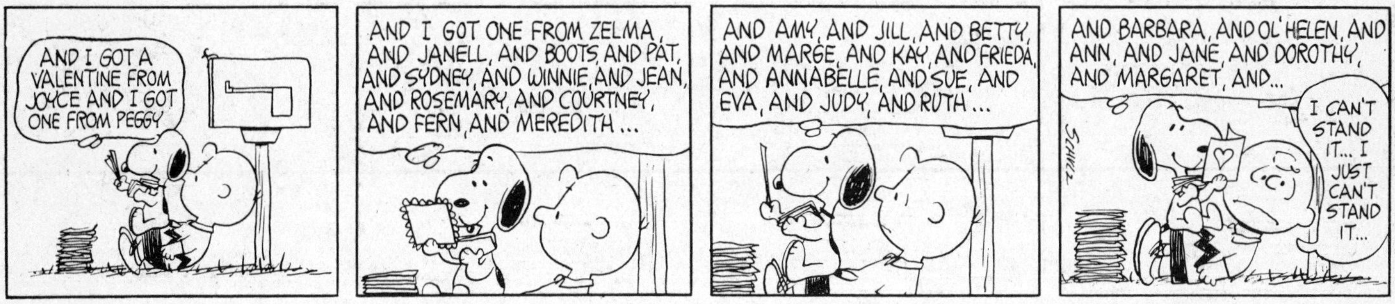
AND I GOT A VALENTINE FROM JOYCE AND I GOT ONE FROM PEGGY
AND I GOT ONE FROM ZELMA, AND JANELL, AND BOOTS, AND PAT, AND SYDNEY, AND WINNIE, AND JEAN, AND ROSEMARY, AND COURTNEY, AND FERN, AND MEREDITH ...
AND AMY, AND JILL, AND BETTY, AND MARGE, AND KAY, AND FRIEDA, AND ANNABELLE, AND SUE, AND EVA, AND JUDY, AND RUTH ...
AND BARBARA, AND OL' HELEN, AND ANN, AND JANE, AND DOROTHY, AND MARGARET, AND...
I CAN'T STAND IT... I JUST CAN'T STAND IT...
SCHULZ

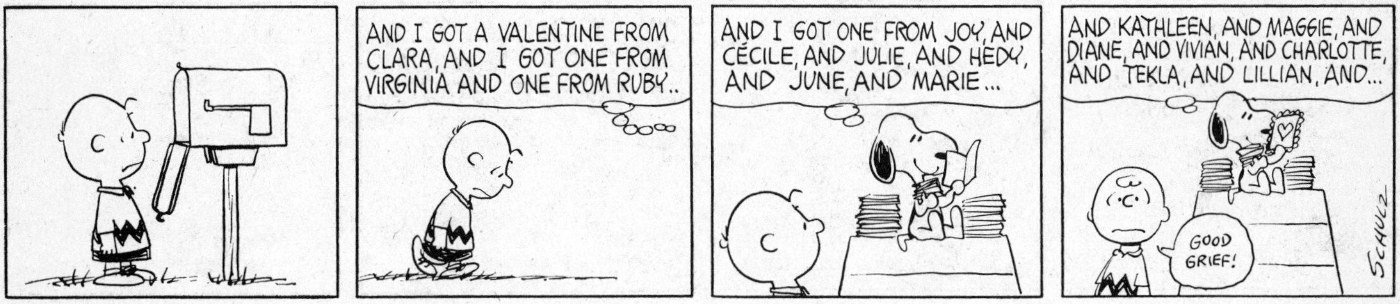
AND I GOT A VALENTINE FROM CLARA, AND I GOT ONE FROM VIRGINIA AND ONE FROM RUBY..
AND I GOT ONE FROM JOY, AND CÉCILE, AND JULIE, AND HEDY, AND JUNE, AND MARIE ...
AND KATHLEEN, AND MAGGIE, AND DIANE, AND VIVIAN, AND CHARLOTTE, AND TEKLA, AND LILLIAN, AND...
GOOD GRIEF!
SCHULZ

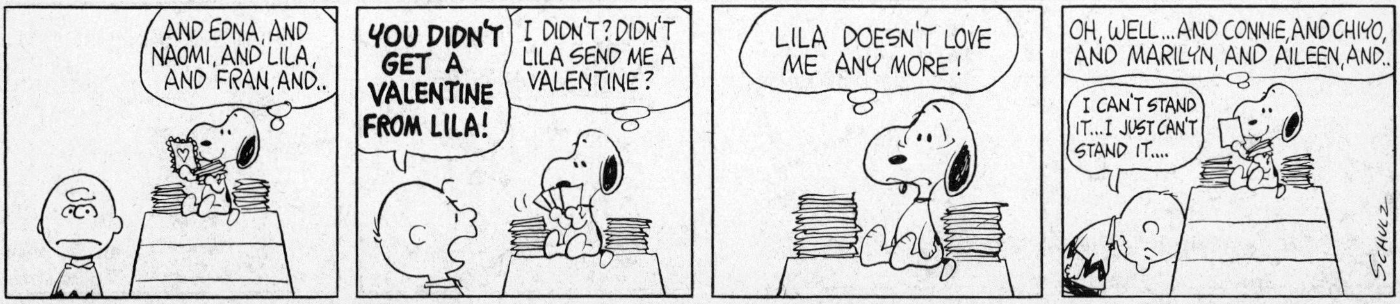
AND EDNA, AND NAOMI, AND LILA, AND FRAN, AND..
YOU DIDN'T GET A VALENTINE FROM LILA!
I DIDN'T? DIDN'T LILA SEND ME A VALENTINE?
LILA DOESN'T LOVE ME ANY MORE!
OH, WELL... AND CONNIE, AND CHIYO, AND MARILYN, AND AILEEN, AND..
I CAN'T STAND IT... I JUST CAN'T STAND IT....
SCHULZ

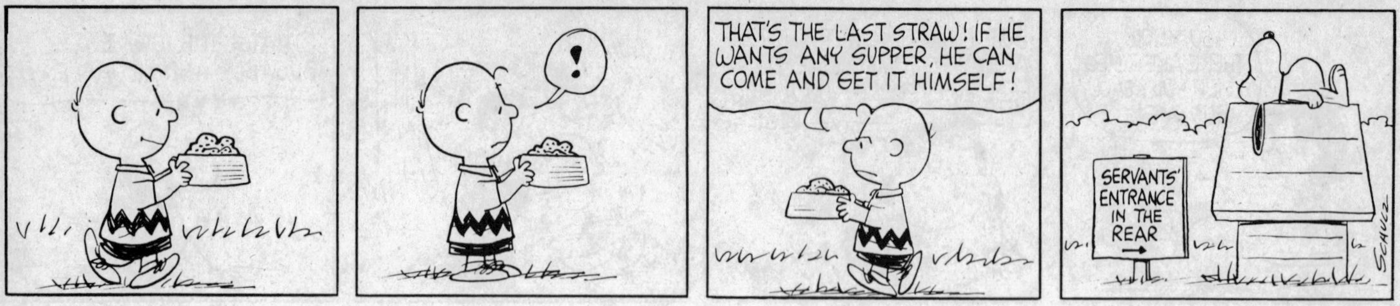
!
THAT'S THE LAST STRAW! IF HE WANTS ANY SUPPER, HE CAN COME AND GET IT HIMSELF!
SERVANTS' ENTRANCE IN THE REAR
SCHULZ

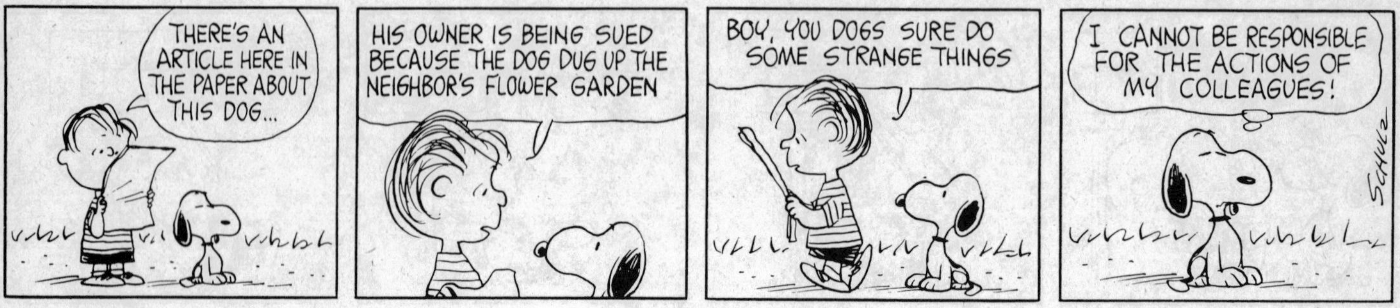
THERE'S AN ARTICLE HERE IN THE PAPER ABOUT THIS DOG...
HIS OWNER IS BEING SUED BECAUSE THE DOG DUG UP THE NEIGHBOR'S FLOWER GARDEN
BOY, YOU DOGS SURE DO SOME STRANGE THINGS
I CANNOT BE RESPONSIBLE FOR THE ACTIONS OF MY COLLEAGUES!
SCHULZ

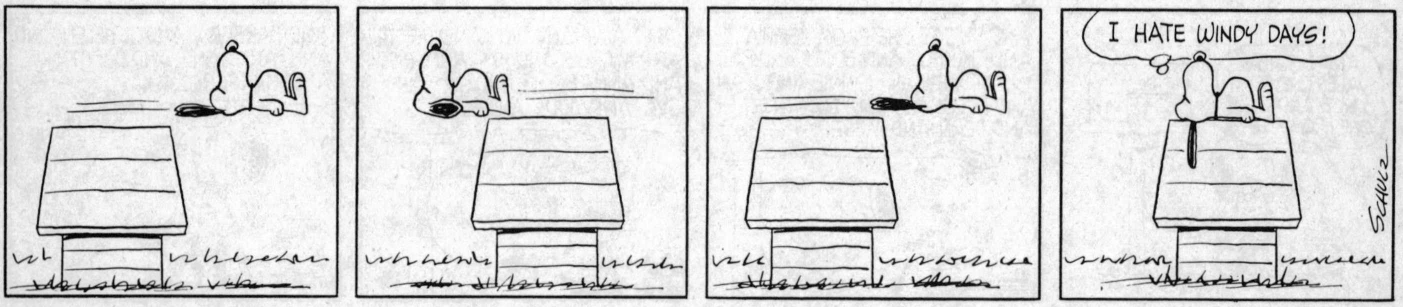
I HATE WINDY DAYS!
SCHULZ

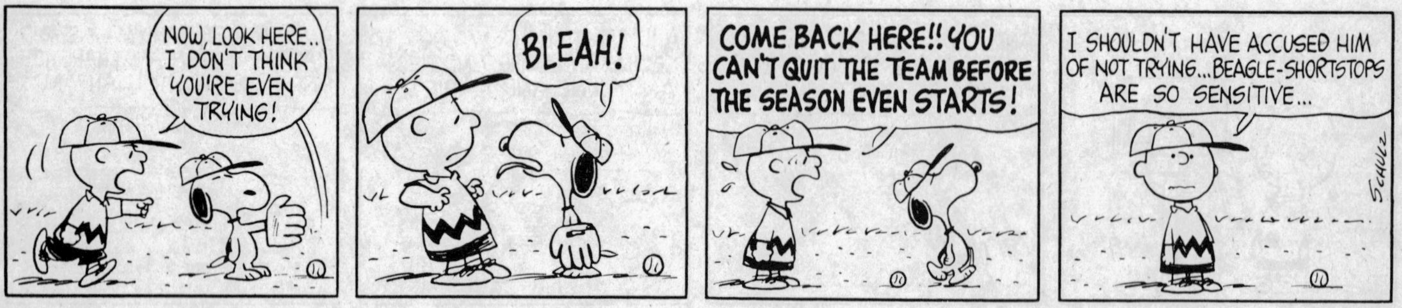
NOW, LOOK HERE.. I DON'T THINK YOU'RE EVEN TRYING!
BLEAH!
COME BACK HERE!! YOU CAN'T QUIT THE TEAM BEFORE THE SEASON EVEN STARTS!
I SHOULDN'T HAVE ACCUSED HIM OF NOT TRYING...BEAGLE-SHORTSTOPS ARE SO SENSITIVE...
SCHULZ

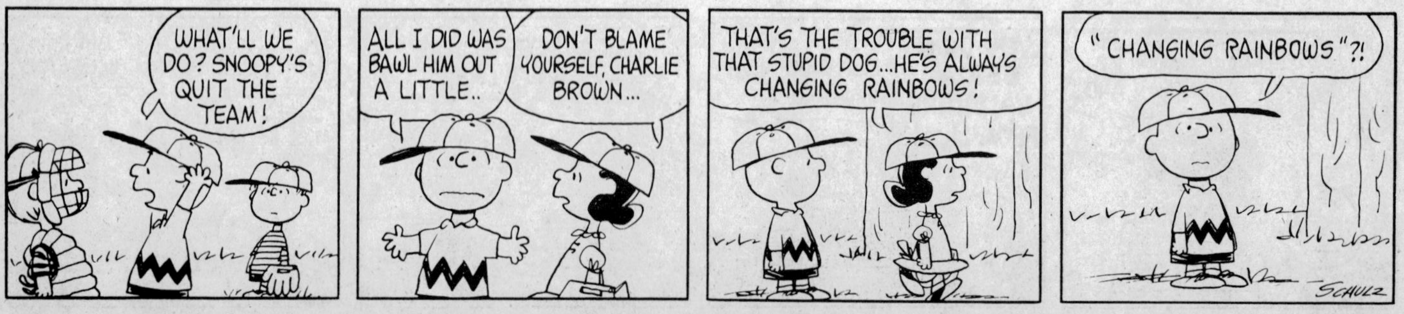
WHAT'LL WE DO? SNOOPY'S QUIT THE TEAM!
ALL I DID WAS BAWL HIM OUT A LITTLE..
DON'T BLAME YOURSELF, CHARLIE BROWN...
THAT'S THE TROUBLE WITH THAT STUPID DOG...HE'S ALWAYS CHANGING RAINBOWS!
"CHANGING RAINBOWS"?!
SCHULZ

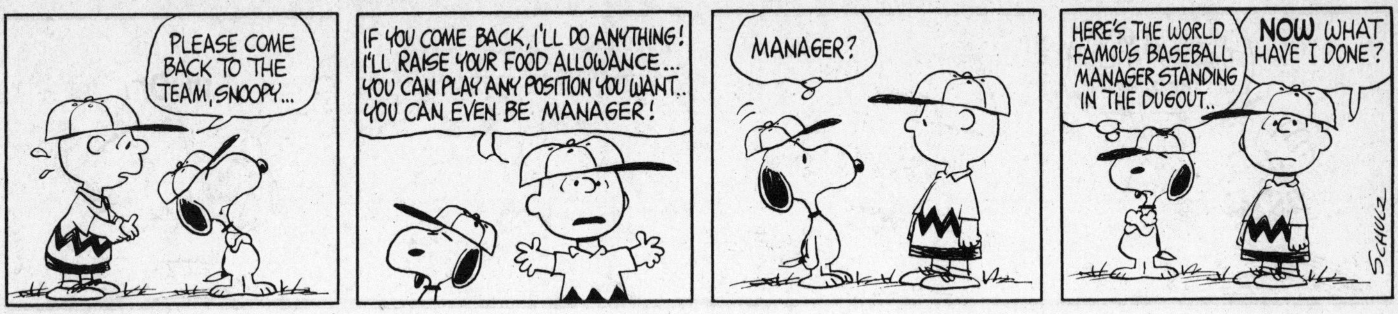
PLEASE COME BACK TO THE TEAM, SNOOPY...
IF YOU COME BACK, I'LL DO ANYTHING! I'LL RAISE YOUR FOOD ALLOWANCE... YOU CAN PLAY ANY POSITION YOU WANT.. YOU CAN EVEN BE MANAGER!
MANAGER?
HERE'S THE WORLD FAMOUS BASEBALL MANAGER STANDING IN THE DUGOUT..
NOW WHAT HAVE I DONE?
SCHULZ

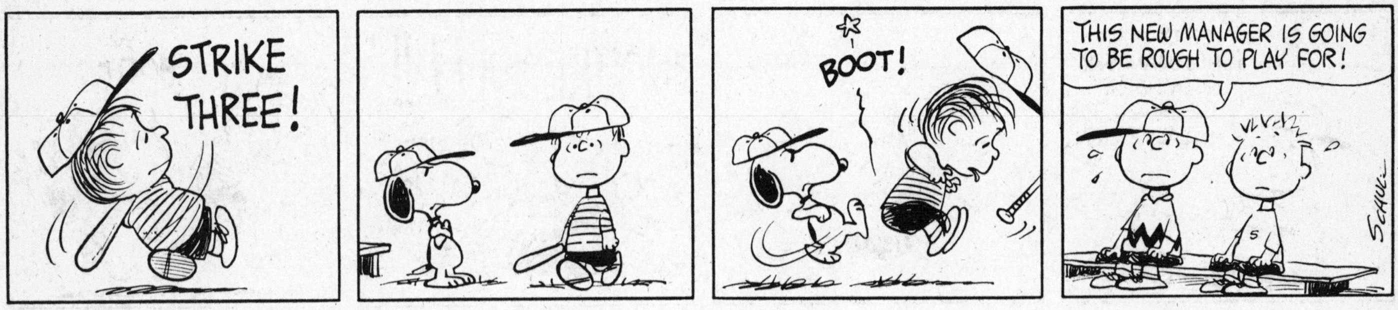
STRIKE THREE!
BOOT!
THIS NEW MANAGER IS GOING TO BE ROUGH TO PLAY FOR!
SCHULZ

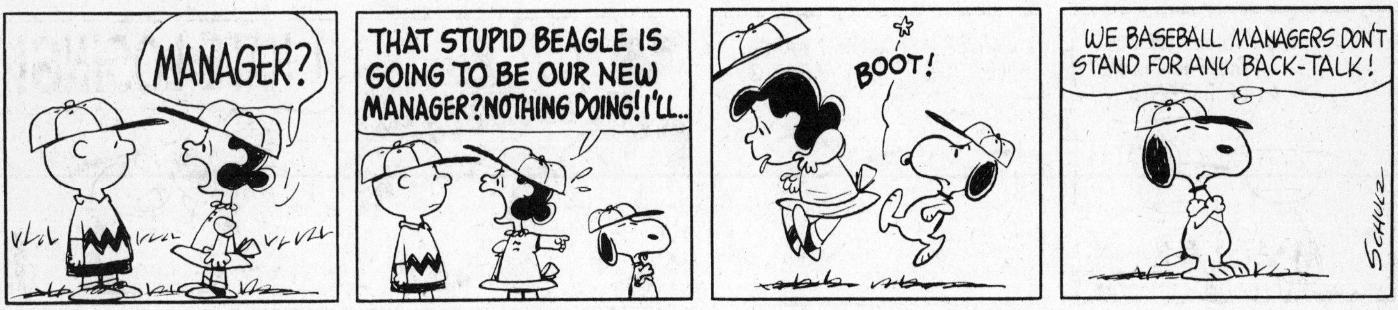
MANAGER?
THAT STUPID BEAGLE IS GOING TO BE OUR NEW MANAGER? NOTHING DOING! I'LL..
BOOT!
WE BASEBALL MANAGERS DON'T STAND FOR ANY BACK-TALK!
SCHULZ

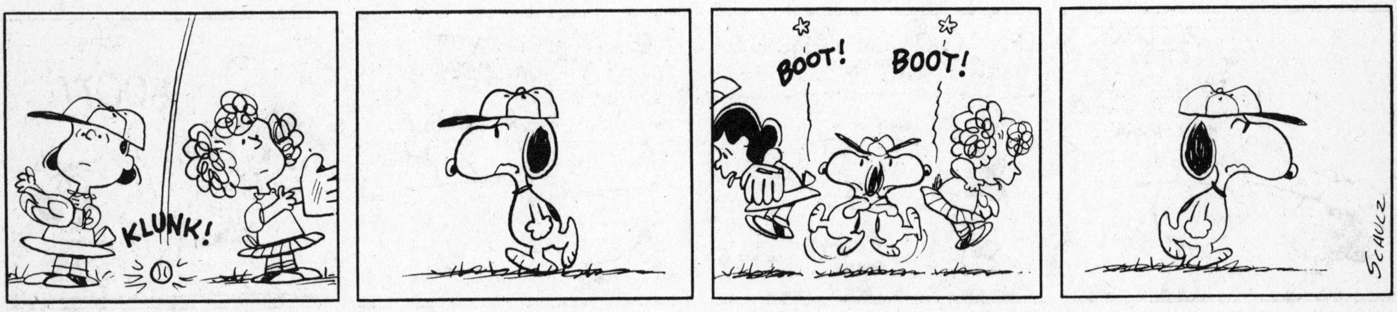
KLUNK!
BOOT!
BOOT!
SCHULZ

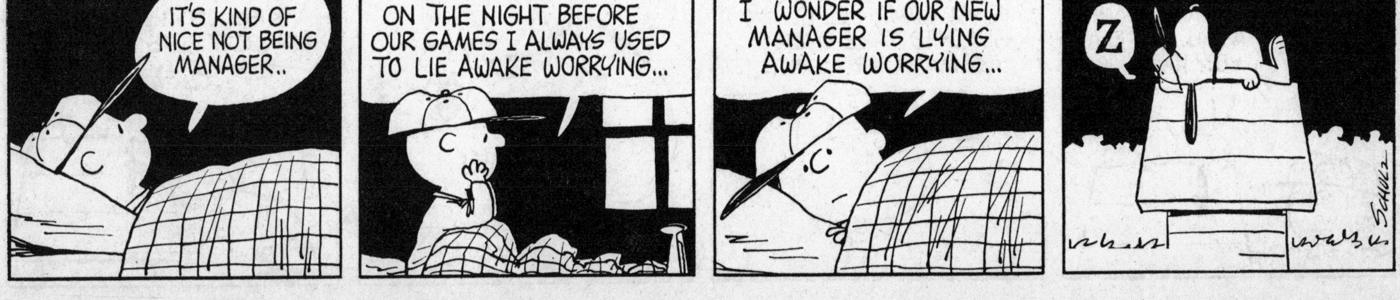
IT'S KIND OF NICE NOT BEING MANAGER..
ON THE NIGHT BEFORE OUR GAMES I ALWAYS USED TO LIE AWAKE WORRYING...
I WONDER IF OUR NEW MANAGER IS LYING AWAKE WORRYING...
Z
SCHULZ

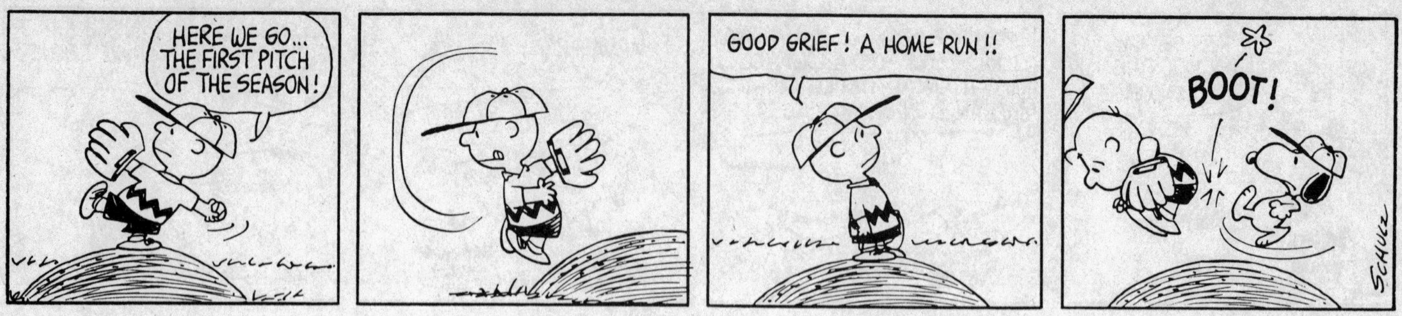
HERE WE GO... THE FIRST PITCH OF THE SEASON!
GOOD GRIEF! A HOME RUN!!
BOOT!
SCHULZ

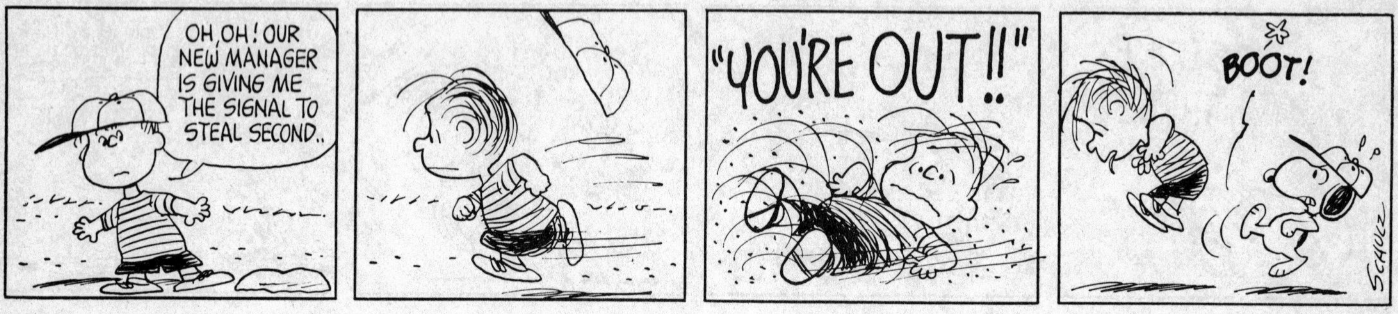
OH, OH! OUR NEW MANAGER IS GIVING ME THE SIGNAL TO STEAL SECOND..
"YOU'RE OUT!!"
BOOT!
SCHULZ

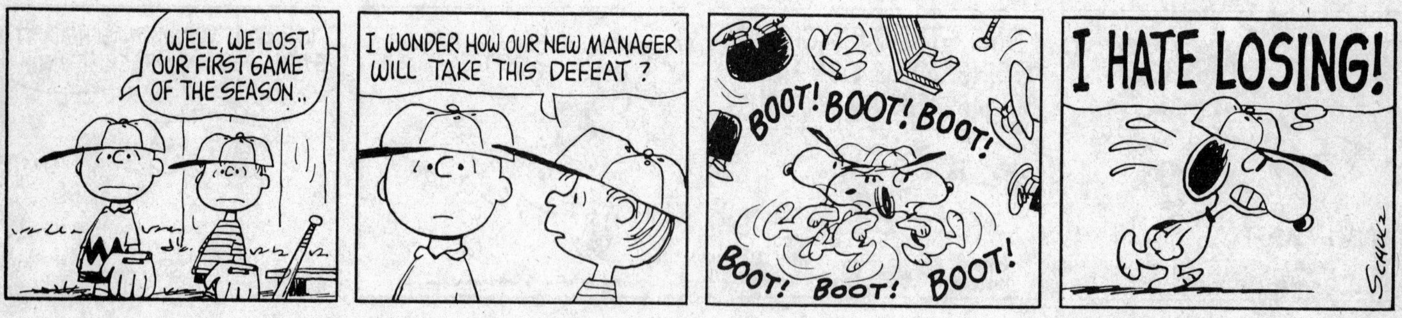
WELL, WE LOST OUR FIRST GAME OF THE SEASON..
I WONDER HOW OUR NEW MANAGER WILL TAKE THIS DEFEAT?
BOOT! BOOT! BOOT!
BOOT! BOOT! BOOT!
I HATE LOSING!
SCHULZ

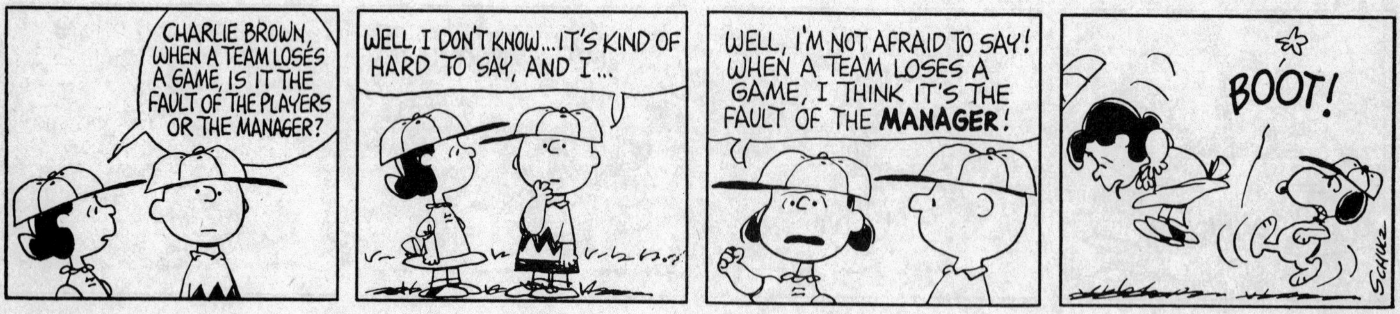
CHARLIE BROWN, WHEN A TEAM LOSES A GAME, IS IT THE FAULT OF THE PLAYERS OR THE MANAGER?
WELL, I DON'T KNOW...IT'S KIND OF HARD TO SAY, AND I...
WELL, I'M NOT AFRAID TO SAY! WHEN A TEAM LOSES A GAME, I THINK IT'S THE FAULT OF THE MANAGER!
BOOT!
SCHULZ

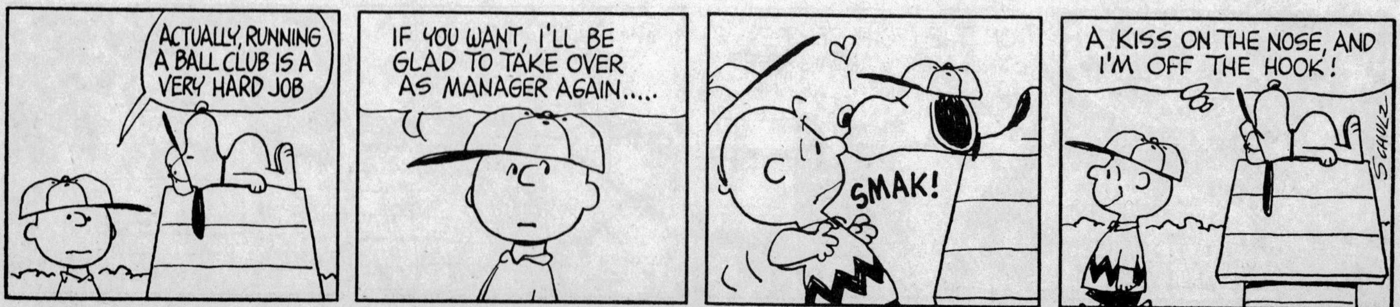
ACTUALLY, RUNNING A BALL CLUB IS A VERY HARD JOB
IF YOU WANT, I'LL BE GLAD TO TAKE OVER AS MANAGER AGAIN.....
SMAK!
A KISS ON THE NOSE, AND I'M OFF THE HOOK!
SCHULZ

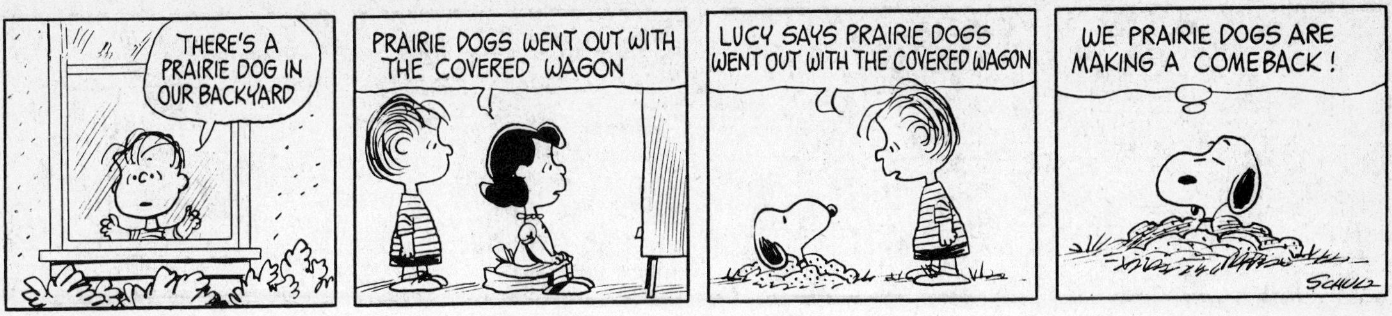
THERE'S A PRAIRIE DOG IN OUR BACKYARD
PRAIRIE DOGS WENT OUT WITH THE COVERED WAGON
LUCY SAYS PRAIRIE DOGS WENT OUT WITH THE COVERED WAGON
WE PRAIRIE DOGS ARE MAKING A COMEBACK !
SCHULZ

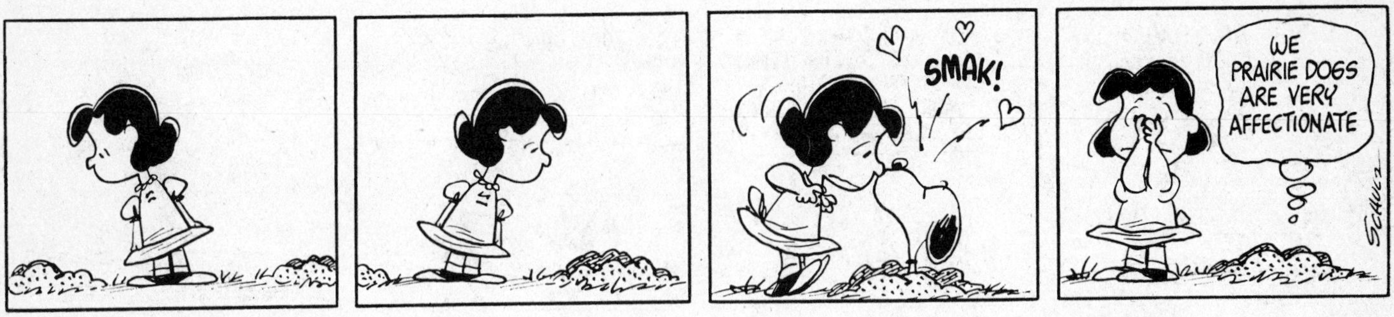
SMAK!
WE PRAIRIE DOGS ARE VERY AFFECTIONATE
SCHULZ

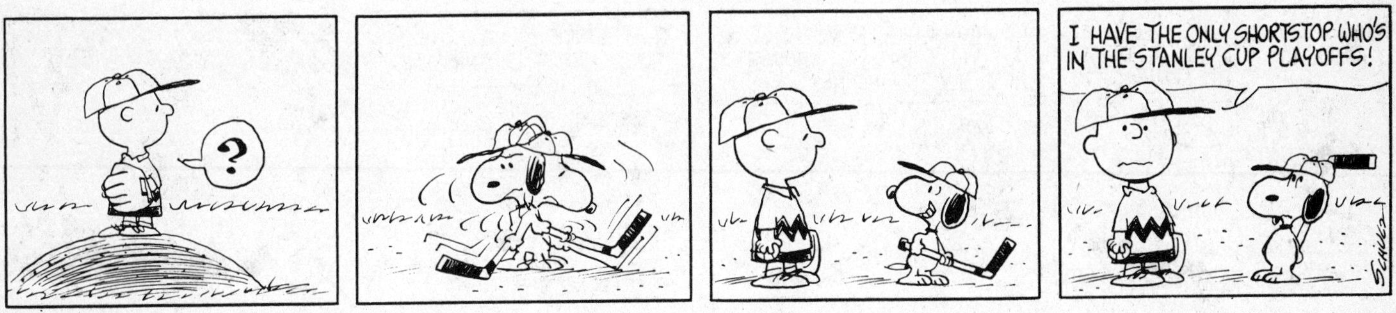
?
I HAVE THE ONLY SHORTSTOP WHO'S IN THE STANLEY CUP PLAYOFFS !
SCHULZ

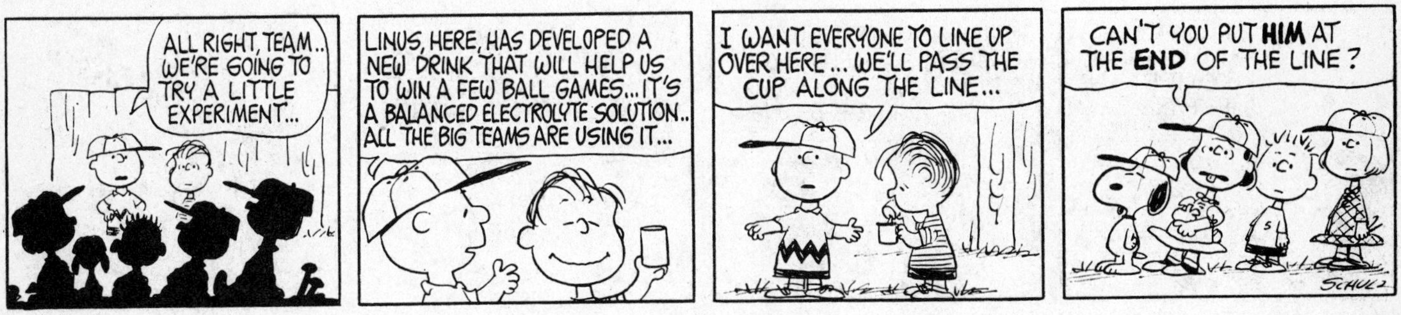
ALL RIGHT, TEAM.. WE'RE GOING TO TRY A LITTLE EXPERIMENT...
LINUS, HERE, HAS DEVELOPED A NEW DRINK THAT WILL HELP US TO WIN A FEW BALL GAMES... IT'S A BALANCED ELECTROLYTE SOLUTION.. ALL THE BIG TEAMS ARE USING IT...
I WANT EVERYONE TO LINE UP OVER HERE ... WE'LL PASS THE CUP ALONG THE LINE...
CAN'T YOU PUT HIM AT THE END OF THE LINE ?
SCHULZ

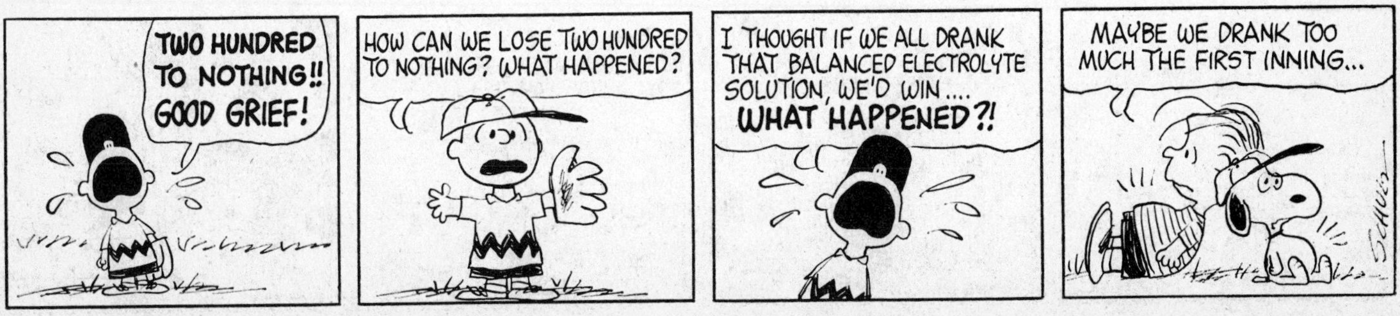
TWO HUNDRED TO NOTHING!! GOOD GRIEF!
HOW CAN WE LOSE TWO HUNDRED TO NOTHING? WHAT HAPPENED?
I THOUGHT IF WE ALL DRANK THAT BALANCED ELECTROLYTE SOLUTION, WE'D WIN .... WHAT HAPPENED ?!
MAYBE WE DRANK TOO MUCH THE FIRST INNING...
SCHULZ

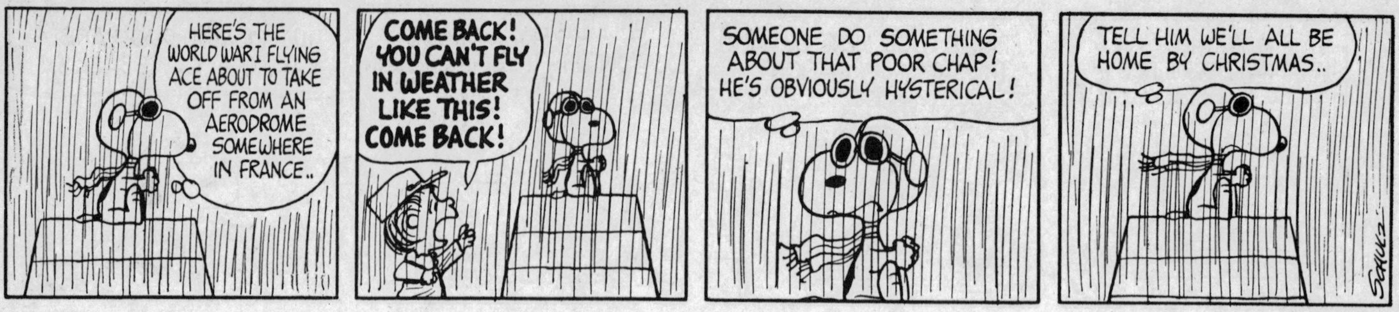
HERE'S THE WORLD WAR I FLYING ACE ABOUT TO TAKE OFF FROM AN AERODROME SOMEWHERE IN FRANCE..
COME BACK! YOU CAN'T FLY IN WEATHER LIKE THIS! COME BACK!
SOMEONE DO SOMETHING ABOUT THAT POOR CHAP! HE'S OBVIOUSLY HYSTERICAL!
TELL HIM WE'LL ALL BE HOME BY CHRISTMAS..
SCHULZ

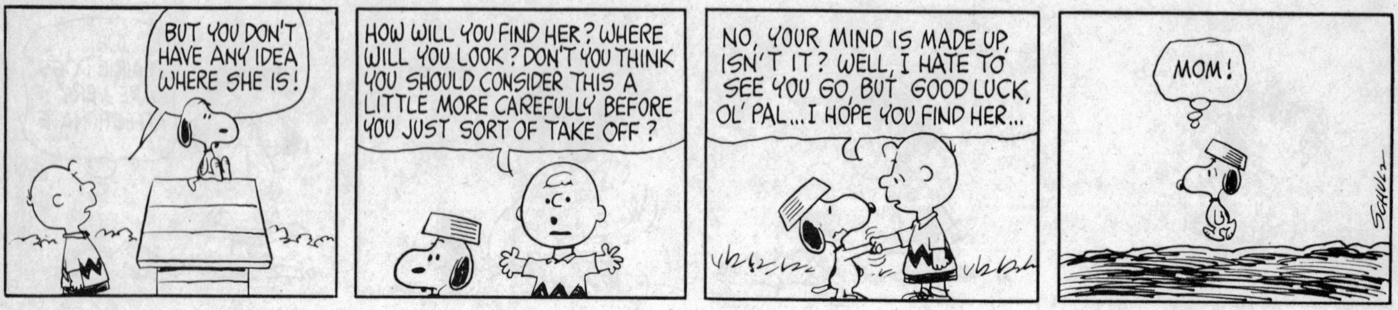
BUT YOU DON'T HAVE ANY IDEA WHERE SHE IS!
HOW WILL YOU FIND HER? WHERE WILL YOU LOOK? DON'T YOU THINK YOU SHOULD CONSIDER THIS A LITTLE MORE CAREFULLY BEFORE YOU JUST SORT OF TAKE OFF?
NO, YOUR MIND IS MADE UP, ISN'T IT? WELL, I HATE TO SEE YOU GO, BUT GOOD LUCK, OL' PAL... I HOPE YOU FIND HER...
MOM!
SCHULZ

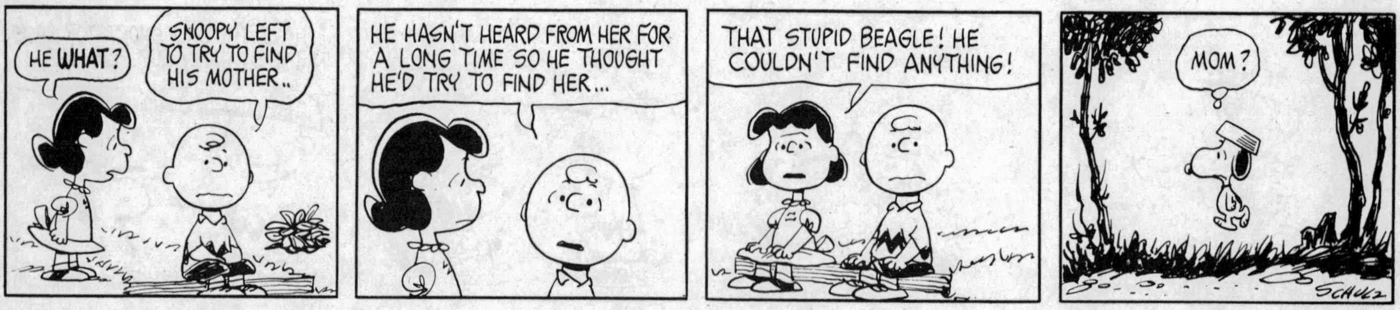
HE WHAT?
SNOOPY LEFT TO TRY TO FIND HIS MOTHER..
HE HASN'T HEARD FROM HER FOR A LONG TIME SO HE THOUGHT HE'D TRY TO FIND HER...
THAT STUPID BEAGLE! HE COULDN'T FIND ANYTHING!
MOM?
SCHULZ

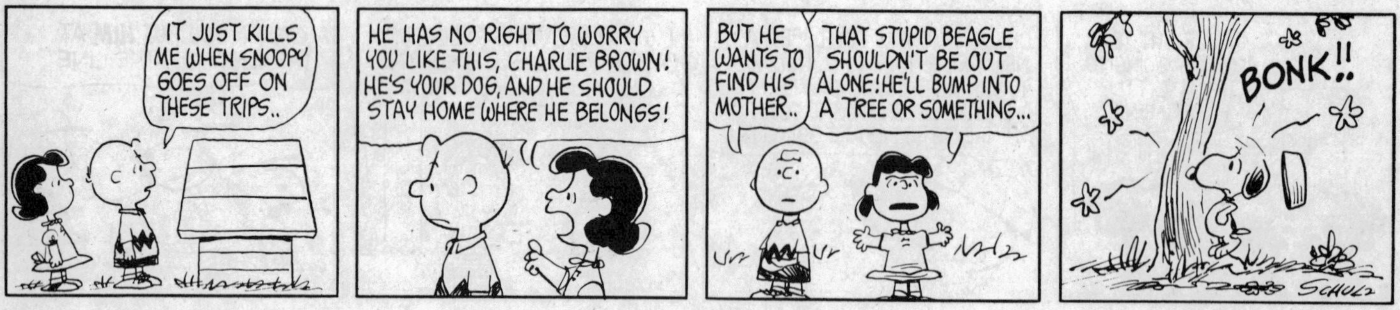
IT JUST KILLS ME WHEN SNOOPY GOES OFF ON THESE TRIPS..
HE HAS NO RIGHT TO WORRY YOU LIKE THIS, CHARLIE BROWN! HE'S YOUR DOG, AND HE SHOULD STAY HOME WHERE HE BELONGS!
BUT HE WANTS TO FIND HIS MOTHER..
THAT STUPID BEAGLE SHOULDN'T BE OUT ALONE! HE'LL BUMP INTO A TREE OR SOMETHING...
BONK!!
SCHULZ

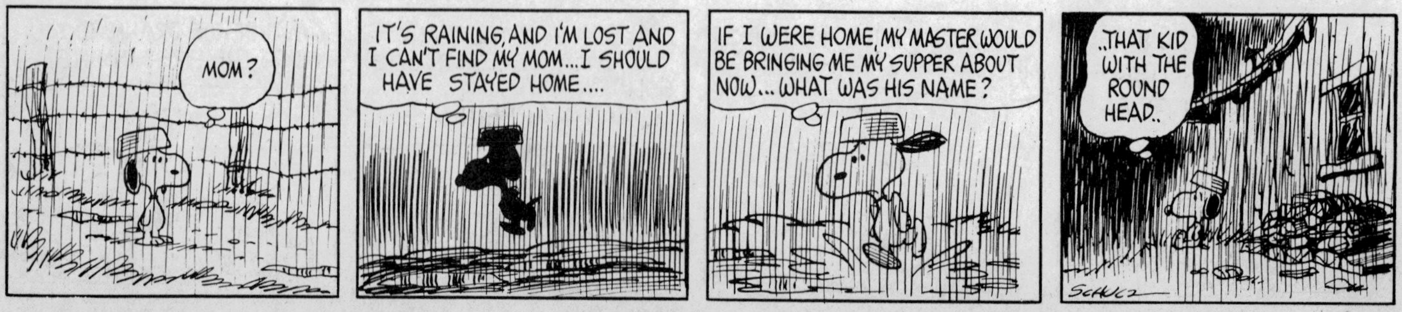
MOM?
IT'S RAINING, AND I'M LOST AND I CAN'T FIND MY MOM... I SHOULD HAVE STAYED HOME....
IF I WERE HOME, MY MASTER WOULD BE BRINGING ME MY SUPPER ABOUT NOW... WHAT WAS HIS NAME?
..THAT KID WITH THE ROUND HEAD..
SCHULZ

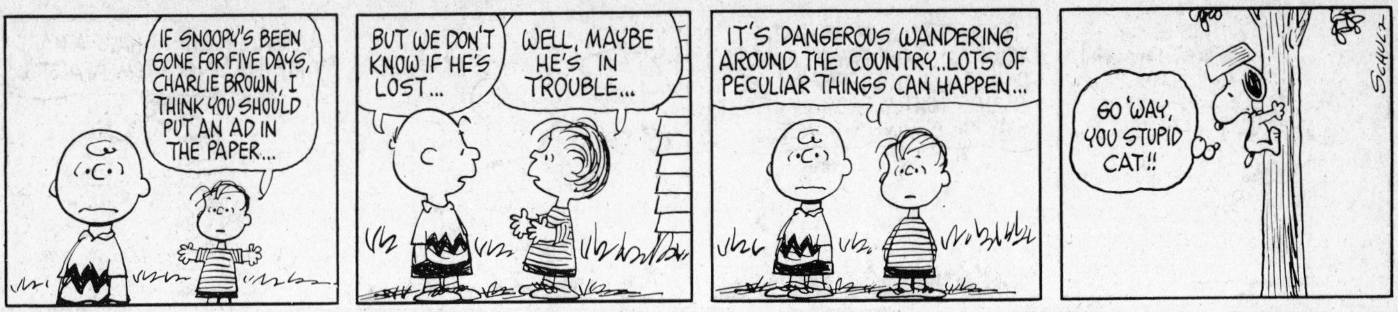
IF SNOOPY'S BEEN GONE FOR FIVE DAYS, CHARLIE BROWN, I THINK YOU SHOULD PUT AN AD IN THE PAPER...
BUT WE DON'T KNOW IF HE'S LOST...
WELL, MAYBE HE'S IN TROUBLE...
IT'S DANGEROUS WANDERING AROUND THE COUNTRY..LOTS OF PECULIAR THINGS CAN HAPPEN...
GO 'WAY, YOU STUPID CAT!!
SCHULZ

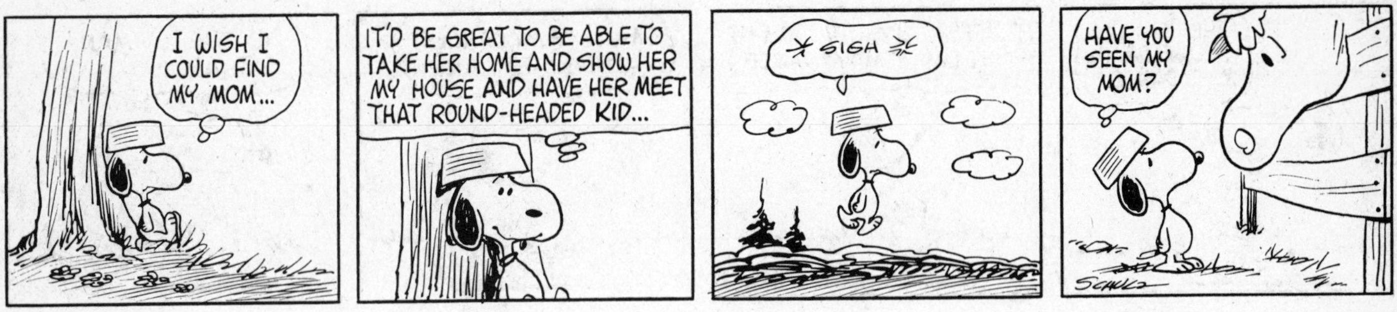
I WISH I COULD FIND MY MOM...
IT'D BE GREAT TO BE ABLE TO TAKE HER HOME AND SHOW HER MY HOUSE AND HAVE HER MEET THAT ROUND-HEADED KID...
SIGH
HAVE YOU SEEN MY MOM?
SCHULZ

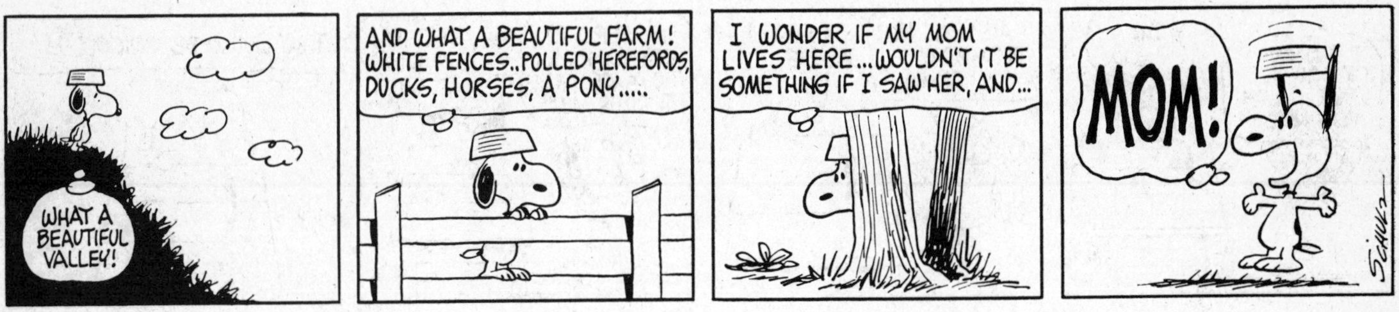
WHAT A BEAUTIFUL VALLEY!
AND WHAT A BEAUTIFUL FARM! WHITE FENCES..POLLED HEREFORDS, DUCKS, HORSES, A PONY.....
I WONDER IF MY MOM LIVES HERE...WOULDN'T IT BE SOMETHING IF I SAW HER, AND...
MOM!
SCHULZ

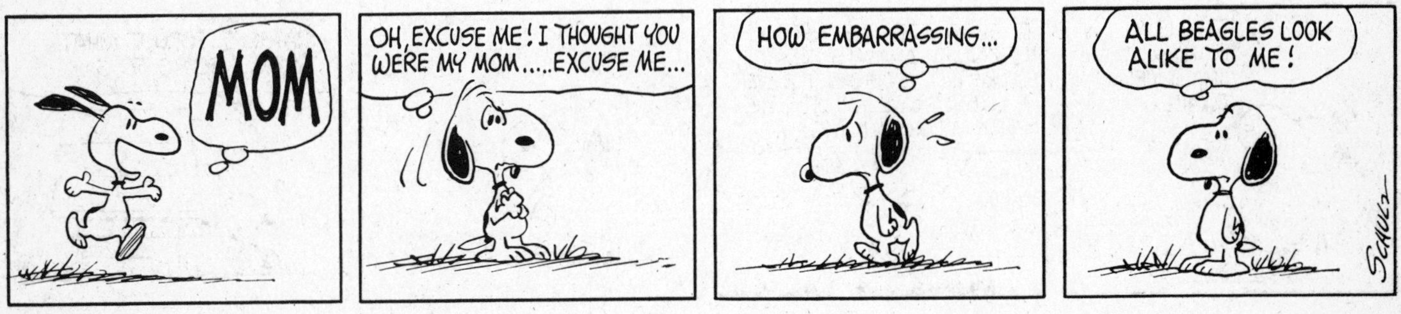
MOM
OH, EXCUSE ME! I THOUGHT YOU WERE MY MOM.....EXCUSE ME...
HOW EMBARRASSING...
ALL BEAGLES LOOK ALIKE TO ME!
SCHULZ

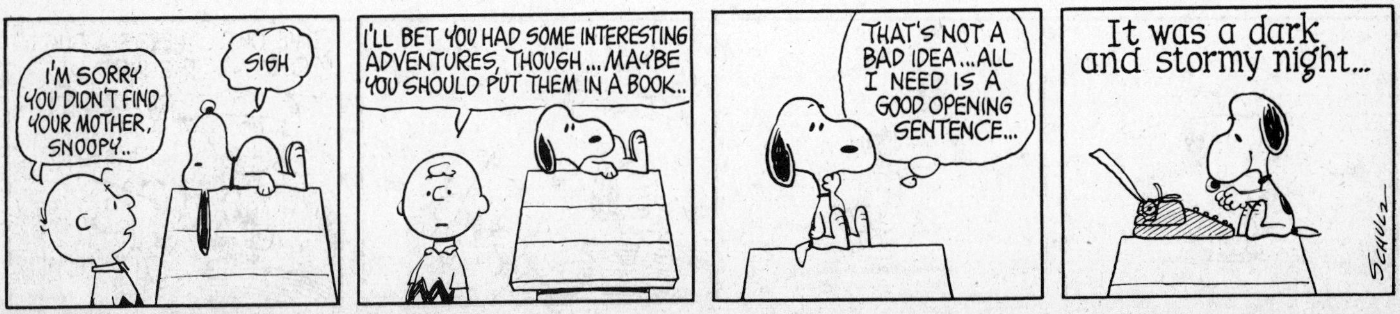
I'M SORRY YOU DIDN'T FIND YOUR MOTHER, SNOOPY..
SIGH
I'LL BET YOU HAD SOME INTERESTING ADVENTURES, THOUGH... MAYBE YOU SHOULD PUT THEM IN A BOOK..
THAT'S NOT A BAD IDEA...ALL I NEED IS A GOOD OPENING SENTENCE...
It was a dark and stormy night...
SCHULZ

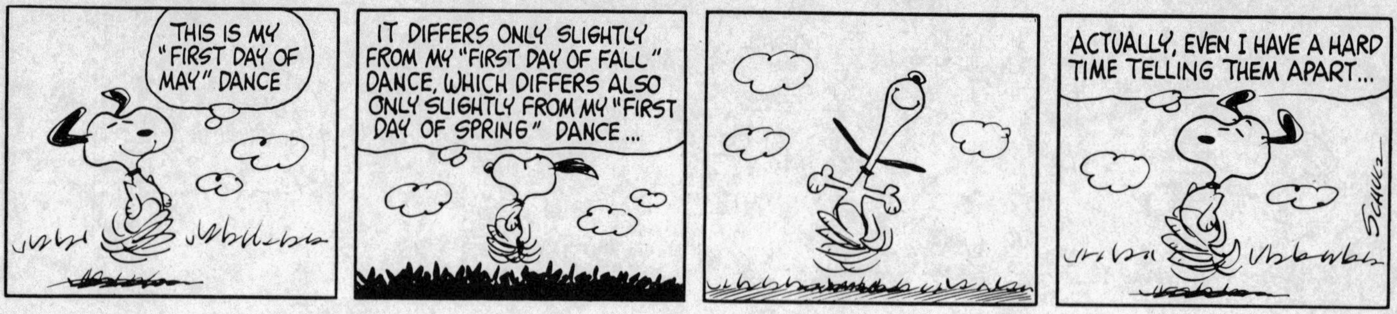
THIS IS MY "FIRST DAY OF MAY" DANCE
IT DIFFERS ONLY SLIGHTLY FROM MY "FIRST DAY OF FALL" DANCE, WHICH DIFFERS ALSO ONLY SLIGHTLY FROM MY "FIRST DAY OF SPRING" DANCE...
ACTUALLY, EVEN I HAVE A HARD TIME TELLING THEM APART...

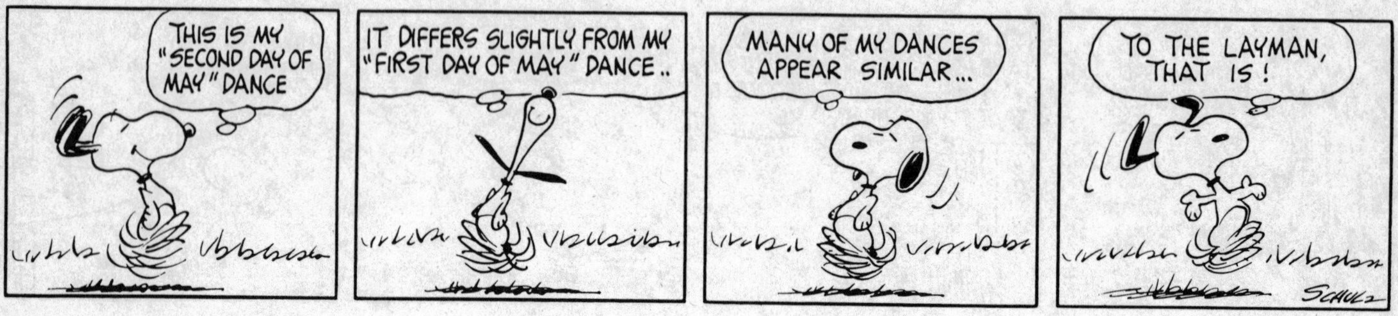
THIS IS MY "SECOND DAY OF MAY" DANCE
IT DIFFERS SLIGHTLY FROM MY "FIRST DAY OF MAY" DANCE..
MANY OF MY DANCES APPEAR SIMILAR...
TO THE LAYMAN, THAT IS!

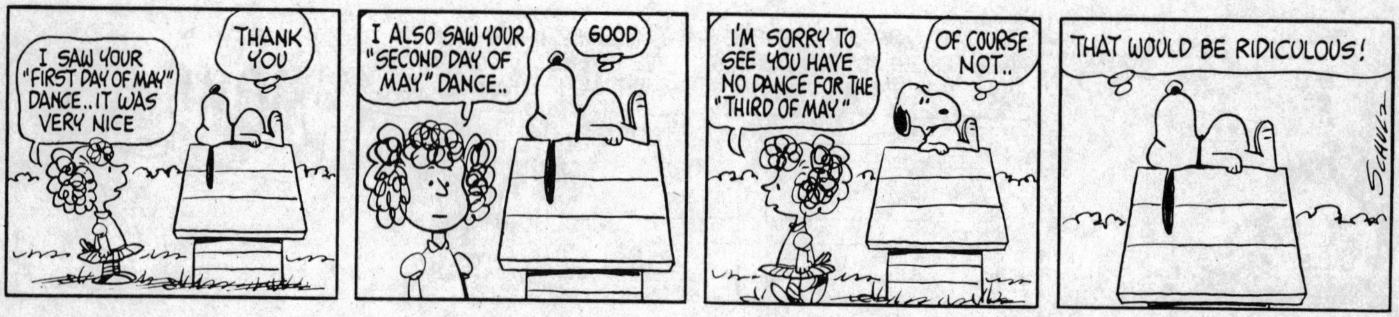
I SAW YOUR "FIRST DAY OF MAY" DANCE..IT WAS VERY NICE
THANK YOU
I ALSO SAW YOUR "SECOND DAY OF MAY" DANCE..
GOOD
I'M SORRY TO SEE YOU HAVE NO DANCE FOR THE "THIRD OF MAY"
OF COURSE NOT..
THAT WOULD BE RIDICULOUS!

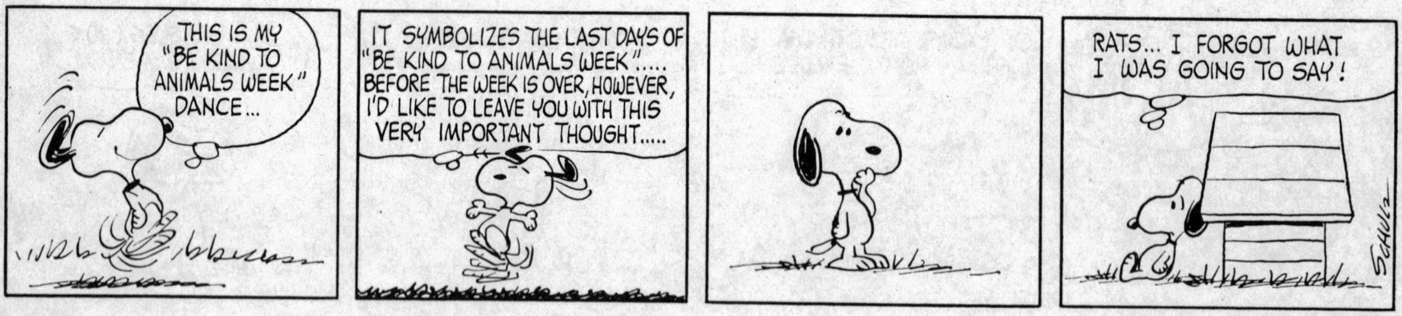
THIS IS MY "BE KIND TO ANIMALS WEEK" DANCE...
IT SYMBOLIZES THE LAST DAYS OF "BE KIND TO ANIMALS WEEK"..... BEFORE THE WEEK IS OVER, HOWEVER, I'D LIKE TO LEAVE YOU WITH THIS VERY IMPORTANT THOUGHT.....
RATS... I FORGOT WHAT I WAS GOING TO SAY!

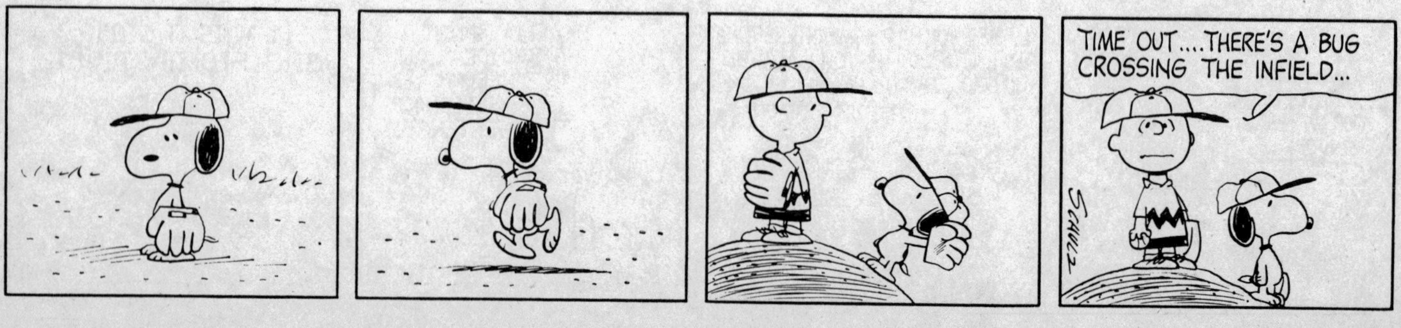
TIME OUT....THERE'S A BUG CROSSING THE INFIELD...

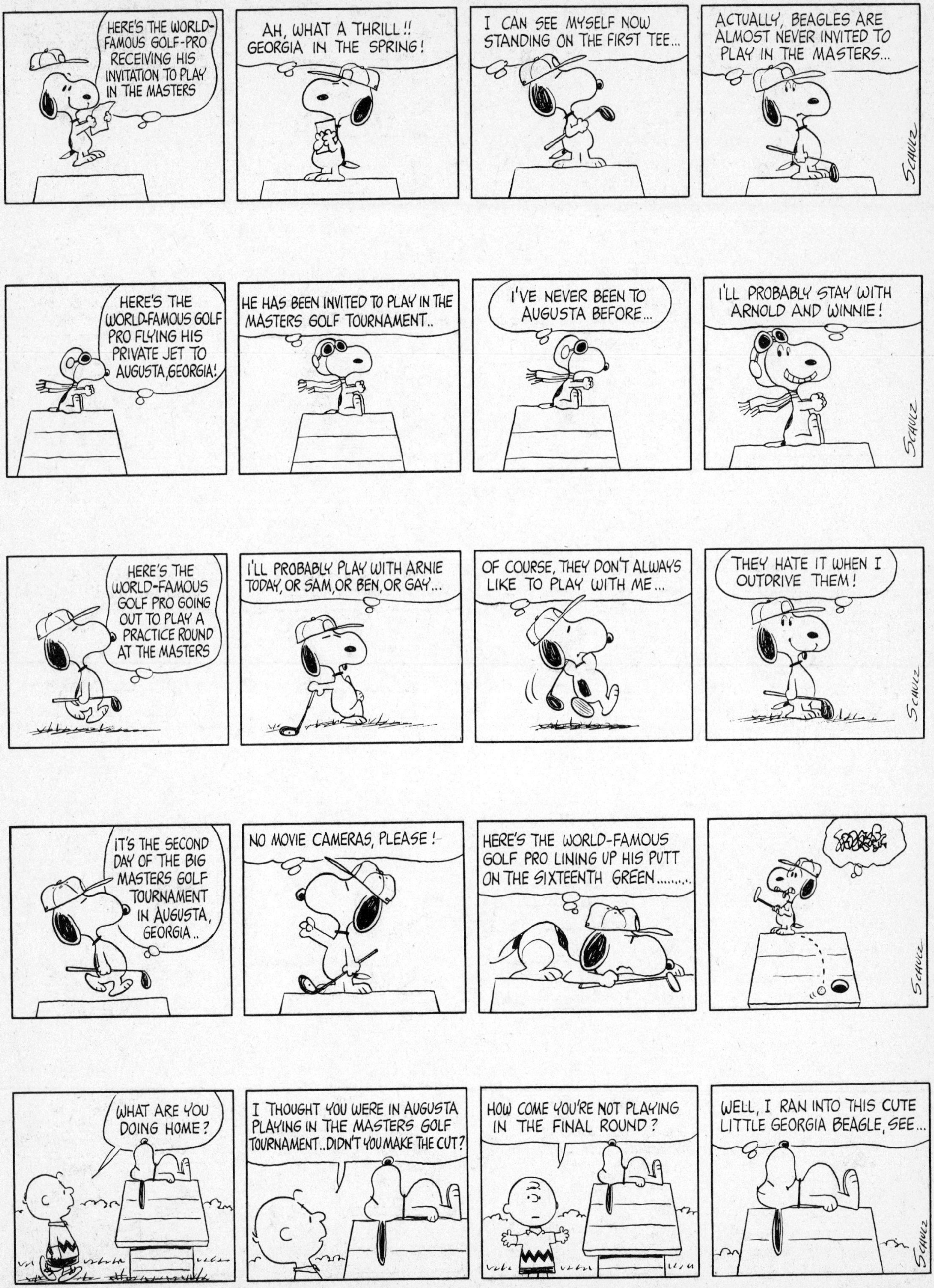
HERE'S THE WORLD-FAMOUS GOLF-PRO RECEIVING HIS INVITATION TO PLAY IN THE MASTERS
AH, WHAT A THRILL !! GEORGIA IN THE SPRING !
I CAN SEE MYSELF NOW STANDING ON THE FIRST TEE...
ACTUALLY, BEAGLES ARE ALMOST NEVER INVITED TO PLAY IN THE MASTERS...
SCHULZ
HERE'S THE WORLD-FAMOUS GOLF PRO FLYING HIS PRIVATE JET TO AUGUSTA, GEORGIA !
HE HAS BEEN INVITED TO PLAY IN THE MASTERS GOLF TOURNAMENT..
I'VE NEVER BEEN TO AUGUSTA BEFORE...
I'LL PROBABLY STAY WITH ARNOLD AND WINNIE !
SCHULZ
HERE'S THE WORLD-FAMOUS GOLF PRO GOING OUT TO PLAY A PRACTICE ROUND AT THE MASTERS
I'LL PROBABLY PLAY WITH ARNIE TODAY, OR SAM, OR BEN, OR GAY...
OF COURSE, THEY DON'T ALWAYS LIKE TO PLAY WITH ME...
THEY HATE IT WHEN I OUTDRIVE THEM !
SCHULZ
IT'S THE SECOND DAY OF THE BIG MASTERS GOLF TOURNAMENT IN AUGUSTA, GEORGIA..
NO MOVIE CAMERAS, PLEASE !
HERE'S THE WORLD-FAMOUS GOLF PRO LINING UP HIS PUTT ON THE SIXTEENTH GREEN.........
SCHULZ
WHAT ARE YOU DOING HOME ?
I THOUGHT YOU WERE IN AUGUSTA PLAYING IN THE MASTERS GOLF TOURNAMENT..DIDN'T YOU MAKE THE CUT ?
HOW COME YOU'RE NOT PLAYING IN THE FINAL ROUND ?
WELL, I RAN INTO THIS CUTE LITTLE GEORGIA BEAGLE, SEE...
SCHULZ

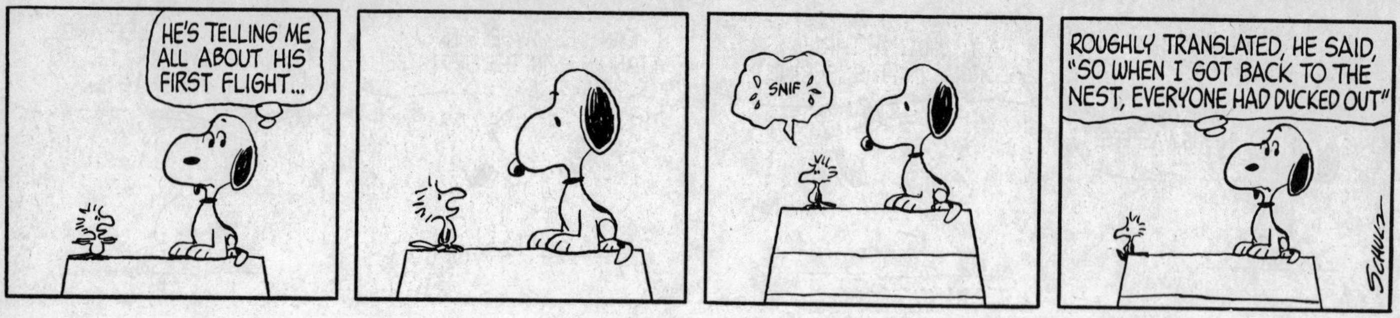
HE'S TELLING ME ALL ABOUT HIS FIRST FLIGHT...
SNIF
ROUGHLY TRANSLATED, HE SAID, "SO WHEN I GOT BACK TO THE NEST, EVERYONE HAD DUCKED OUT"
SCHULZ

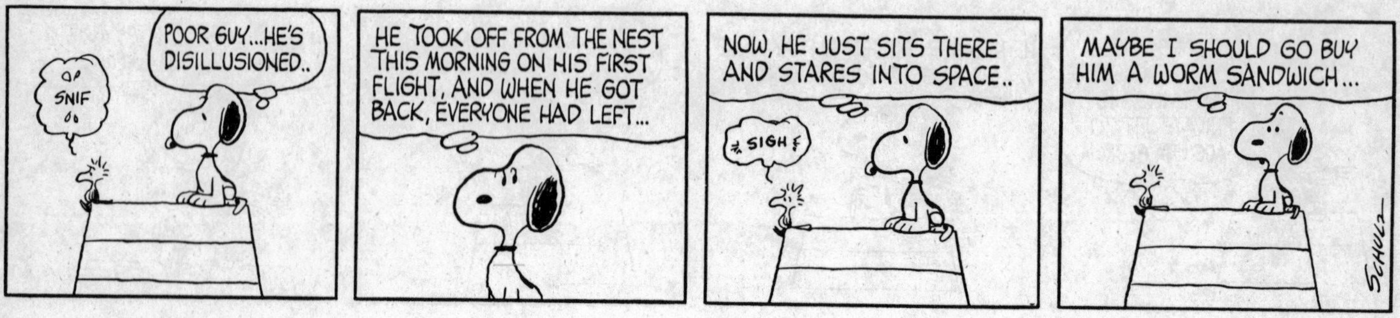
SNIF
POOR GUY...HE'S DISILLUSIONED..
HE TOOK OFF FROM THE NEST THIS MORNING ON HIS FIRST FLIGHT, AND WHEN HE GOT BACK, EVERYONE HAD LEFT...
NOW, HE JUST SITS THERE AND STARES INTO SPACE..
SIGH
MAYBE I SHOULD GO BUY HIM A WORM SANDWICH...
SCHULZ

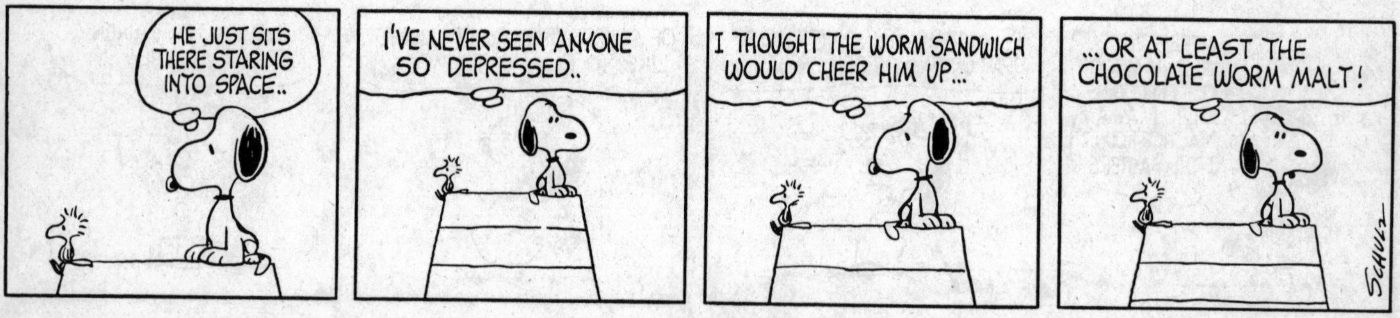
HE JUST SITS THERE STARING INTO SPACE..
I'VE NEVER SEEN ANYONE SO DEPRESSED..
I THOUGHT THE WORM SANDWICH WOULD CHEER HIM UP...
...OR AT LEAST THE CHOCOLATE WORM MALT!
SCHULZ

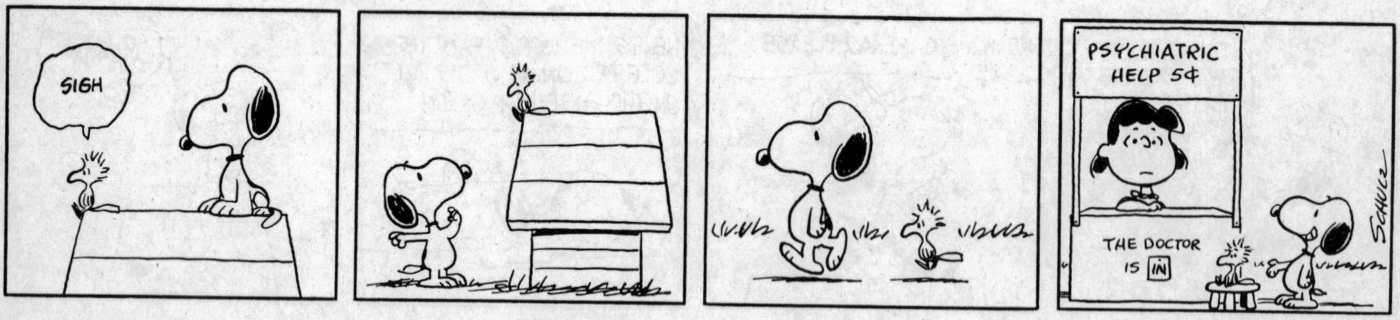
SIGH
PSYCHIATRIC HELP 5¢
THE DOCTOR IS IN
SCHULZ

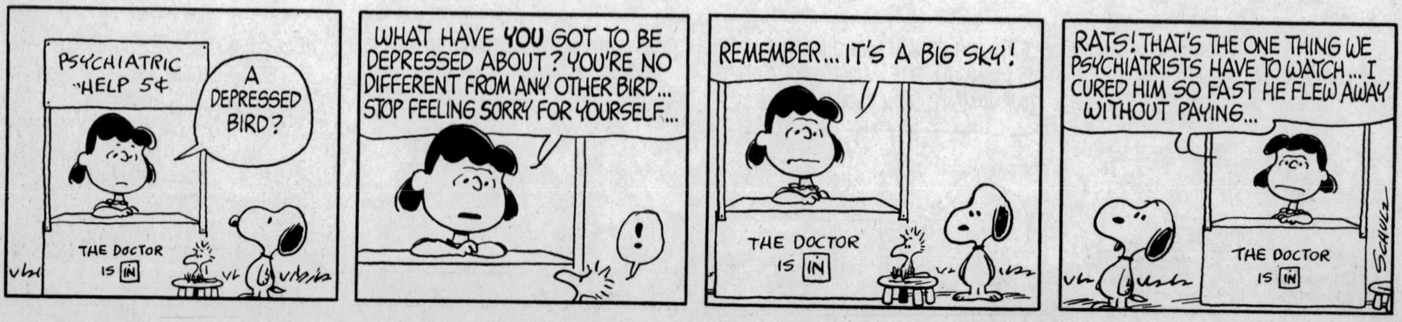
PSYCHIATRIC HELP 5¢
A DEPRESSED BIRD?
THE DOCTOR IS IN
WHAT HAVE YOU GOT TO BE DEPRESSED ABOUT? YOU'RE NO DIFFERENT FROM ANY OTHER BIRD... STOP FEELING SORRY FOR YOURSELF...
!
REMEMBER... IT'S A BIG SKY!
THE DOCTOR IS IN
RATS! THAT'S THE ONE THING WE PSYCHIATRISTS HAVE TO WATCH... I CURED HIM SO FAST HE FLEW AWAY WITHOUT PAYING...
THE DOCTOR IS IN
SCHULZ

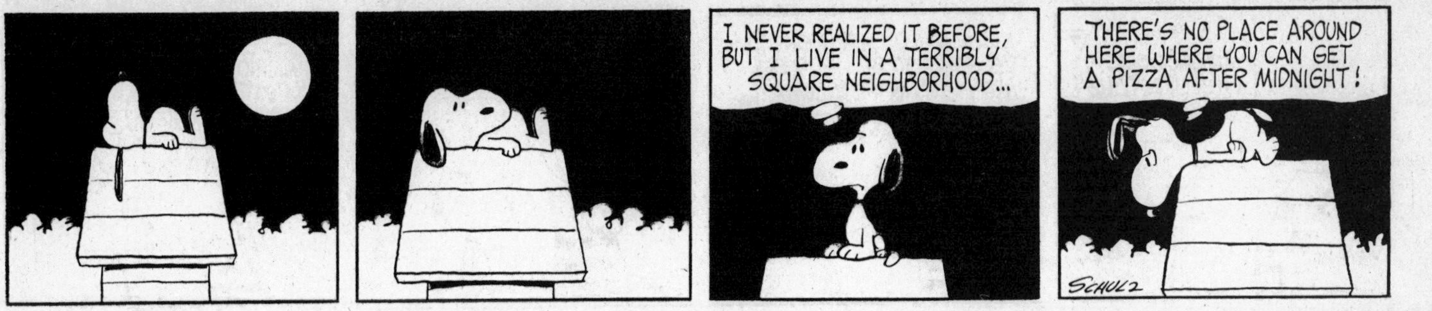
I NEVER REALIZED IT BEFORE, BUT I LIVE IN A TERRIBLY SQUARE NEIGHBORHOOD...
THERE'S NO PLACE AROUND HERE WHERE YOU CAN GET A PIZZA AFTER MIDNIGHT!

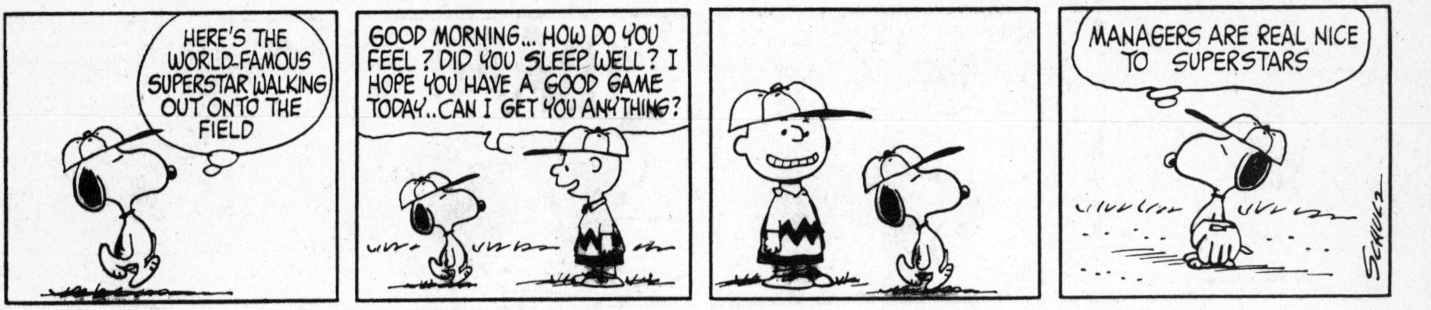
HERE'S THE WORLD-FAMOUS SUPERSTAR WALKING OUT ONTO THE FIELD
GOOD MORNING... HOW DO YOU FEEL? DID YOU SLEEP WELL? I HOPE YOU HAVE A GOOD GAME TODAY..CAN I GET YOU ANYTHING?
MANAGERS ARE REAL NICE TO SUPERSTARS

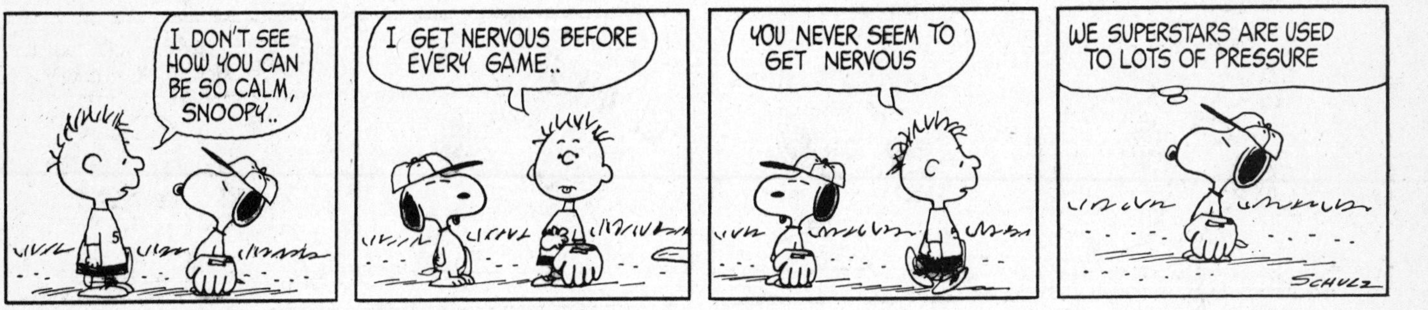
I DON'T SEE HOW YOU CAN BE SO CALM, SNOOPY..
I GET NERVOUS BEFORE EVERY GAME..
YOU NEVER SEEM TO GET NERVOUS
WE SUPERSTARS ARE USED TO LOTS OF PRESSURE

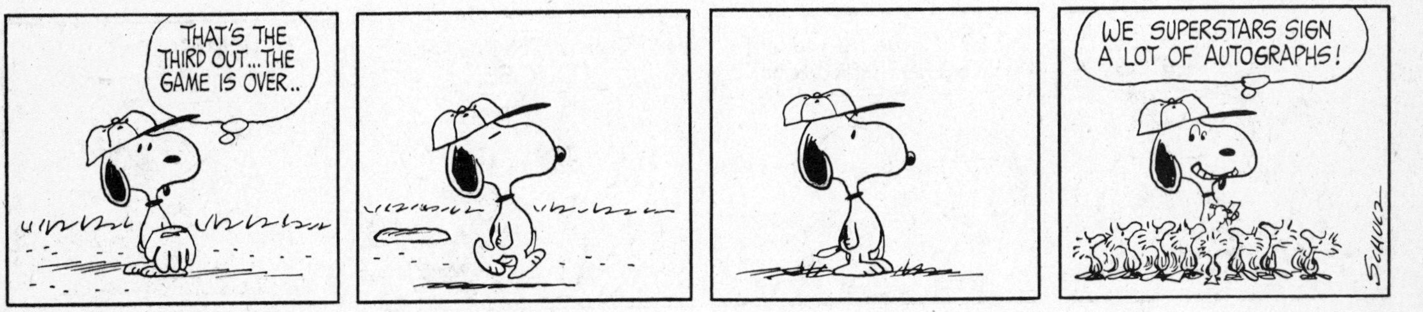
THAT'S THE THIRD OUT...THE GAME IS OVER..
WE SUPERSTARS SIGN A LOT OF AUTOGRAPHS!

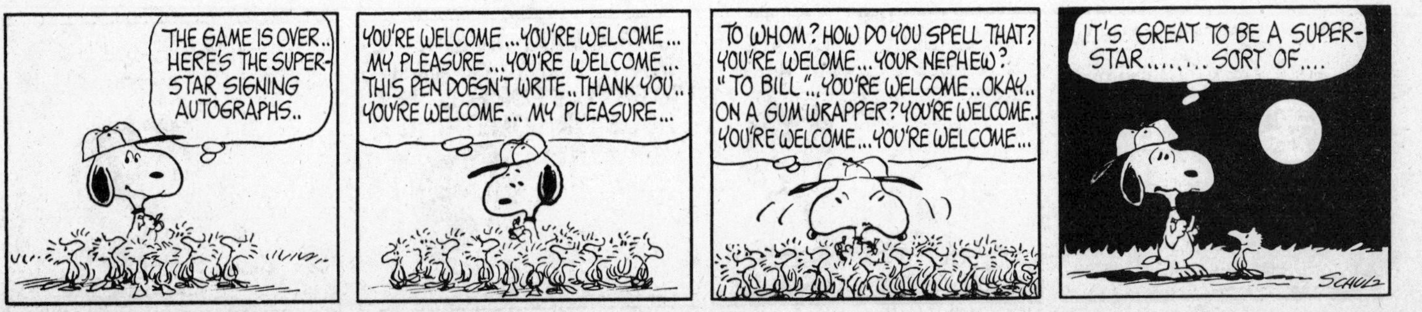
THE GAME IS OVER.. HERE'S THE SUPER-STAR SIGNING AUTOGRAPHS..
YOU'RE WELCOME...YOU'RE WELCOME... MY PLEASURE...YOU'RE WELCOME... THIS PEN DOESN'T WRITE..THANK YOU.. YOU'RE WELCOME... MY PLEASURE...
TO WHOM? HOW DO YOU SPELL THAT? YOU'RE WELOME...YOUR NEPHEW? "TO BILL"..YOU'RE WELCOME..OKAY.. ON A GUM WRAPPER? YOU'RE WELCOME.. YOU'RE WELCOME...YOU'RE WELCOME...
IT'S GREAT TO BE A SUPER-STAR...... SORT OF....

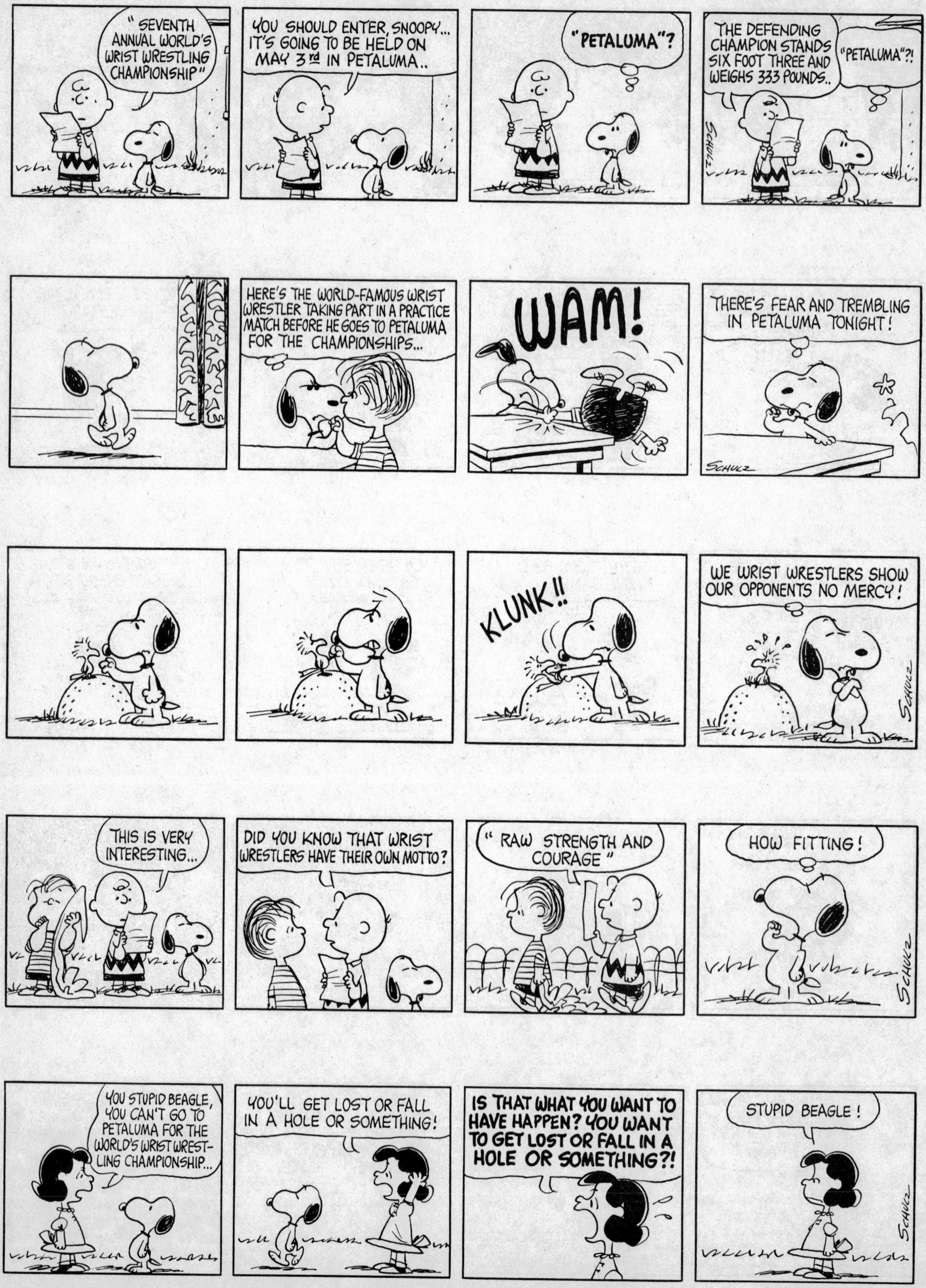
" SEVENTH ANNUAL WORLD'S WRIST WRESTLING CHAMPIONSHIP"
YOU SHOULD ENTER, SNOOPY... IT'S GOING TO BE HELD ON MAY 3rd IN PETALUMA..
"PETALUMA"?
THE DEFENDING CHAMPION STANDS SIX FOOT THREE AND WEIGHS 333 POUNDS..
"PETALUMA"?!
SCHULZ
HERE'S THE WORLD-FAMOUS WRIST WRESTLER TAKING PART IN A PRACTICE MATCH BEFORE HE GOES TO PETALUMA FOR THE CHAMPIONSHIPS...
WAM!
THERE'S FEAR AND TREMBLING IN PETALUMA TONIGHT!
SCHULZ
KLUNK!!
WE WRIST WRESTLERS SHOW OUR OPPONENTS NO MERCY!
SCHULZ
THIS IS VERY INTERESTING...
DID YOU KNOW THAT WRIST WRESTLERS HAVE THEIR OWN MOTTO?
" RAW STRENGTH AND COURAGE "
HOW FITTING!
SCHULZ
YOU STUPID BEAGLE, YOU CAN'T GO TO PETALUMA FOR THE WORLD'S WRIST WRESTLING CHAMPIONSHIP...
YOU'LL GET LOST OR FALL IN A HOLE OR SOMETHING!
IS THAT WHAT YOU WANT TO HAVE HAPPEN? YOU WANT TO GET LOST OR FALL IN A HOLE OR SOMETHING?!
STUPID BEAGLE!
SCHULZ

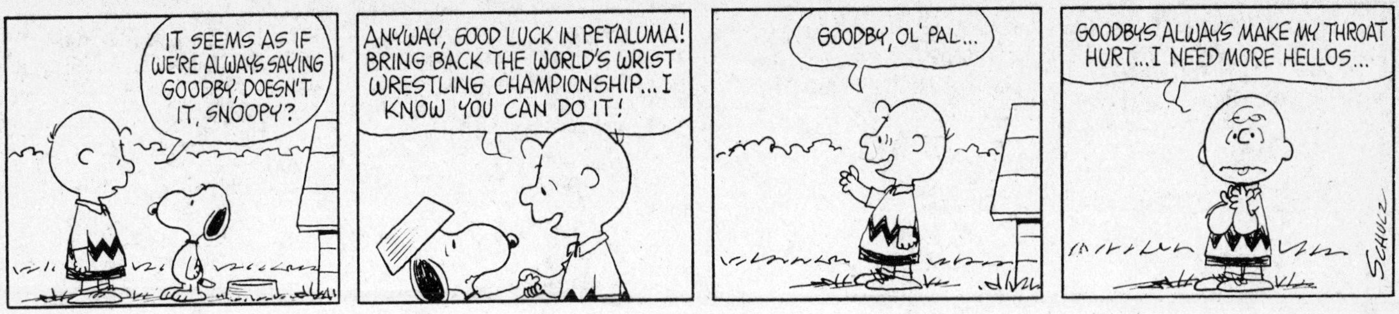
IT SEEMS AS IF WE'RE ALWAYS SAYING GOODBY, DOESN'T IT, SNOOPY?
ANYWAY, GOOD LUCK IN PETALUMA! BRING BACK THE WORLD'S WRIST WRESTLING CHAMPIONSHIP... I KNOW YOU CAN DO IT!
GOODBY, OL' PAL...
GOODBYS ALWAYS MAKE MY THROAT HURT... I NEED MORE HELLOS...
SCHULZ

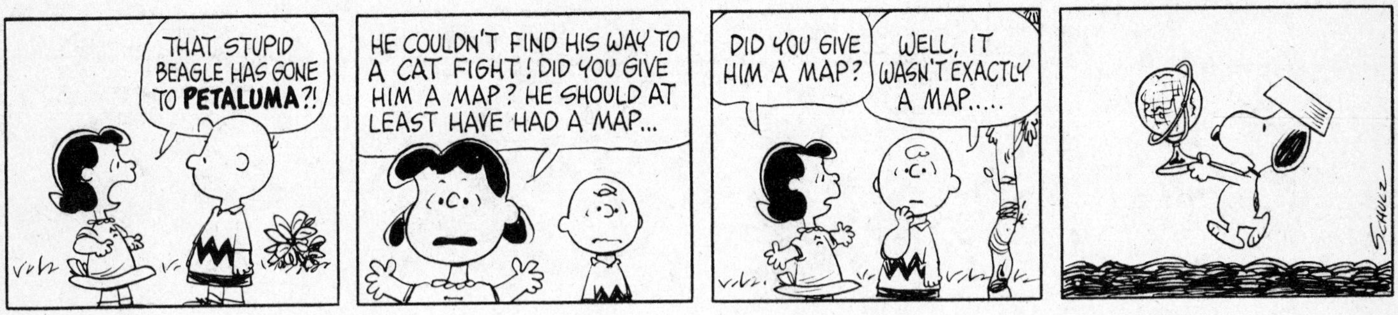
THAT STUPID BEAGLE HAS GONE TO **PETALUMA**?!
HE COULDN'T FIND HIS WAY TO A CAT FIGHT! DID YOU GIVE HIM A MAP? HE SHOULD AT LEAST HAVE HAD A MAP...
DID YOU GIVE HIM A MAP?
WELL, IT WASN'T EXACTLY A MAP.....
SCHULZ

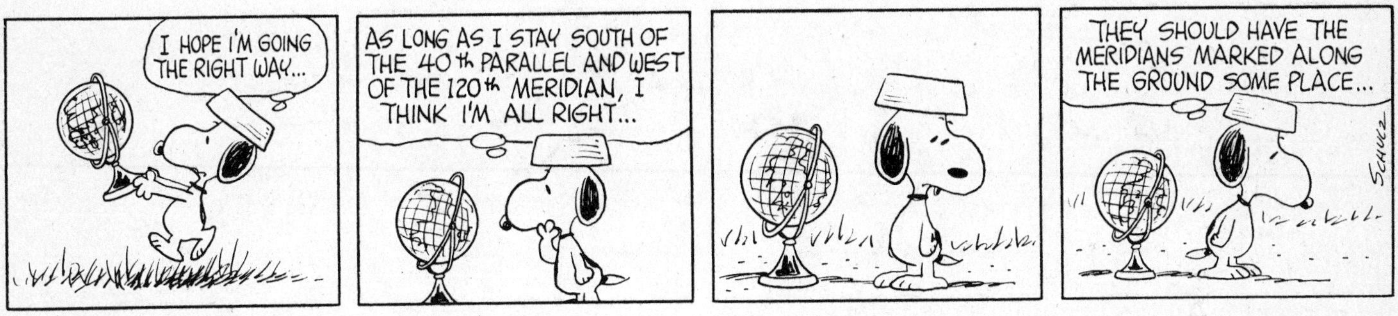
I HOPE I'M GOING THE RIGHT WAY...
AS LONG AS I STAY SOUTH OF THE 40th PARALLEL AND WEST OF THE 120th MERIDIAN, I THINK I'M ALL RIGHT...
THEY SHOULD HAVE THE MERIDIANS MARKED ALONG THE GROUND SOME PLACE...
SCHULZ

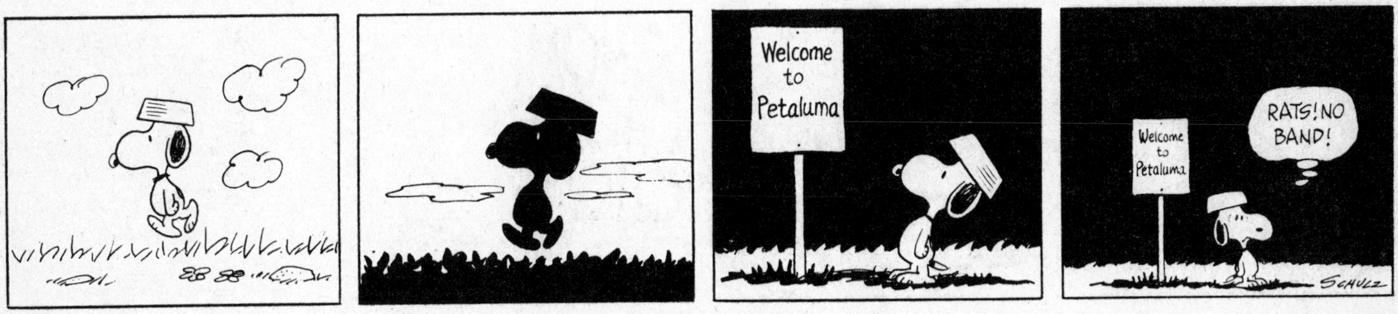
Welcome to Petaluma
Welcome to Petaluma
RATS! NO BAND!
SCHULZ

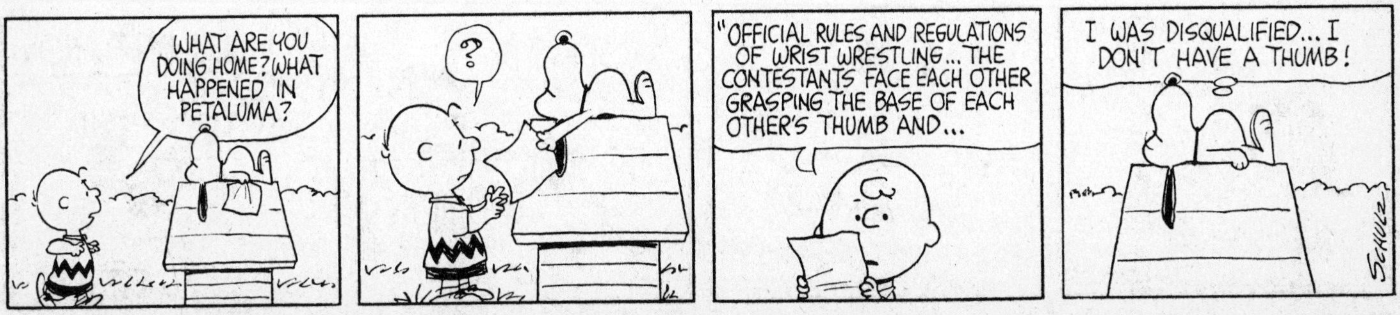
WHAT ARE YOU DOING HOME? WHAT HAPPENED IN PETALUMA?
?
"OFFICIAL RULES AND REGULATIONS OF WRIST WRESTLING... THE CONTESTANTS FACE EACH OTHER GRASPING THE BASE OF EACH OTHER'S THUMB AND...
I WAS DISQUALIFIED... I DON'T HAVE A THUMB!
SCHULZ

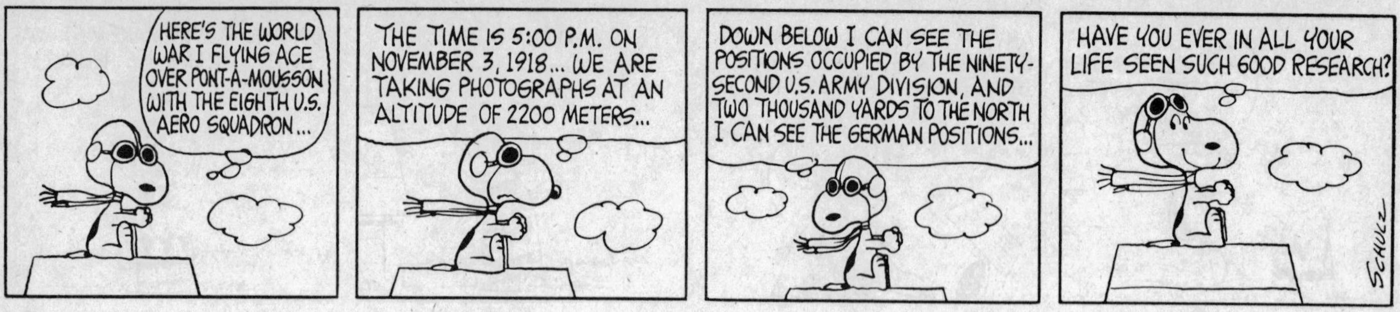
HERE'S THE WORLD WAR I FLYING ACE OVER PONT-À-MOUSSON WITH THE EIGHTH U.S. AERO SQUADRON...
THE TIME IS 5:00 P.M. ON NOVEMBER 3, 1918... WE ARE TAKING PHOTOGRAPHS AT AN ALTITUDE OF 2200 METERS...
DOWN BELOW I CAN SEE THE POSITIONS OCCUPIED BY THE NINETY-SECOND U.S. ARMY DIVISION, AND TWO THOUSAND YARDS TO THE NORTH I CAN SEE THE GERMAN POSITIONS...
HAVE YOU EVER IN ALL YOUR LIFE SEEN SUCH GOOD RESEARCH?
SCHULZ

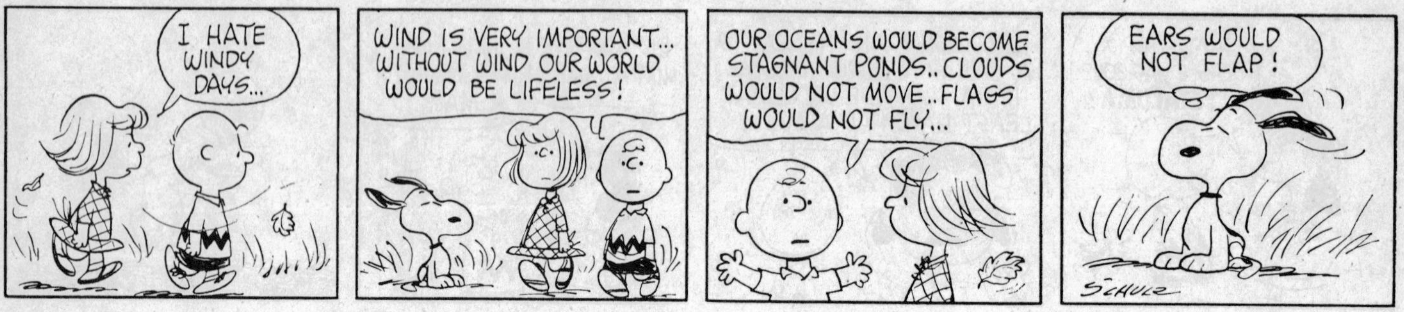
I HATE WINDY DAYS...
WIND IS VERY IMPORTANT... WITHOUT WIND OUR WORLD WOULD BE LIFELESS!
OUR OCEANS WOULD BECOME STAGNANT PONDS.. CLOUDS WOULD NOT MOVE.. FLAGS WOULD NOT FLY...
EARS WOULD NOT FLAP!
SCHULZ

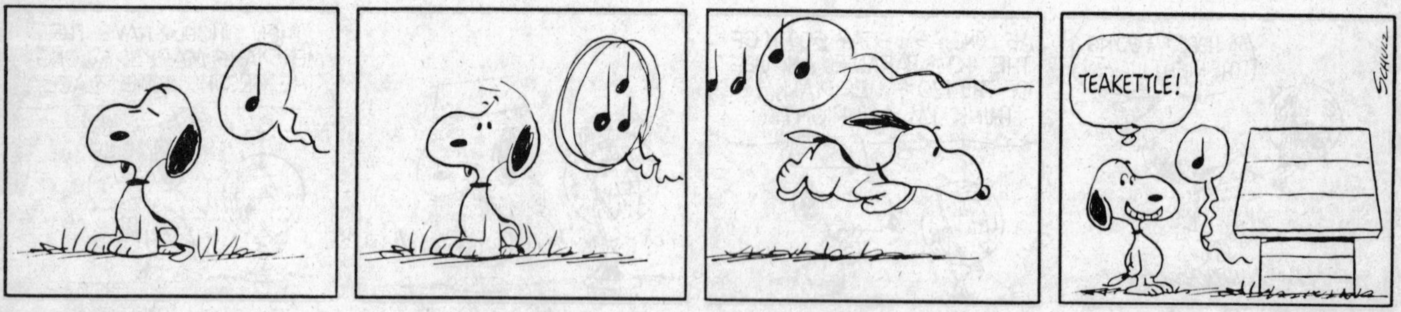
TEAKETTLE!
SCHULZ

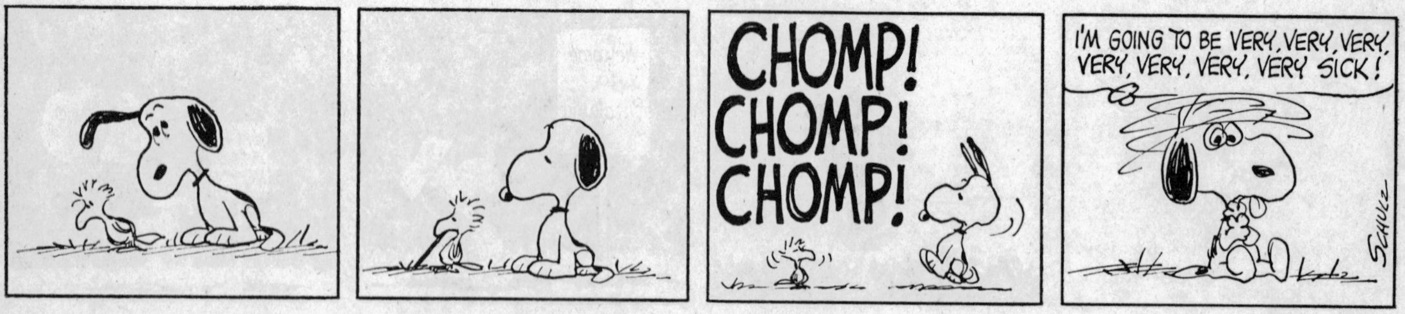
CHOMP! CHOMP! CHOMP!
I'M GOING TO BE VERY, VERY, VERY, VERY, VERY, VERY, VERY SICK!
SCHULZ

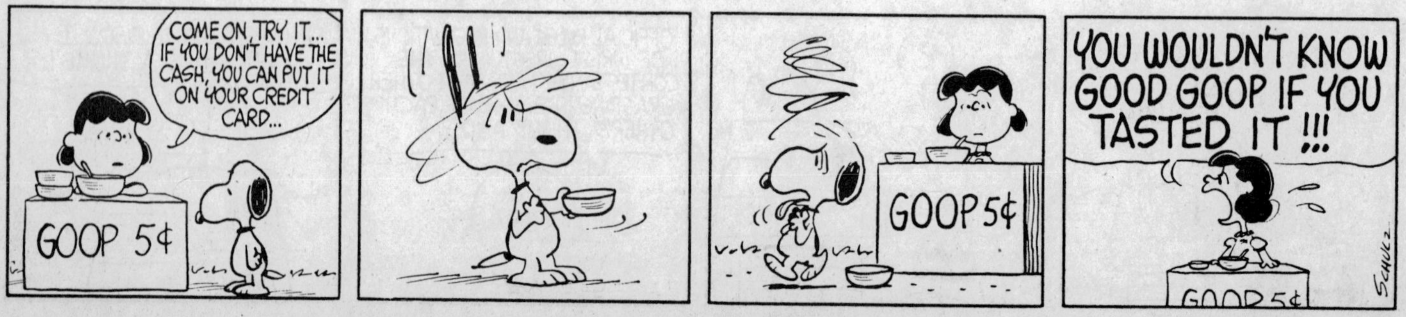
COME ON, TRY IT... IF YOU DON'T HAVE THE CASH, YOU CAN PUT IT ON YOUR CREDIT CARD...
GOOP 5¢
GOOP 5¢
YOU WOULDN'T KNOW GOOD GOOP IF YOU TASTED IT !!!
SCHULZ

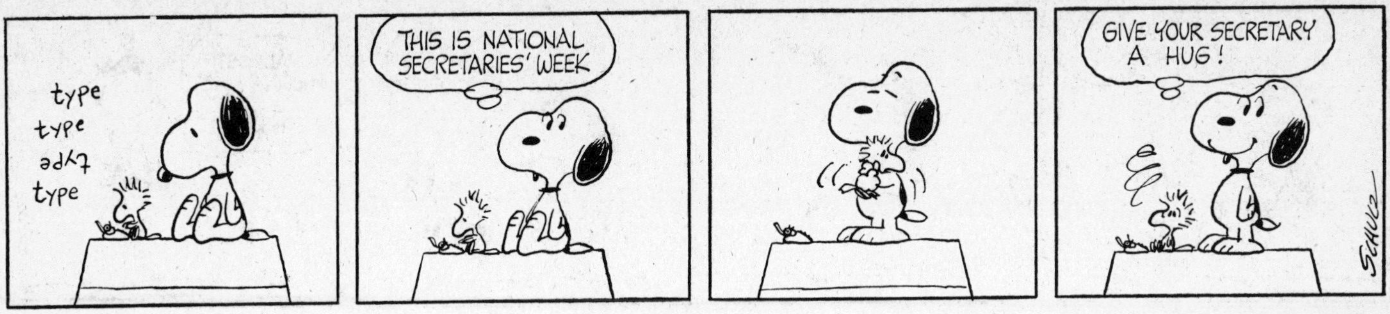
type type type type
THIS IS NATIONAL SECRETARIES' WEEK
GIVE YOUR SECRETARY A HUG!
SCHULZ

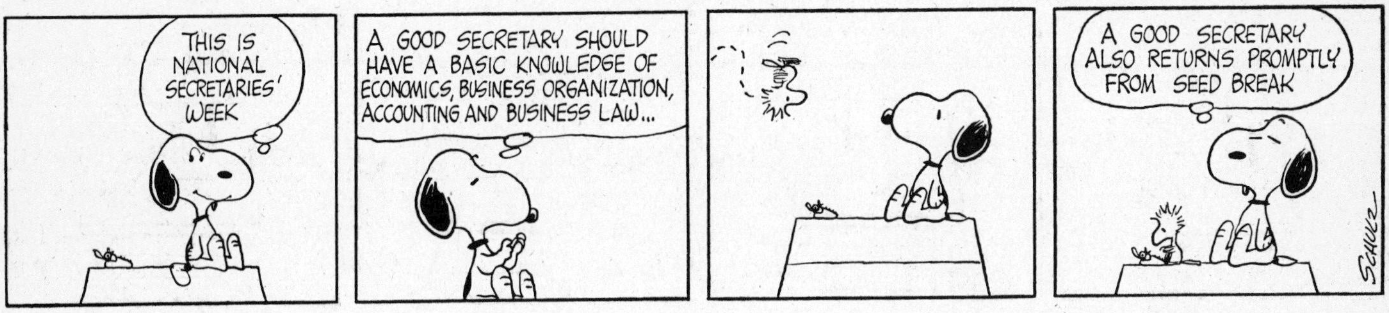
THIS IS NATIONAL SECRETARIES' WEEK
A GOOD SECRETARY SHOULD HAVE A BASIC KNOWLEDGE OF ECONOMICS, BUSINESS ORGANIZATION, ACCOUNTING AND BUSINESS LAW...
A GOOD SECRETARY ALSO RETURNS PROMPTLY FROM SEED BREAK
SCHULZ

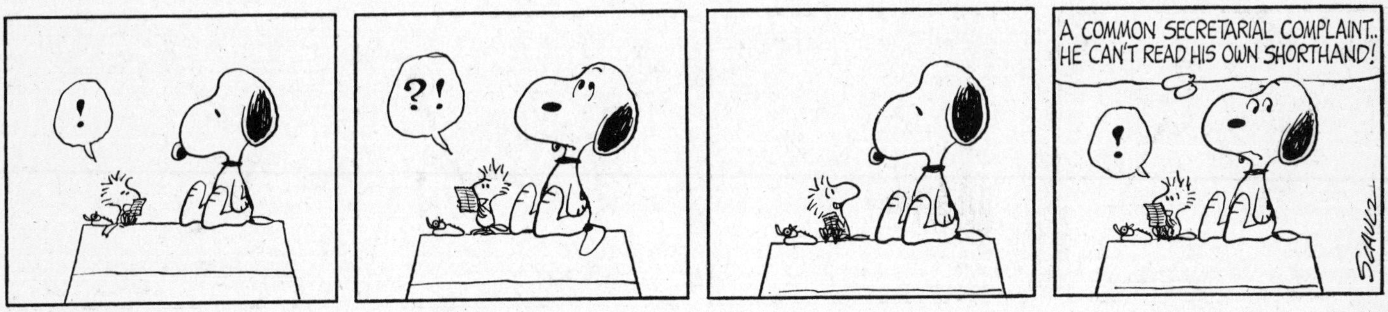
!
?!
A COMMON SECRETARIAL COMPLAINT.. HE CAN'T READ HIS OWN SHORTHAND!
!
SCHULZ

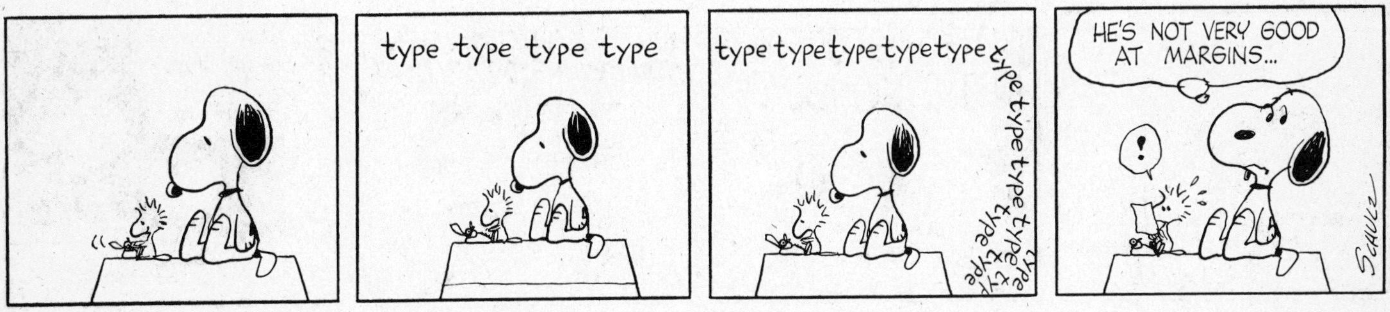
type type type type
type type type type type
HE'S NOT VERY GOOD AT MARGINS...
!
SCHULZ

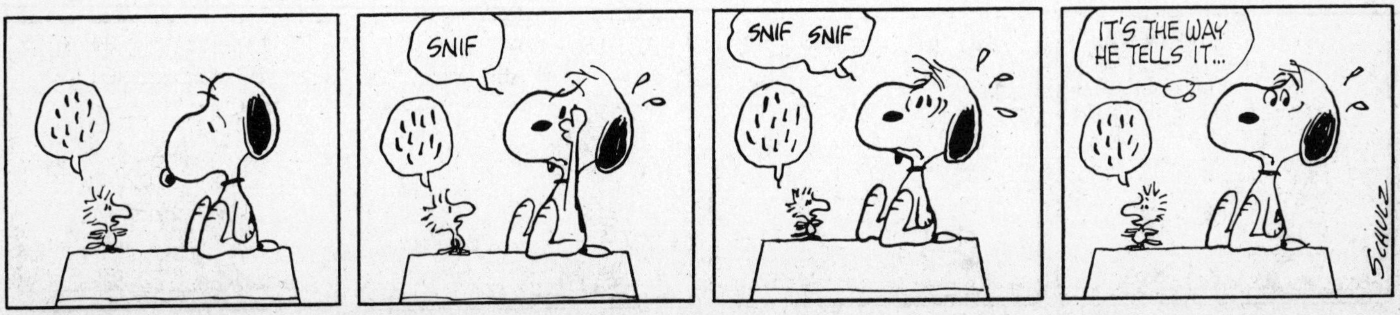
SNIF
SNIF SNIF
IT'S THE WAY HE TELLS IT...
SCHULZ

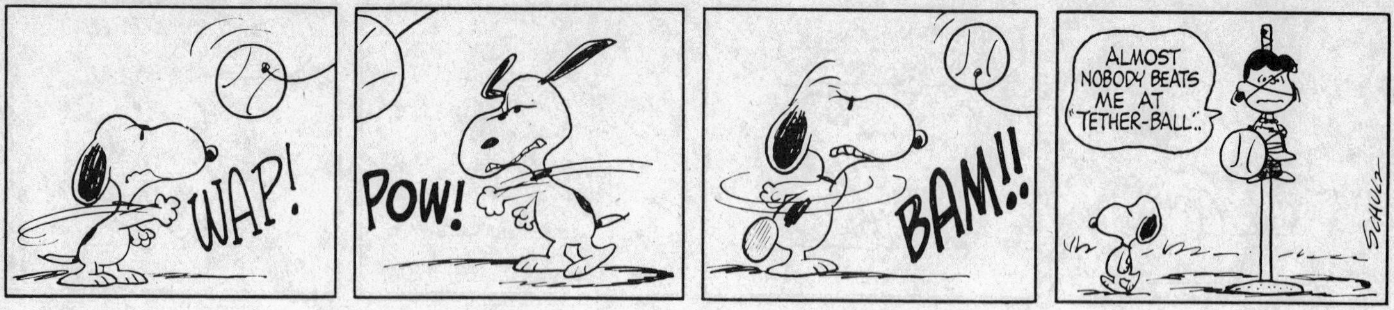
WAP!
POW!
BAM!!
ALMOST NOBODY BEATS ME AT "TETHER-BALL"..

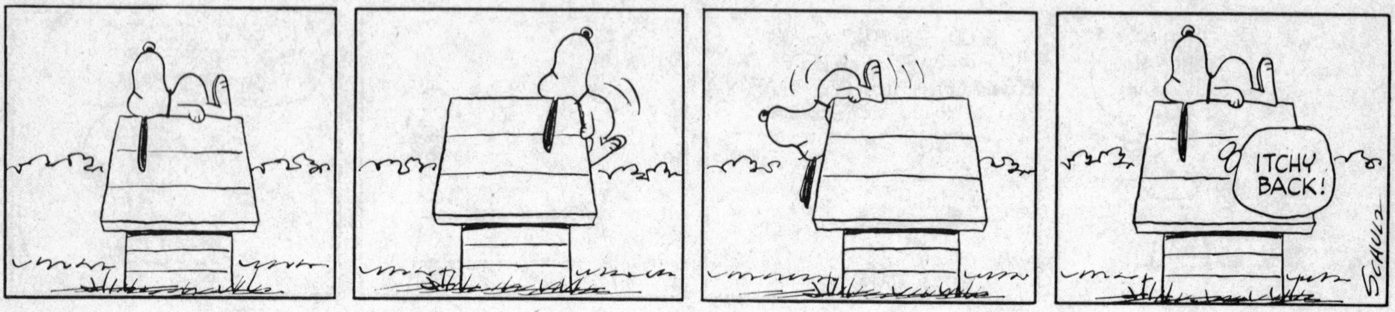
ITCHY BACK!

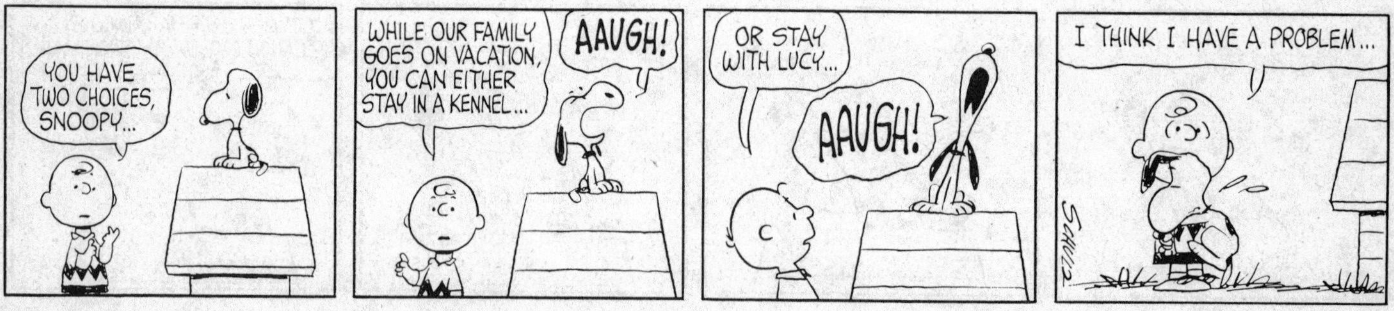
YOU HAVE TWO CHOICES, SNOOPY...
WHILE OUR FAMILY GOES ON VACATION, YOU CAN EITHER STAY IN A KENNEL...
AAUGH!
OR STAY WITH LUCY...
AAUGH!
I THINK I HAVE A PROBLEM...

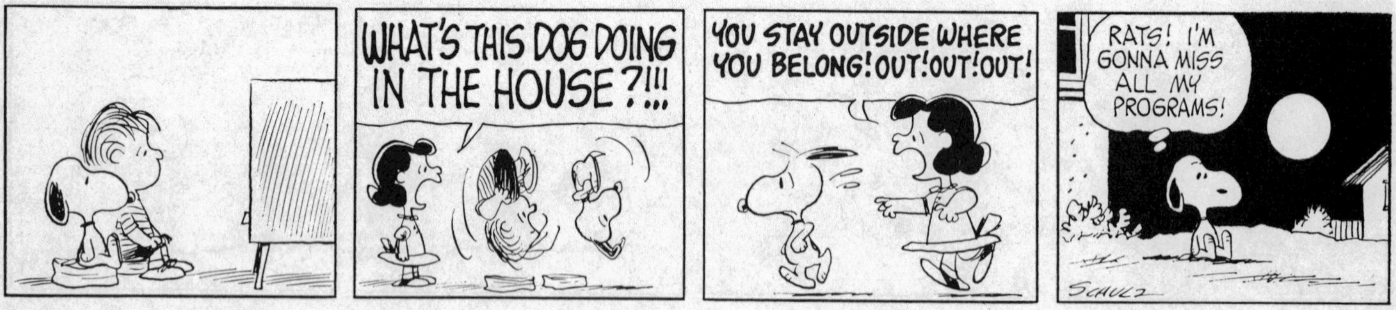
WHAT'S THIS DOG DOING IN THE HOUSE?!!!
YOU STAY OUTSIDE WHERE YOU BELONG! OUT! OUT! OUT!
RATS! I'M GONNA MISS ALL MY PROGRAMS!

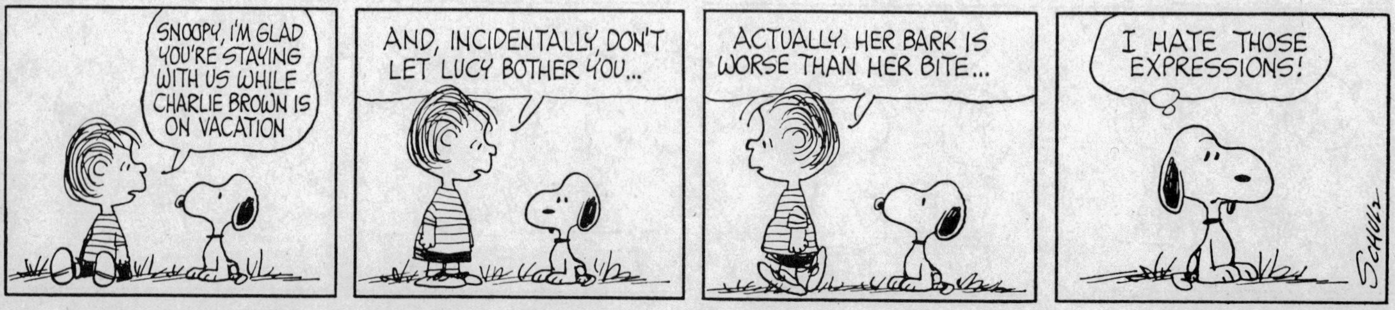
SNOOPY, I'M GLAD YOU'RE STAYING WITH US WHILE CHARLIE BROWN IS ON VACATION
AND, INCIDENTALLY, DON'T LET LUCY BOTHER YOU...
ACTUALLY, HER BARK IS WORSE THAN HER BITE...
I HATE THOSE EXPRESSIONS!

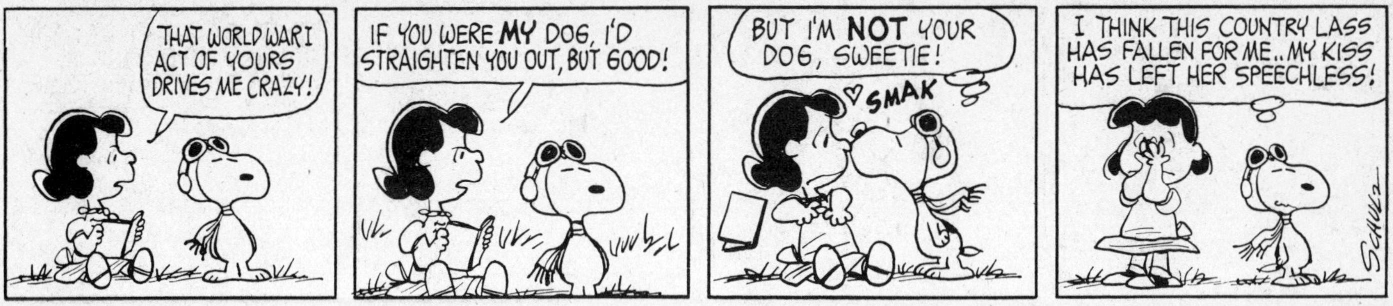
THAT WORLD WAR I ACT OF YOURS DRIVES ME CRAZY!
IF YOU WERE MY DOG, I'D STRAIGHTEN YOU OUT, BUT GOOD!
BUT I'M NOT YOUR DOG, SWEETIE!
SMAK
I THINK THIS COUNTRY LASS HAS FALLEN FOR ME.. MY KISS HAS LEFT HER SPEECHLESS!
SCHULZ

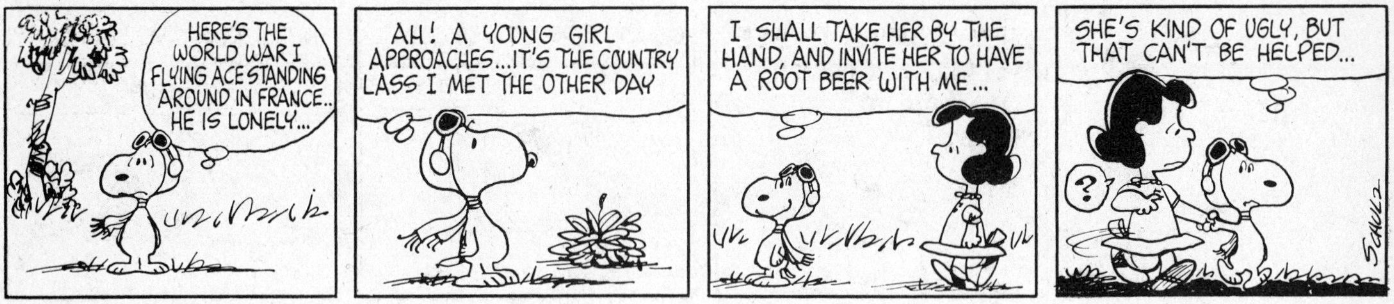
HERE'S THE WORLD WAR I FLYING ACE STANDING AROUND IN FRANCE.. HE IS LONELY...
AH! A YOUNG GIRL APPROACHES...IT'S THE COUNTRY LASS I MET THE OTHER DAY
I SHALL TAKE HER BY THE HAND, AND INVITE HER TO HAVE A ROOT BEER WITH ME...
SHE'S KIND OF UGLY, BUT THAT CAN'T BE HELPED...
?
SCHULZ

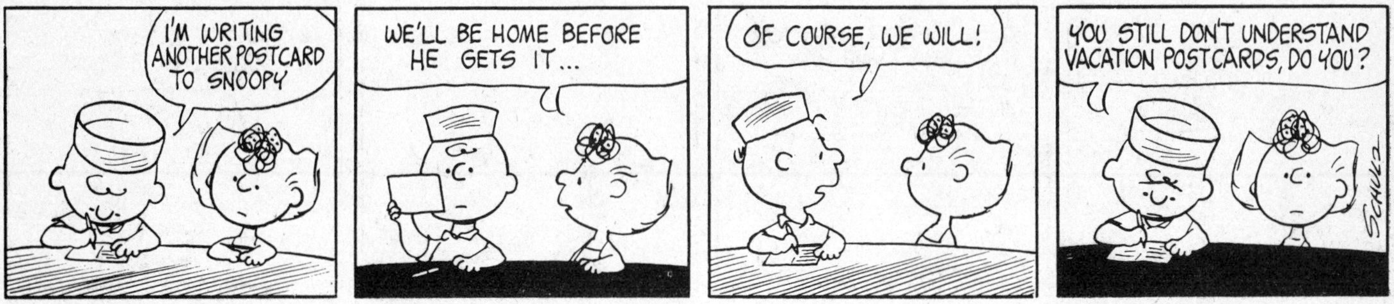
I'M WRITING ANOTHER POSTCARD TO SNOOPY
WE'LL BE HOME BEFORE HE GETS IT...
OF COURSE, WE WILL!
YOU STILL DON'T UNDERSTAND VACATION POSTCARDS, DO YOU?
SCHULZ

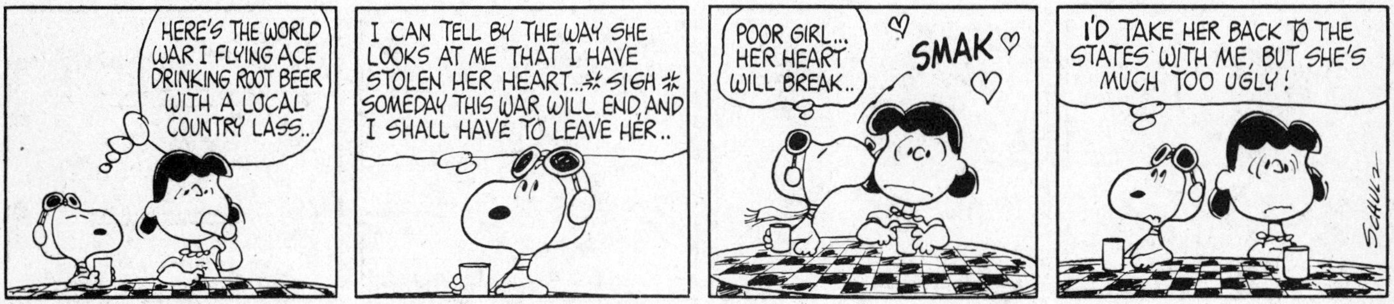
HERE'S THE WORLD WAR I FLYING ACE DRINKING ROOT BEER WITH A LOCAL COUNTRY LASS..
I CAN TELL BY THE WAY SHE LOOKS AT ME THAT I HAVE STOLEN HER HEART...* SIGH * SOMEDAY THIS WAR WILL END, AND I SHALL HAVE TO LEAVE HER..
POOR GIRL... HER HEART WILL BREAK..
SMAK
I'D TAKE HER BACK TO THE STATES WITH ME, BUT SHE'S MUCH TOO UGLY!
SCHULZ

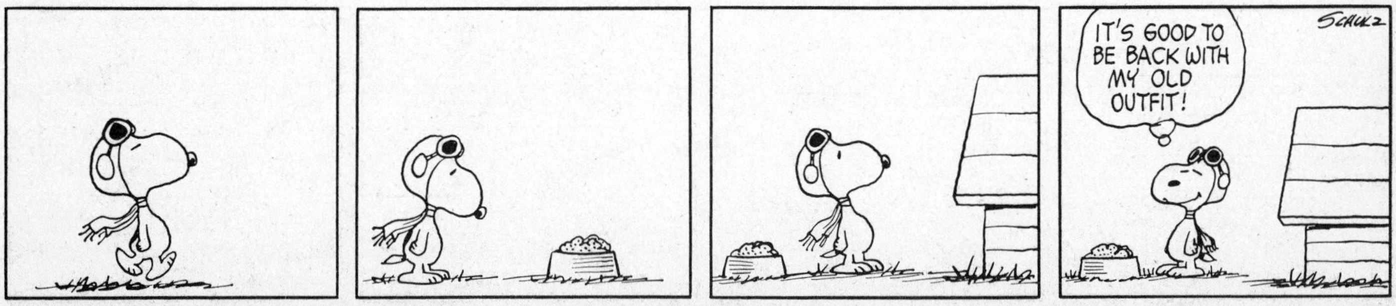
SCHULZ
IT'S GOOD TO BE BACK WITH MY OLD OUTFIT!

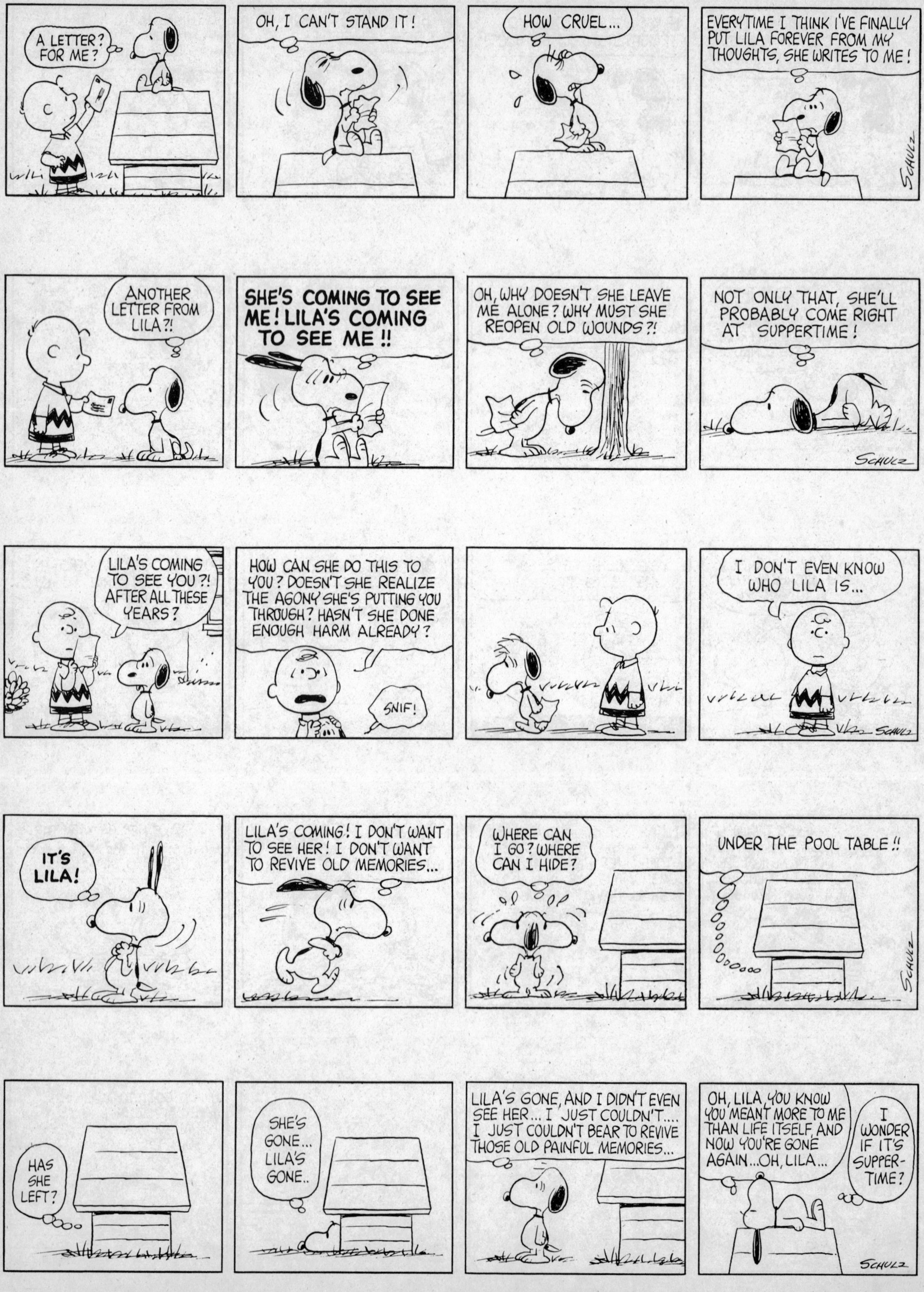
A LETTER? FOR ME?
OH, I CAN'T STAND IT!
HOW CRUEL...
EVERYTIME I THINK I'VE FINALLY PUT LILA FOREVER FROM MY THOUGHTS, SHE WRITES TO ME!
SCHULZ
ANOTHER LETTER FROM LILA?!
SHE'S COMING TO SEE ME! LILA'S COMING TO SEE ME!!
OH, WHY DOESN'T SHE LEAVE ME ALONE? WHY MUST SHE REOPEN OLD WOUNDS?!
NOT ONLY THAT, SHE'LL PROBABLY COME RIGHT AT SUPPERTIME!
SCHULZ
LILA'S COMING TO SEE YOU?! AFTER ALL THESE YEARS?
HOW CAN SHE DO THIS TO YOU? DOESN'T SHE REALIZE THE AGONY SHE'S PUTTING YOU THROUGH? HASN'T SHE DONE ENOUGH HARM ALREADY?
SNIF!
I DON'T EVEN KNOW WHO LILA IS...
SCHULZ
IT'S LILA!
LILA'S COMING! I DON'T WANT TO SEE HER! I DON'T WANT TO REVIVE OLD MEMORIES...
WHERE CAN I GO? WHERE CAN I HIDE?
UNDER THE POOL TABLE!!
SCHULZ
HAS SHE LEFT?
SHE'S GONE... LILA'S GONE..
LILA'S GONE, AND I DIDN'T EVEN SEE HER... I JUST COULDN'T.... I JUST COULDN'T BEAR TO REVIVE THOSE OLD PAINFUL MEMORIES...
OH, LILA, YOU KNOW YOU MEANT MORE TO ME THAN LIFE ITSELF, AND NOW YOU'RE GONE AGAIN...OH, LILA...
I WONDER IF IT'S SUPPER-TIME?
SCHULZ

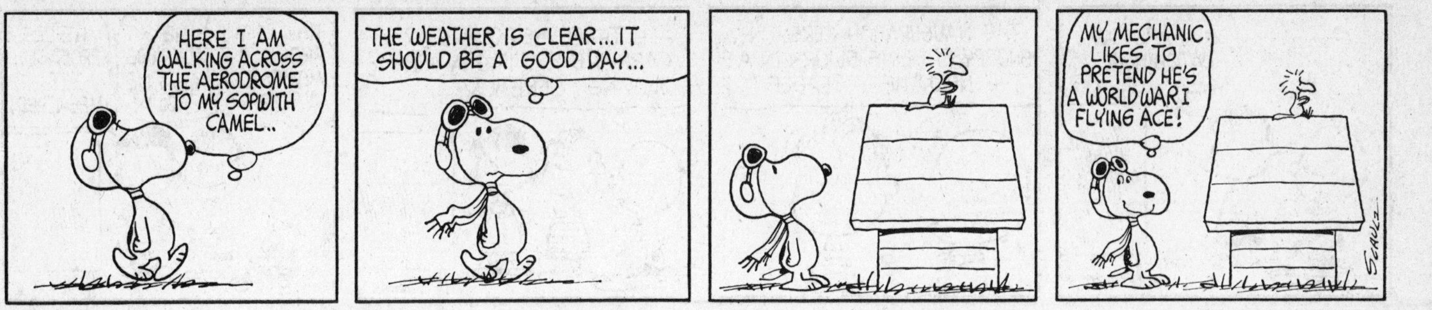
HERE I AM WALKING ACROSS THE AERODROME TO MY SOPWITH CAMEL..
THE WEATHER IS CLEAR... IT SHOULD BE A GOOD DAY...
MY MECHANIC LIKES TO PRETEND HE'S A WORLD WAR I FLYING ACE!
SCHULZ

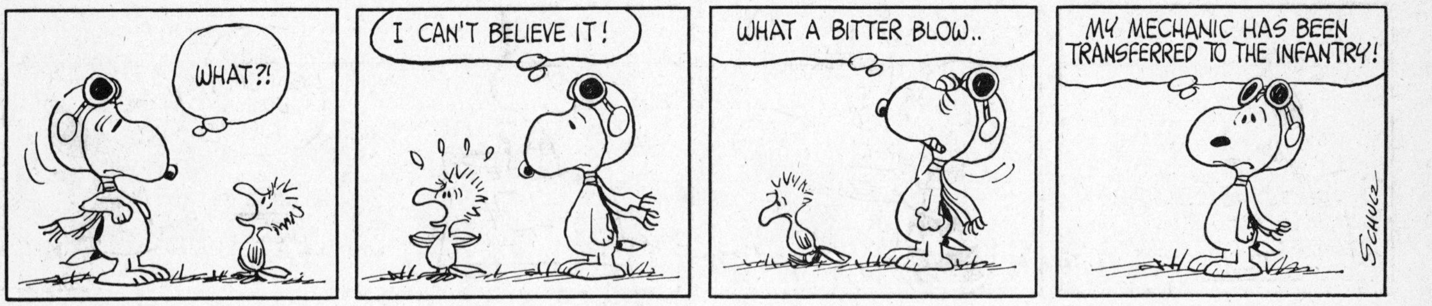
WHAT?!
I CAN'T BELIEVE IT!
WHAT A BITTER BLOW..
MY MECHANIC HAS BEEN TRANSFERRED TO THE INFANTRY!
SCHULZ

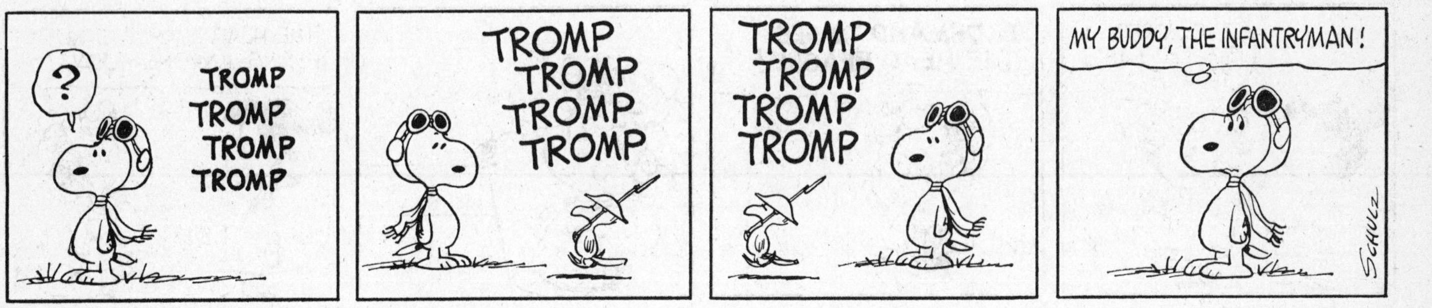
?
TROMP TROMP TROMP TROMP
TROMP TROMP TROMP TROMP
TROMP TROMP TROMP TROMP
MY BUDDY, THE INFANTRYMAN!
SCHULZ

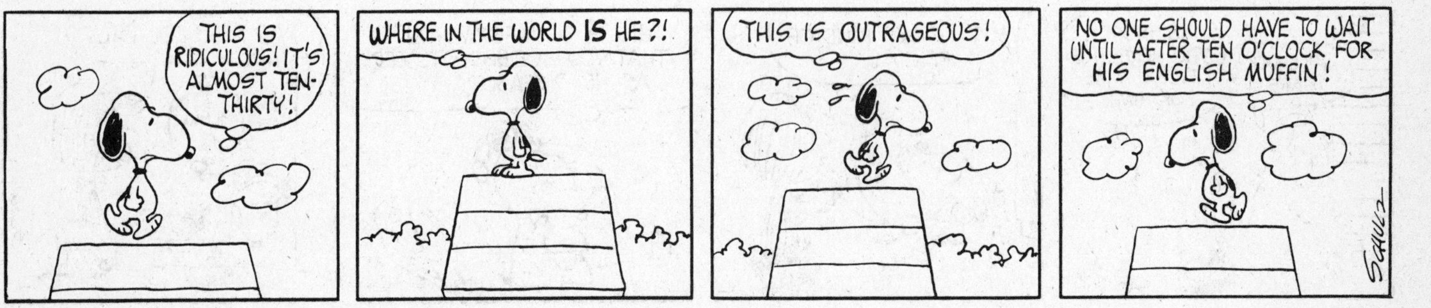
THIS IS RIDICULOUS! IT'S ALMOST TEN-THIRTY!
WHERE IN THE WORLD IS HE?!
THIS IS OUTRAGEOUS!
NO ONE SHOULD HAVE TO WAIT UNTIL AFTER TEN O'CLOCK FOR HIS ENGLISH MUFFIN!
SCHULZ

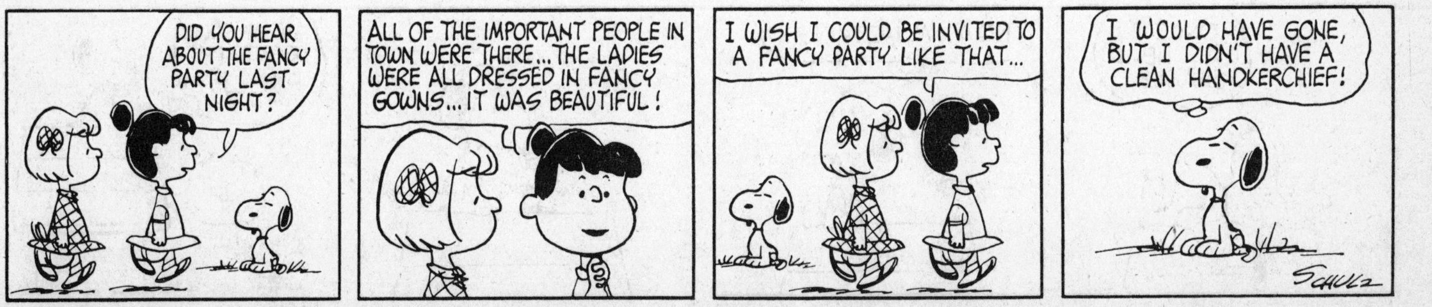
DID YOU HEAR ABOUT THE FANCY PARTY LAST NIGHT?
ALL OF THE IMPORTANT PEOPLE IN TOWN WERE THERE... THE LADIES WERE ALL DRESSED IN FANCY GOWNS... IT WAS BEAUTIFUL!
I WISH I COULD BE INVITED TO A FANCY PARTY LIKE THAT...
I WOULD HAVE GONE, BUT I DIDN'T HAVE A CLEAN HANDKERCHIEF!
SCHULZ

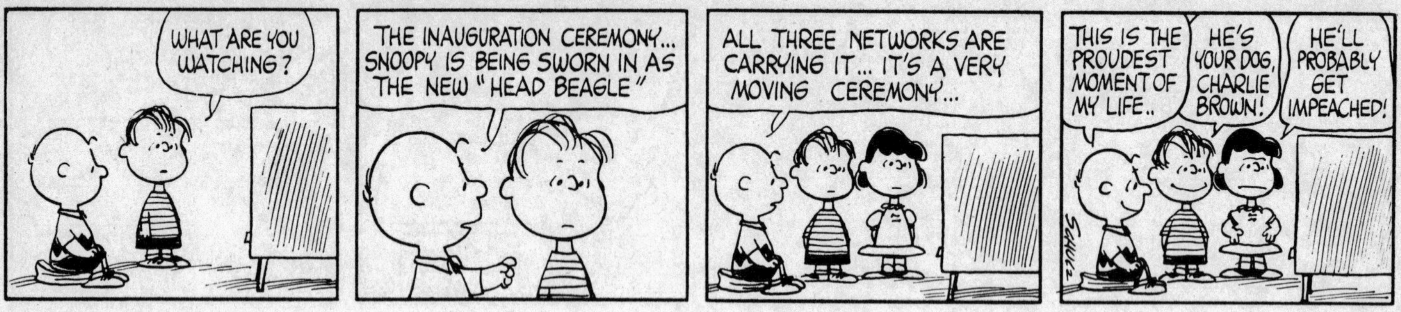
WHAT ARE YOU WATCHING?
THE INAUGURATION CEREMONY... SNOOPY IS BEING SWORN IN AS THE NEW "HEAD BEAGLE"
ALL THREE NETWORKS ARE CARRYING IT... IT'S A VERY MOVING CEREMONY...
THIS IS THE PROUDEST MOMENT OF MY LIFE..
HE'S YOUR DOG, CHARLIE BROWN!
HE'LL PROBABLY GET IMPEACHED!
SCHULZ

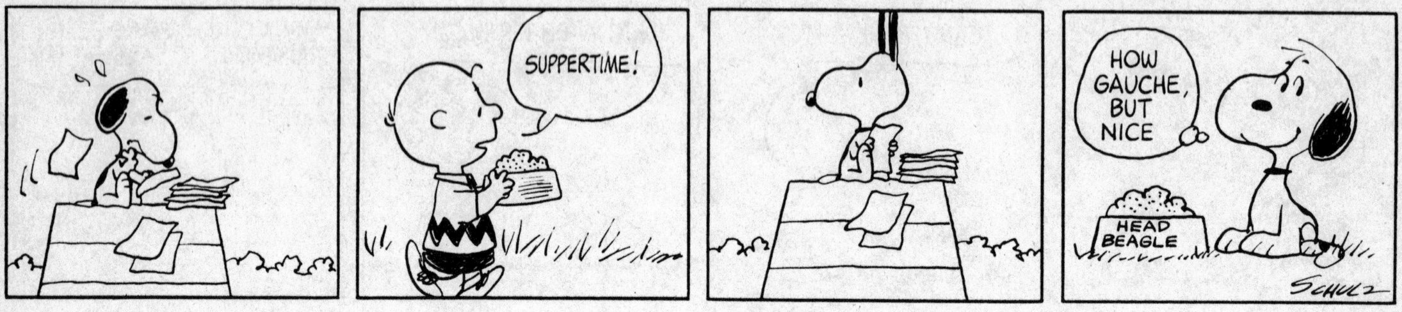
SUPPERTIME!
HOW GAUCHE, BUT NICE
HEAD BEAGLE
SCHULZ

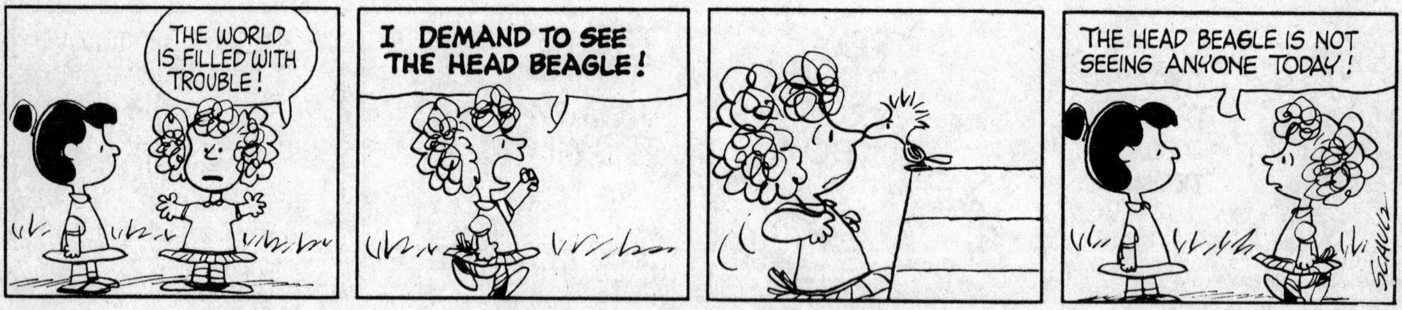
THE WORLD IS FILLED WITH TROUBLE!
I DEMAND TO SEE THE HEAD BEAGLE!
THE HEAD BEAGLE IS NOT SEEING ANYONE TODAY!
SCHULZ

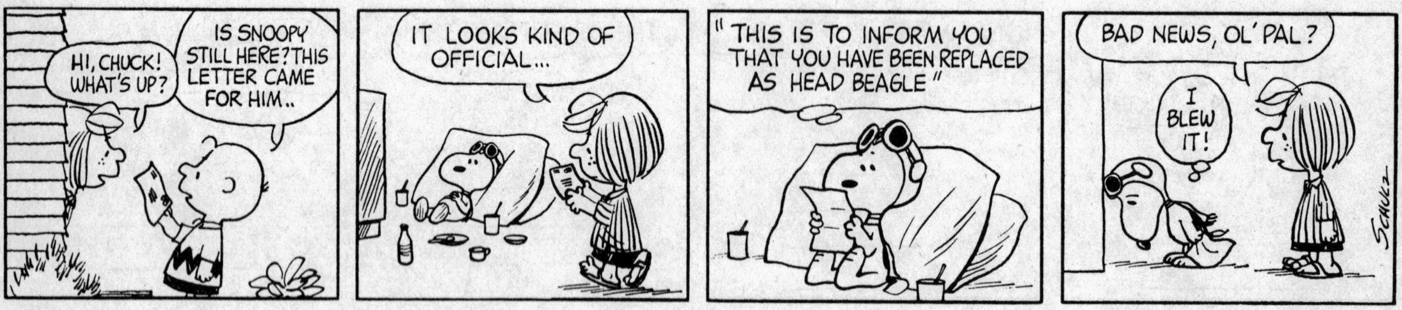
HI, CHUCK! WHAT'S UP?
IS SNOOPY STILL HERE? THIS LETTER CAME FOR HIM..
IT LOOKS KIND OF OFFICIAL...
"THIS IS TO INFORM YOU THAT YOU HAVE BEEN REPLACED AS HEAD BEAGLE"
BAD NEWS, OL' PAL?
I BLEW IT!
SCHULZ

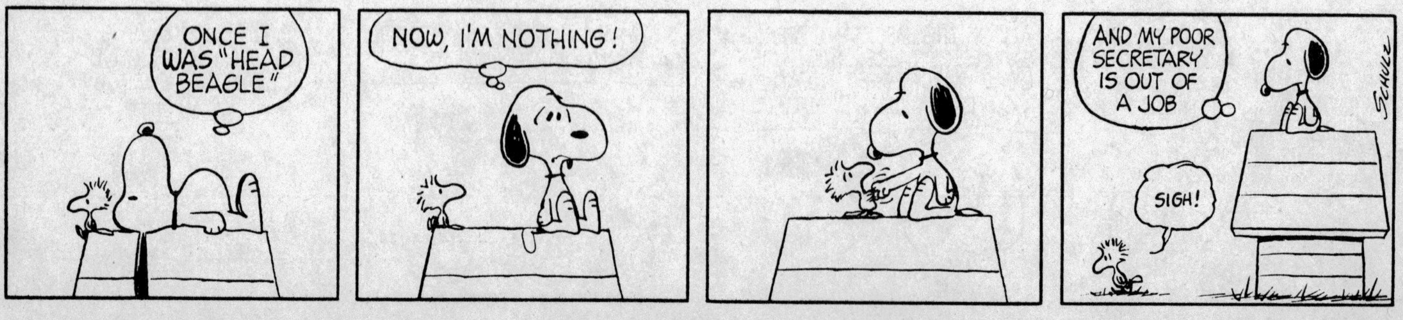
ONCE I WAS "HEAD BEAGLE"
NOW, I'M NOTHING!
AND MY POOR SECRETARY IS OUT OF A JOB
SIGH!
SCHULZ

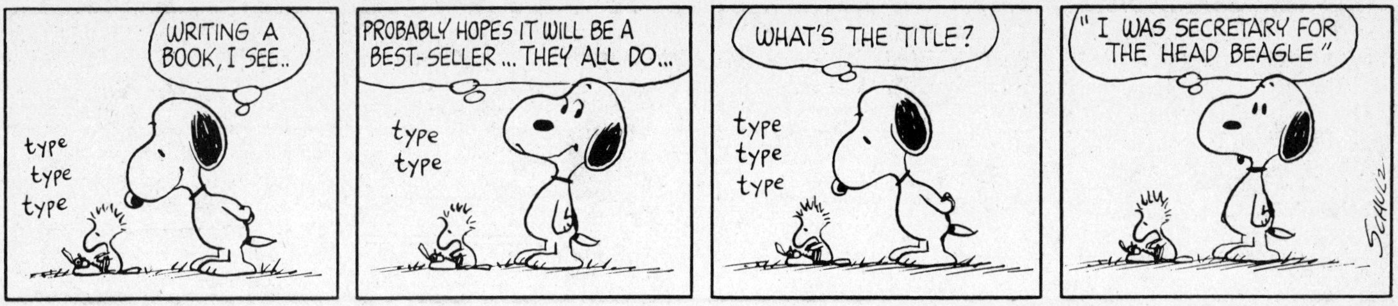
WRITING A BOOK, I SEE..
type type type
PROBABLY HOPES IT WILL BE A BEST-SELLER ... THEY ALL DO...
type type
WHAT'S THE TITLE?
type type type
" I WAS SECRETARY FOR THE HEAD BEAGLE "
SCHULZ

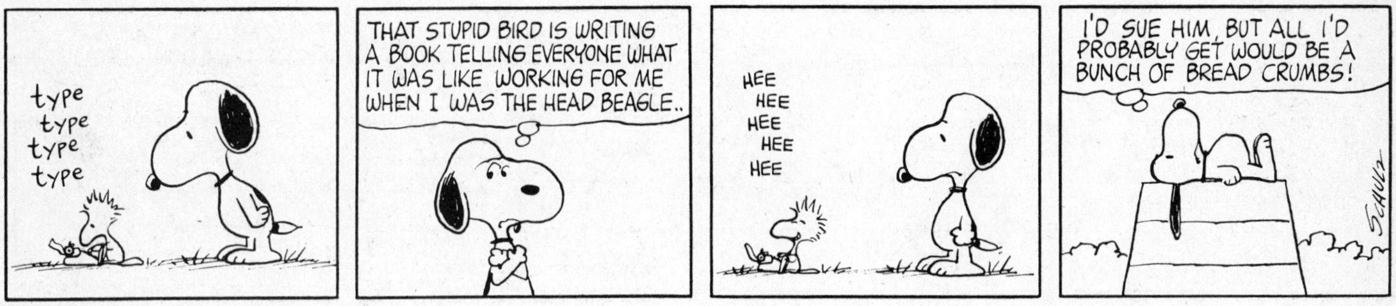
type type type type
THAT STUPID BIRD IS WRITING A BOOK TELLING EVERYONE WHAT IT WAS LIKE WORKING FOR ME WHEN I WAS THE HEAD BEAGLE..
HEE HEE HEE HEE HEE
I'D SUE HIM, BUT ALL I'D PROBABLY GET WOULD BE A BUNCH OF BREAD CRUMBS!
SCHULZ

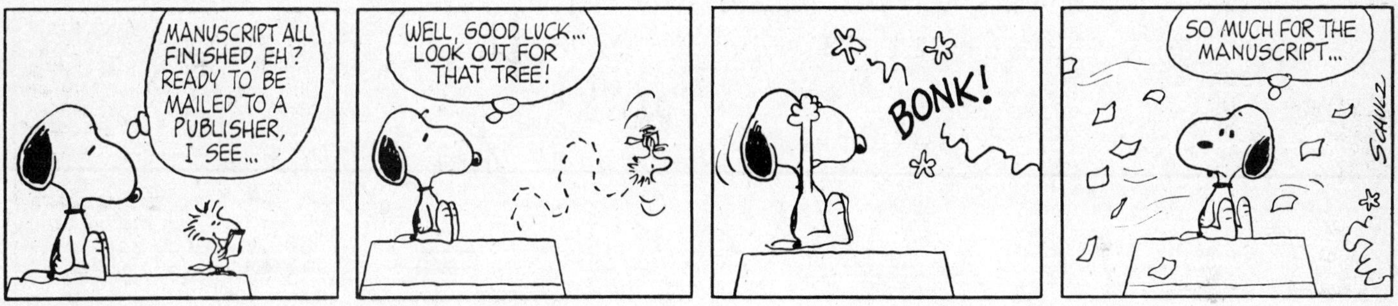
MANUSCRIPT ALL FINISHED, EH? READY TO BE MAILED TO A PUBLISHER, I SEE...
WELL, GOOD LUCK... LOOK OUT FOR THAT TREE!
BONK!
SO MUCH FOR THE MANUSCRIPT...
SCHULZ

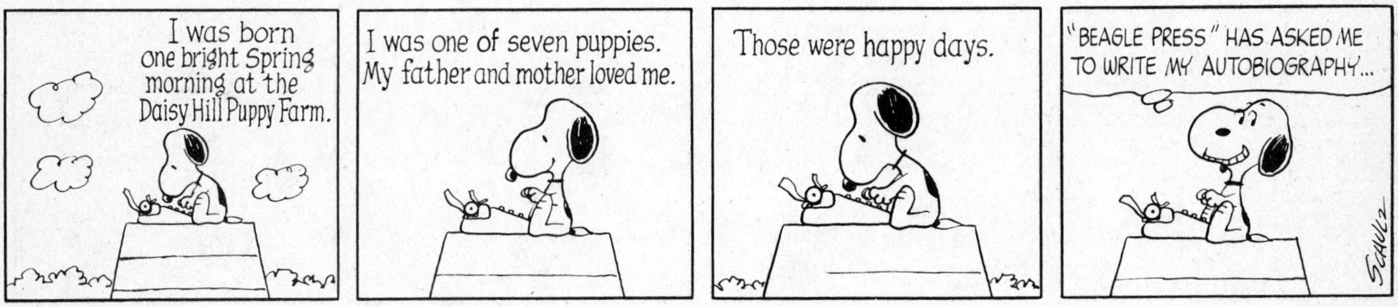
I was born one bright Spring morning at the Daisy Hill Puppy Farm.
I was one of seven puppies. My father and mother loved me.
Those were happy days.
"BEAGLE PRESS" HAS ASKED ME TO WRITE MY AUTOBIOGRAPHY...
SCHULZ

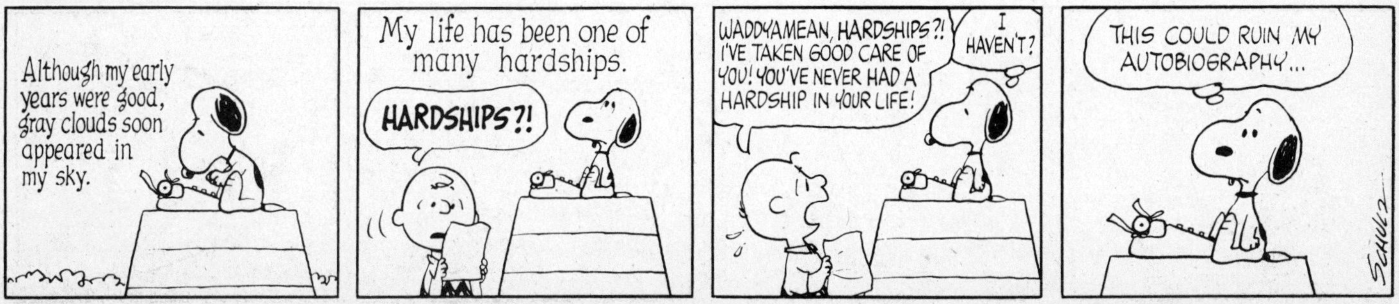
Although my early years were good, gray clouds soon appeared in my sky.
My life has been one of many hardships.
HARDSHIPS?!
WADDYAMEAN, HARDSHIPS?! I'VE TAKEN GOOD CARE OF YOU! YOU'VE NEVER HAD A HARDSHIP IN YOUR LIFE!
I HAVEN'T?
THIS COULD RUIN MY AUTOBIOGRAPHY...
SCHULZ

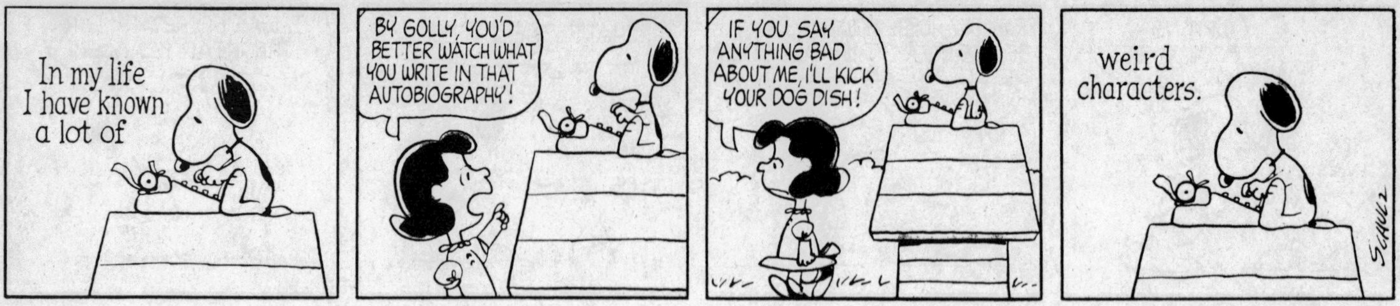
In my life I have known a lot of
BY GOLLY, YOU'D BETTER WATCH WHAT YOU WRITE IN THAT AUTOBIOGRAPHY!
IF YOU SAY ANYTHING BAD ABOUT ME, I'LL KICK YOUR DOG DISH!
weird characters.
SCHULZ

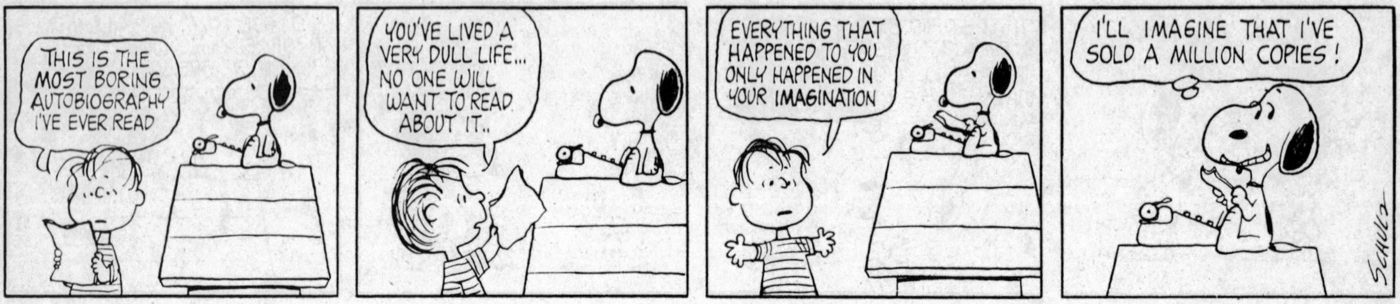
THIS IS THE MOST BORING AUTOBIOGRAPHY I'VE EVER READ
YOU'VE LIVED A VERY DULL LIFE... NO ONE WILL WANT TO READ ABOUT IT..
EVERYTHING THAT HAPPENED TO YOU ONLY HAPPENED IN YOUR IMAGINATION
I'LL IMAGINE THAT I'VE SOLD A MILLION COPIES!
SCHULZ

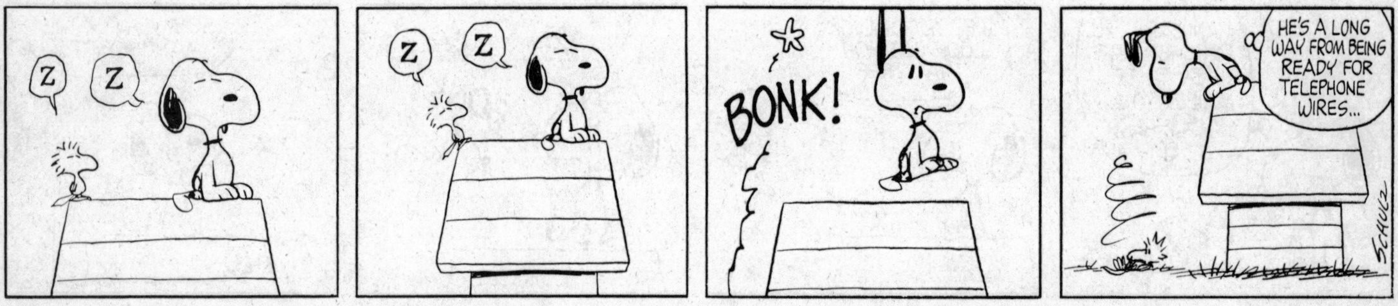
Z Z
Z Z
BONK!
HE'S A LONG WAY FROM BEING READY FOR TELEPHONE WIRES...
SCHULZ

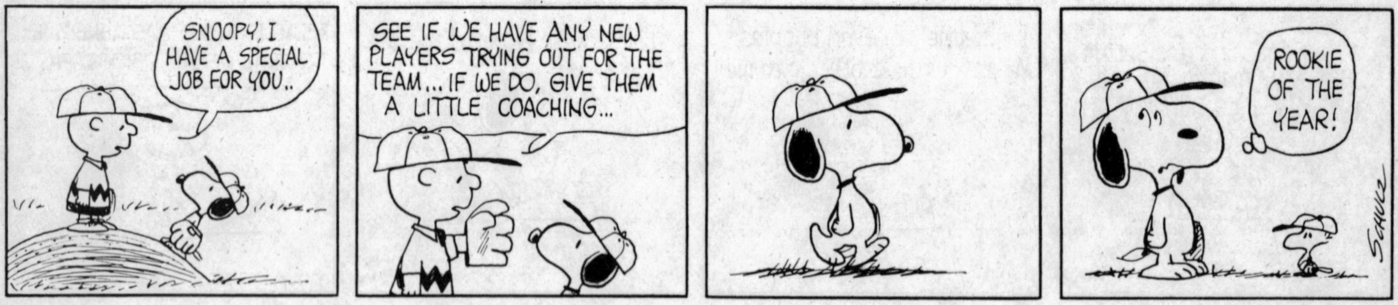
SNOOPY, I HAVE A SPECIAL JOB FOR YOU..
SEE IF WE HAVE ANY NEW PLAYERS TRYING OUT FOR THE TEAM... IF WE DO, GIVE THEM A LITTLE COACHING...
ROOKIE OF THE YEAR!
SCHULZ

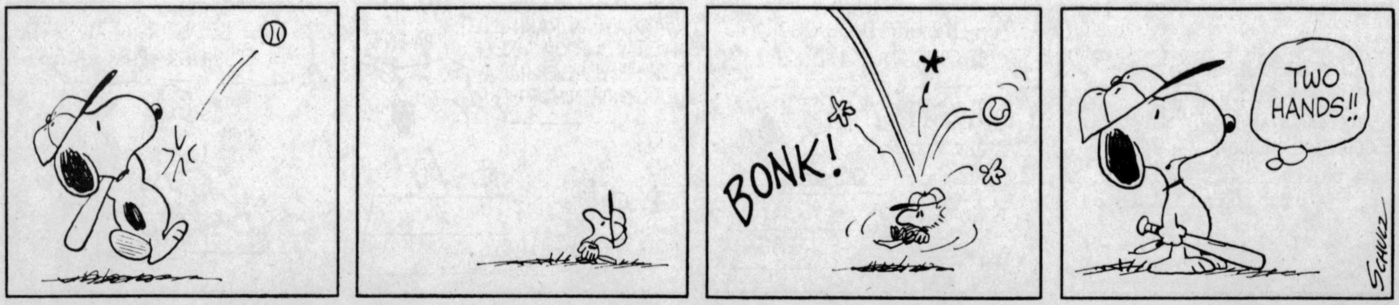
BONK!
TWO HANDS!!
SCHULZ

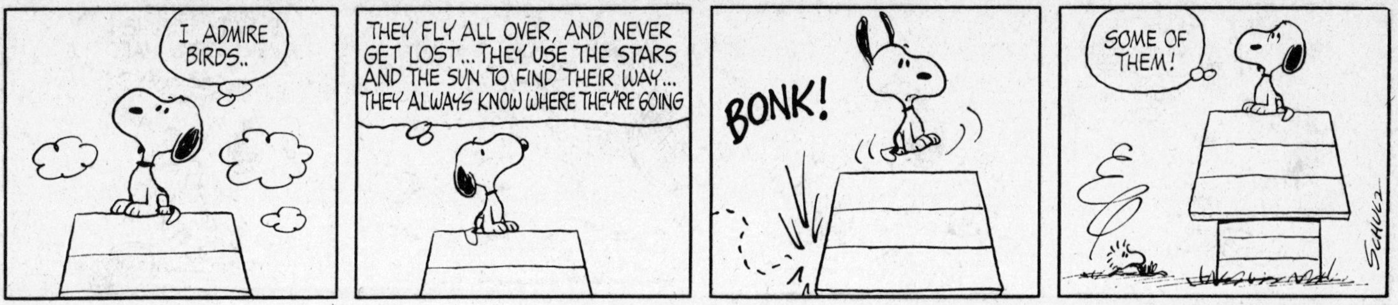
I ADMIRE BIRDS..
THEY FLY ALL OVER, AND NEVER GET LOST...THEY USE THE STARS AND THE SUN TO FIND THEIR WAY... THEY ALWAYS KNOW WHERE THEY'RE GOING
BONK!
SOME OF THEM!
SCHULZ

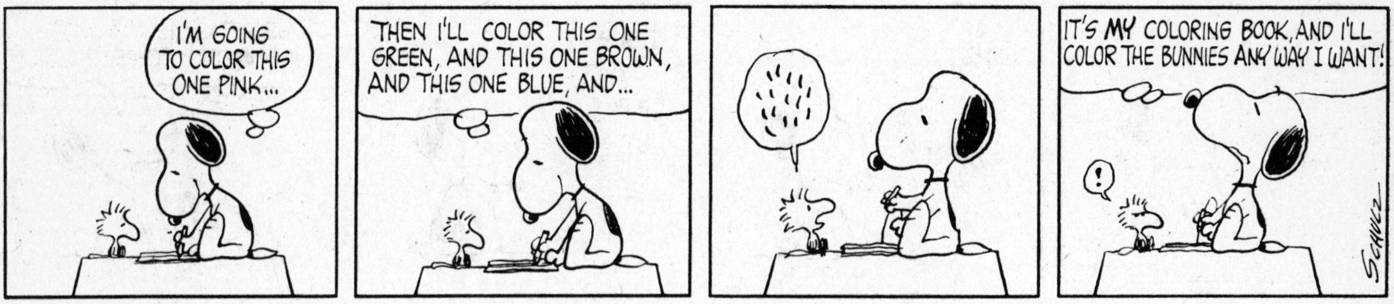
I'M GOING TO COLOR THIS ONE PINK...
THEN I'LL COLOR THIS ONE GREEN, AND THIS ONE BROWN, AND THIS ONE BLUE, AND...
!
IT'S MY COLORING BOOK, AND I'LL COLOR THE BUNNIES ANY WAY I WANT!
SCHULZ

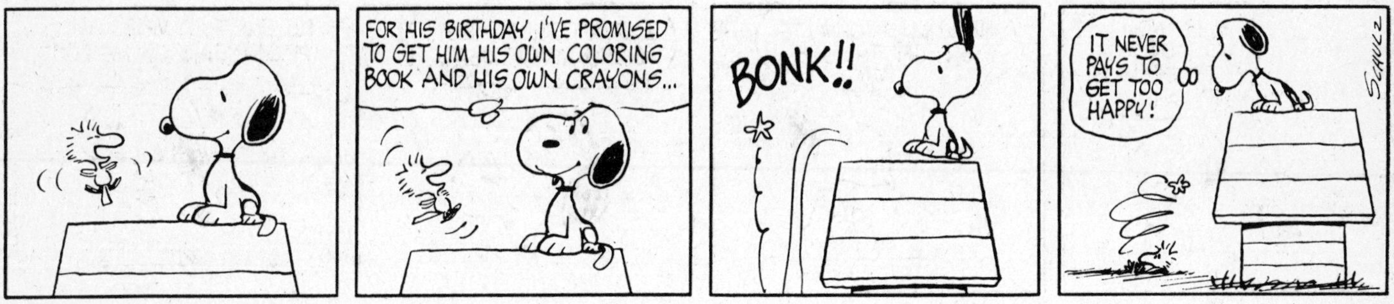
FOR HIS BIRTHDAY, I'VE PROMISED TO GET HIM HIS OWN COLORING BOOK AND HIS OWN CRAYONS...
BONK!!
IT NEVER PAYS TO GET TOO HAPPY!
SCHULZ

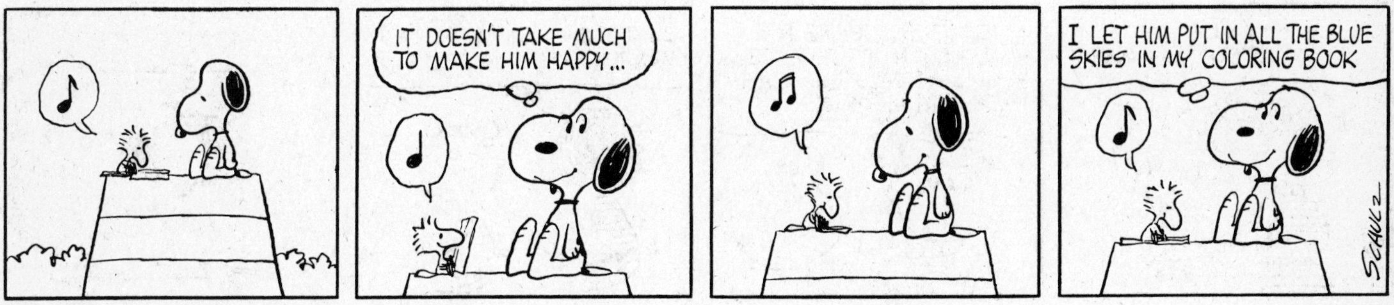
IT DOESN'T TAKE MUCH TO MAKE HIM HAPPY...
I LET HIM PUT IN ALL THE BLUE SKIES IN MY COLORING BOOK
SCHULZ

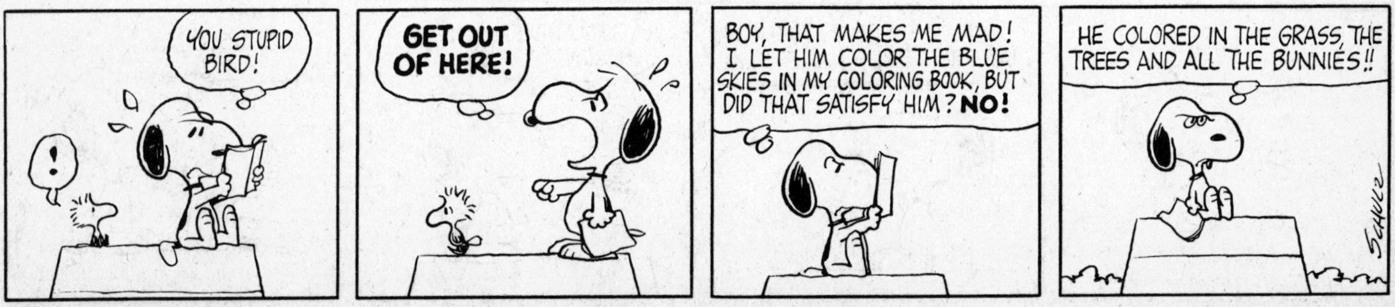
YOU STUPID BIRD!
!
GET OUT OF HERE!
BOY, THAT MAKES ME MAD! I LET HIM COLOR THE BLUE SKIES IN MY COLORING BOOK, BUT DID THAT SATISFY HIM? NO!
HE COLORED IN THE GRASS, THE TREES AND ALL THE BUNNIES!!
SCHULZ

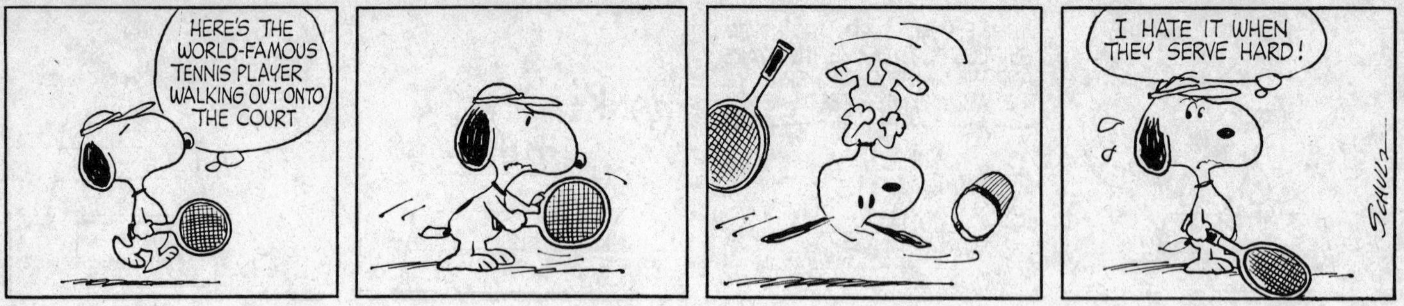
HERE'S THE WORLD-FAMOUS TENNIS PLAYER WALKING OUT ONTO THE COURT
I HATE IT WHEN THEY SERVE HARD!
SCHULZ

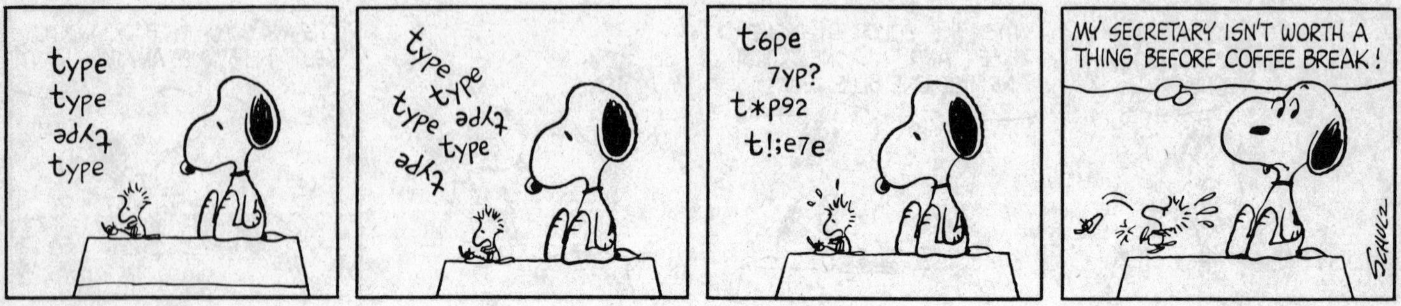
type
type
type
type
type
type
type
t6pe
7yp?
t*p92
t!;e7e
MY SECRETARY ISN'T WORTH A THING BEFORE COFFEE BREAK!
SCHULZ

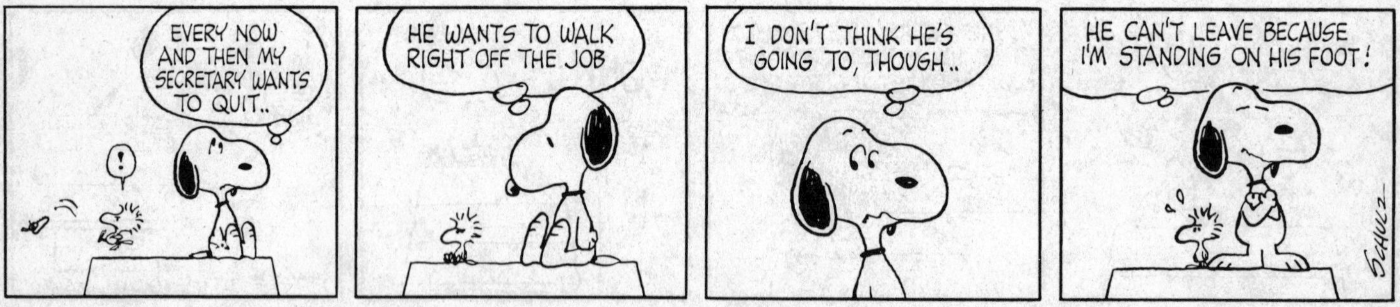
EVERY NOW AND THEN MY SECRETARY WANTS TO QUIT..
!
HE WANTS TO WALK RIGHT OFF THE JOB
I DON'T THINK HE'S GOING TO, THOUGH..
HE CAN'T LEAVE BECAUSE I'M STANDING ON HIS FOOT!
SCHULZ

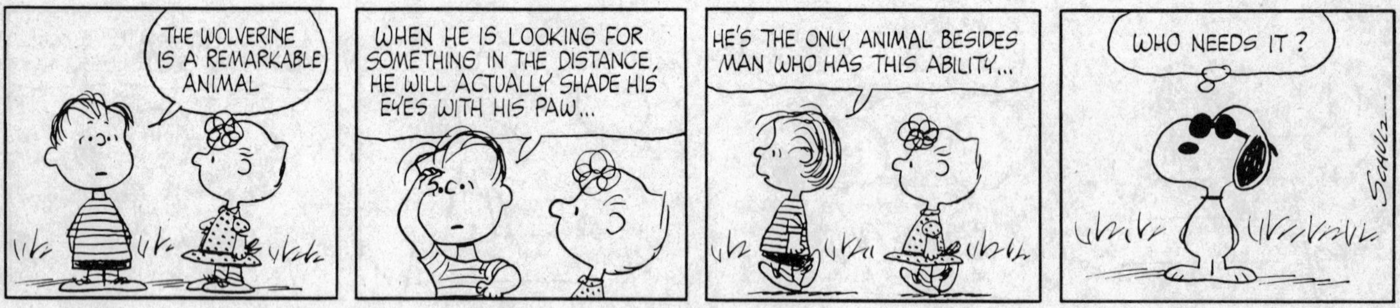
THE WOLVERINE IS A REMARKABLE ANIMAL
WHEN HE IS LOOKING FOR SOMETHING IN THE DISTANCE, HE WILL ACTUALLY SHADE HIS EYES WITH HIS PAW...
HE'S THE ONLY ANIMAL BESIDES MAN WHO HAS THIS ABILITY...
WHO NEEDS IT?
SCHULZ

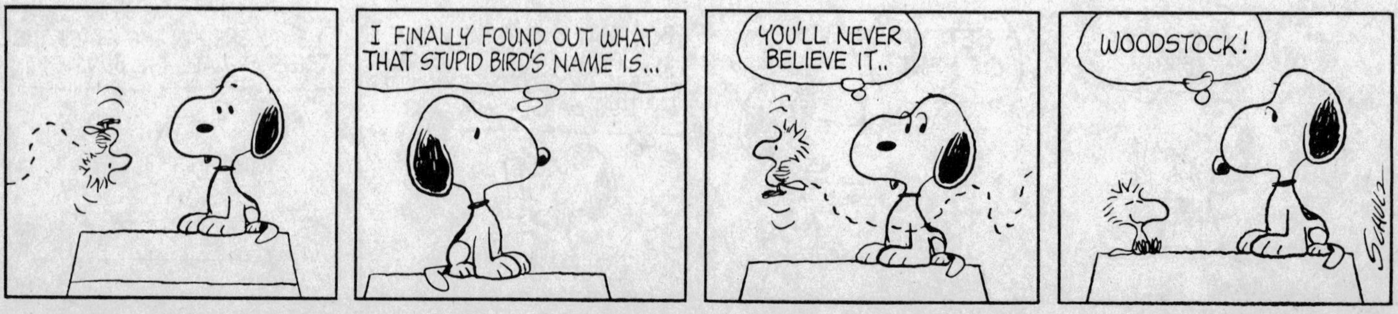
I FINALLY FOUND OUT WHAT THAT STUPID BIRD'S NAME IS...
YOU'LL NEVER BELIEVE IT..
WOODSTOCK!
SCHULZ

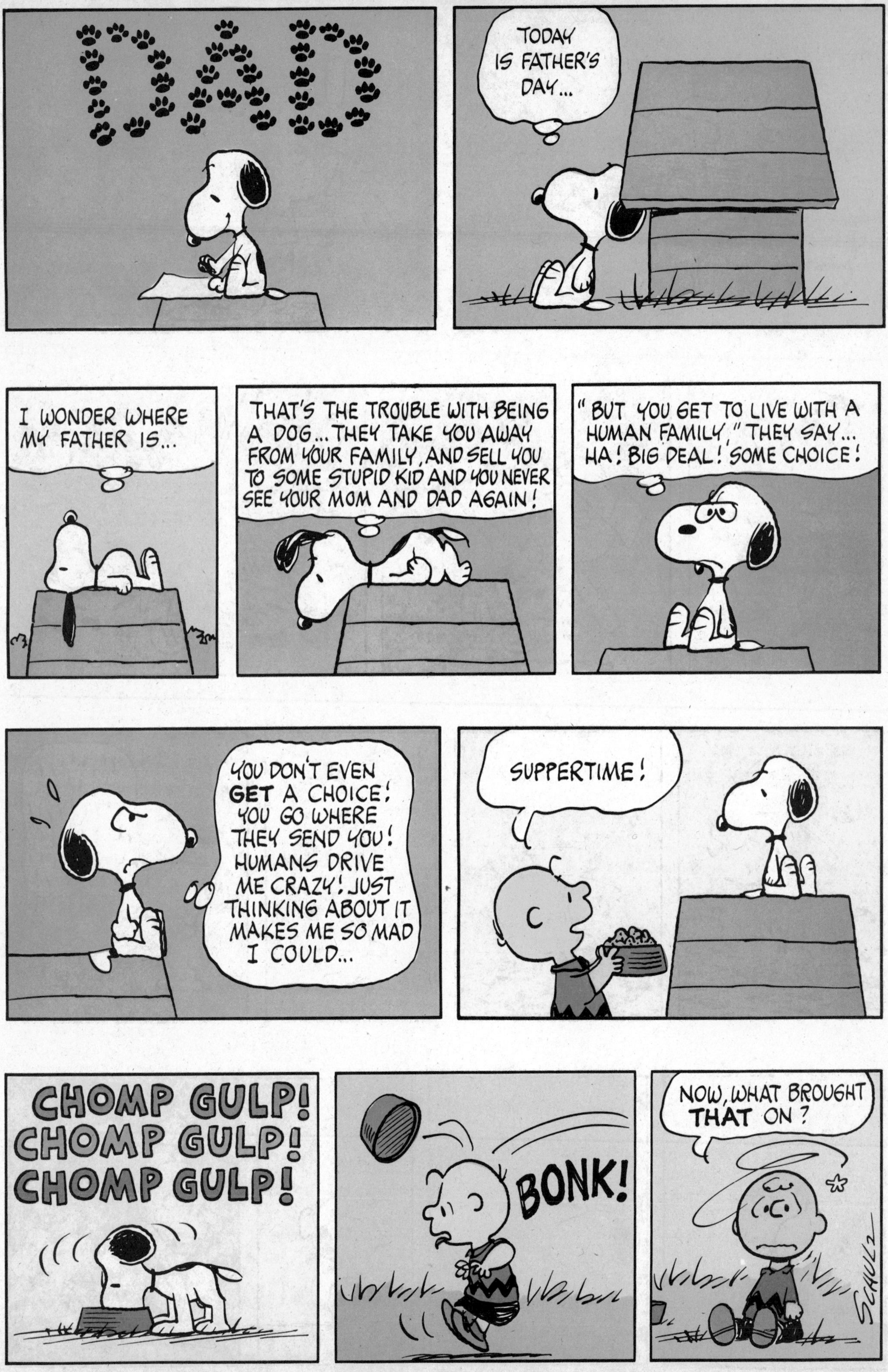
DAD
TODAY IS FATHER'S DAY...
I WONDER WHERE MY FATHER IS...
THAT'S THE TROUBLE WITH BEING A DOG... THEY TAKE YOU AWAY FROM YOUR FAMILY, AND SELL YOU TO SOME STUPID KID AND YOU NEVER SEE YOUR MOM AND DAD AGAIN!
"BUT YOU GET TO LIVE WITH A HUMAN FAMILY," THEY SAY... HA! BIG DEAL! SOME CHOICE!
YOU DON'T EVEN **GET** A CHOICE! YOU GO WHERE THEY SEND YOU! HUMANS DRIVE ME CRAZY! JUST THINKING ABOUT IT MAKES ME SO MAD I COULD...
SUPPERTIME!
CHOMP GULP! CHOMP GULP! CHOMP GULP!
BONK!
NOW, WHAT BROUGHT **THAT** ON?
SCHULZ

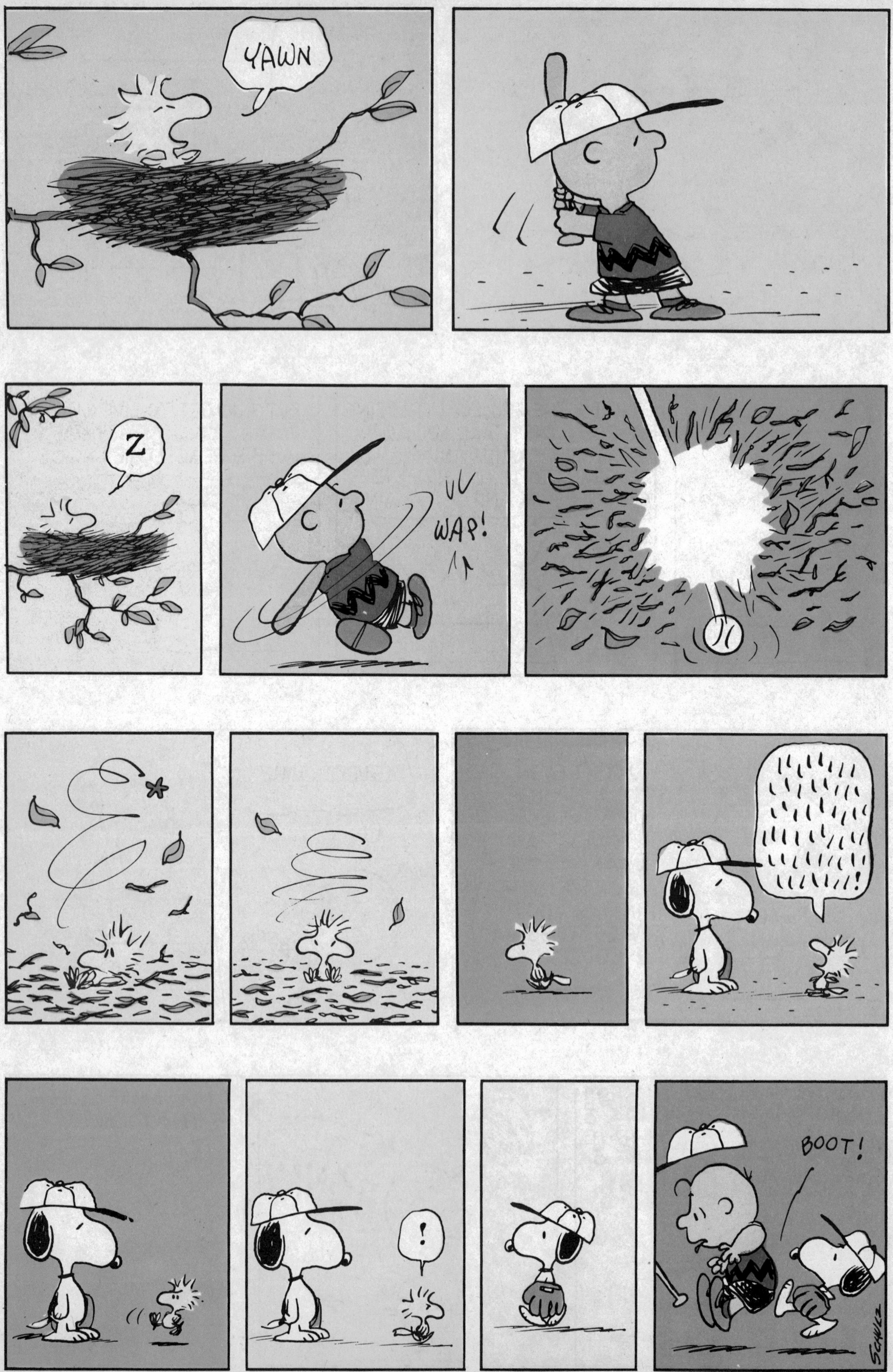
YAWN
Z
WAP!
!
BOOT!
SCHULZ

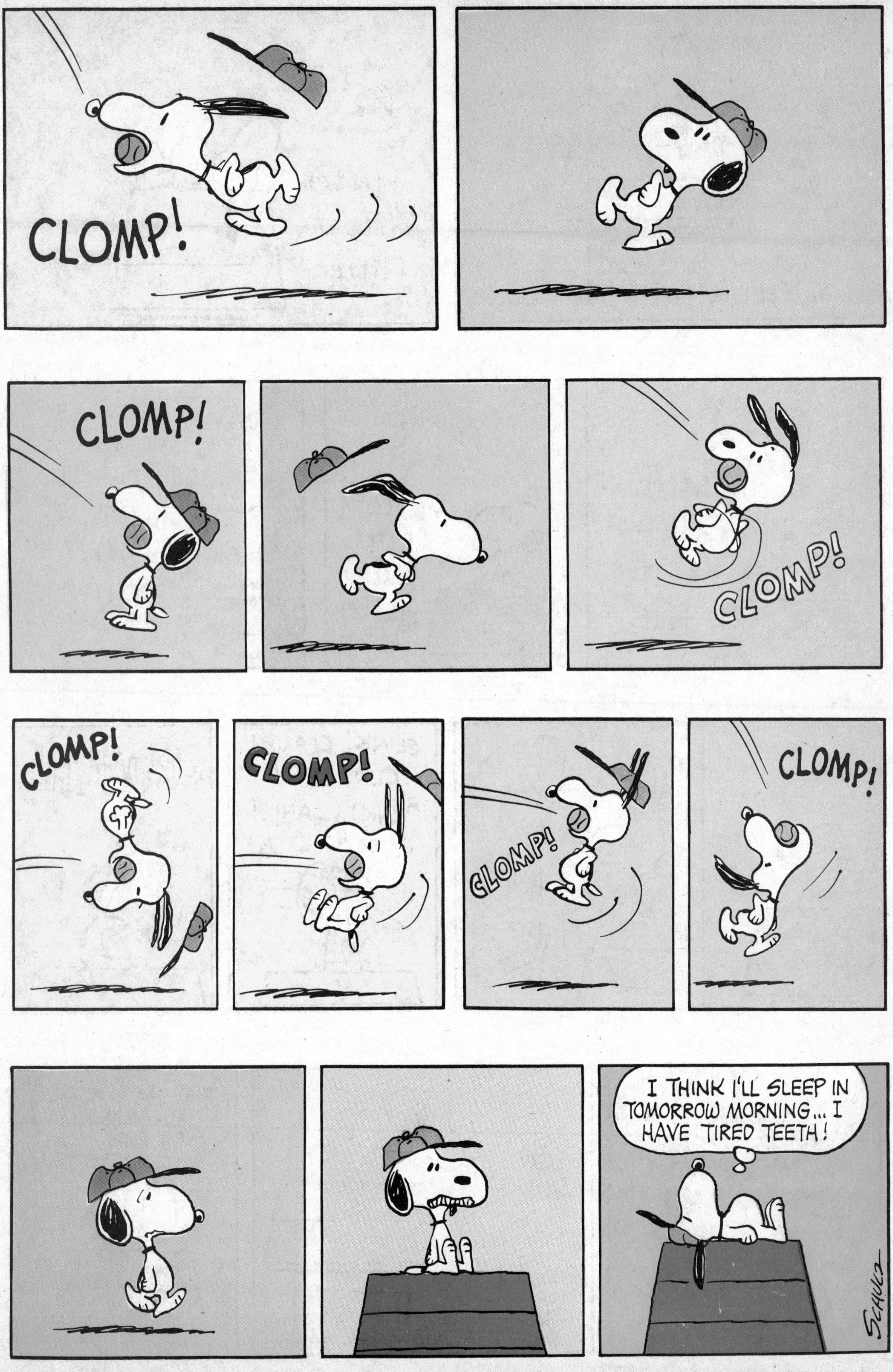
CLOMP!
CLOMP!
CLOMP!
CLOMP!
CLOMP!
CLOMP!
CLOMP!
I THINK I'LL SLEEP IN TOMORROW MORNING... I HAVE TIRED TEETH!
SCHULZ

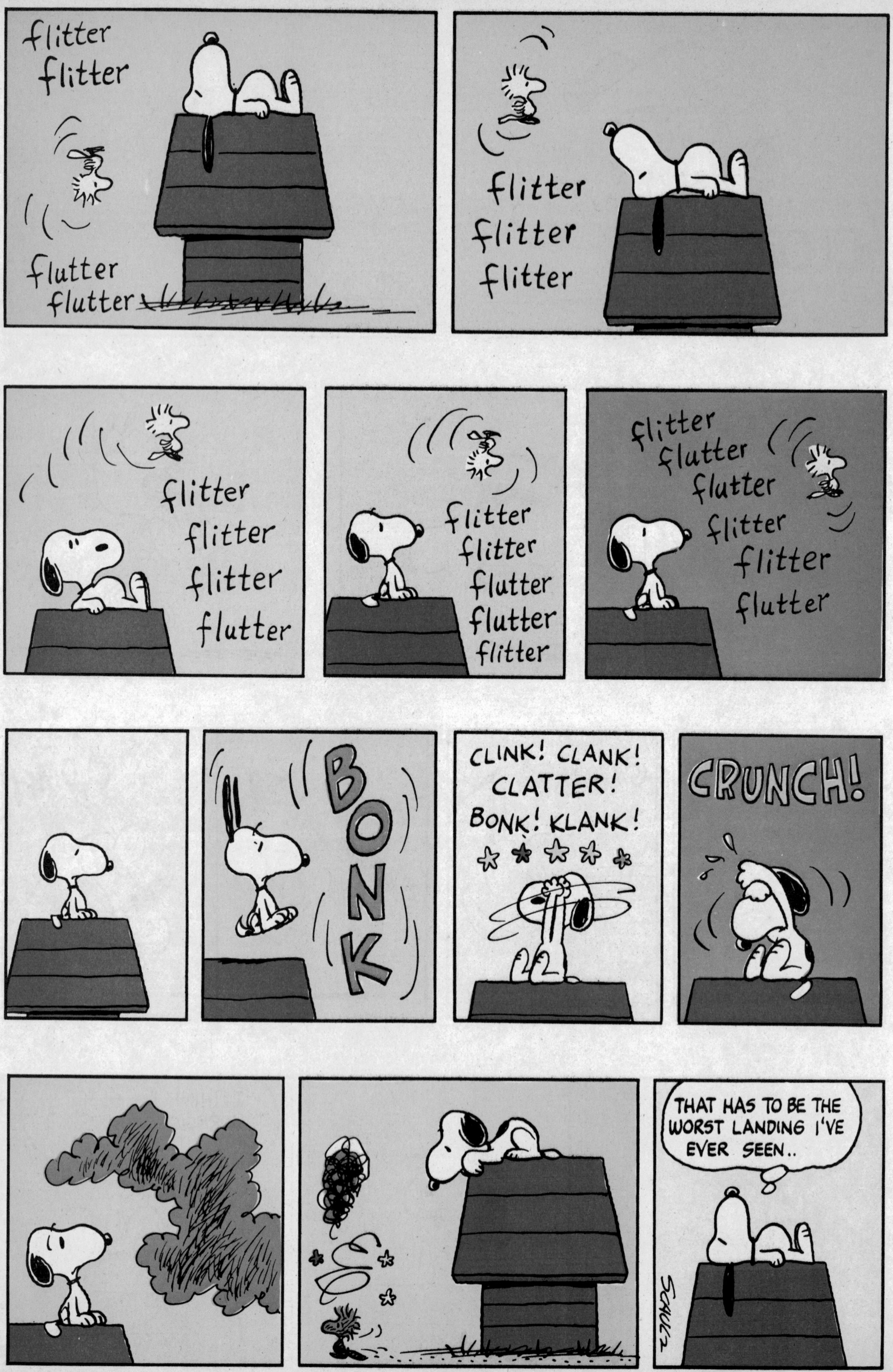
flitter
flitter
flutter
flutter
flitter
flitter
flitter
flitter
flitter
flitter
flutter
flitter
flitter
flutter
flutter
flitter
flitter
flutter
flutter
flitter
flitter
flutter
BONK
CLINK! CLANK!
CLATTER!
BONK! KLANK!
CRUNCH!
THAT HAS TO BE THE
WORST LANDING I'VE
EVER SEEN..
SCHULZ

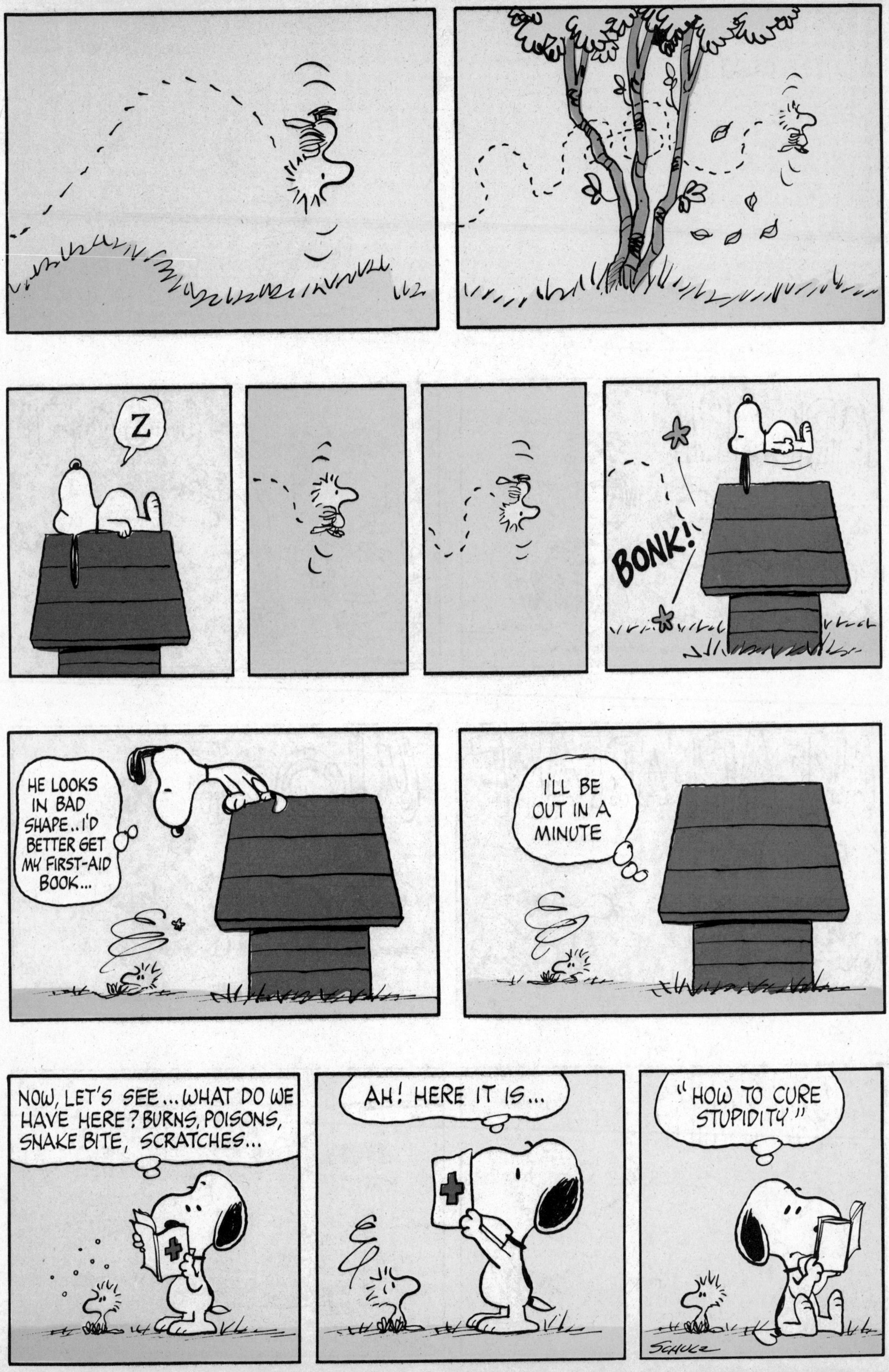
Z
BONK!
HE LOOKS IN BAD SHAPE..I'D BETTER GET MY FIRST-AID BOOK...
I'LL BE OUT IN A MINUTE
NOW, LET'S SEE...WHAT DO WE HAVE HERE? BURNS, POISONS, SNAKE BITE, SCRATCHES...
AH! HERE IT IS...
"HOW TO CURE STUPIDITY"
SCHULZ

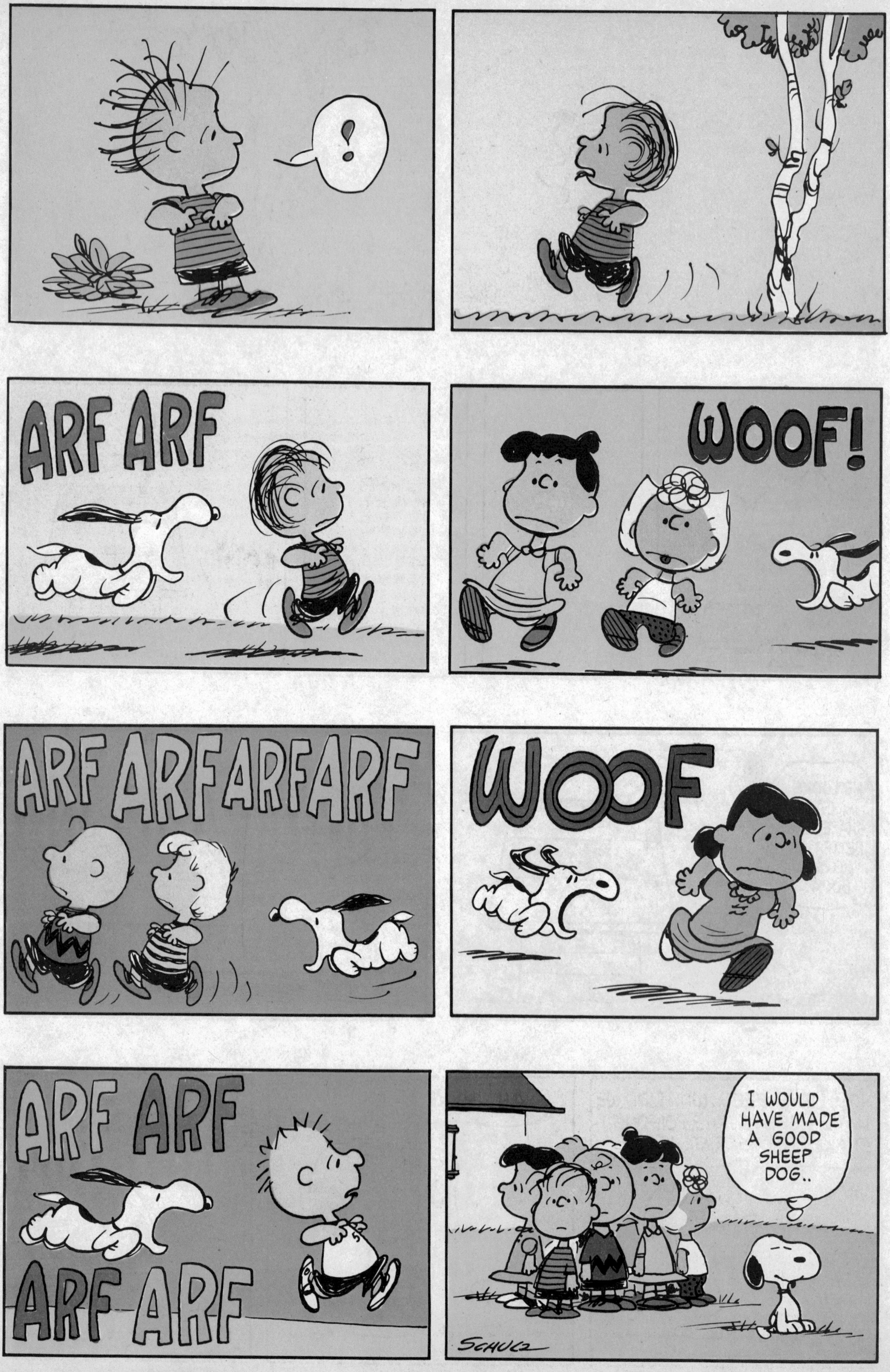
!
ARF ARF
WOOF!
ARF ARF ARF ARF
WOOF
ARF ARF
ARF ARF
I WOULD HAVE MADE A GOOD SHEEP DOG..
SCHULZ

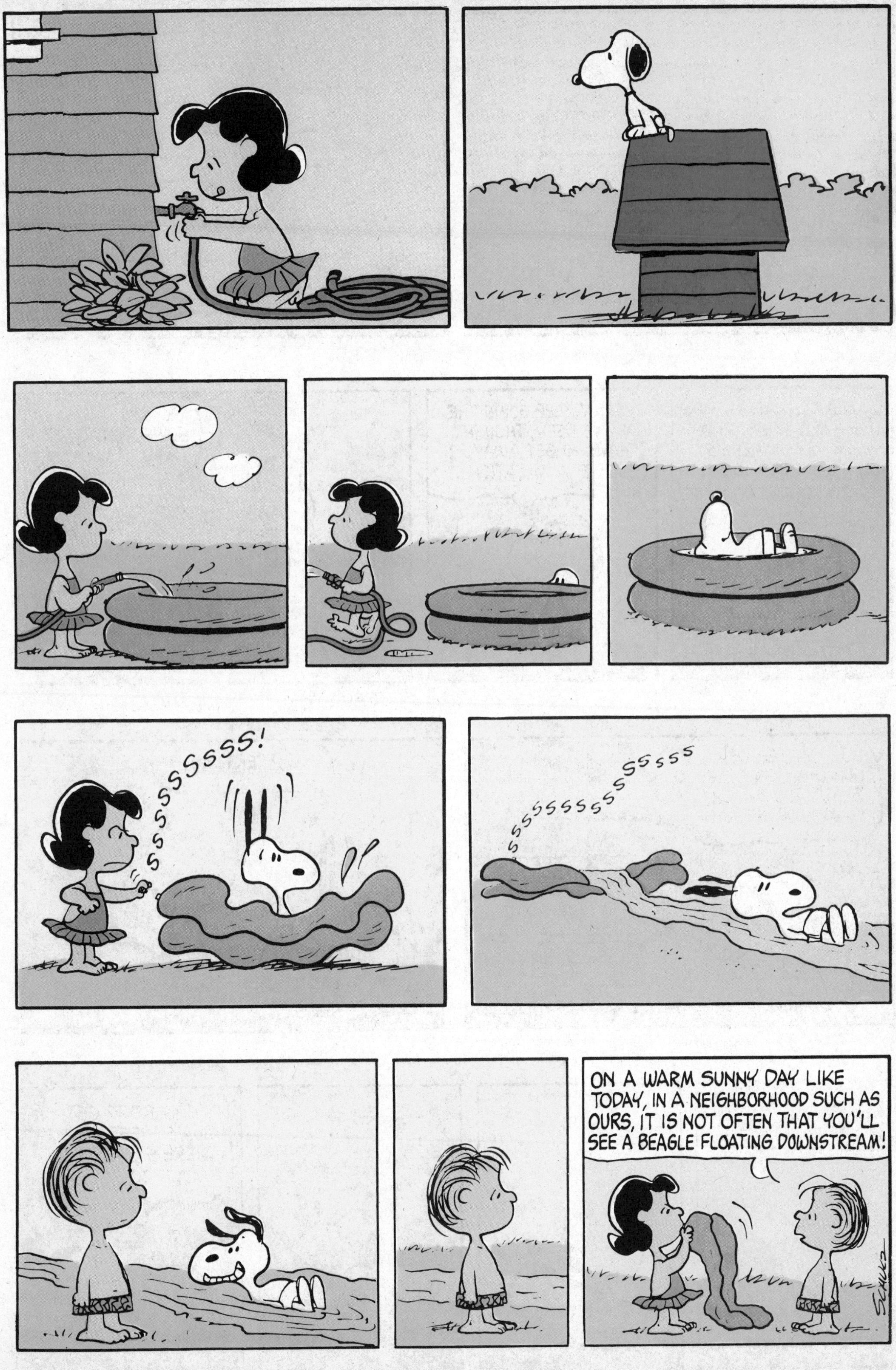
SSSSSSS!
SSSSSSSSSSSSSSSS
ON A WARM SUNNY DAY LIKE TODAY, IN A NEIGHBORHOOD SUCH AS OURS, IT IS NOT OFTEN THAT YOU'LL SEE A BEAGLE FLOATING DOWNSTREAM!
SCHULZ

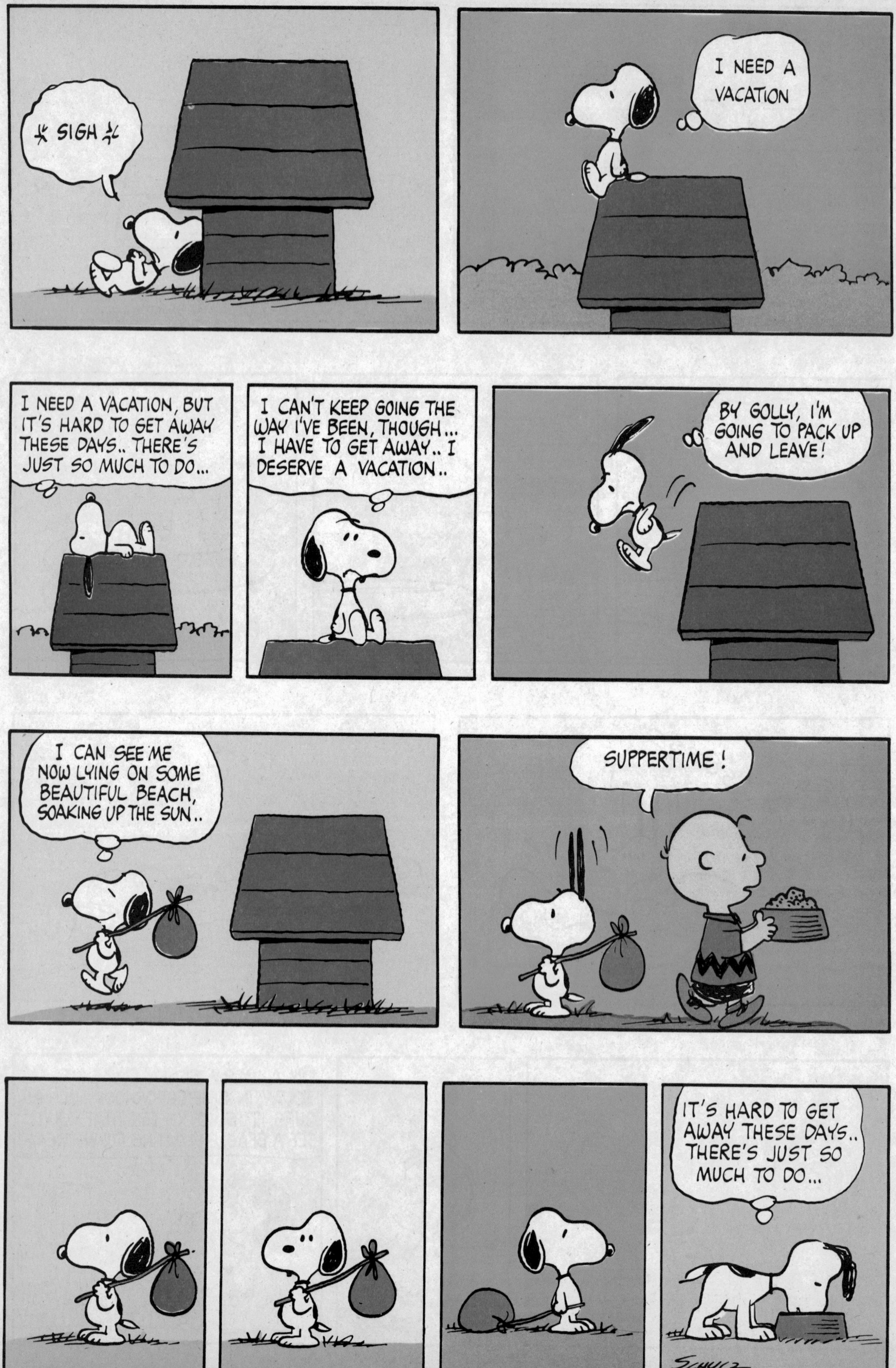
* SIGH *
I NEED A VACATION
I NEED A VACATION, BUT IT'S HARD TO GET AWAY THESE DAYS.. THERE'S JUST SO MUCH TO DO...
I CAN'T KEEP GOING THE WAY I'VE BEEN, THOUGH... I HAVE TO GET AWAY.. I DESERVE A VACATION..
BY GOLLY, I'M GOING TO PACK UP AND LEAVE!
I CAN SEE ME NOW LYING ON SOME BEAUTIFUL BEACH, SOAKING UP THE SUN..
SUPPERTIME!
IT'S HARD TO GET AWAY THESE DAYS.. THERE'S JUST SO MUCH TO DO...
SCHULZ

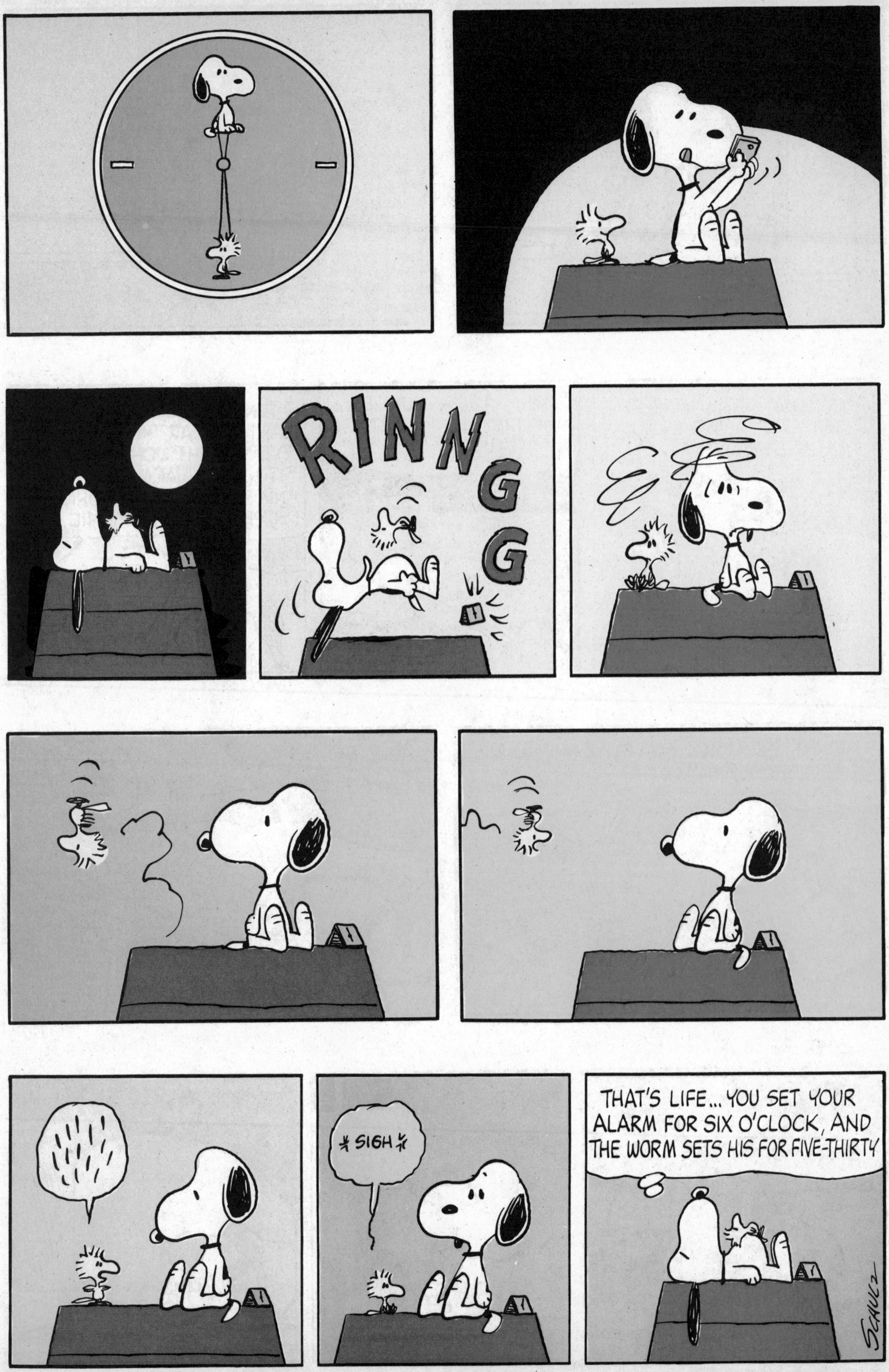
RINNGG
* SIGH *
THAT'S LIFE... YOU SET YOUR ALARM FOR SIX O'CLOCK, AND THE WORM SETS HIS FOR FIVE-THIRTY
SCHULZ

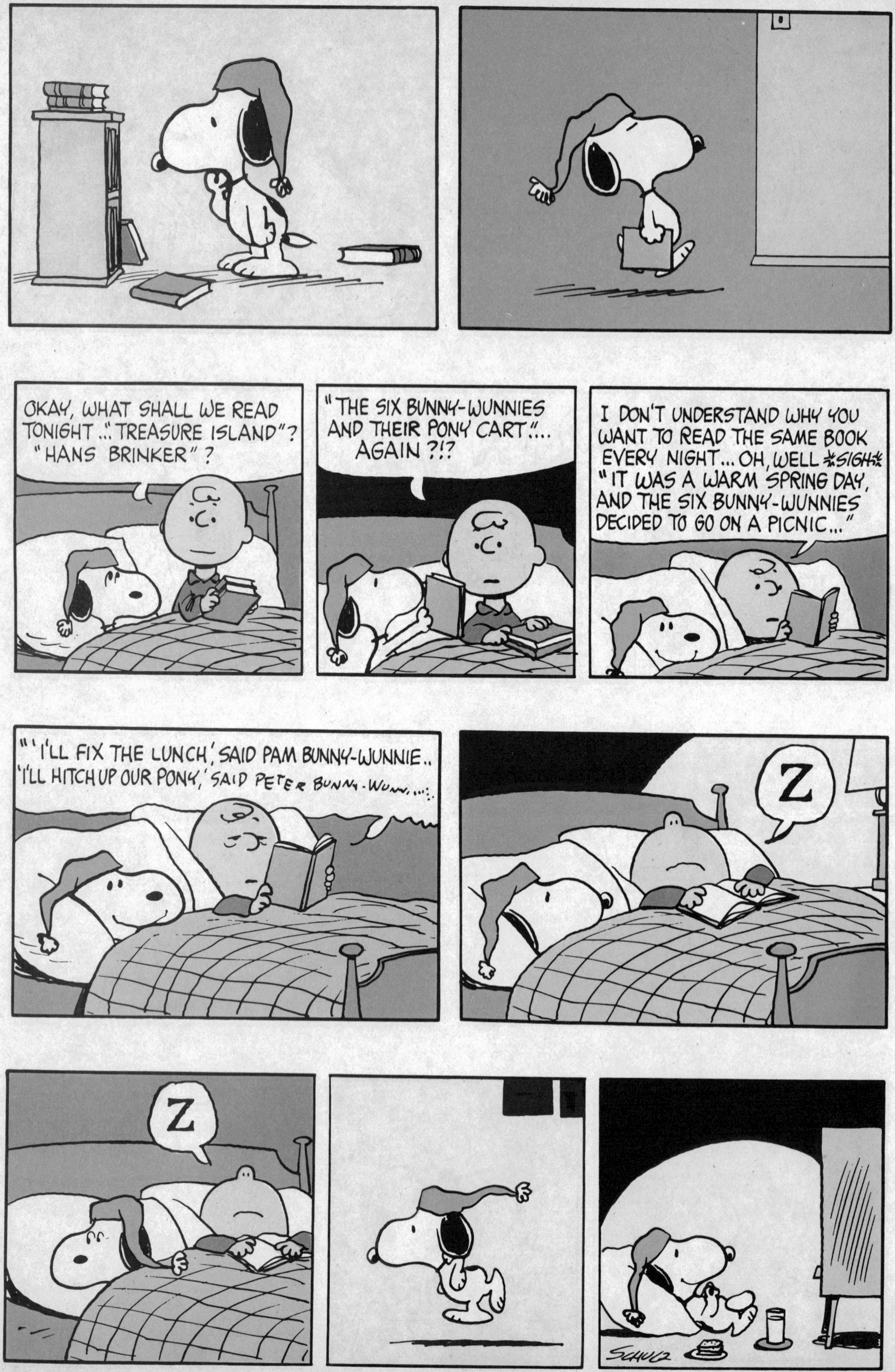
OKAY, WHAT SHALL WE READ TONIGHT..."TREASURE ISLAND"? "HANS BRINKER"?
"THE SIX BUNNY-WUNNIES AND THEIR PONY CART"... AGAIN ?!?
I DON'T UNDERSTAND WHY YOU WANT TO READ THE SAME BOOK EVERY NIGHT... OH, WELL *SIGH* "IT WAS A WARM SPRING DAY, AND THE SIX BUNNY-WUNNIES DECIDED TO GO ON A PICNIC..."
"'I'LL FIX THE LUNCH,' SAID PAM BUNNY-WUNNIE.. 'I'LL HITCH UP OUR PONY,' SAID PETER BUNNY-WUNN...
Z
Z
SCHULZ

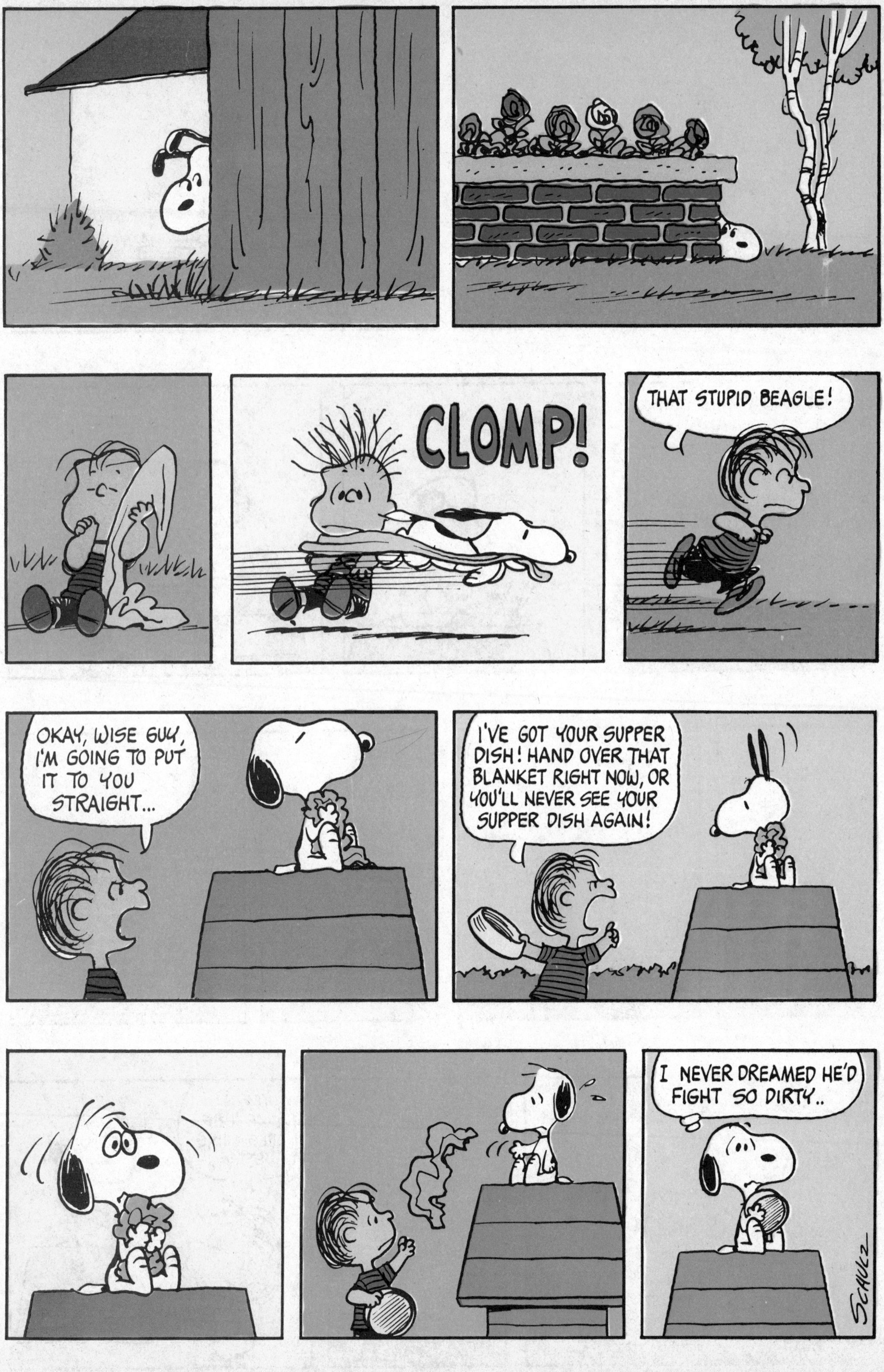
CLOMP!
THAT STUPID BEAGLE!
OKAY, WISE GUY, I'M GOING TO PUT IT TO YOU STRAIGHT...
I'VE GOT YOUR SUPPER DISH! HAND OVER THAT BLANKET RIGHT NOW, OR YOU'LL NEVER SEE YOUR SUPPER DISH AGAIN!
I NEVER DREAMED HE'D FIGHT SO DIRTY..
SCHULZ

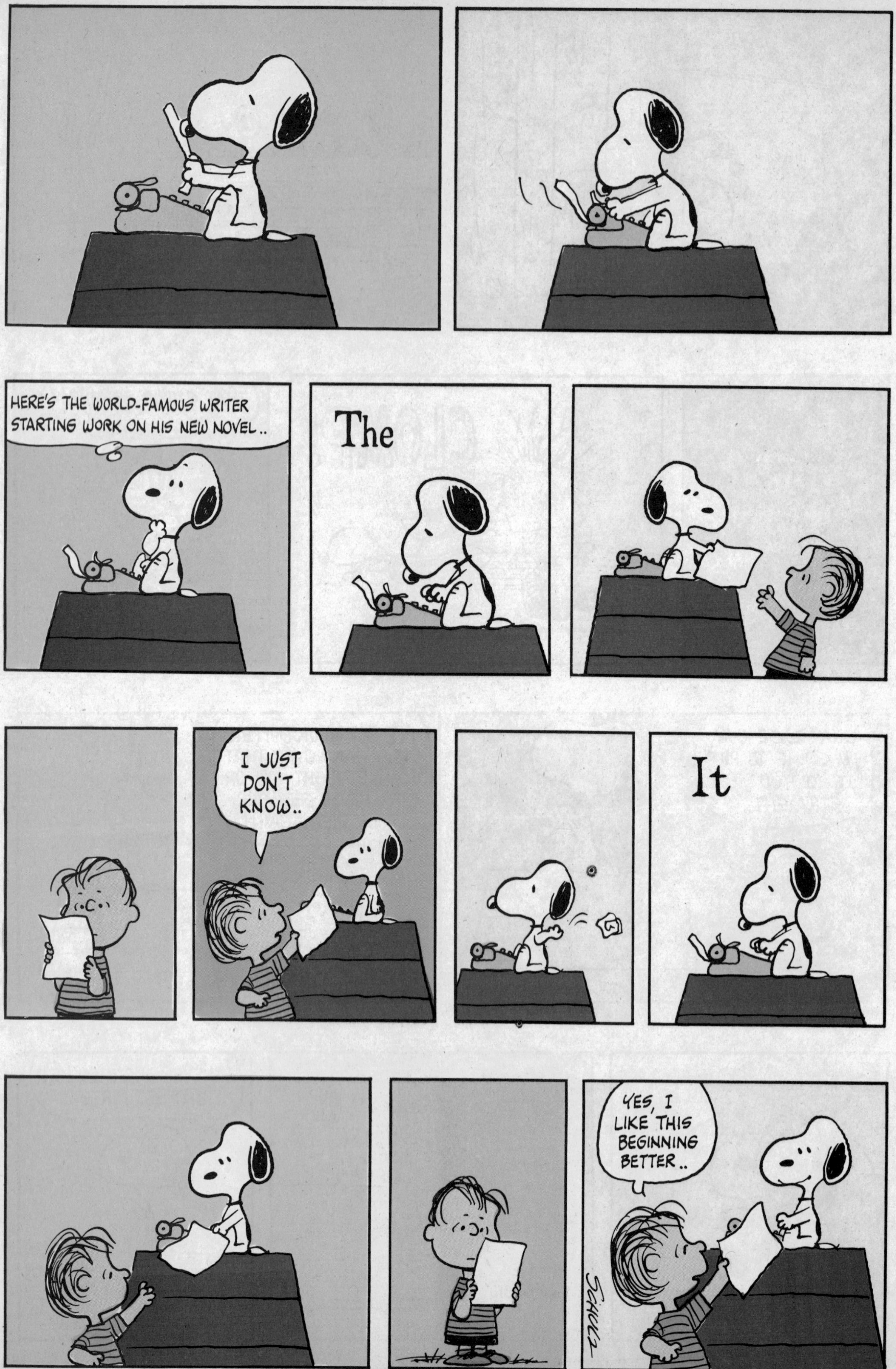

HERE'S THE WORLD-FAMOUS WRITER STARTING WORK ON HIS NEW NOVEL..
The
I JUST DON'T KNOW..
It
YES, I LIKE THIS BEGINNING BETTER..
SCHULZ

The
The Cabin. A short story
I DON'T UNDERSTAND YOU..
FIRST, YOU WERE GOING TO WRITE A NOVEL..
NOW, YOU'RE WORKING ON A SHORT STORY..
I DON'T UNDERSTAND WHY YOU STOPPED WRITING YOUR NOVEL TO WORK ON A SHORT STORY..
SCHULZ
I ONLY HAVE ONE SHEET OF PAPER!

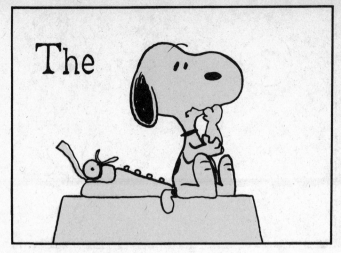

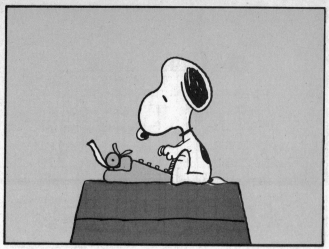

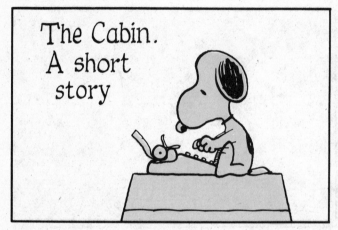

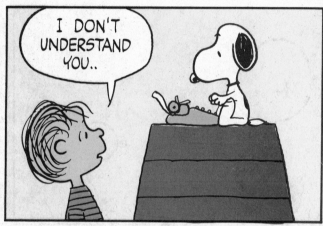

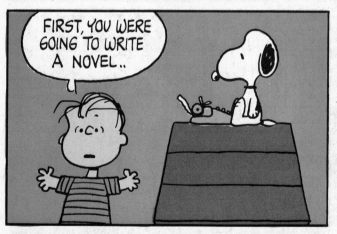

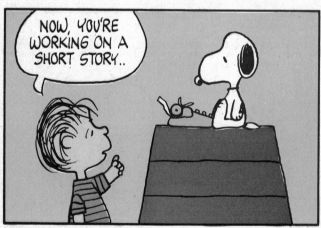

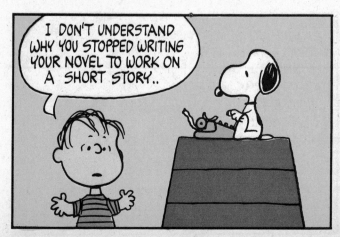

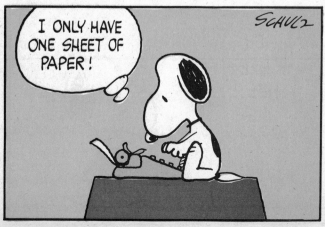

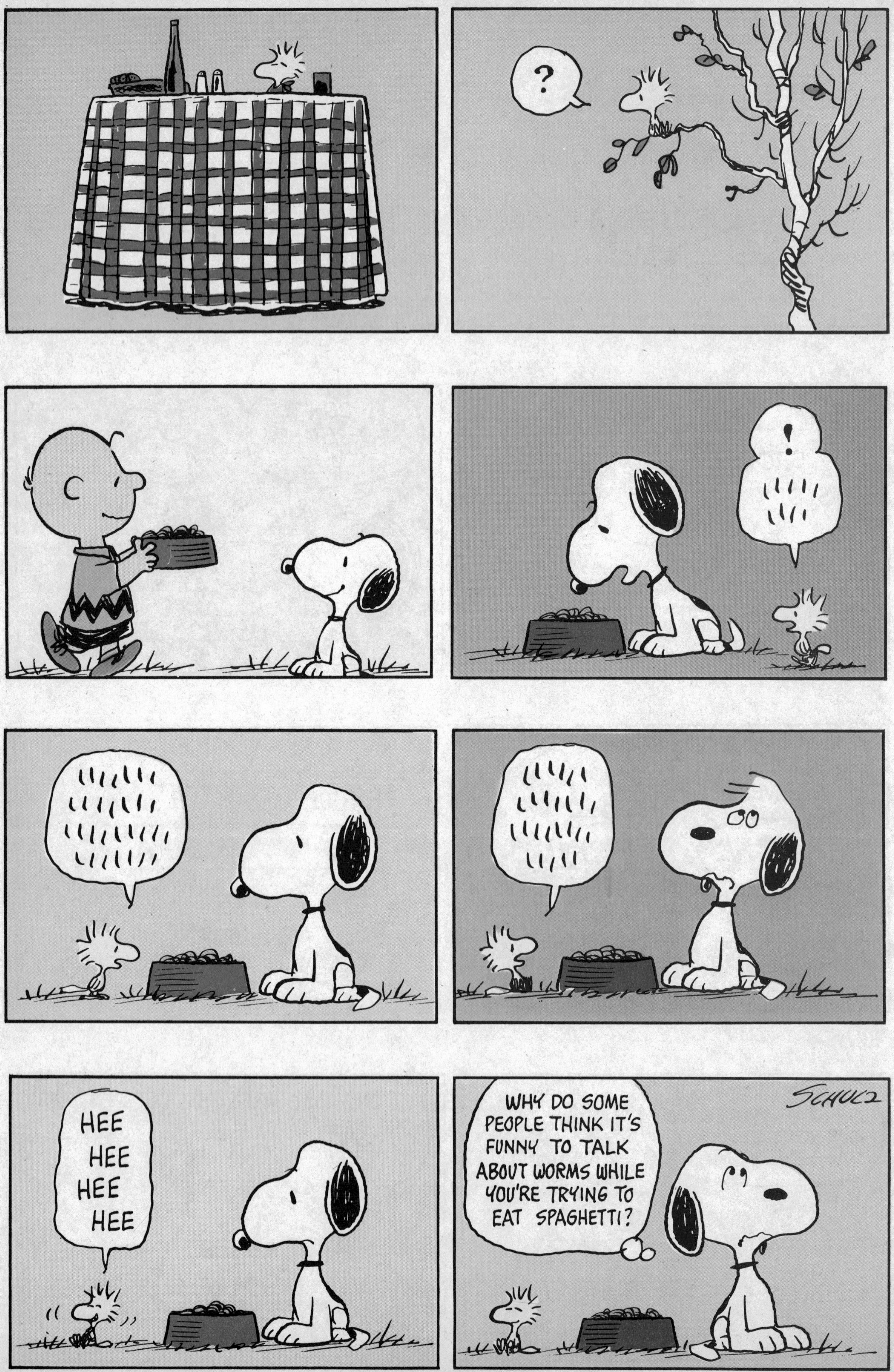
?
!
HEE
HEE
HEE
HEE
WHY DO SOME PEOPLE THINK IT'S FUNNY TO TALK ABOUT WORMS WHILE YOU'RE TRYING TO EAT SPAGHETTI?
SCHULZ

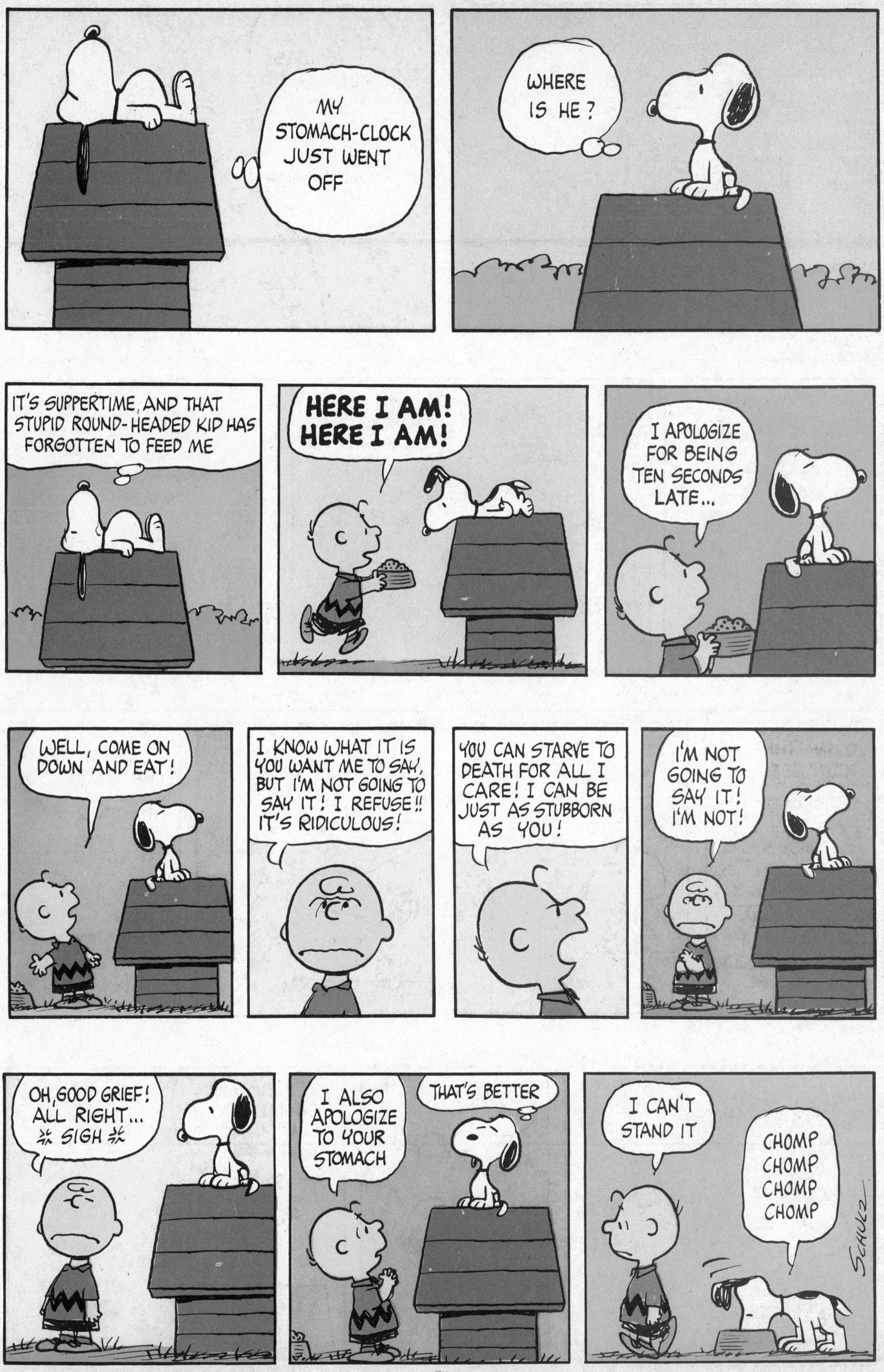
MY STOMACH-CLOCK JUST WENT OFF
WHERE IS HE?
IT'S SUPPERTIME, AND THAT STUPID ROUND-HEADED KID HAS FORGOTTEN TO FEED ME
HERE I AM! HERE I AM!
I APOLOGIZE FOR BEING TEN SECONDS LATE...
WELL, COME ON DOWN AND EAT!
I KNOW WHAT IT IS YOU WANT ME TO SAY, BUT I'M NOT GOING TO SAY IT! I REFUSE!! IT'S RIDICULOUS!
YOU CAN STARVE TO DEATH FOR ALL I CARE! I CAN BE JUST AS STUBBORN AS YOU!
I'M NOT GOING TO SAY IT! I'M NOT!
OH, GOOD GRIEF! ALL RIGHT... SIGH
I ALSO APOLOGIZE TO YOUR STOMACH
THAT'S BETTER
I CAN'T STAND IT
CHOMP CHOMP CHOMP CHOMP
SCHULZ

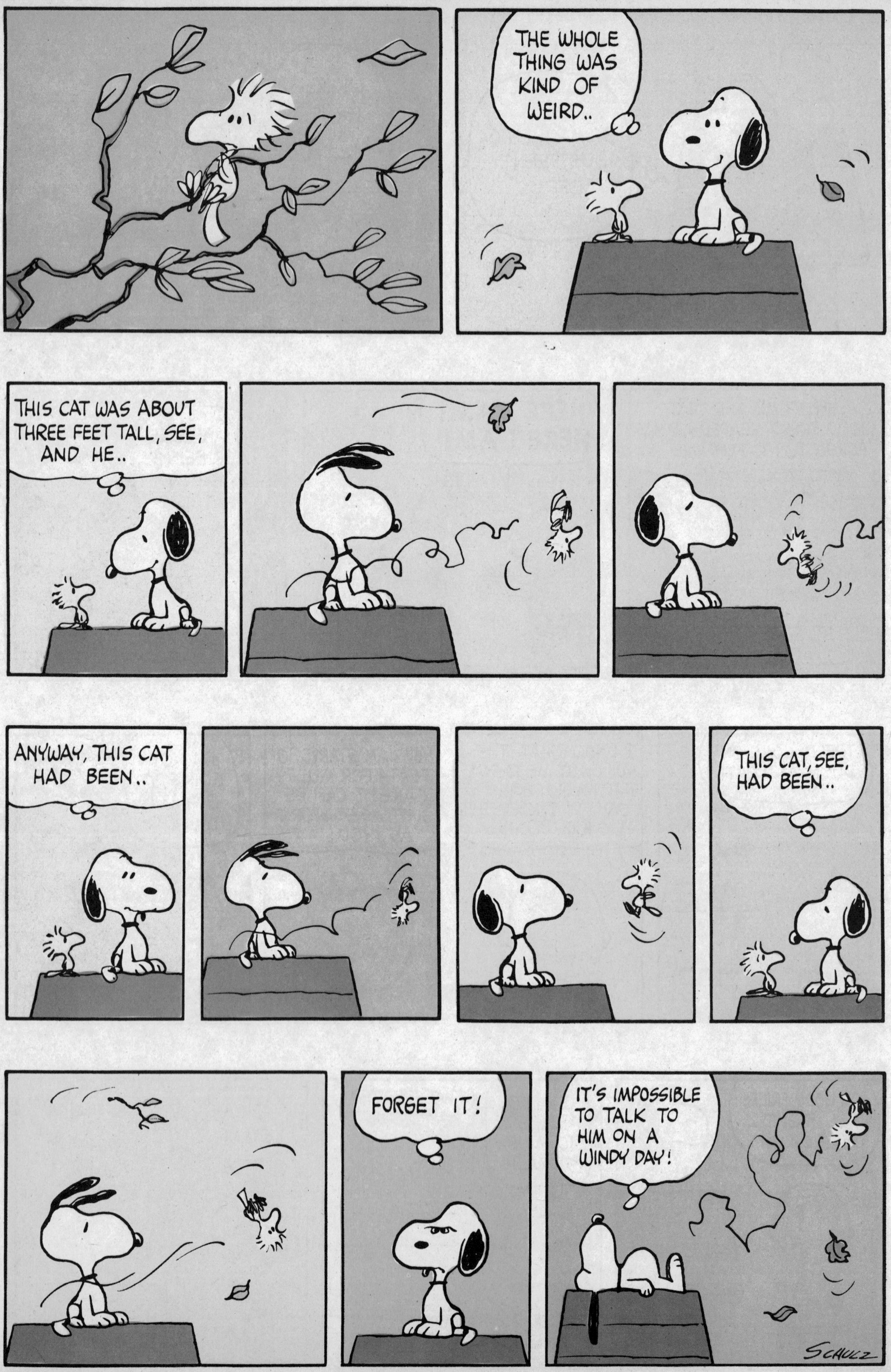
THE WHOLE THING WAS KIND OF WEIRD..
THIS CAT WAS ABOUT THREE FEET TALL, SEE, AND HE..
ANYWAY, THIS CAT HAD BEEN..
THIS CAT, SEE, HAD BEEN..
FORGET IT!
IT'S IMPOSSIBLE TO TALK TO HIM ON A WINDY DAY!
SCHULZ

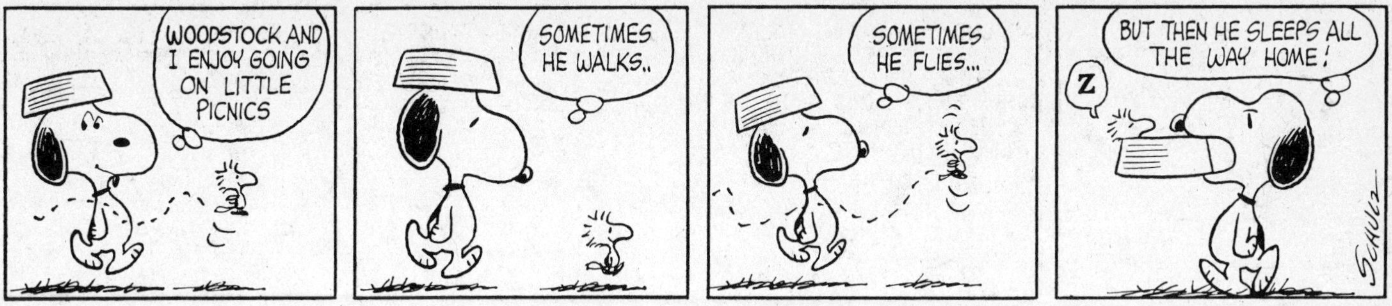
WOODSTOCK AND I ENJOY GOING ON LITTLE PICNICS
SOMETIMES HE WALKS..
SOMETIMES HE FLIES...
Z
BUT THEN HE SLEEPS ALL THE WAY HOME!
SCHULZ

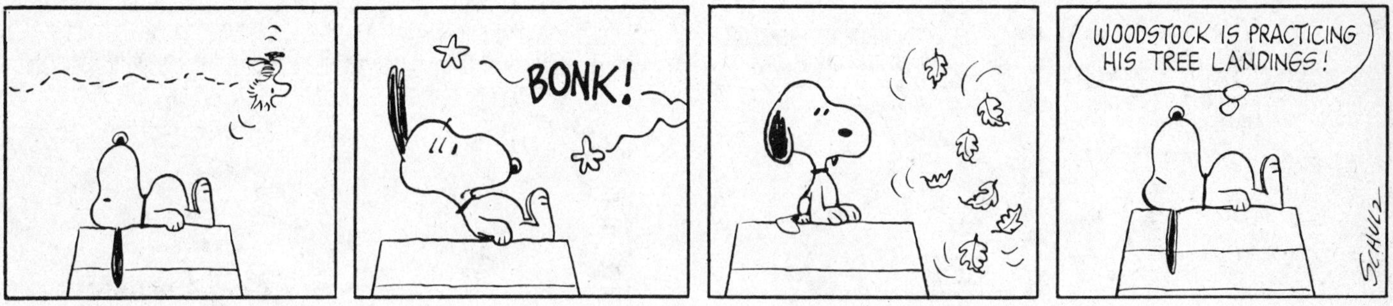
BONK!
WOODSTOCK IS PRACTICING HIS TREE LANDINGS!
SCHULZ

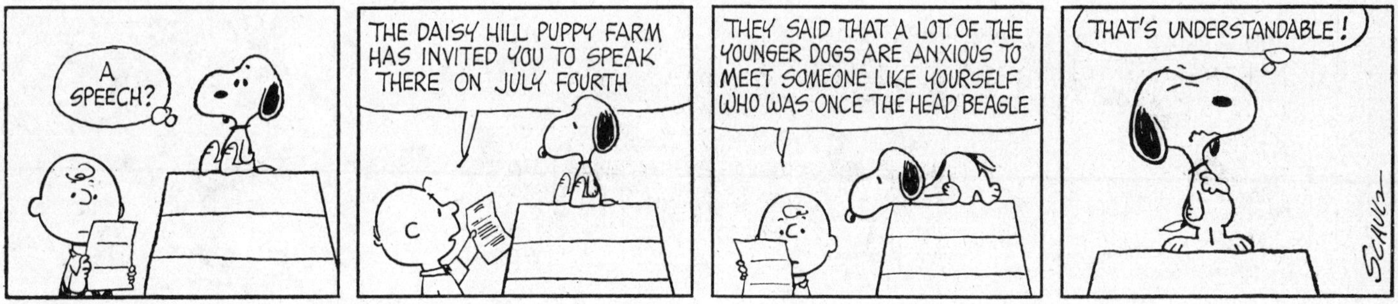
A SPEECH?
THE DAISY HILL PUPPY FARM HAS INVITED YOU TO SPEAK THERE ON JULY FOURTH
THEY SAID THAT A LOT OF THE YOUNGER DOGS ARE ANXIOUS TO MEET SOMEONE LIKE YOURSELF WHO WAS ONCE THE HEAD BEAGLE
THAT'S UNDERSTANDABLE!
SCHULZ

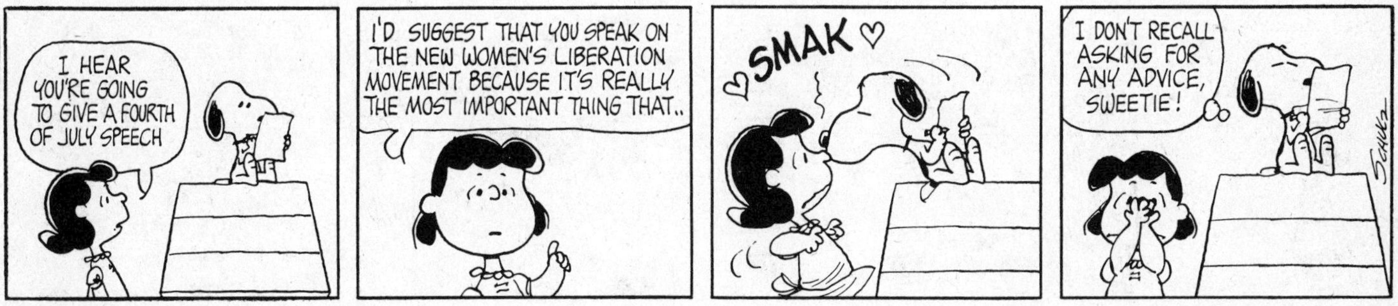
I HEAR YOU'RE GOING TO GIVE A FOURTH OF JULY SPEECH
I'D SUGGEST THAT YOU SPEAK ON THE NEW WOMEN'S LIBERATION MOVEMENT BECAUSE IT'S REALLY THE MOST IMPORTANT THING THAT..
SMAK
I DON'T RECALL ASKING FOR ANY ADVICE, SWEETIE!
SCHULZ

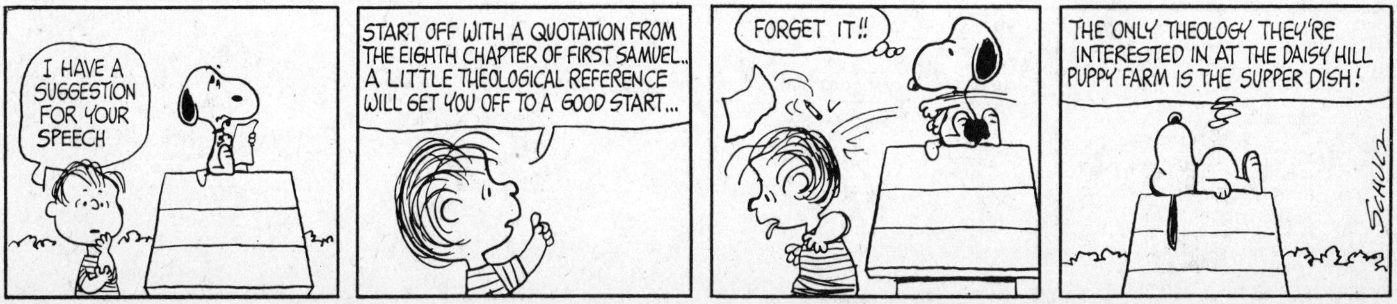
I HAVE A SUGGESTION FOR YOUR SPEECH
START OFF WITH A QUOTATION FROM THE EIGHTH CHAPTER OF FIRST SAMUEL.. A LITTLE THEOLOGICAL REFERENCE WILL GET YOU OFF TO A GOOD START...
FORGET IT!!
THE ONLY THEOLOGY THEY'RE INTERESTED IN AT THE DAISY HILL PUPPY FARM IS THE SUPPER DISH!
SCHULZ

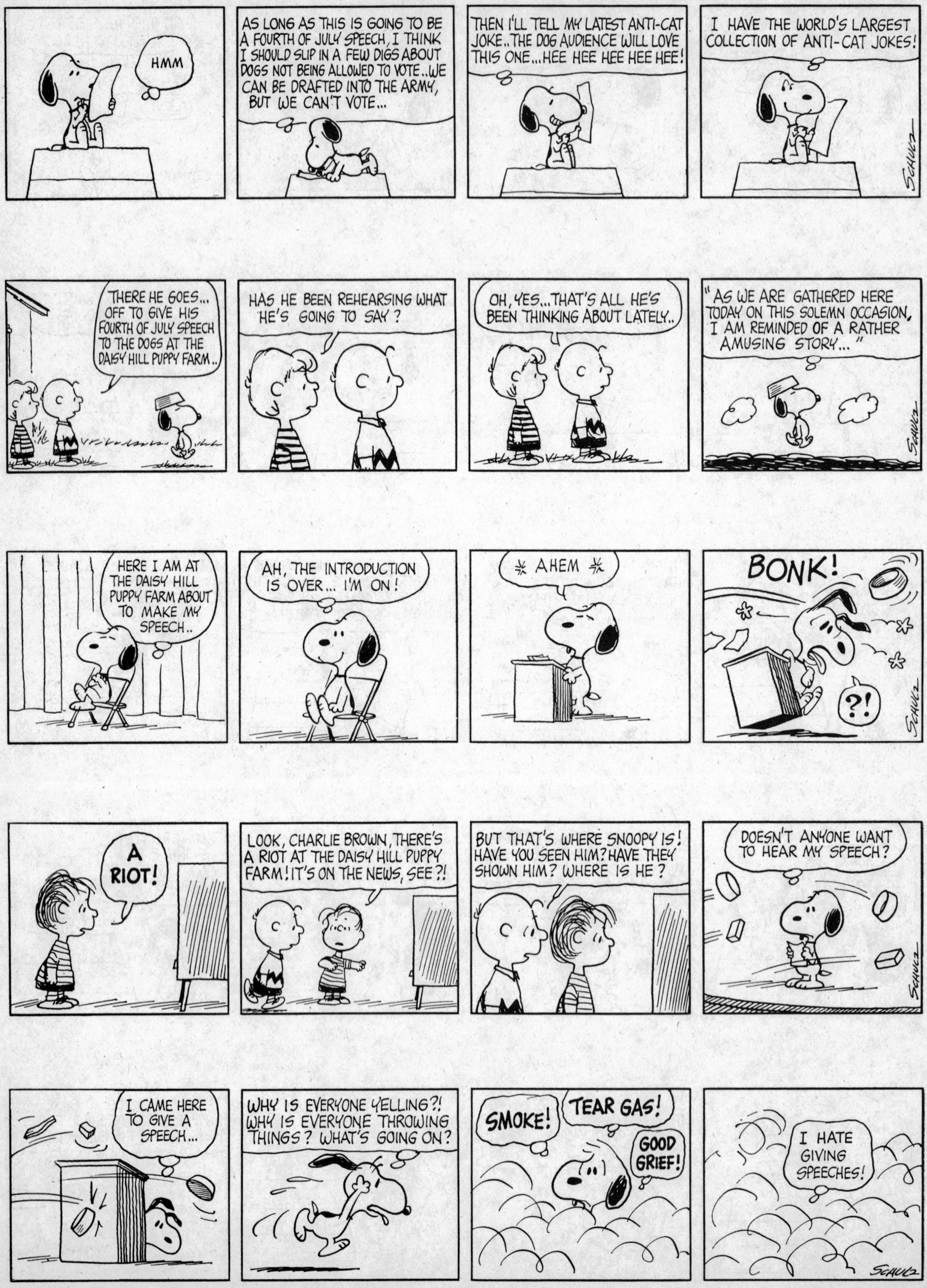
HMM
AS LONG AS THIS IS GOING TO BE A FOURTH OF JULY SPEECH, I THINK I SHOULD SLIP IN A FEW DIGS ABOUT DOGS NOT BEING ALLOWED TO VOTE..WE CAN BE DRAFTED INTO THE ARMY, BUT WE CAN'T VOTE...
THEN I'LL TELL MY LATEST ANTI-CAT JOKE..THE DOG AUDIENCE WILL LOVE THIS ONE...HEE HEE HEE HEE HEE!
I HAVE THE WORLD'S LARGEST COLLECTION OF ANTI-CAT JOKES!
THERE HE GOES... OFF TO GIVE HIS FOURTH OF JULY SPEECH TO THE DOGS AT THE DAISY HILL PUPPY FARM..
HAS HE BEEN REHEARSING WHAT HE'S GOING TO SAY?
OH, YES...THAT'S ALL HE'S BEEN THINKING ABOUT LATELY..
"AS WE ARE GATHERED HERE TODAY ON THIS SOLEMN OCCASION, I AM REMINDED OF A RATHER AMUSING STORY..."
HERE I AM AT THE DAISY HILL PUPPY FARM ABOUT TO MAKE MY SPEECH..
AH, THE INTRODUCTION IS OVER... I'M ON!
AHEM
BONK!
?!
A RIOT!
LOOK, CHARLIE BROWN, THERE'S A RIOT AT THE DAISY HILL PUPPY FARM! IT'S ON THE NEWS, SEE?!
BUT THAT'S WHERE SNOOPY IS! HAVE YOU SEEN HIM? HAVE THEY SHOWN HIM? WHERE IS HE?
DOESN'T ANYONE WANT TO HEAR MY SPEECH?
I CAME HERE TO GIVE A SPEECH...
WHY IS EVERYONE YELLING?! WHY IS EVERYONE THROWING THINGS? WHAT'S GOING ON?
SMOKE!
TEAR GAS!
GOOD GRIEF!
I HATE GIVING SPEECHES!
SCHULZ

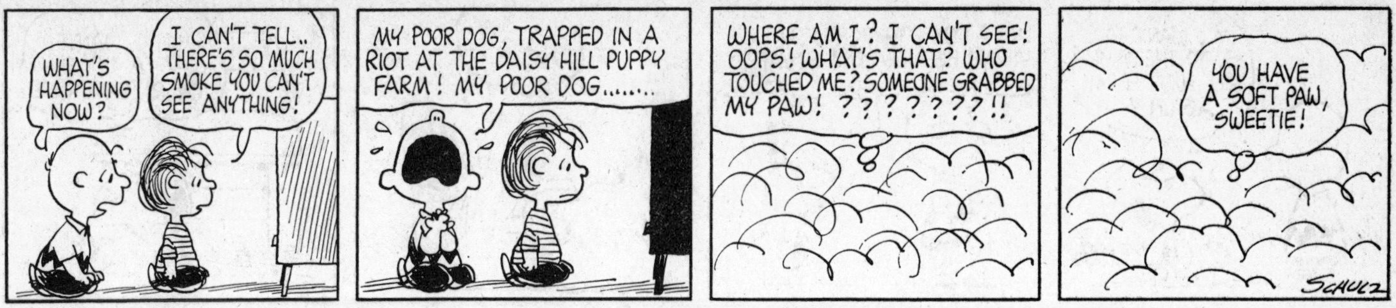
WHAT'S HAPPENING NOW?
I CAN'T TELL.. THERE'S SO MUCH SMOKE YOU CAN'T SEE ANYTHING!
MY POOR DOG, TRAPPED IN A RIOT AT THE DAISY HILL PUPPY FARM! MY POOR DOG.......
WHERE AM I? I CAN'T SEE! OOPS! WHAT'S THAT? WHO TOUCHED ME? SOMEONE GRABBED MY PAW! ????????!!
YOU HAVE A SOFT PAW, SWEETIE!
SCHULZ

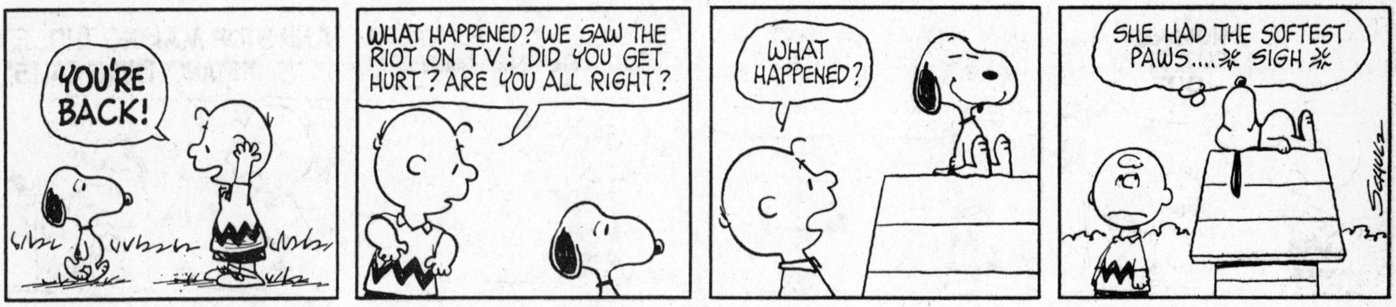
YOU'RE BACK!
WHAT HAPPENED? WE SAW THE RIOT ON TV! DID YOU GET HURT? ARE YOU ALL RIGHT?
WHAT HAPPENED?
SHE HAD THE SOFTEST PAWS.... ✻ SIGH ✻
SCHULZ

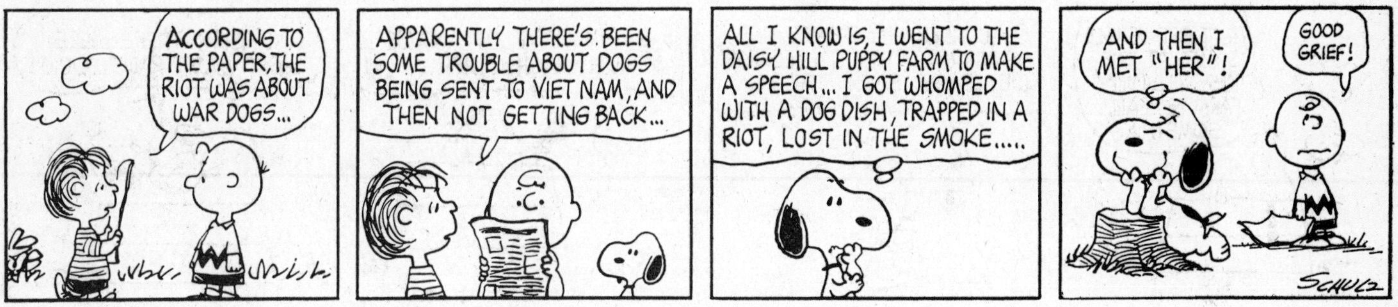
ACCORDING TO THE PAPER, THE RIOT WAS ABOUT WAR DOGS...
APPARENTLY THERE'S BEEN SOME TROUBLE ABOUT DOGS BEING SENT TO VIET NAM, AND THEN NOT GETTING BACK...
ALL I KNOW IS, I WENT TO THE DAISY HILL PUPPY FARM TO MAKE A SPEECH... I GOT WHOMPED WITH A DOG DISH, TRAPPED IN A RIOT, LOST IN THE SMOKE.....
AND THEN I MET "HER"!
GOOD GRIEF!
SCHULZ

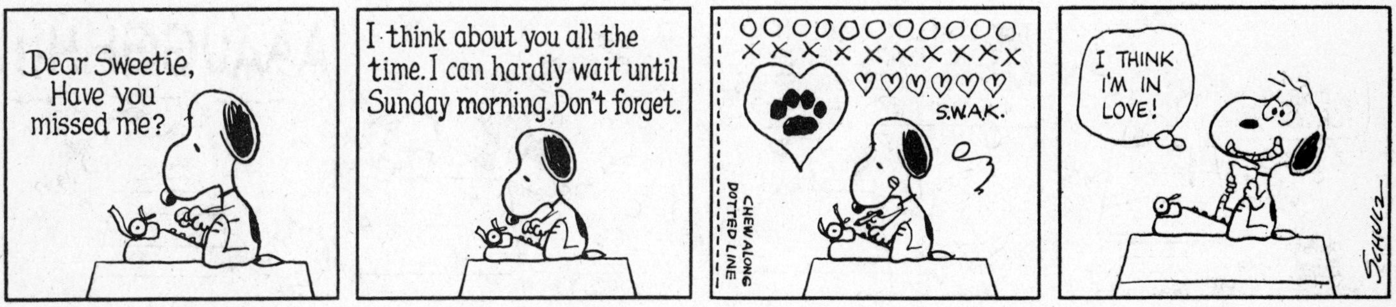
Dear Sweetie,
Have you missed me?
I think about you all the time. I can hardly wait until Sunday morning. Don't forget.
OOOOOOOOOOO
XXXXXXXXXXX
♡♡♡♡♡♡♡
S.W.A.K.
CHEW ALONG DOTTED LINE
I THINK I'M IN LOVE!
SCHULZ

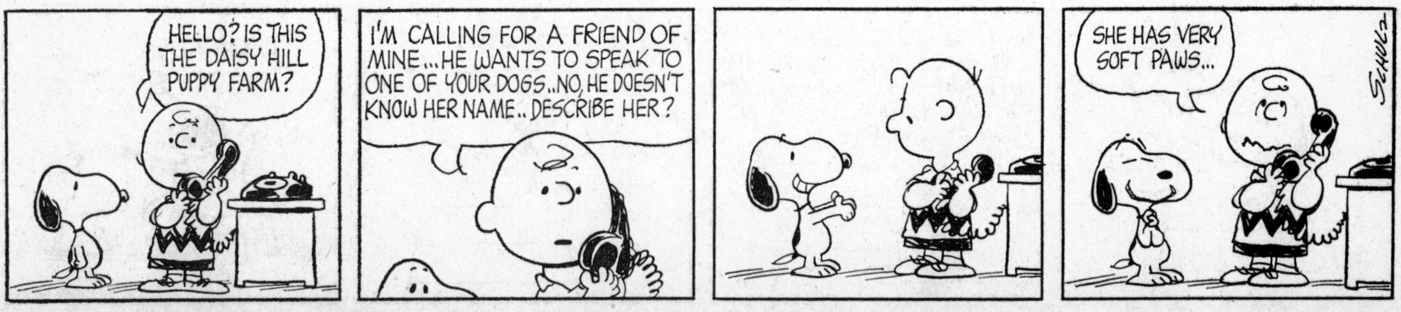
HELLO? IS THIS THE DAISY HILL PUPPY FARM?
I'M CALLING FOR A FRIEND OF MINE... HE WANTS TO SPEAK TO ONE OF YOUR DOGS.. NO, HE DOESN'T KNOW HER NAME.. DESCRIBE HER?
SHE HAS VERY SOFT PAWS...
SCHULZ

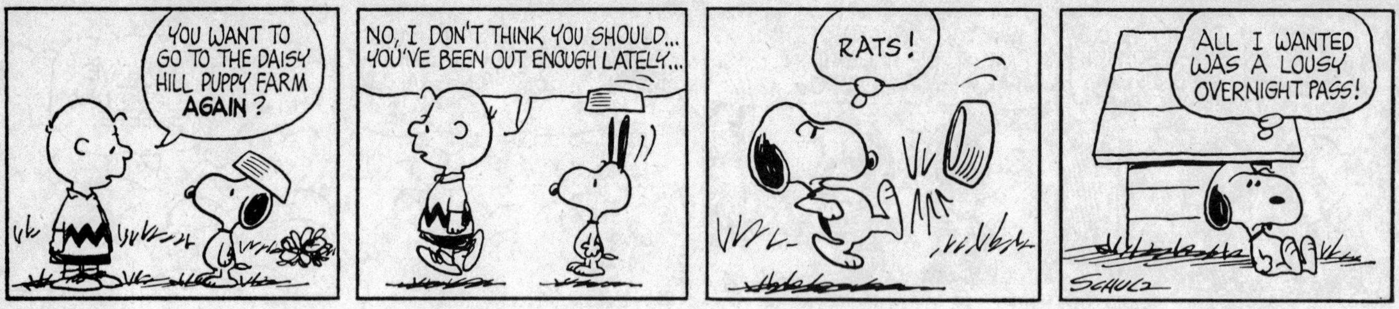
YOU WANT TO GO TO THE DAISY HILL PUPPY FARM AGAIN?
NO, I DON'T THINK YOU SHOULD... YOU'VE BEEN OUT ENOUGH LATELY...
RATS!
ALL I WANTED WAS A LOUSY OVERNIGHT PASS!
SCHULZ

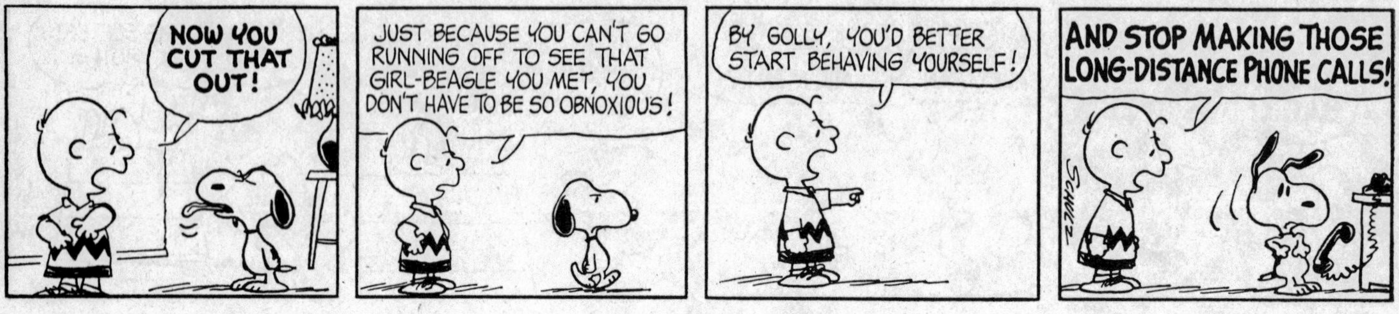
NOW YOU CUT THAT OUT!
JUST BECAUSE YOU CAN'T GO RUNNING OFF TO SEE THAT GIRL-BEAGLE YOU MET, YOU DON'T HAVE TO BE SO OBNOXIOUS!
BY GOLLY, YOU'D BETTER START BEHAVING YOURSELF!
AND STOP MAKING THOSE LONG-DISTANCE PHONE CALLS!
SCHULZ

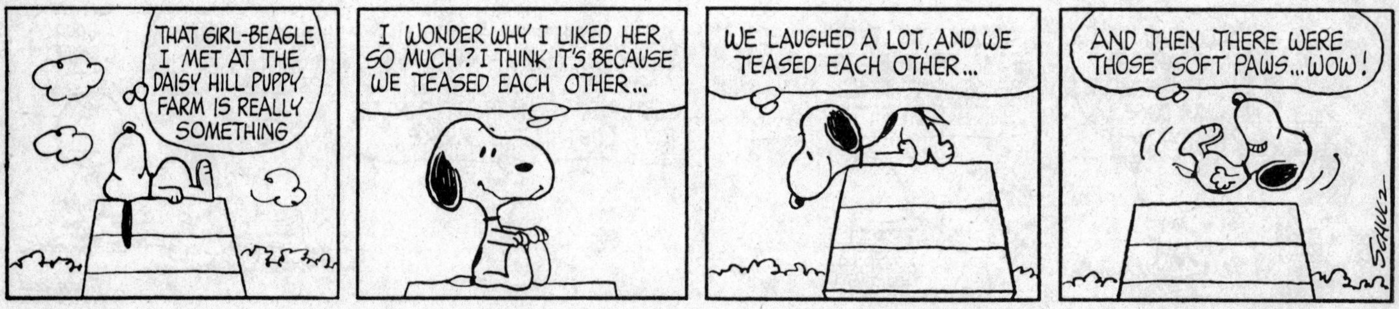
THAT GIRL-BEAGLE I MET AT THE DAISY HILL PUPPY FARM IS REALLY SOMETHING
I WONDER WHY I LIKED HER SO MUCH? I THINK IT'S BECAUSE WE TEASED EACH OTHER...
WE LAUGHED A LOT, AND WE TEASED EACH OTHER...
AND THEN THERE WERE THOSE SOFT PAWS... WOW!
SCHULZ

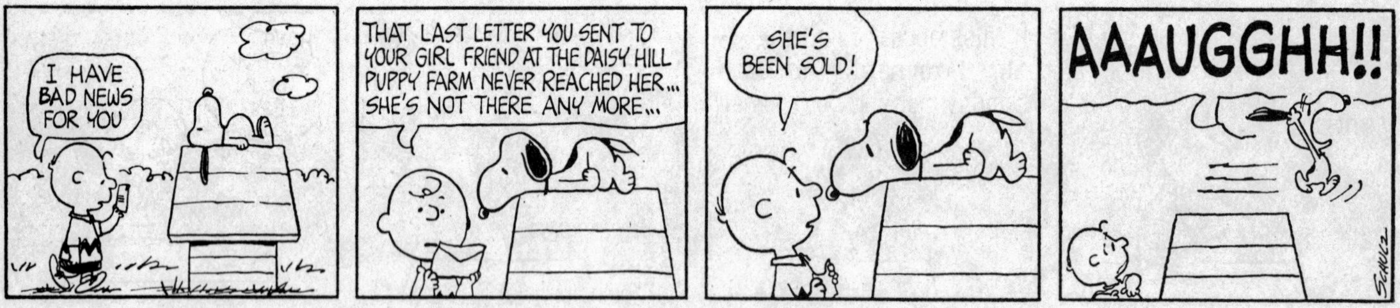
I HAVE BAD NEWS FOR YOU
THAT LAST LETTER YOU SENT TO YOUR GIRL FRIEND AT THE DAISY HILL PUPPY FARM NEVER REACHED HER... SHE'S NOT THERE ANY MORE...
SHE'S BEEN SOLD!
AAAUGGHH!!
SCHULZ

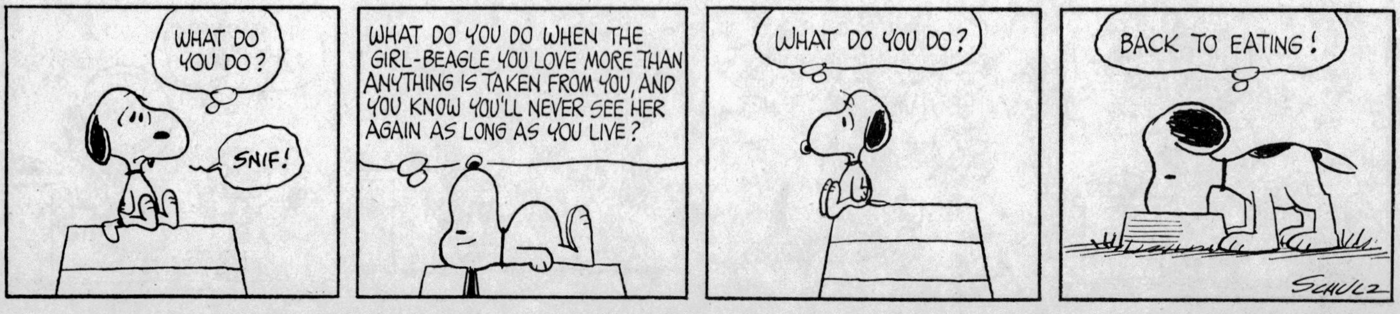
WHAT DO YOU DO?
SNIF!
WHAT DO YOU DO WHEN THE GIRL-BEAGLE YOU LOVE MORE THAN ANYTHING IS TAKEN FROM YOU, AND YOU KNOW YOU'LL NEVER SEE HER AGAIN AS LONG AS YOU LIVE?
WHAT DO YOU DO?
BACK TO EATING!
SCHULZ

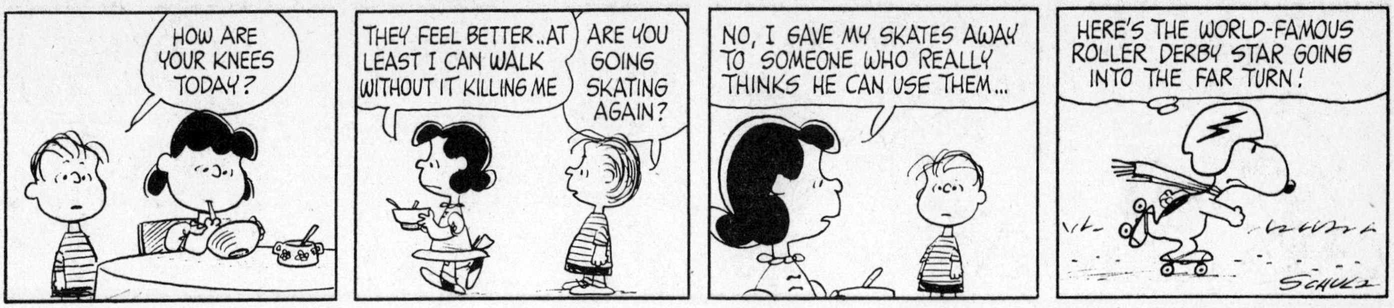
HOW ARE YOUR KNEES TODAY?
THEY FEEL BETTER..AT LEAST I CAN WALK WITHOUT IT KILLING ME
ARE YOU GOING SKATING AGAIN?
NO, I GAVE MY SKATES AWAY TO SOMEONE WHO REALLY THINKS HE CAN USE THEM...
HERE'S THE WORLD-FAMOUS ROLLER DERBY STAR GOING INTO THE FAR TURN!
SCHULZ

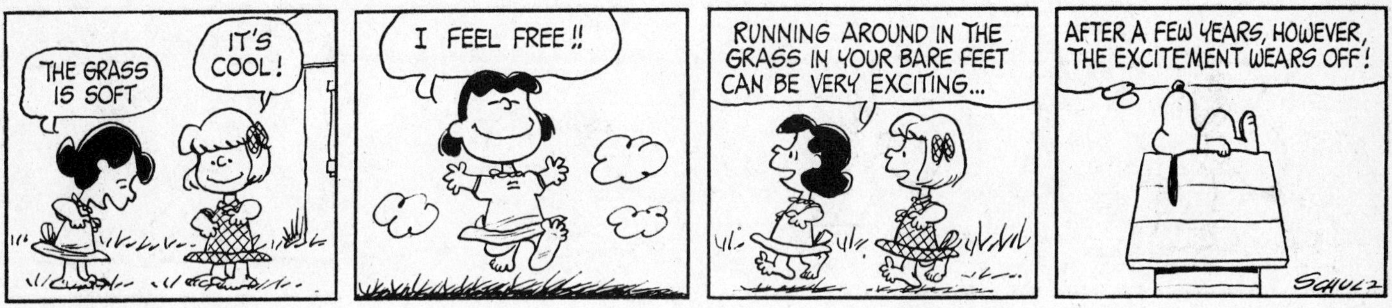
THE GRASS IS SOFT
IT'S COOL!
I FEEL FREE!!
RUNNING AROUND IN THE GRASS IN YOUR BARE FEET CAN BE VERY EXCITING...
AFTER A FEW YEARS, HOWEVER, THE EXCITEMENT WEARS OFF!
SCHULZ

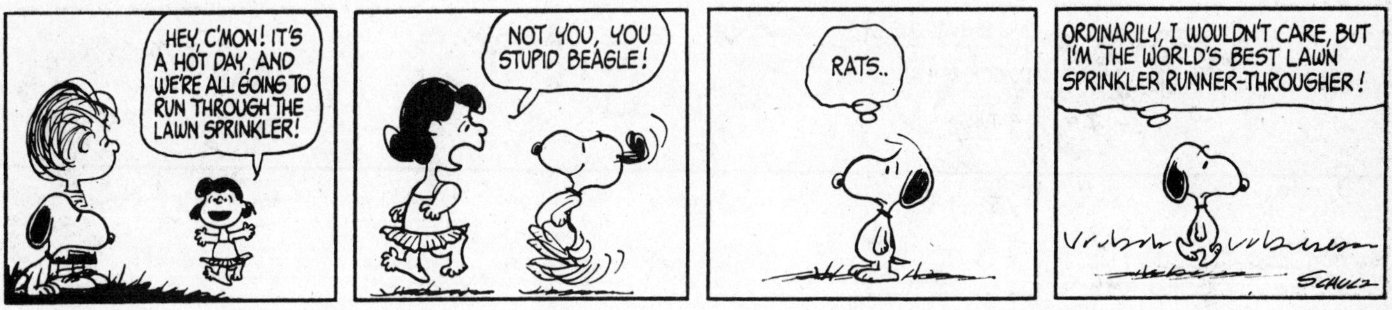
HEY, C'MON! IT'S A HOT DAY, AND WE'RE ALL GOING TO RUN THROUGH THE LAWN SPRINKLER!
NOT YOU, YOU STUPID BEAGLE!
RATS..
ORDINARILY, I WOULDN'T CARE, BUT I'M THE WORLD'S BEST LAWN SPRINKLER RUNNER-THROUGHER!
SCHULZ

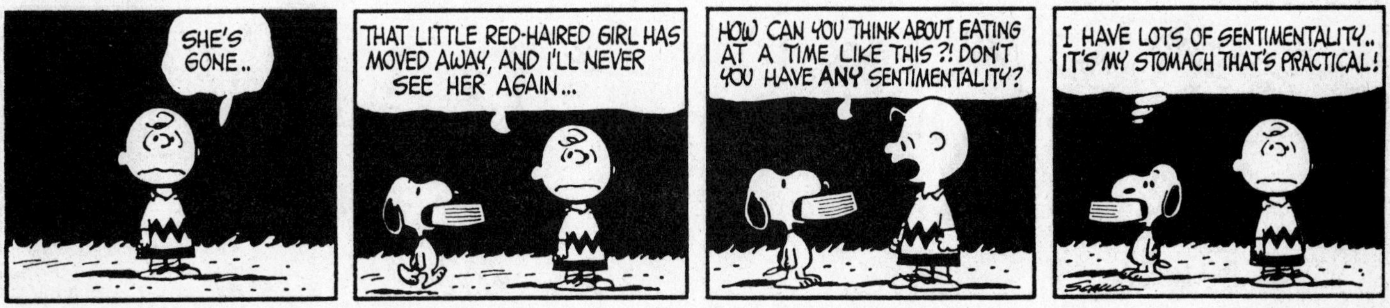
SHE'S GONE..
THAT LITTLE RED-HAIRED GIRL HAS MOVED AWAY, AND I'LL NEVER SEE HER AGAIN...
HOW CAN YOU THINK ABOUT EATING AT A TIME LIKE THIS?! DON'T YOU HAVE ANY SENTIMENTALITY?
I HAVE LOTS OF SENTIMENTALITY.. IT'S MY STOMACH THAT'S PRACTICAL!
SCHULZ

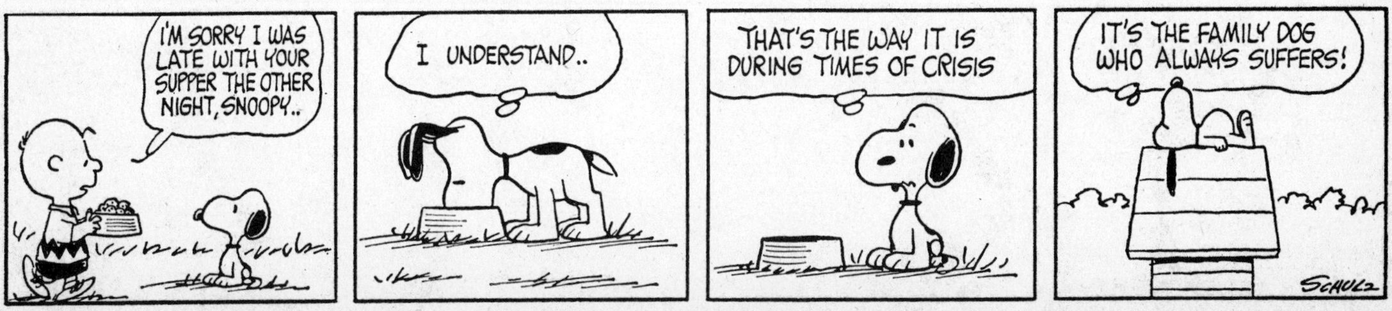
I'M SORRY I WAS LATE WITH YOUR SUPPER THE OTHER NIGHT, SNOOPY..
I UNDERSTAND..
THAT'S THE WAY IT IS DURING TIMES OF CRISIS
IT'S THE FAMILY DOG WHO ALWAYS SUFFERS!
SCHULZ

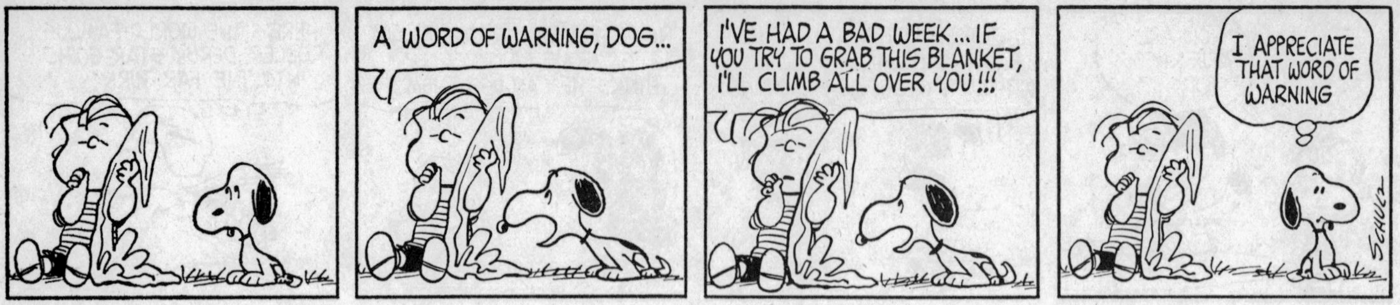
A WORD OF WARNING, DOG...
I'VE HAD A BAD WEEK... IF YOU TRY TO GRAB THIS BLANKET, I'LL CLIMB ALL OVER YOU!!!
I APPRECIATE THAT WORD OF WARNING
SCHULZ

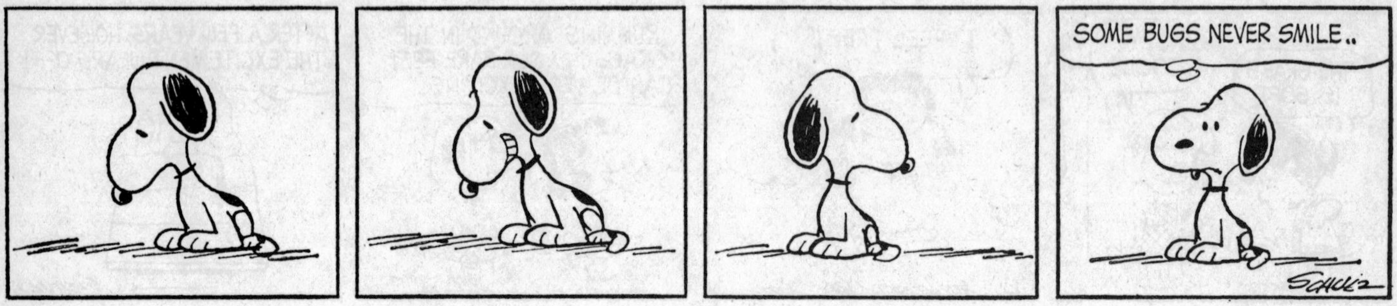
SOME BUGS NEVER SMILE..
SCHULZ

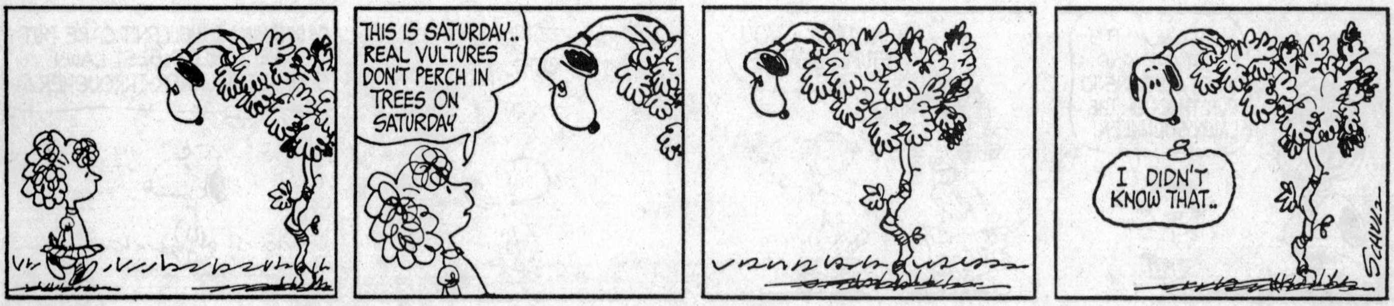
THIS IS SATURDAY.. REAL VULTURES DON'T PERCH IN TREES ON SATURDAY
I DIDN'T KNOW THAT..
SCHULZ

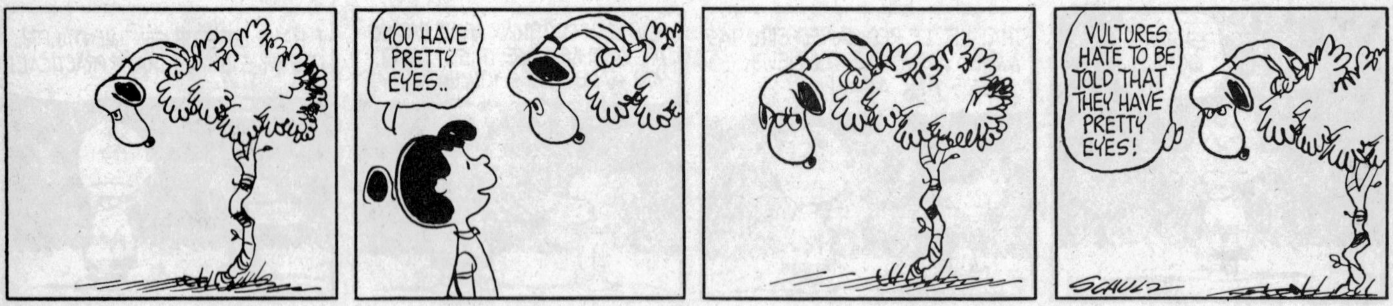
YOU HAVE PRETTY EYES..
VULTURES HATE TO BE TOLD THAT THEY HAVE PRETTY EYES!
SCHULZ

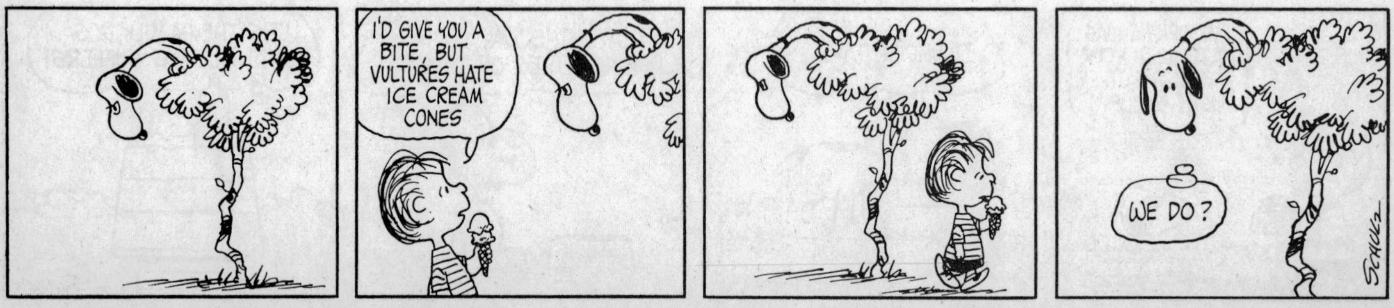
I'D GIVE YOU A BITE, BUT VULTURES HATE ICE CREAM CONES
WE DO?
SCHULZ

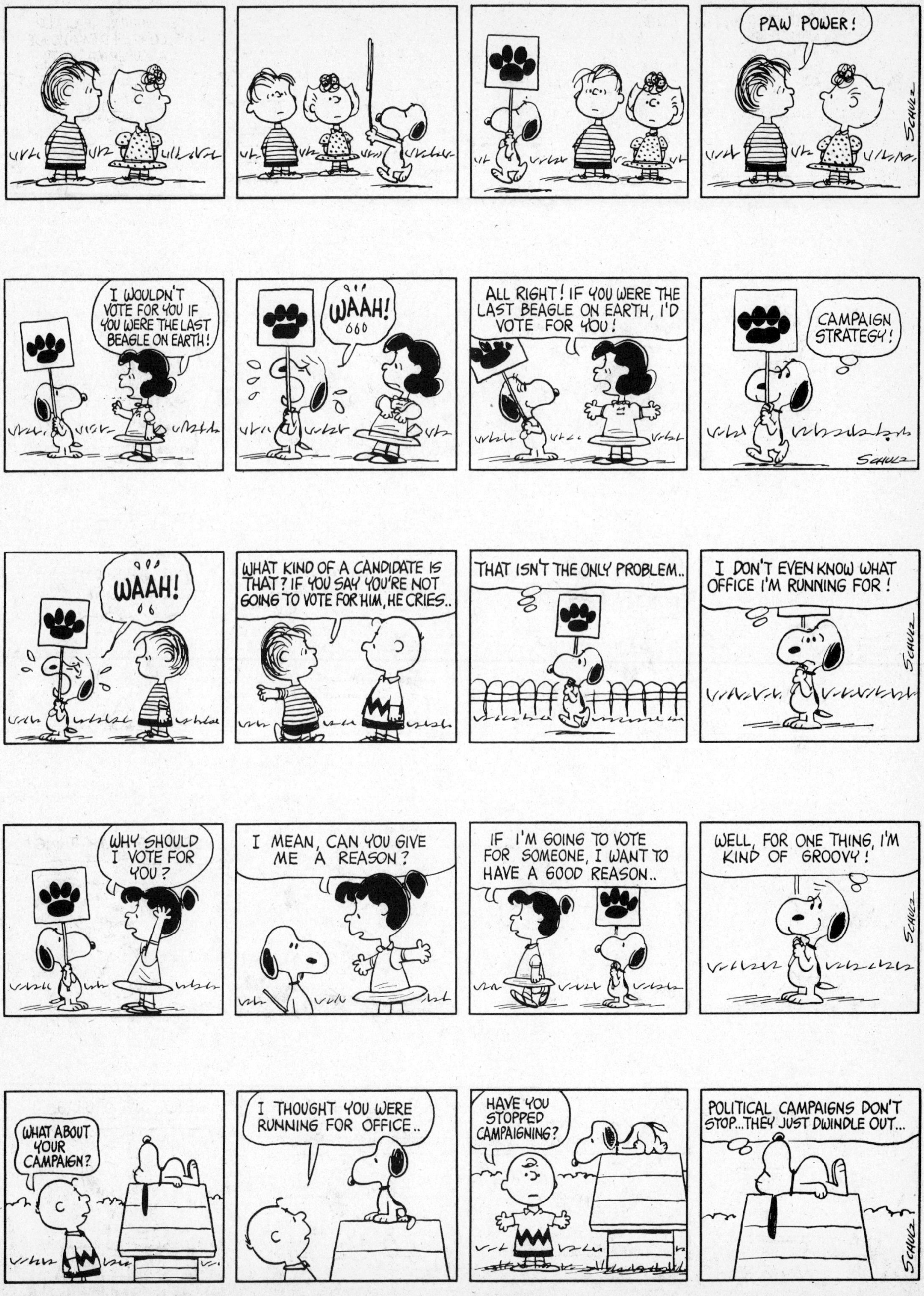
PAW POWER!
SCHULZ
I WOULDN'T VOTE FOR YOU IF YOU WERE THE LAST BEAGLE ON EARTH!
WAAH!
ALL RIGHT! IF YOU WERE THE LAST BEAGLE ON EARTH, I'D VOTE FOR YOU!
CAMPAIGN STRATEGY!
SCHULZ
WAAH!
WHAT KIND OF A CANDIDATE IS THAT? IF YOU SAY YOU'RE NOT GOING TO VOTE FOR HIM, HE CRIES..
THAT ISN'T THE ONLY PROBLEM..
I DON'T EVEN KNOW WHAT OFFICE I'M RUNNING FOR!
SCHULZ
WHY SHOULD I VOTE FOR YOU?
I MEAN, CAN YOU GIVE ME A REASON?
IF I'M GOING TO VOTE FOR SOMEONE, I WANT TO HAVE A GOOD REASON..
WELL, FOR ONE THING, I'M KIND OF GROOVY!
SCHULZ
WHAT ABOUT YOUR CAMPAIGN?
I THOUGHT YOU WERE RUNNING FOR OFFICE..
HAVE YOU STOPPED CAMPAIGNING?
POLITICAL CAMPAIGNS DON'T STOP...THEY JUST DWINDLE OUT...
SCHULZ

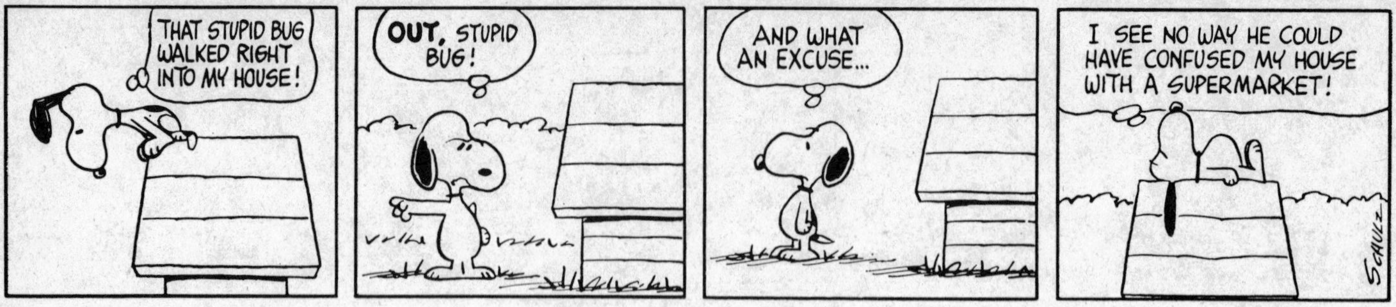
THAT STUPID BUG WALKED RIGHT INTO MY HOUSE!
OUT, STUPID BUG!
AND WHAT AN EXCUSE...
I SEE NO WAY HE COULD HAVE CONFUSED MY HOUSE WITH A SUPERMARKET!
SCHULZ

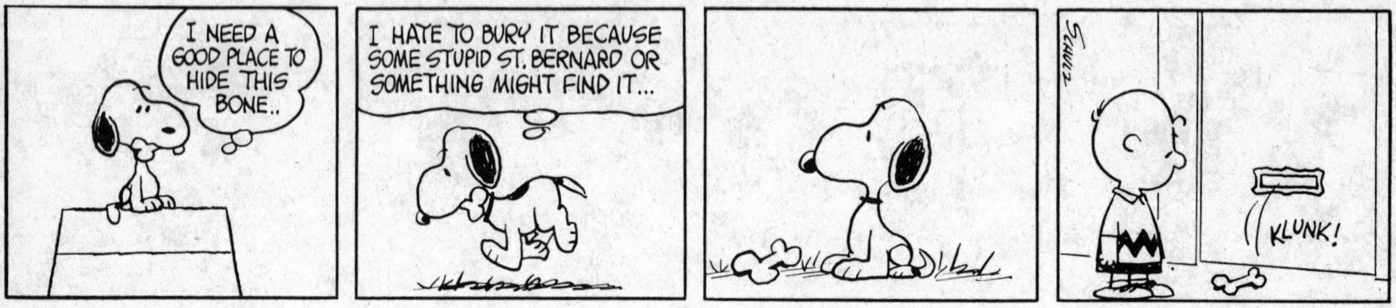
I NEED A GOOD PLACE TO HIDE THIS BONE..
I HATE TO BURY IT BECAUSE SOME STUPID ST. BERNARD OR SOMETHING MIGHT FIND IT...
SCHULZ
KLUNK!

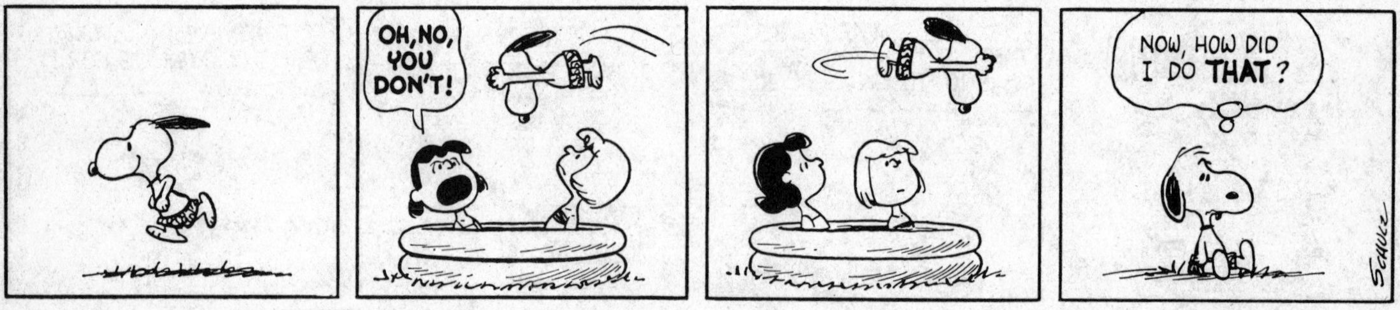
OH, NO, YOU DON'T!
NOW, HOW DID I DO THAT?
SCHULZ

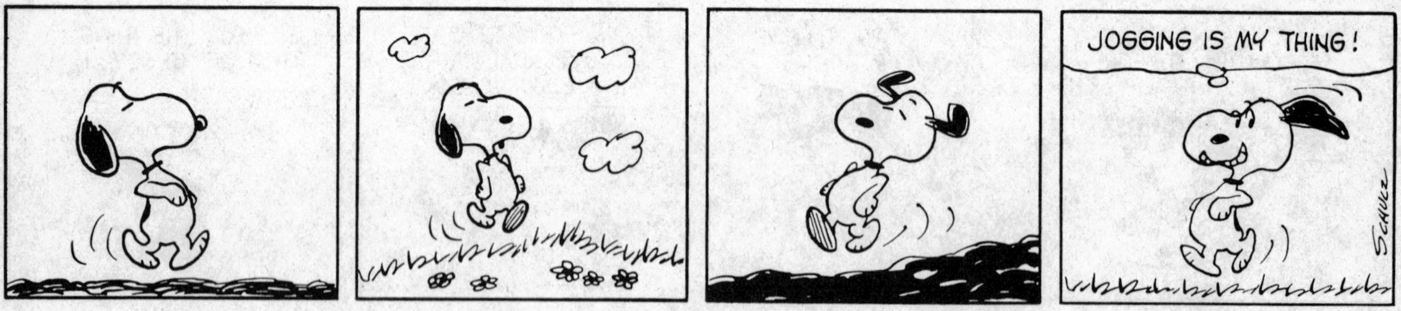
JOGGING IS MY THING!
SCHULZ

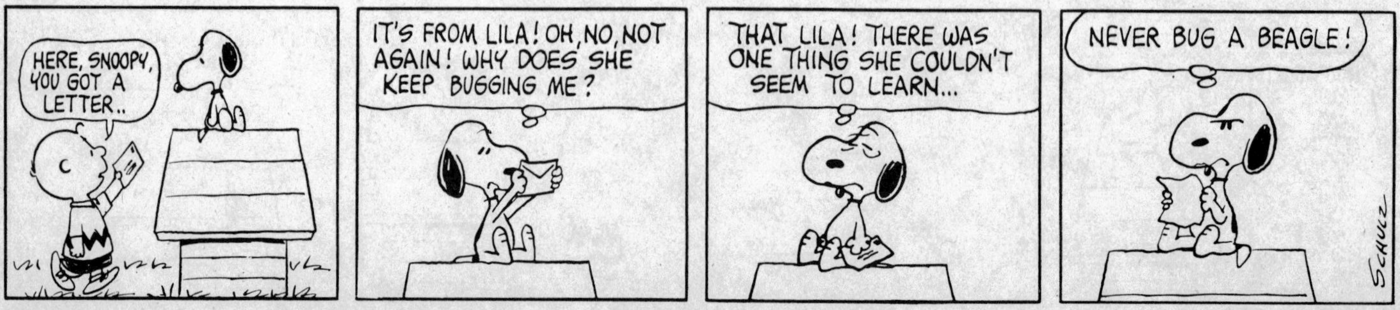
HERE, SNOOPY, YOU GOT A LETTER..
IT'S FROM LILA! OH, NO, NOT AGAIN! WHY DOES SHE KEEP BUGGING ME?
THAT LILA! THERE WAS ONE THING SHE COULDN'T SEEM TO LEARN...
NEVER BUG A BEAGLE!
SCHULZ

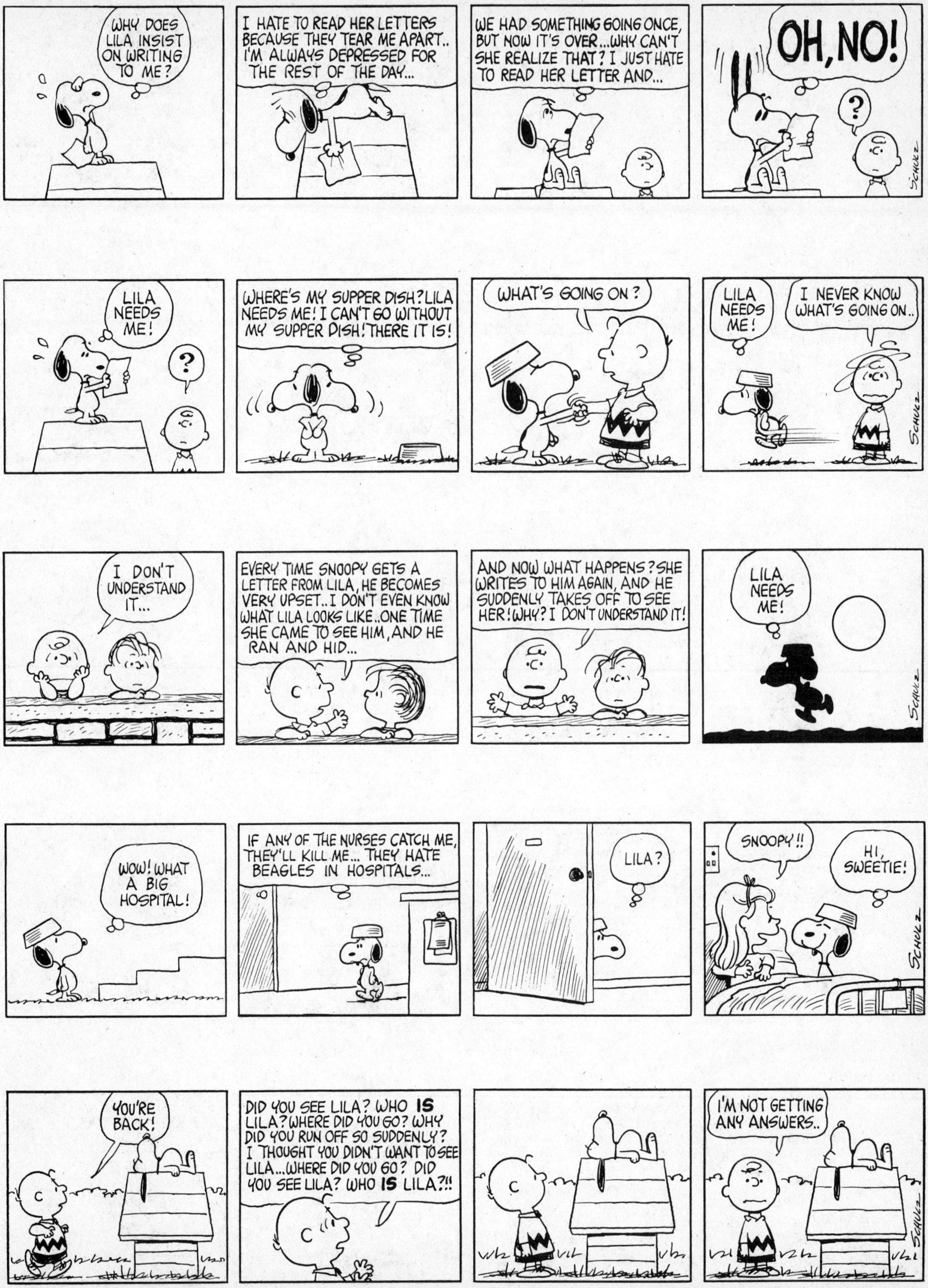
WHY DOES LILA INSIST ON WRITING TO ME?
I HATE TO READ HER LETTERS BECAUSE THEY TEAR ME APART.. I'M ALWAYS DEPRESSED FOR THE REST OF THE DAY...
WE HAD SOMETHING GOING ONCE, BUT NOW IT'S OVER...WHY CAN'T SHE REALIZE THAT? I JUST HATE TO READ HER LETTER AND...
OH, NO!
?
SCHULZ
LILA NEEDS ME!
?
WHERE'S MY SUPPER DISH? LILA NEEDS ME! I CAN'T GO WITHOUT MY SUPPER DISH! THERE IT IS!
WHAT'S GOING ON?
LILA NEEDS ME!
I NEVER KNOW WHAT'S GOING ON..
SCHULZ
I DON'T UNDERSTAND IT...
EVERY TIME SNOOPY GETS A LETTER FROM LILA, HE BECOMES VERY UPSET.. I DON'T EVEN KNOW WHAT LILA LOOKS LIKE..ONE TIME SHE CAME TO SEE HIM, AND HE RAN AND HID...
AND NOW WHAT HAPPENS? SHE WRITES TO HIM AGAIN, AND HE SUDDENLY TAKES OFF TO SEE HER! WHY? I DON'T UNDERSTAND IT!
LILA NEEDS ME!
SCHULZ
WOW! WHAT A BIG HOSPITAL!
IF ANY OF THE NURSES CATCH ME, THEY'LL KILL ME... THEY HATE BEAGLES IN HOSPITALS...
LILA?
SNOOPY!!
HI, SWEETIE!
SCHULZ
YOU'RE BACK!
DID YOU SEE LILA? WHO IS LILA? WHERE DID YOU GO? WHY DID YOU RUN OFF SO SUDDENLY? I THOUGHT YOU DIDN'T WANT TO SEE LILA...WHERE DID YOU GO? DID YOU SEE LILA? WHO IS LILA?!!
I'M NOT GETTING ANY ANSWERS..
SCHULZ

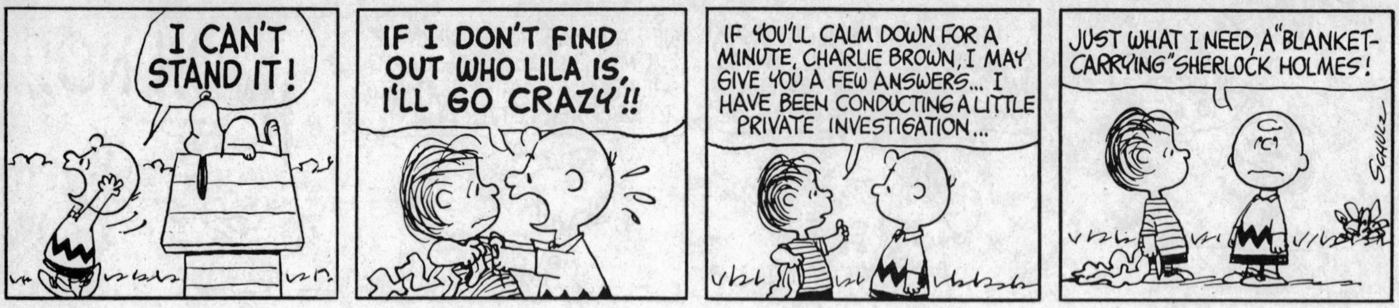
I CAN'T STAND IT!
IF I DON'T FIND OUT WHO LILA IS, I'LL GO CRAZY!!
IF YOU'LL CALM DOWN FOR A MINUTE, CHARLIE BROWN, I MAY GIVE YOU A FEW ANSWERS... I HAVE BEEN CONDUCTING A LITTLE PRIVATE INVESTIGATION...
JUST WHAT I NEED, A "BLANKET-CARRYING" SHERLOCK HOLMES!
SCHULZ

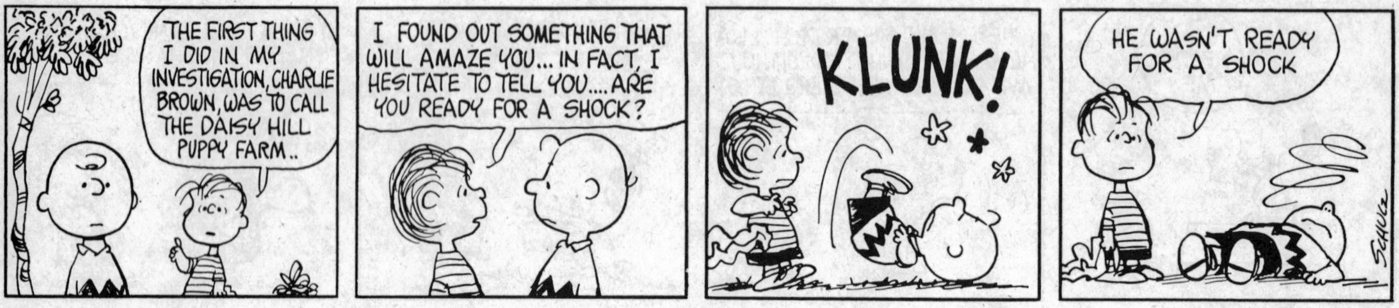
THE FIRST THING I DID IN MY INVESTIGATION, CHARLIE BROWN, WAS TO CALL THE DAISY HILL PUPPY FARM..
I FOUND OUT SOMETHING THAT WILL AMAZE YOU... IN FACT, I HESITATE TO TELL YOU.... ARE YOU READY FOR A SHOCK?
KLUNK!
HE WASN'T READY FOR A SHOCK
SCHULZ

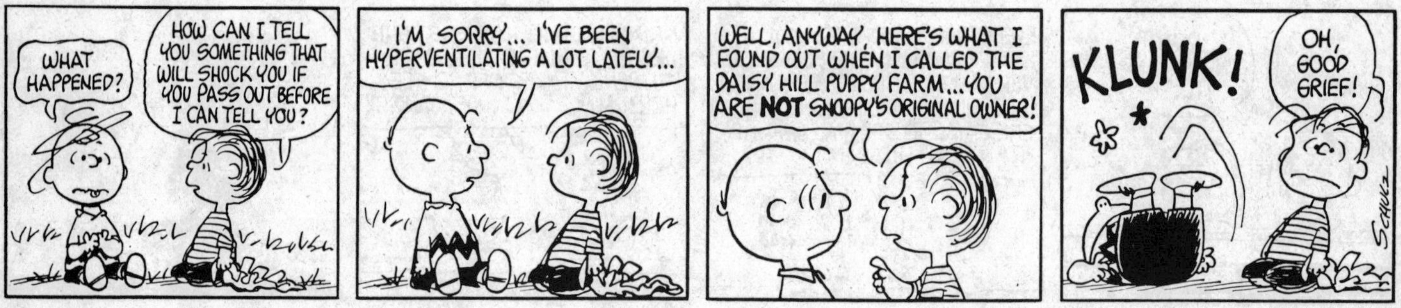
WHAT HAPPENED?
HOW CAN I TELL YOU SOMETHING THAT WILL SHOCK YOU IF YOU PASS OUT BEFORE I CAN TELL YOU?
I'M SORRY... I'VE BEEN HYPERVENTILATING A LOT LATELY...
WELL, ANYWAY, HERE'S WHAT I FOUND OUT WHEN I CALLED THE DAISY HILL PUPPY FARM...YOU ARE NOT SNOOPY'S ORIGINAL OWNER!
KLUNK!
OH, GOOD GRIEF!
SCHULZ

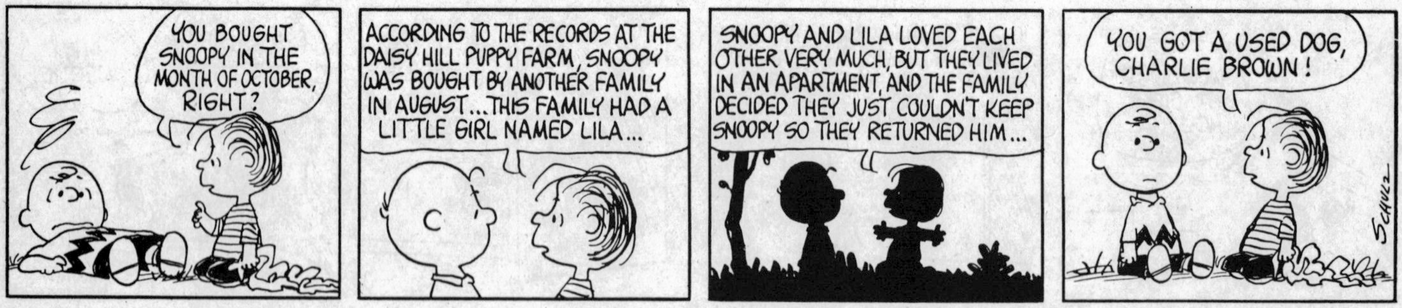
YOU BOUGHT SNOOPY IN THE MONTH OF OCTOBER, RIGHT?
ACCORDING TO THE RECORDS AT THE DAISY HILL PUPPY FARM, SNOOPY WAS BOUGHT BY ANOTHER FAMILY IN AUGUST...THIS FAMILY HAD A LITTLE GIRL NAMED LILA...
SNOOPY AND LILA LOVED EACH OTHER VERY MUCH, BUT THEY LIVED IN AN APARTMENT, AND THE FAMILY DECIDED THEY JUST COULDN'T KEEP SNOOPY SO THEY RETURNED HIM...
YOU GOT A USED DOG, CHARLIE BROWN!
SCHULZ

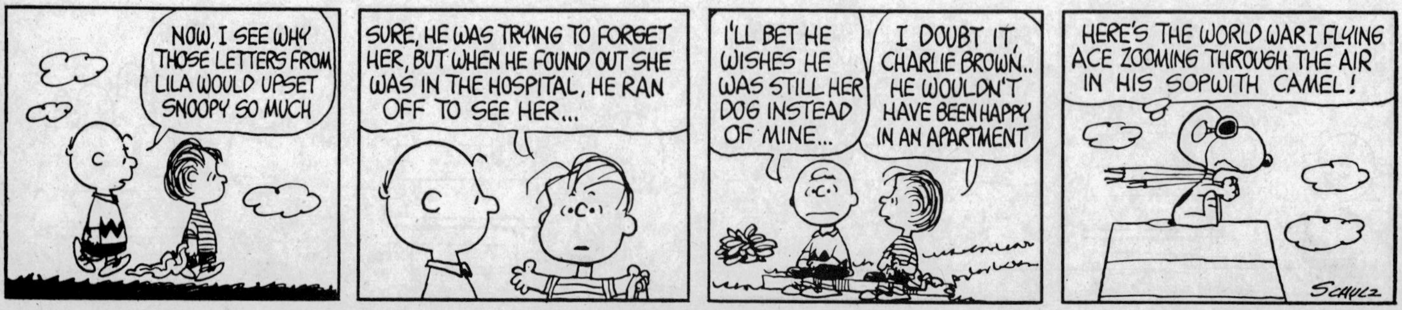
NOW, I SEE WHY THOSE LETTERS FROM LILA WOULD UPSET SNOOPY SO MUCH
SURE, HE WAS TRYING TO FORGET HER, BUT WHEN HE FOUND OUT SHE WAS IN THE HOSPITAL, HE RAN OFF TO SEE HER...
I'LL BET HE WISHES HE WAS STILL HER DOG INSTEAD OF MINE...
I DOUBT IT, CHARLIE BROWN.. HE WOULDN'T HAVE BEEN HAPPY IN AN APARTMENT
HERE'S THE WORLD WAR I FLYING ACE ZOOMING THROUGH THE AIR IN HIS SOPWITH CAMEL!
SCHULZ

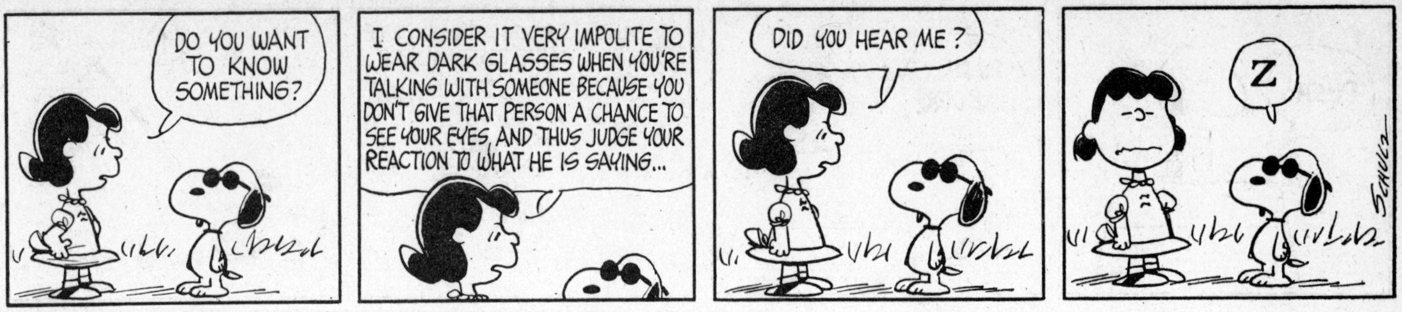
DO YOU WANT TO KNOW SOMETHING?
I CONSIDER IT VERY IMPOLITE TO WEAR DARK GLASSES WHEN YOU'RE TALKING WITH SOMEONE BECAUSE YOU DON'T GIVE THAT PERSON A CHANCE TO SEE YOUR EYES, AND THUS JUDGE YOUR REACTION TO WHAT HE IS SAYING...
DID YOU HEAR ME?
Z
SCHULZ

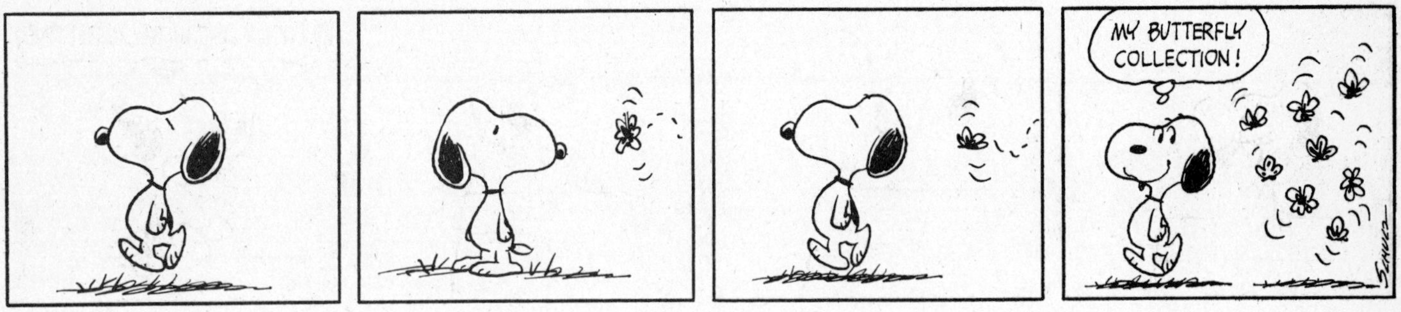
MY BUTTERFLY COLLECTION!
SCHULZ

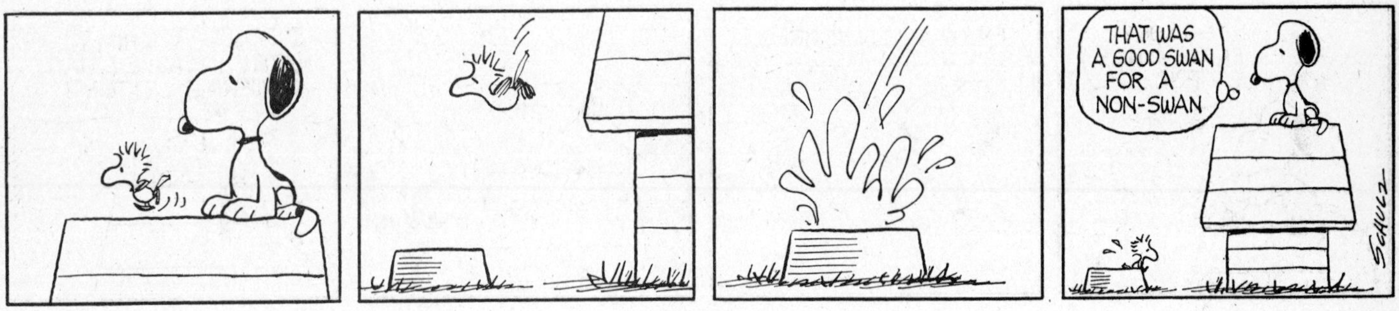
THAT WAS A GOOD SWAN FOR A NON-SWAN
SCHULZ

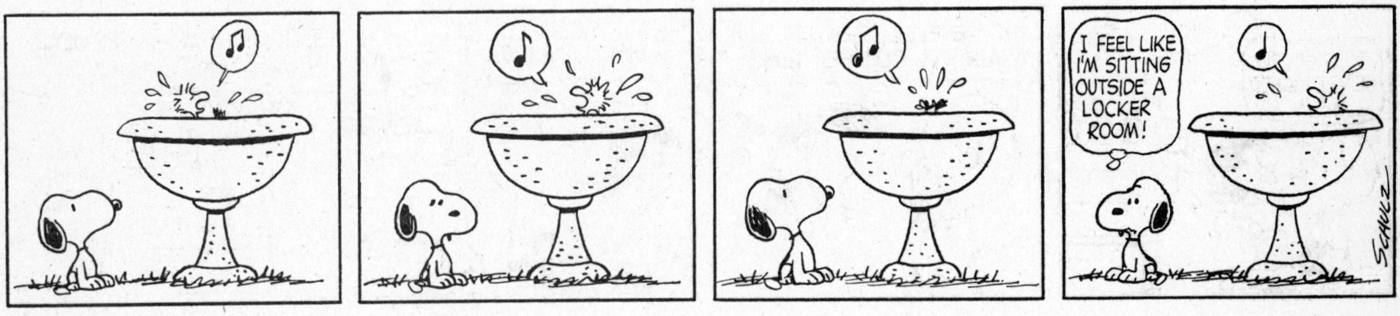
I FEEL LIKE I'M SITTING OUTSIDE A LOCKER ROOM!
SCHULZ

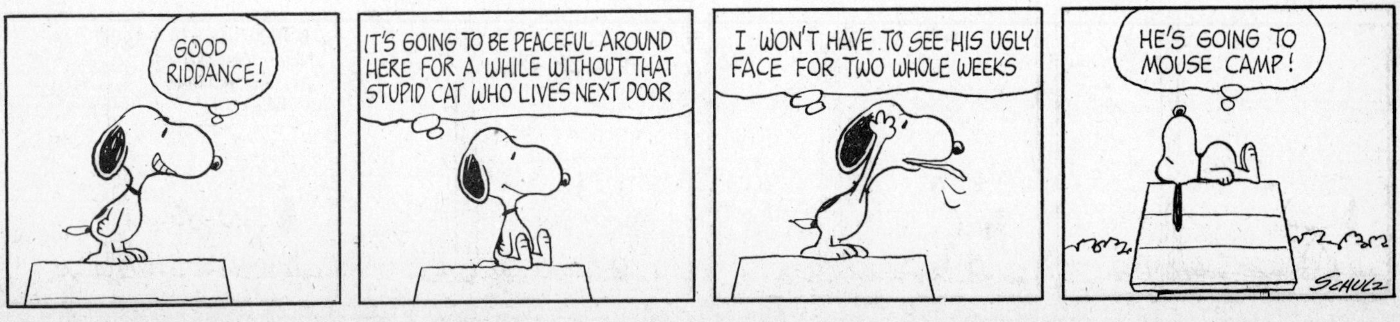
GOOD RIDDANCE!
IT'S GOING TO BE PEACEFUL AROUND HERE FOR A WHILE WITHOUT THAT STUPID CAT WHO LIVES NEXT DOOR
I WON'T HAVE TO SEE HIS UGLY FACE FOR TWO WHOLE WEEKS
HE'S GOING TO MOUSE CAMP!
SCHULZ

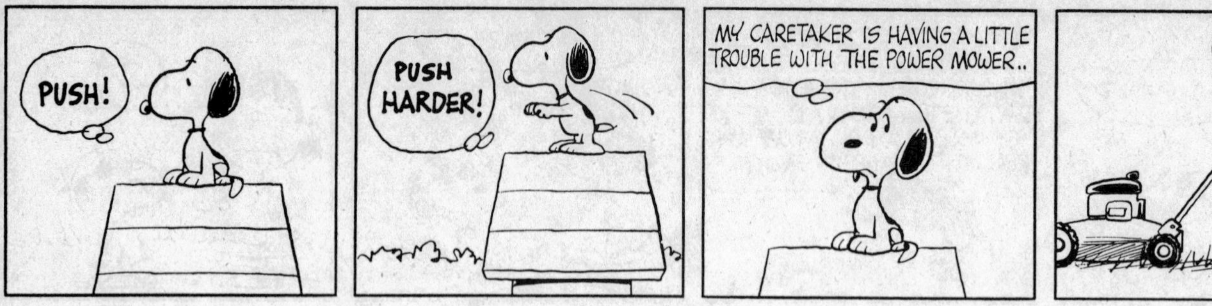
PUSH!
PUSH HARDER!
MY CARETAKER IS HAVING A LITTLE TROUBLE WITH THE POWER MOWER..
!
SCHULZ

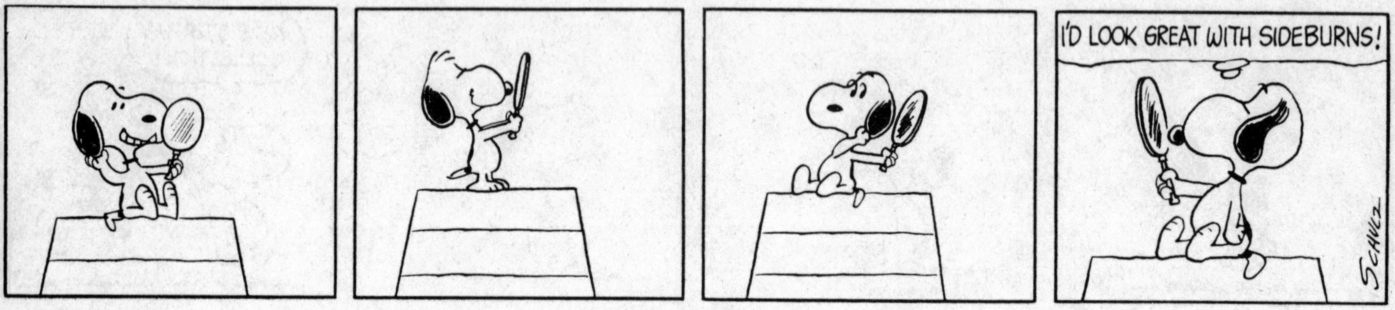
I'D LOOK GREAT WITH SIDEBURNS!
SCHULZ

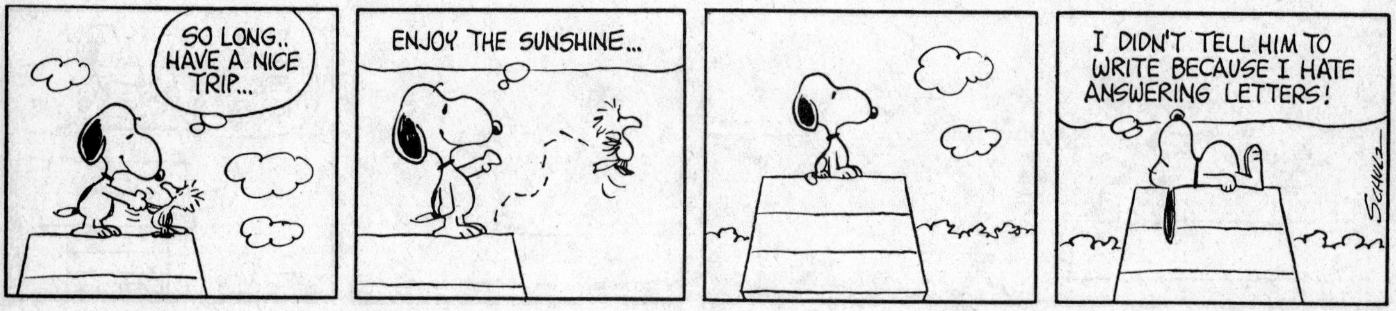
SO LONG.. HAVE A NICE TRIP...
ENJOY THE SUNSHINE...
I DIDN'T TELL HIM TO WRITE BECAUSE I HATE ANSWERING LETTERS!
SCHULZ

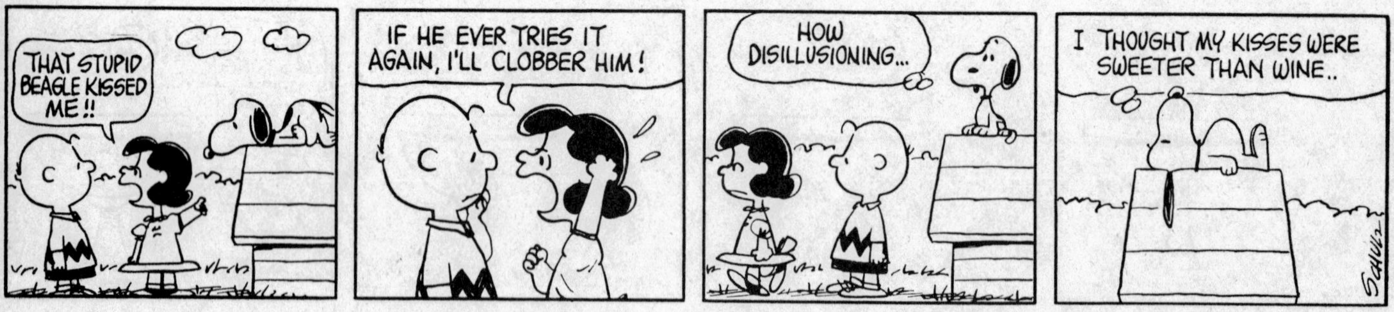
THAT STUPID BEAGLE KISSED ME!!
IF HE EVER TRIES IT AGAIN, I'LL CLOBBER HIM!
HOW DISILLUSIONING...
I THOUGHT MY KISSES WERE SWEETER THAN WINE..
SCHULZ

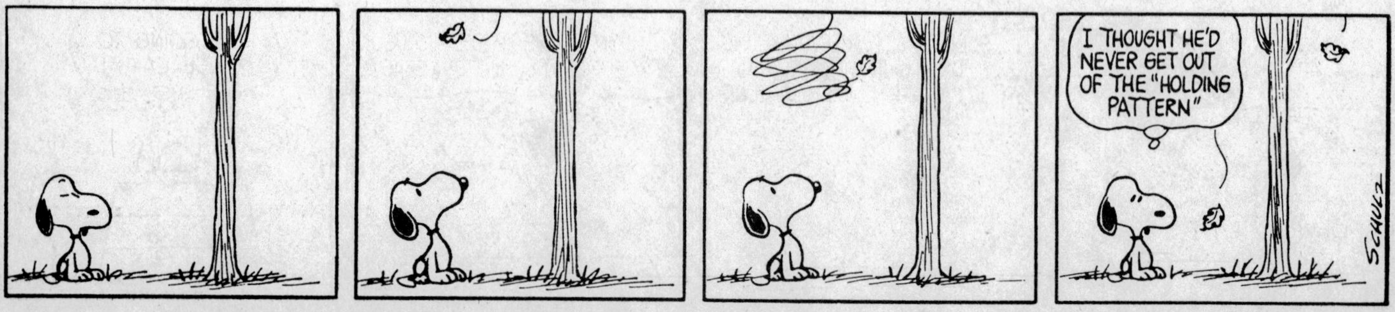
I THOUGHT HE'D NEVER GET OUT OF THE "HOLDING PATTERN"
SCHULZ

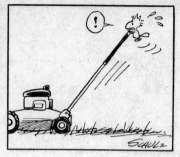

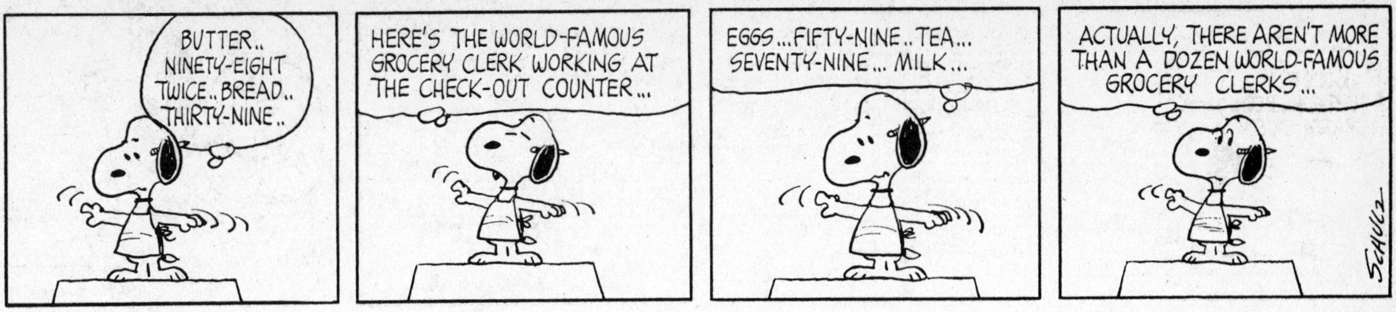
BUTTER.. NINETY-EIGHT TWICE..BREAD.. THIRTY-NINE..
HERE'S THE WORLD-FAMOUS GROCERY CLERK WORKING AT THE CHECK-OUT COUNTER...
EGGS...FIFTY-NINE..TEA... SEVENTY-NINE... MILK...
ACTUALLY, THERE AREN'T MORE THAN A DOZEN WORLD-FAMOUS GROCERY CLERKS...
SCHULZ

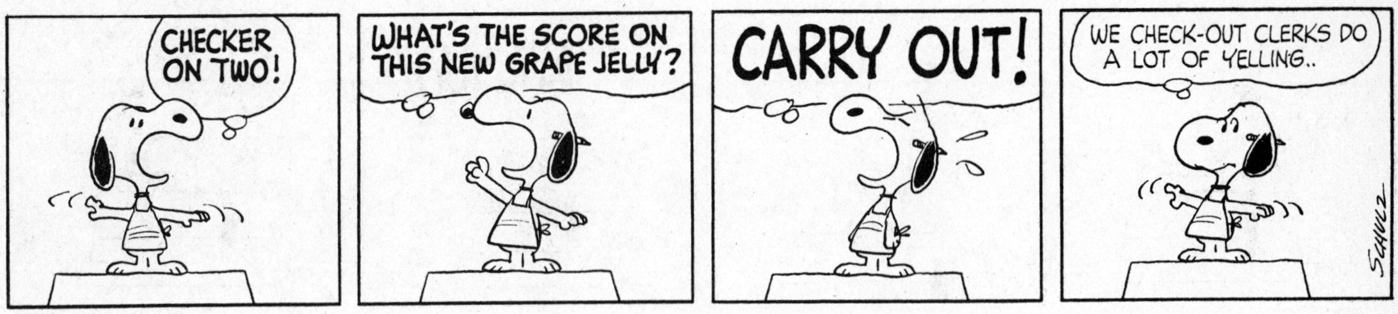
CHECKER ON TWO!
WHAT'S THE SCORE ON THIS NEW GRAPE JELLY?
CARRY OUT!
WE CHECK-OUT CLERKS DO A LOT OF YELLING..
SCHULZ

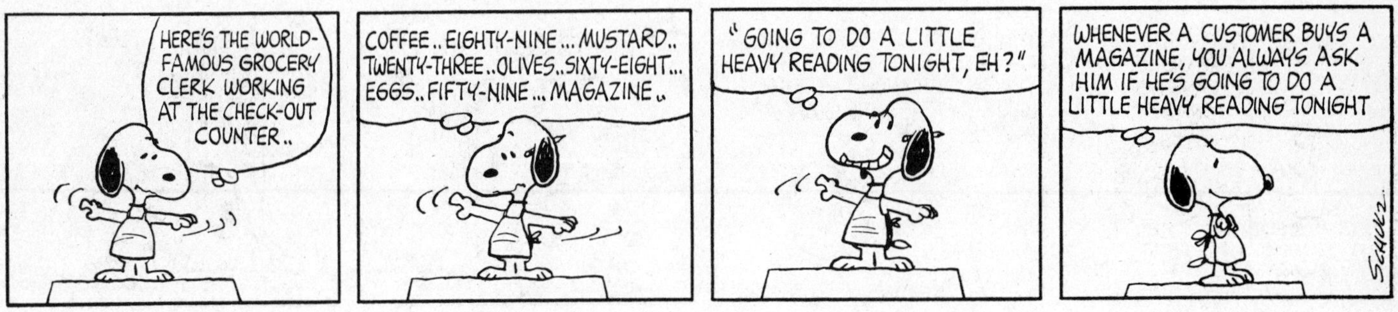
HERE'S THE WORLD-FAMOUS GROCERY CLERK WORKING AT THE CHECK-OUT COUNTER..
COFFEE..EIGHTY-NINE...MUSTARD.. TWENTY-THREE..OLIVES..SIXTY-EIGHT... EGGS..FIFTY-NINE...MAGAZINE..
"GOING TO DO A LITTLE HEAVY READING TONIGHT, EH?"
WHENEVER A CUSTOMER BUYS A MAGAZINE, YOU ALWAYS ASK HIM IF HE'S GOING TO DO A LITTLE HEAVY READING TONIGHT
SCHULZ

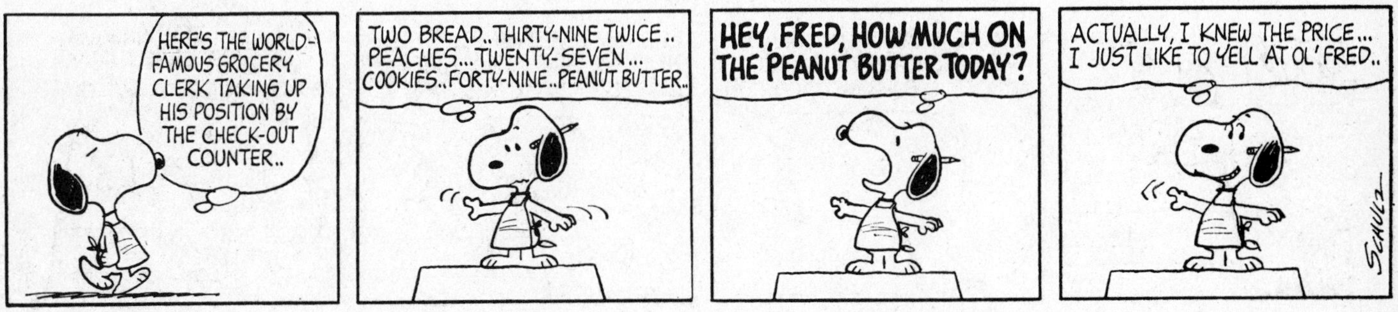
HERE'S THE WORLD-FAMOUS GROCERY CLERK TAKING UP HIS POSITION BY THE CHECK-OUT COUNTER..
TWO BREAD..THIRTY-NINE TWICE.. PEACHES...TWENTY-SEVEN... COOKIES..FORTY-NINE..PEANUT BUTTER..
HEY, FRED, HOW MUCH ON THE PEANUT BUTTER TODAY?
ACTUALLY, I KNEW THE PRICE... I JUST LIKE TO YELL AT OL' FRED..
SCHULZ

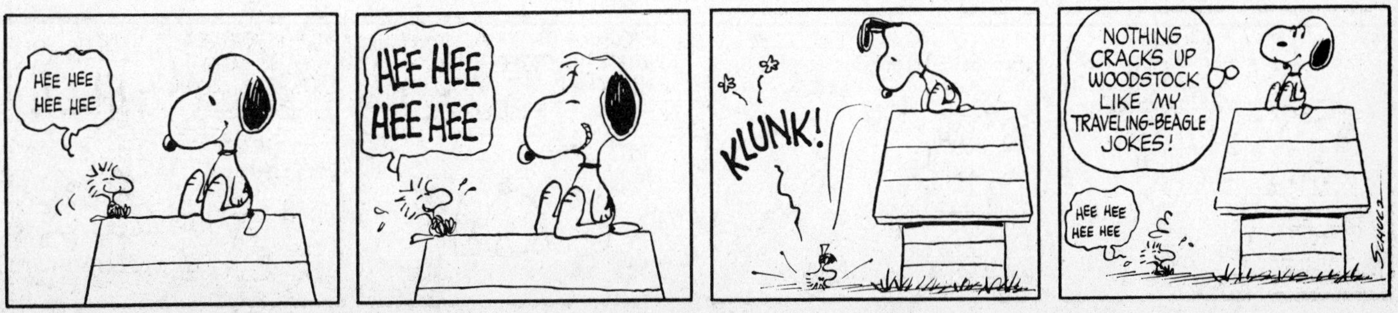
HEE HEE HEE HEE
HEE HEE HEE HEE
KLUNK!
NOTHING CRACKS UP WOODSTOCK LIKE MY TRAVELING-BEAGLE JOKES!
HEE HEE HEE HEE
SCHULZ

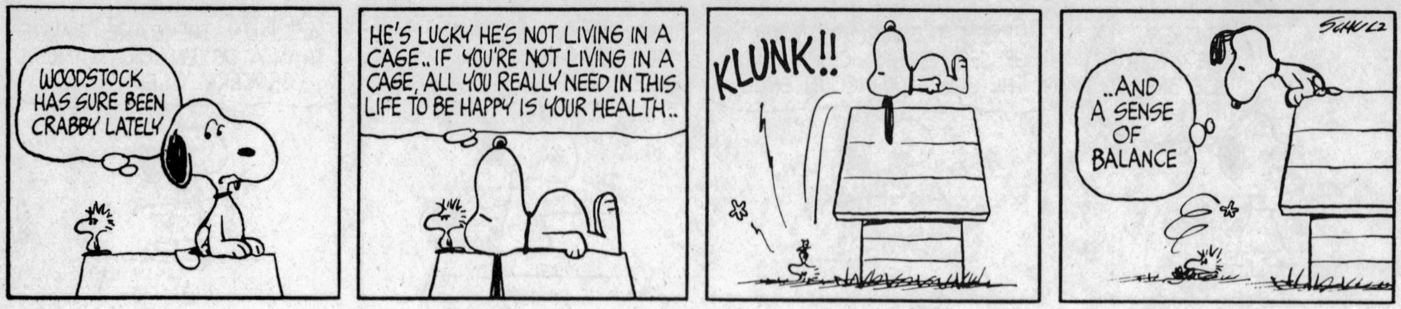
WOODSTOCK HAS SURE BEEN CRABBY LATELY
HE'S LUCKY HE'S NOT LIVING IN A CAGE.. IF YOU'RE NOT LIVING IN A CAGE, ALL YOU REALLY NEED IN THIS LIFE TO BE HAPPY IS YOUR HEALTH..
KLUNK!!
..AND A SENSE OF BALANCE
SCHULZ

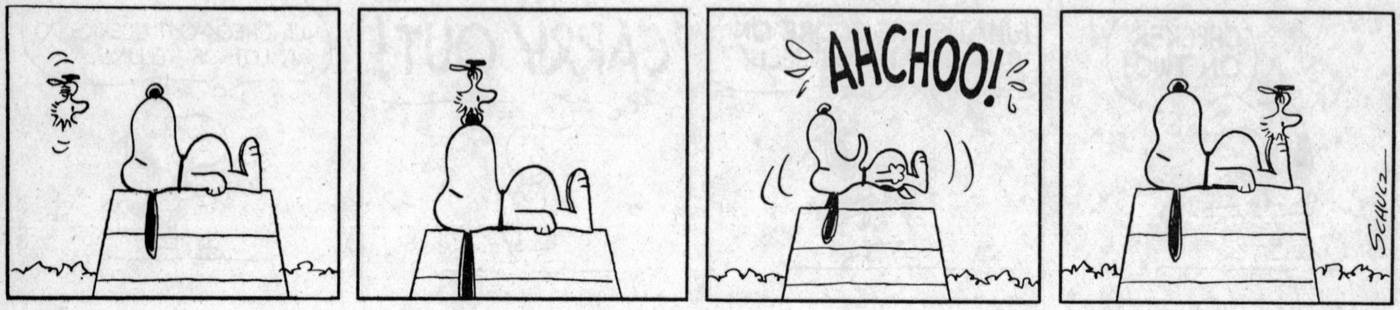
AHCHOO!
SCHULZ

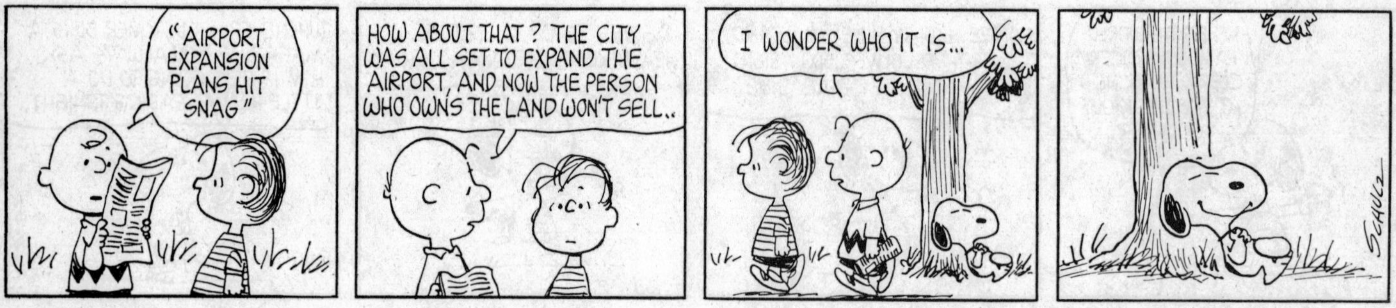
"AIRPORT EXPANSION PLANS HIT SNAG"
HOW ABOUT THAT? THE CITY WAS ALL SET TO EXPAND THE AIRPORT, AND NOW THE PERSON WHO OWNS THE LAND WON'T SELL..
I WONDER WHO IT IS...
SCHULZ

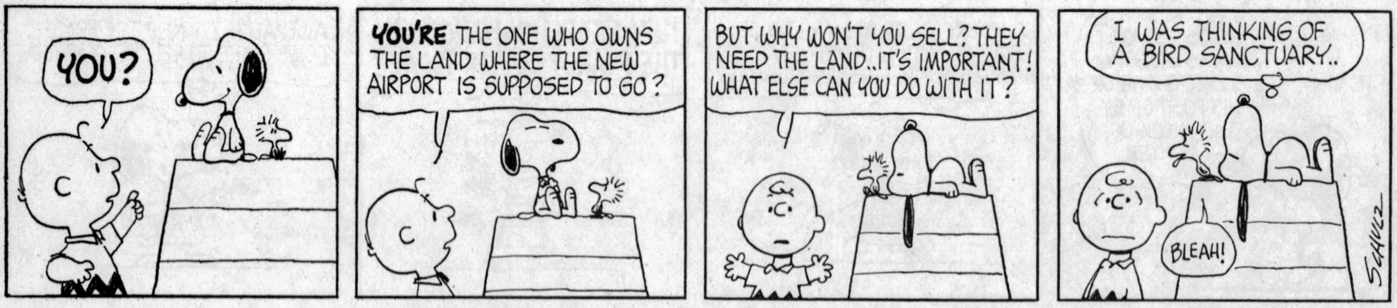
YOU?
YOU'RE THE ONE WHO OWNS THE LAND WHERE THE NEW AIRPORT IS SUPPOSED TO GO?
BUT WHY WON'T YOU SELL? THEY NEED THE LAND..IT'S IMPORTANT! WHAT ELSE CAN YOU DO WITH IT?
I WAS THINKING OF A BIRD SANCTUARY..
BLEAH!
SCHULZ

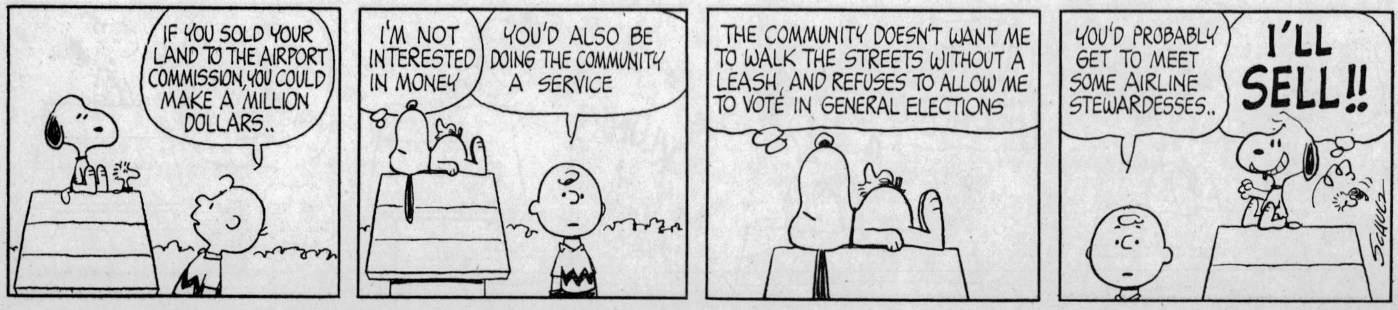
IF YOU SOLD YOUR LAND TO THE AIRPORT COMMISSION, YOU COULD MAKE A MILLION DOLLARS..
I'M NOT INTERESTED IN MONEY
YOU'D ALSO BE DOING THE COMMUNITY A SERVICE
THE COMMUNITY DOESN'T WANT ME TO WALK THE STREETS WITHOUT A LEASH, AND REFUSES TO ALLOW ME TO VOTE IN GENERAL ELECTIONS
YOU'D PROBABLY GET TO MEET SOME AIRLINE STEWARDESSES..
I'LL SELL!!
SCHULZ

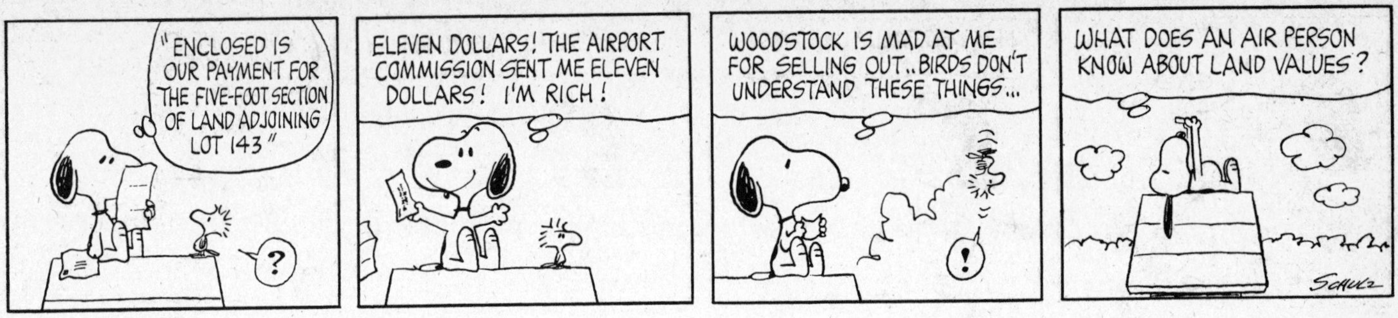
"ENCLOSED IS OUR PAYMENT FOR THE FIVE-FOOT SECTION OF LAND ADJOINING LOT 143"
?
ELEVEN DOLLARS! THE AIRPORT COMMISSION SENT ME ELEVEN DOLLARS! I'M RICH!
WOODSTOCK IS MAD AT ME FOR SELLING OUT.. BIRDS DON'T UNDERSTAND THESE THINGS...
!
WHAT DOES AN AIR PERSON KNOW ABOUT LAND VALUES?

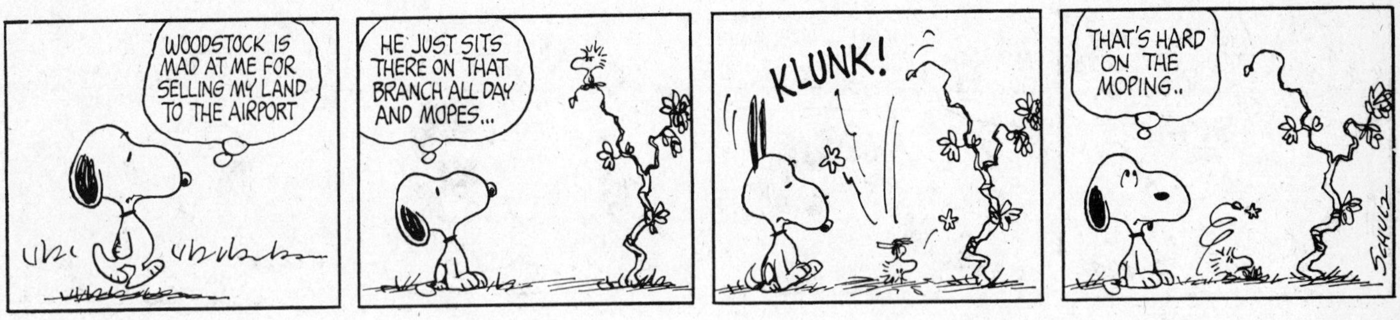
WOODSTOCK IS MAD AT ME FOR SELLING MY LAND TO THE AIRPORT
HE JUST SITS THERE ON THAT BRANCH ALL DAY AND MOPES...
KLUNK!
THAT'S HARD ON THE MOPING..

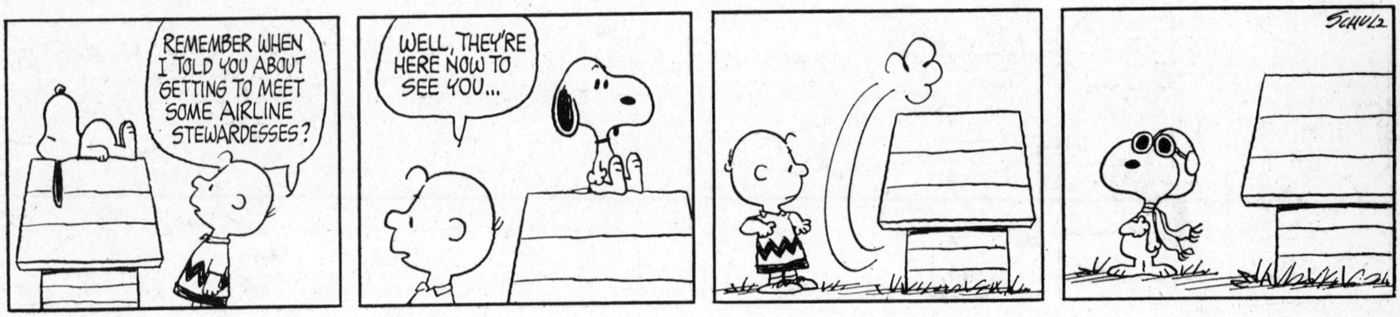
REMEMBER WHEN I TOLD YOU ABOUT GETTING TO MEET SOME AIRLINE STEWARDESSES?
WELL, THEY'RE HERE NOW TO SEE YOU...

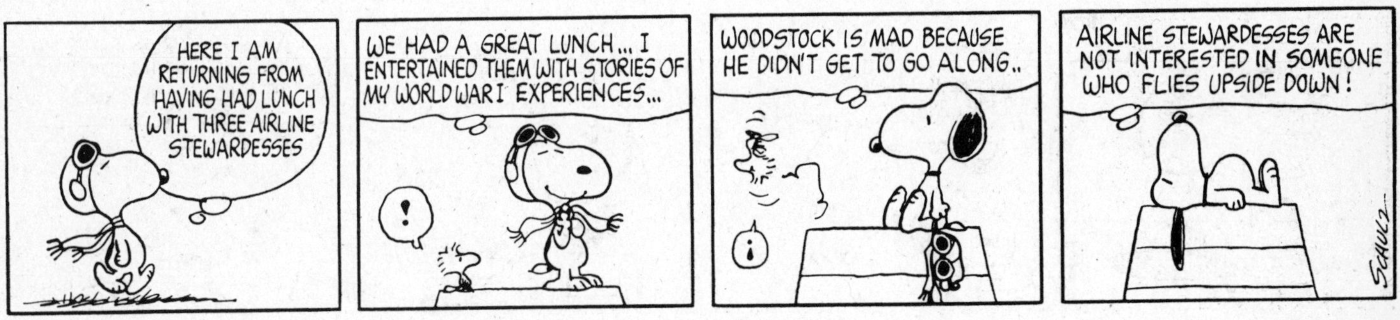
HERE I AM RETURNING FROM HAVING HAD LUNCH WITH THREE AIRLINE STEWARDESSES
WE HAD A GREAT LUNCH... I ENTERTAINED THEM WITH STORIES OF MY WORLD WAR I EXPERIENCES...
!
WOODSTOCK IS MAD BECAUSE HE DIDN'T GET TO GO ALONG..
AIRLINE STEWARDESSES ARE NOT INTERESTED IN SOMEONE WHO FLIES UPSIDE DOWN!

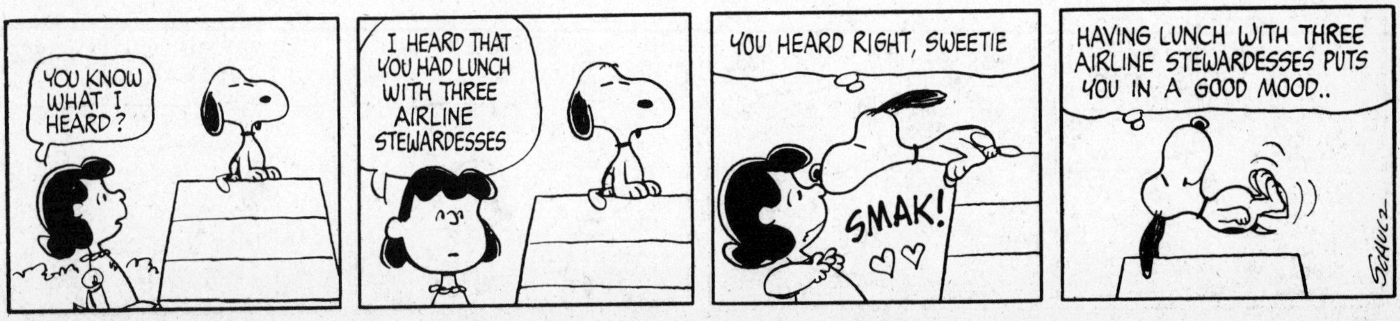
YOU KNOW WHAT I HEARD?
I HEARD THAT YOU HAD LUNCH WITH THREE AIRLINE STEWARDESSES
YOU HEARD RIGHT, SWEETIE
SMAK!
HAVING LUNCH WITH THREE AIRLINE STEWARDESSES PUTS YOU IN A GOOD MOOD..

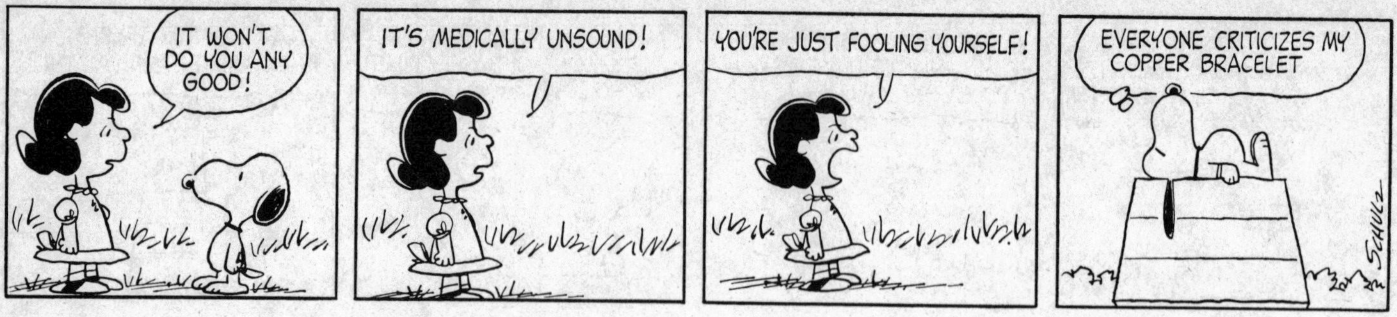
IT WON'T DO YOU ANY GOOD!
IT'S MEDICALLY UNSOUND!
YOU'RE JUST FOOLING YOURSELF!
EVERYONE CRITICIZES MY COPPER BRACELET
SCHULZ

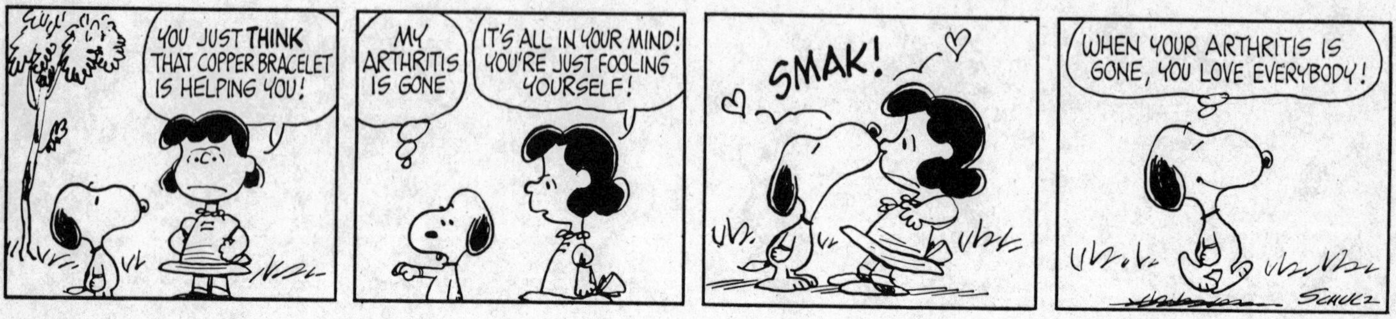
YOU JUST THINK THAT COPPER BRACELET IS HELPING YOU!
MY ARTHRITIS IS GONE
IT'S ALL IN YOUR MIND! YOU'RE JUST FOOLING YOURSELF!
SMAK!
WHEN YOUR ARTHRITIS IS GONE, YOU LOVE EVERYBODY!
SCHULZ

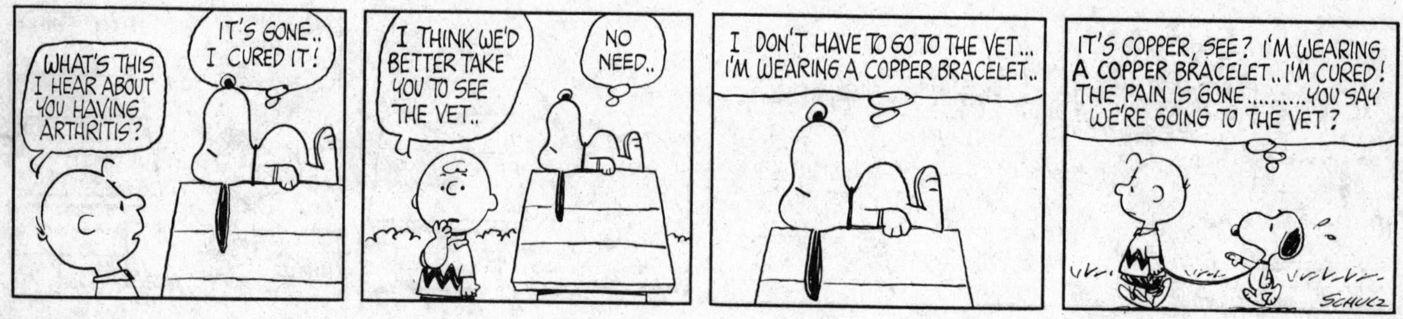
WHAT'S THIS I HEAR ABOUT YOU HAVING ARTHRITIS?
IT'S GONE.. I CURED IT!
I THINK WE'D BETTER TAKE YOU TO SEE THE VET..
NO NEED..
I DON'T HAVE TO GO TO THE VET... I'M WEARING A COPPER BRACELET..
IT'S COPPER, SEE? I'M WEARING A COPPER BRACELET.. I'M CURED! THE PAIN IS GONE.........YOU SAY WE'RE GOING TO THE VET?
SCHULZ

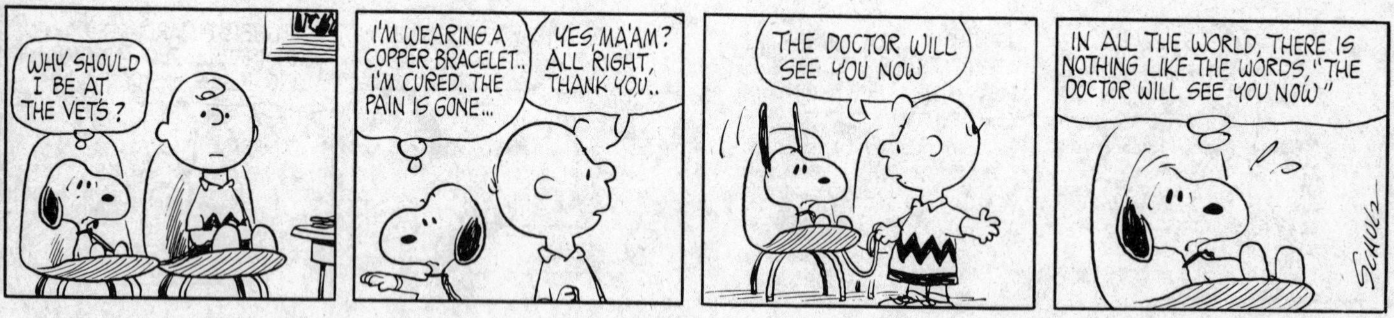
WHY SHOULD I BE AT THE VET'S?
I'M WEARING A COPPER BRACELET.. I'M CURED.. THE PAIN IS GONE...
YES, MA'AM? ALL RIGHT, THANK YOU..
THE DOCTOR WILL SEE YOU NOW
IN ALL THE WORLD, THERE IS NOTHING LIKE THE WORDS, "THE DOCTOR WILL SEE YOU NOW"
SCHULZ

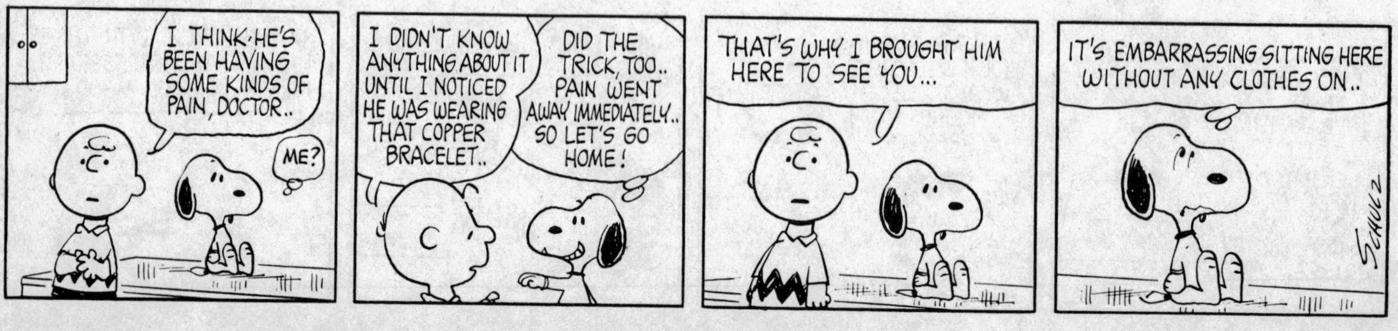
I THINK HE'S BEEN HAVING SOME KINDS OF PAIN, DOCTOR..
ME?
I DIDN'T KNOW ANYTHING ABOUT IT UNTIL I NOTICED HE WAS WEARING THAT COPPER BRACELET..
DID THE TRICK, TOO.. PAIN WENT AWAY IMMEDIATELY.. SO LET'S GO HOME!
THAT'S WHY I BROUGHT HIM HERE TO SEE YOU...
IT'S EMBARRASSING SITTING HERE WITHOUT ANY CLOTHES ON..
SCHULZ

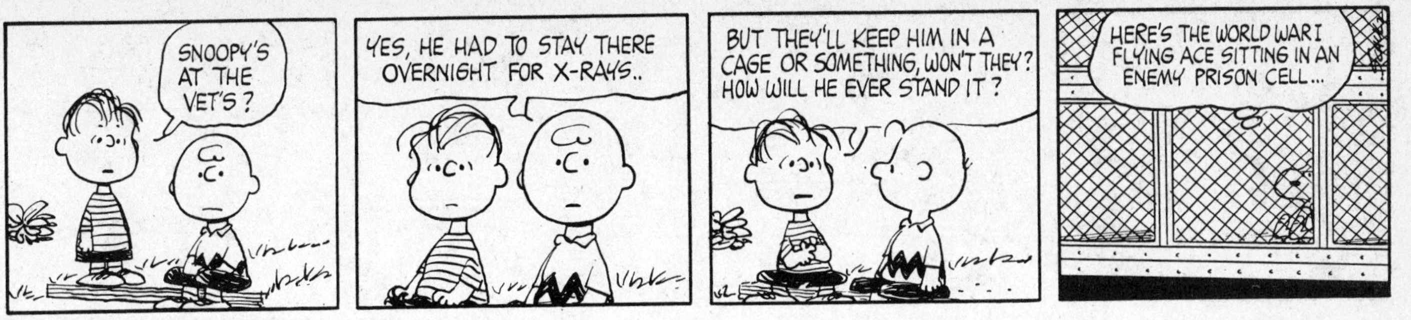
SNOPPY'S AT THE VET'S ?
YES, HE HAD TO STAY THERE OVERNIGHT FOR X-RAYS..
BUT THEY'LL KEEP HIM IN A CAGE OR SOMETHING, WON'T THEY? HOW WILL HE EVER STAND IT ?
HERE'S THE WORLD WAR I FLYING ACE SITTING IN AN ENEMY PRISON CELL...

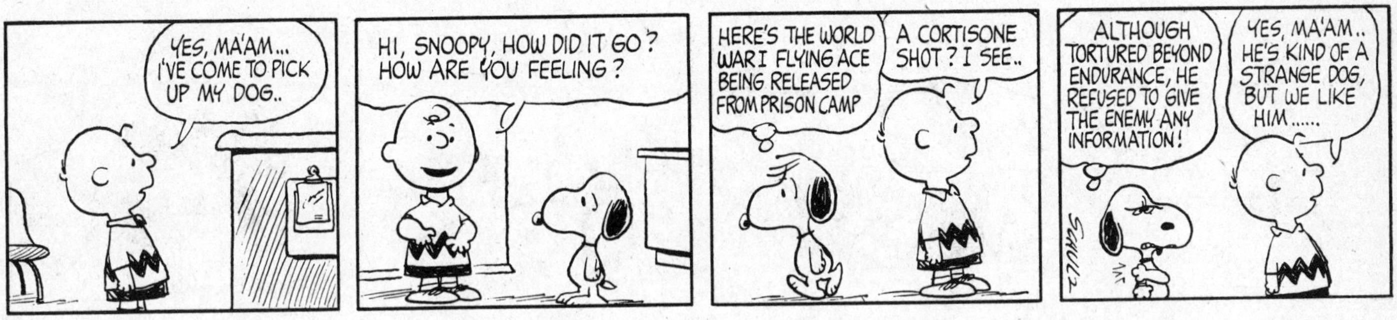
YES, MA'AM... I'VE COME TO PICK UP MY DOG..
HI, SNOOPY, HOW DID IT GO? HOW ARE YOU FEELING ?
HERE'S THE WORLD WAR I FLYING ACE BEING RELEASED FROM PRISON CAMP
A CORTISONE SHOT? I SEE..
ALTHOUGH TORTURED BEYOND ENDURANCE, HE REFUSED TO GIVE THE ENEMY ANY INFORMATION!
YES, MA'AM.. HE'S KIND OF A STRANGE DOG, BUT WE LIKE HIM......

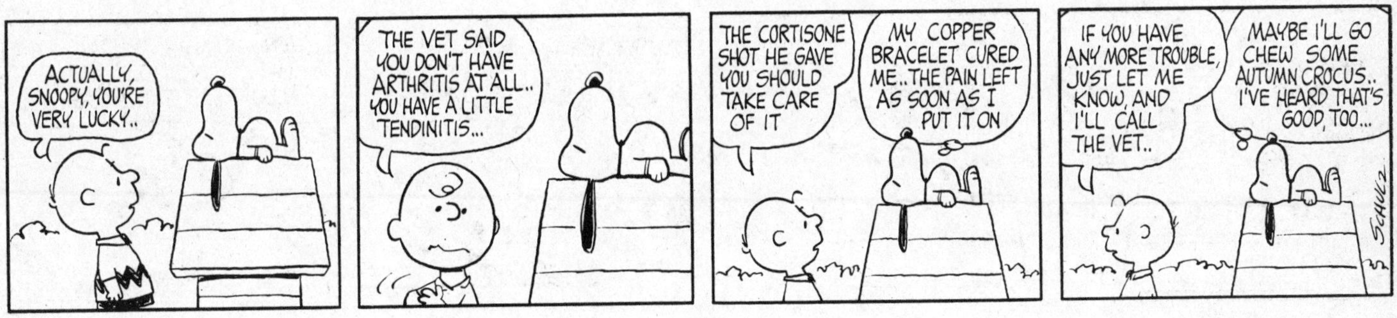
ACTUALLY, SNOOPY, YOU'RE VERY LUCKY..
THE VET SAID YOU DON'T HAVE ARTHRITIS AT ALL.. YOU HAVE A LITTLE TENDINITIS...
THE CORTISONE SHOT HE GAVE YOU SHOULD TAKE CARE OF IT
MY COPPER BRACELET CURED ME.. THE PAIN LEFT AS SOON AS I PUT IT ON
IF YOU HAVE ANY MORE TROUBLE, JUST LET ME KNOW, AND I'LL CALL THE VET..
MAYBE I'LL GO CHEW SOME AUTUMN CROCUS.. I'VE HEARD THAT'S GOOD, TOO...

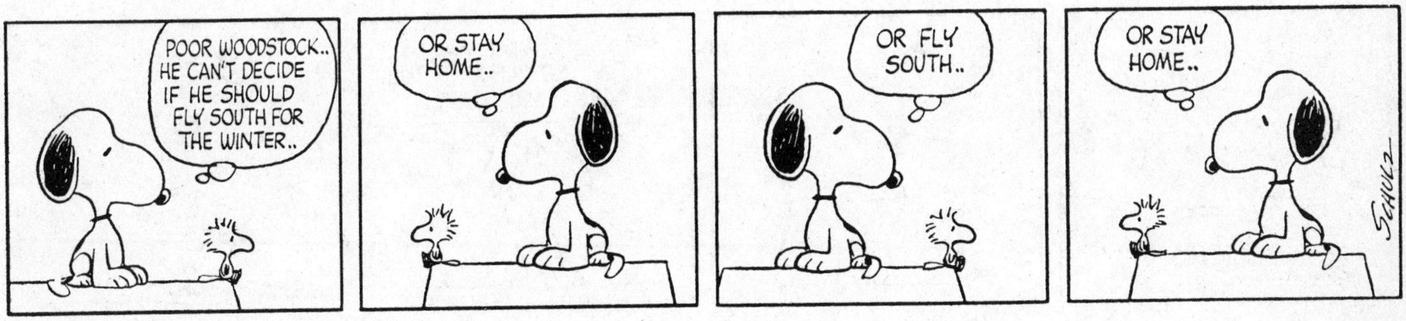
POOR WOODSTOCK.. HE CAN'T DECIDE IF HE SHOULD FLY SOUTH FOR THE WINTER..
OR STAY HOME..
OR FLY SOUTH..
OR STAY HOME..

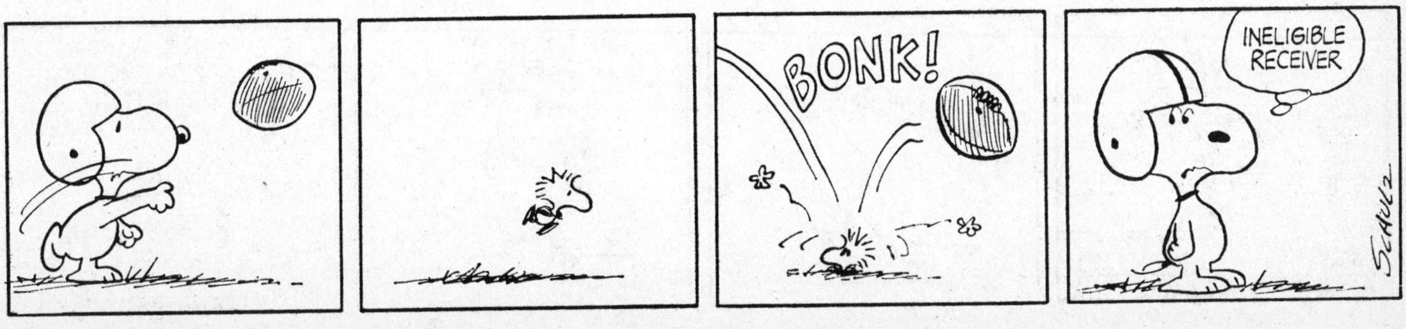
BONK!
INELIGIBLE RECEIVER

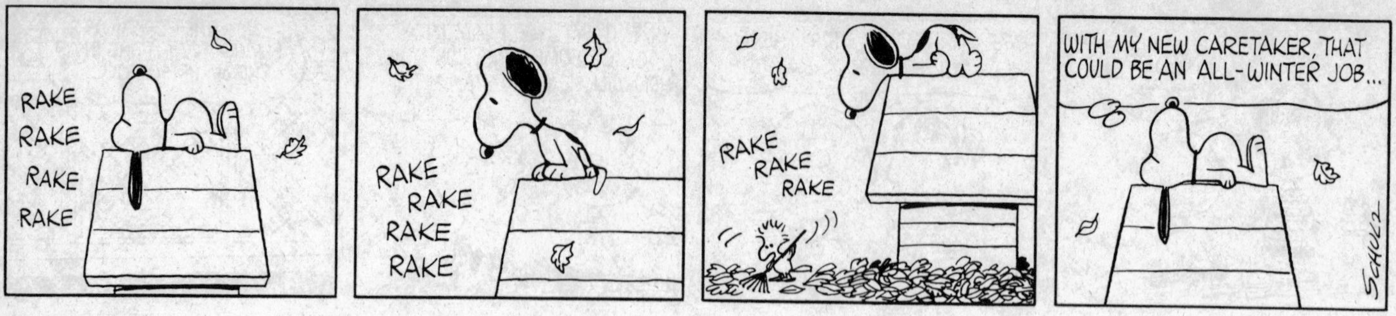
RAKE RAKE RAKE RAKE
RAKE RAKE RAKE RAKE
RAKE RAKE RAKE
WITH MY NEW CARETAKER, THAT COULD BE AN ALL-WINTER JOB...
SCHULZ

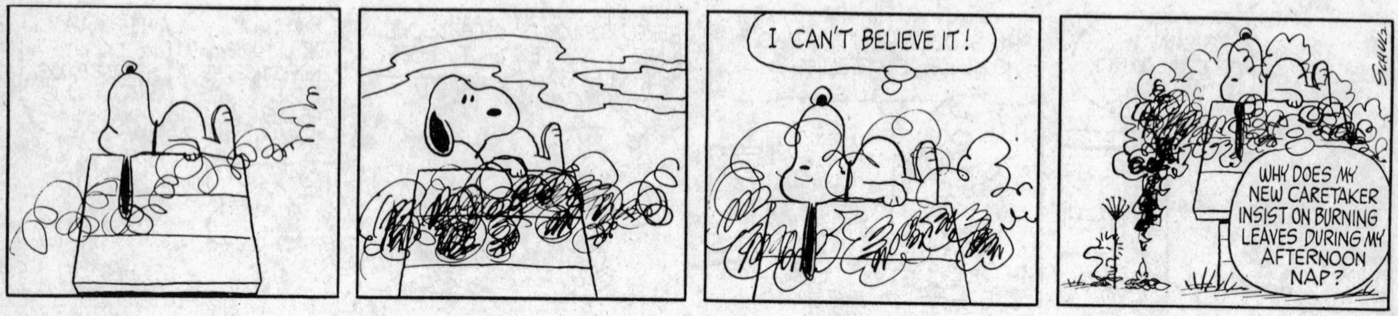
I CAN'T BELIEVE IT!
WHY DOES MY NEW CARETAKER INSIST ON BURNING LEAVES DURING MY AFTERNOON NAP?
SCHULZ

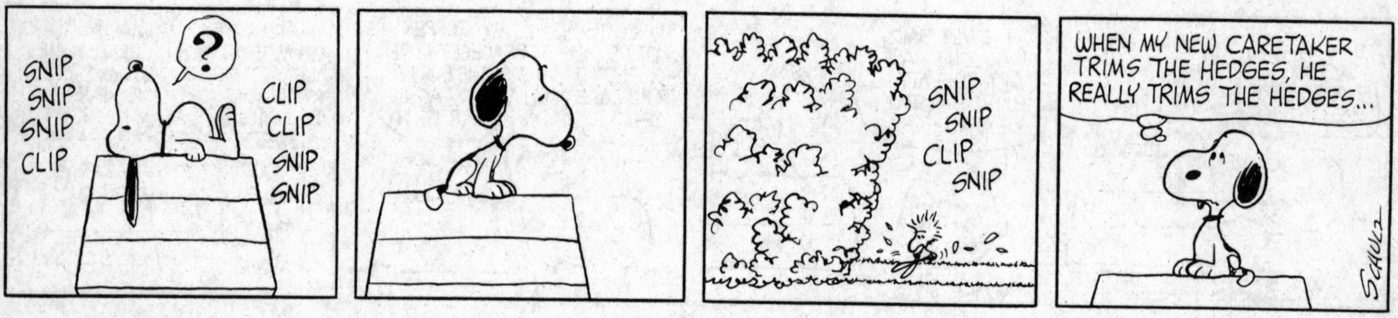
SNIP SNIP SNIP CLIP
?
CLIP CLIP SNIP SNIP
SNIP SNIP CLIP SNIP
WHEN MY NEW CARETAKER TRIMS THE HEDGES, HE REALLY TRIMS THE HEDGES...
SCHULZ

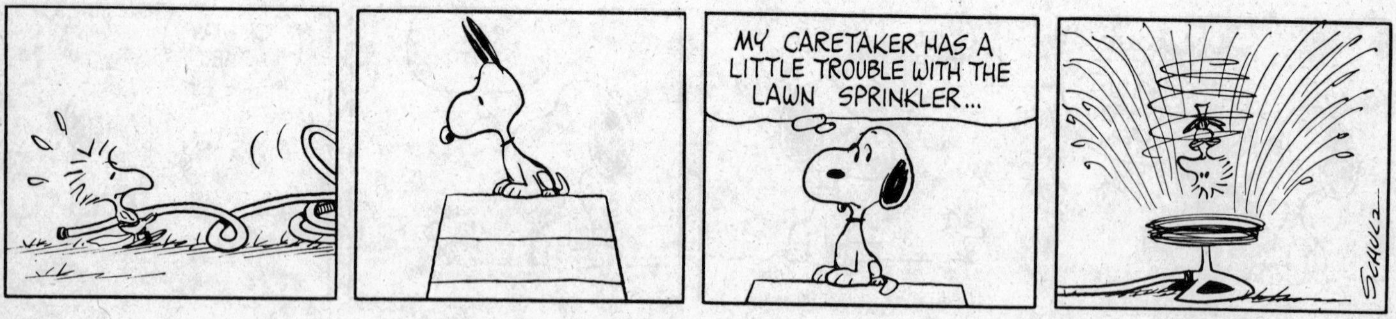
MY CARETAKER HAS A LITTLE TROUBLE WITH THE LAWN SPRINKLER...
SCHULZ

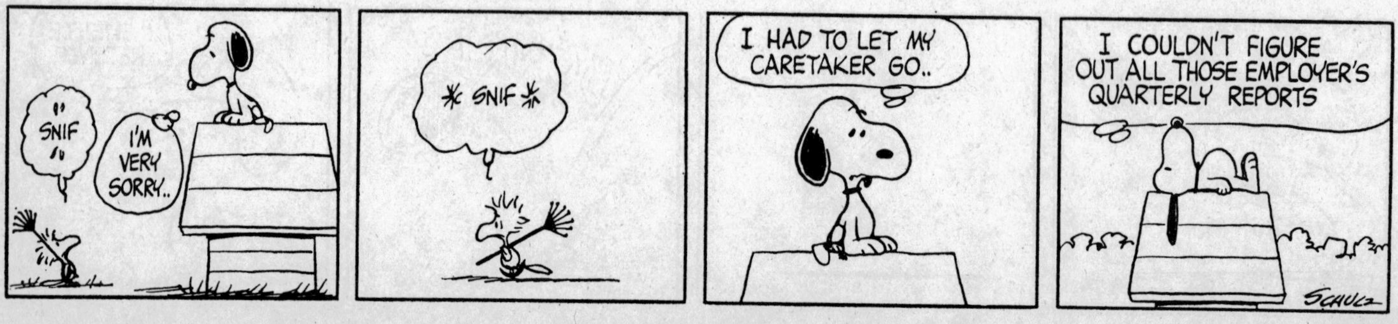
SNIF
I'M VERY SORRY..
SNIF
I HAD TO LET MY CARETAKER GO..
I COULDN'T FIGURE OUT ALL THOSE EMPLOYER'S QUARTERLY REPORTS
SCHULZ

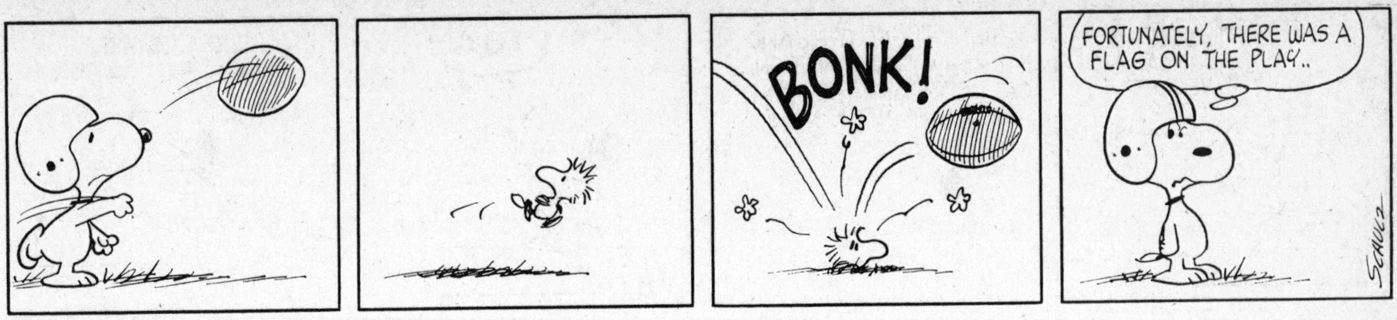
BONK!
FORTUNATELY, THERE WAS A FLAG ON THE PLAY..
SCHULZ

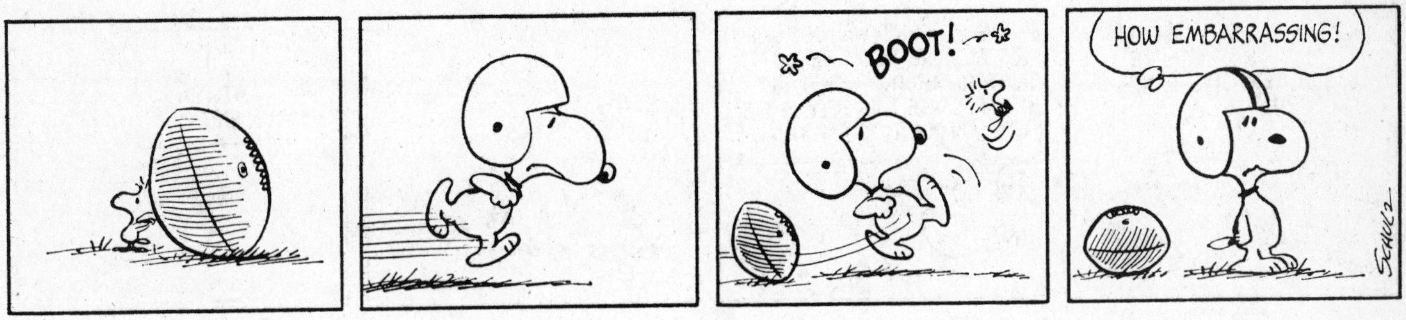
BOOT!
HOW EMBARRASSING!
SCHULZ

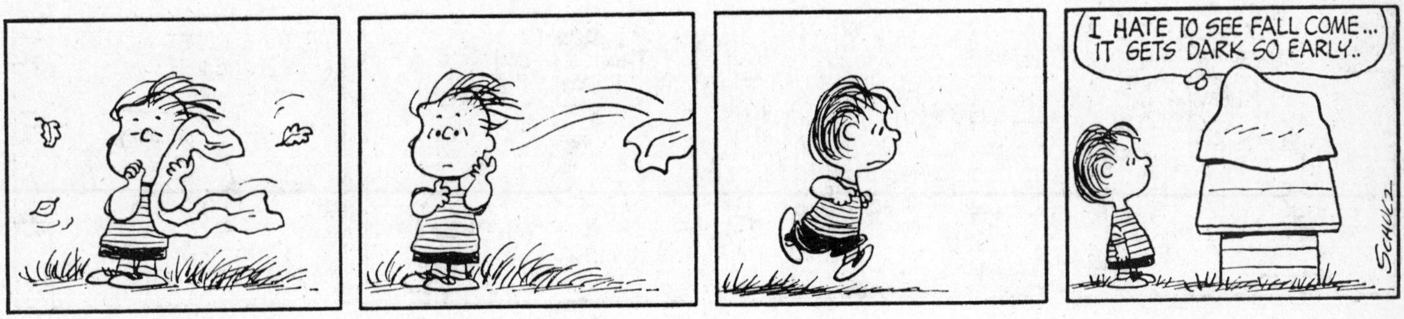
I HATE TO SEE FALL COME... IT GETS DARK SO EARLY..
SCHULZ

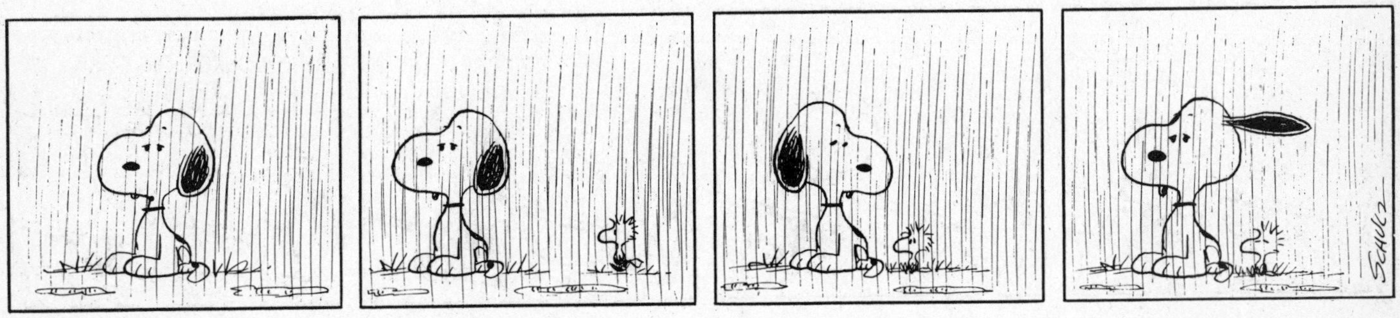
SCHULZ

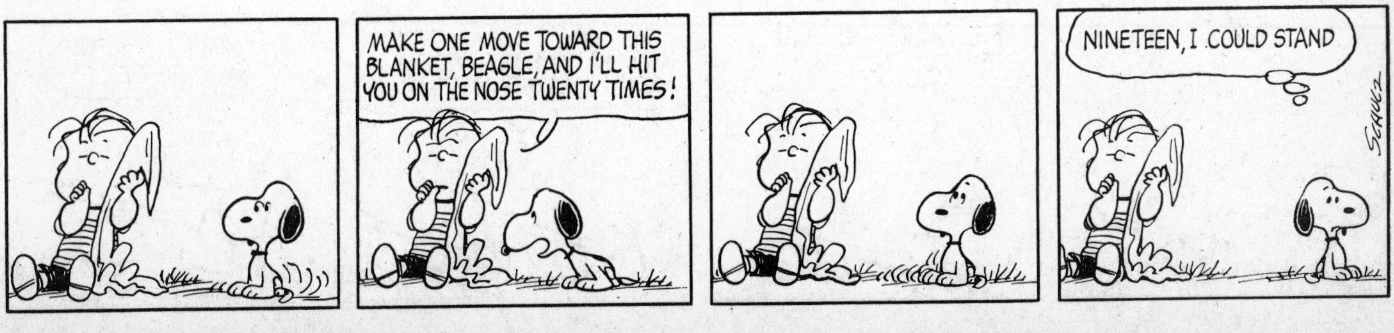
MAKE ONE MOVE TOWARD THIS BLANKET, BEAGLE, AND I'LL HIT YOU ON THE NOSE TWENTY TIMES!
NINETEEN, I COULD STAND
SCHULZ

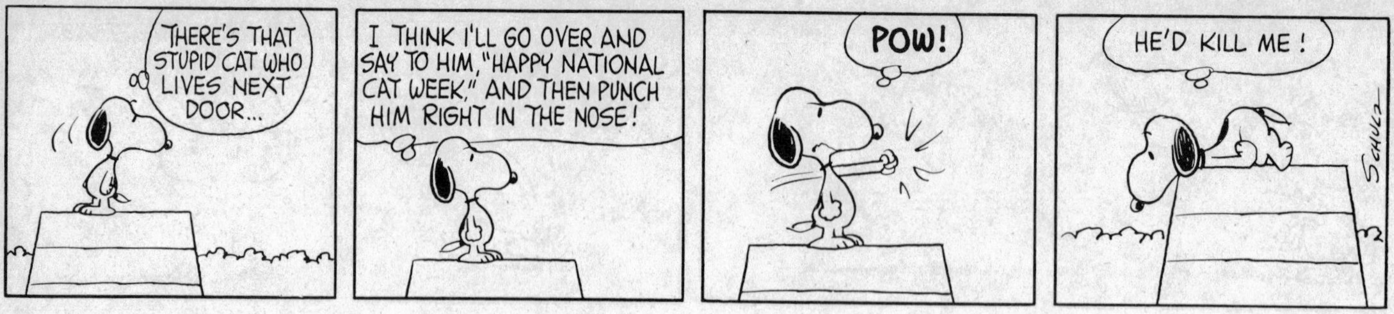
THERE'S THAT STUPID CAT WHO LIVES NEXT DOOR...
I THINK I'LL GO OVER AND SAY TO HIM, "HAPPY NATIONAL CAT WEEK," AND THEN PUNCH HIM RIGHT IN THE NOSE!
POW!
HE'D KILL ME!
SCHULZ

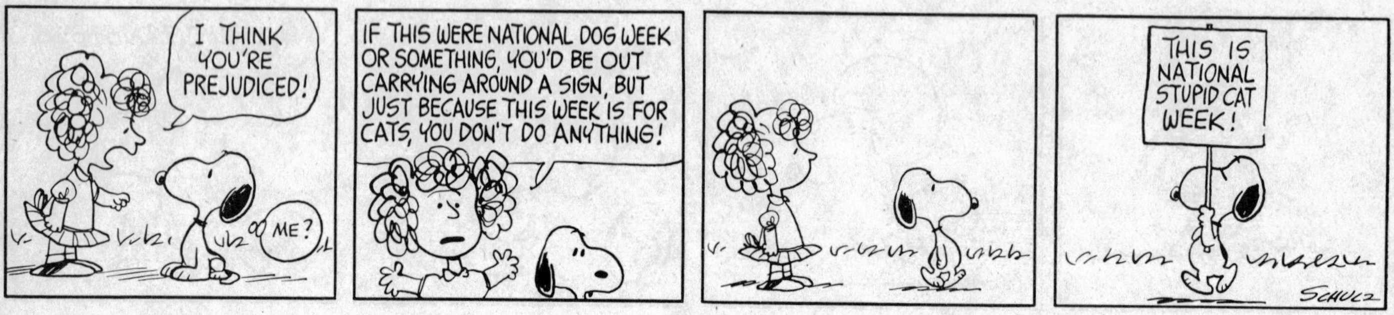
I THINK YOU'RE PREJUDICED!
ME?
IF THIS WERE NATIONAL DOG WEEK OR SOMETHING, YOU'D BE OUT CARRYING AROUND A SIGN, BUT JUST BECAUSE THIS WEEK IS FOR CATS, YOU DON'T DO ANYTHING!
THIS IS NATIONAL STUPID CAT WEEK!
SCHULZ

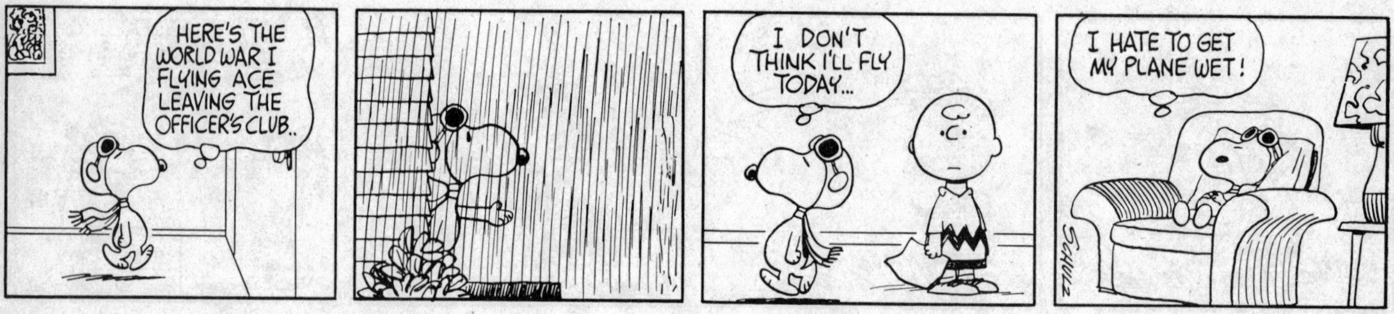
HERE'S THE WORLD WAR I FLYING ACE LEAVING THE OFFICER'S CLUB..
I DON'T THINK I'LL FLY TODAY...
I HATE TO GET MY PLANE WET!
SCHULZ

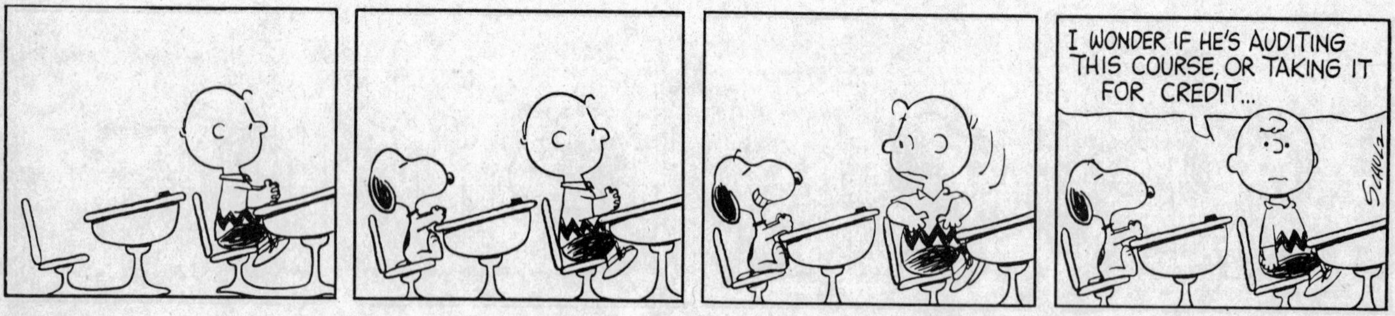
I WONDER IF HE'S AUDITING THIS COURSE, OR TAKING IT FOR CREDIT...
SCHULZ

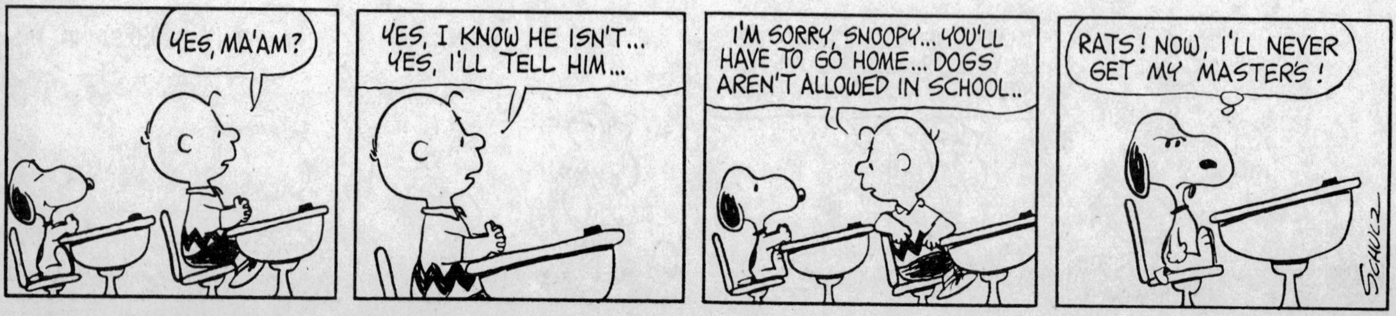
YES, MA'AM?
YES, I KNOW HE ISN'T... YES, I'LL TELL HIM...
I'M SORRY, SNOOPY... YOU'LL HAVE TO GO HOME... DOGS AREN'T ALLOWED IN SCHOOL..
RATS! NOW, I'LL NEVER GET MY MASTER'S!
SCHULZ

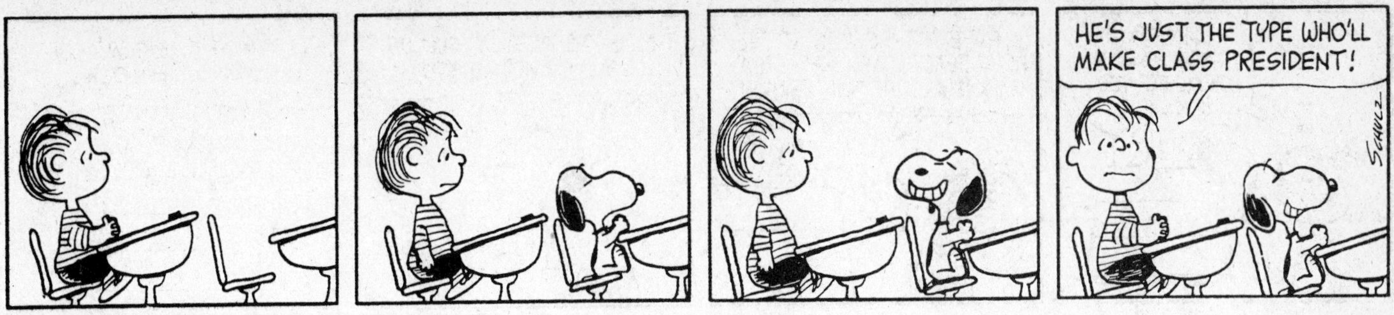
HE'S JUST THE TYPE WHO'LL MAKE CLASS PRESIDENT!
SCHULZ

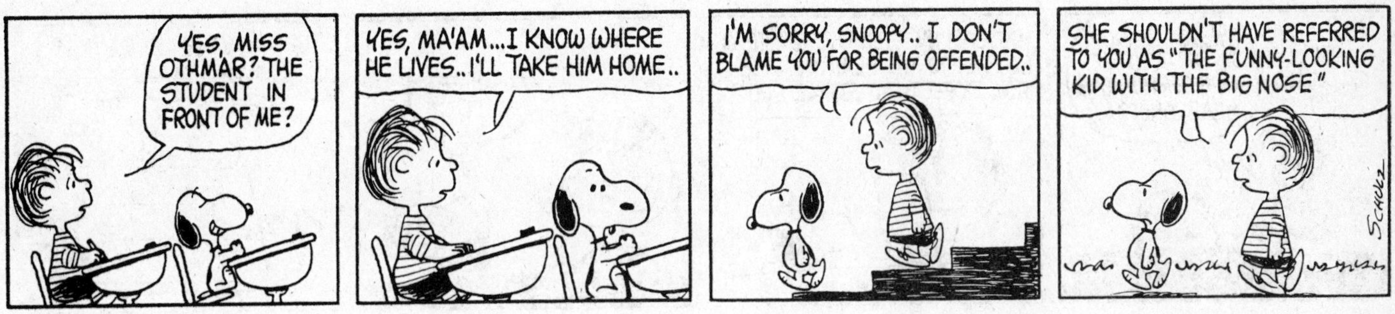
YES, MISS OTHMAR? THE STUDENT IN FRONT OF ME?
YES, MA'AM...I KNOW WHERE HE LIVES..I'LL TAKE HIM HOME..
I'M SORRY, SNOOPY.. I DON'T BLAME YOU FOR BEING OFFENDED..
SHE SHOULDN'T HAVE REFERRED TO YOU AS "THE FUNNY-LOOKING KID WITH THE BIG NOSE"
SCHULZ

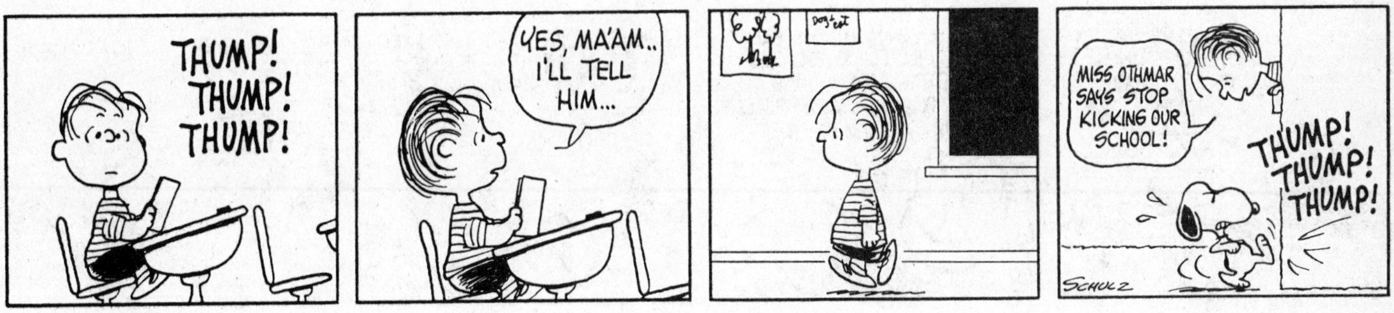
THUMP! THUMP! THUMP!
YES, MA'AM.. I'LL TELL HIM...
MISS OTHMAR SAYS STOP KICKING OUR SCHOOL!
THUMP! THUMP! THUMP!
SCHULZ

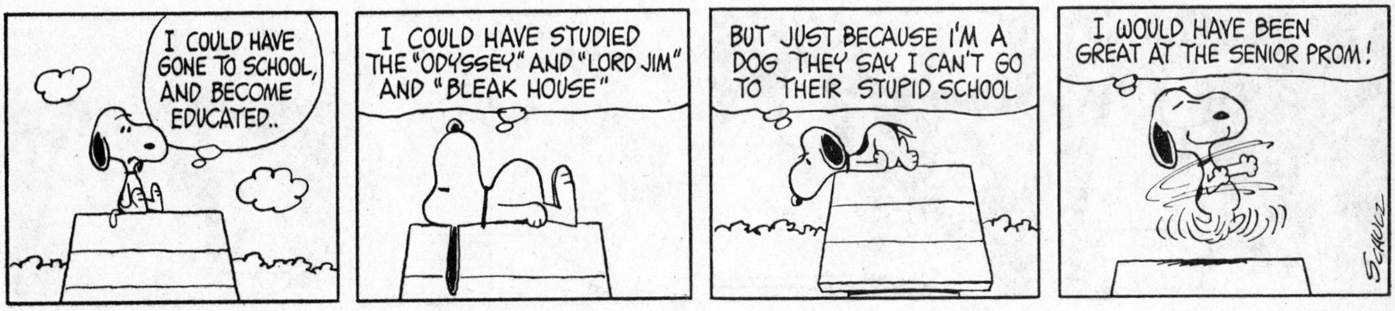
I COULD HAVE GONE TO SCHOOL, AND BECOME EDUCATED..
I COULD HAVE STUDIED THE "ODYSSEY" AND "LORD JIM" AND "BLEAK HOUSE"
BUT JUST BECAUSE I'M A DOG THEY SAY I CAN'T GO TO THEIR STUPID SCHOOL
I WOULD HAVE BEEN GREAT AT THE SENIOR PROM!
SCHULZ

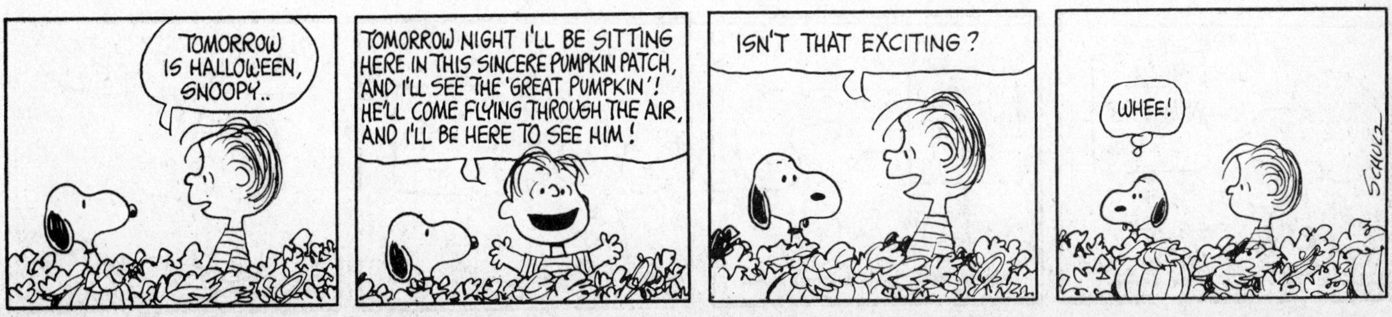
TOMORROW IS HALLOWEEN, SNOOPY..
TOMORROW NIGHT I'LL BE SITTING HERE IN THIS SINCERE PUMPKIN PATCH, AND I'LL SEE THE 'GREAT PUMPKIN'! HE'LL COME FLYING THROUGH THE AIR, AND I'LL BE HERE TO SEE HIM!
ISN'T THAT EXCITING?
WHEE!
SCHULZ

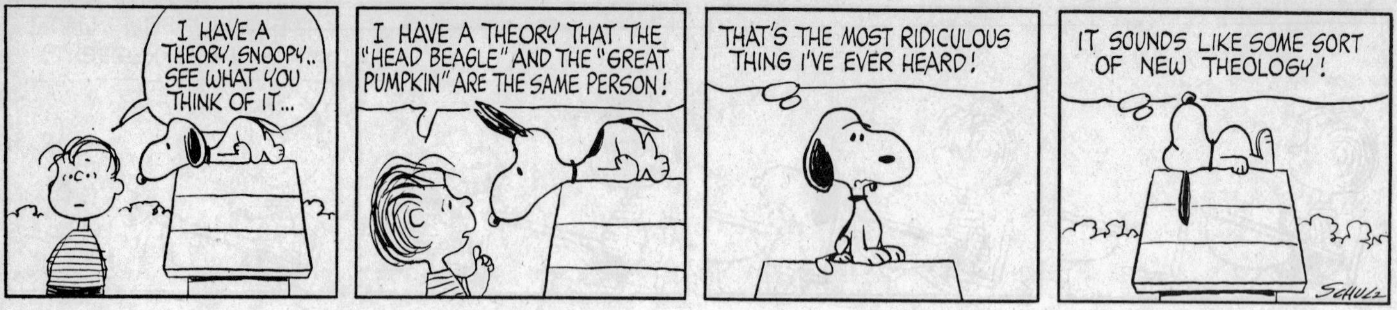
I HAVE A THEORY, SNOOPY.. SEE WHAT YOU THINK OF IT...
I HAVE A THEORY THAT THE "HEAD BEAGLE" AND THE "GREAT PUMPKIN" ARE THE SAME PERSON!
THAT'S THE MOST RIDICULOUS THING I'VE EVER HEARD!
IT SOUNDS LIKE SOME SORT OF NEW THEOLOGY!
SCHULZ

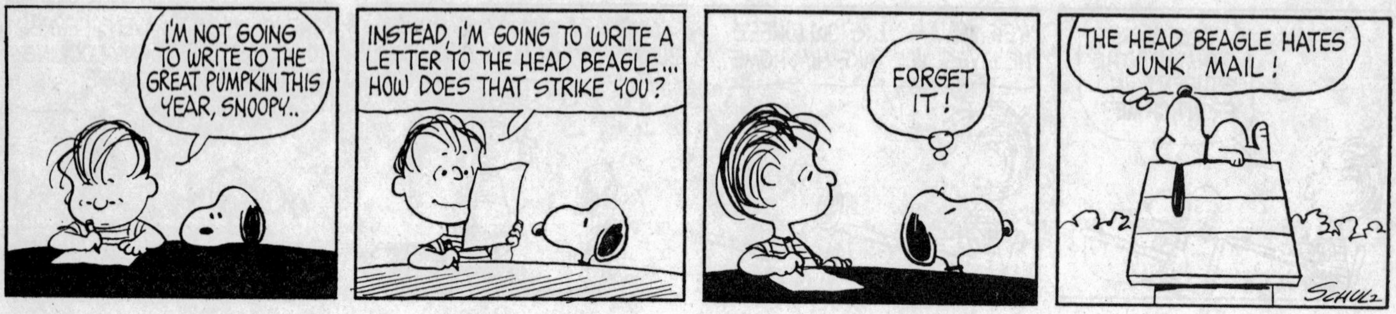
I'M NOT GOING TO WRITE TO THE GREAT PUMPKIN THIS YEAR, SNOOPY..
INSTEAD, I'M GOING TO WRITE A LETTER TO THE HEAD BEAGLE... HOW DOES THAT STRIKE YOU?
FORGET IT!
THE HEAD BEAGLE HATES JUNK MAIL!
SCHULZ

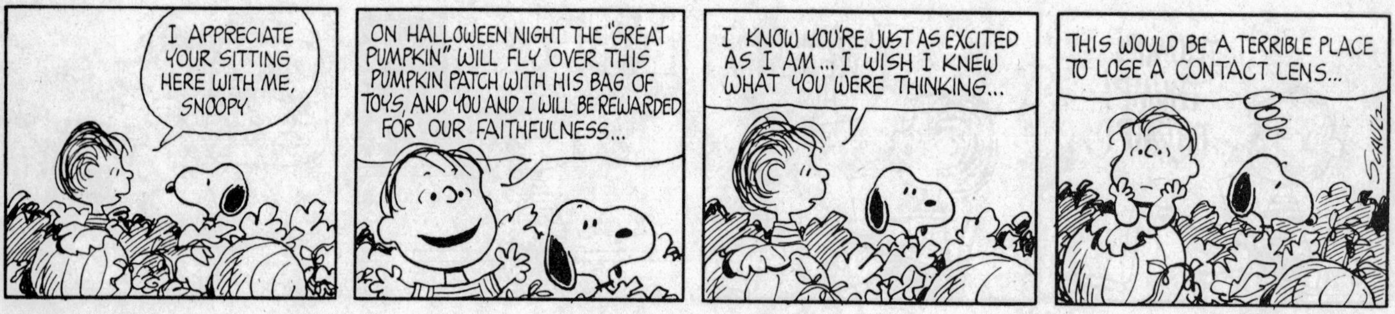
I APPRECIATE YOUR SITTING HERE WITH ME, SNOOPY
ON HALLOWEEN NIGHT THE "GREAT PUMPKIN" WILL FLY OVER THIS PUMPKIN PATCH WITH HIS BAG OF TOYS, AND YOU AND I WILL BE REWARDED FOR OUR FAITHFULNESS...
I KNOW YOU'RE JUST AS EXCITED AS I AM... I WISH I KNEW WHAT YOU WERE THINKING...
THIS WOULD BE A TERRIBLE PLACE TO LOSE A CONTACT LENS...
SCHULZ

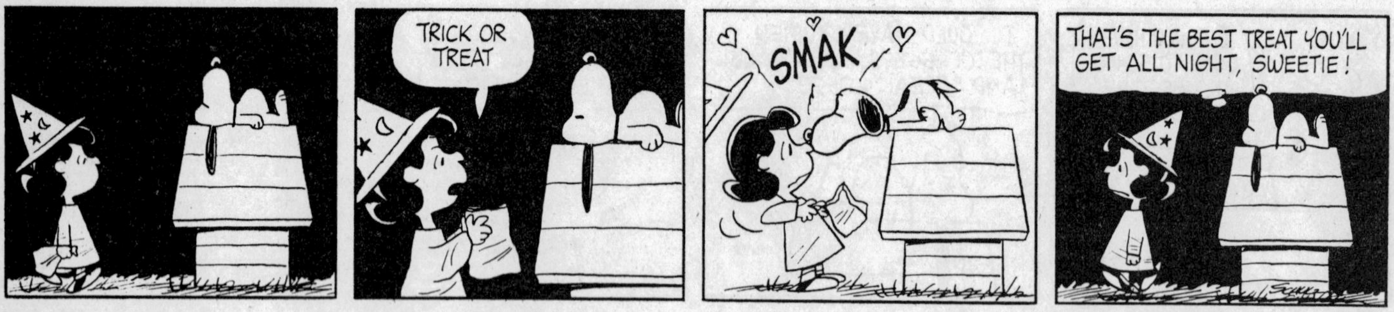
TRICK OR TREAT
SMAK
THAT'S THE BEST TREAT YOU'LL GET ALL NIGHT, SWEETIE!

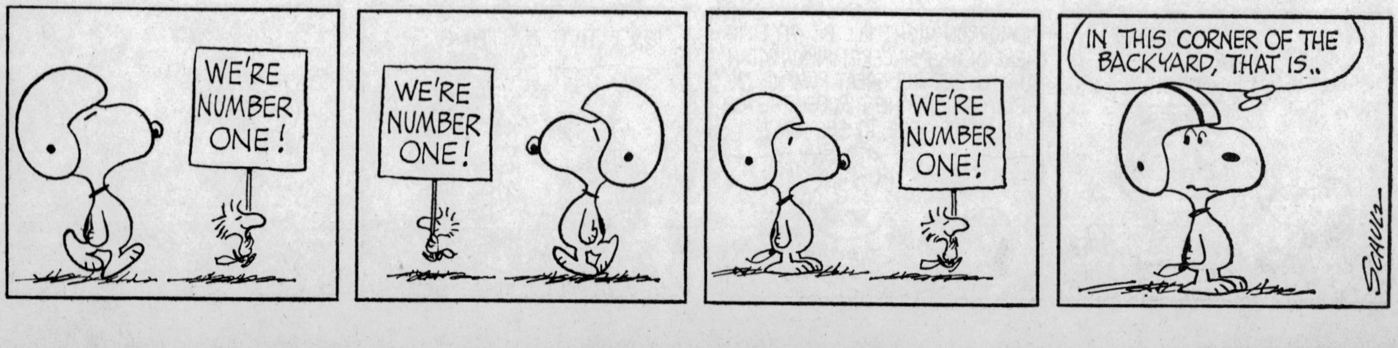
WE'RE NUMBER ONE!
WE'RE NUMBER ONE!
WE'RE NUMBER ONE!
IN THIS CORNER OF THE BACKYARD, THAT IS..
SCHULZ

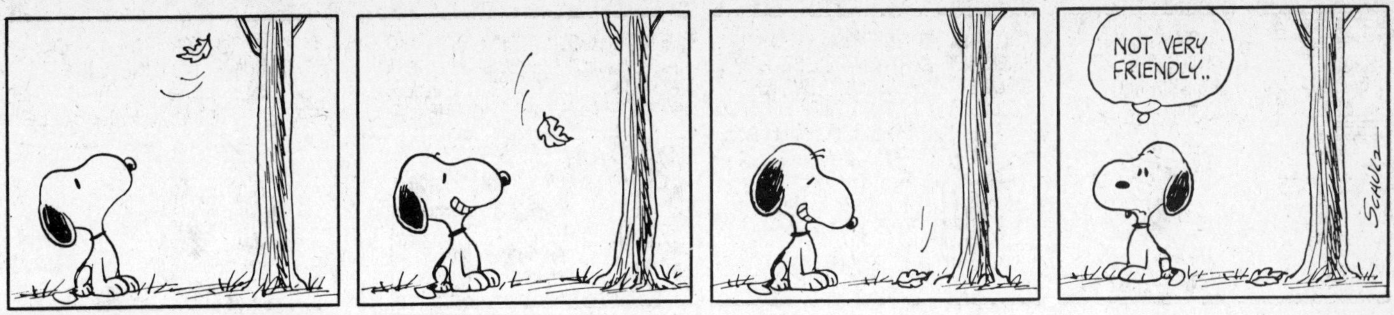
NOT VERY FRIENDLY..
SCHULZ

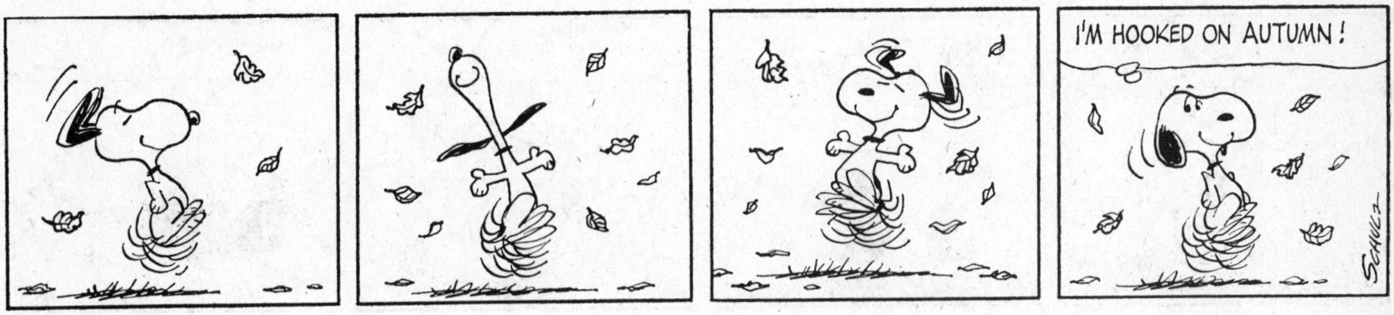
I'M HOOKED ON AUTUMN!
SCHULZ

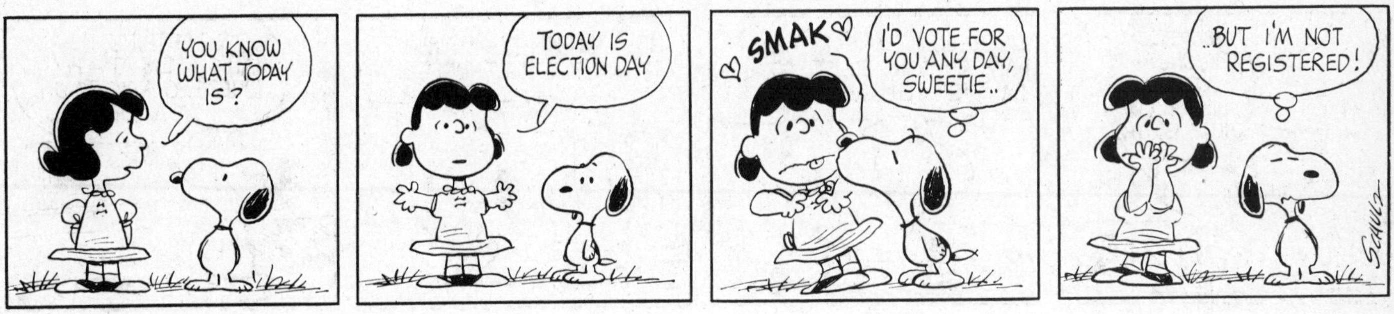
YOU KNOW WHAT TODAY IS?
TODAY IS ELECTION DAY
SMAK
I'D VOTE FOR YOU ANY DAY, SWEETIE..
..BUT I'M NOT REGISTERED!
SCHULZ

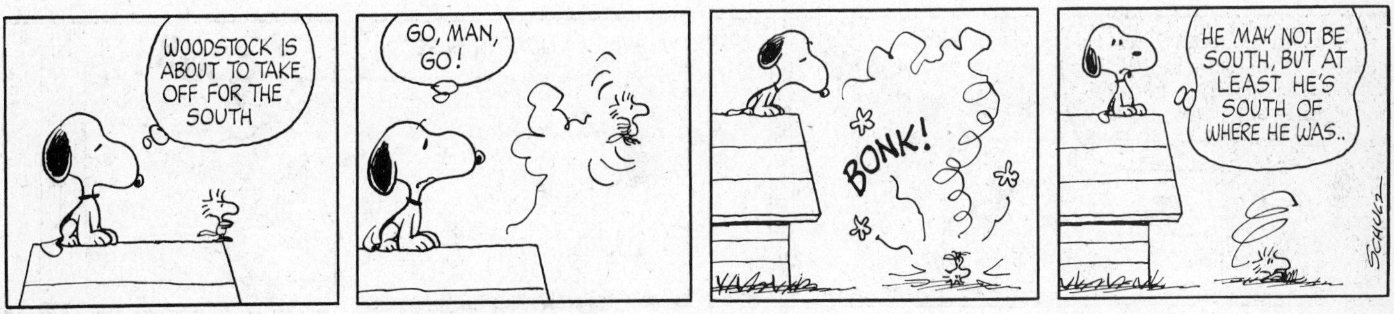
WOODSTOCK IS ABOUT TO TAKE OFF FOR THE SOUTH
GO, MAN, GO!
BONK!
HE MAY NOT BE SOUTH, BUT AT LEAST HE'S SOUTH OF WHERE HE WAS..
SCHULZ

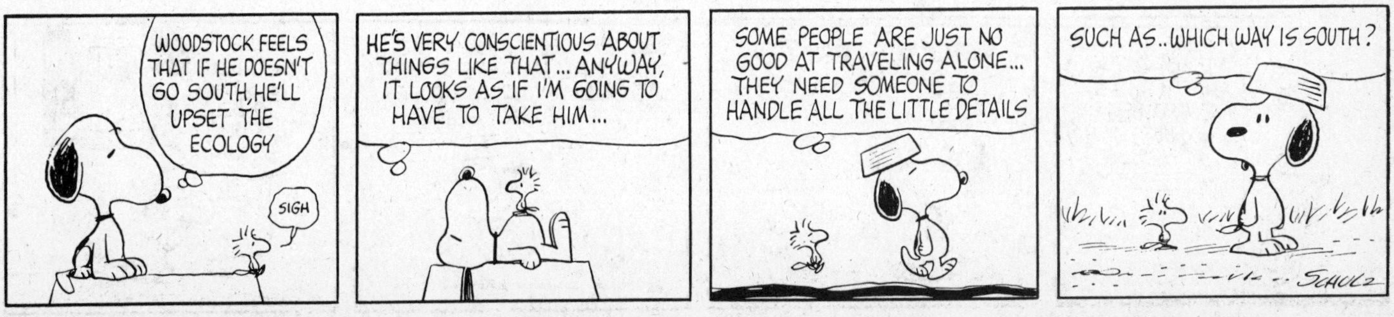
WOODSTOCK FEELS THAT IF HE DOESN'T GO SOUTH, HE'LL UPSET THE ECOLOGY
SIGH
HE'S VERY CONSCIENTIOUS ABOUT THINGS LIKE THAT... ANYWAY, IT LOOKS AS IF I'M GOING TO HAVE TO TAKE HIM...
SOME PEOPLE ARE JUST NO GOOD AT TRAVELING ALONE... THEY NEED SOMEONE TO HANDLE ALL THE LITTLE DETAILS
SUCH AS.. WHICH WAY IS SOUTH?
SCHULZ

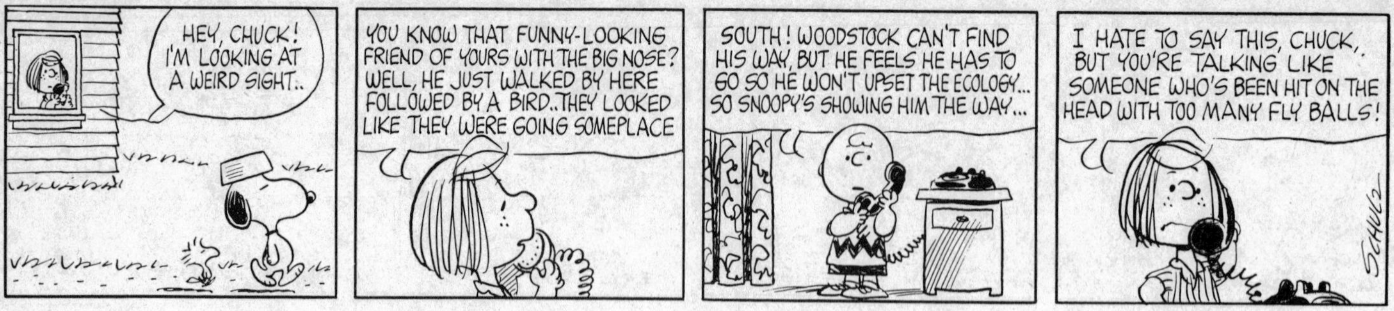
HEY, CHUCK! I'M LOOKING AT A WEIRD SIGHT..
YOU KNOW THAT FUNNY-LOOKING FRIEND OF YOURS WITH THE BIG NOSE? WELL, HE JUST WALKED BY HERE FOLLOWED BY A BIRD..THEY LOOKED LIKE THEY WERE GOING SOMEPLACE
SOUTH! WOODSTOCK CAN'T FIND HIS WAY, BUT HE FEELS HE HAS TO GO SO HE WON'T UPSET THE ECOLOGY... SO SNOOPY'S SHOWING HIM THE WAY...
I HATE TO SAY THIS, CHUCK, BUT YOU'RE TALKING LIKE SOMEONE WHO'S BEEN HIT ON THE HEAD WITH TOO MANY FLY BALLS!
SCHULZ

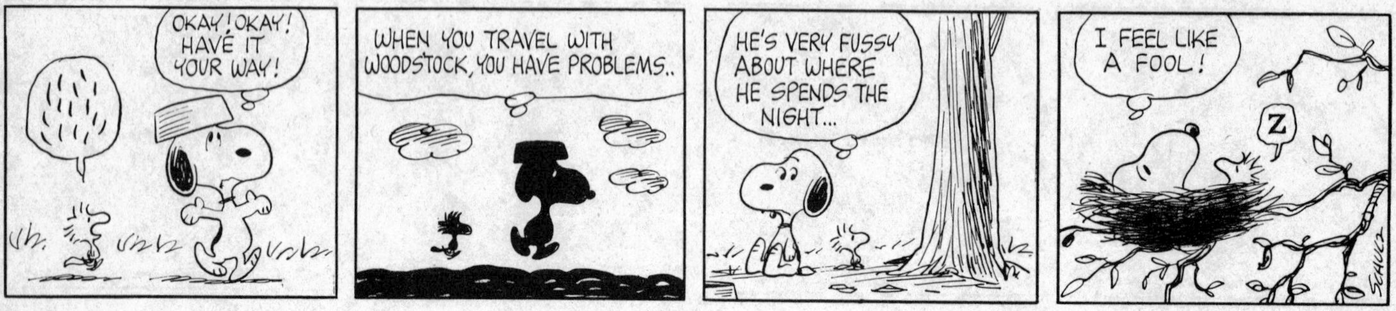
OKAY! OKAY! HAVE IT YOUR WAY!
WHEN YOU TRAVEL WITH WOODSTOCK, YOU HAVE PROBLEMS..
HE'S VERY FUSSY ABOUT WHERE HE SPENDS THE NIGHT...
I FEEL LIKE A FOOL!
Z
SCHULZ

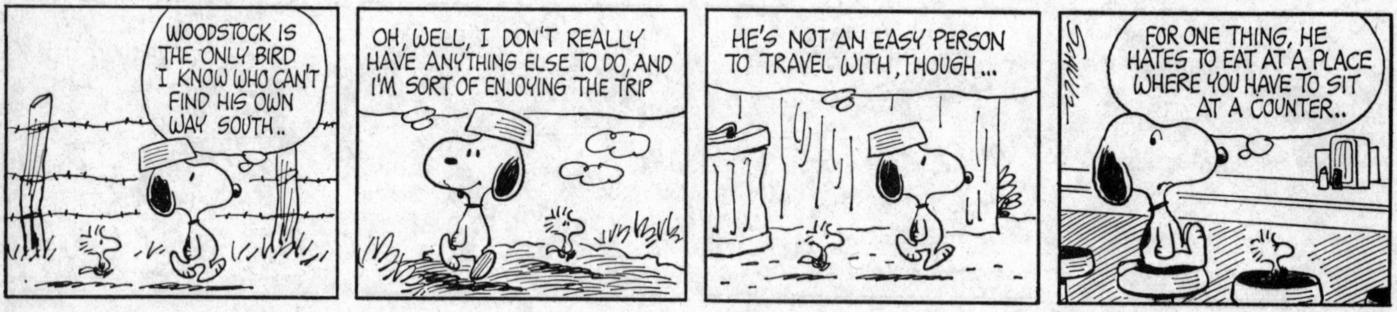
WOODSTOCK IS THE ONLY BIRD I KNOW WHO CAN'T FIND HIS OWN WAY SOUTH..
OH, WELL, I DON'T REALLY HAVE ANYTHING ELSE TO DO, AND I'M SORT OF ENJOYING THE TRIP
HE'S NOT AN EASY PERSON TO TRAVEL WITH, THOUGH...
SCHULZ
FOR ONE THING, HE HATES TO EAT AT A PLACE WHERE YOU HAVE TO SIT AT A COUNTER..

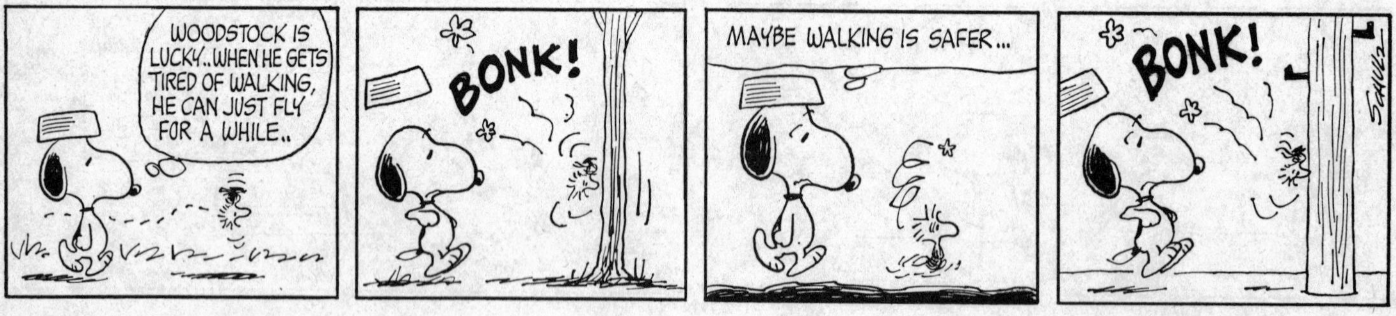
WOODSTOCK IS LUCKY..WHEN HE GETS TIRED OF WALKING, HE CAN JUST FLY FOR A WHILE..
BONK!
MAYBE WALKING IS SAFER...
BONK!
SCHULZ

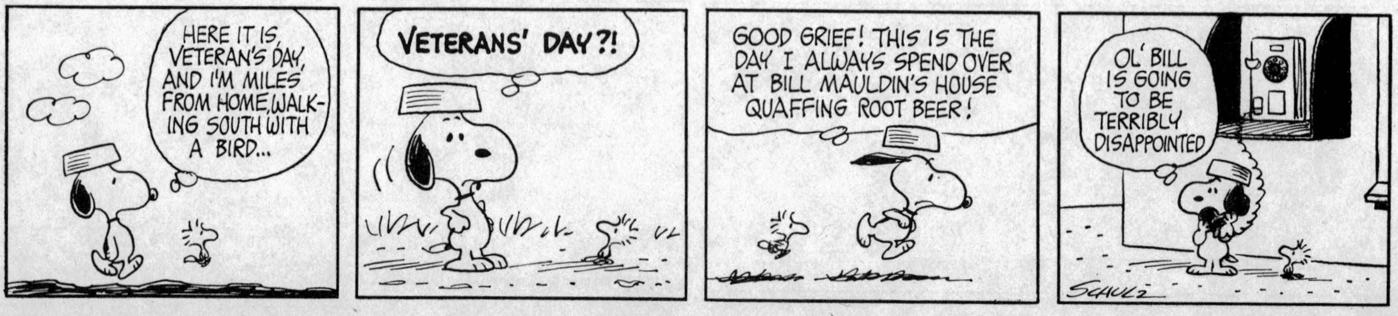
HERE IT IS, VETERAN'S DAY, AND I'M MILES FROM HOME, WALKING SOUTH WITH A BIRD...
VETERANS' DAY?!
GOOD GRIEF! THIS IS THE DAY I ALWAYS SPEND OVER AT BILL MAULDIN'S HOUSE QUAFFING ROOT BEER!
OL' BILL IS GOING TO BE TERRIBLY DISAPPOINTED
SCHULZ

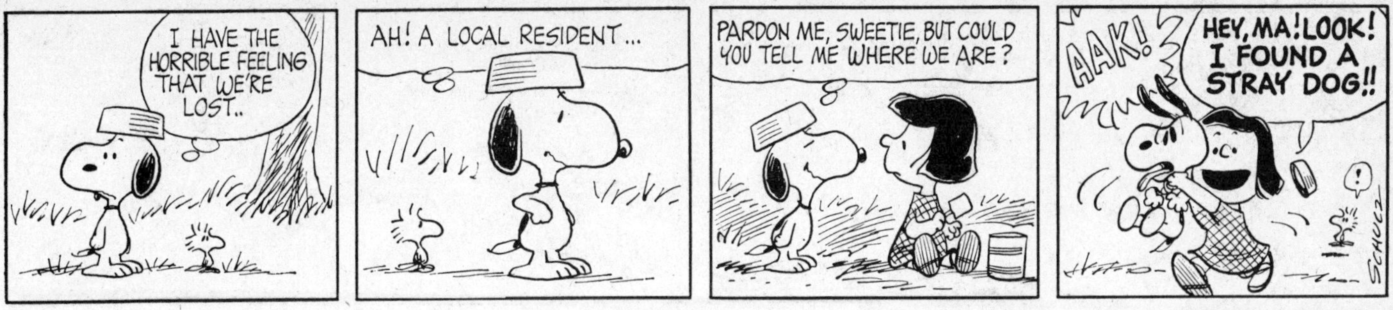
I HAVE THE HORRIBLE FEELING THAT WE'RE LOST..
AH! A LOCAL RESIDENT...
PARDON ME, SWEETIE, BUT COULD YOU TELL ME WHERE WE ARE?
AAK!
HEY, MA! LOOK! I FOUND A STRAY DOG!!
!

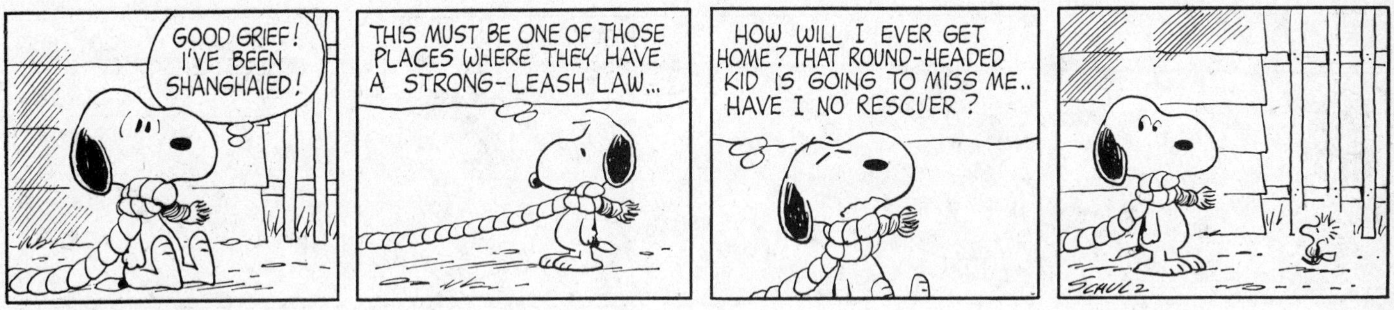
GOOD GRIEF! I'VE BEEN SHANGHAIED!
THIS MUST BE ONE OF THOSE PLACES WHERE THEY HAVE A STRONG-LEASH LAW...
HOW WILL I EVER GET HOME? THAT ROUND-HEADED KID IS GOING TO MISS ME.. HAVE I NO RESCUER?

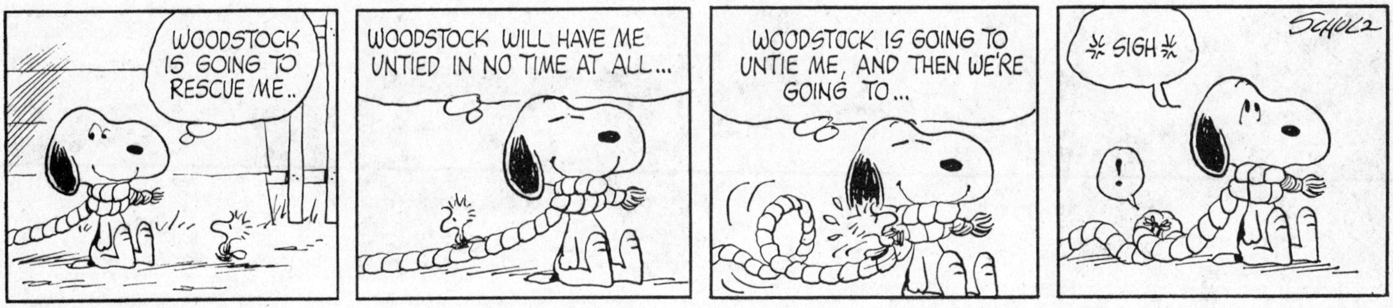
WOODSTOCK IS GOING TO RESCUE ME..
WOODSTOCK WILL HAVE ME UNTIED IN NO TIME AT ALL...
WOODSTOCK IS GOING TO UNTIE ME, AND THEN WE'RE GOING TO...
SIGH
!

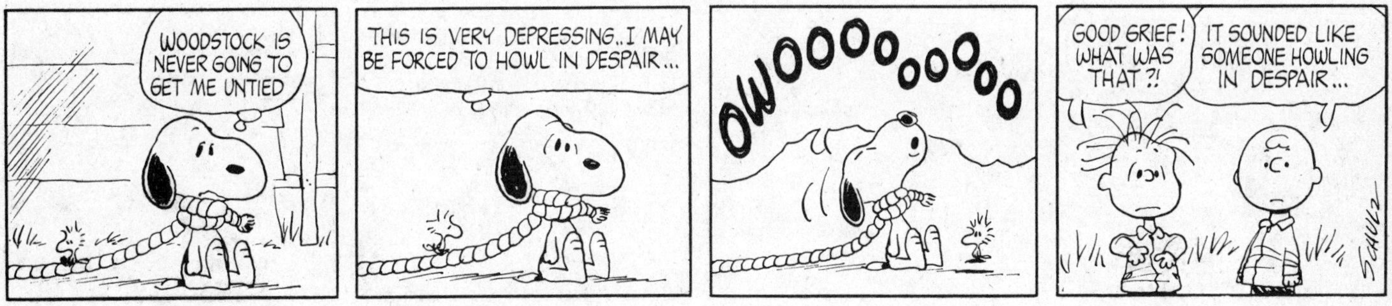
WOODSTOCK IS NEVER GOING TO GET ME UNTIED
THIS IS VERY DEPRESSING..I MAY BE FORCED TO HOWL IN DESPAIR...
OWOOOOOOOOO
GOOD GRIEF! WHAT WAS THAT?!
IT SOUNDED LIKE SOMEONE HOWLING IN DESPAIR...

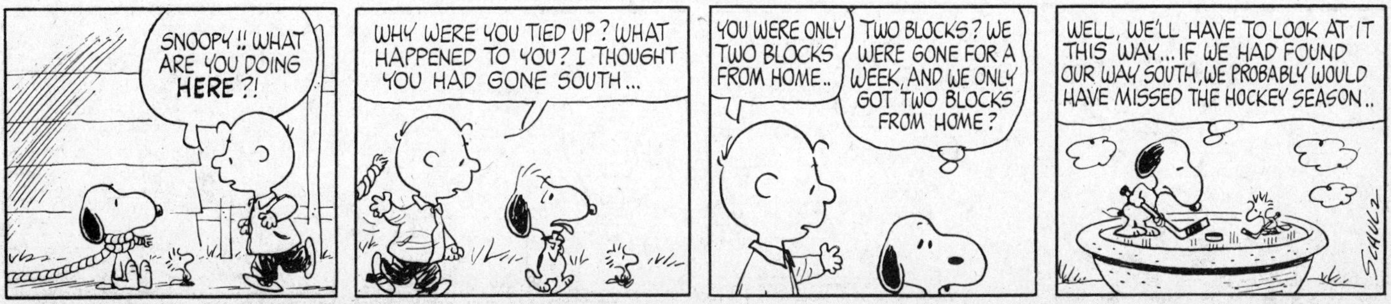
SNOOPY!! WHAT ARE YOU DOING HERE?!
WHY WERE YOU TIED UP? WHAT HAPPENED TO YOU? I THOUGHT YOU HAD GONE SOUTH...
YOU WERE ONLY TWO BLOCKS FROM HOME..
TWO BLOCKS? WE WERE GONE FOR A WEEK, AND WE ONLY GOT TWO BLOCKS FROM HOME?
WELL, WE'LL HAVE TO LOOK AT IT THIS WAY... IF WE HAD FOUND OUR WAY SOUTH, WE PROBABLY WOULD HAVE MISSED THE HOCKEY SEASON..

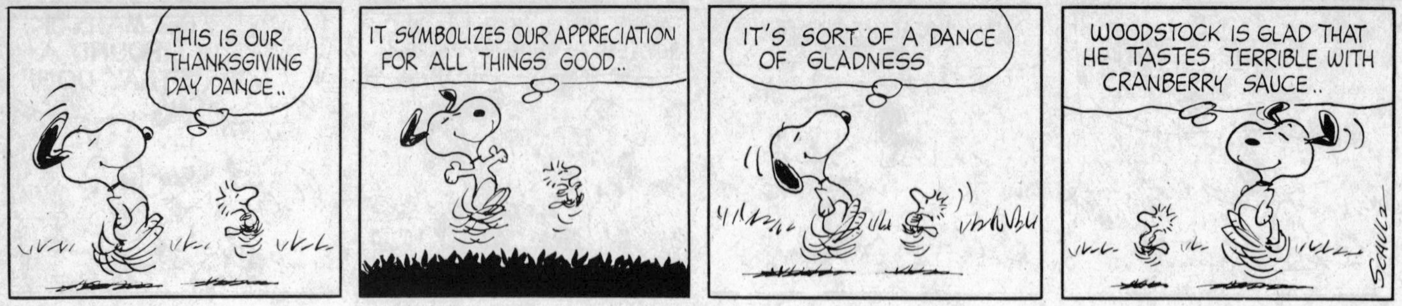
THIS IS OUR THANKSGIVING DAY DANCE..
IT SYMBOLIZES OUR APPRECIATION FOR ALL THINGS GOOD..
IT'S SORT OF A DANCE OF GLADNESS
WOODSTOCK IS GLAD THAT HE TASTES TERRIBLE WITH CRANBERRY SAUCE..
SCHULZ

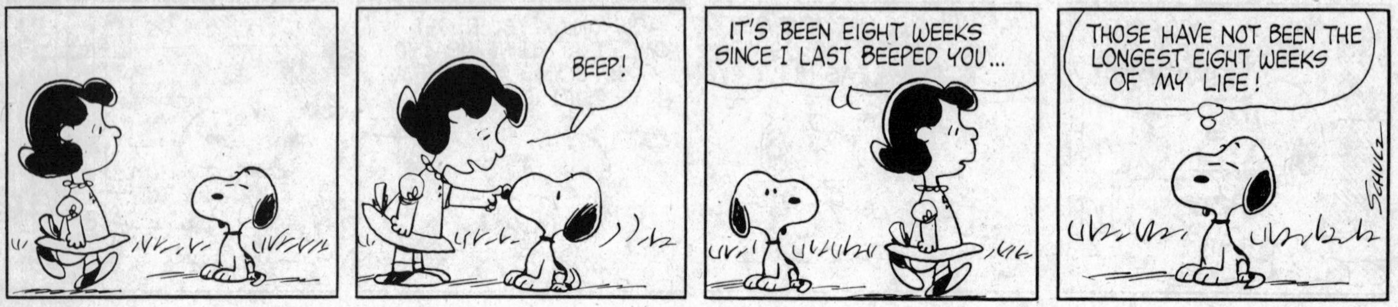
BEEP!
IT'S BEEN EIGHT WEEKS SINCE I LAST BEEPED YOU...
THOSE HAVE NOT BEEN THE LONGEST EIGHT WEEKS OF MY LIFE!
SCHULZ

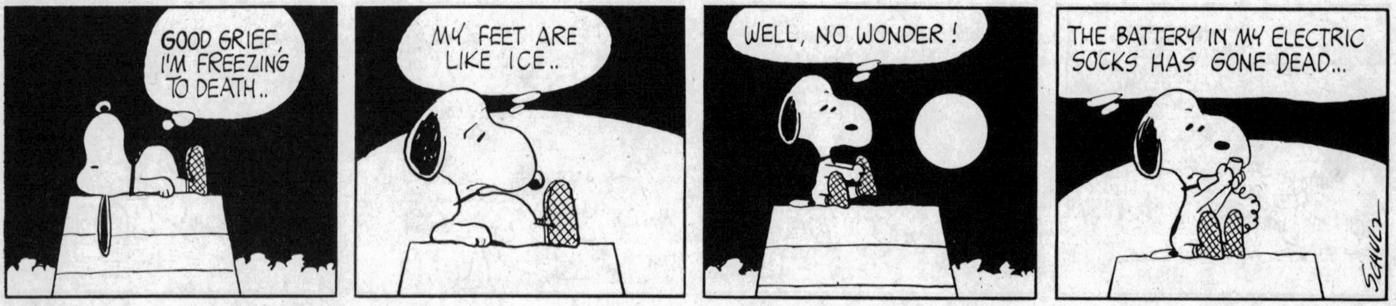
GOOD GRIEF, I'M FREEZING TO DEATH..
MY FEET ARE LIKE ICE..
WELL, NO WONDER!
THE BATTERY IN MY ELECTRIC SOCKS HAS GONE DEAD...
SCHULZ

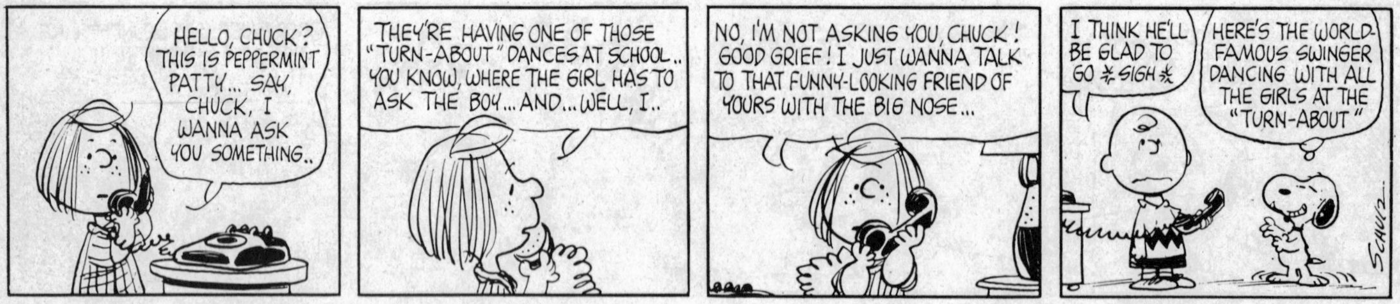
HELLO, CHUCK? THIS IS PEPPERMINT PATTY... SAY, CHUCK, I WANNA ASK YOU SOMETHING..
THEY'RE HAVING ONE OF THOSE "TURN-ABOUT" DANCES AT SCHOOL.. YOU KNOW, WHERE THE GIRL HAS TO ASK THE BOY... AND... WELL, I..
NO, I'M NOT ASKING YOU, CHUCK! GOOD GRIEF! I JUST WANNA TALK TO THAT FUNNY-LOOKING FRIEND OF YOURS WITH THE BIG NOSE...
I THINK HE'LL BE GLAD TO GO *SIGH*
HERE'S THE WORLD-FAMOUS SWINGER DANCING WITH ALL THE GIRLS AT THE "TURN-ABOUT"
SCHULZ

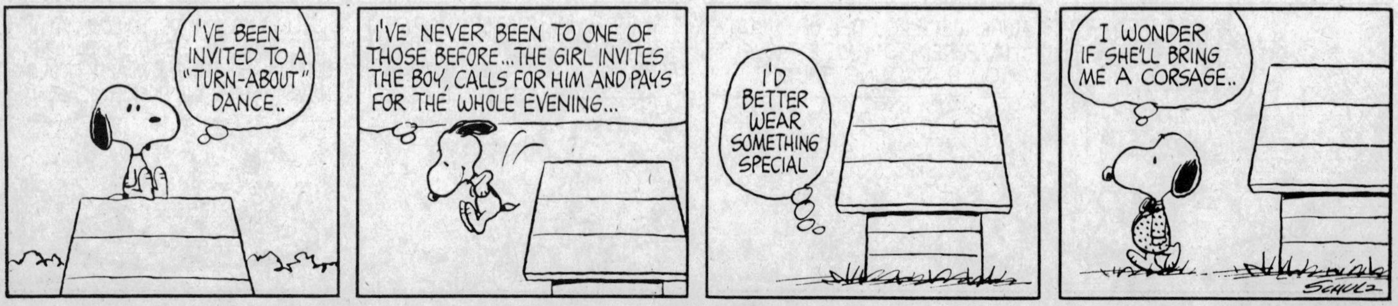
I'VE BEEN INVITED TO A "TURN-ABOUT" DANCE..
I'VE NEVER BEEN TO ONE OF THOSE BEFORE... THE GIRL INVITES THE BOY, CALLS FOR HIM AND PAYS FOR THE WHOLE EVENING...
I'D BETTER WEAR SOMETHING SPECIAL
I WONDER IF SHE'LL BRING ME A CORSAGE..
SCHULZ

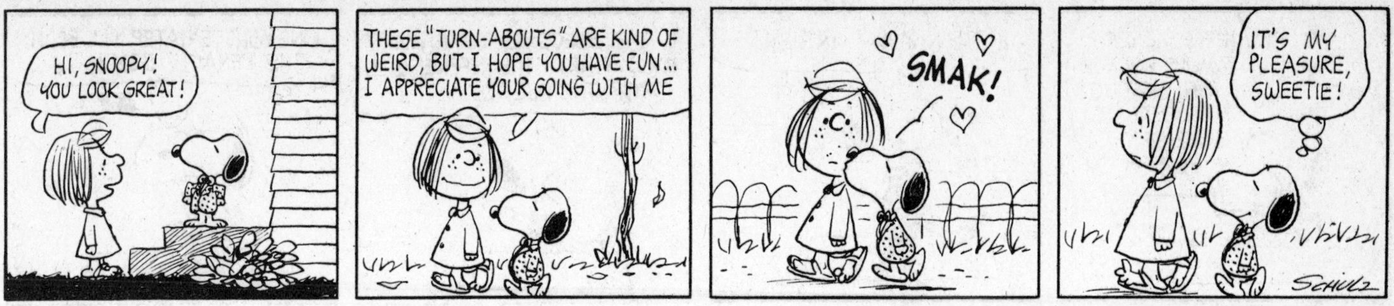
HI, SNOOPY! YOU LOOK GREAT!
THESE "TURN-ABOUTS" ARE KIND OF WEIRD, BUT I HOPE YOU HAVE FUN... I APPRECIATE YOUR GOING WITH ME
SMAK!
IT'S MY PLEASURE, SWEETIE!

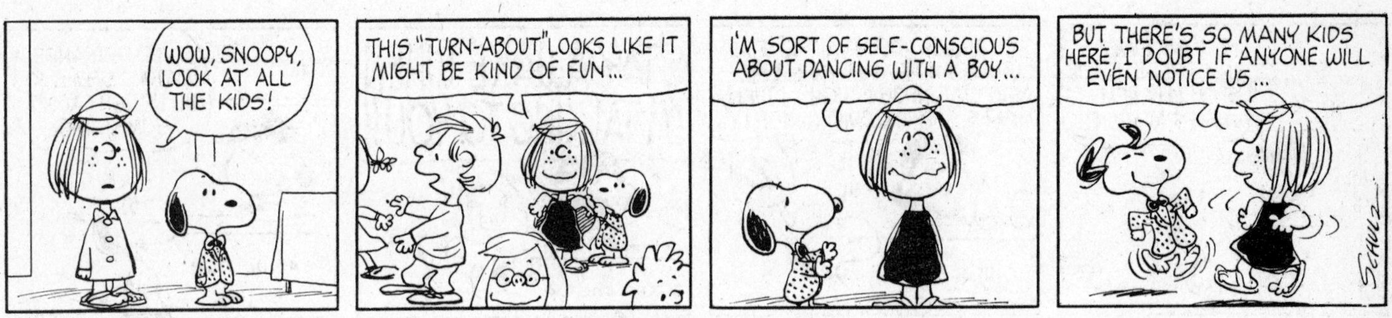
WOW, SNOOPY, LOOK AT ALL THE KIDS!
THIS "TURN-ABOUT" LOOKS LIKE IT MIGHT BE KIND OF FUN...
I'M SORT OF SELF-CONSCIOUS ABOUT DANCING WITH A BOY...
BUT THERE'S SO MANY KIDS HERE, I DOUBT IF ANYONE WILL EVEN NOTICE US...

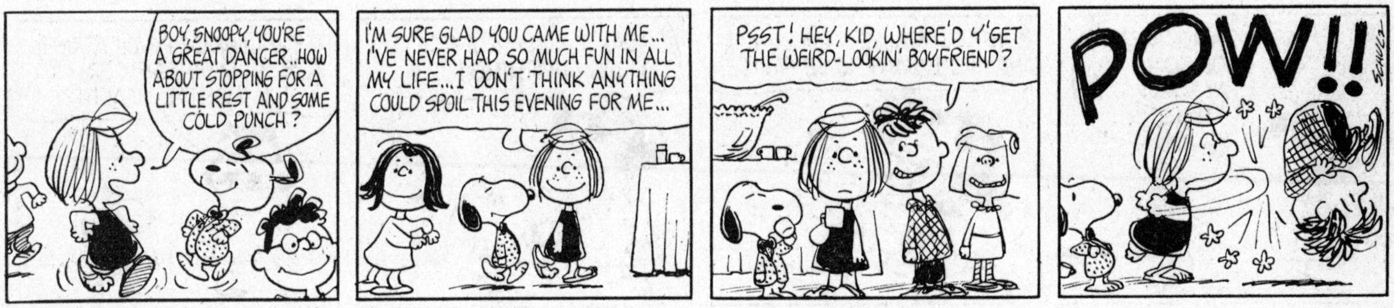
BOY, SNOOPY, YOU'RE A GREAT DANCER..HOW ABOUT STOPPING FOR A LITTLE REST AND SOME COLD PUNCH?
I'M SURE GLAD YOU CAME WITH ME... I'VE NEVER HAD SO MUCH FUN IN ALL MY LIFE...I DON'T THINK ANYTHING COULD SPOIL THIS EVENING FOR ME...
PSST! HEY, KID, WHERE'D Y'GET THE WEIRD-LOOKIN' BOYFRIEND?
POW!!

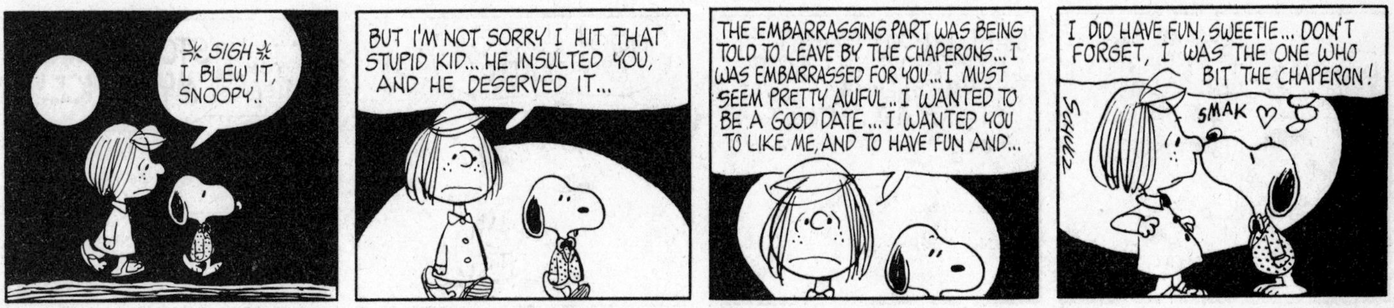
SIGH I BLEW IT, SNOOPY..
BUT I'M NOT SORRY I HIT THAT STUPID KID... HE INSULTED YOU, AND HE DESERVED IT...
THE EMBARRASSING PART WAS BEING TOLD TO LEAVE BY THE CHAPERONS... I WAS EMBARRASSED FOR YOU... I MUST SEEM PRETTY AWFUL.. I WANTED TO BE A GOOD DATE... I WANTED YOU TO LIKE ME, AND TO HAVE FUN AND...
I DID HAVE FUN, SWEETIE... DON'T FORGET, I WAS THE ONE WHO BIT THE CHAPERON!
SMAK

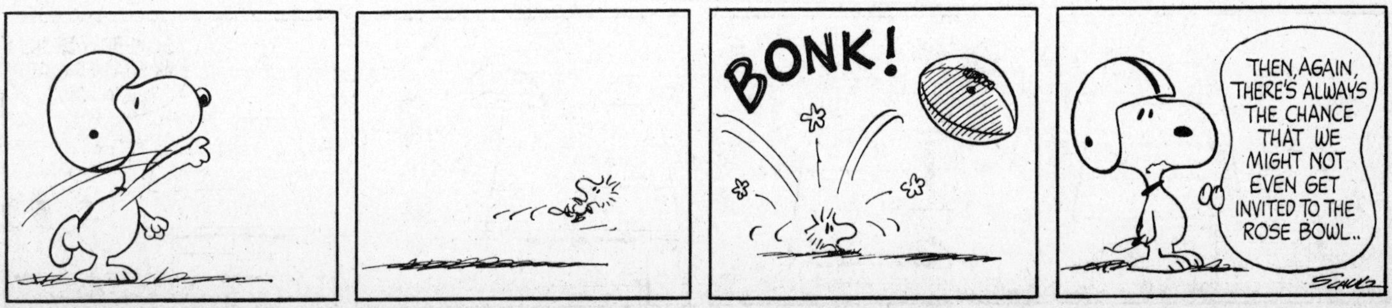
BONK!
THEN, AGAIN, THERE'S ALWAYS THE CHANCE THAT WE MIGHT NOT EVEN GET INVITED TO THE ROSE BOWL..

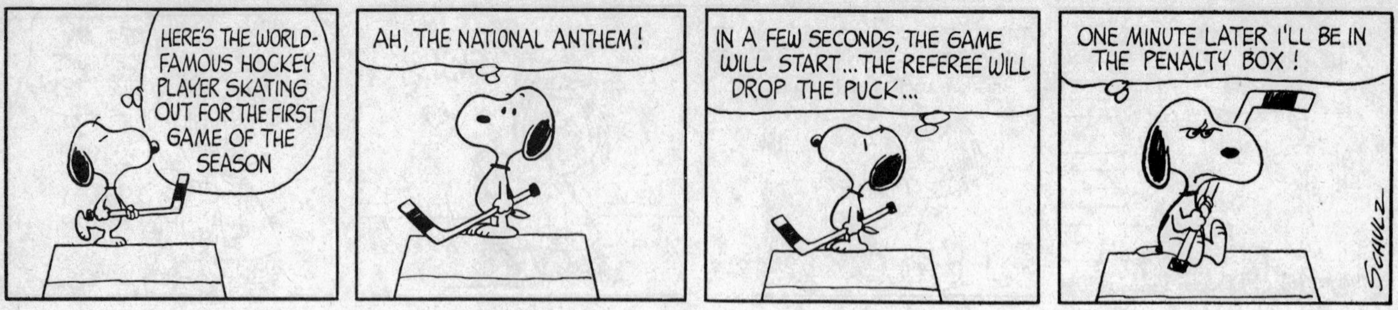
HERE'S THE WORLD-FAMOUS HOCKEY PLAYER SKATING OUT FOR THE FIRST GAME OF THE SEASON
AH, THE NATIONAL ANTHEM!
IN A FEW SECONDS, THE GAME WILL START...THE REFEREE WILL DROP THE PUCK...
ONE MINUTE LATER I'LL BE IN THE PENALTY BOX!
SCHULZ

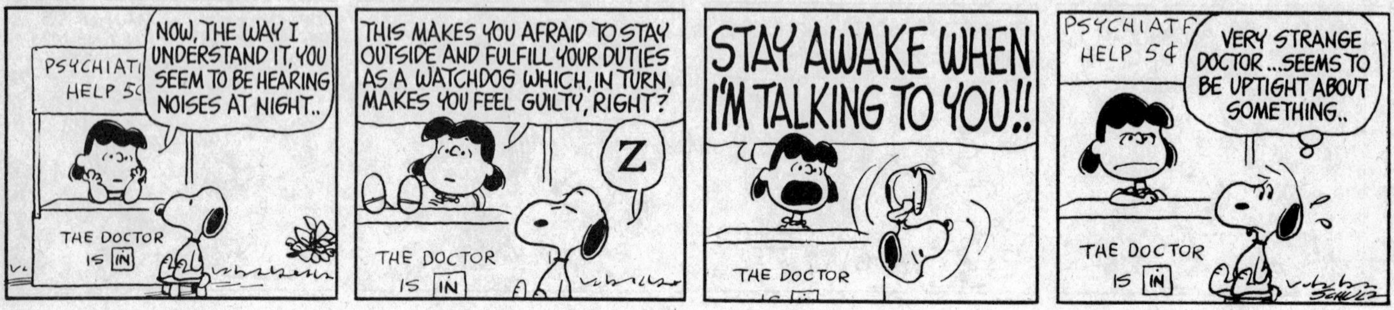
PSYCHIATRI
HELP 5¢
THE DOCTOR IS IN
NOW, THE WAY I UNDERSTAND IT, YOU SEEM TO BE HEARING NOISES AT NIGHT..
THIS MAKES YOU AFRAID TO STAY OUTSIDE AND FULFILL YOUR DUTIES AS A WATCHDOG WHICH, IN TURN, MAKES YOU FEEL GUILTY, RIGHT?
Z
THE DOCTOR IS IN
STAY AWAKE WHEN I'M TALKING TO YOU!!
THE DOCTOR
PSYCHIATR
HELP 5¢
VERY STRANGE DOCTOR...SEEMS TO BE UPTIGHT ABOUT SOMETHING..
THE DOCTOR IS IN
SCHULZ

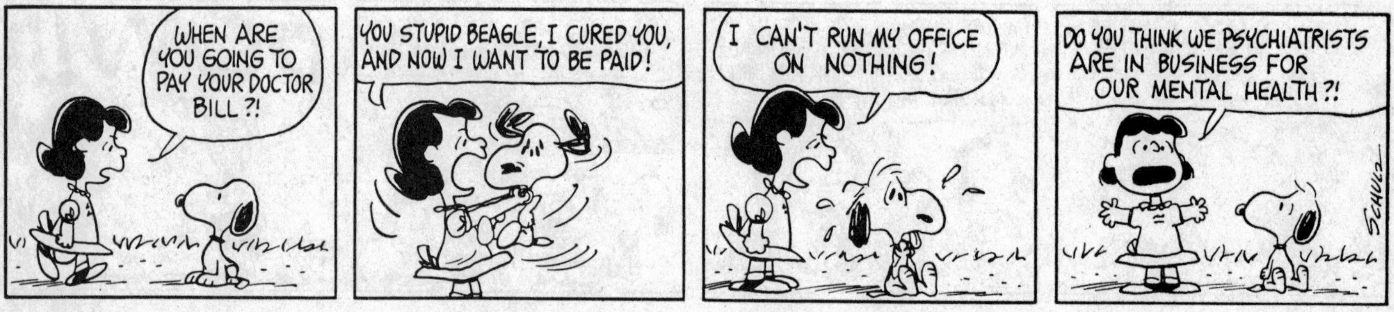
WHEN ARE YOU GOING TO PAY YOUR DOCTOR BILL?!
YOU STUPID BEAGLE, I CURED YOU, AND NOW I WANT TO BE PAID!
I CAN'T RUN MY OFFICE ON NOTHING!
DO YOU THINK WE PSYCHIATRISTS ARE IN BUSINESS FOR OUR MENTAL HEALTH?!
SCHULZ

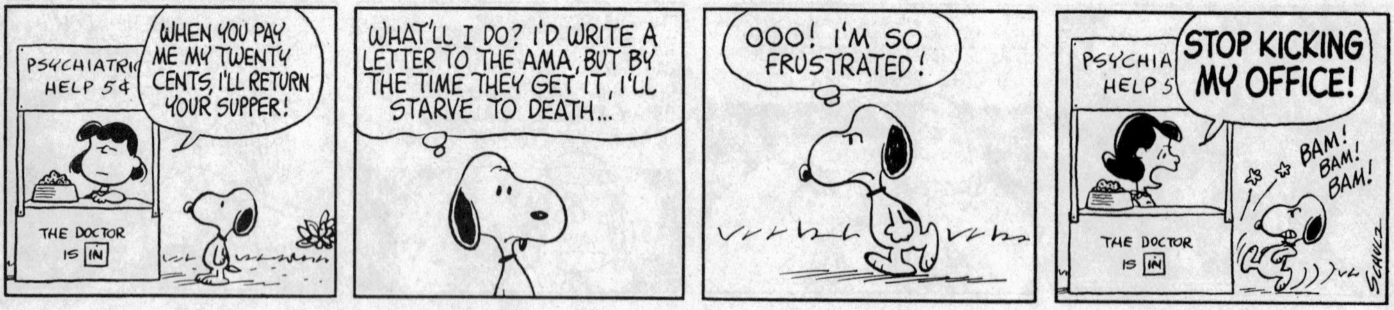
PSYCHIATRI
HELP 5¢
THE DOCTOR IS IN
WHEN YOU PAY ME MY TWENTY CENTS, I'LL RETURN YOUR SUPPER!
WHAT'LL I DO? I'D WRITE A LETTER TO THE AMA, BUT BY THE TIME THEY GET IT, I'LL STARVE TO DEATH...
OOO! I'M SO FRUSTRATED!
PSYCHIA
HELP 5
STOP KICKING MY OFFICE!
BAM! BAM! BAM!
THE DOCTOR IS IN
SCHULZ

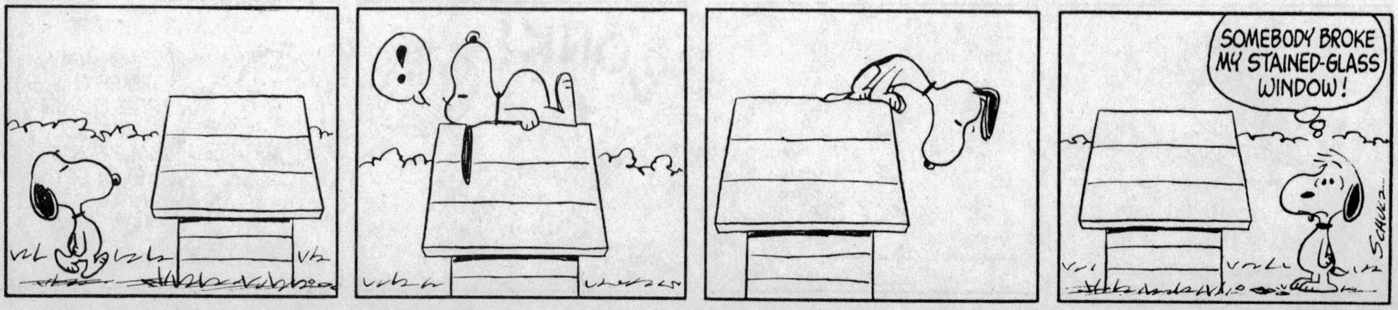
!
SOMEBODY BROKE MY STAINED-GLASS WINDOW!
SCHULZ

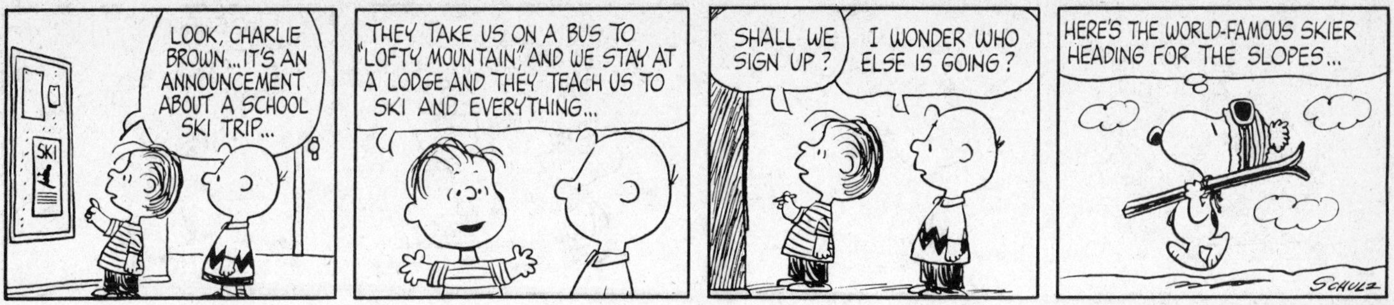
LOOK, CHARLIE BROWN...IT'S AN ANNOUNCEMENT ABOUT A SCHOOL SKI TRIP...
SKI
THEY TAKE US ON A BUS TO "LOFTY MOUNTAIN," AND WE STAY AT A LODGE AND THEY TEACH US TO SKI AND EVERYTHING...
SHALL WE SIGN UP?
I WONDER WHO ELSE IS GOING?
HERE'S THE WORLD-FAMOUS SKIER HEADING FOR THE SLOPES...
SCHULZ

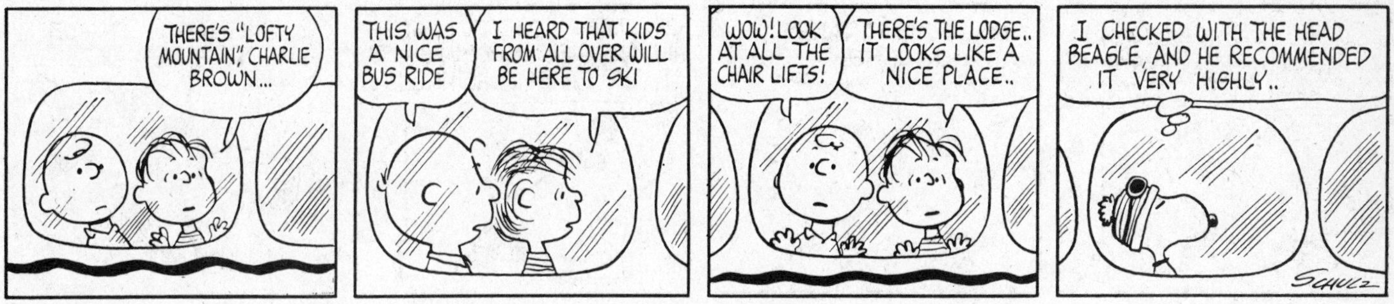
THERE'S "LOFTY MOUNTAIN," CHARLIE BROWN...
THIS WAS A NICE BUS RIDE
I HEARD THAT KIDS FROM ALL OVER WILL BE HERE TO SKI
WOW! LOOK AT ALL THE CHAIR LIFTS!
THERE'S THE LODGE.. IT LOOKS LIKE A NICE PLACE..
I CHECKED WITH THE HEAD BEAGLE, AND HE RECOMMENDED IT VERY HIGHLY..
SCHULZ

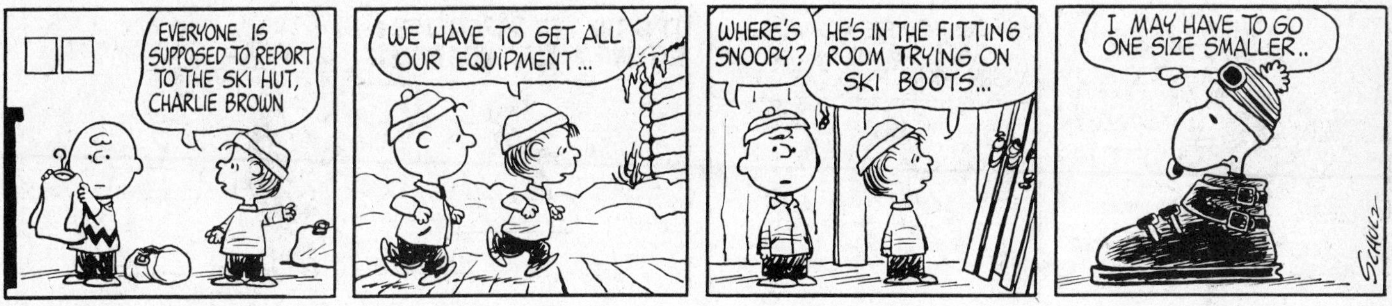
EVERYONE IS SUPPOSED TO REPORT TO THE SKI HUT, CHARLIE BROWN
WE HAVE TO GET ALL OUR EQUIPMENT...
WHERE'S SNOOPY?
HE'S IN THE FITTING ROOM TRYING ON SKI BOOTS...
I MAY HAVE TO GO ONE SIZE SMALLER..
SCHULZ

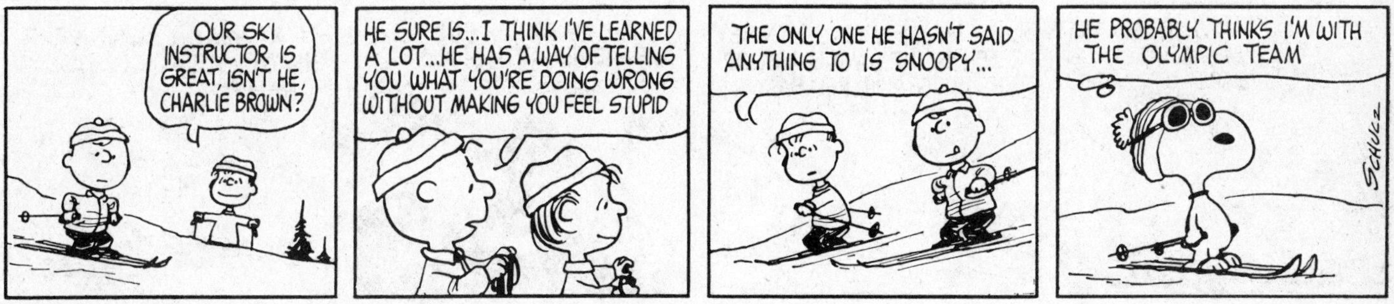
OUR SKI INSTRUCTOR IS GREAT, ISN'T HE, CHARLIE BROWN?
HE SURE IS...I THINK I'VE LEARNED A LOT...HE HAS A WAY OF TELLING YOU WHAT YOU'RE DOING WRONG WITHOUT MAKING YOU FEEL STUPID
THE ONLY ONE HE HASN'T SAID ANYTHING TO IS SNOOPY...
HE PROBABLY THINKS I'M WITH THE OLYMPIC TEAM
SCHULZ

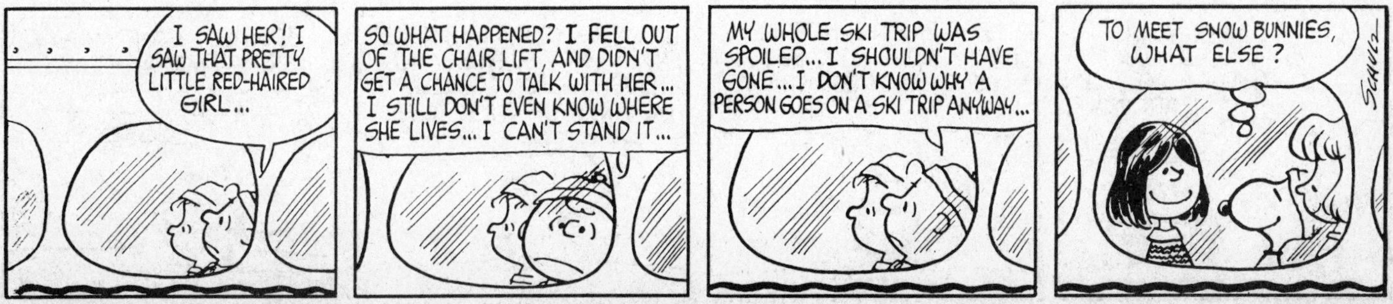
I SAW HER! I SAW THAT PRETTY LITTLE RED-HAIRED GIRL...
SO WHAT HAPPENED? I FELL OUT OF THE CHAIR LIFT, AND DIDN'T GET A CHANCE TO TALK WITH HER... I STILL DON'T EVEN KNOW WHERE SHE LIVES... I CAN'T STAND IT...
MY WHOLE SKI TRIP WAS SPOILED... I SHOULDN'T HAVE GONE... I DON'T KNOW WHY A PERSON GOES ON A SKI TRIP ANYWAY...
TO MEET SNOW BUNNIES, WHAT ELSE?
SCHULZ

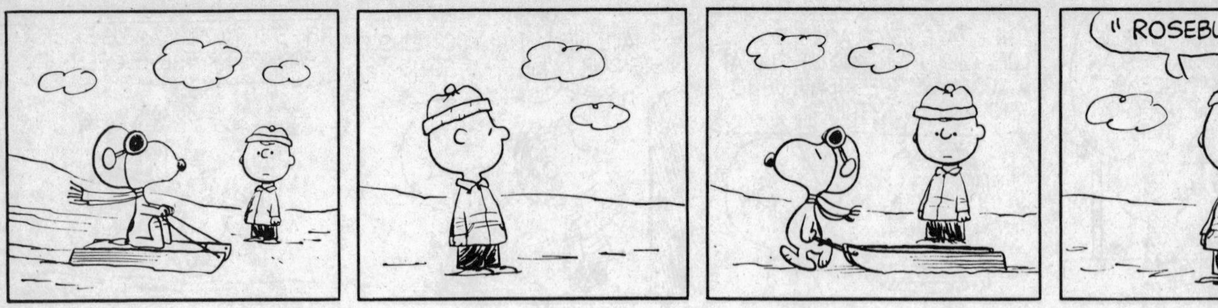
"ROSEBUD"?
SCHULZ

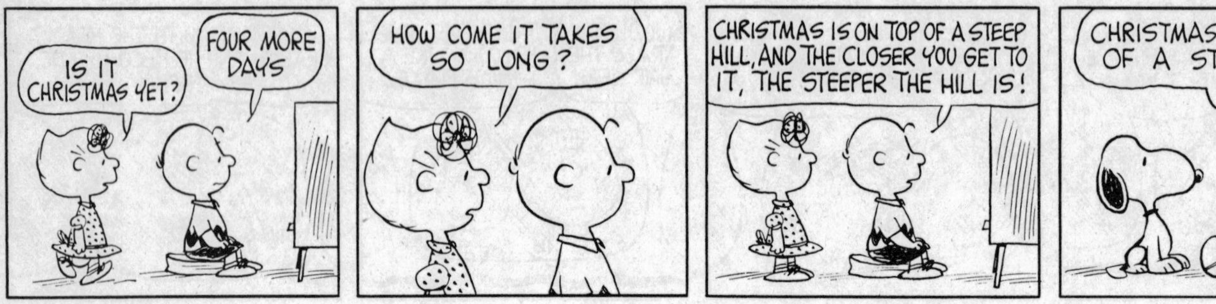
IS IT CHRISTMAS YET?
FOUR MORE DAYS
HOW COME IT TAKES SO LONG?
CHRISTMAS IS ON TOP OF A STEEP HILL, AND THE CLOSER YOU GET TO IT, THE STEEPER THE HILL IS!
CHRISTMAS IS ON TOP OF A STEEP HILL!
SCHULZ

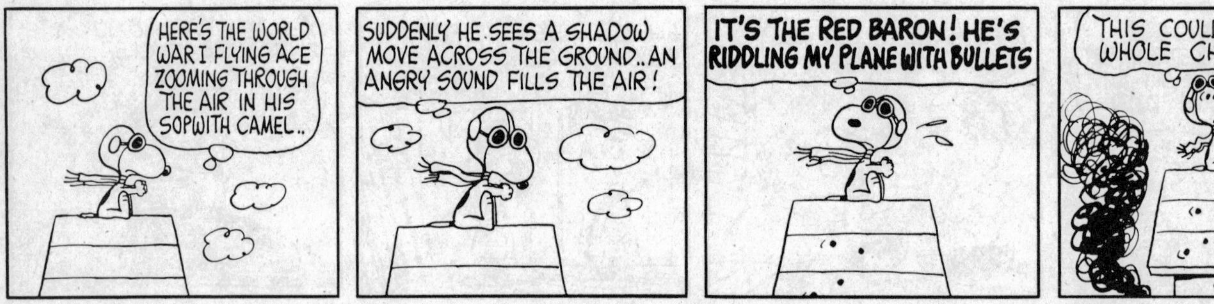
HERE'S THE WORLD WAR I FLYING ACE ZOOMING THROUGH THE AIR IN HIS SOPWITH CAMEL..
SUDDENLY HE SEES A SHADOW MOVE ACROSS THE GROUND..AN ANGRY SOUND FILLS THE AIR!
IT'S THE RED BARON! HE'S RIDDLING MY PLANE WITH BULLETS
THIS COULD RUIN MY WHOLE CHRISTMAS!
SCHULZ

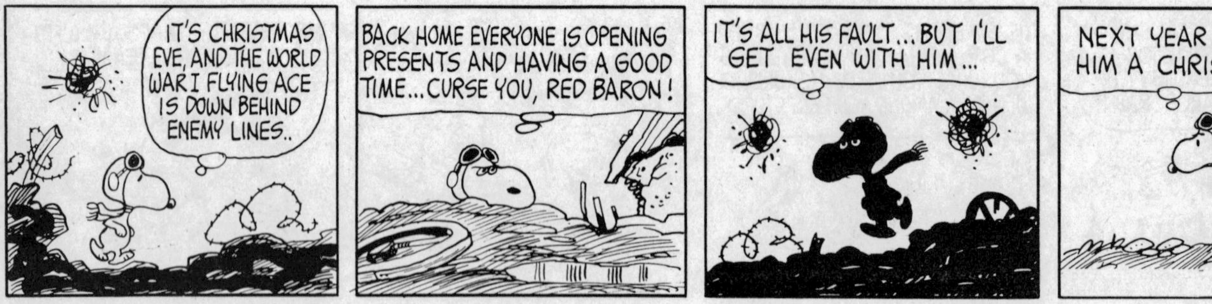
IT'S CHRISTMAS EVE, AND THE WORLD WAR I FLYING ACE IS DOWN BEHIND ENEMY LINES..
BACK HOME EVERYONE IS OPENING PRESENTS AND HAVING A GOOD TIME...CURSE YOU, RED BARON!
IT'S ALL HIS FAULT...BUT I'LL GET EVEN WITH HIM...
NEXT YEAR I WON'T SEND HIM A CHRISTMAS CARD!
SCHULZ

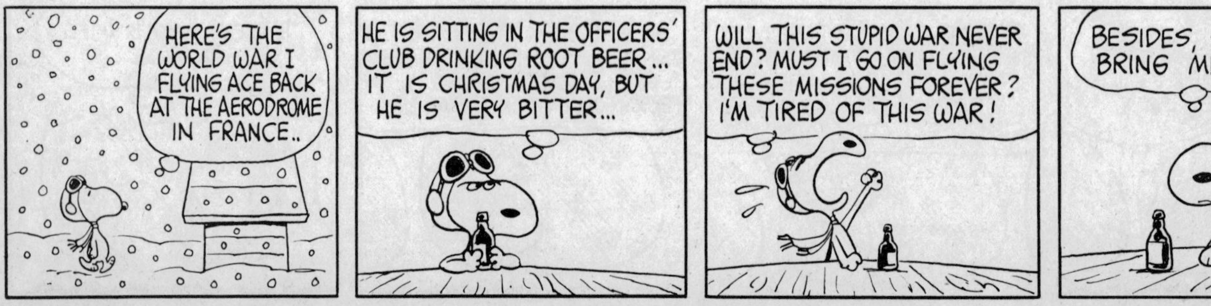
HERE'S THE WORLD WAR I FLYING ACE BACK AT THE AERODROME IN FRANCE..
HE IS SITTING IN THE OFFICERS' CLUB DRINKING ROOT BEER... IT IS CHRISTMAS DAY, BUT HE IS VERY BITTER...
WILL THIS STUPID WAR NEVER END? MUST I GO ON FLYING THESE MISSIONS FOREVER? I'M TIRED OF THIS WAR!
BESIDES, SANTY DIDN'T BRING ME ANYTHING..
SCHULZ

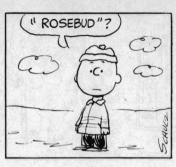

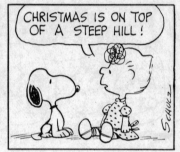

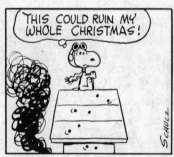

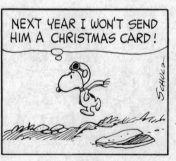

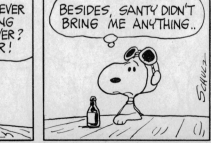

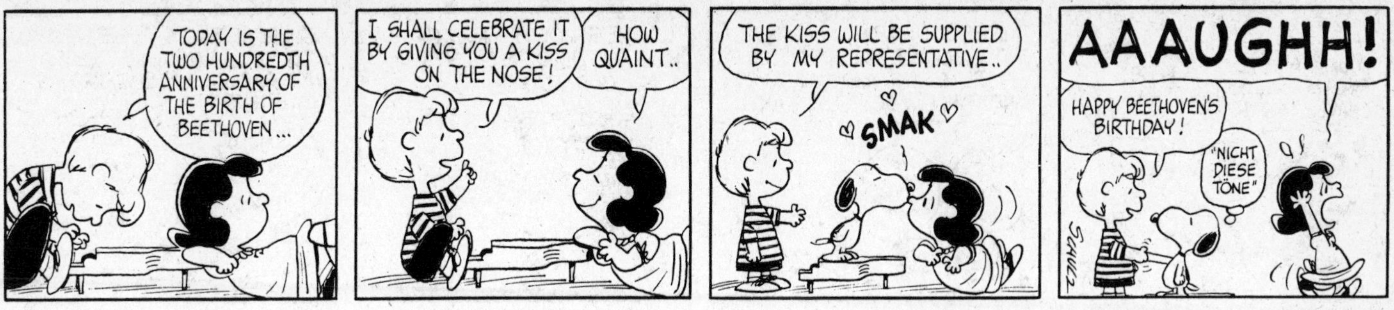
TODAY IS THE TWO HUNDREDTH ANNIVERSARY OF THE BIRTH OF BEETHOVEN ...
I SHALL CELEBRATE IT BY GIVING YOU A KISS ON THE NOSE!
HOW QUAINT..
THE KISS WILL BE SUPPLIED BY MY REPRESENTATIVE..
SMAK
AAAUGHH!
HAPPY BEETHOVEN'S BIRTHDAY!
"NICHT DIESE TÖNE"
SCHULZ

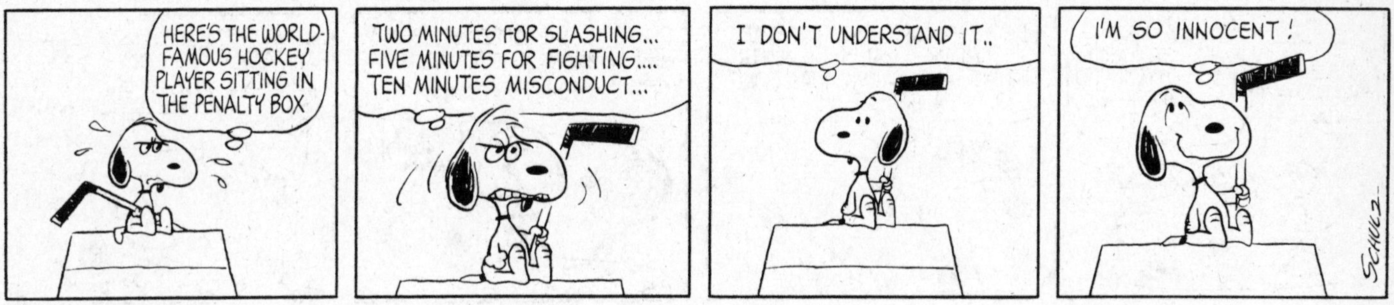
HERE'S THE WORLD-FAMOUS HOCKEY PLAYER SITTING IN THE PENALTY BOX
TWO MINUTES FOR SLASHING... FIVE MINUTES FOR FIGHTING.... TEN MINUTES MISCONDUCT...
I DON'T UNDERSTAND IT..
I'M SO INNOCENT!
SCHULZ

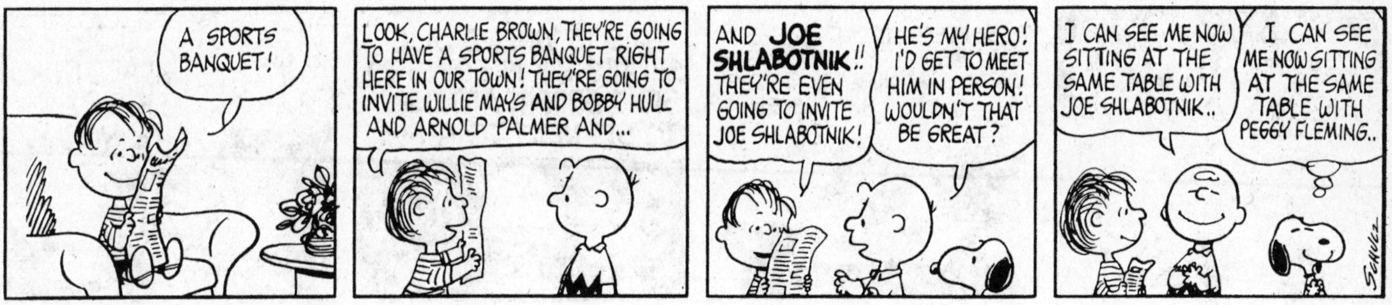
A SPORTS BANQUET!
LOOK, CHARLIE BROWN, THEY'RE GOING TO HAVE A SPORTS BANQUET RIGHT HERE IN OUR TOWN! THEY'RE GOING TO INVITE WILLIE MAYS AND BOBBY HULL AND ARNOLD PALMER AND...
AND JOE SHLABOTNIK!! THEY'RE EVEN GOING TO INVITE JOE SHLABOTNIK!
HE'S MY HERO! I'D GET TO MEET HIM IN PERSON! WOULDN'T THAT BE GREAT?
I CAN SEE ME NOW SITTING AT THE SAME TABLE WITH JOE SHLABOTNIK..
I CAN SEE ME NOW SITTING AT THE SAME TABLE WITH PEGGY FLEMING..
SCHULZ

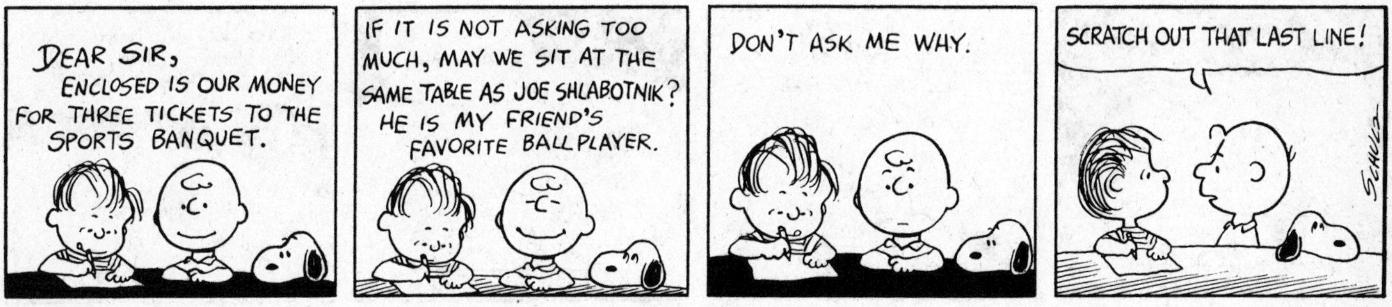
DEAR SIR, ENCLOSED IS OUR MONEY FOR THREE TICKETS TO THE SPORTS BANQUET.
IF IT IS NOT ASKING TOO MUCH, MAY WE SIT AT THE SAME TABLE AS JOE SHLABOTNIK? HE IS MY FRIEND'S FAVORITE BALLPLAYER.
DON'T ASK ME WHY.
SCRATCH OUT THAT LAST LINE!
SCHULZ

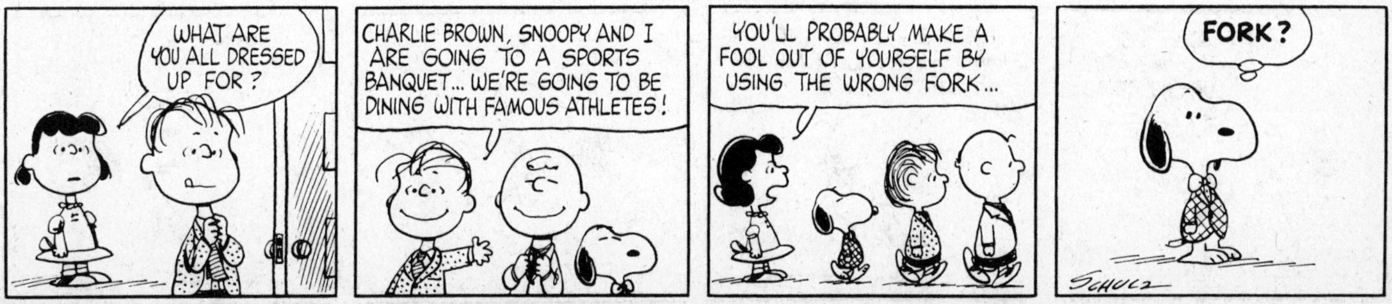
WHAT ARE YOU ALL DRESSED UP FOR?
CHARLIE BROWN, SNOOPY AND I ARE GOING TO A SPORTS BANQUET... WE'RE GOING TO BE DINING WITH FAMOUS ATHLETES!
YOU'LL PROBABLY MAKE A FOOL OUT OF YOURSELF BY USING THE WRONG FORK...
FORK?
SCHULZ

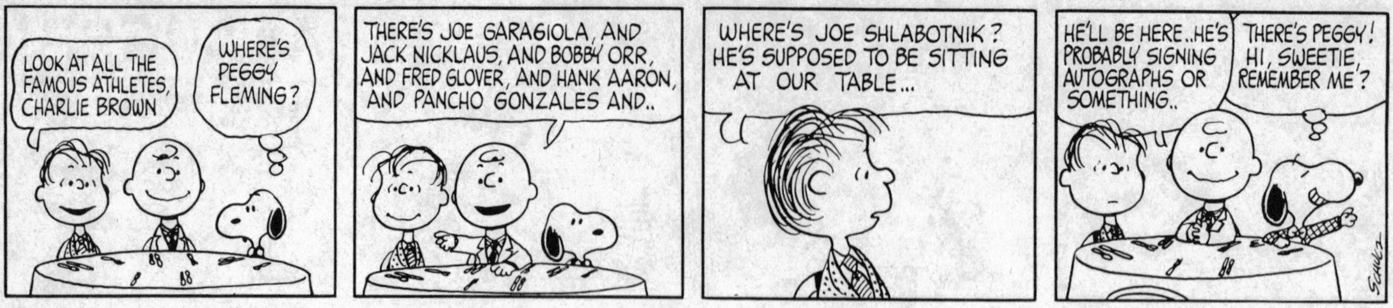
LOOK AT ALL THE FAMOUS ATHLETES, CHARLIE BROWN
WHERE'S PEGGY FLEMING?
THERE'S JOE GARAGIOLA, AND JACK NICKLAUS, AND BOBBY ORR, AND FRED GLOVER, AND HANK AARON, AND PANCHO GONZALES AND..
WHERE'S JOE SHLABOTNIK? HE'S SUPPOSED TO BE SITTING AT OUR TABLE...
HE'LL BE HERE..HE'S PROBABLY SIGNING AUTOGRAPHS OR SOMETHING..
THERE'S PEGGY! HI, SWEETIE, REMEMBER ME?
SCHULZ

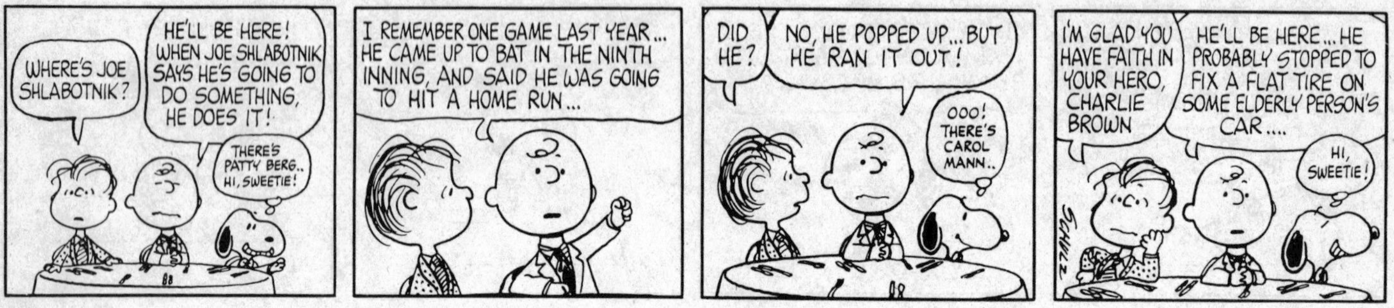
WHERE'S JOE SHLABOTNIK?
HE'LL BE HERE! WHEN JOE SHLABOTNIK SAYS HE'S GOING TO DO SOMETHING, HE DOES IT!
THERE'S PATTY BERG.. HI, SWEETIE!
I REMEMBER ONE GAME LAST YEAR... HE CAME UP TO BAT IN THE NINTH INNING, AND SAID HE WAS GOING TO HIT A HOME RUN...
DID HE?
NO, HE POPPED UP... BUT HE RAN IT OUT!
OOO! THERE'S CAROL MANN..
I'M GLAD YOU HAVE FAITH IN YOUR HERO, CHARLIE BROWN
HE'LL BE HERE... HE PROBABLY STOPPED TO FIX A FLAT TIRE ON SOME ELDERLY PERSON'S CAR....
HI, SWEETIE!
SCHULZ

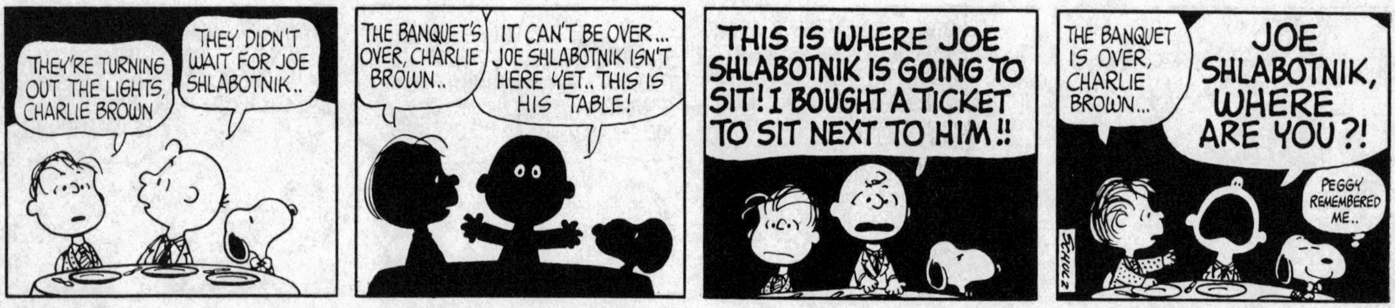
THEY'RE TURNING OUT THE LIGHTS, CHARLIE BROWN
THEY DIDN'T WAIT FOR JOE SHLABOTNIK..
THE BANQUET'S OVER, CHARLIE BROWN..
IT CAN'T BE OVER... JOE SHLABOTNIK ISN'T HERE YET.. THIS IS HIS TABLE!
THIS IS WHERE JOE SHLABOTNIK IS GOING TO SIT! I BOUGHT A TICKET TO SIT NEXT TO HIM!!
THE BANQUET IS OVER, CHARLIE BROWN...
JOE SHLABOTNIK, WHERE ARE YOU?!
PEGGY REMEMBERED ME..
SCHULZ

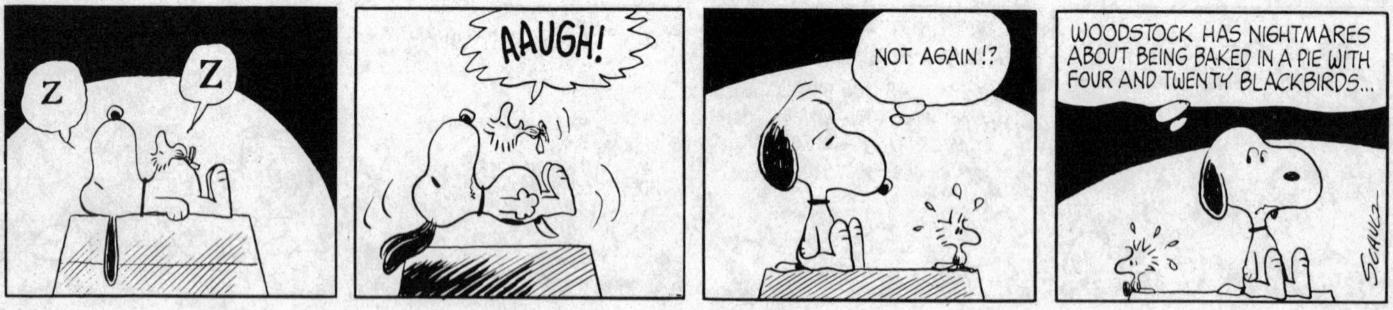
Z
Z
AAUGH!
NOT AGAIN!?
WOODSTOCK HAS NIGHTMARES ABOUT BEING BAKED IN A PIE WITH FOUR AND TWENTY BLACKBIRDS...
SCHULZ

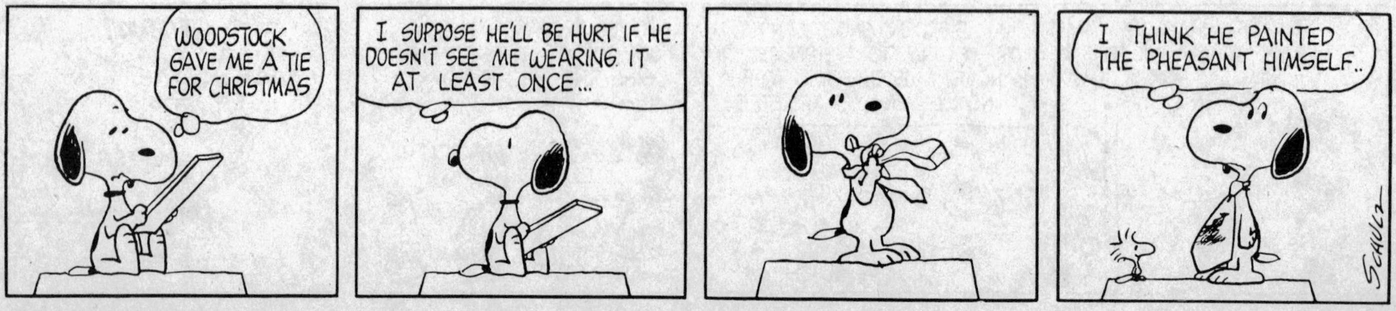
WOODSTOCK GAVE ME A TIE FOR CHRISTMAS
I SUPPOSE HE'LL BE HURT IF HE DOESN'T SEE ME WEARING IT AT LEAST ONCE...
I THINK HE PAINTED THE PHEASANT HIMSELF..
SCHULZ

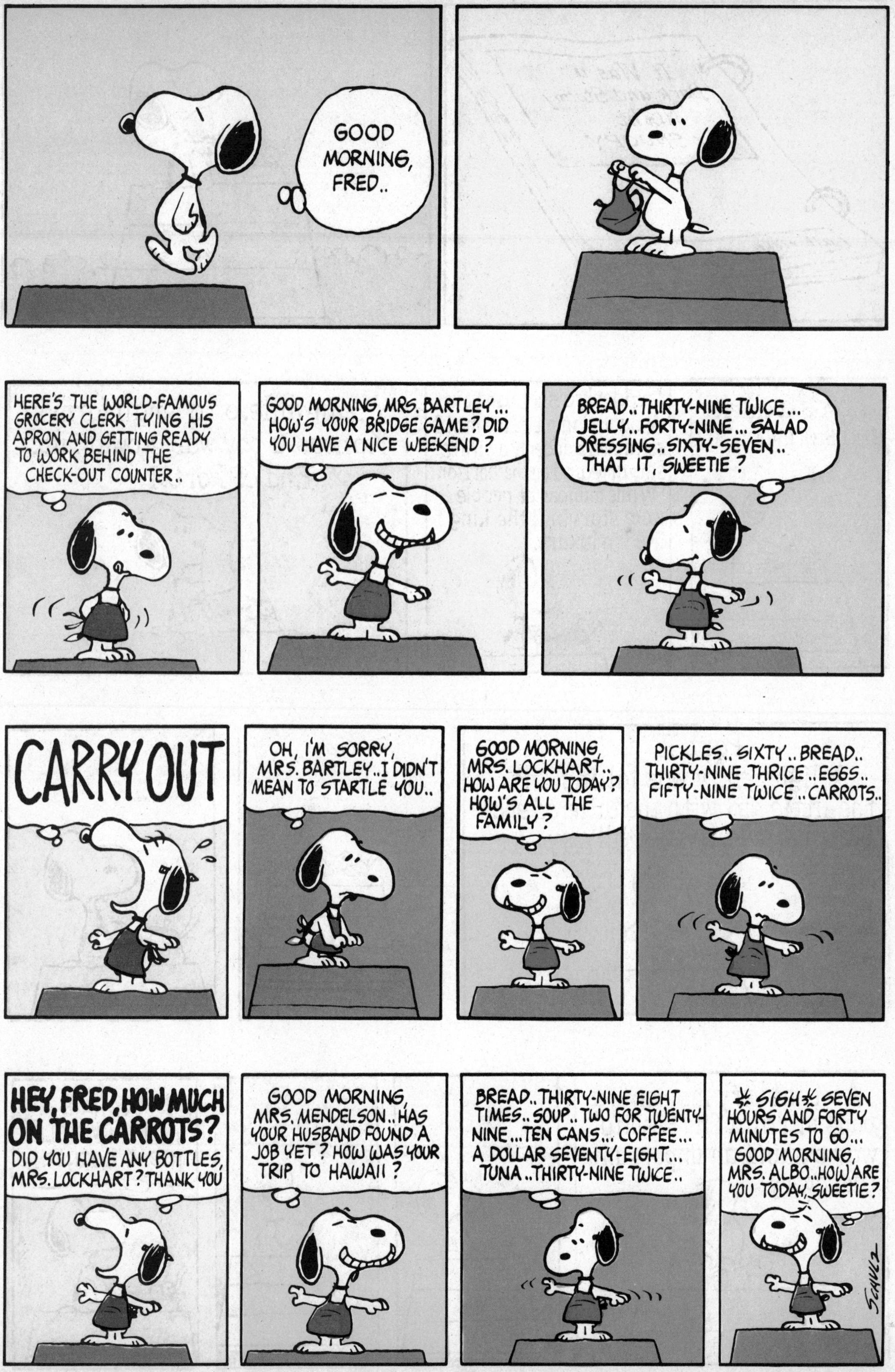
GOOD MORNING, FRED..
HERE'S THE WORLD-FAMOUS GROCERY CLERK TYING HIS APRON AND GETTING READY TO WORK BEHIND THE CHECK-OUT COUNTER..
GOOD MORNING, MRS. BARTLEY... HOW'S YOUR BRIDGE GAME? DID YOU HAVE A NICE WEEKEND?
BREAD.. THIRTY-NINE TWICE... JELLY.. FORTY-NINE... SALAD DRESSING.. SIXTY-SEVEN.. THAT IT, SWEETIE?
CARRY OUT
OH, I'M SORRY, MRS. BARTLEY.. I DIDN'T MEAN TO STARTLE YOU..
GOOD MORNING, MRS. LOCKHART.. HOW ARE YOU TODAY? HOW'S ALL THE FAMILY?
PICKLES.. SIXTY.. BREAD.. THIRTY-NINE THRICE.. EGGS.. FIFTY-NINE TWICE.. CARROTS..
HEY, FRED, HOW MUCH ON THE CARROTS?
DID YOU HAVE ANY BOTTLES, MRS. LOCKHART? THANK YOU
GOOD MORNING, MRS. MENDELSON.. HAS YOUR HUSBAND FOUND A JOB YET? HOW WAS YOUR TRIP TO HAWAII?
BREAD.. THIRTY-NINE EIGHT TIMES.. SOUP.. TWO FOR TWENTY-NINE... TEN CANS... COFFEE... A DOLLAR SEVENTY-EIGHT... TUNA.. THIRTY-NINE TWICE..
SIGH SEVEN HOURS AND FORTY MINUTES TO GO... GOOD MORNING, MRS. ALBO.. HOW ARE YOU TODAY, SWEETIE?
SCHULZ

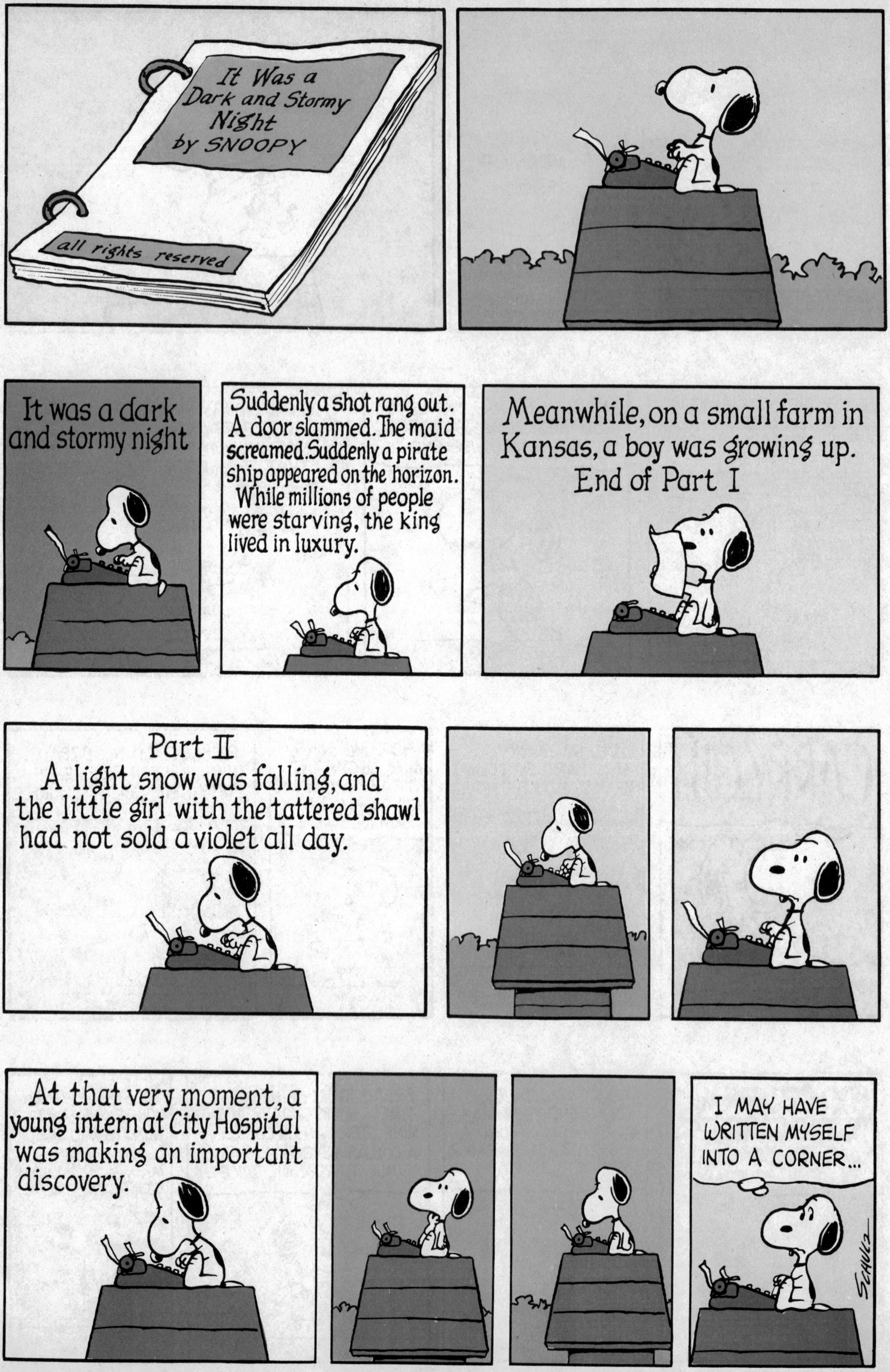
It Was a Dark and Stormy Night by SNOOPY
all rights reserved
It was a dark and stormy night
Suddenly a shot rang out. A door slammed. The maid screamed. Suddenly a pirate ship appeared on the horizon. While millions of people were starving, the king lived in luxury.
Meanwhile, on a small farm in Kansas, a boy was growing up. End of Part I
Part II A light snow was falling, and the little girl with the tattered shawl had not sold a violet all day.
At that very moment, a young intern at City Hospital was making an important discovery.
I MAY HAVE WRITTEN MYSELF INTO A CORNER...
SCHULZ

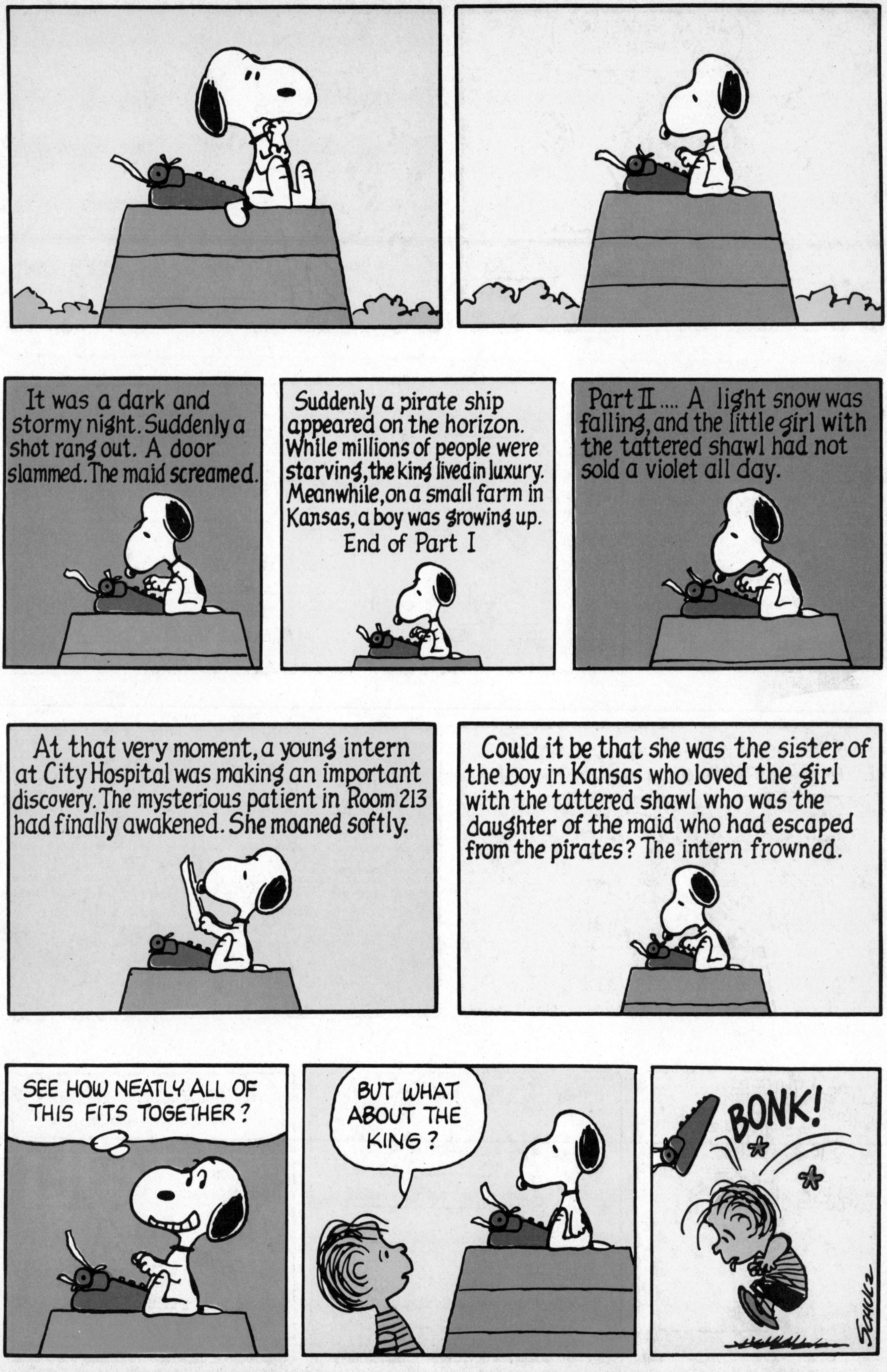
It was a dark and stormy night. Suddenly a shot rang out. A door slammed. The maid screamed.
Suddenly a pirate ship appeared on the horizon. While millions of people were starving, the king lived in luxury. Meanwhile, on a small farm in Kansas, a boy was growing up.
End of Part I
Part II .... A light snow was falling, and the little girl with the tattered shawl had not sold a violet all day.
At that very moment, a young intern at City Hospital was making an important discovery. The mysterious patient in Room 213 had finally awakened. She moaned softly.
Could it be that she was the sister of the boy in Kansas who loved the girl with the tattered shawl who was the daughter of the maid who had escaped from the pirates? The intern frowned.
SEE HOW NEATLY ALL OF THIS FITS TOGETHER?
BUT WHAT ABOUT THE KING?
BONK!
SCHULZ

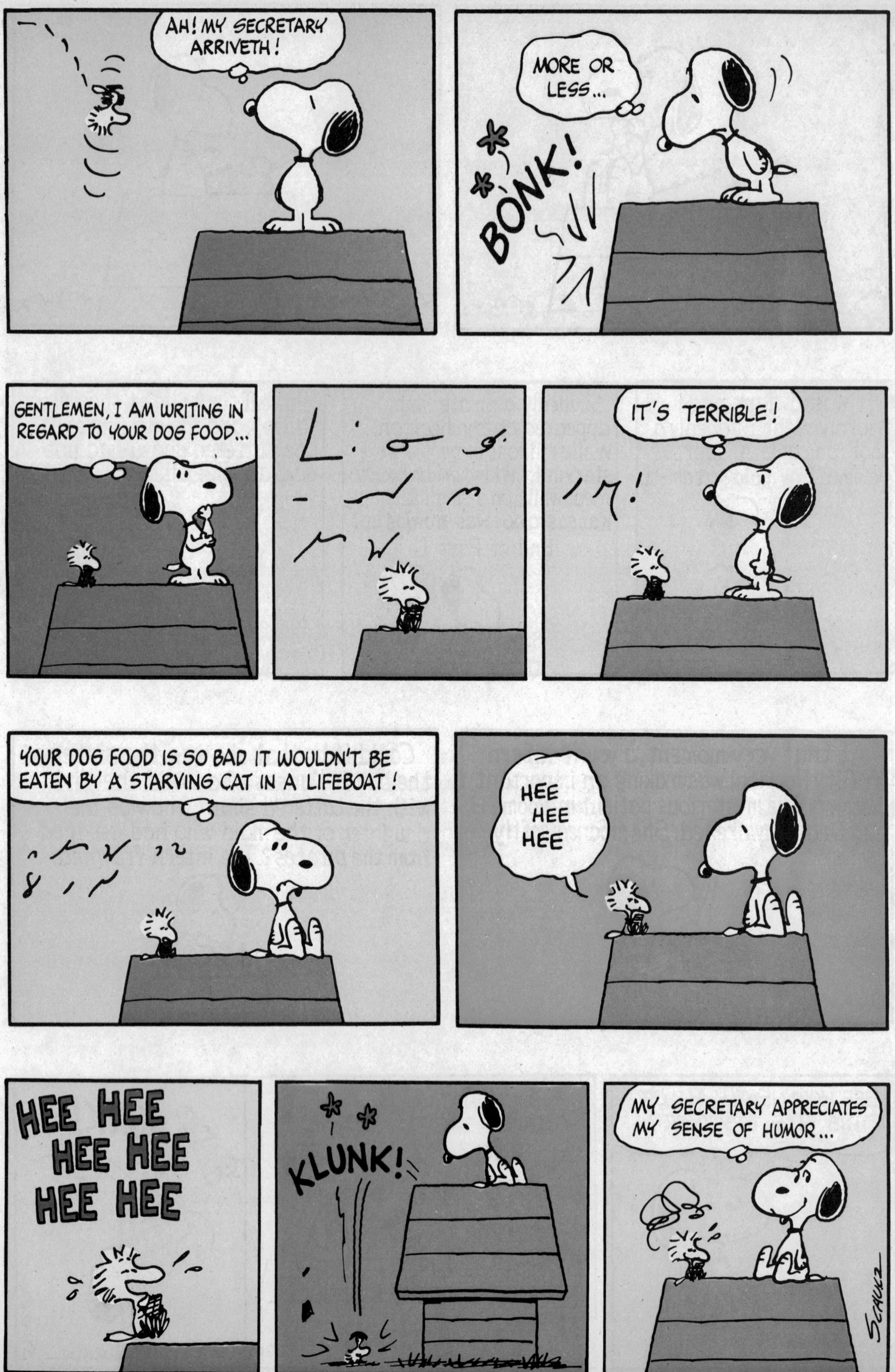
AH! MY SECRETARY ARRIVETH!
MORE OR LESS...
BONK!
GENTLEMEN, I AM WRITING IN REGARD TO YOUR DOG FOOD...
IT'S TERRIBLE!
YOUR DOG FOOD IS SO BAD IT WOULDN'T BE EATEN BY A STARVING CAT IN A LIFEBOAT!
HEE HEE HEE
HEE HEE
HEE HEE
HEE HEE
KLUNK!
MY SECRETARY APPRECIATES MY SENSE OF HUMOR...
SCHULZ

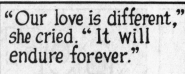

"Our love is different," she cried. "It will endure forever."

AH! MY SECRETARY WITH THE MORNING MAIL...

Dear Contributor, Thank you for submitting your manuscript. We regret that it does not suit our present needs.

ANOTHER REJECTION SLIP...

RATS!

OH, WELL, TAKE IT AND FILE IT WITH THE OTHERS...

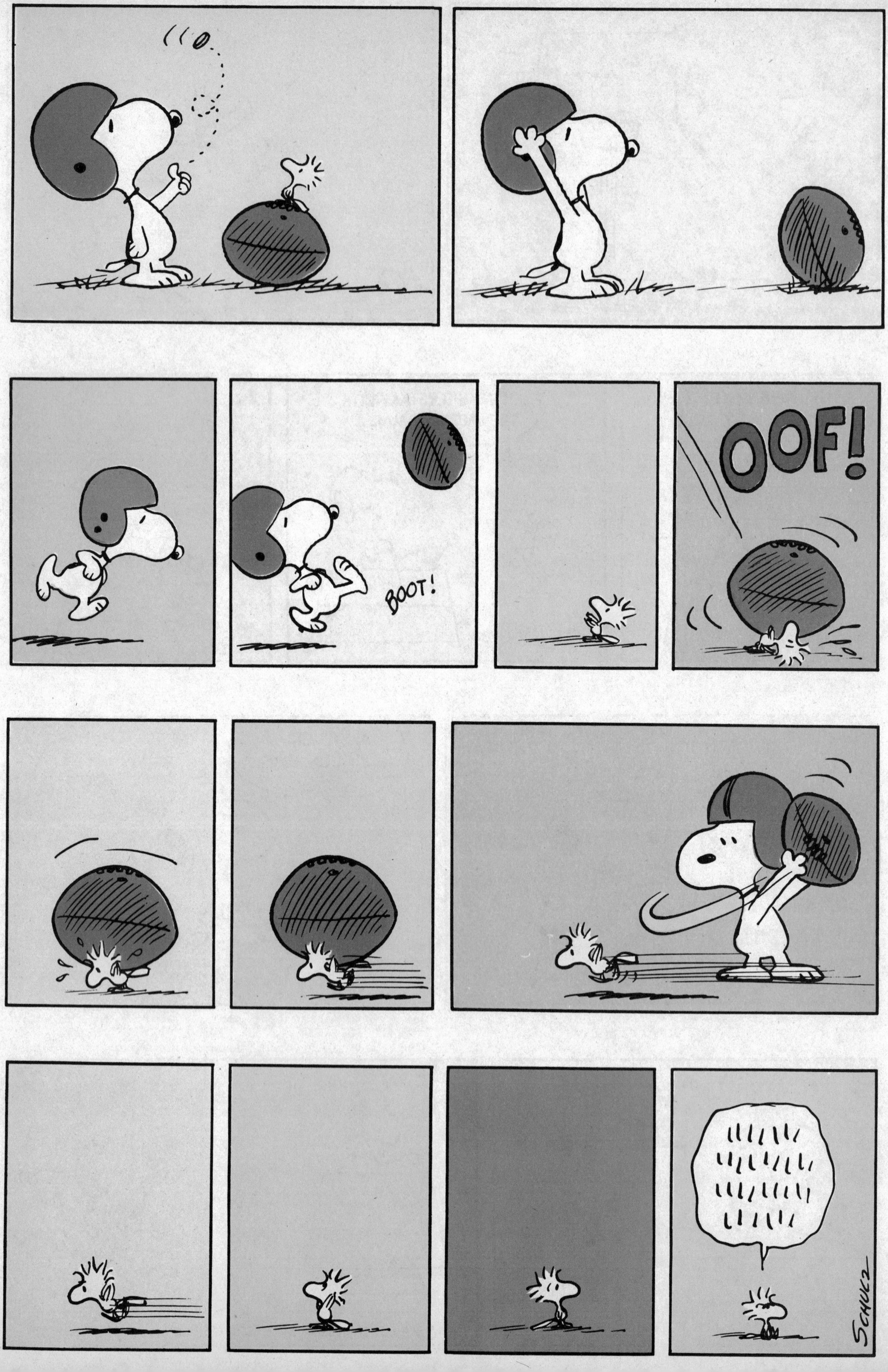

BOOT!
OOF!
SCHULZ

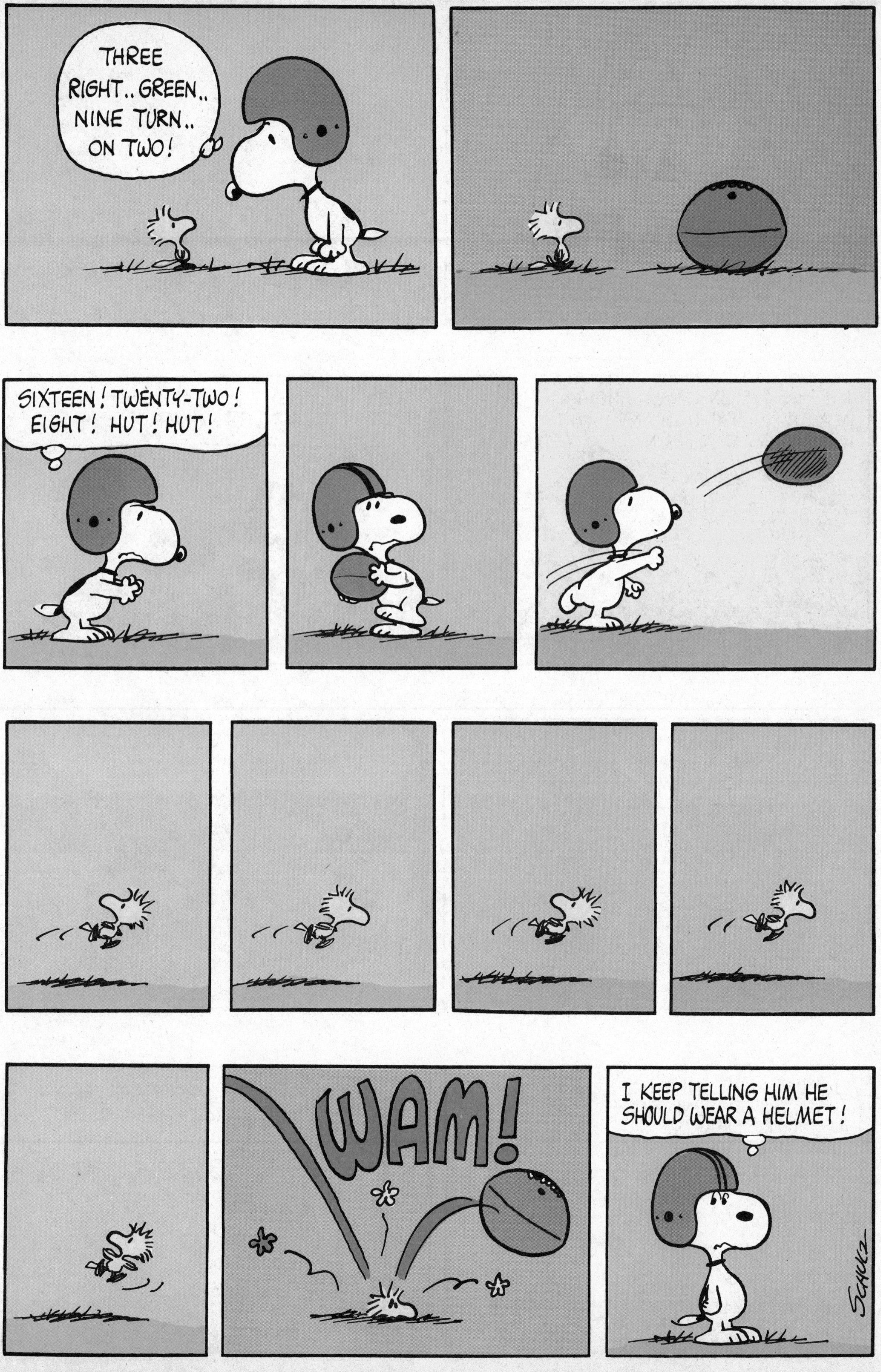
THREE RIGHT.. GREEN.. NINE TURN.. ON TWO!
SIXTEEN! TWENTY-TWO! EIGHT! HUT! HUT!
WAM!
I KEEP TELLING HIM HE SHOULD WEAR A HELMET!
SCHULZ

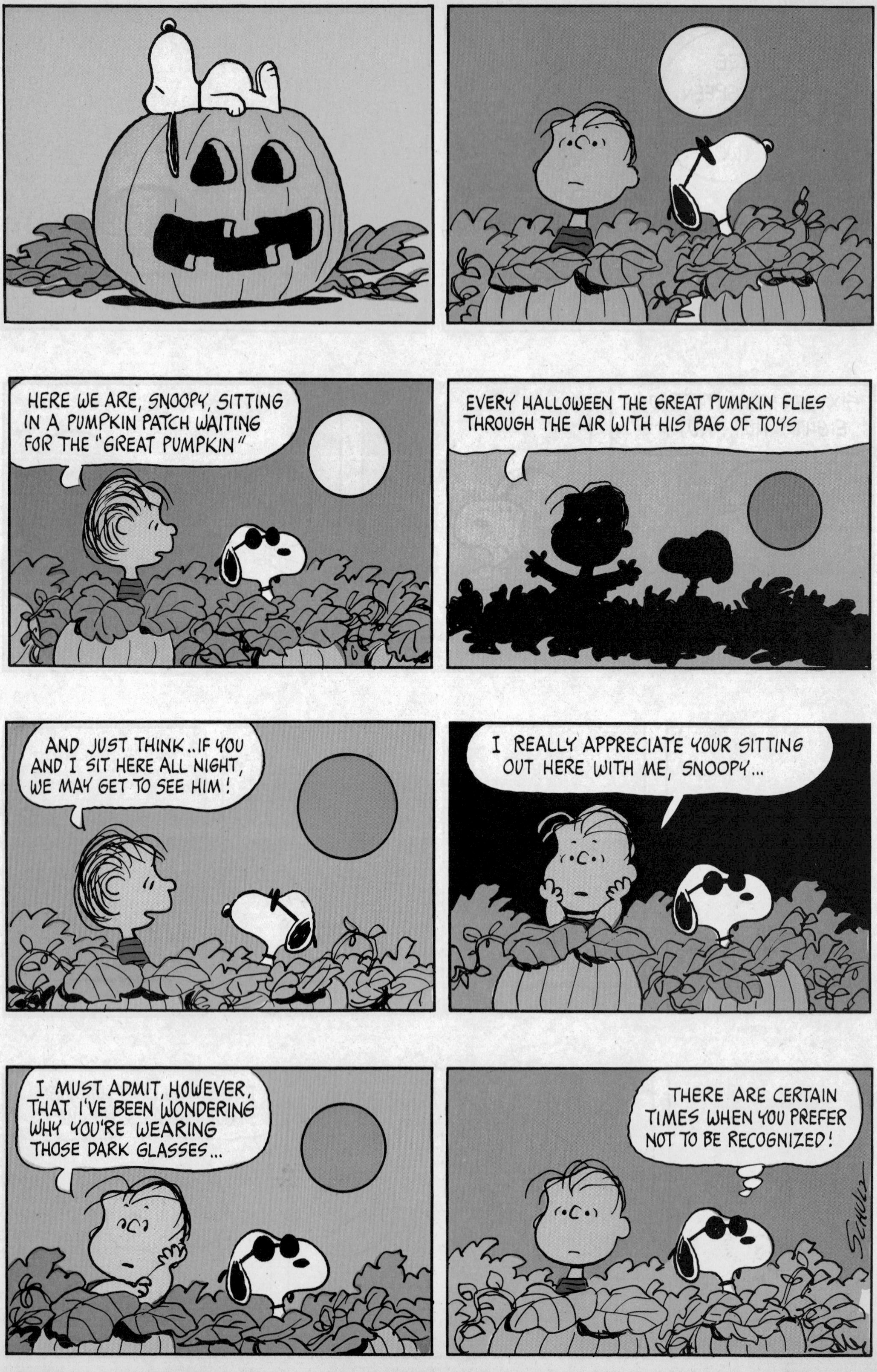
HERE WE ARE, SNOOPY, SITTING IN A PUMPKIN PATCH WAITING FOR THE "GREAT PUMPKIN"
EVERY HALLOWEEN THE GREAT PUMPKIN FLIES THROUGH THE AIR WITH HIS BAG OF TOYS
AND JUST THINK..IF YOU AND I SIT HERE ALL NIGHT, WE MAY GET TO SEE HIM!
I REALLY APPRECIATE YOUR SITTING OUT HERE WITH ME, SNOOPY...
I MUST ADMIT, HOWEVER, THAT I'VE BEEN WONDERING WHY YOU'RE WEARING THOSE DARK GLASSES...
THERE ARE CERTAIN TIMES WHEN YOU PREFER NOT TO BE RECOGNIZED!
SCHULZ

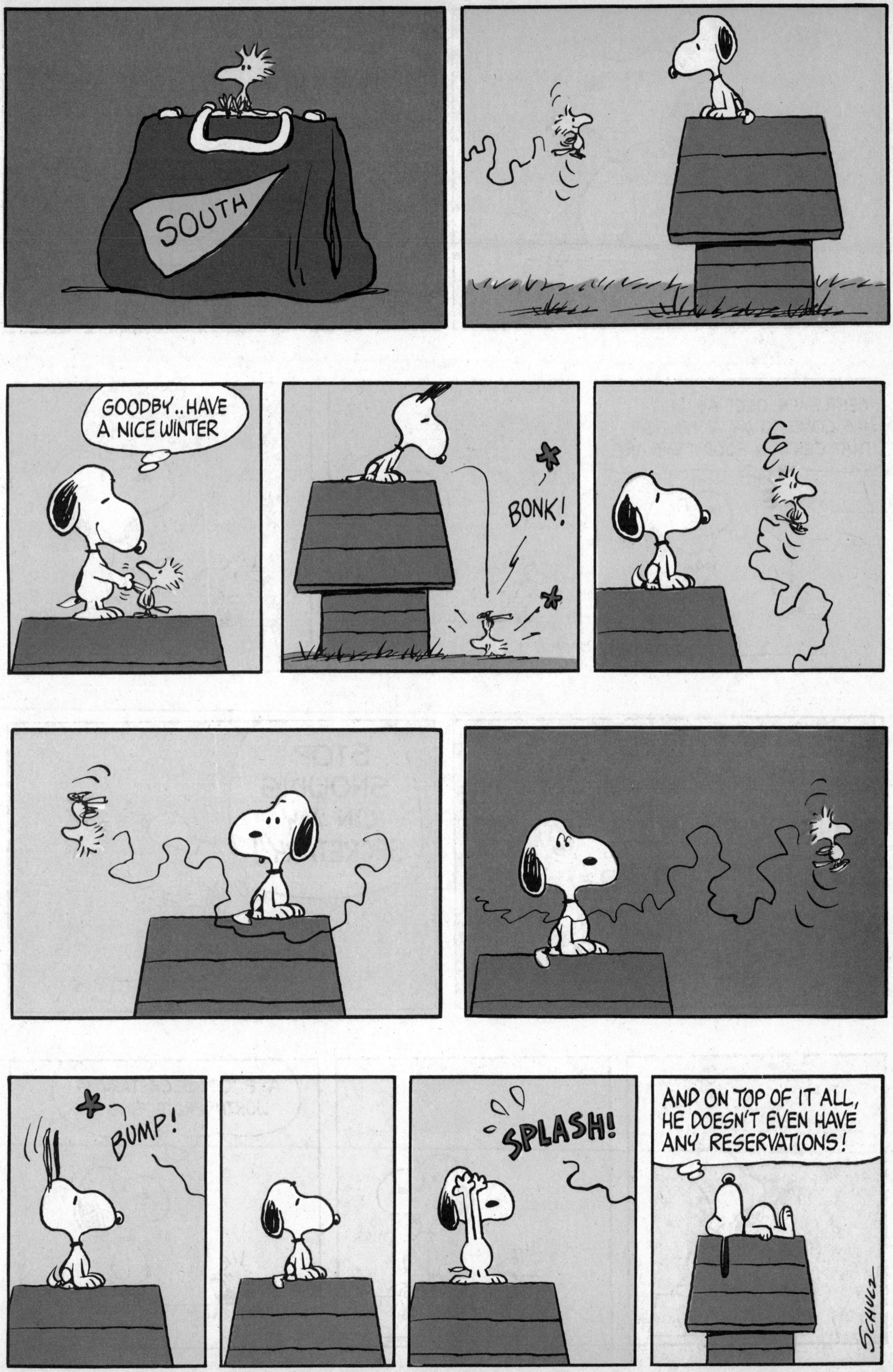
SOUTH
GOODBY..HAVE A NICE WINTER
BONK!
BUMP!
SPLASH!
AND ON TOP OF IT ALL, HE DOESN'T EVEN HAVE ANY RESERVATIONS!
SCHULZ

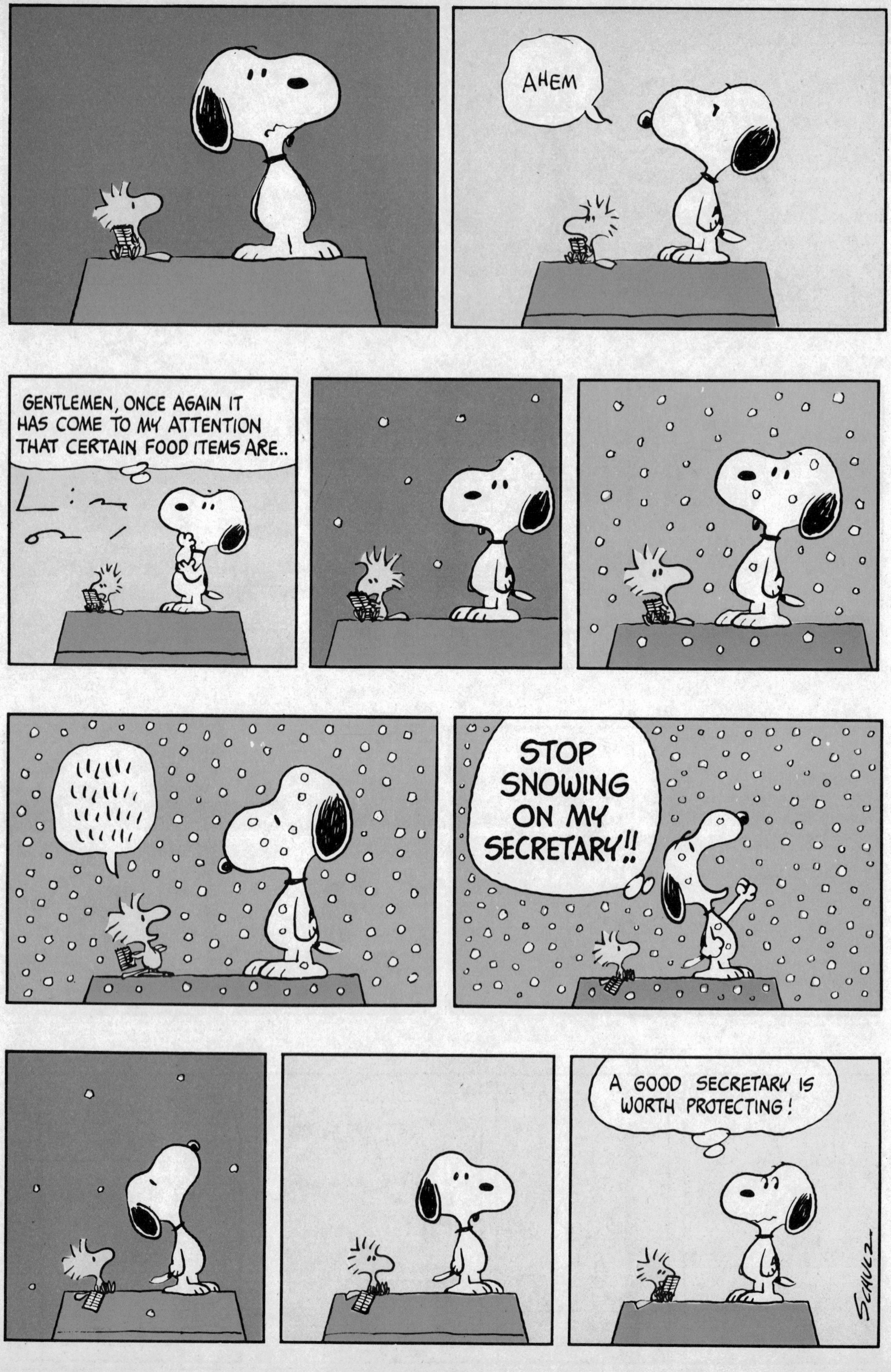
AHEM
GENTLEMEN, ONCE AGAIN IT HAS COME TO MY ATTENTION THAT CERTAIN FOOD ITEMS ARE..
STOP SNOWING ON MY SECRETARY!!
A GOOD SECRETARY IS WORTH PROTECTING!
SCHULZ

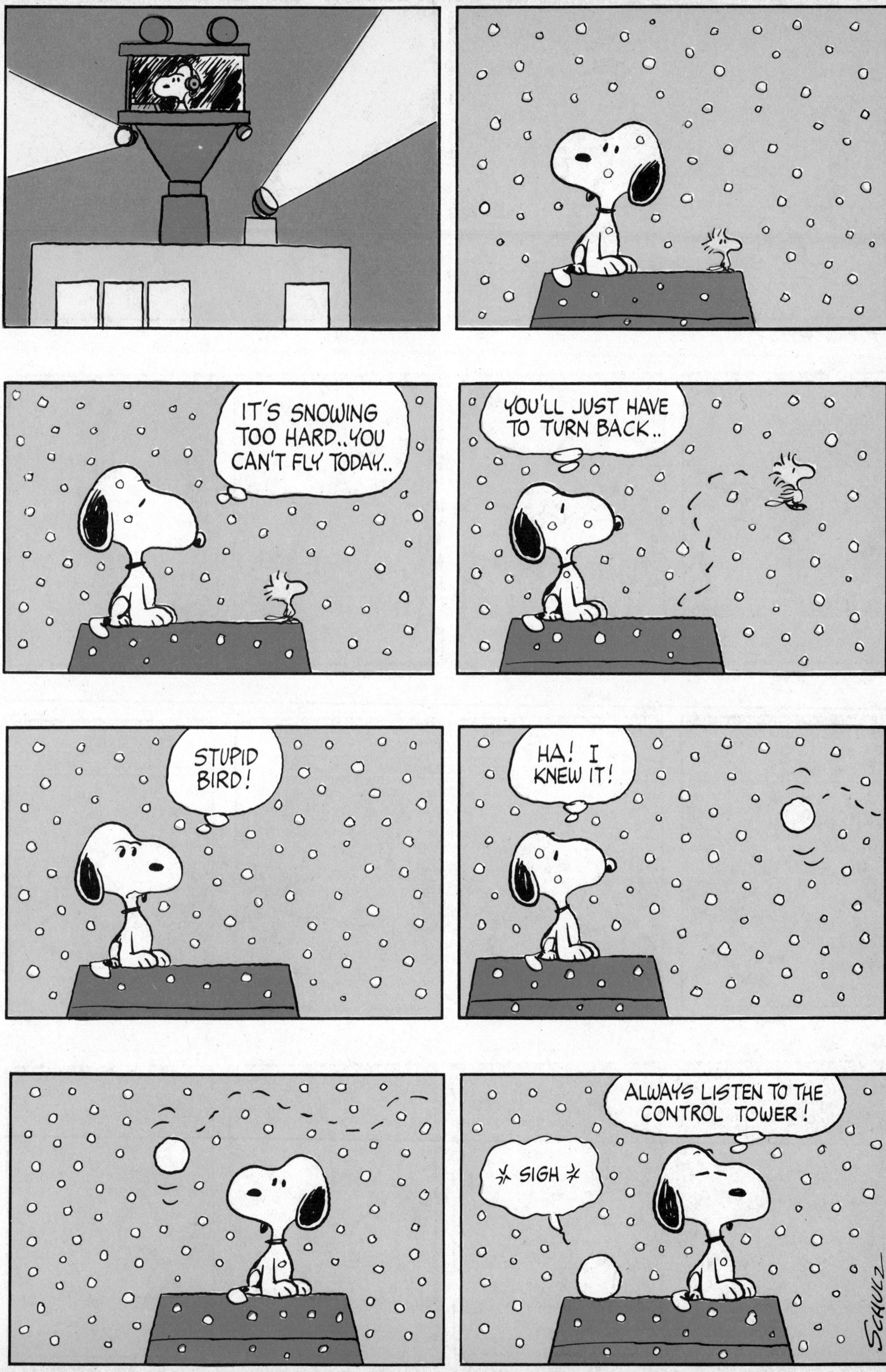
IT'S SNOWING TOO HARD..YOU CAN'T FLY TODAY..
YOU'LL JUST HAVE TO TURN BACK..
STUPID BIRD!
HA! I KNEW IT!
ALWAYS LISTEN TO THE CONTROL TOWER!
* SIGH *
SCHULZ

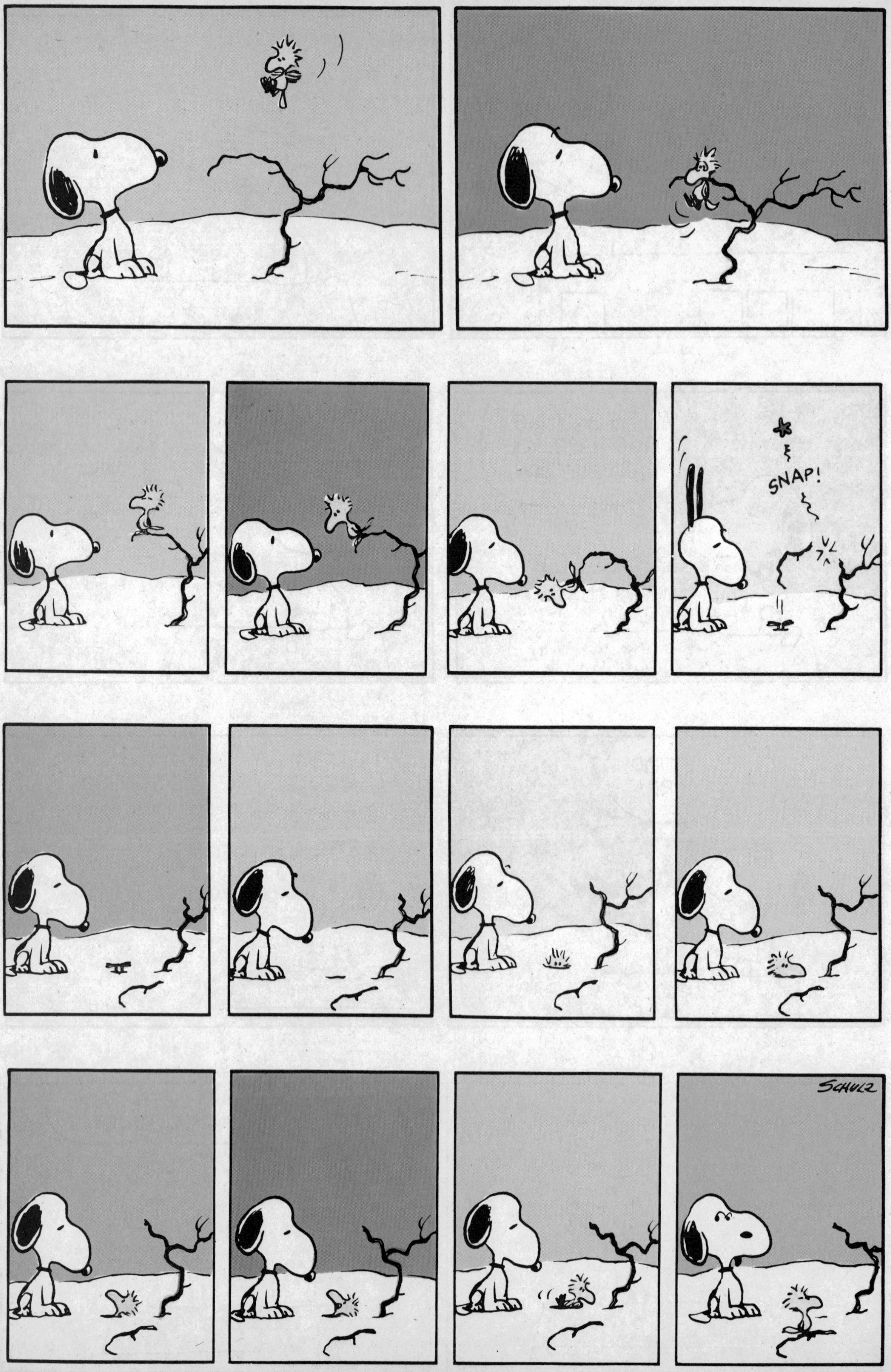
SNAP!
SCHULZ

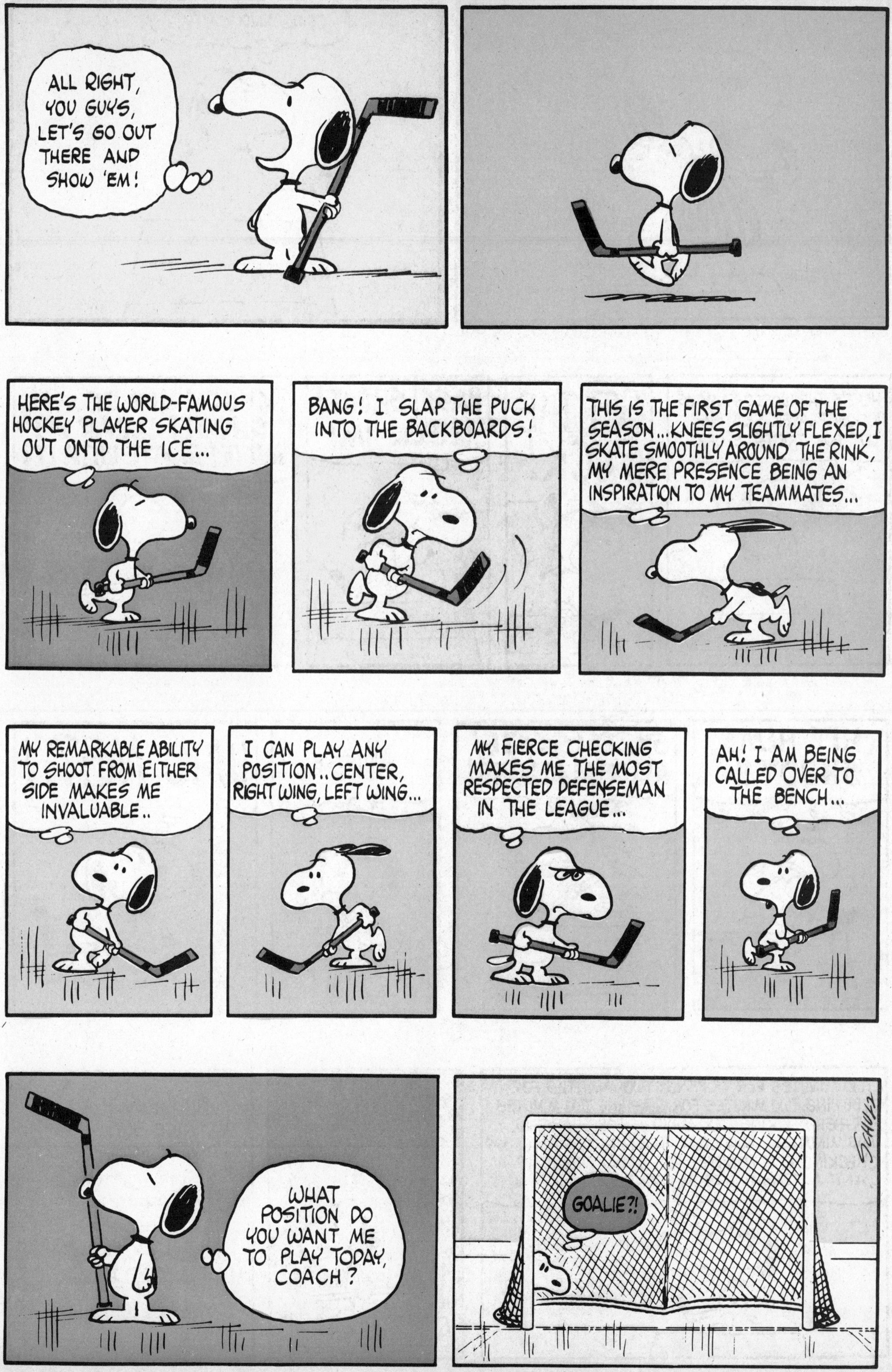
ALL RIGHT, YOU GUYS, LET'S GO OUT THERE AND SHOW 'EM!
HERE'S THE WORLD-FAMOUS HOCKEY PLAYER SKATING OUT ONTO THE ICE...
BANG! I SLAP THE PUCK INTO THE BACKBOARDS!
THIS IS THE FIRST GAME OF THE SEASON...KNEES SLIGHTLY FLEXED, I SKATE SMOOTHLY AROUND THE RINK, MY MERE PRESENCE BEING AN INSPIRATION TO MY TEAMMATES...
MY REMARKABLE ABILITY TO SHOOT FROM EITHER SIDE MAKES ME INVALUABLE..
I CAN PLAY ANY POSITION..CENTER, RIGHT WING, LEFT WING...
MY FIERCE CHECKING MAKES ME THE MOST RESPECTED DEFENSEMAN IN THE LEAGUE...
AH! I AM BEING CALLED OVER TO THE BENCH...
WHAT POSITION DO YOU WANT ME TO PLAY TODAY, COACH?
GOALIE?!
SCHULZ

COOL AND CALM..

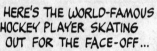
HERE'S THE WORLD-FAMOUS HOCKEY PLAYER SKATING OUT FOR THE FACE-OFF...

GET THE PUCK!

PASS! SHOOT! CHECK 'IM!

KNOCK HIM DOWN! SHOOT! CLEAR IT! MOVE! SKATE WITH IT!

HIT HIM! SHOOT!!

SKATE! SKATE! ALLONS! ALLONS!

A WHISTLE!

WHO, ME??!

TWO MINUTES FOR TRIPPING, TWO MINUTES FOR ELBOWING, TWO MINUTES FOR SLASHING, TWO MINUTES FOR HIGH-STICKING, TWO MINUTES FOR CHARGING, TWO MINUTES FOR HOLDING, TWO MINUTES FOR CROSS CHECKING, FIVE MINUTES FOR BOARD CHECKING AND A TEN-MINUTE MISCONDUCT...

BUT I'M SUCH A NICE GUY...

SCHULZ

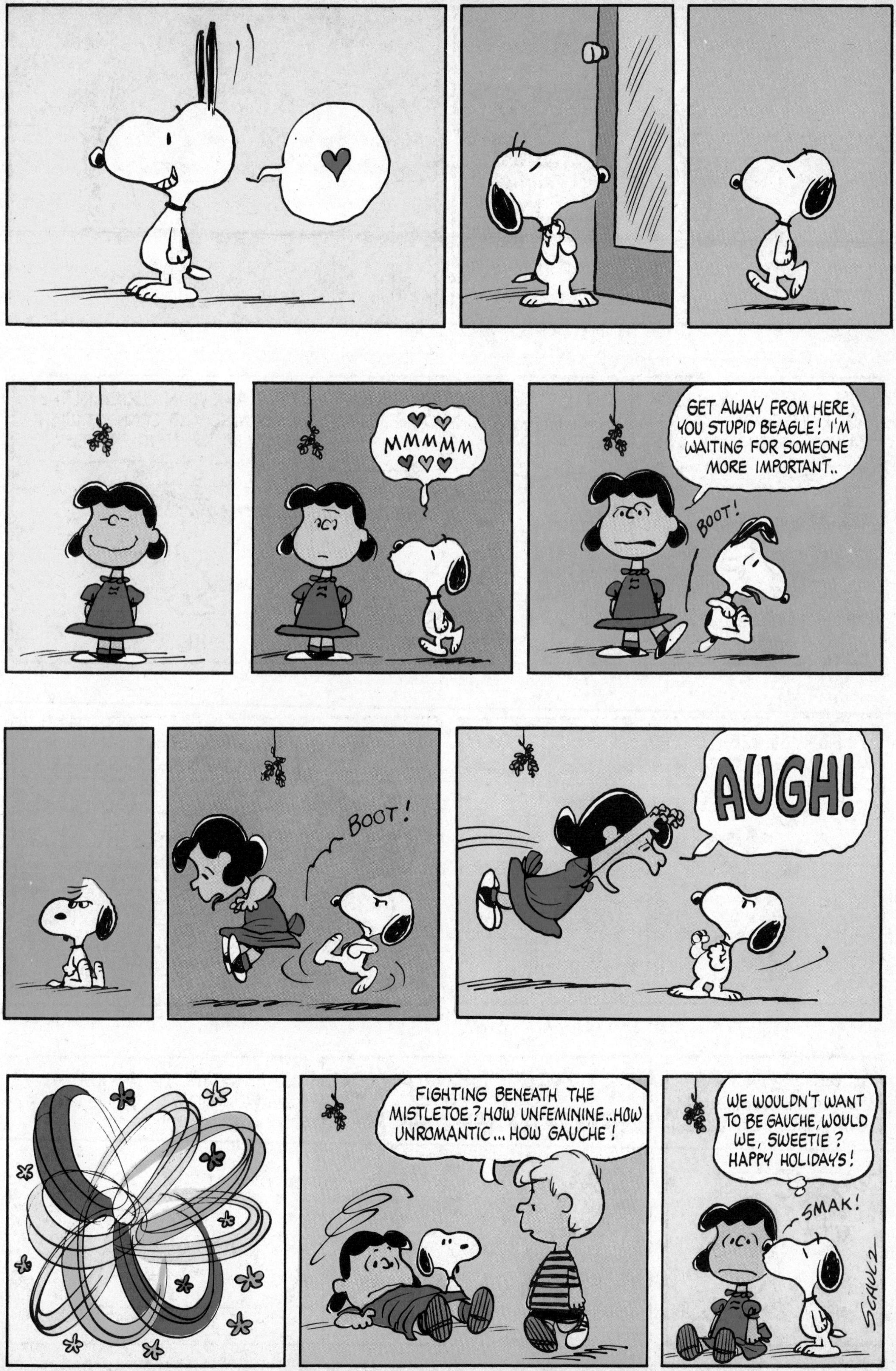
MMMMM
GET AWAY FROM HERE, YOU STUPID BEAGLE! I'M WAITING FOR SOMEONE MORE IMPORTANT..
BOOT!
BOOT!
AUGH!
FIGHTING BENEATH THE MISTLETOE? HOW UNFEMININE..HOW UNROMANTIC... HOW GAUCHE!
WE WOULDN'T WANT TO BE GAUCHE, WOULD WE, SWEETIE? HAPPY HOLIDAYS!
SMAK!
SCHULZ

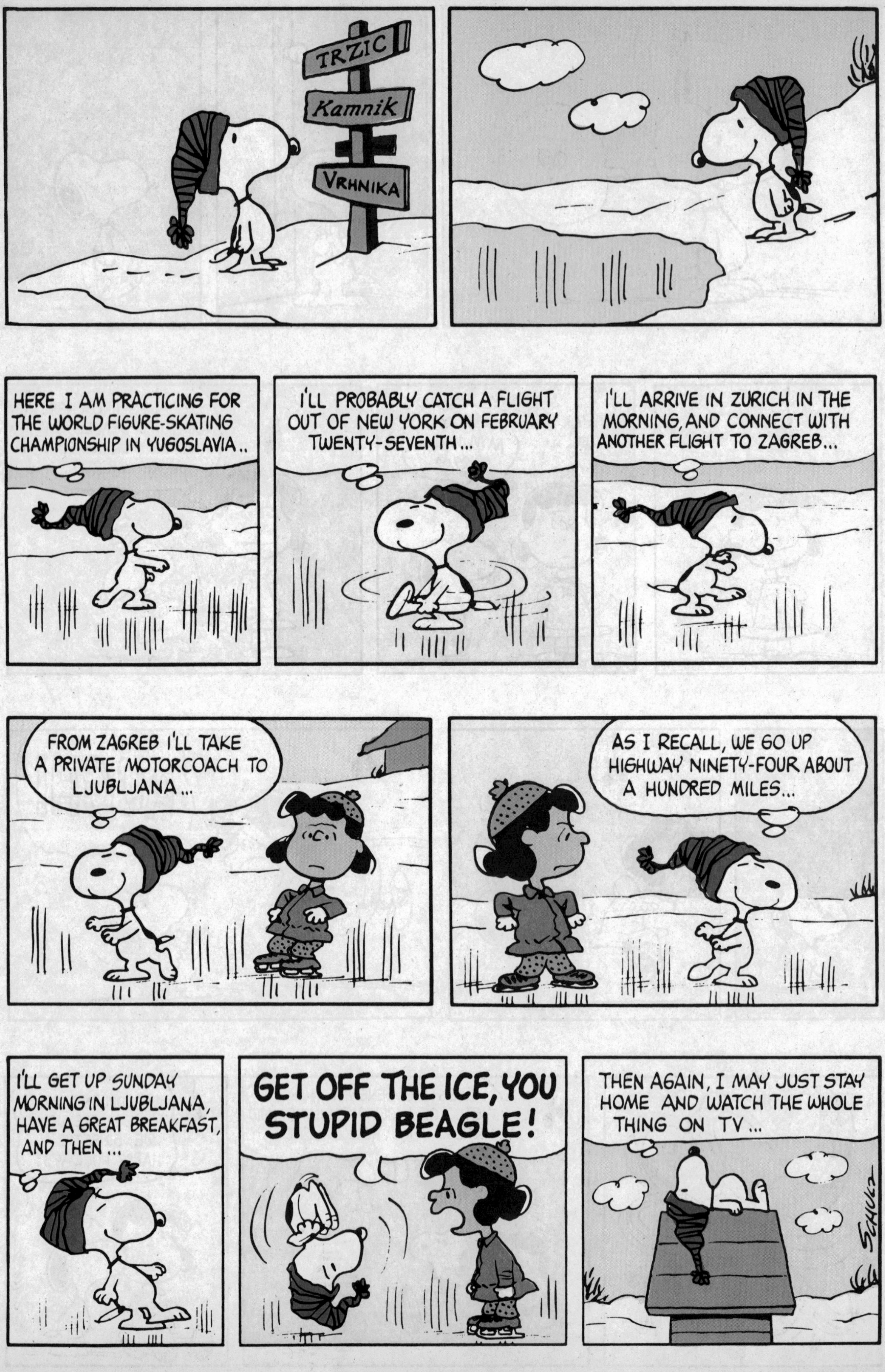
TRZIC
Kamnik
VRHNIKA
HERE I AM PRACTICING FOR THE WORLD FIGURE-SKATING CHAMPIONSHIP IN YUGOSLAVIA..
I'LL PROBABLY CATCH A FLIGHT OUT OF NEW YORK ON FEBRUARY TWENTY-SEVENTH...
I'LL ARRIVE IN ZURICH IN THE MORNING, AND CONNECT WITH ANOTHER FLIGHT TO ZAGREB...
FROM ZAGREB I'LL TAKE A PRIVATE MOTORCOACH TO LJUBLJANA...
AS I RECALL, WE GO UP HIGHWAY NINETY-FOUR ABOUT A HUNDRED MILES...
I'LL GET UP SUNDAY MORNING IN LJUBLJANA, HAVE A GREAT BREAKFAST, AND THEN...
GET OFF THE ICE, YOU STUPID BEAGLE!
THEN AGAIN, I MAY JUST STAY HOME AND WATCH THE WHOLE THING ON TV...
SCHULZ

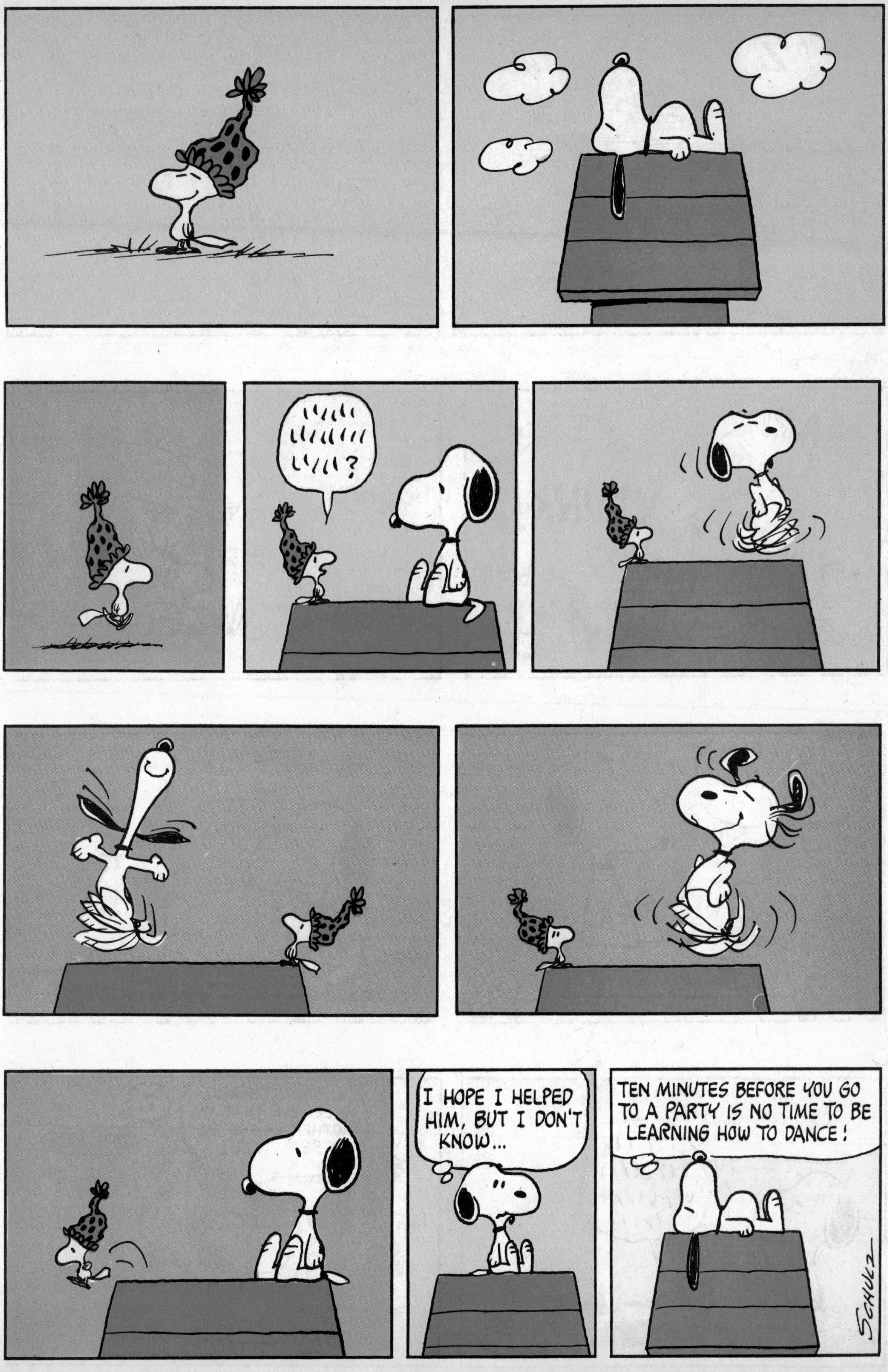

I HOPE I HELPED HIM, BUT I DON'T KNOW...
TEN MINUTES BEFORE YOU GO TO A PARTY IS NO TIME TO BE LEARNING HOW TO DANCE!
SCHULZ

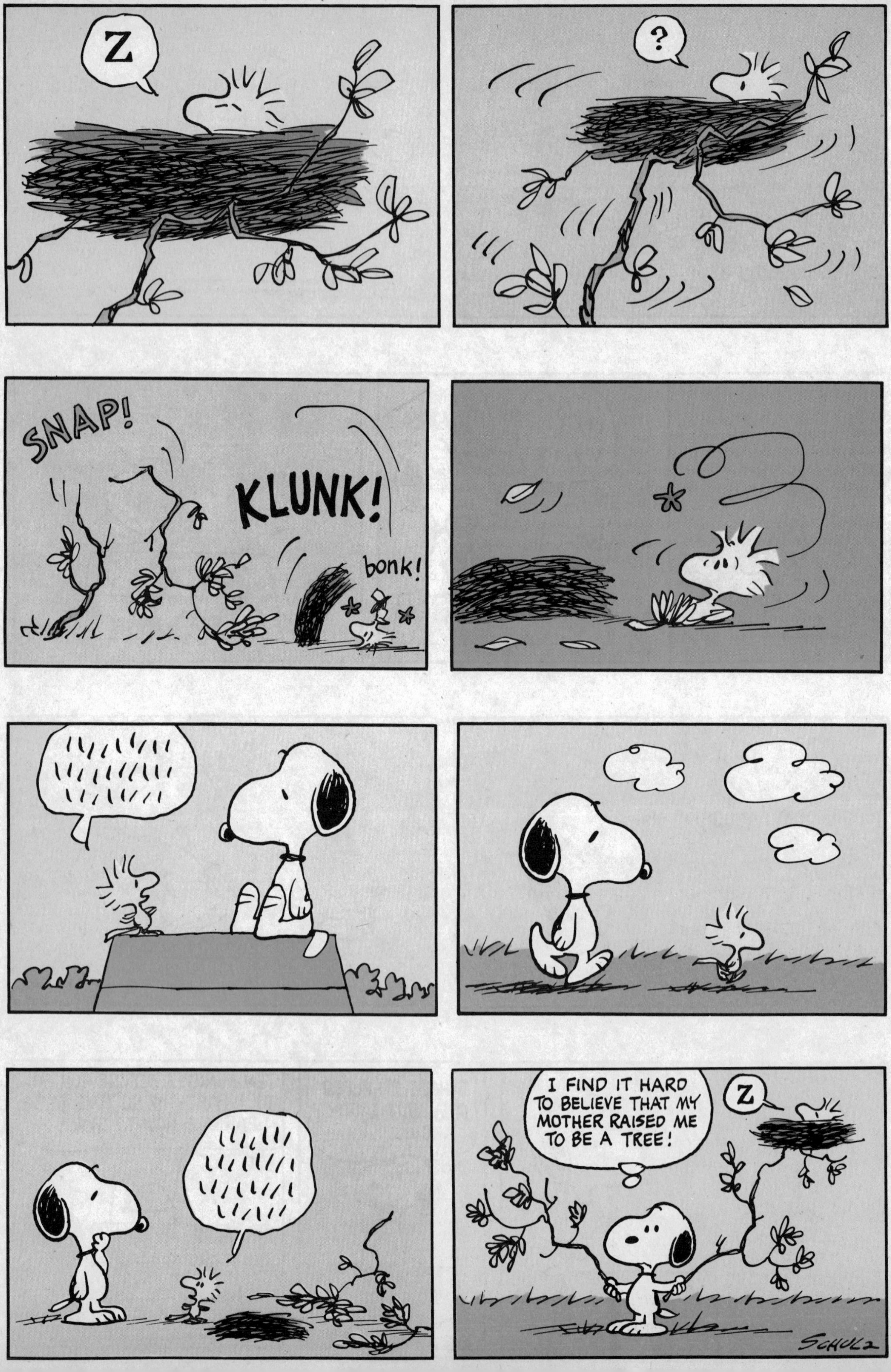
Z
?
SNAP!
KLUNK!
bonk!
I FIND IT HARD TO BELIEVE THAT MY MOTHER RAISED ME TO BE A TREE!
Z
SCHULZ

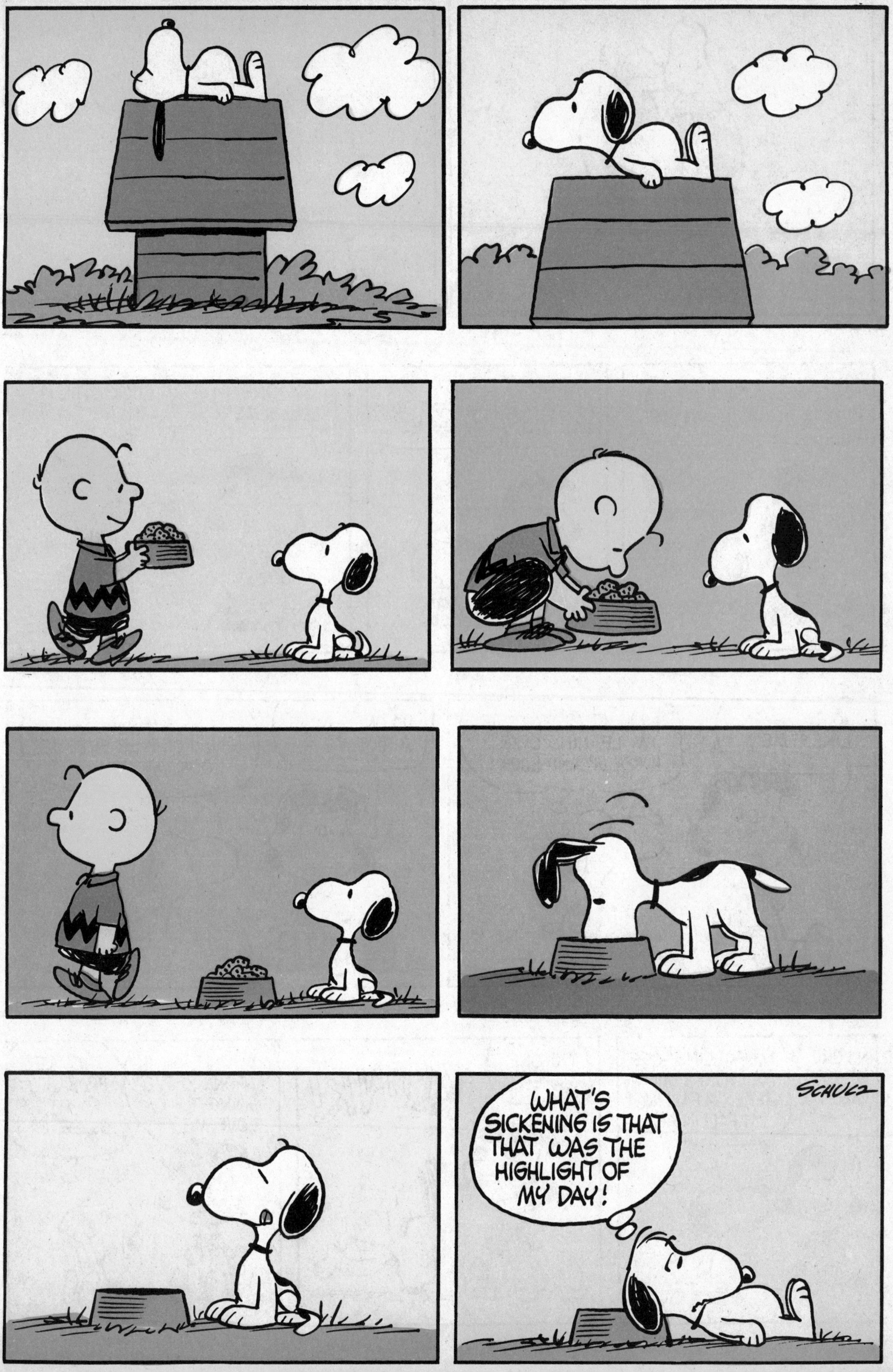
SCHULZ
WHAT'S SICKENING IS THAT THAT WAS THE HIGHLIGHT OF MY DAY!

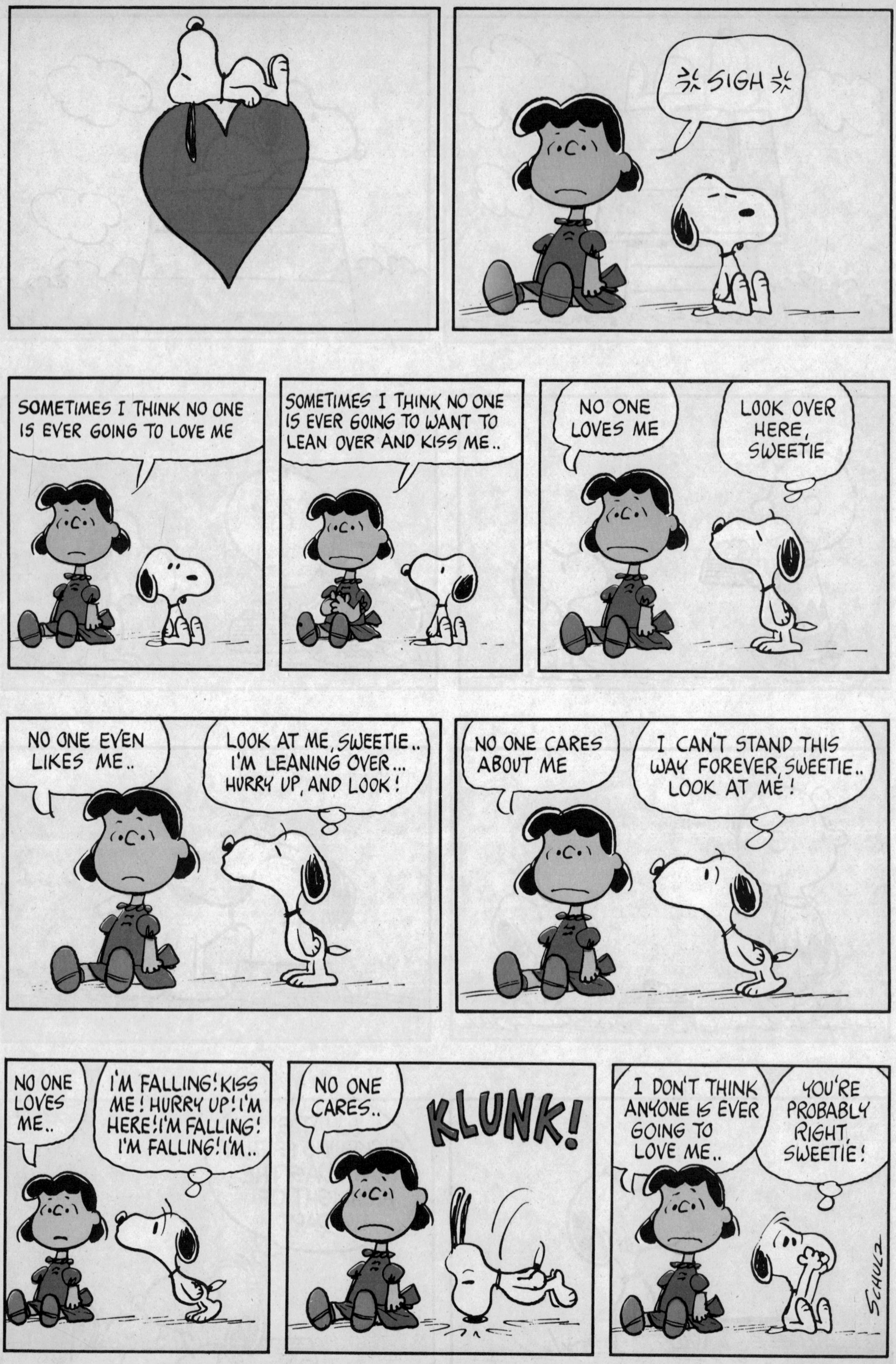
SIGH
SOMETIMES I THINK NO ONE IS EVER GOING TO LOVE ME
SOMETIMES I THINK NO ONE IS EVER GOING TO WANT TO LEAN OVER AND KISS ME..
NO ONE LOVES ME
LOOK OVER HERE, SWEETIE
NO ONE EVEN LIKES ME..
LOOK AT ME, SWEETIE.. I'M LEANING OVER... HURRY UP, AND LOOK!
NO ONE CARES ABOUT ME
I CAN'T STAND THIS WAY FOREVER, SWEETIE.. LOOK AT ME!
NO ONE LOVES ME..
I'M FALLING! KISS ME! HURRY UP! I'M HERE! I'M FALLING! I'M FALLING! I'M..
NO ONE CARES..
KLUNK!
I DON'T THINK ANYONE IS EVER GOING TO LOVE ME..
YOU'RE PROBABLY RIGHT, SWEETIE!
SCHULZ

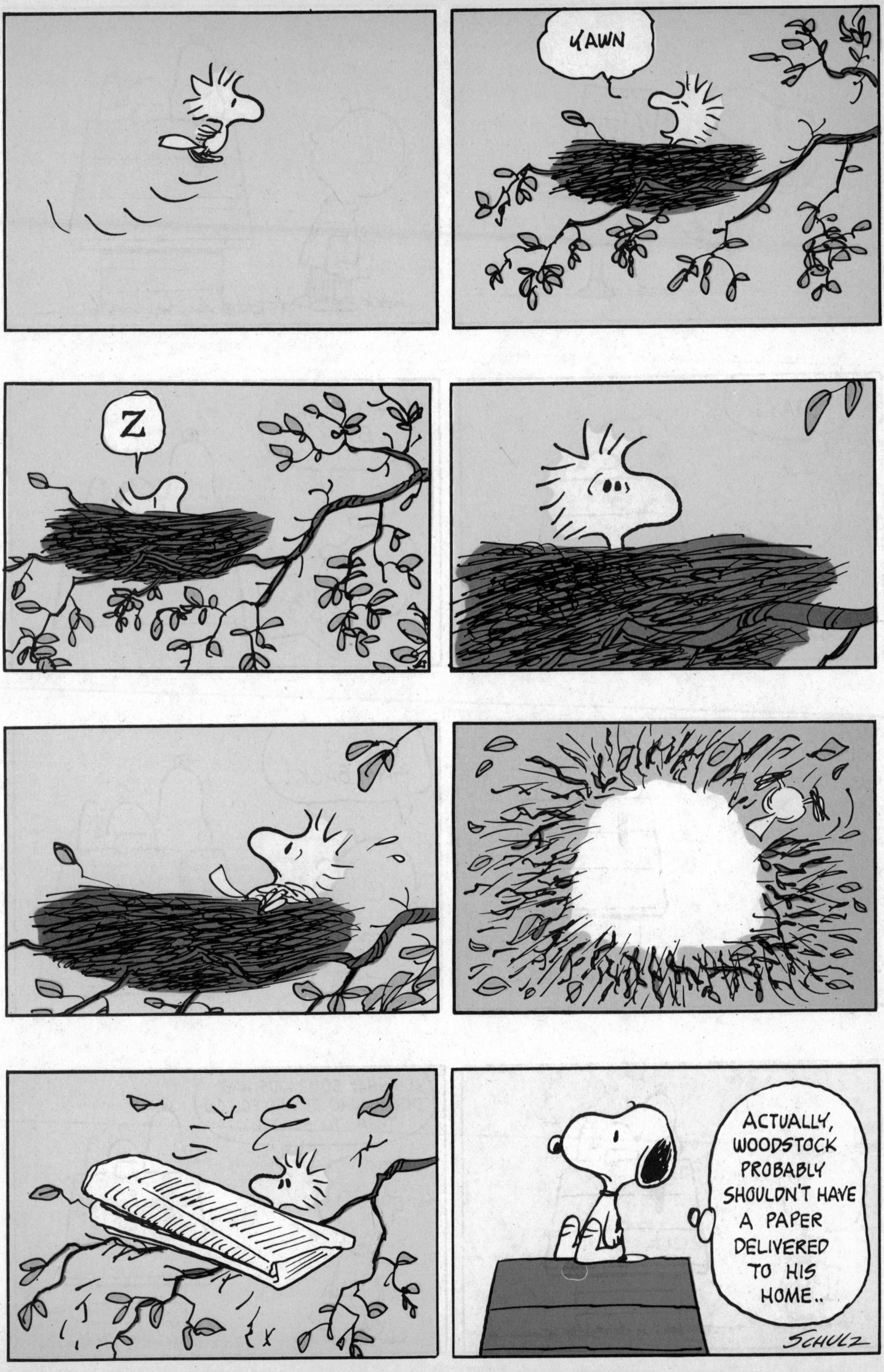
KAWN
Z
ACTUALLY, WOODSTOCK PROBABLY SHOULDN'T HAVE A PAPER DELIVERED TO HIS HOME..
SCHULZ

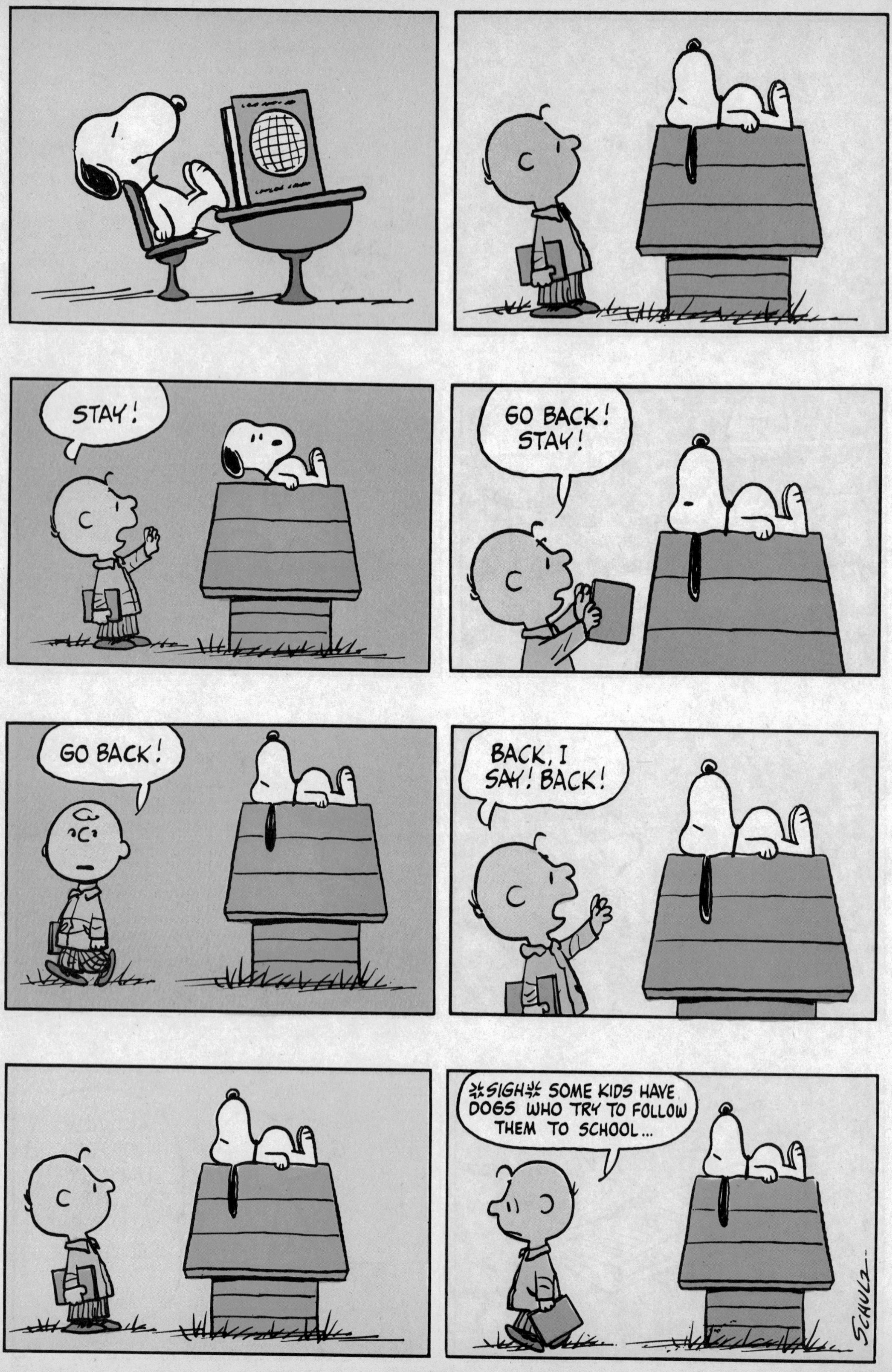
STAY!
GO BACK! STAY!
GO BACK!
BACK, I SAY! BACK!
SIGH SOME KIDS HAVE DOGS WHO TRY TO FOLLOW THEM TO SCHOOL...
SCHULZ

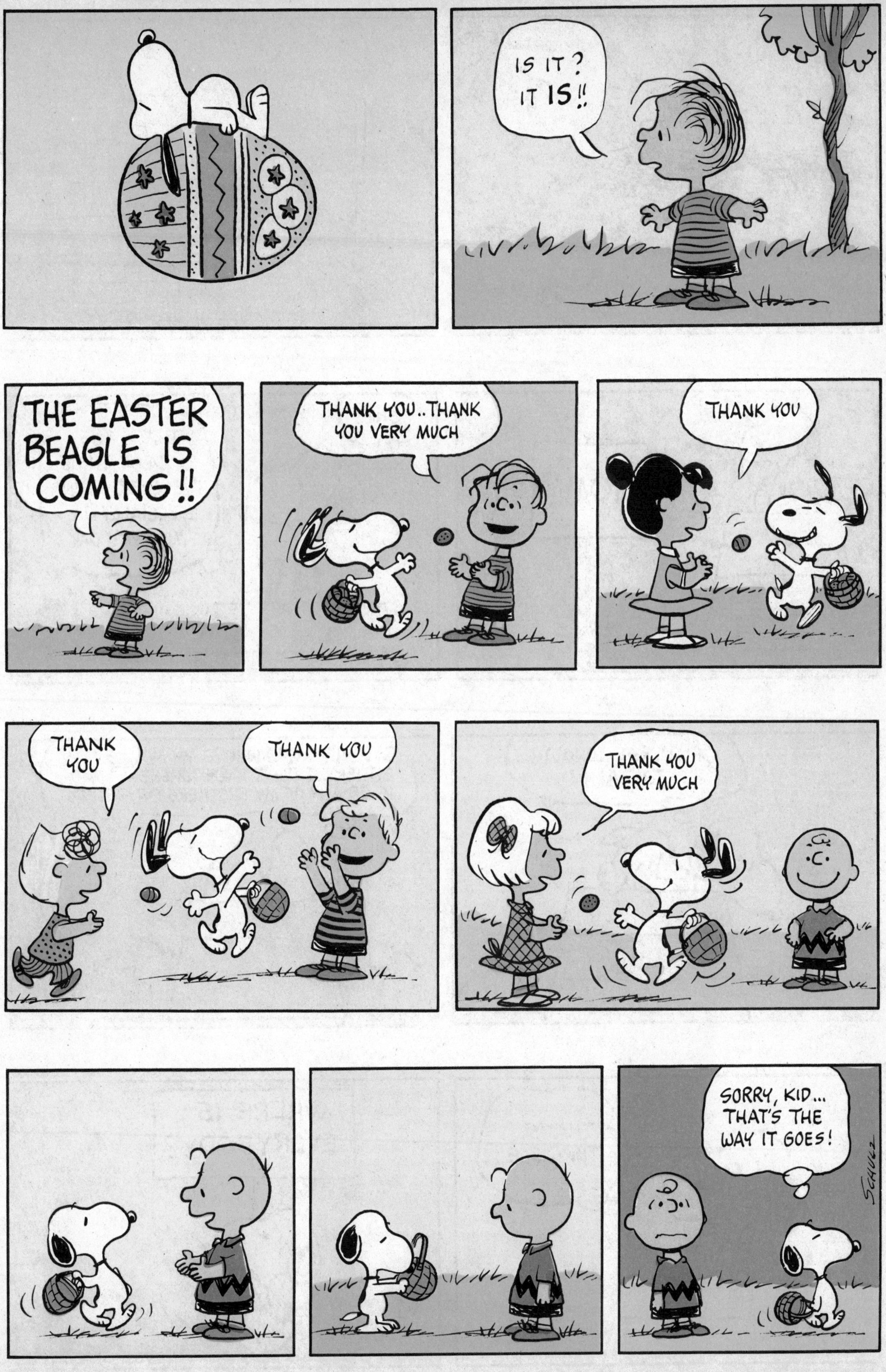
IS IT ?
IT IS !!
THE EASTER BEAGLE IS COMING !!
THANK YOU..THANK YOU VERY MUCH
THANK YOU
THANK YOU
THANK YOU
THANK YOU VERY MUCH
SORRY, KID... THAT'S THE WAY IT GOES!
SCHULZ

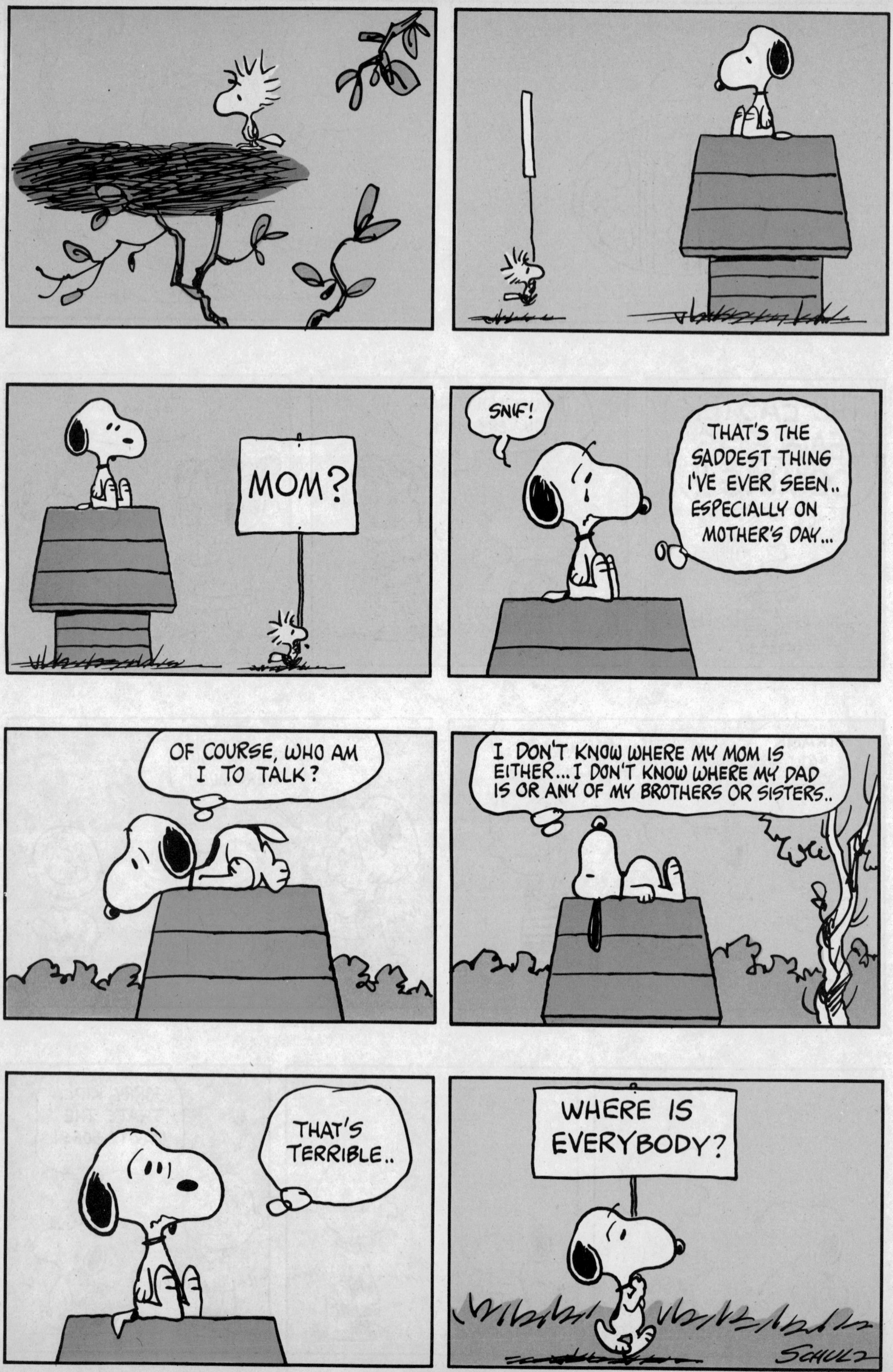
MOM?
SNIF!
THAT'S THE SADDEST THING I'VE EVER SEEN.. ESPECIALLY ON MOTHER'S DAY...
OF COURSE, WHO AM I TO TALK?
I DON'T KNOW WHERE MY MOM IS EITHER... I DON'T KNOW WHERE MY DAD IS OR ANY OF MY BROTHERS OR SISTERS..
THAT'S TERRIBLE..
WHERE IS EVERYBODY?
SCHULZ

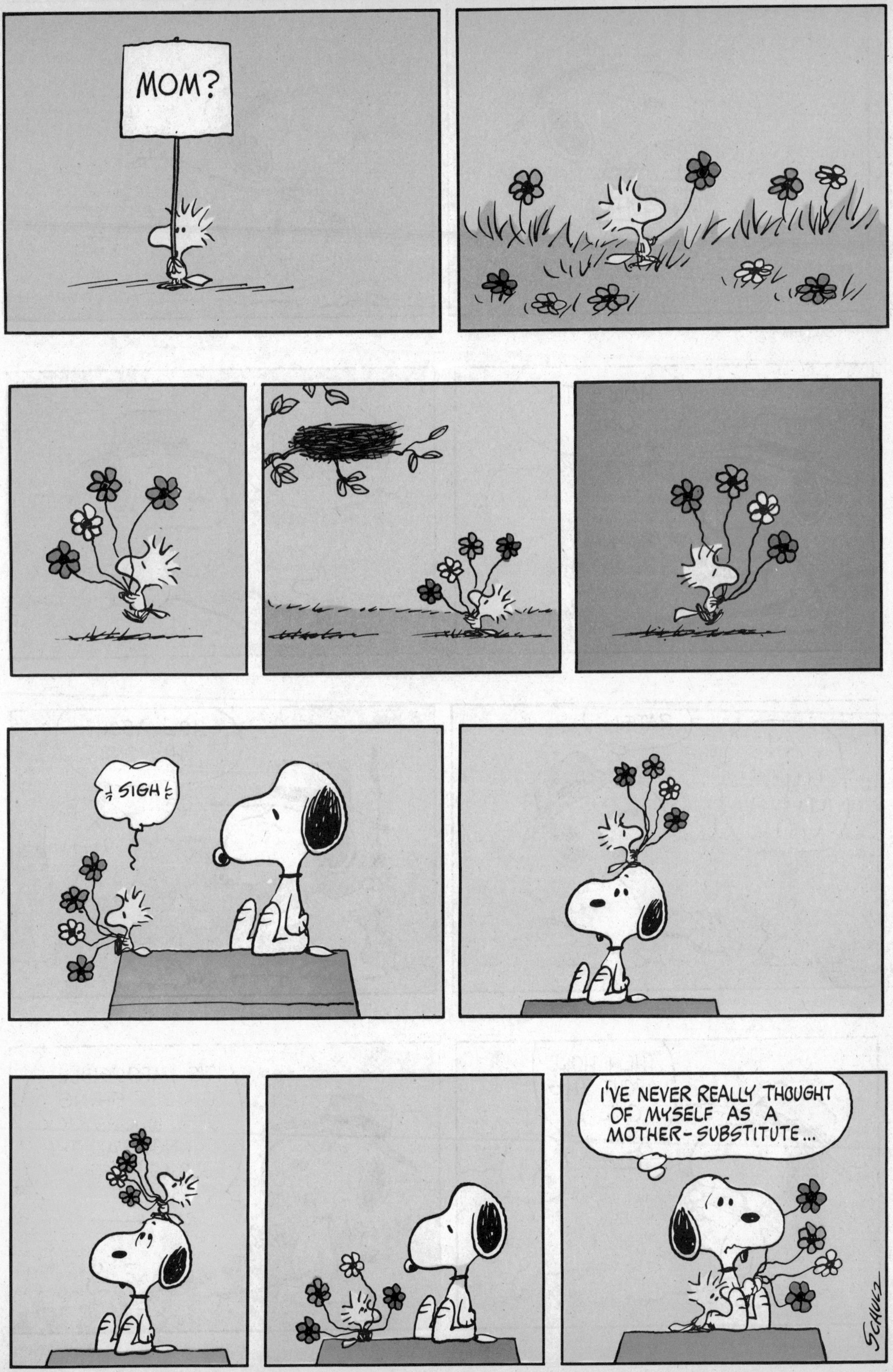
MOM?
SIGH
I'VE NEVER REALLY THOUGHT OF MYSELF AS A MOTHER-SUBSTITUTE...
SCHULZ

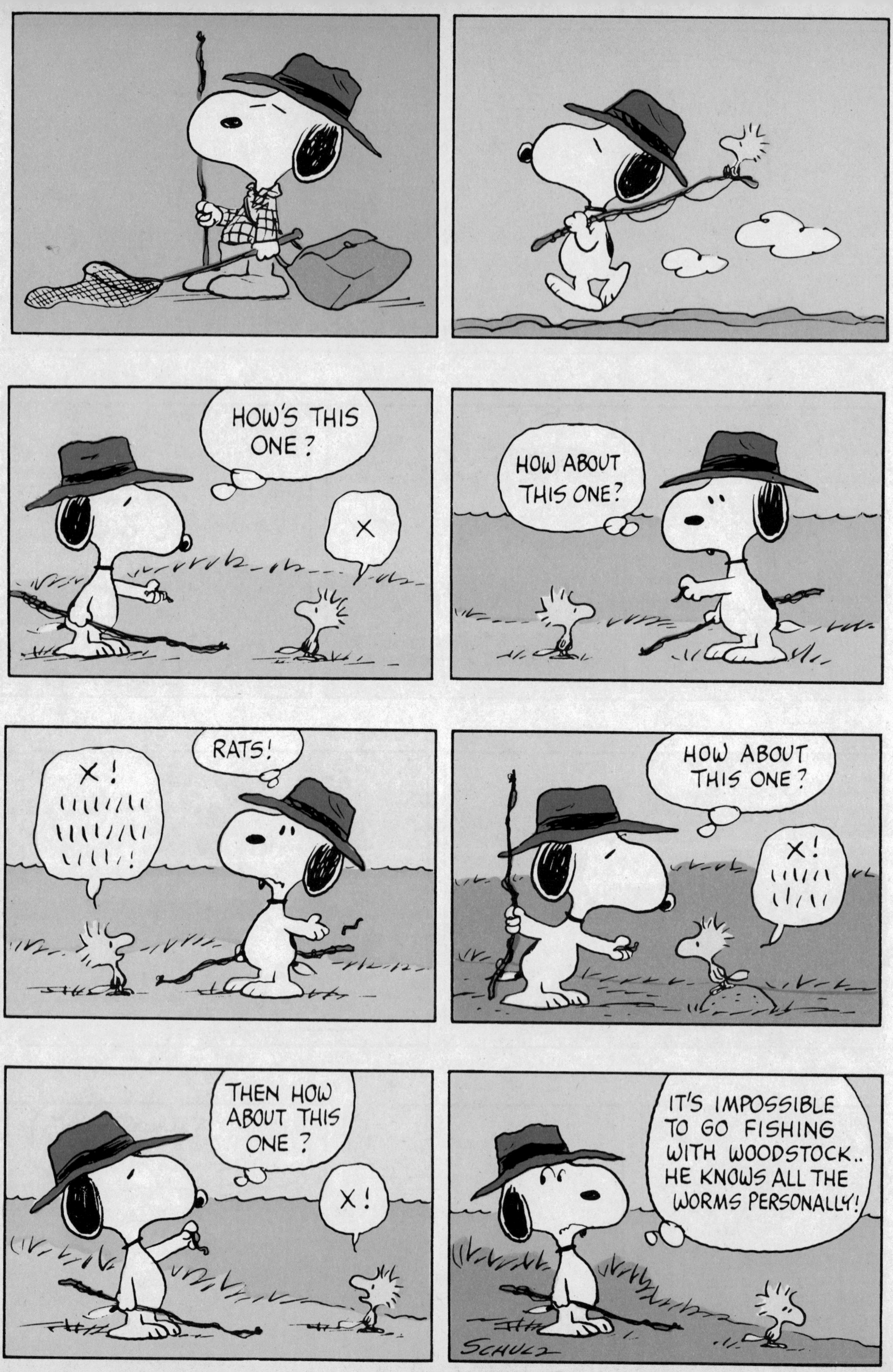
HOW'S THIS ONE ?
X
HOW ABOUT THIS ONE?
RATS!
X !
HOW ABOUT THIS ONE ?
X!
THEN HOW ABOUT THIS ONE ?
X !
IT'S IMPOSSIBLE TO GO FISHING WITH WOODSTOCK.. HE KNOWS ALL THE WORMS PERSONALLY!
SCHULZ

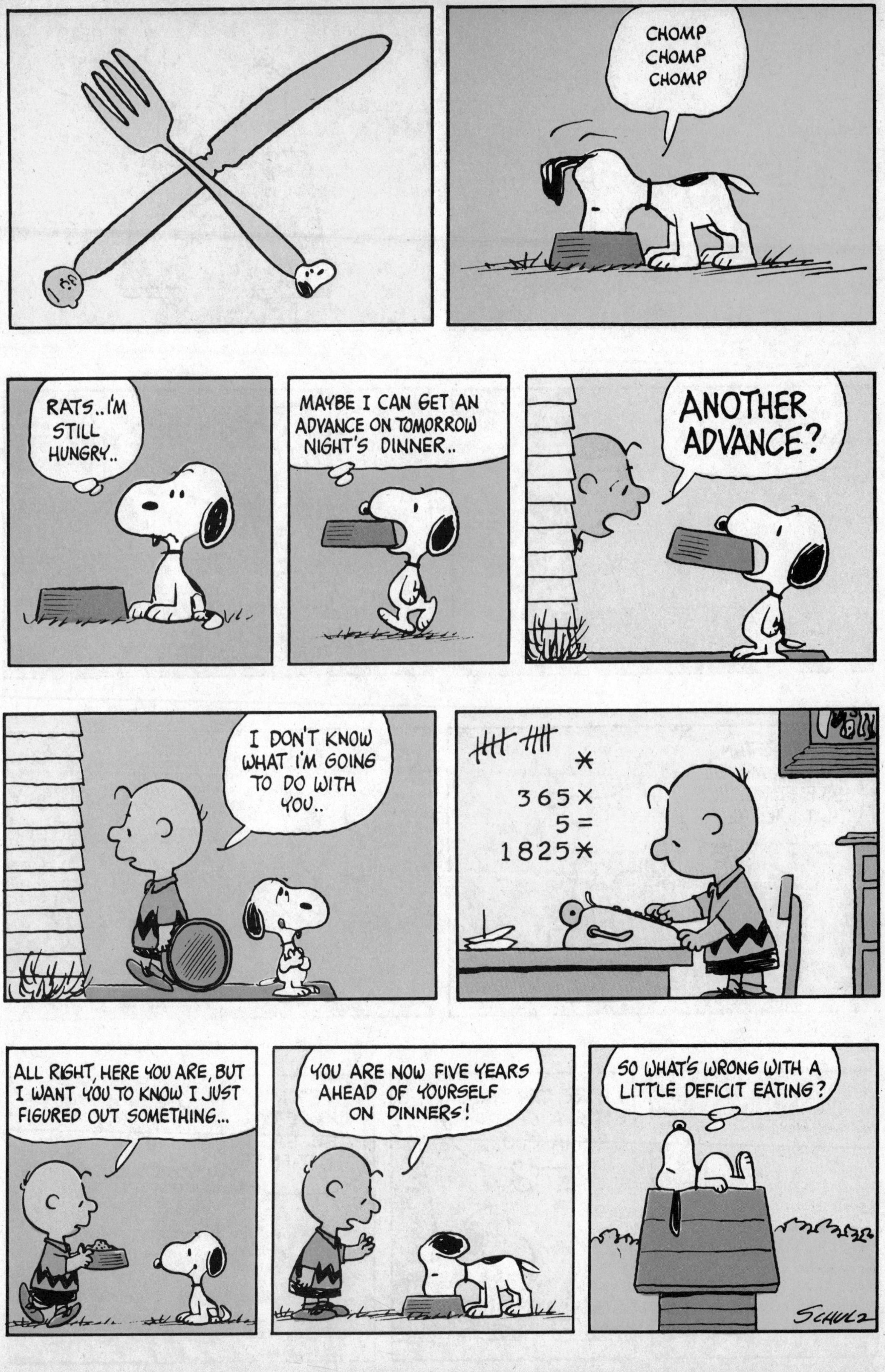
CHOMP
CHOMP
CHOMP
RATS..I'M STILL HUNGRY..
MAYBE I CAN GET AN ADVANCE ON TOMORROW NIGHT'S DINNER..
ANOTHER ADVANCE?
I DON'T KNOW WHAT I'M GOING TO DO WITH YOU..
365×
5=
1825*
ALL RIGHT, HERE YOU ARE, BUT I WANT YOU TO KNOW I JUST FIGURED OUT SOMETHING...
YOU ARE NOW FIVE YEARS AHEAD OF YOURSELF ON DINNERS!
SO WHAT'S WRONG WITH A LITTLE DEFICIT EATING?
SCHULZ

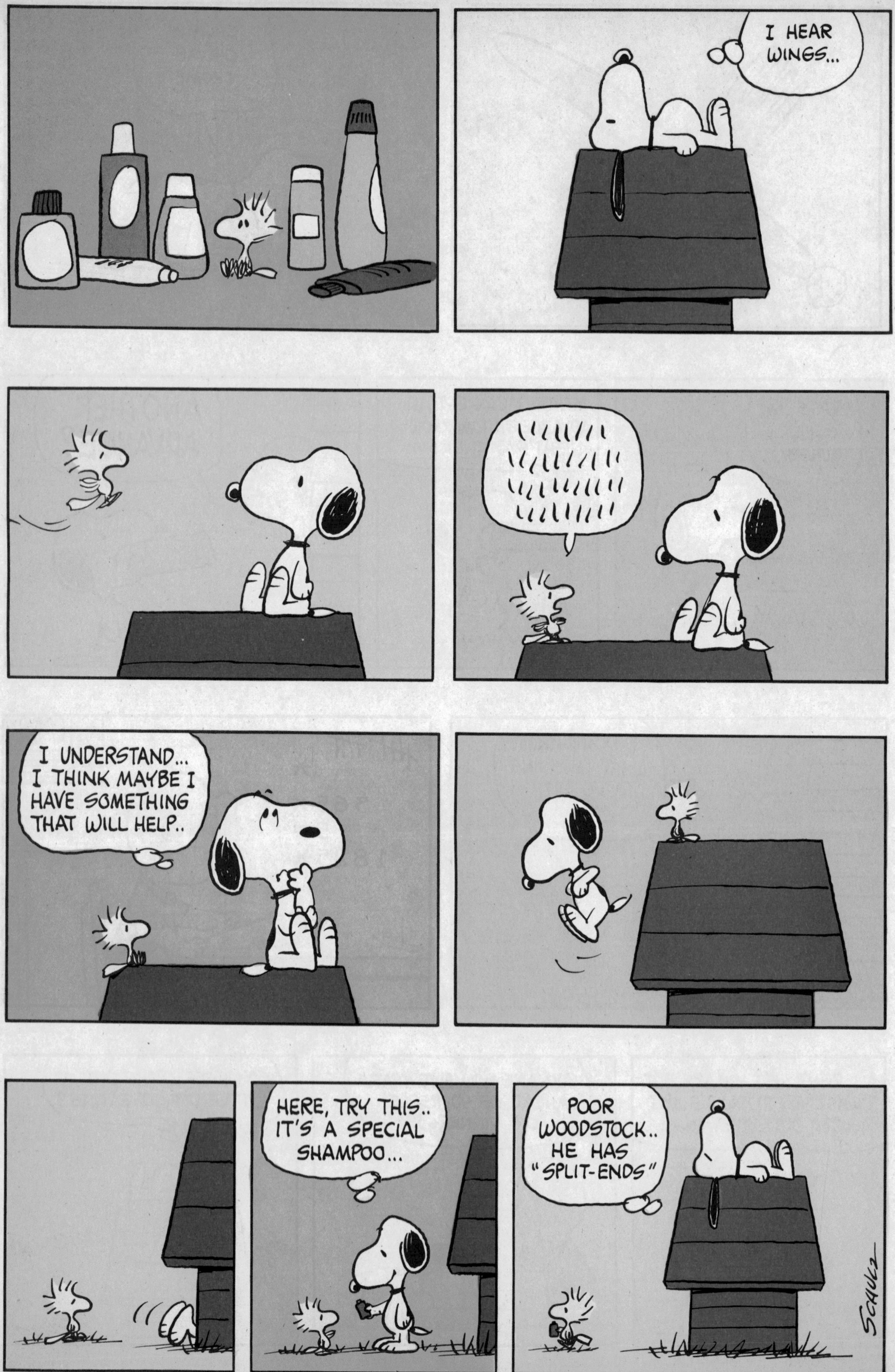
I HEAR WINGS...
I UNDERSTAND... I THINK MAYBE I HAVE SOMETHING THAT WILL HELP..
HERE, TRY THIS.. IT'S A SPECIAL SHAMPOO...
POOR WOODSTOCK.. HE HAS "SPLIT-ENDS"
SCHULZ

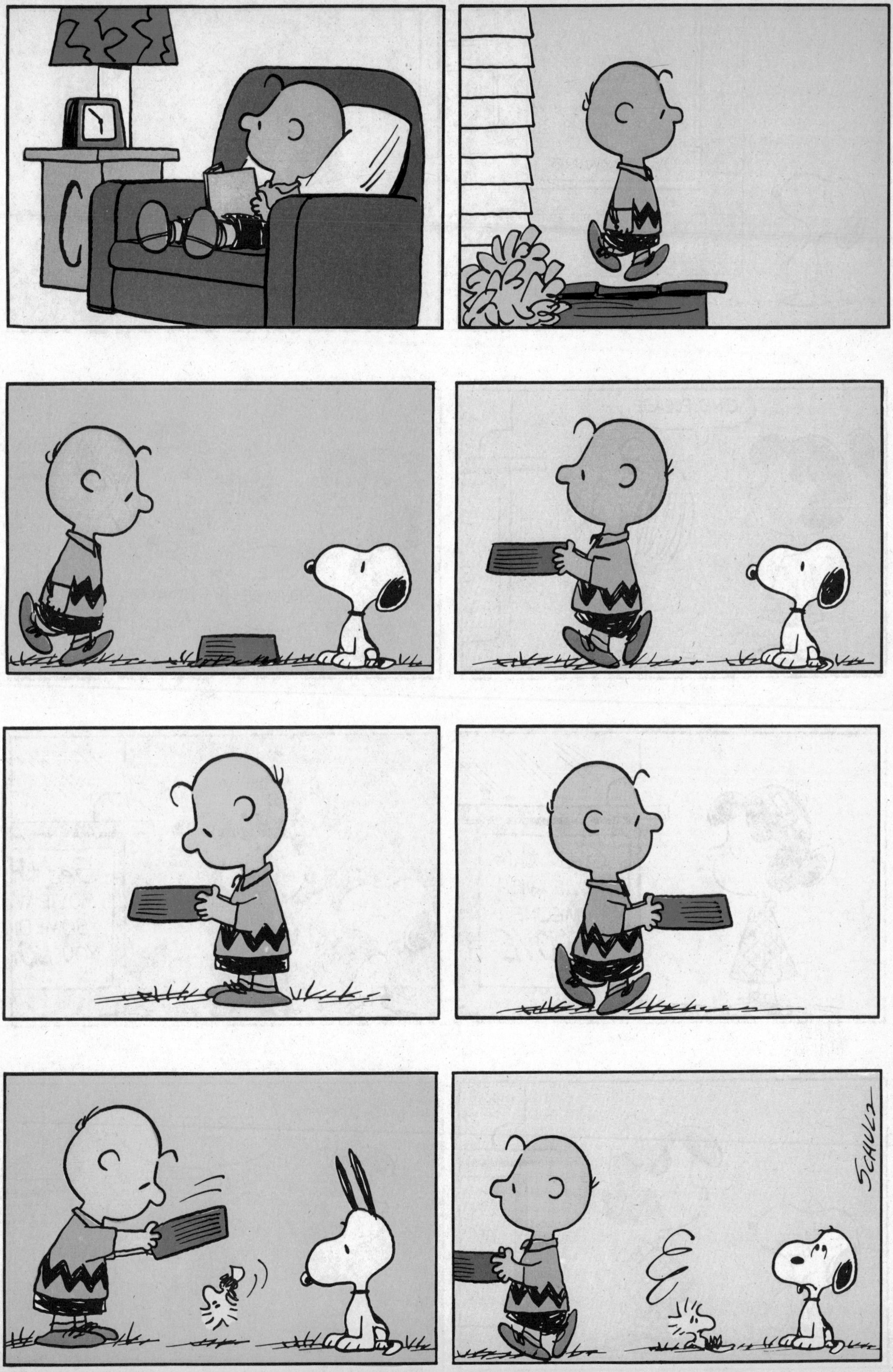
SCHULZ

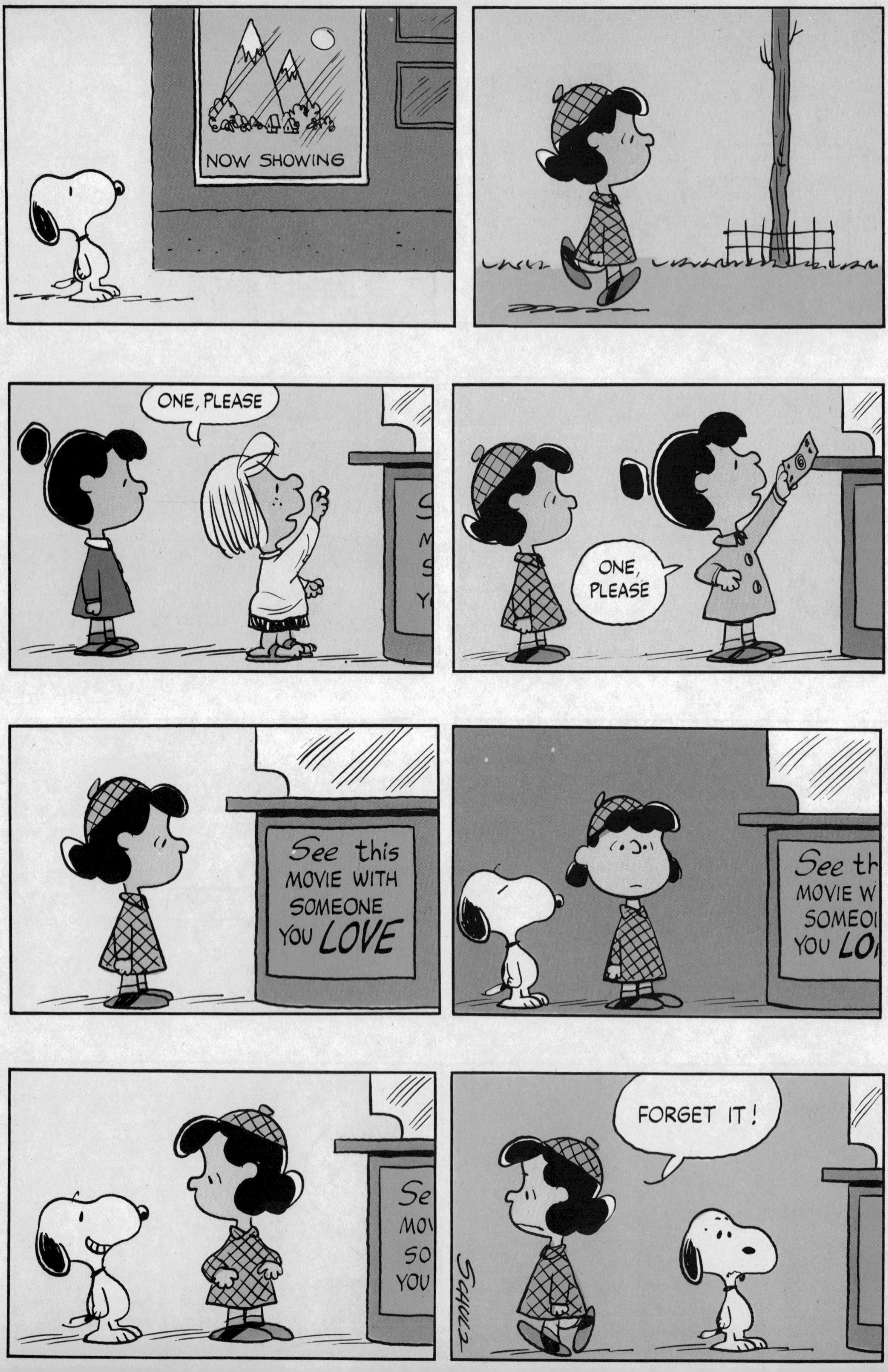
NOW SHOWING
ONE, PLEASE
ONE, PLEASE
See this MOVIE WITH SOMEONE YOU LOVE
FORGET IT!
SCHULZ

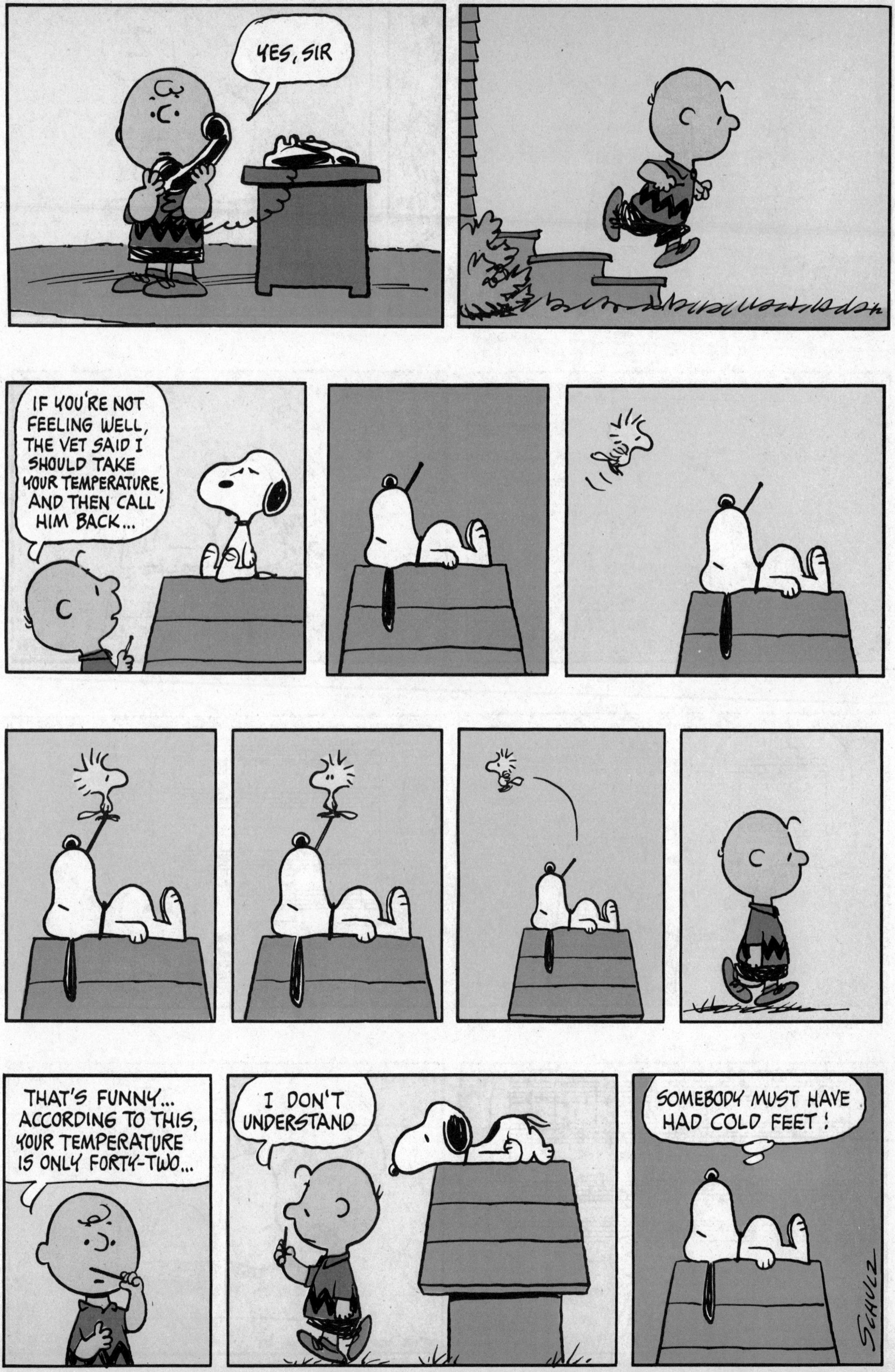
YES, SIR
IF YOU'RE NOT FEELING WELL, THE VET SAID I SHOULD TAKE YOUR TEMPERATURE, AND THEN CALL HIM BACK...
THAT'S FUNNY... ACCORDING TO THIS, YOUR TEMPERATURE IS ONLY FORTY-TWO...
I DON'T UNDERSTAND
SOMEBODY MUST HAVE HAD COLD FEET!
SCHULZ

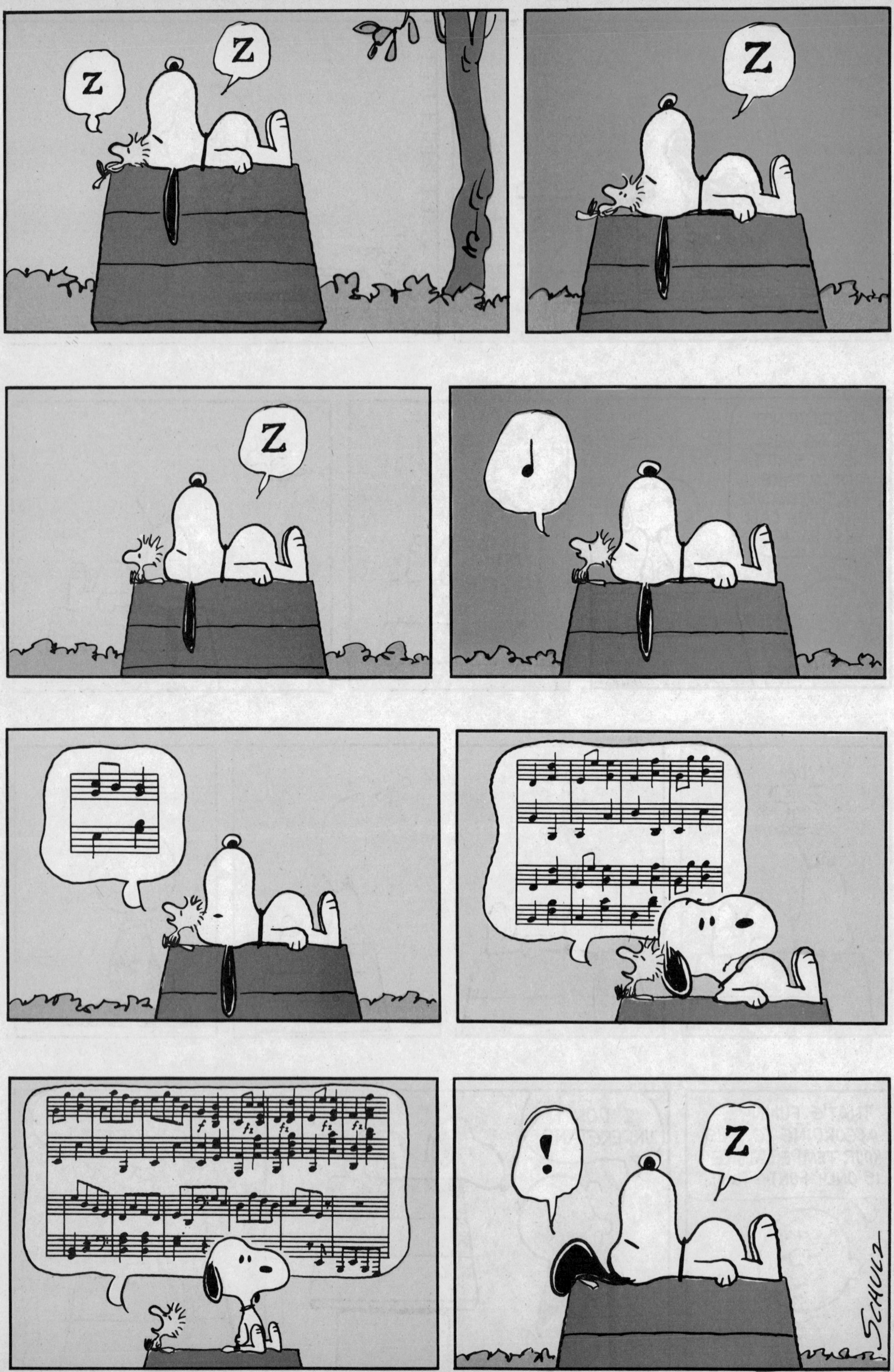
Z
Z
Z
Z
!
Z
SCHULZ

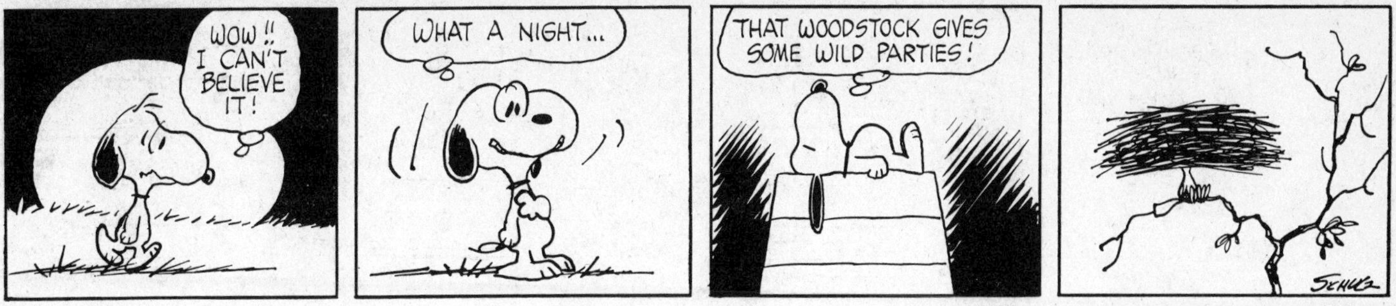
WOW!! I CAN'T BELIEVE IT!
WHAT A NIGHT...
THAT WOODSTOCK GIVES SOME WILD PARTIES!
SCHULZ

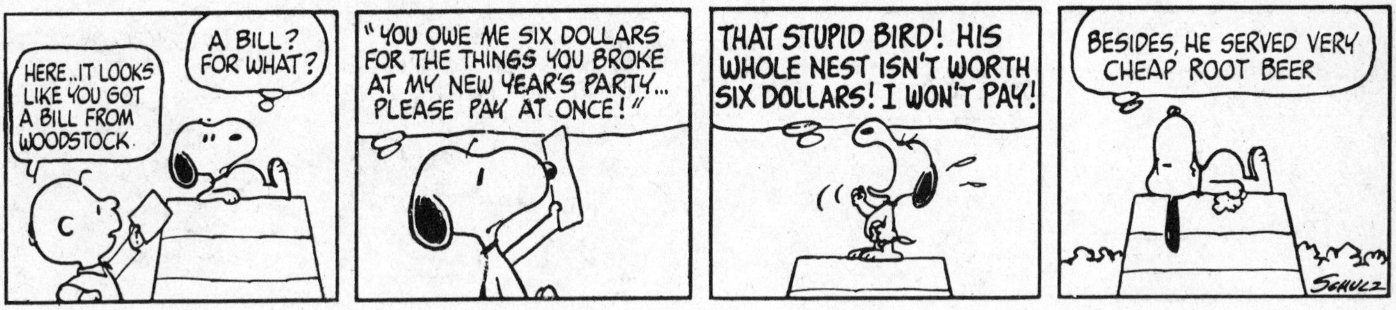
HERE...IT LOOKS LIKE YOU GOT A BILL FROM WOODSTOCK.
A BILL? FOR WHAT?
"YOU OWE ME SIX DOLLARS FOR THE THINGS YOU BROKE AT MY NEW YEAR'S PARTY... PLEASE PAY AT ONCE!"
THAT STUPID BIRD! HIS WHOLE NEST ISN'T WORTH SIX DOLLARS! I WON'T PAY!
BESIDES, HE SERVED VERY CHEAP ROOT BEER
SCHULZ

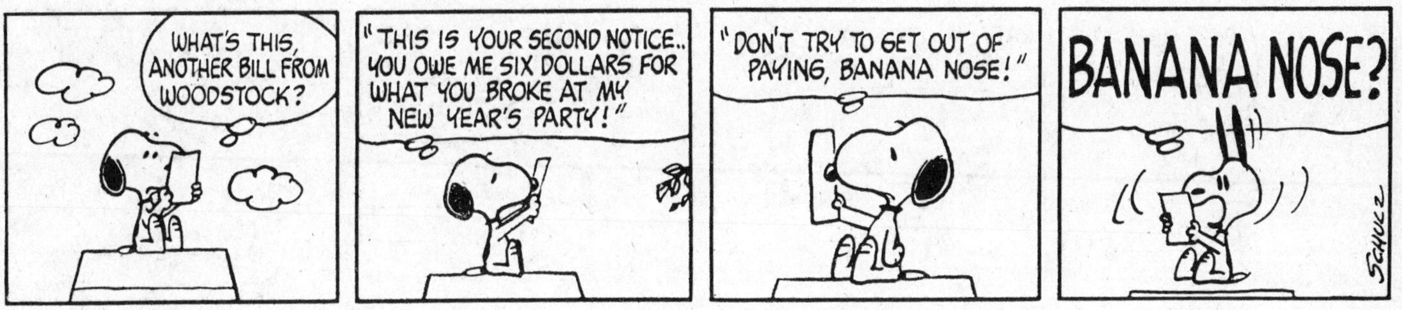
WHAT'S THIS, ANOTHER BILL FROM WOODSTOCK?
"THIS IS YOUR SECOND NOTICE.. YOU OWE ME SIX DOLLARS FOR WHAT YOU BROKE AT MY NEW YEAR'S PARTY!"
"DON'T TRY TO GET OUT OF PAYING, BANANA NOSE!"
BANANA NOSE?
SCHULZ

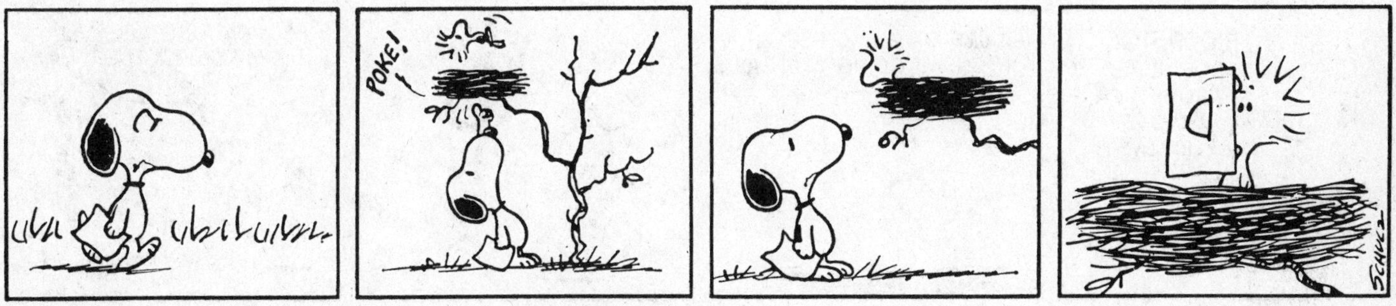
POKE!
SCHULZ

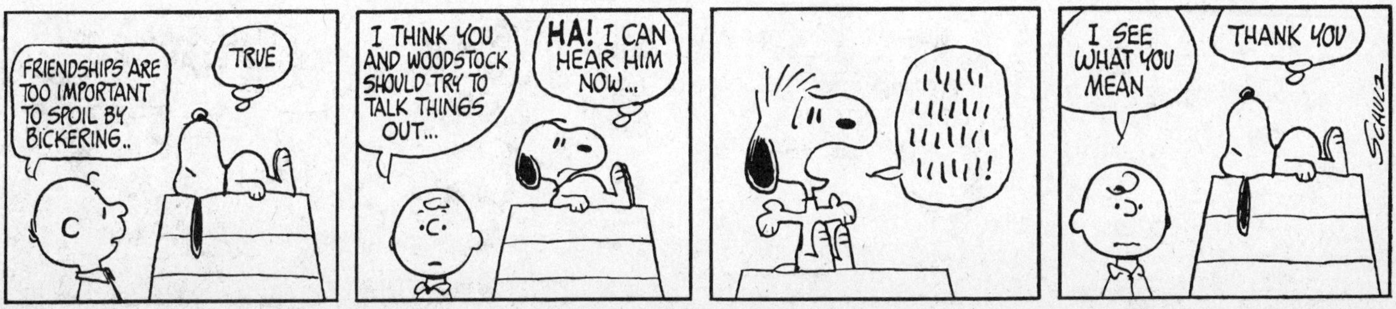
FRIENDSHIPS ARE TOO IMPORTANT TO SPOIL BY BICKERING..
TRUE
I THINK YOU AND WOODSTOCK SHOULD TRY TO TALK THINGS OUT...
HA! I CAN HEAR HIM NOW...
I SEE WHAT YOU MEAN
THANK YOU
SCHULZ

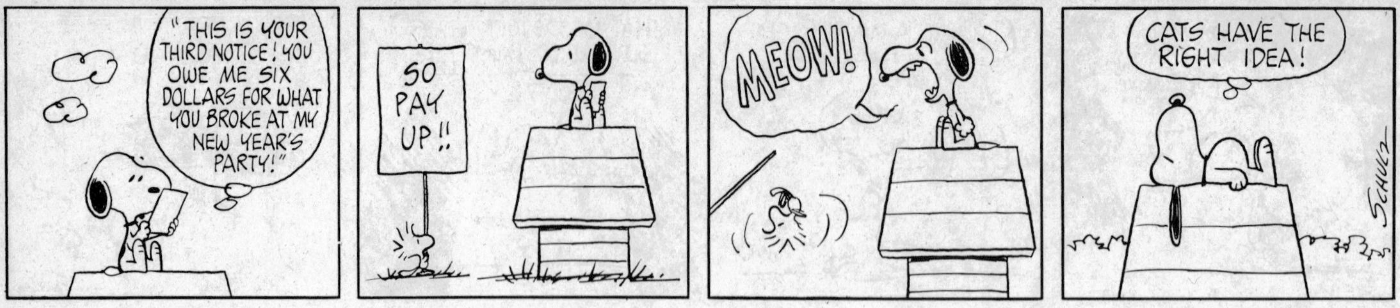
"THIS IS YOUR THIRD NOTICE! YOU OWE ME SIX DOLLARS FOR WHAT YOU BROKE AT MY NEW YEAR'S PARTY!"
SO PAY UP!!
MEOW!
CATS HAVE THE RIGHT IDEA!
SCHULZ

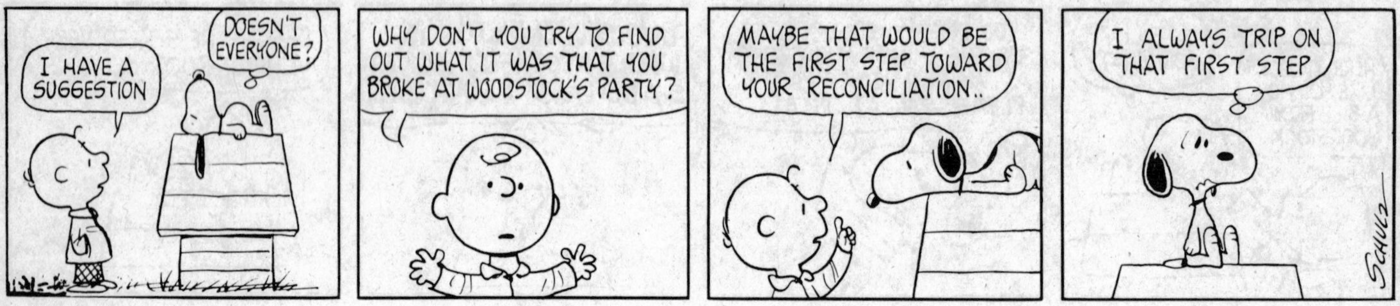
I HAVE A SUGGESTION
DOESN'T EVERYONE?
WHY DON'T YOU TRY TO FIND OUT WHAT IT WAS THAT YOU BROKE AT WOODSTOCK'S PARTY?
MAYBE THAT WOULD BE THE FIRST STEP TOWARD YOUR RECONCILIATION..
I ALWAYS TRIP ON THAT FIRST STEP
SCHULZ

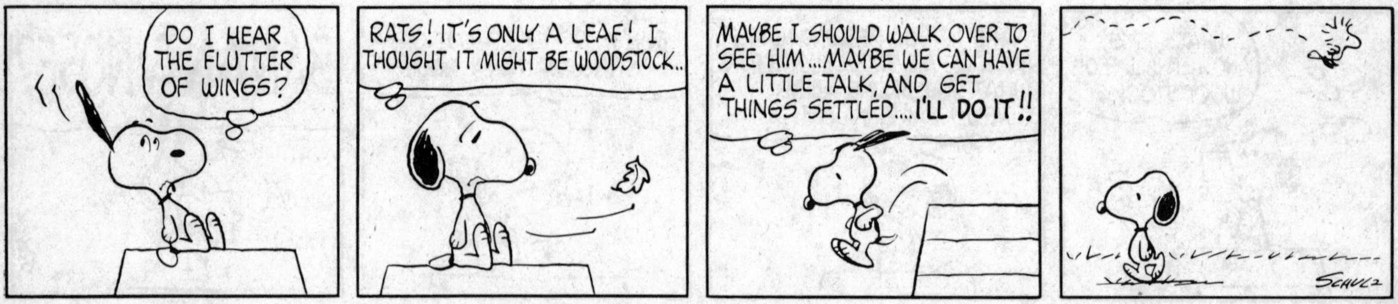
DO I HEAR THE FLUTTER OF WINGS?
RATS! IT'S ONLY A LEAF! I THOUGHT IT MIGHT BE WOODSTOCK..
MAYBE I SHOULD WALK OVER TO SEE HIM...MAYBE WE CAN HAVE A LITTLE TALK, AND GET THINGS SETTLED....I'LL DO IT!!
SCHULZ

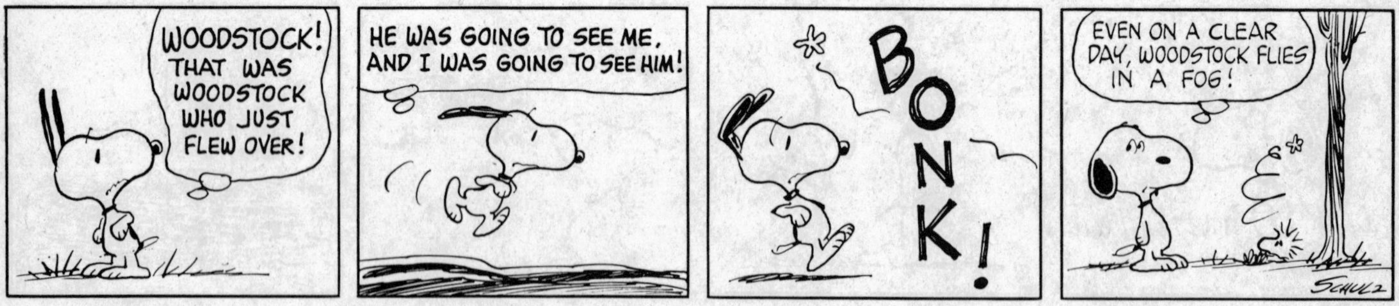
WOODSTOCK! THAT WAS WOODSTOCK WHO JUST FLEW OVER!
HE WAS GOING TO SEE ME, AND I WAS GOING TO SEE HIM!
BONK!
EVEN ON A CLEAR DAY, WOODSTOCK FLIES IN A FOG!
SCHULZ

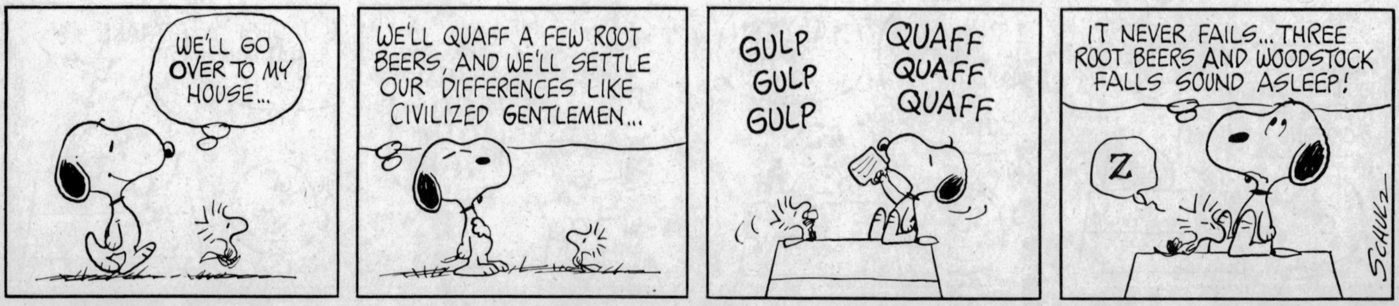
WE'LL GO OVER TO MY HOUSE...
WE'LL QUAFF A FEW ROOT BEERS, AND WE'LL SETTLE OUR DIFFERENCES LIKE CIVILIZED GENTLEMEN...
GULP GULP GULP
QUAFF QUAFF QUAFF
IT NEVER FAILS...THREE ROOT BEERS AND WOODSTOCK FALLS SOUND ASLEEP!
Z
SCHULZ

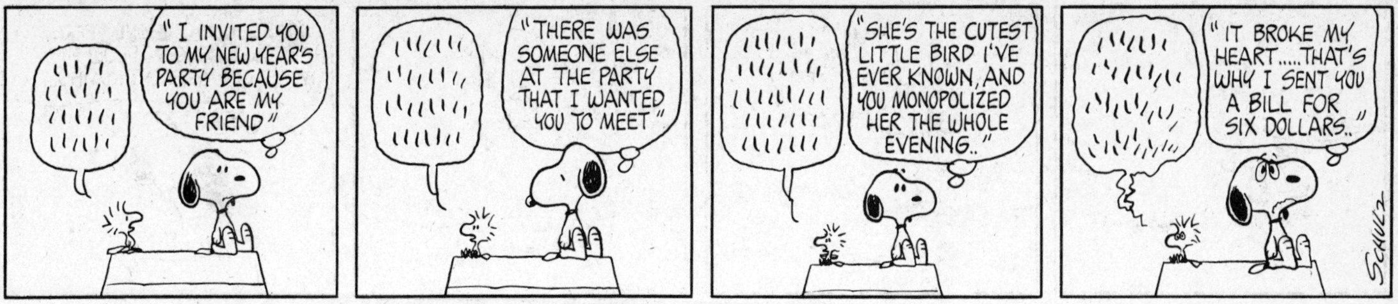
"I INVITED YOU TO MY NEW YEAR'S PARTY BECAUSE YOU ARE MY FRIEND"
"THERE WAS SOMEONE ELSE AT THE PARTY THAT I WANTED YOU TO MEET"
"SHE'S THE CUTEST LITTLE BIRD I'VE EVER KNOWN, AND YOU MONOPOLIZED HER THE WHOLE EVENING.."
"IT BROKE MY HEART.....THAT'S WHY I SENT YOU A BILL FOR SIX DOLLARS.."
SCHULZ

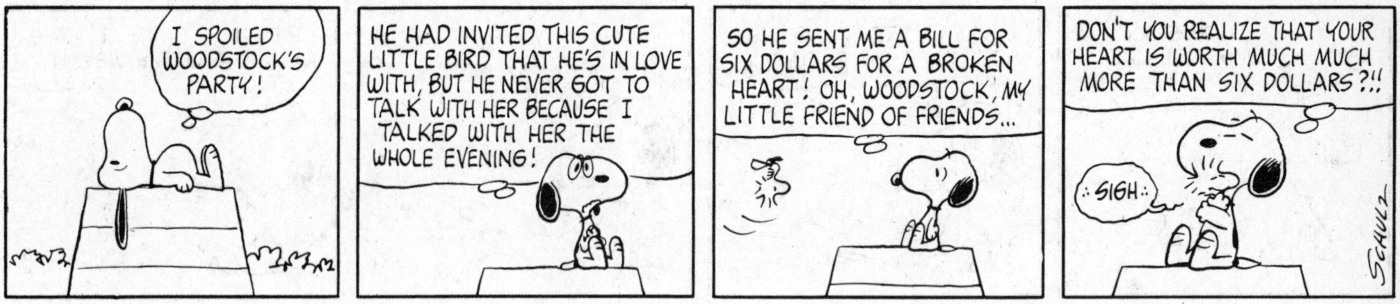
I SPOILED WOODSTOCK'S PARTY!
HE HAD INVITED THIS CUTE LITTLE BIRD THAT HE'S IN LOVE WITH, BUT HE NEVER GOT TO TALK WITH HER BECAUSE I TALKED WITH HER THE WHOLE EVENING!
SO HE SENT ME A BILL FOR SIX DOLLARS FOR A BROKEN HEART! OH, WOODSTOCK, MY LITTLE FRIEND OF FRIENDS...
DON'T YOU REALIZE THAT YOUR HEART IS WORTH MUCH MUCH MORE THAN SIX DOLLARS?!!
SIGH
SCHULZ

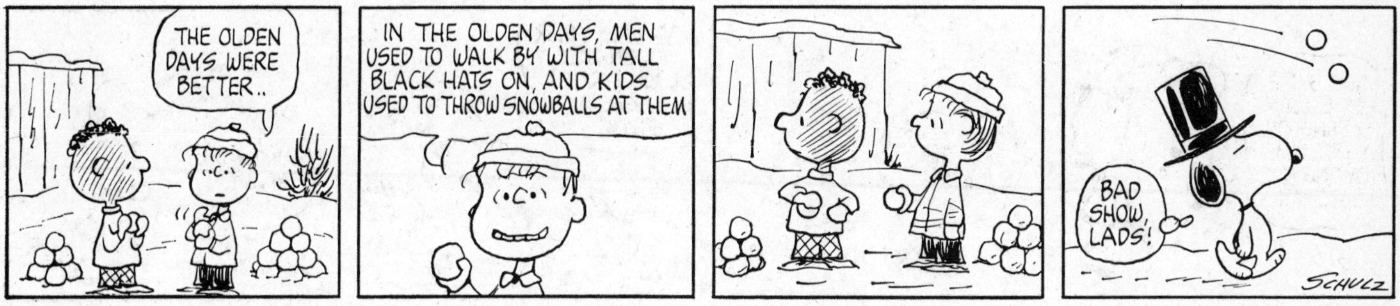
THE OLDEN DAYS WERE BETTER..
IN THE OLDEN DAYS, MEN USED TO WALK BY WITH TALL BLACK HATS ON, AND KIDS USED TO THROW SNOWBALLS AT THEM
BAD SHOW, LADS!
SCHULZ

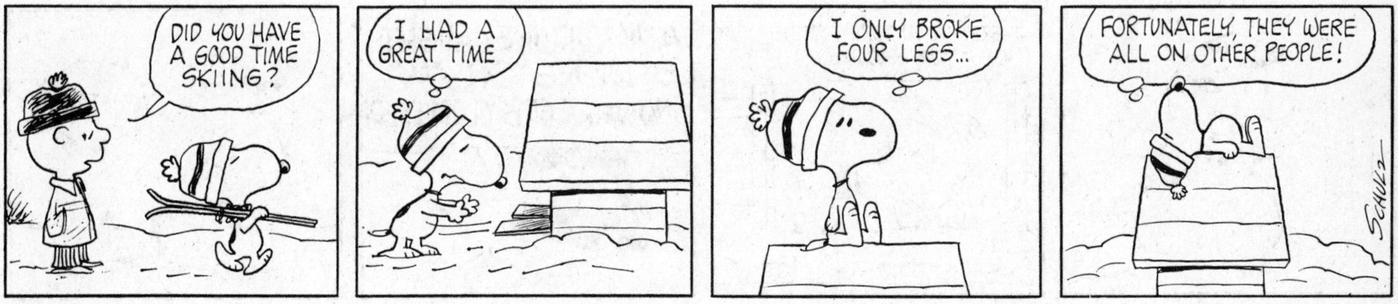
DID YOU HAVE A GOOD TIME SKIING?
I HAD A GREAT TIME
I ONLY BROKE FOUR LEGS...
FORTUNATELY, THEY WERE ALL ON OTHER PEOPLE!
SCHULZ

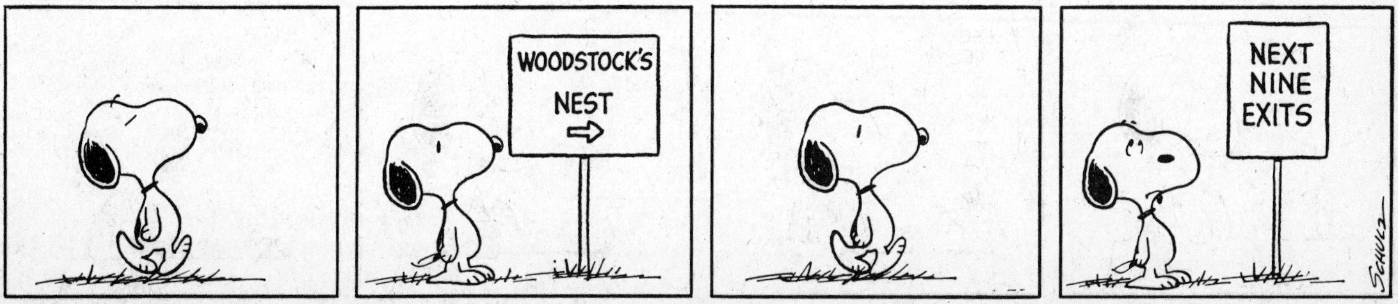
WOODSTOCK'S NEST
NEXT NINE EXITS
SCHULZ

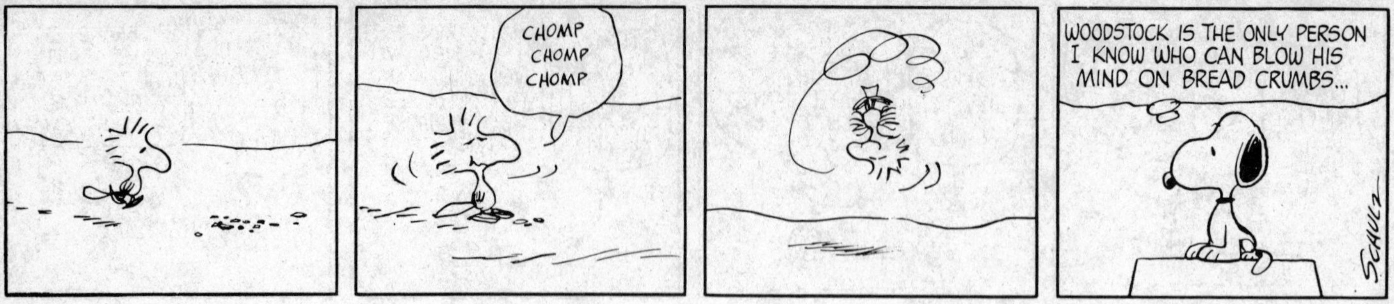
CHOMP CHOMP CHOMP
WOODSTOCK IS THE ONLY PERSON I KNOW WHO CAN BLOW HIS MIND ON BREAD CRUMBS...
SCHULZ

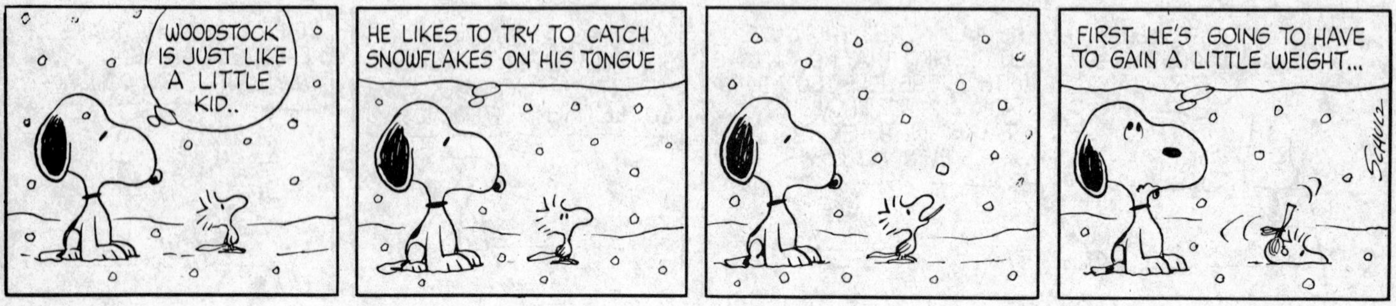
WOODSTOCK IS JUST LIKE A LITTLE KID..
HE LIKES TO TRY TO CATCH SNOWFLAKES ON HIS TONGUE
FIRST HE'S GOING TO HAVE TO GAIN A LITTLE WEIGHT...
SCHULZ

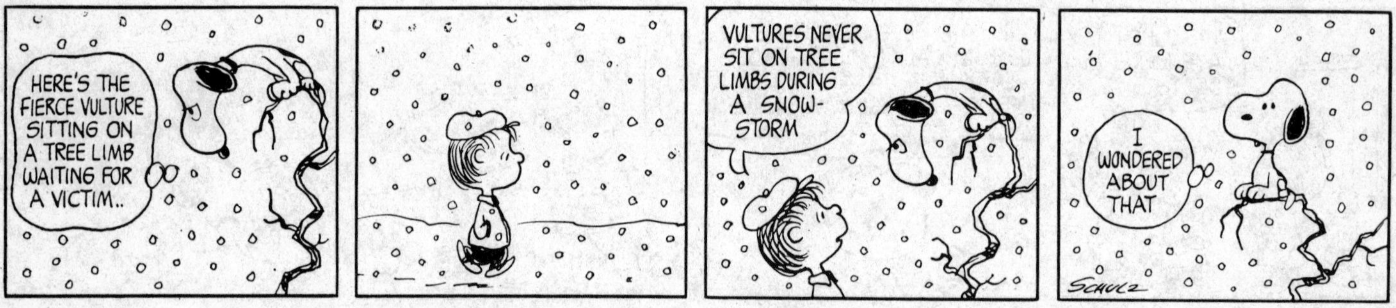
HERE'S THE FIERCE VULTURE SITTING ON A TREE LIMB WAITING FOR A VICTIM..
VULTURES NEVER SIT ON TREE LIMBS DURING A SNOW-STORM
I WONDERED ABOUT THAT
SCHULZ

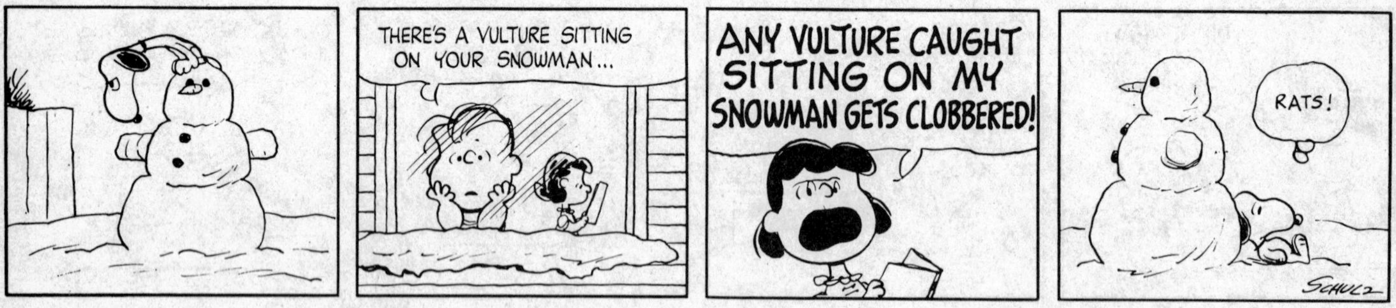
THERE'S A VULTURE SITTING ON YOUR SNOWMAN...
ANY VULTURE CAUGHT SITTING ON MY SNOWMAN GETS CLOBBERED!
RATS!
SCHULZ

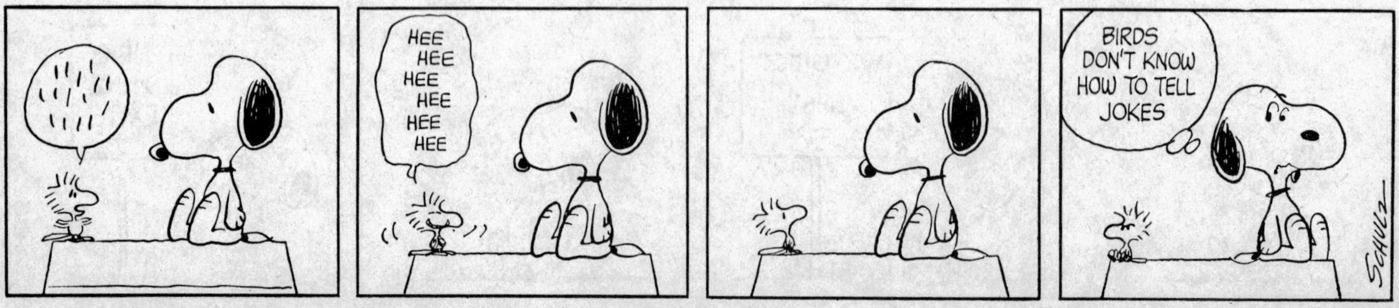
HEE HEE HEE HEE HEE HEE
BIRDS DON'T KNOW HOW TO TELL JOKES
SCHULZ

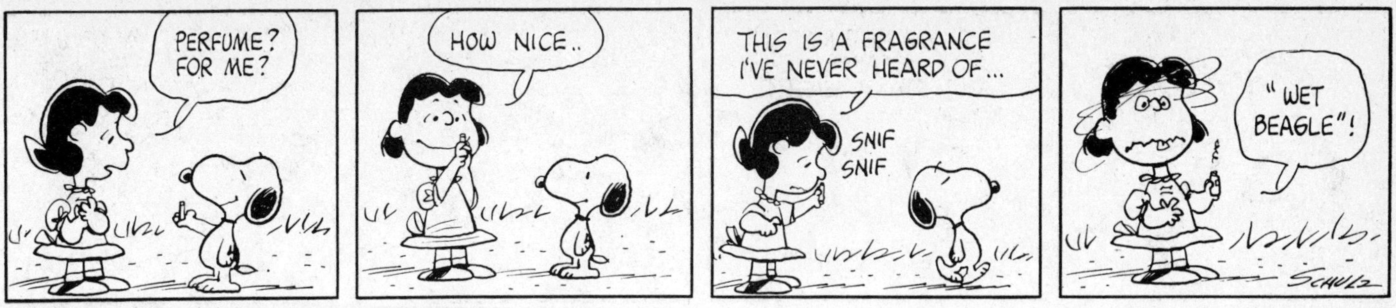
PERFUME? FOR ME?
HOW NICE..
THIS IS A FRAGRANCE I'VE NEVER HEARD OF...
SNIF SNIF
"WET BEAGLE"!
SCHULZ

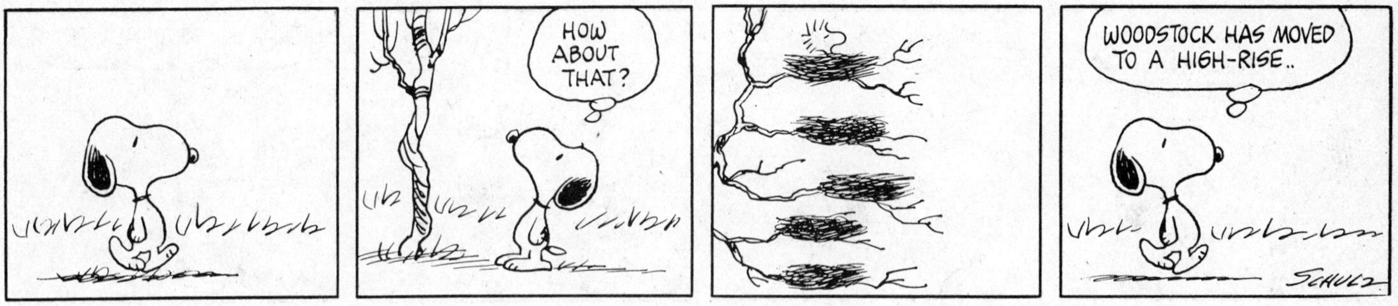
HOW ABOUT THAT?
WOODSTOCK HAS MOVED TO A HIGH-RISE..
SCHULZ

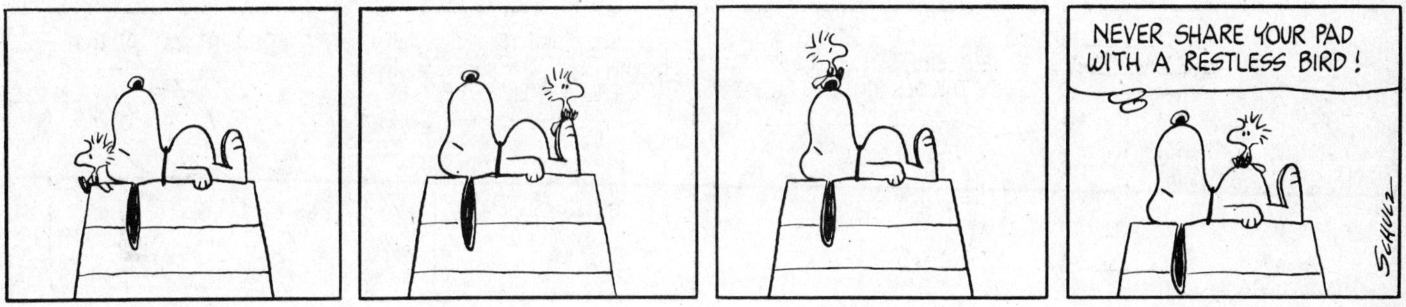
NEVER SHARE YOUR PAD WITH A RESTLESS BIRD!
SCHULZ

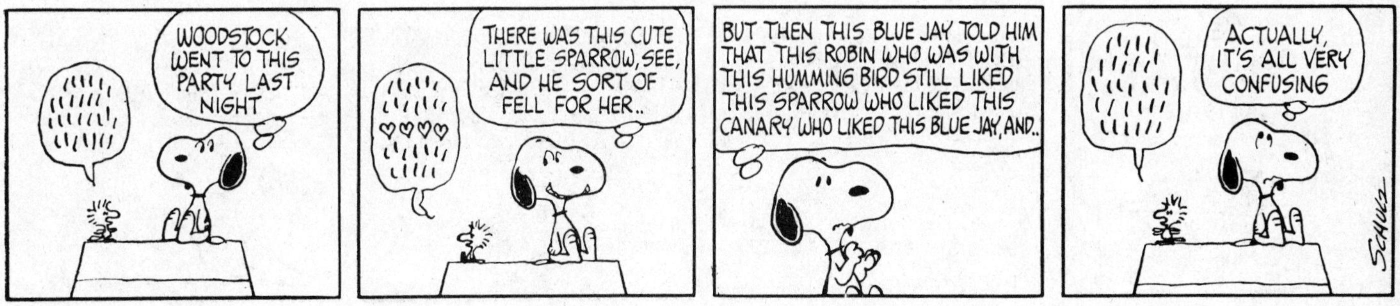
WOODSTOCK WENT TO THIS PARTY LAST NIGHT
THERE WAS THIS CUTE LITTLE SPARROW, SEE, AND HE SORT OF FELL FOR HER..
BUT THEN THIS BLUE JAY TOLD HIM THAT THIS ROBIN WHO WAS WITH THIS HUMMING BIRD STILL LIKED THIS SPARROW WHO LIKED THIS CANARY WHO LIKED THIS BLUE JAY, AND..
ACTUALLY, IT'S ALL VERY CONFUSING
SCHULZ

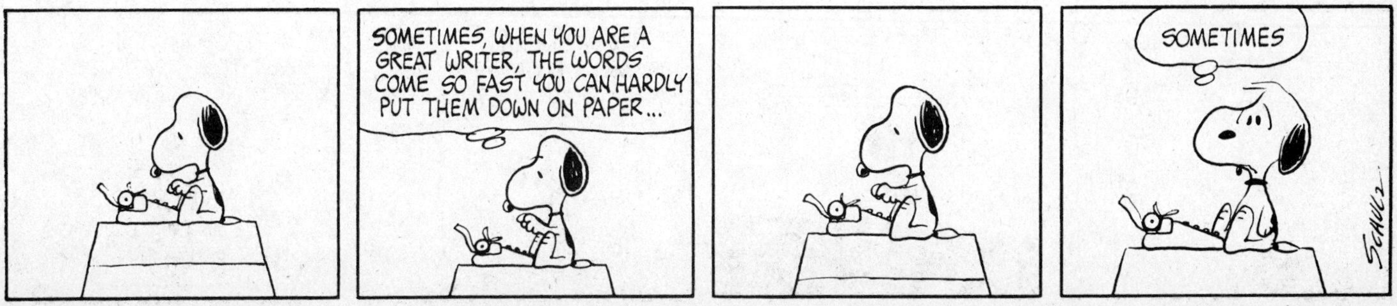
SOMETIMES, WHEN YOU ARE A GREAT WRITER, THE WORDS COME SO FAST YOU CAN HARDLY PUT THEM DOWN ON PAPER...
SOMETIMES
SCHULZ

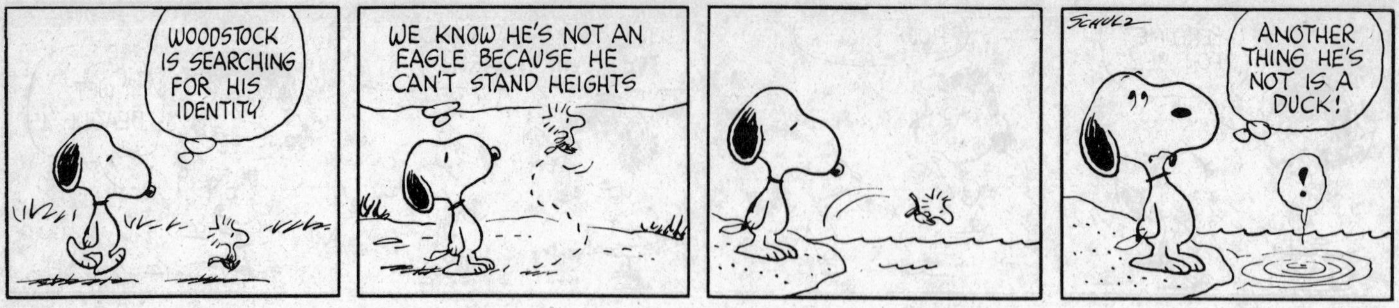
WOODSTOCK IS SEARCHING FOR HIS IDENTITY
WE KNOW HE'S NOT AN EAGLE BECAUSE HE CAN'T STAND HEIGHTS
SCHULZ
ANOTHER THING HE'S NOT IS A DUCK!
!

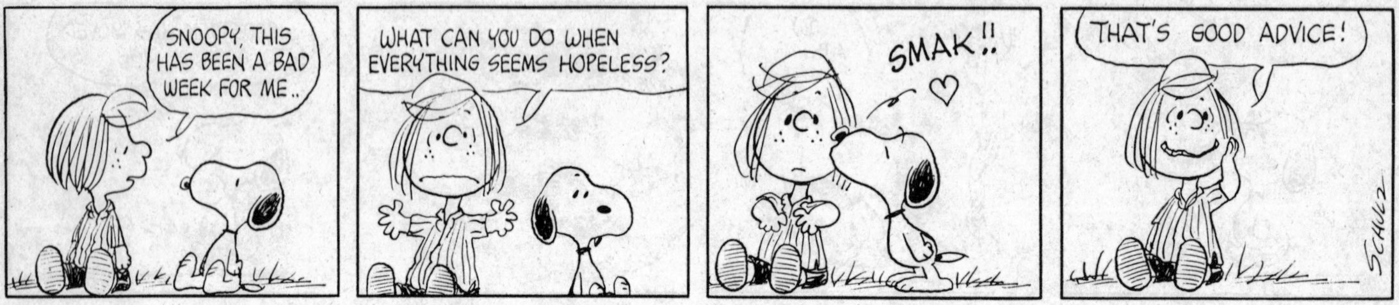
SNOOPY, THIS HAS BEEN A BAD WEEK FOR ME..
WHAT CAN YOU DO WHEN EVERYTHING SEEMS HOPELESS?
SMAK!!
THAT'S GOOD ADVICE!
SCHULZ

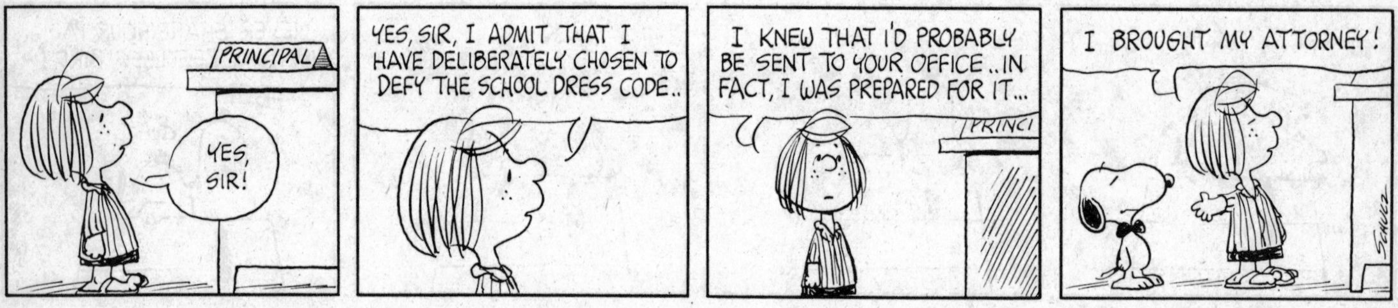
PRINCIPAL
YES, SIR!
YES, SIR, I ADMIT THAT I HAVE DELIBERATELY CHOSEN TO DEFY THE SCHOOL DRESS CODE..
I KNEW THAT I'D PROBABLY BE SENT TO YOUR OFFICE..IN FACT, I WAS PREPARED FOR IT...
PRINCI
I BROUGHT MY ATTORNEY!
SCHULZ

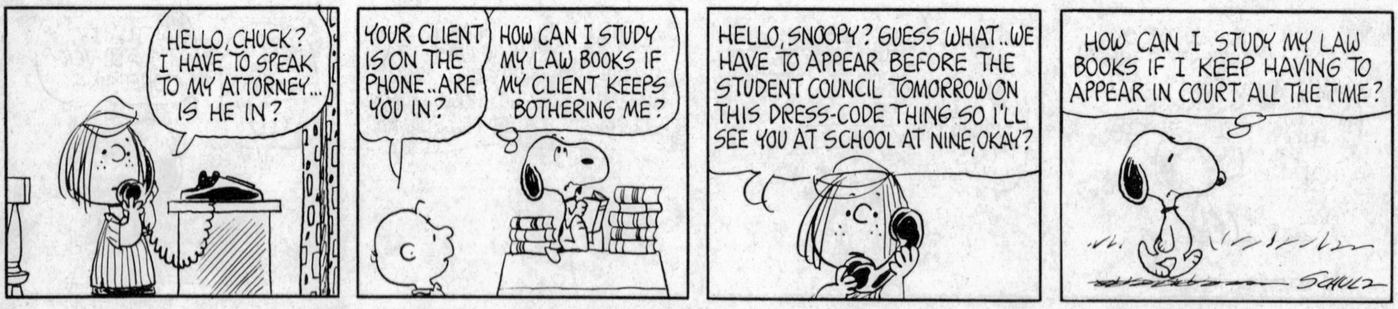
HELLO, CHUCK? I HAVE TO SPEAK TO MY ATTORNEY... IS HE IN?
YOUR CLIENT IS ON THE PHONE..ARE YOU IN?
HOW CAN I STUDY MY LAW BOOKS IF MY CLIENT KEEPS BOTHERING ME?
HELLO, SNOOPY? GUESS WHAT..WE HAVE TO APPEAR BEFORE THE STUDENT COUNCIL TOMORROW ON THIS DRESS-CODE THING SO I'LL SEE YOU AT SCHOOL AT NINE, OKAY?
HOW CAN I STUDY MY LAW BOOKS IF I KEEP HAVING TO APPEAR IN COURT ALL THE TIME?
SCHULZ

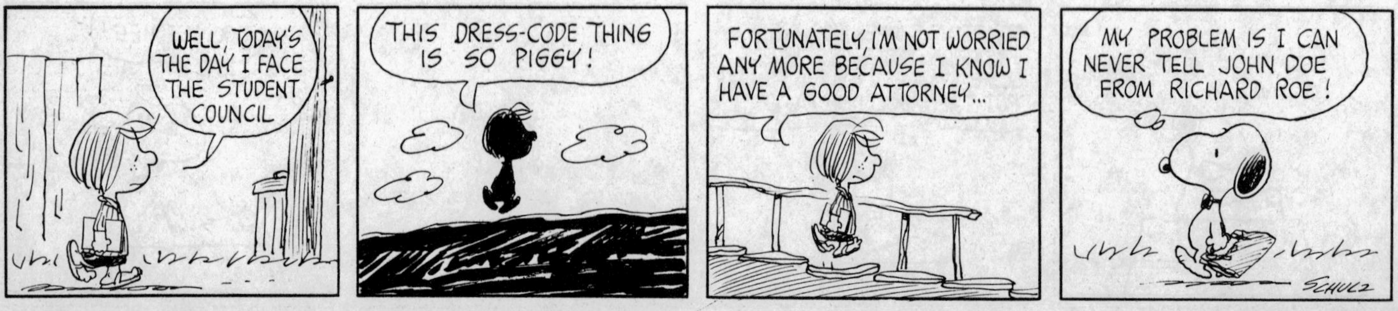
WELL, TODAY'S THE DAY I FACE THE STUDENT COUNCIL
THIS DRESS-CODE THING IS SO PIGGY!
FORTUNATELY, I'M NOT WORRIED ANY MORE BECAUSE I KNOW I HAVE A GOOD ATTORNEY...
MY PROBLEM IS I CAN NEVER TELL JOHN DOE FROM RICHARD ROE!
SCHULZ

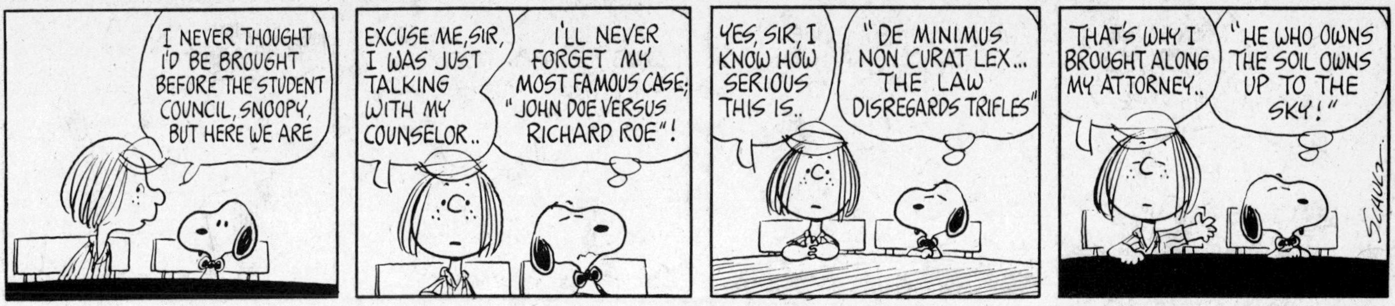
I NEVER THOUGHT I'D BE BROUGHT BEFORE THE STUDENT COUNCIL, SNOOPY, BUT HERE WE ARE
EXCUSE ME, SIR, I WAS JUST TALKING WITH MY COUNSELOR..
I'LL NEVER FORGET MY MOST FAMOUS CASE; "JOHN DOE VERSUS RICHARD ROE"!
YES, SIR, I KNOW HOW SERIOUS THIS IS..
"DE MINIMUS NON CURAT LEX... THE LAW DISREGARDS TRIFLES"
THAT'S WHY I BROUGHT ALONG MY ATTORNEY..
"HE WHO OWNS THE SOIL OWNS UP TO THE SKY!"
SCHULZ

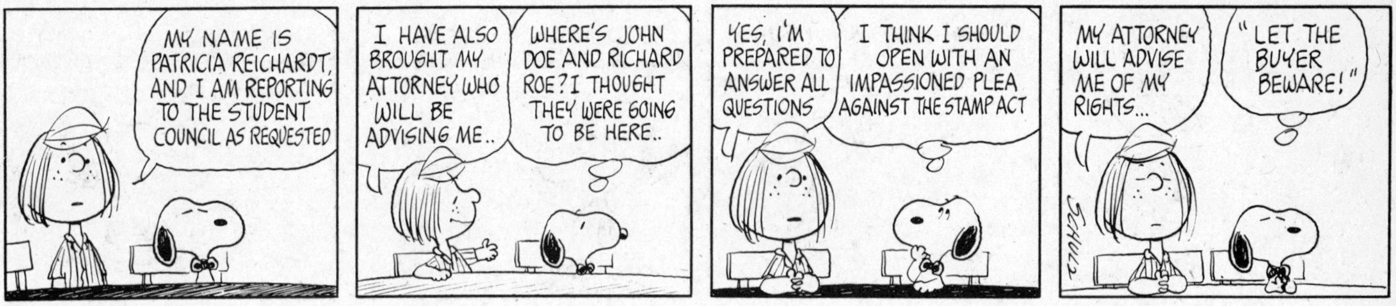
MY NAME IS PATRICIA REICHARDT, AND I AM REPORTING TO THE STUDENT COUNCIL AS REQUESTED
I HAVE ALSO BROUGHT MY ATTORNEY WHO WILL BE ADVISING ME..
WHERE'S JOHN DOE AND RICHARD ROE? I THOUGHT THEY WERE GOING TO BE HERE..
YES, I'M PREPARED TO ANSWER ALL QUESTIONS
I THINK I SHOULD OPEN WITH AN IMPASSIONED PLEA AGAINST THE STAMP ACT
MY ATTORNEY WILL ADVISE ME OF MY RIGHTS...
"LET THE BUYER BEWARE!"
SCHULZ

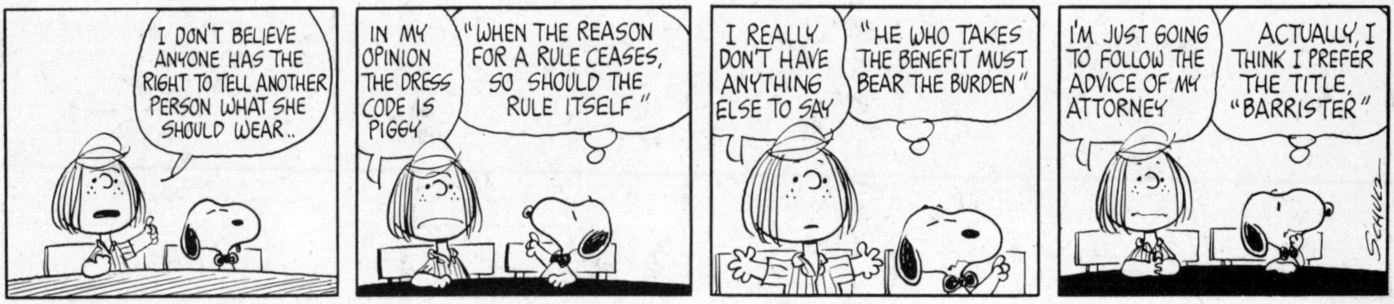
I DON'T BELIEVE ANYONE HAS THE RIGHT TO TELL ANOTHER PERSON WHAT SHE SHOULD WEAR..
IN MY OPINION THE DRESS CODE IS PIGGY
"WHEN THE REASON FOR A RULE CEASES, SO SHOULD THE RULE ITSELF"
I REALLY DON'T HAVE ANYTHING ELSE TO SAY
"HE WHO TAKES THE BENEFIT MUST BEAR THE BURDEN"
I'M JUST GOING TO FOLLOW THE ADVICE OF MY ATTORNEY
ACTUALLY, I THINK I PREFER THE TITLE, "BARRISTER"
SCHULZ

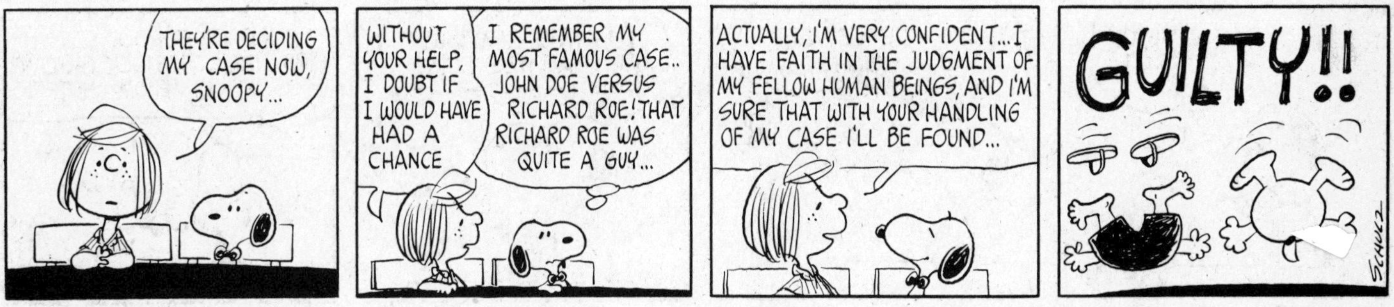
THEY'RE DECIDING MY CASE NOW, SNOOPY...
WITHOUT YOUR HELP, I DOUBT IF I WOULD HAVE HAD A CHANCE
I REMEMBER MY MOST FAMOUS CASE.. JOHN DOE VERSUS RICHARD ROE! THAT RICHARD ROE WAS QUITE A GUY...
ACTUALLY, I'M VERY CONFIDENT... I HAVE FAITH IN THE JUDGMENT OF MY FELLOW HUMAN BEINGS, AND I'M SURE THAT WITH YOUR HANDLING OF MY CASE I'LL BE FOUND...
GUILTY!!
SCHULZ

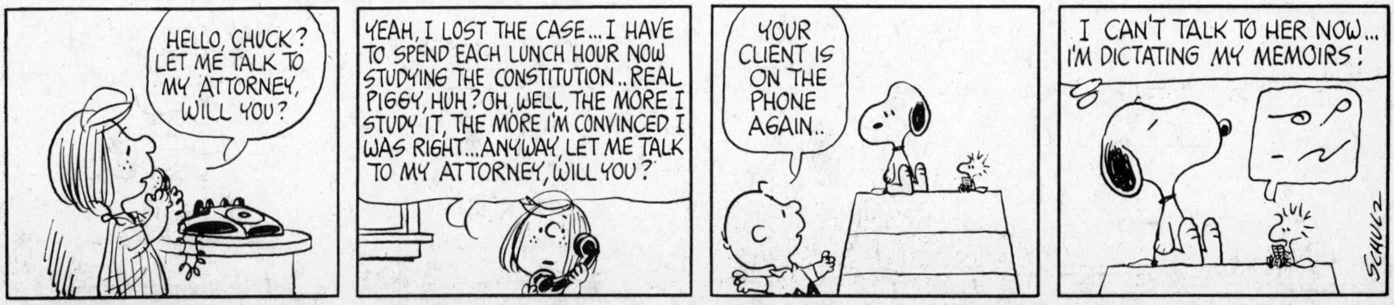
HELLO, CHUCK? LET ME TALK TO MY ATTORNEY, WILL YOU?
YEAH, I LOST THE CASE... I HAVE TO SPEND EACH LUNCH HOUR NOW STUDYING THE CONSTITUTION.. REAL PIGGY, HUH? OH, WELL, THE MORE I STUDY IT, THE MORE I'M CONVINCED I WAS RIGHT... ANYWAY, LET ME TALK TO MY ATTORNEY, WILL YOU?
YOUR CLIENT IS ON THE PHONE AGAIN..
I CAN'T TALK TO HER NOW... I'M DICTATING MY MEMOIRS!
SCHULZ

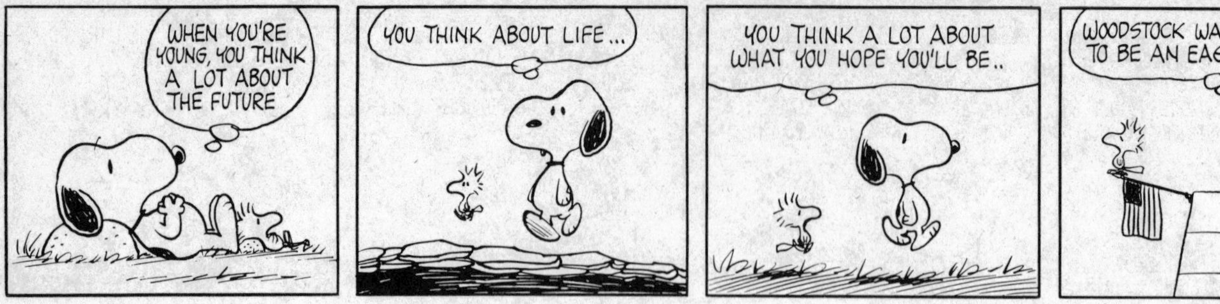
WHEN YOU'RE YOUNG, YOU THINK A LOT ABOUT THE FUTURE
YOU THINK ABOUT LIFE...
YOU THINK A LOT ABOUT WHAT YOU HOPE YOU'LL BE..
WOODSTOCK WANTS TO BE AN EAGLE
SCHULZ

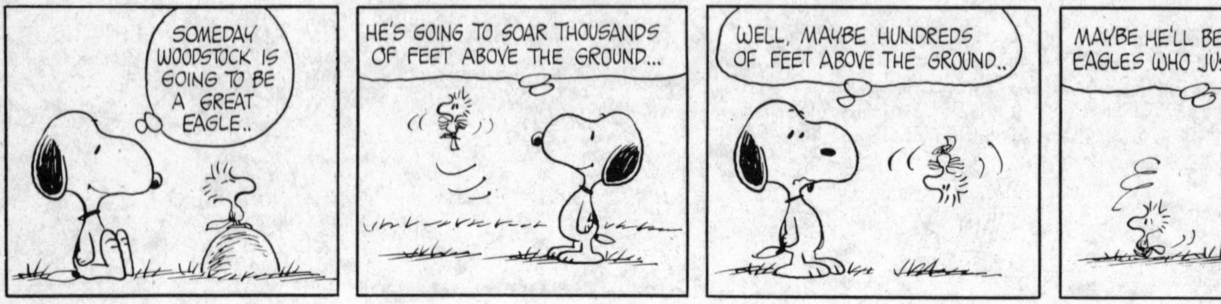
SOMEDAY WOODSTOCK IS GOING TO BE A GREAT EAGLE..
HE'S GOING TO SOAR THOUSANDS OF FEET ABOVE THE GROUND...
WELL, MAYBE HUNDREDS OF FEET ABOVE THE GROUND..
MAYBE HE'LL BE ONE OF THOSE EAGLES WHO JUST WALK AROUND
SCHULZ

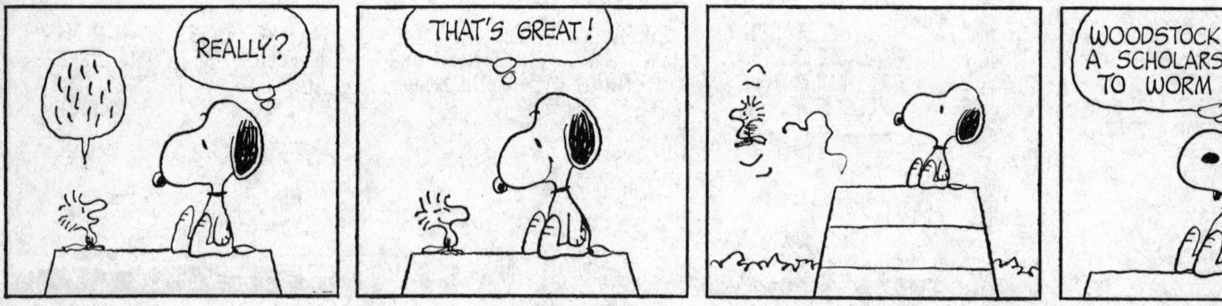
REALLY?
THAT'S GREAT!
WOODSTOCK JUST GOT A SCHOLARSHIP TO GO TO WORM SCHOOL!
SCHULZ

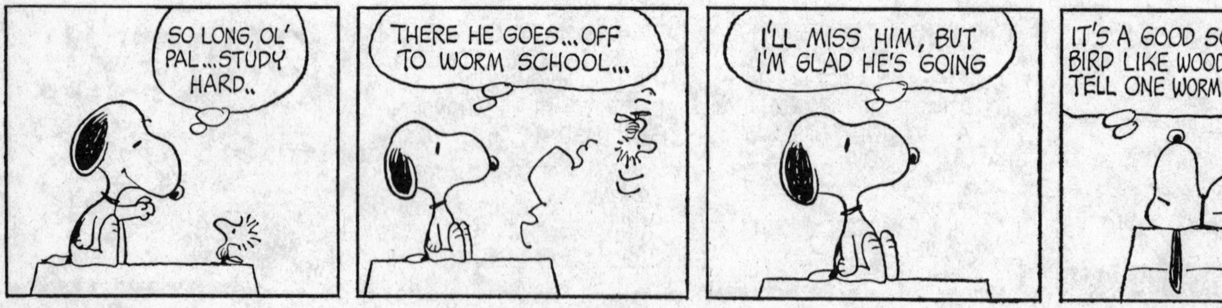
SO LONG, OL' PAL...STUDY HARD..
THERE HE GOES...OFF TO WORM SCHOOL...
I'LL MISS HIM, BUT I'M GLAD HE'S GOING
IT'S A GOOD SCHOOL FOR A BIRD LIKE WOODSTOCK WHO CAN'T TELL ONE WORM FROM ANOTHER
SCHULZ

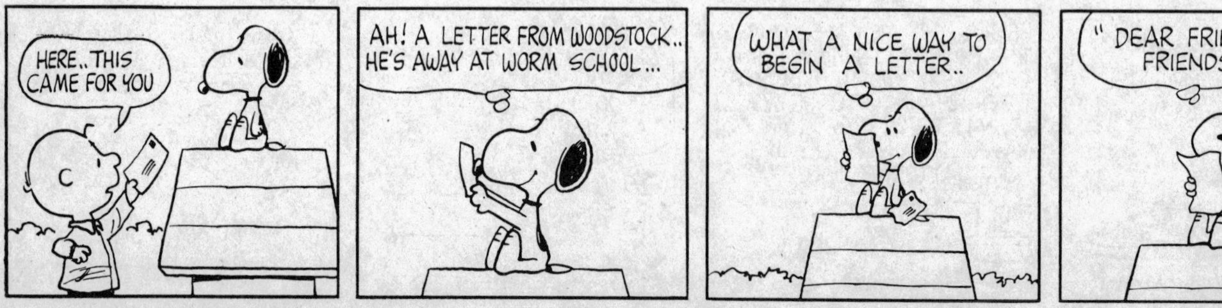
HERE..THIS CAME FOR YOU
AH! A LETTER FROM WOODSTOCK.. HE'S AWAY AT WORM SCHOOL...
WHAT A NICE WAY TO BEGIN A LETTER..
" DEAR FRIEND OF FRIENDS..."
SCHULZ

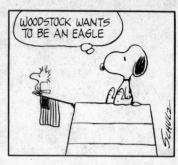

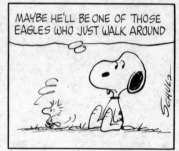

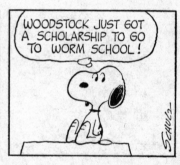

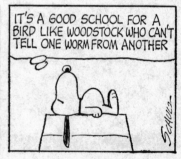

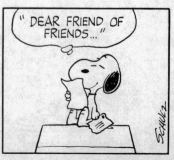

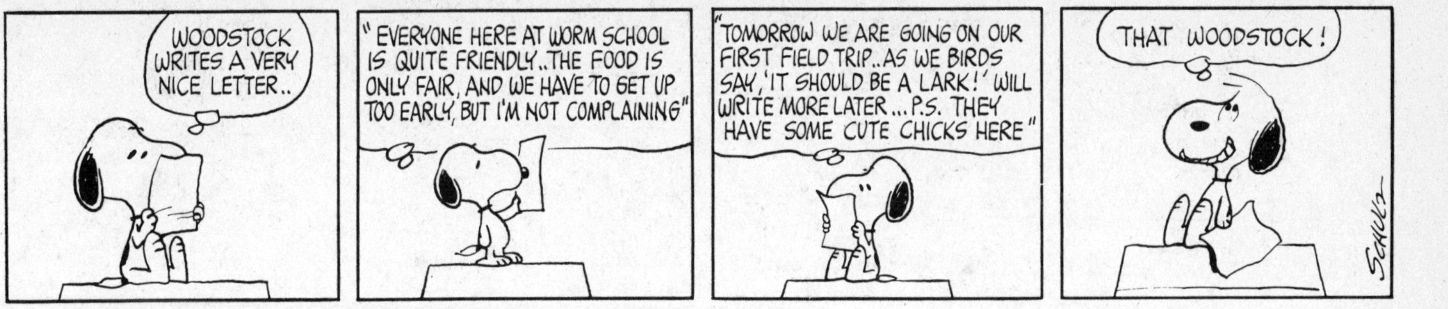
WOODSTOCK WRITES A VERY NICE LETTER..
"EVERYONE HERE AT WORM SCHOOL IS QUITE FRIENDLY..THE FOOD IS ONLY FAIR, AND WE HAVE TO GET UP TOO EARLY, BUT I'M NOT COMPLAINING"
"TOMORROW WE ARE GOING ON OUR FIRST FIELD TRIP..AS WE BIRDS SAY, 'IT SHOULD BE A LARK!' WILL WRITE MORE LATER ... P.S. THEY HAVE SOME CUTE CHICKS HERE"
THAT WOODSTOCK!
SCHULZ

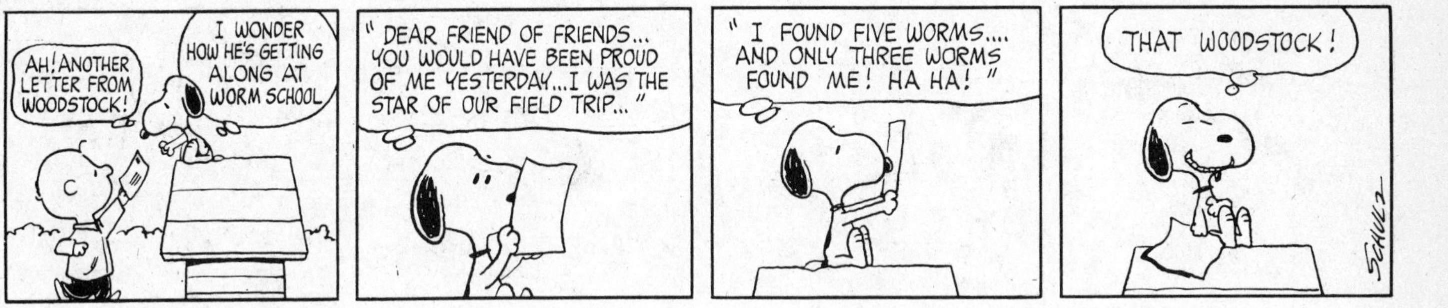
AH! ANOTHER LETTER FROM WOODSTOCK!
I WONDER HOW HE'S GETTING ALONG AT WORM SCHOOL
" DEAR FRIEND OF FRIENDS... YOU WOULD HAVE BEEN PROUD OF ME YESTERDAY...I WAS THE STAR OF OUR FIELD TRIP... "
" I FOUND FIVE WORMS.... AND ONLY THREE WORMS FOUND ME! HA HA! "
THAT WOODSTOCK!
SCHULZ

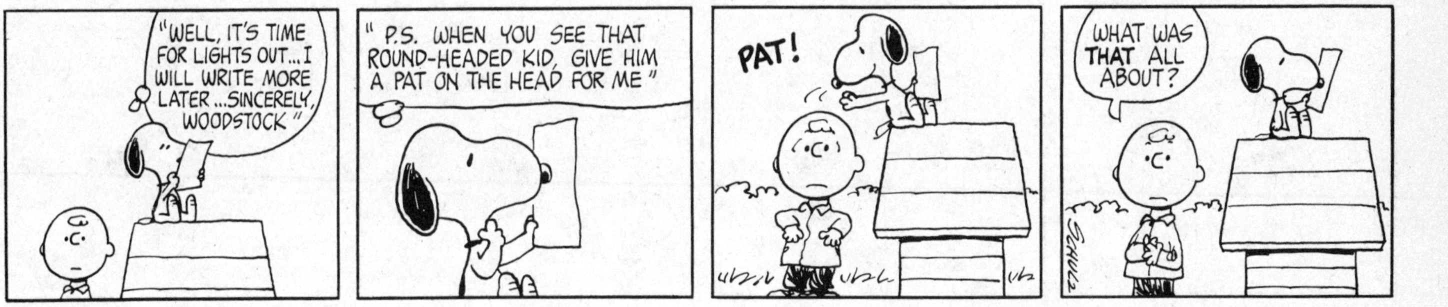
"WELL, IT'S TIME FOR LIGHTS OUT...I WILL WRITE MORE LATER ...SINCERELY, WOODSTOCK"
" P.S. WHEN YOU SEE THAT ROUND-HEADED KID, GIVE HIM A PAT ON THE HEAD FOR ME "
PAT!
WHAT WAS THAT ALL ABOUT?
SCHULZ

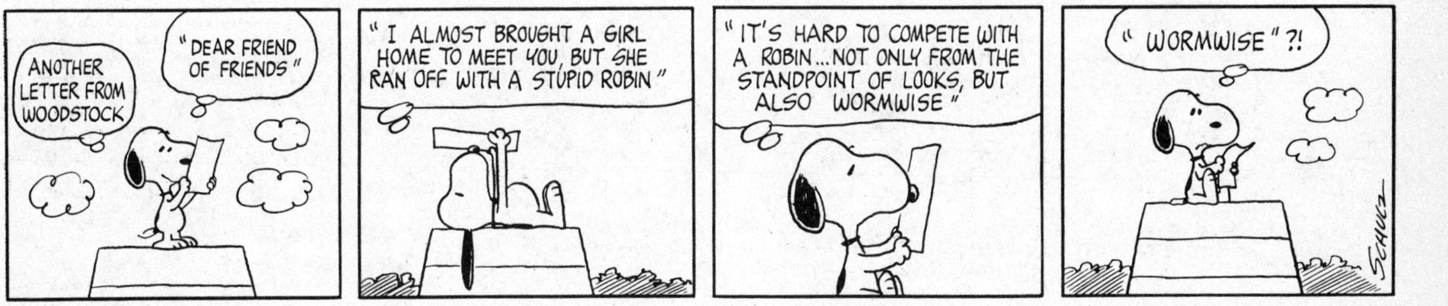
ANOTHER LETTER FROM WOODSTOCK
"DEAR FRIEND OF FRIENDS"
" I ALMOST BROUGHT A GIRL HOME TO MEET YOU, BUT SHE RAN OFF WITH A STUPID ROBIN "
" IT'S HARD TO COMPETE WITH A ROBIN...NOT ONLY FROM THE STANDPOINT OF LOOKS, BUT ALSO WORMWISE "
" WORMWISE " ?!
SCHULZ

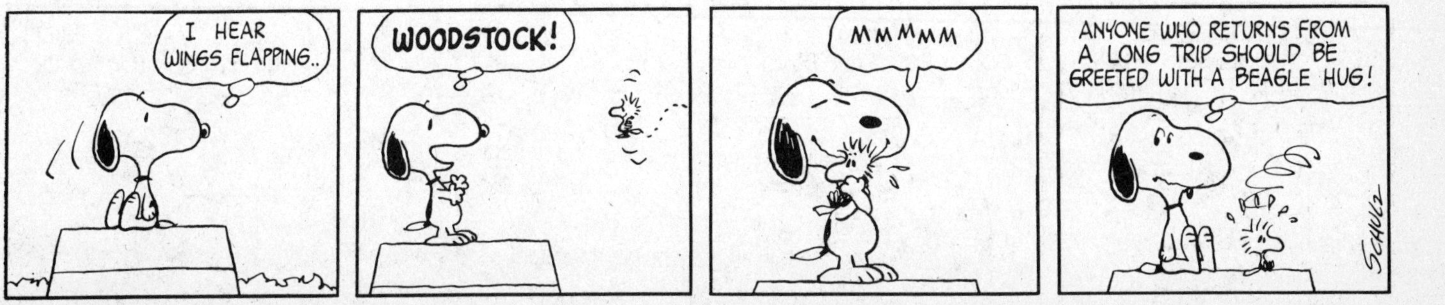
I HEAR WINGS FLAPPING..
WOODSTOCK!
MMMMM
ANYONE WHO RETURNS FROM A LONG TRIP SHOULD BE GREETED WITH A BEAGLE HUG!
SCHULZ

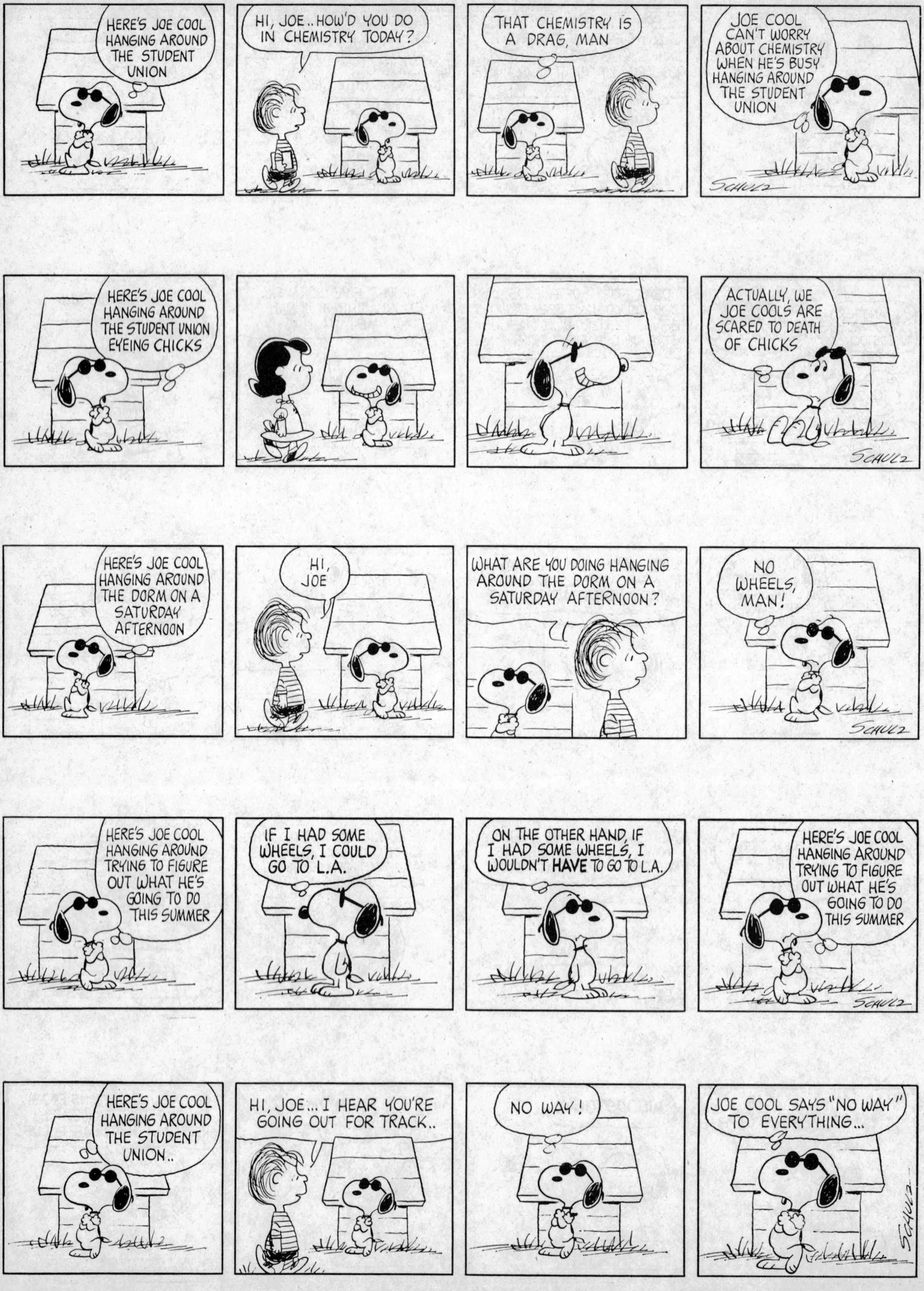
HERE'S JOE COOL HANGING AROUND THE STUDENT UNION
HI, JOE.. HOW'D YOU DO IN CHEMISTRY TODAY?
THAT CHEMISTRY IS A DRAG, MAN
JOE COOL CAN'T WORRY ABOUT CHEMISTRY WHEN HE'S BUSY HANGING AROUND THE STUDENT UNION
SCHULZ
HERE'S JOE COOL HANGING AROUND THE STUDENT UNION EYEING CHICKS
ACTUALLY, WE JOE COOLS ARE SCARED TO DEATH OF CHICKS
SCHULZ
HERE'S JOE COOL HANGING AROUND THE DORM ON A SATURDAY AFTERNOON
HI, JOE
WHAT ARE YOU DOING HANGING AROUND THE DORM ON A SATURDAY AFTERNOON?
NO WHEELS, MAN!
SCHULZ
HERE'S JOE COOL HANGING AROUND TRYING TO FIGURE OUT WHAT HE'S GOING TO DO THIS SUMMER
IF I HAD SOME WHEELS, I COULD GO TO L.A.
ON THE OTHER HAND, IF I HAD SOME WHEELS, I WOULDN'T HAVE TO GO TO L.A.
HERE'S JOE COOL HANGING AROUND TRYING TO FIGURE OUT WHAT HE'S GOING TO DO THIS SUMMER
SCHULZ
HERE'S JOE COOL HANGING AROUND THE STUDENT UNION..
HI, JOE... I HEAR YOU'RE GOING OUT FOR TRACK..
NO WAY!
JOE COOL SAYS "NO WAY" TO EVERYTHING...
SCHULZ

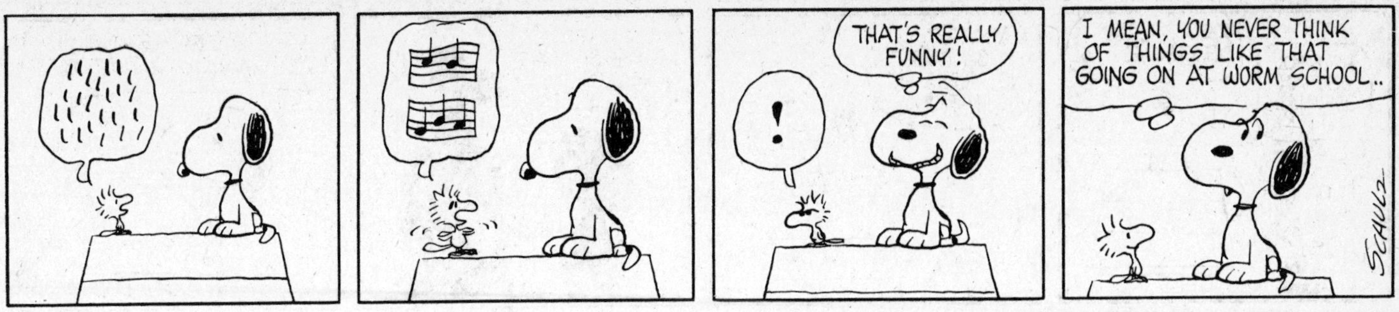
THAT'S REALLY FUNNY!
I MEAN, YOU NEVER THINK OF THINGS LIKE THAT GOING ON AT WORM SCHOOL..
SCHULZ

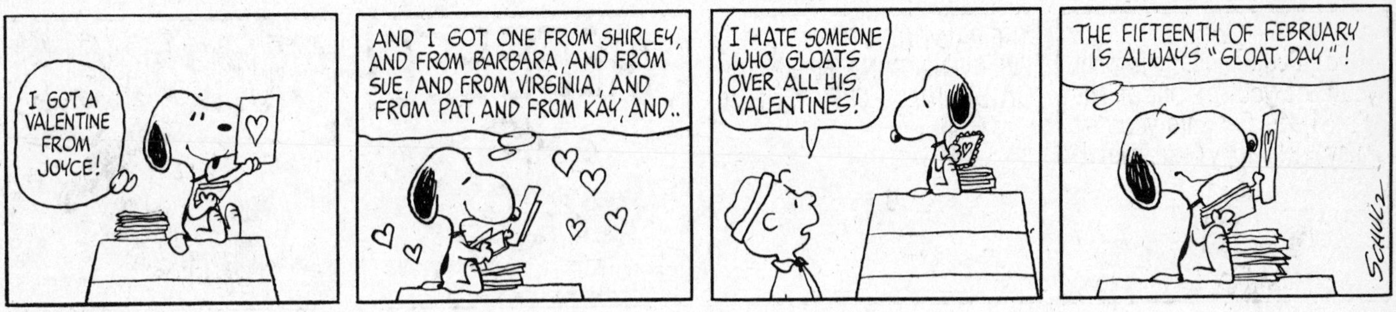
I GOT A VALENTINE FROM JOYCE!
AND I GOT ONE FROM SHIRLEY, AND FROM BARBARA, AND FROM SUE, AND FROM VIRGINIA, AND FROM PAT, AND FROM KAY, AND..
I HATE SOMEONE WHO GLOATS OVER ALL HIS VALENTINES!
THE FIFTEENTH OF FEBRUARY IS ALWAYS "GLOAT DAY"!
SCHULZ

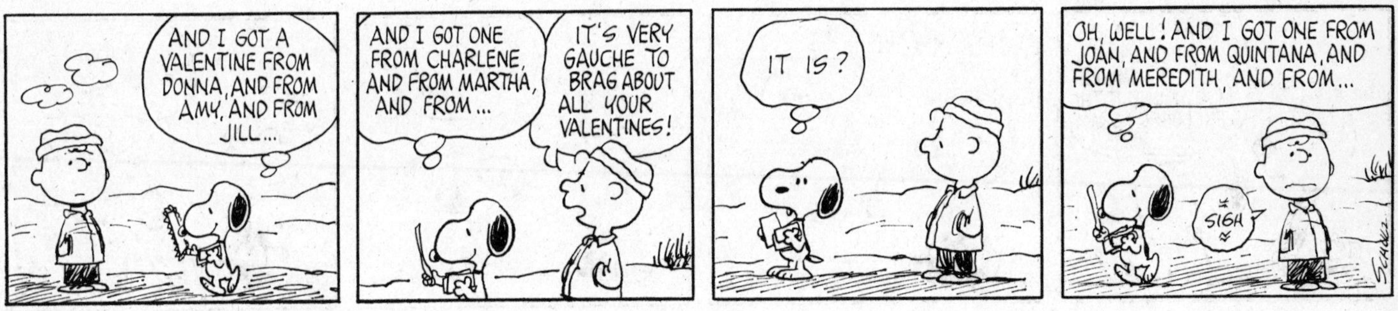
AND I GOT A VALENTINE FROM DONNA, AND FROM AMY, AND FROM JILL...
AND I GOT ONE FROM CHARLENE, AND FROM MARTHA, AND FROM...
IT'S VERY GAUCHE TO BRAG ABOUT ALL YOUR VALENTINES!
IT IS?
OH, WELL! AND I GOT ONE FROM JOAN, AND FROM QUINTANA, AND FROM MEREDITH, AND FROM...
SIGH
SCHULZ

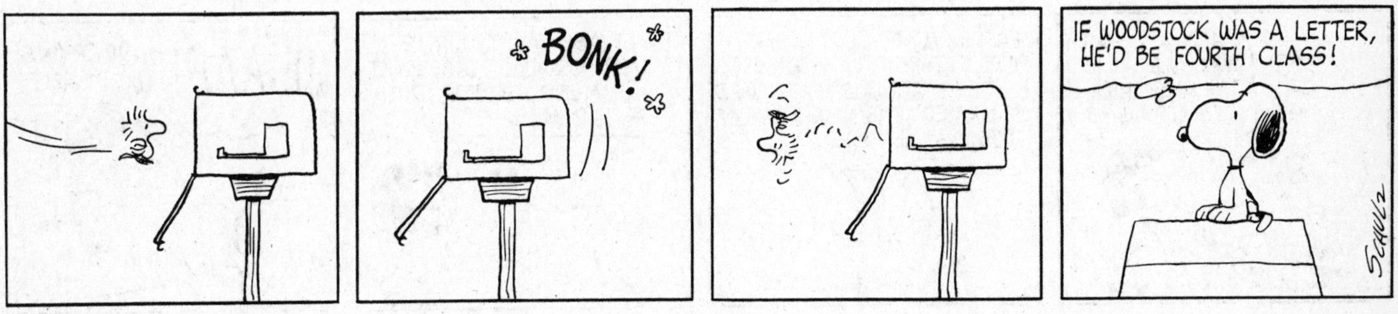
BONK!
IF WOODSTOCK WAS A LETTER, HE'D BE FOURTH CLASS!
SCHULZ

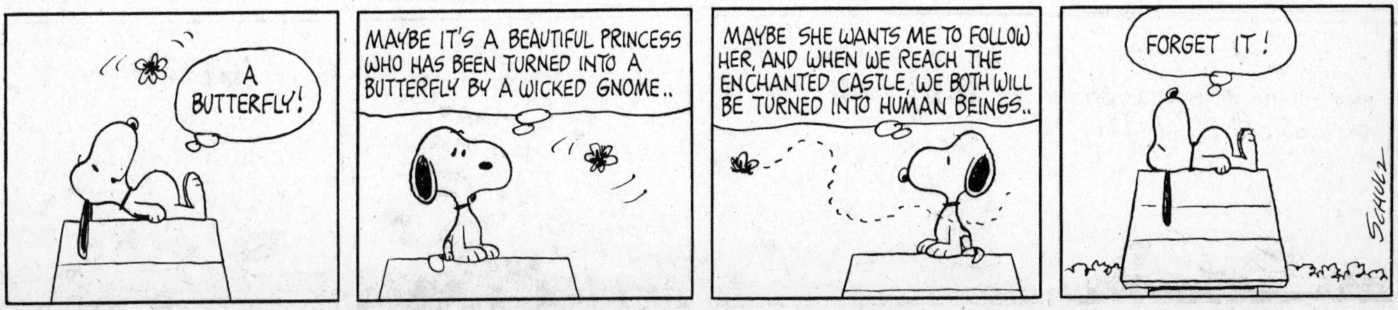
A BUTTERFLY!
MAYBE IT'S A BEAUTIFUL PRINCESS WHO HAS BEEN TURNED INTO A BUTTERFLY BY A WICKED GNOME..
MAYBE SHE WANTS ME TO FOLLOW HER, AND WHEN WE REACH THE ENCHANTED CASTLE, WE BOTH WILL BE TURNED INTO HUMAN BEINGS..
FORGET IT!
SCHULZ

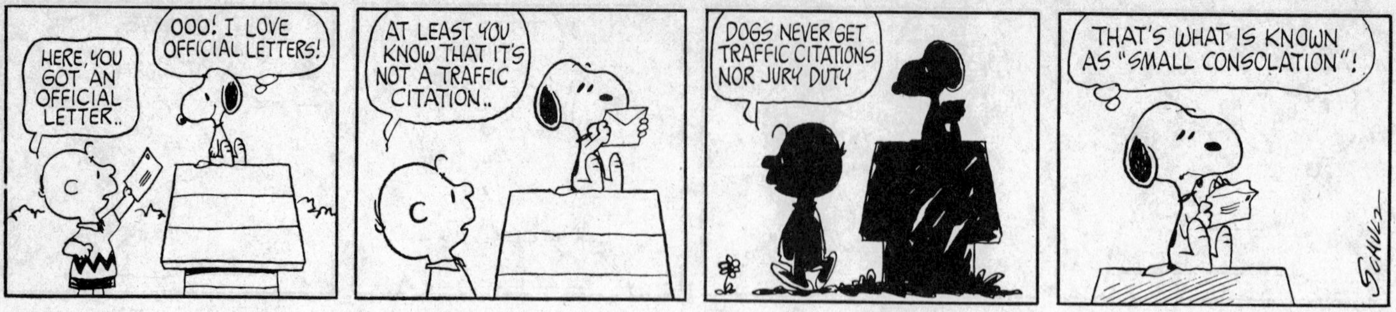
HERE, YOU GOT AN OFFICIAL LETTER..
OOO! I LOVE OFFICIAL LETTERS!
AT LEAST YOU KNOW THAT IT'S NOT A TRAFFIC CITATION..
DOGS NEVER GET TRAFFIC CITATIONS NOR JURY DUTY
THAT'S WHAT IS KNOWN AS "SMALL CONSOLATION"!
SCHULZ

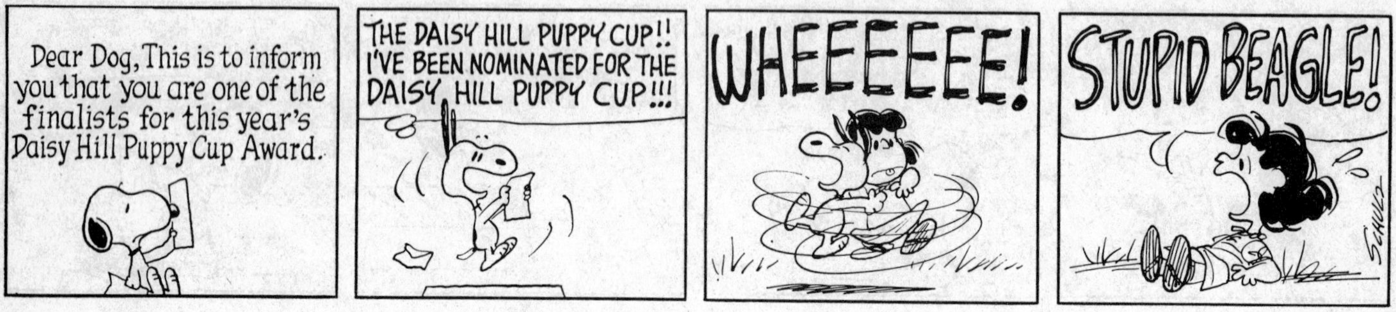
Dear Dog, This is to inform you that you are one of the finalists for this year's Daisy Hill Puppy Cup Award.
THE DAISY HILL PUPPY CUP!! I'VE BEEN NOMINATED FOR THE DAISY HILL PUPPY CUP!!!
WHEEEEEEE!
STUPID BEAGLE!
SCHULZ

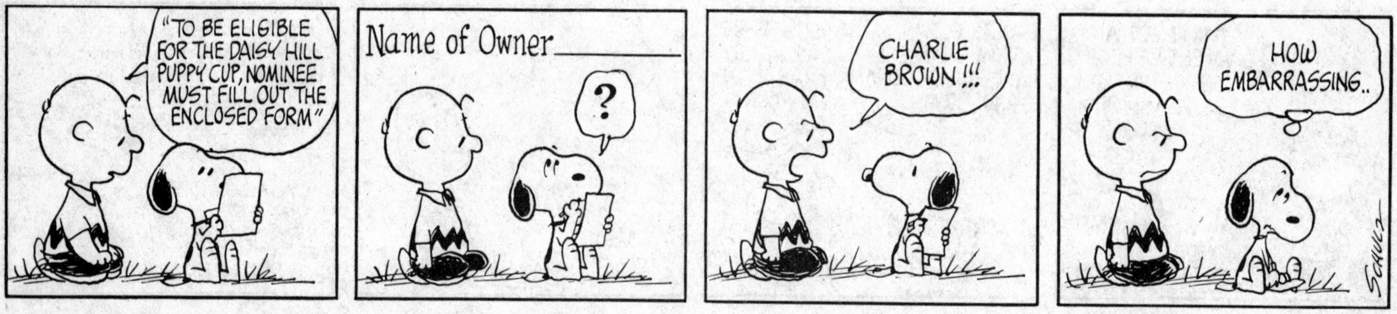
"TO BE ELIGIBLE FOR THE DAISY HILL PUPPY CUP, NOMINEE MUST FILL OUT THE ENCLOSED FORM"
Name of Owner
?
CHARLIE BROWN!!!
HOW EMBARRASSING..
SCHULZ

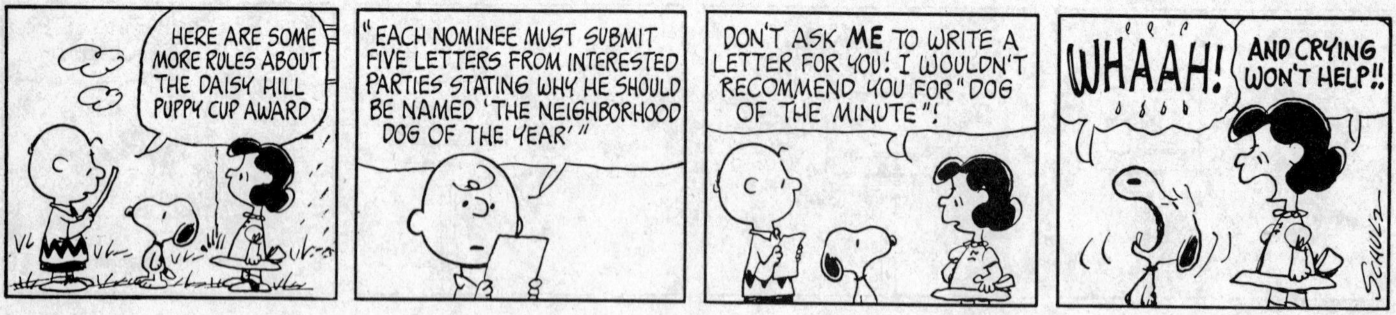
HERE ARE SOME MORE RULES ABOUT THE DAISY HILL PUPPY CUP AWARD
"EACH NOMINEE MUST SUBMIT FIVE LETTERS FROM INTERESTED PARTIES STATING WHY HE SHOULD BE NAMED 'THE NEIGHBORHOOD DOG OF THE YEAR'"
DON'T ASK ME TO WRITE A LETTER FOR YOU! I WOULDN'T RECOMMEND YOU FOR "DOG OF THE MINUTE"!
WHAAH!
AND CRYING WON'T HELP!!
SCHULZ

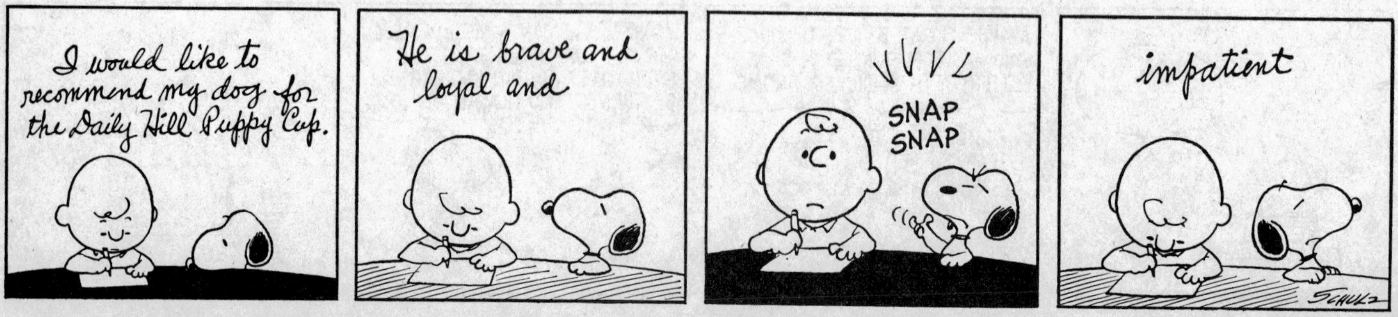
I would like to recommend my dog for the Daily Hill Puppy Cup.
He is brave and loyal and
SNAP SNAP
impatient
SCHULZ

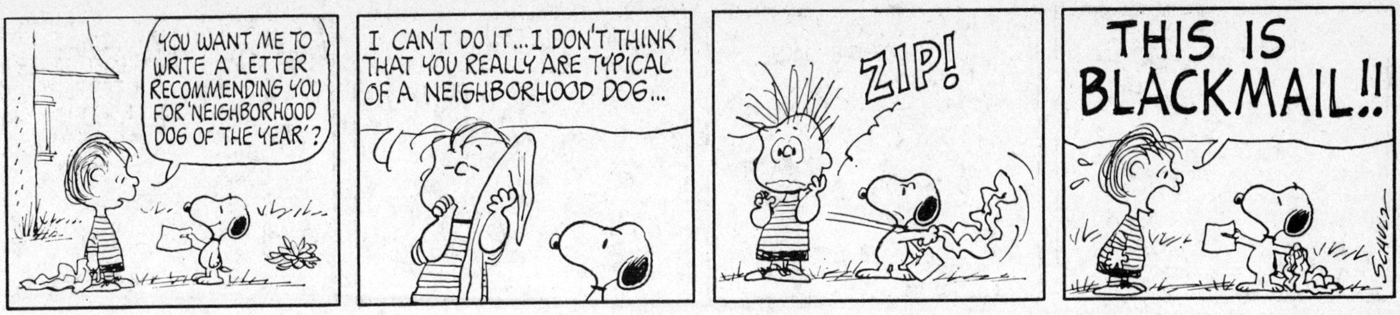
YOU WANT ME TO WRITE A LETTER RECOMMENDING YOU FOR 'NEIGHBORHOOD DOG OF THE YEAR'?
I CAN'T DO IT...I DON'T THINK THAT YOU REALLY ARE TYPICAL OF A NEIGHBORHOOD DOG...
ZIP!
THIS IS BLACKMAIL!!
SCHULZ

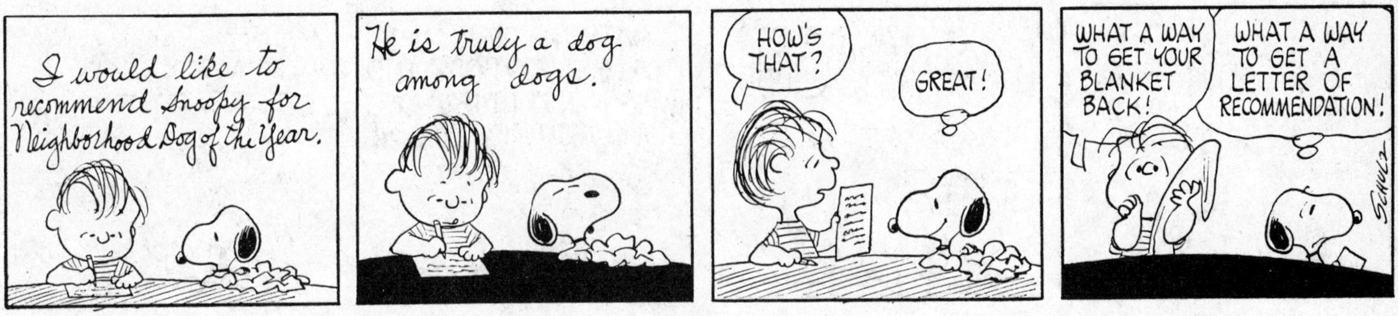
I would like to recommend Snoopy for Neighborhood Dog of the Year.
He is truly a dog among dogs.
HOW'S THAT?
GREAT!
WHAT A WAY TO GET YOUR BLANKET BACK!
WHAT A WAY TO GET A LETTER OF RECOMMENDATION!
SCHULZ

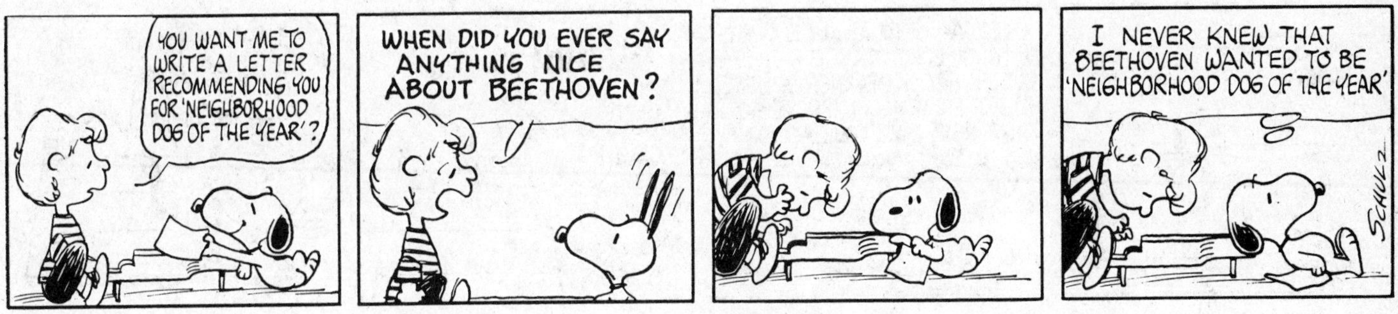
YOU WANT ME TO WRITE A LETTER RECOMMENDING YOU FOR 'NEIGHBORHOOD DOG OF THE YEAR'?
WHEN DID YOU EVER SAY ANYTHING NICE ABOUT BEETHOVEN?
I NEVER KNEW THAT BEETHOVEN WANTED TO BE 'NEIGHBORHOOD DOG OF THE YEAR'
SCHULZ

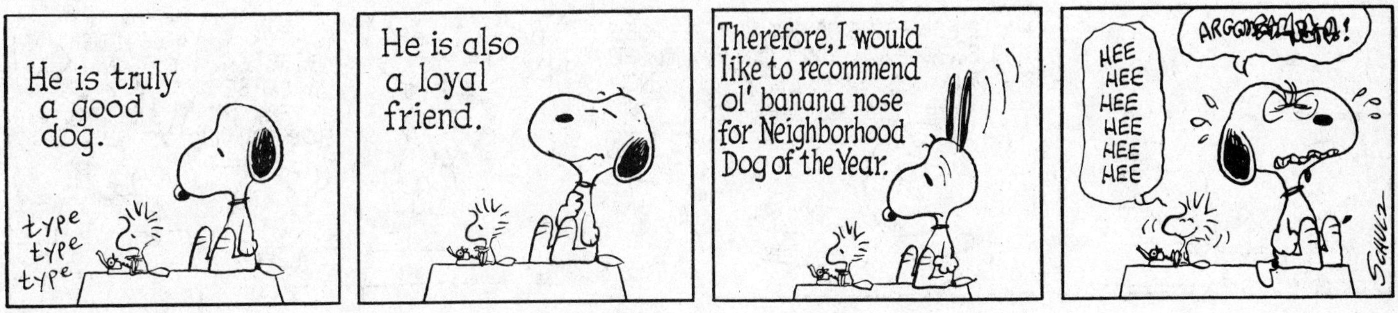
He is truly a good dog.
type type type
He is also a loyal friend.
Therefore, I would like to recommend ol' banana nose for Neighborhood Dog of the Year.
HEE HEE HEE HEE HEE HEE
SCHULZ

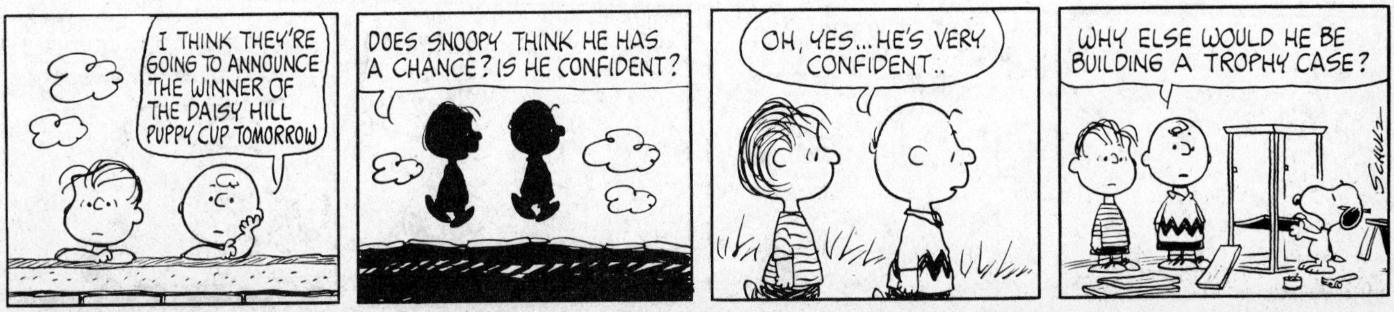
I THINK THEY'RE GOING TO ANNOUNCE THE WINNER OF THE DAISY HILL PUPPY CUP TOMORROW
DOES SNOOPY THINK HE HAS A CHANCE? IS HE CONFIDENT?
OH, YES...HE'S VERY CONFIDENT..
WHY ELSE WOULD HE BE BUILDING A TROPHY CASE?
SCHULZ

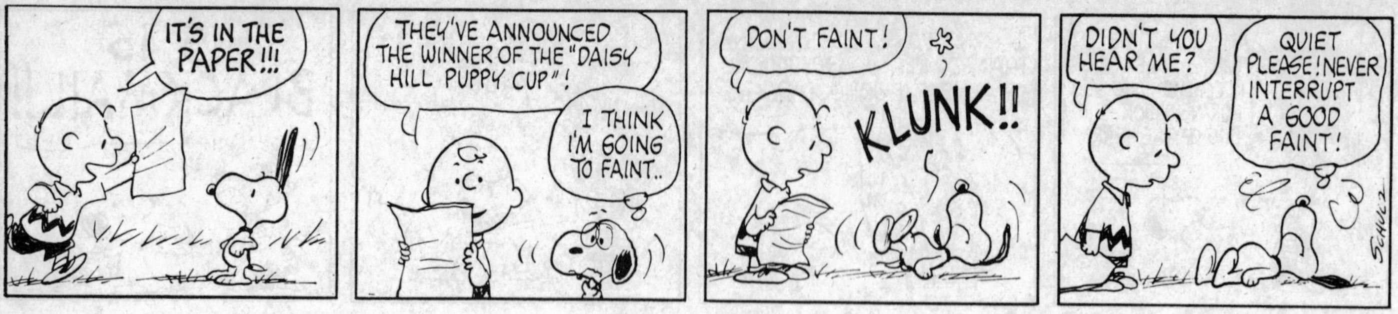
IT'S IN THE PAPER!!!
THEY'VE ANNOUNCED THE WINNER OF THE "DAISY HILL PUPPY CUP"!
I THINK I'M GOING TO FAINT..
DON'T FAINT!
KLUNK!!
DIDN'T YOU HEAR ME?
QUIET PLEASE! NEVER INTERRUPT A GOOD FAINT!
SCHULZ

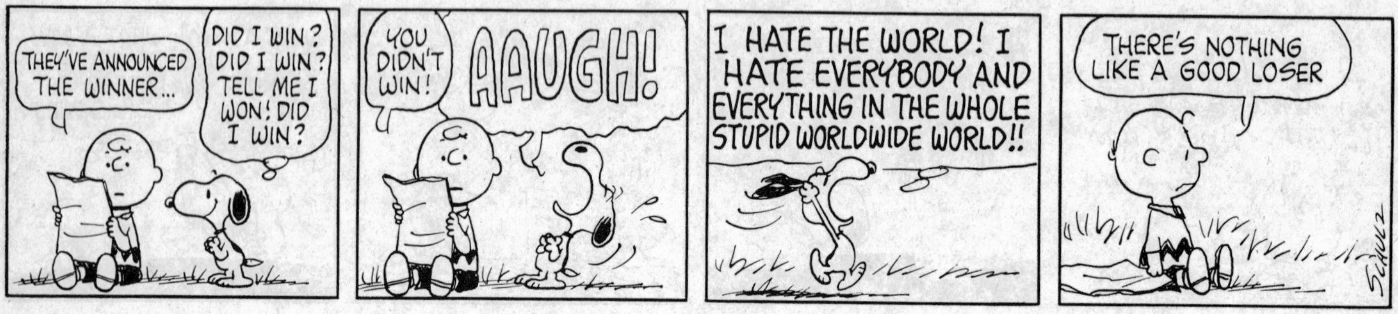
THEY'VE ANNOUNCED THE WINNER...
DID I WIN? DID I WIN? TELL ME I WON! DID I WIN?
YOU DIDN'T WIN!
AAUGH!
I HATE THE WORLD! I HATE EVERYBODY AND EVERYTHING IN THE WHOLE STUPID WORLDWIDE WORLD!!
THERE'S NOTHING LIKE A GOOD LOSER
SCHULZ

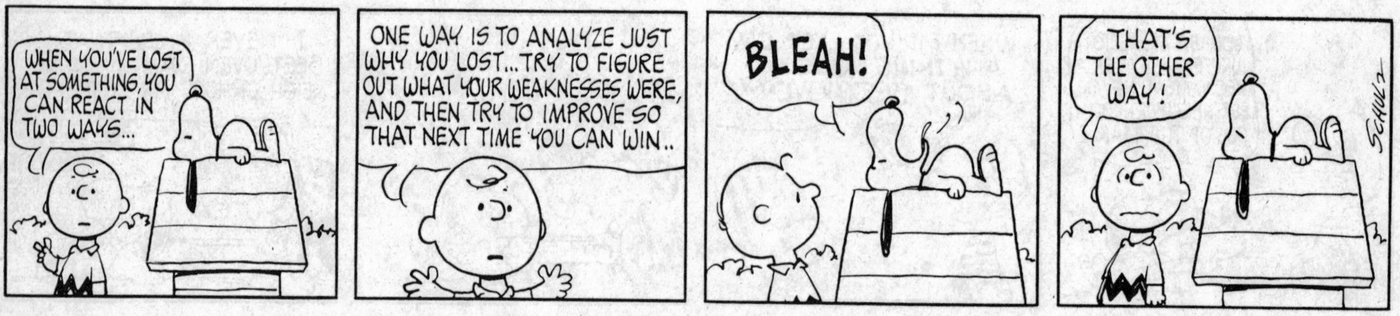
WHEN YOU'VE LOST AT SOMETHING, YOU CAN REACT IN TWO WAYS...
ONE WAY IS TO ANALYZE JUST WHY YOU LOST...TRY TO FIGURE OUT WHAT YOUR WEAKNESSES WERE, AND THEN TRY TO IMPROVE SO THAT NEXT TIME YOU CAN WIN..
BLEAH!
THAT'S THE OTHER WAY!
SCHULZ

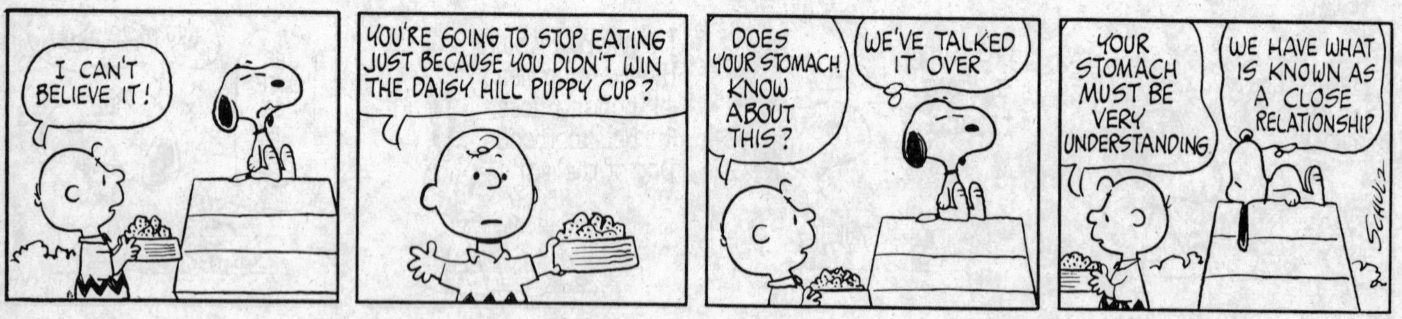
I CAN'T BELIEVE IT!
YOU'RE GOING TO STOP EATING JUST BECAUSE YOU DIDN'T WIN THE DAISY HILL PUPPY CUP?
DOES YOUR STOMACH KNOW ABOUT THIS?
WE'VE TALKED IT OVER
YOUR STOMACH MUST BE VERY UNDERSTANDING
WE HAVE WHAT IS KNOWN AS A CLOSE RELATIONSHIP
SCHULZ

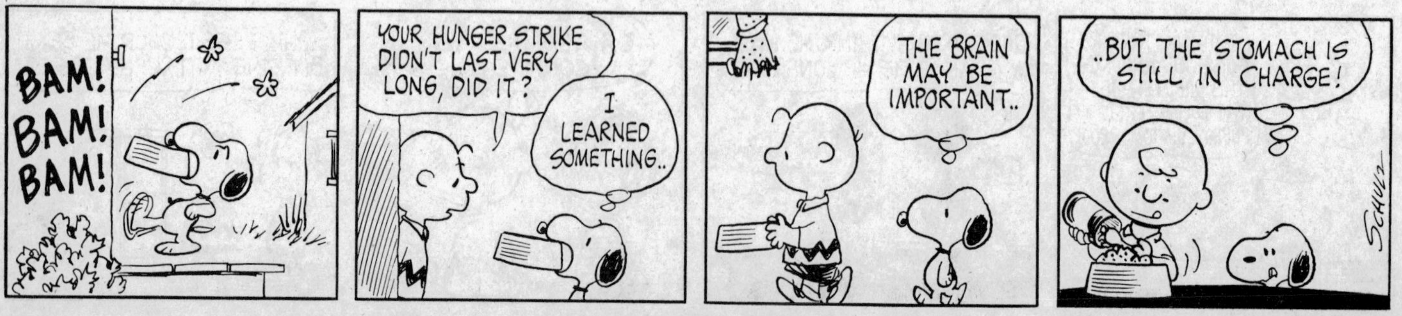
BAM! BAM! BAM!
YOUR HUNGER STRIKE DIDN'T LAST VERY LONG, DID IT?
I LEARNED SOMETHING..
THE BRAIN MAY BE IMPORTANT..
..BUT THE STOMACH IS STILL IN CHARGE!
SCHULZ

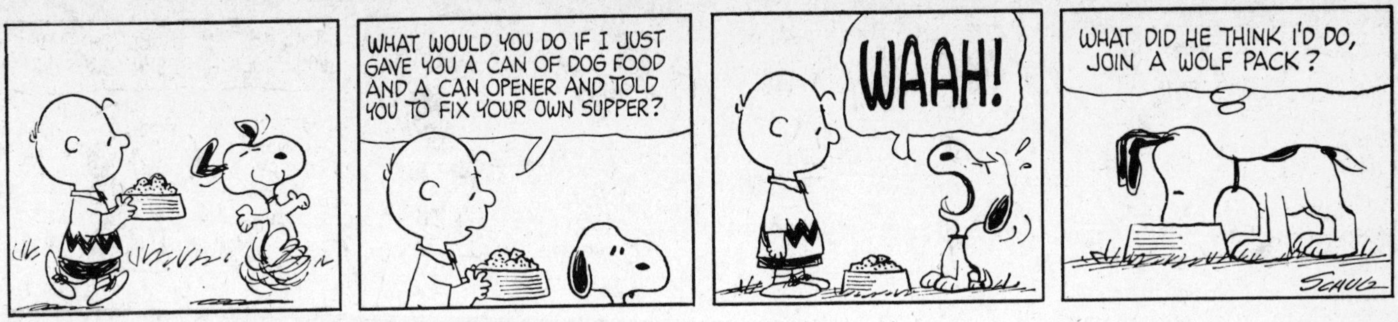
WHAT WOULD YOU DO IF I JUST GAVE YOU A CAN OF DOG FOOD AND A CAN OPENER AND TOLD YOU TO FIX YOUR OWN SUPPER?
WAAH!
WHAT DID HE THINK I'D DO, JOIN A WOLF PACK?
SCHULZ

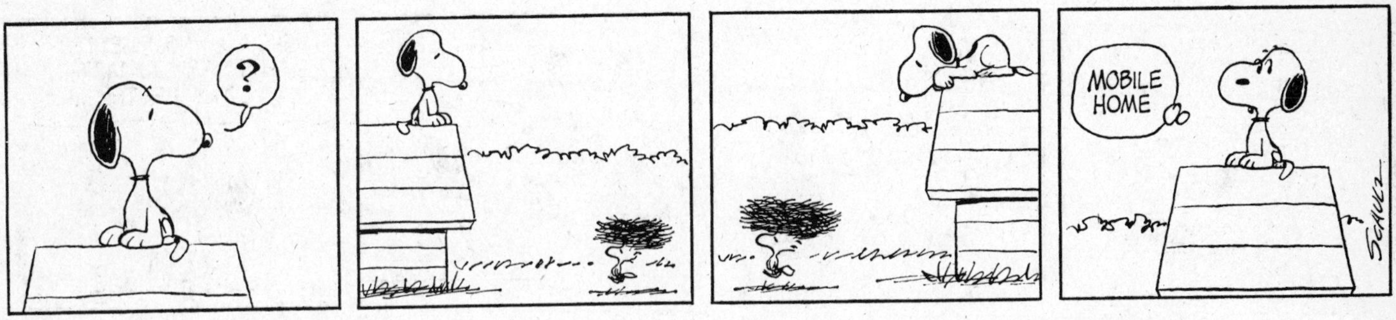
?
MOBILE HOME
SCHULZ

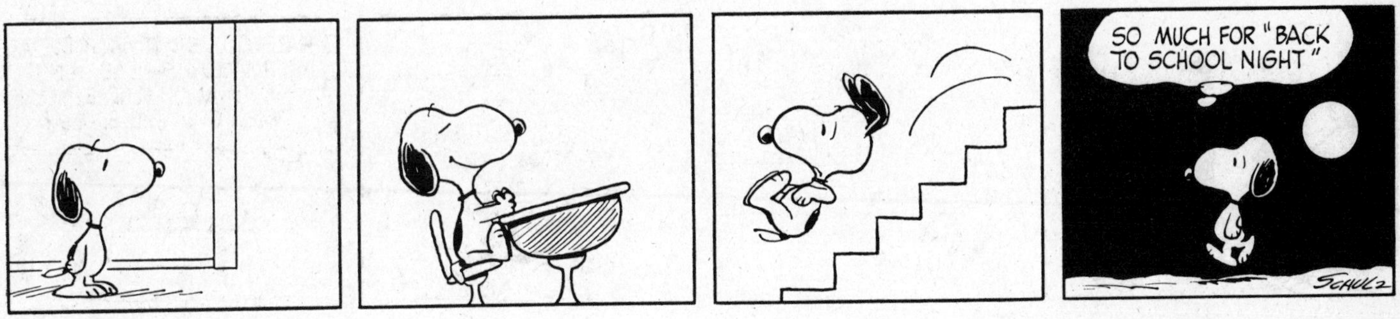
SO MUCH FOR "BACK TO SCHOOL NIGHT"
SCHULZ

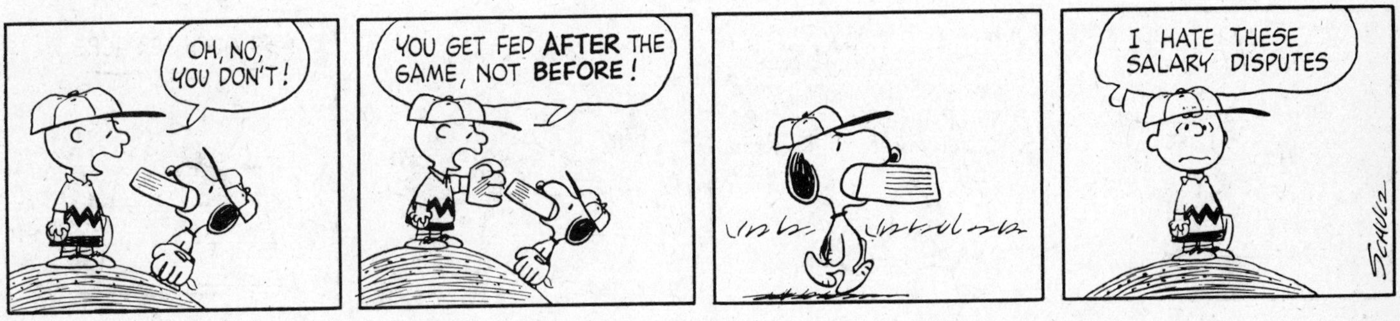
OH, NO, YOU DON'T!
YOU GET FED AFTER THE GAME, NOT BEFORE!
I HATE THESE SALARY DISPUTES
SCHULZ

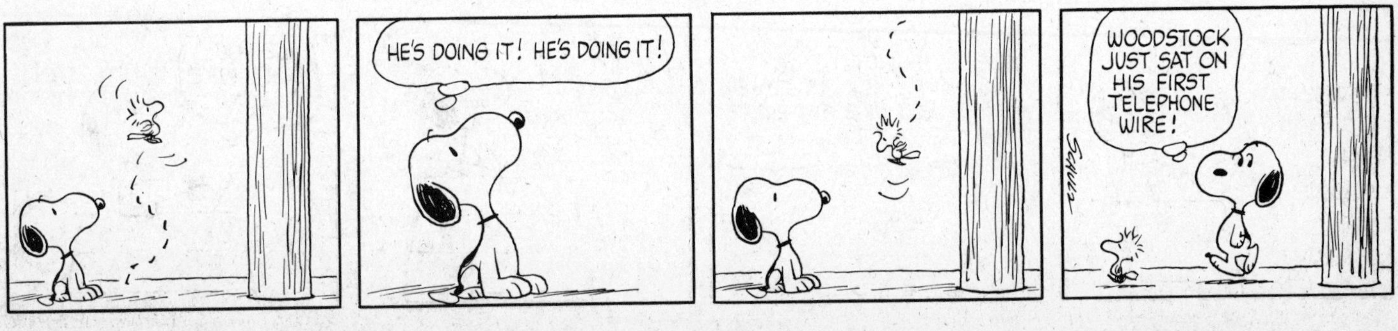
HE'S DOING IT! HE'S DOING IT!
WOODSTOCK JUST SAT ON HIS FIRST TELEPHONE WIRE!
SCHULZ

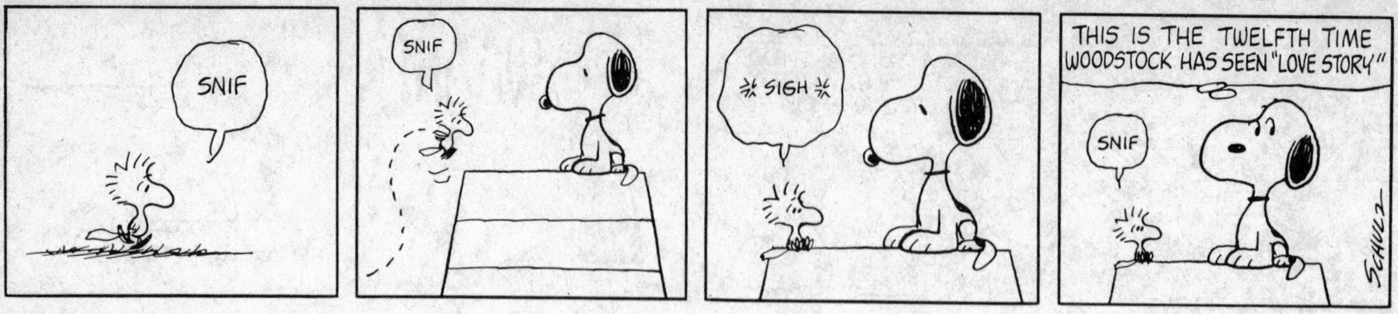
SNIF
SNIF
✳ SIGH ✳
THIS IS THE TWELFTH TIME WOODSTOCK HAS SEEN "LOVE STORY"
SNIF
SCHULZ

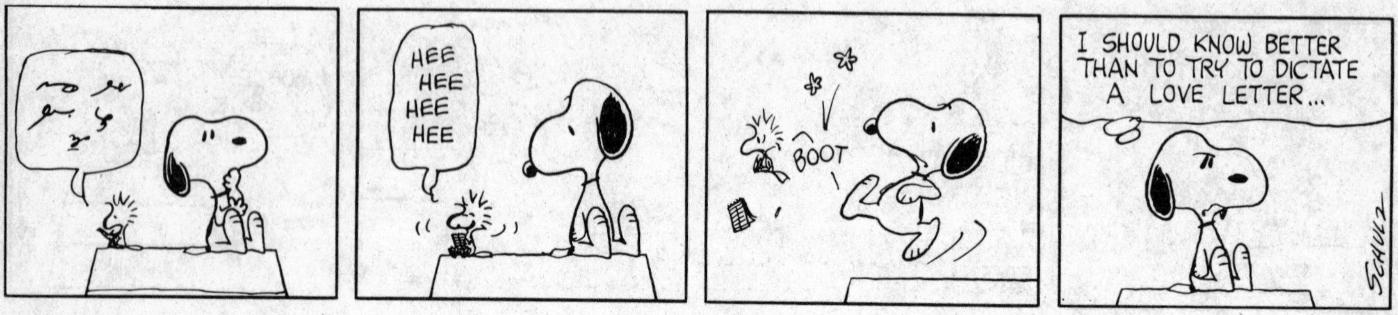
HEE HEE HEE HEE
BOOT
I SHOULD KNOW BETTER THAN TO TRY TO DICTATE A LOVE LETTER...
SCHULZ

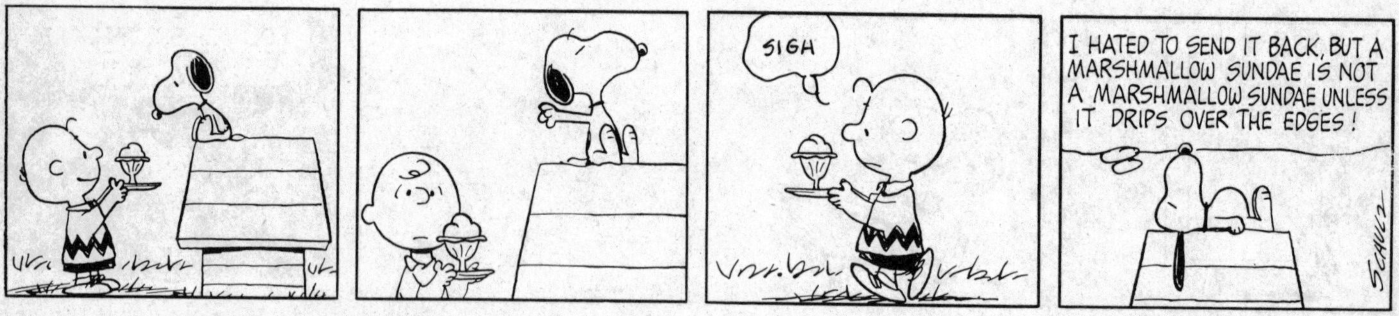
SIGH
I HATED TO SEND IT BACK, BUT A MARSHMALLOW SUNDAE IS NOT A MARSHMALLOW SUNDAE UNLESS IT DRIPS OVER THE EDGES!
SCHULZ

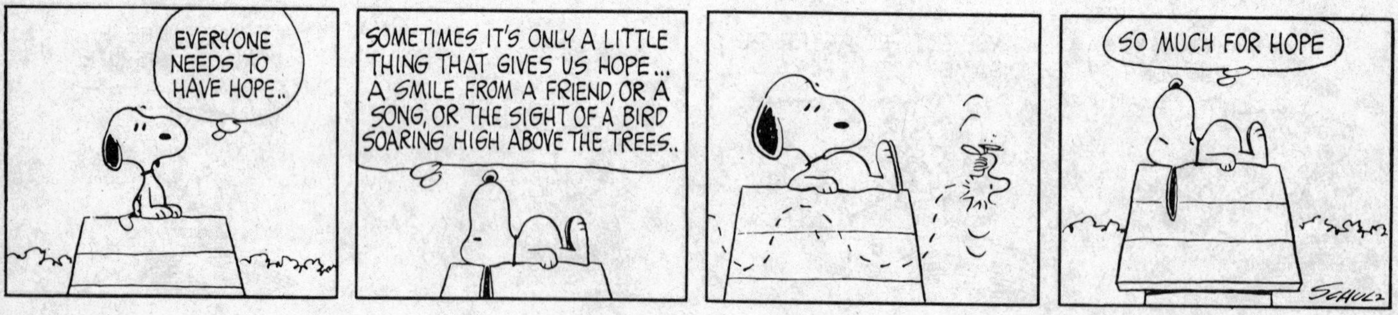
EVERYONE NEEDS TO HAVE HOPE..
SOMETIMES IT'S ONLY A LITTLE THING THAT GIVES US HOPE... A SMILE FROM A FRIEND, OR A SONG, OR THE SIGHT OF A BIRD SOARING HIGH ABOVE THE TREES..
SO MUCH FOR HOPE
SCHULZ

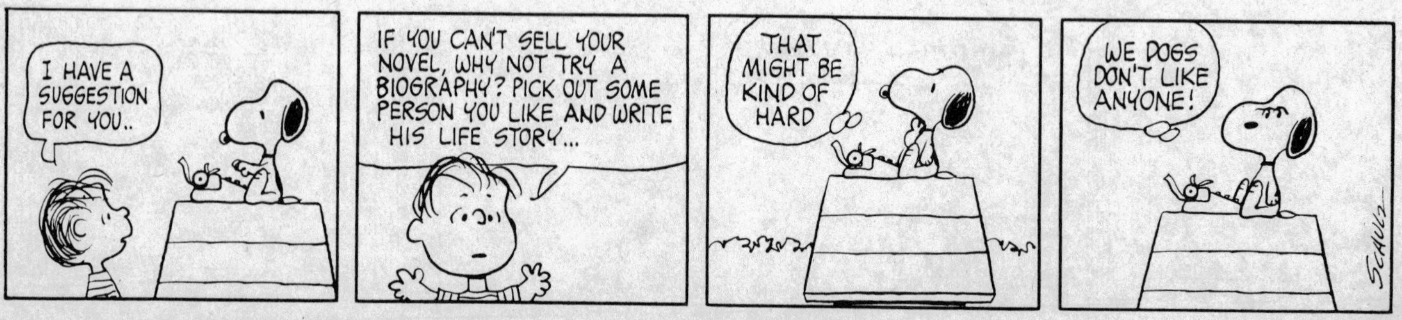
I HAVE A SUGGESTION FOR YOU..
IF YOU CAN'T SELL YOUR NOVEL, WHY NOT TRY A BIOGRAPHY? PICK OUT SOME PERSON YOU LIKE AND WRITE HIS LIFE STORY...
THAT MIGHT BE KIND OF HARD
WE DOGS DON'T LIKE ANYONE!
SCHULZ

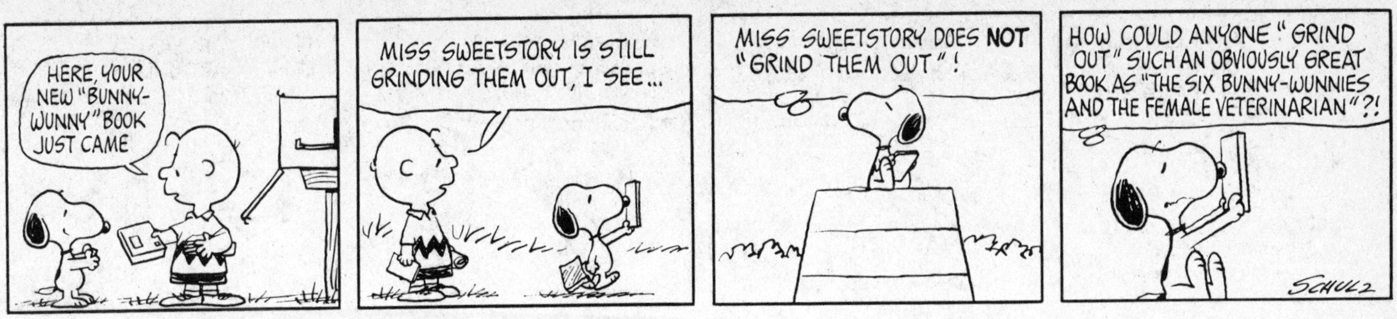
HERE, YOUR NEW "BUNNY-WUNNY" BOOK JUST CAME
MISS SWEETSTORY IS STILL GRINDING THEM OUT, I SEE...
MISS SWEETSTORY DOES NOT "GRIND THEM OUT"!
HOW COULD ANYONE "GRIND OUT" SUCH AN OBVIOUSLY GREAT BOOK AS "THE SIX BUNNY-WUNNIES AND THE FEMALE VETERINARIAN"?!
SCHULZ

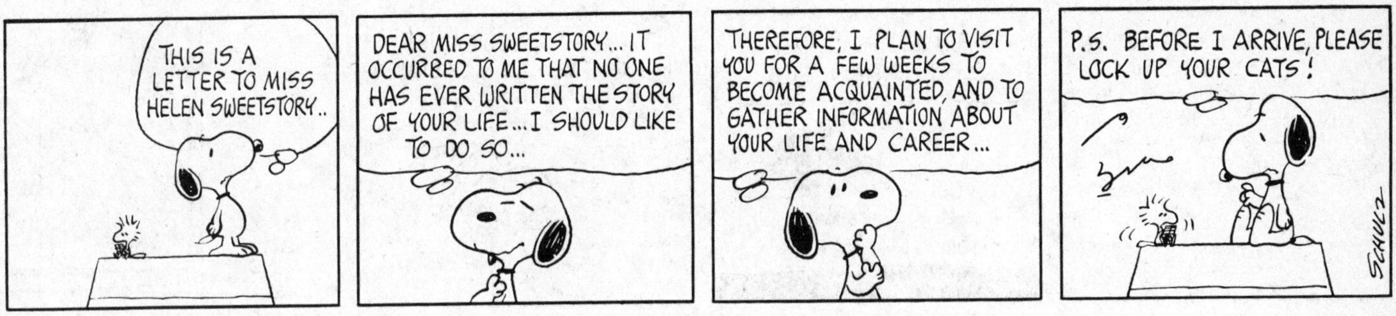
THIS IS A LETTER TO MISS HELEN SWEETSTORY..
DEAR MISS SWEETSTORY... IT OCCURRED TO ME THAT NO ONE HAS EVER WRITTEN THE STORY OF YOUR LIFE...I SHOULD LIKE TO DO SO...
THEREFORE, I PLAN TO VISIT YOU FOR A FEW WEEKS TO BECOME ACQUAINTED, AND TO GATHER INFORMATION ABOUT YOUR LIFE AND CAREER...
P.S. BEFORE I ARRIVE, PLEASE LOCK UP YOUR CATS!
SCHULZ

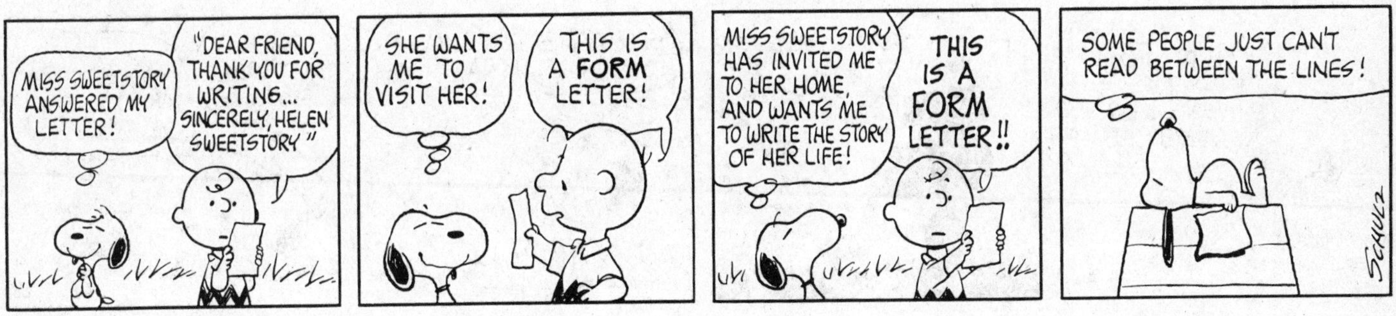
MISS SWEETSTORY ANSWERED MY LETTER!
"DEAR FRIEND, THANK YOU FOR WRITING... SINCERELY, HELEN SWEETSTORY"
SHE WANTS ME TO VISIT HER!
THIS IS A FORM LETTER!
MISS SWEETSTORY HAS INVITED ME TO HER HOME, AND WANTS ME TO WRITE THE STORY OF HER LIFE!
THIS IS A FORM LETTER!!
SOME PEOPLE JUST CAN'T READ BETWEEN THE LINES!
SCHULZ

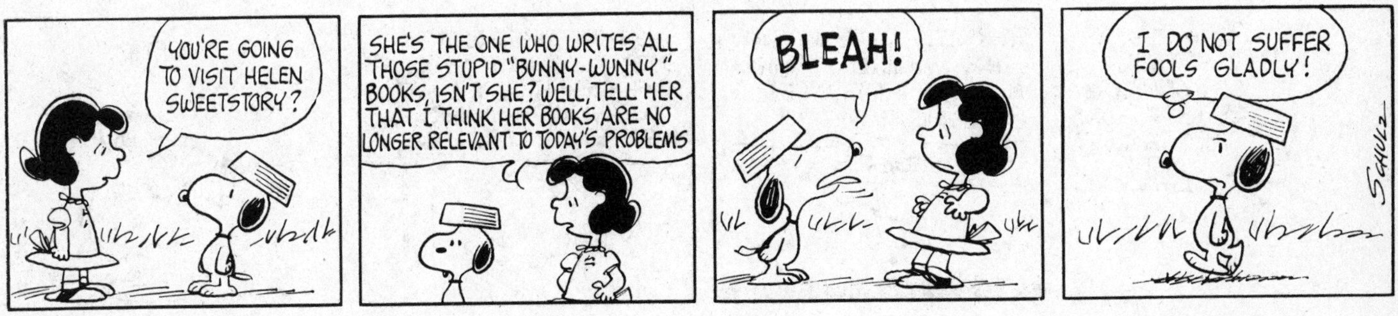
YOU'RE GOING TO VISIT HELEN SWEETSTORY?
SHE'S THE ONE WHO WRITES ALL THOSE STUPID "BUNNY-WUNNY" BOOKS, ISN'T SHE? WELL, TELL HER THAT I THINK HER BOOKS ARE NO LONGER RELEVANT TO TODAY'S PROBLEMS
BLEAH!
I DO NOT SUFFER FOOLS GLADLY!
SCHULZ

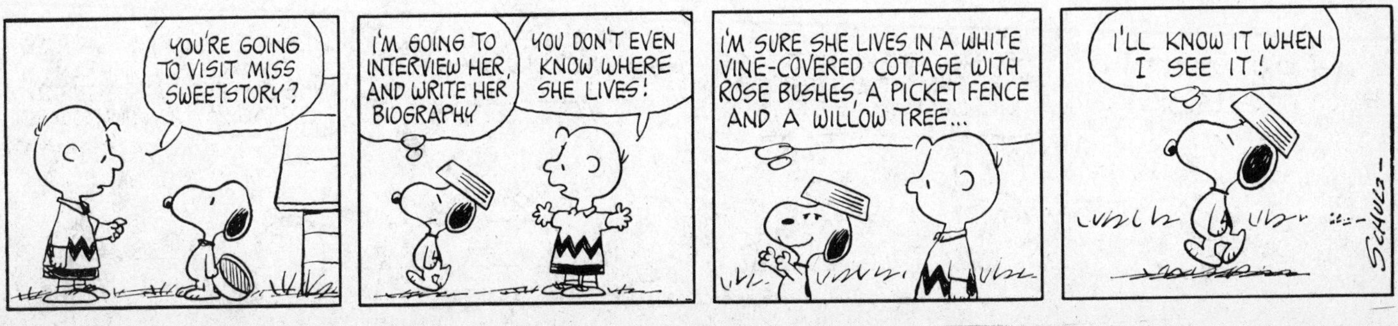
YOU'RE GOING TO VISIT MISS SWEETSTORY?
I'M GOING TO INTERVIEW HER, AND WRITE HER BIOGRAPHY
YOU DON'T EVEN KNOW WHERE SHE LIVES!
I'M SURE SHE LIVES IN A WHITE VINE-COVERED COTTAGE WITH ROSE BUSHES, A PICKET FENCE AND A WILLOW TREE...
I'LL KNOW IT WHEN I SEE IT!
SCHULZ

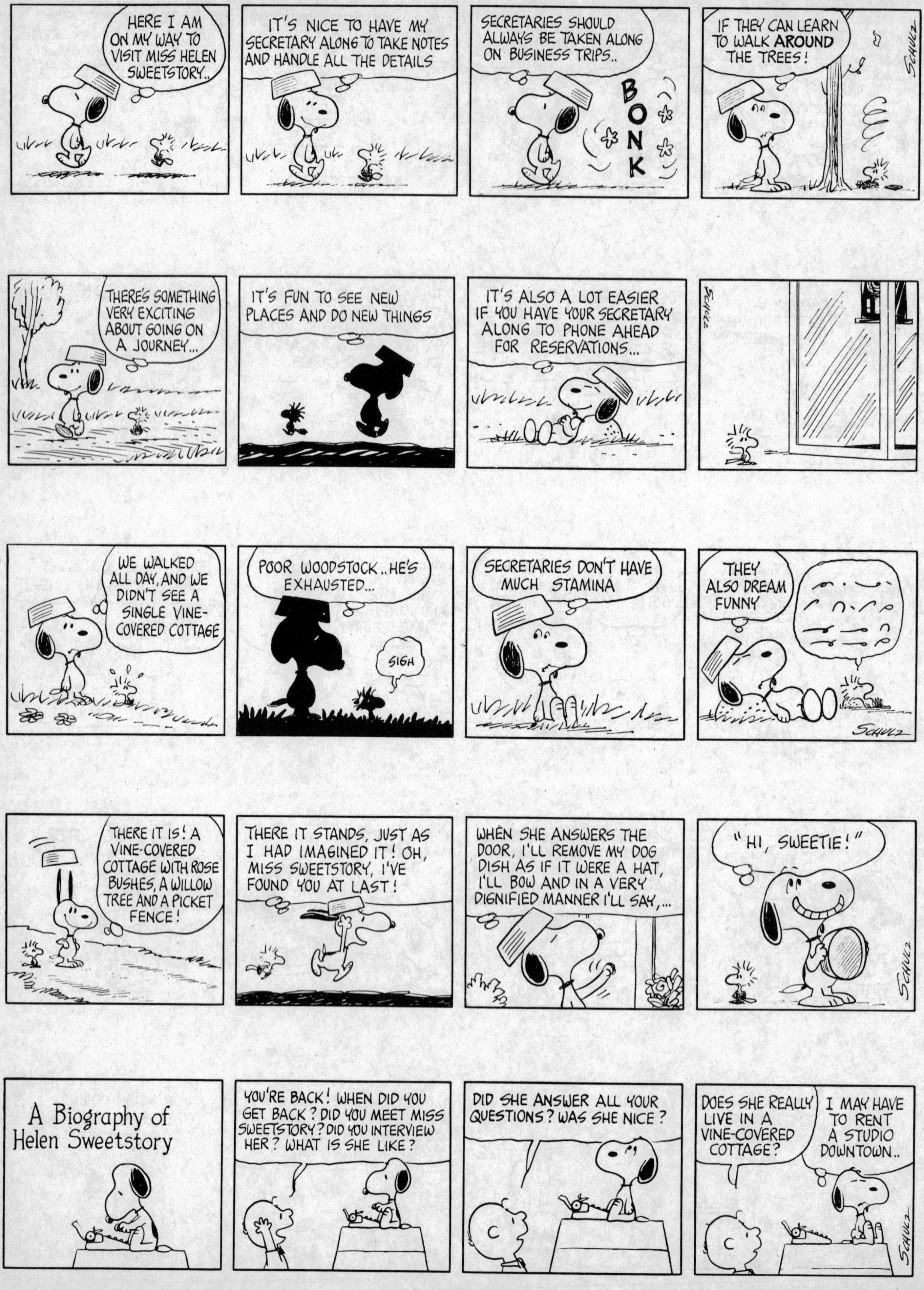
HERE I AM ON MY WAY TO VISIT MISS HELEN SWEETSTORY..
IT'S NICE TO HAVE MY SECRETARY ALONG TO TAKE NOTES AND HANDLE ALL THE DETAILS
SECRETARIES SHOULD ALWAYS BE TAKEN ALONG ON BUSINESS TRIPS..
BONK
IF THEY CAN LEARN TO WALK **AROUND** THE TREES!
SCHULZ
THERE'S SOMETHING VERY EXCITING ABOUT GOING ON A JOURNEY...
IT'S FUN TO SEE NEW PLACES AND DO NEW THINGS
IT'S ALSO A LOT EASIER IF YOU HAVE YOUR SECRETARY ALONG TO PHONE AHEAD FOR RESERVATIONS...
SCHULZ
WE WALKED ALL DAY, AND WE DIDN'T SEE A SINGLE VINE-COVERED COTTAGE
POOR WOODSTOCK..HE'S EXHAUSTED...
SIGH
SECRETARIES DON'T HAVE MUCH STAMINA
THEY ALSO DREAM FUNNY
SCHULZ
THERE IT IS! A VINE-COVERED COTTAGE WITH ROSE BUSHES, A WILLOW TREE AND A PICKET FENCE!
THERE IT STANDS, JUST AS I HAD IMAGINED IT! OH, MISS SWEETSTORY, I'VE FOUND YOU AT LAST!
WHEN SHE ANSWERS THE DOOR, I'LL REMOVE MY DOG DISH AS IF IT WERE A HAT, I'LL BOW AND IN A VERY DIGNIFIED MANNER I'LL SAY,...
"HI, SWEETIE!"
SCHULZ
A Biography of Helen Sweetstory
YOU'RE BACK! WHEN DID YOU GET BACK? DID YOU MEET MISS SWEETSTORY? DID YOU INTERVIEW HER? WHAT IS SHE LIKE?
DID SHE ANSWER ALL YOUR QUESTIONS? WAS SHE NICE?
DOES SHE REALLY LIVE IN A VINE-COVERED COTTAGE?
I MAY HAVE TO RENT A STUDIO DOWNTOWN..
SCHULZ

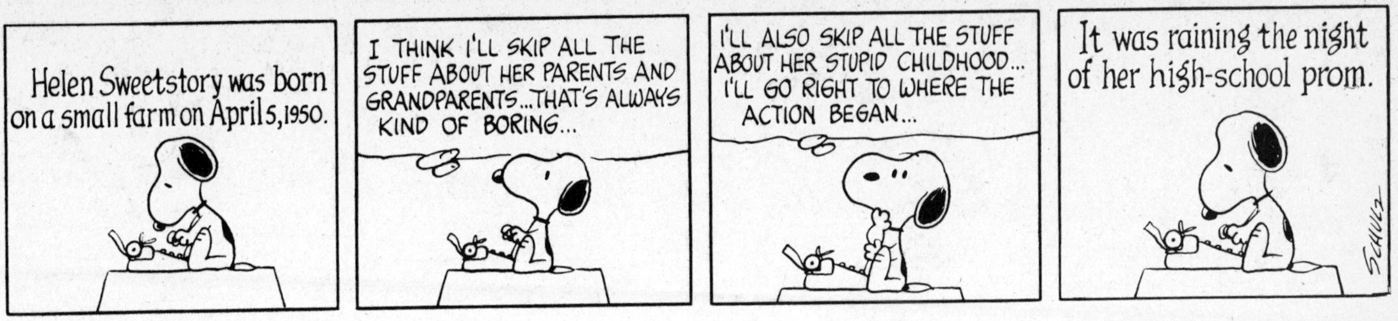
Helen Sweetstory was born on a small farm on April 5, 1950.
I THINK I'LL SKIP ALL THE STUFF ABOUT HER PARENTS AND GRANDPARENTS...THAT'S ALWAYS KIND OF BORING...
I'LL ALSO SKIP ALL THE STUFF ABOUT HER STUPID CHILDHOOD... I'LL GO RIGHT TO WHERE THE ACTION BEGAN...
It was raining the night of her high-school prom.
SCHULZ

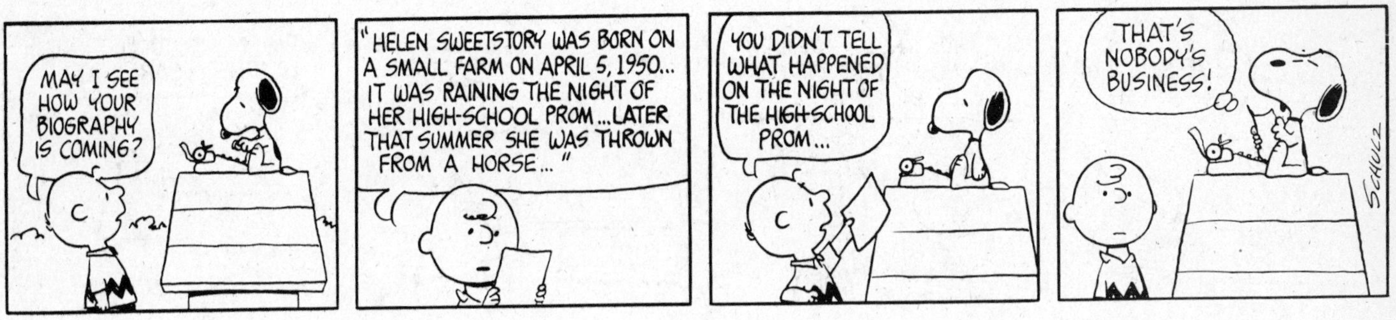
MAY I SEE HOW YOUR BIOGRAPHY IS COMING?
"HELEN SWEETSTORY WAS BORN ON A SMALL FARM ON APRIL 5, 1950... IT WAS RAINING THE NIGHT OF HER HIGH-SCHOOL PROM...LATER THAT SUMMER SHE WAS THROWN FROM A HORSE..."
YOU DIDN'T TELL WHAT HAPPENED ON THE NIGHT OF THE HIGH-SCHOOL PROM...
THAT'S NOBODY'S BUSINESS!
SCHULZ

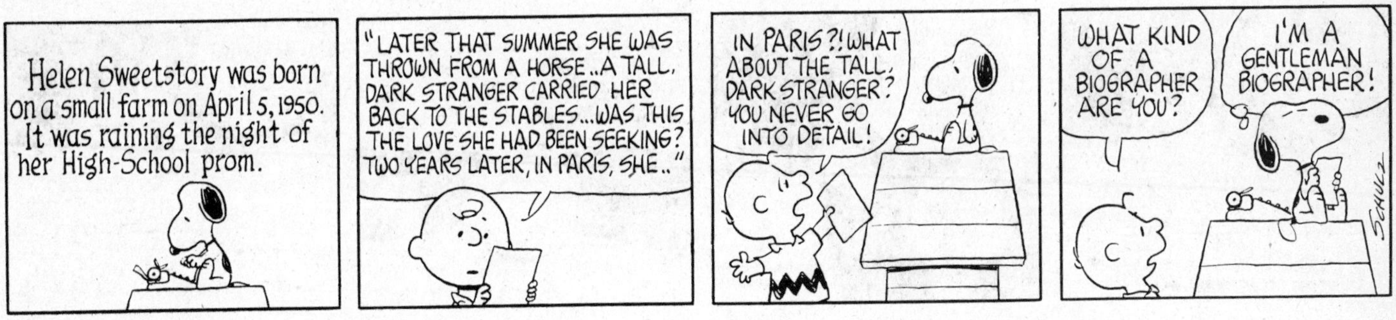
Helen Sweetstory was born on a small farm on April 5, 1950. It was raining the night of her High-School prom.
"LATER THAT SUMMER SHE WAS THROWN FROM A HORSE..A TALL, DARK STRANGER CARRIED HER BACK TO THE STABLES...WAS THIS THE LOVE SHE HAD BEEN SEEKING? TWO YEARS LATER, IN PARIS, SHE.."
IN PARIS?! WHAT ABOUT THE TALL, DARK STRANGER? YOU NEVER GO INTO DETAIL!
WHAT KIND OF A BIOGRAPHER ARE YOU?
I'M A GENTLEMAN BIOGRAPHER!
SCHULZ

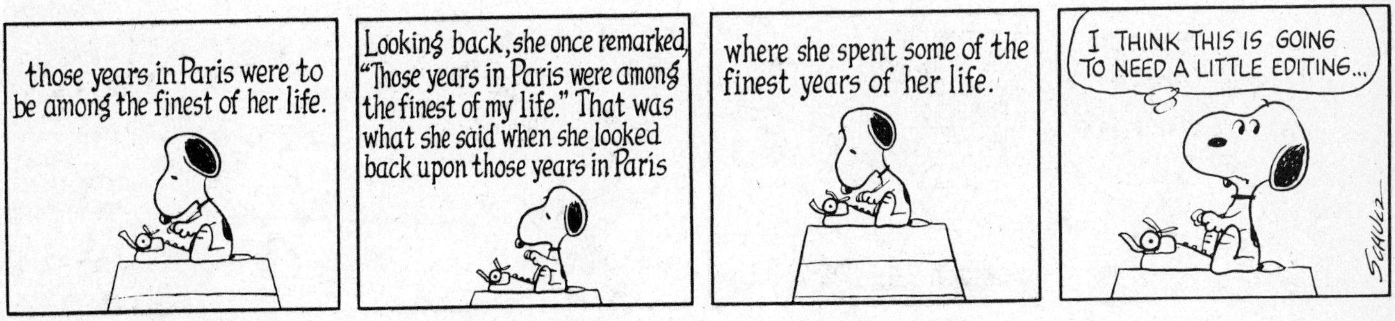
those years in Paris were to be among the finest of her life.
Looking back, she once remarked, "Those years in Paris were among the finest of my life." That was what she said when she looked back upon those years in Paris
where she spent some of the finest years of her life.
I THINK THIS IS GOING TO NEED A LITTLE EDITING...
SCHULZ

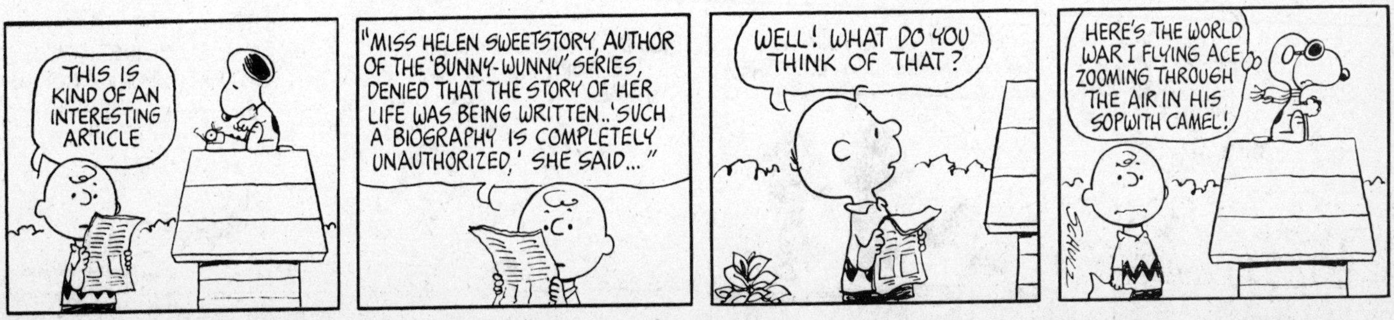
THIS IS KIND OF AN INTERESTING ARTICLE
"MISS HELEN SWEETSTORY, AUTHOR OF THE 'BUNNY-WUNNY' SERIES, DENIED THAT THE STORY OF HER LIFE WAS BEING WRITTEN..'SUCH A BIOGRAPHY IS COMPLETELY UNAUTHORIZED,' SHE SAID..."
WELL! WHAT DO YOU THINK OF THAT?
HERE'S THE WORLD WAR I FLYING ACE ZOOMING THROUGH THE AIR IN HIS SOPWITH CAMEL!
SCHULZ

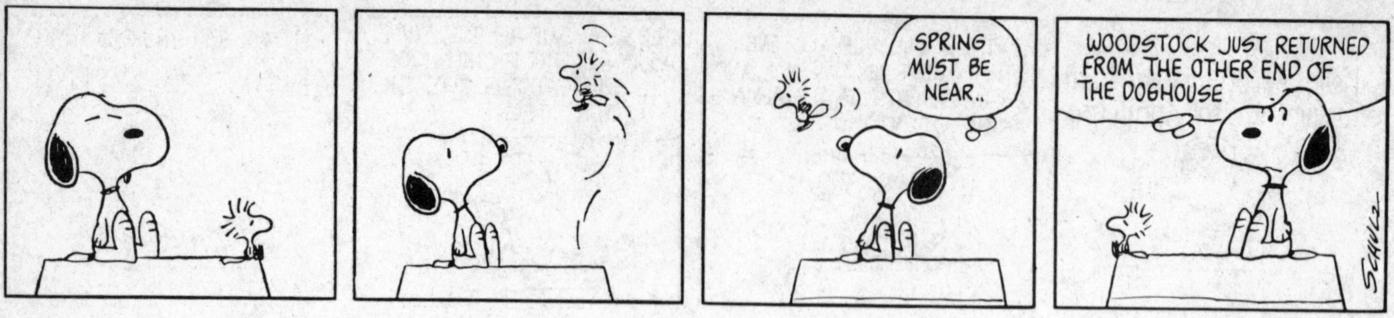
SPRING MUST BE NEAR..
WOODSTOCK JUST RETURNED FROM THE OTHER END OF THE DOGHOUSE
SCHULZ

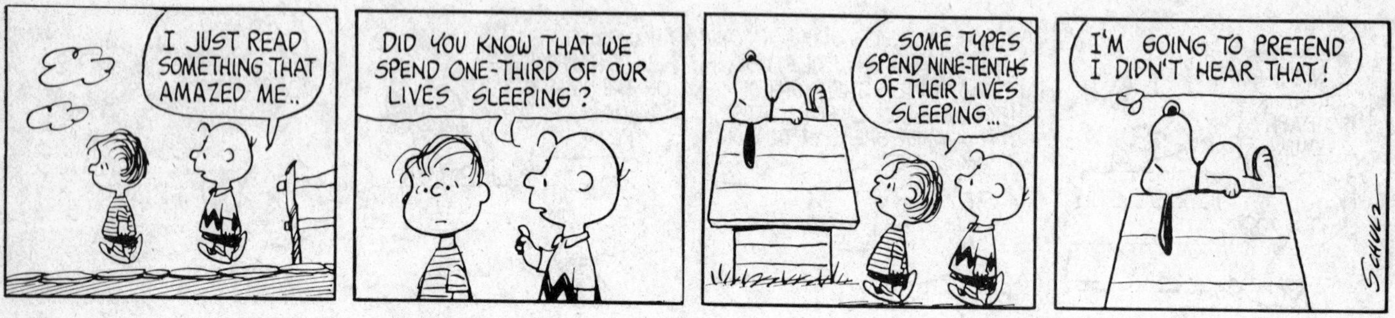
I JUST READ SOMETHING THAT AMAZED ME..
DID YOU KNOW THAT WE SPEND ONE-THIRD OF OUR LIVES SLEEPING ?
SOME TYPES SPEND NINE-TENTHS OF THEIR LIVES SLEEPING...
I'M GOING TO PRETEND I DIDN'T HEAR THAT!
SCHULZ

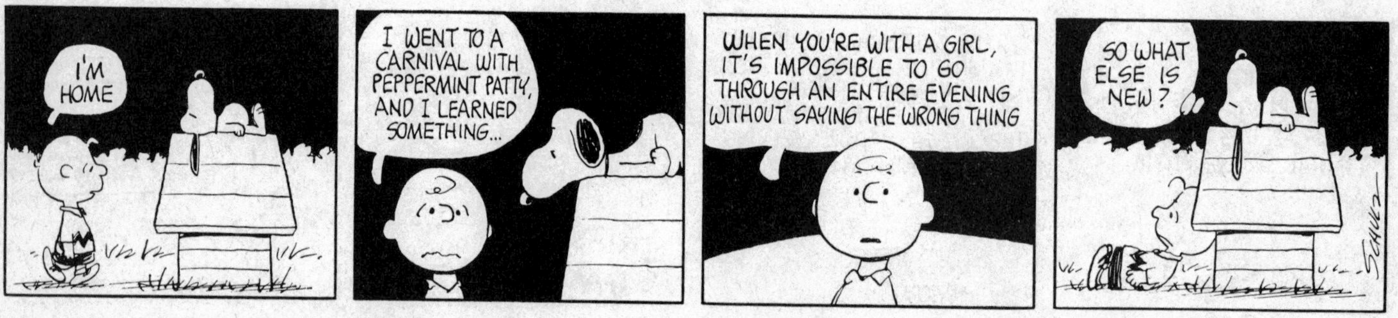
I'M HOME
I WENT TO A CARNIVAL WITH PEPPERMINT PATTY, AND I LEARNED SOMETHING...
WHEN YOU'RE WITH A GIRL, IT'S IMPOSSIBLE TO GO THROUGH AN ENTIRE EVENING WITHOUT SAYING THE WRONG THING
SO WHAT ELSE IS NEW ?
SCHULZ

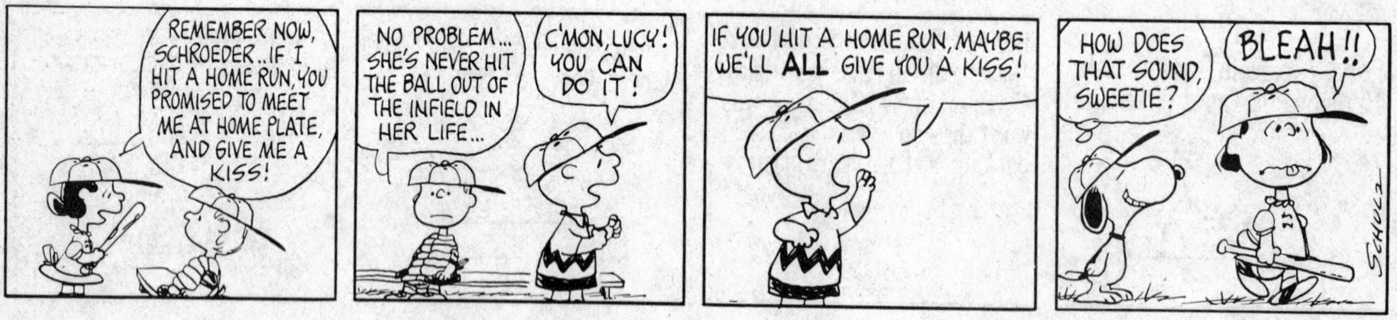
REMEMBER NOW, SCHROEDER..IF I HIT A HOME RUN, YOU PROMISED TO MEET ME AT HOME PLATE, AND GIVE ME A KISS!
NO PROBLEM... SHE'S NEVER HIT THE BALL OUT OF THE INFIELD IN HER LIFE...
C'MON, LUCY! YOU CAN DO IT!
IF YOU HIT A HOME RUN, MAYBE WE'LL ALL GIVE YOU A KISS!
HOW DOES THAT SOUND, SWEETIE ?
BLEAH!!
SCHULZ

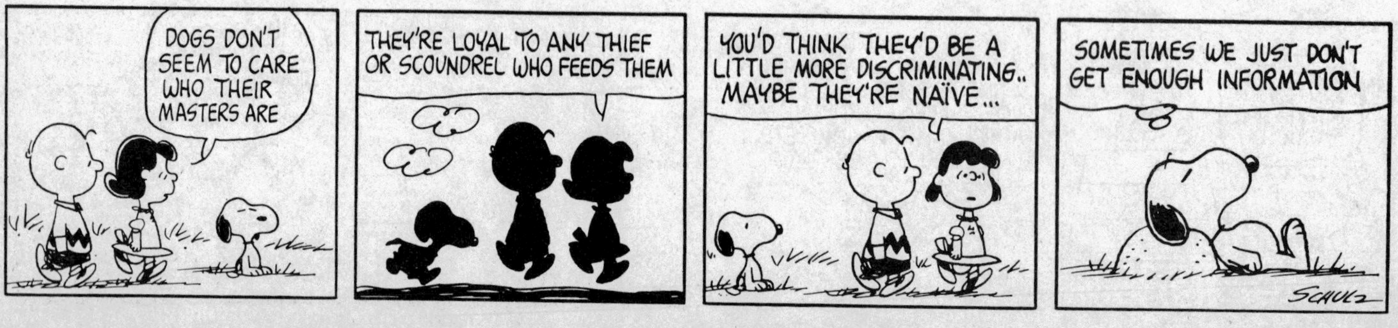
DOGS DON'T SEEM TO CARE WHO THEIR MASTERS ARE
THEY'RE LOYAL TO ANY THIEF OR SCOUNDREL WHO FEEDS THEM
YOU'D THINK THEY'D BE A LITTLE MORE DISCRIMINATING.. MAYBE THEY'RE NAÏVE...
SOMETIMES WE JUST DON'T GET ENOUGH INFORMATION
SCHULZ

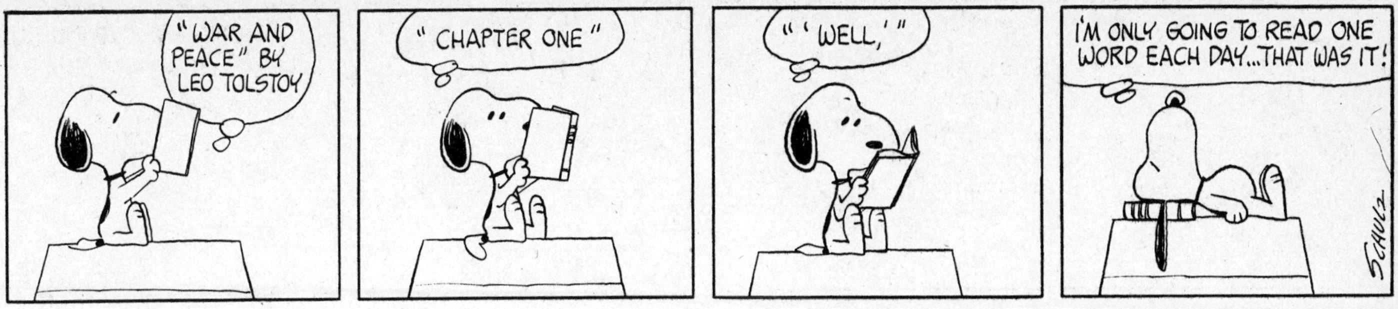
"WAR AND PEACE" BY LEO TOLSTOY
" CHAPTER ONE "
" ' WELL, ' "
I'M ONLY GOING TO READ ONE WORD EACH DAY...THAT WAS IT!
SCHULZ

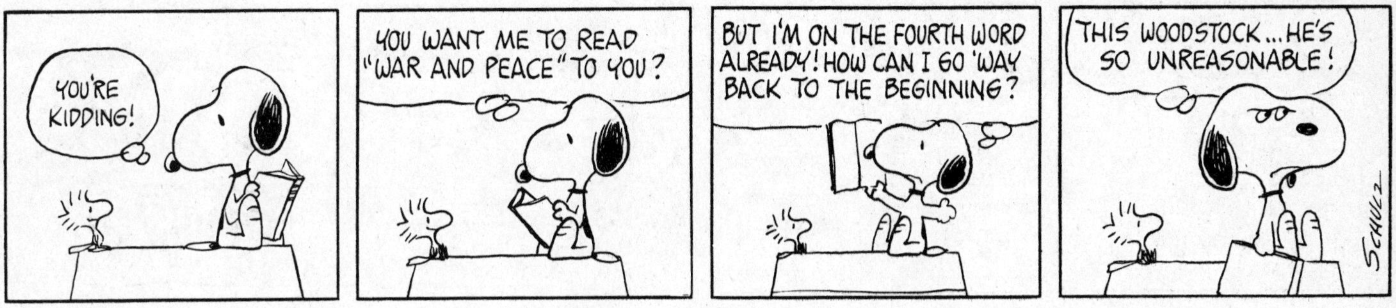
YOU'RE KIDDING!
YOU WANT ME TO READ "WAR AND PEACE" TO YOU?
BUT I'M ON THE FOURTH WORD ALREADY! HOW CAN I GO 'WAY BACK TO THE BEGINNING?
THIS WOODSTOCK...HE'S SO UNREASONABLE!
SCHULZ

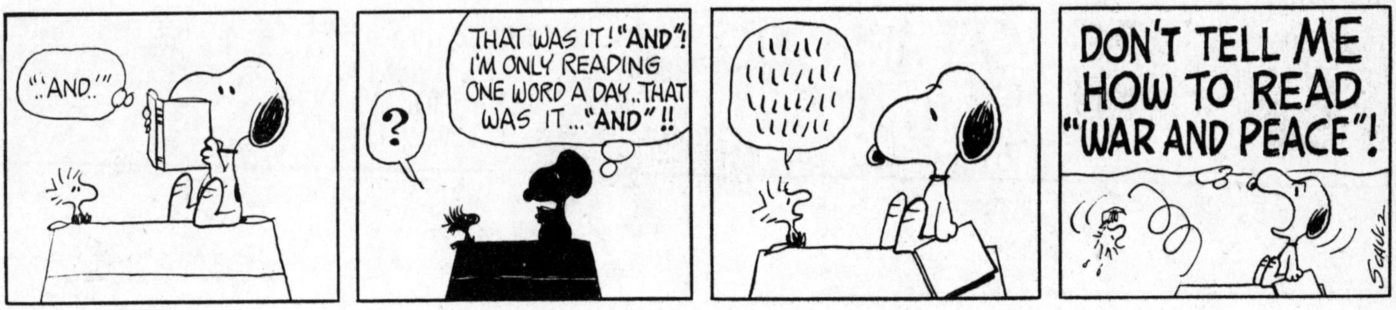
"..AND.."
?
THAT WAS IT! "AND"! I'M ONLY READING ONE WORD A DAY..THAT WAS IT..."AND"!!
DON'T TELL ME HOW TO READ "WAR AND PEACE"!
SCHULZ

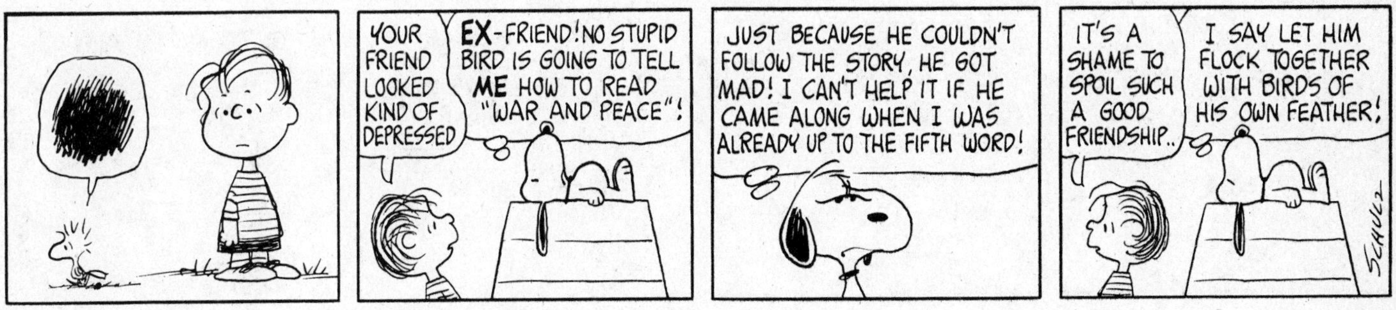
YOUR FRIEND LOOKED KIND OF DEPRESSED
EX-FRIEND! NO STUPID BIRD IS GOING TO TELL ME HOW TO READ "WAR AND PEACE"!
JUST BECAUSE HE COULDN'T FOLLOW THE STORY, HE GOT MAD! I CAN'T HELP IT IF HE CAME ALONG WHEN I WAS ALREADY UP TO THE FIFTH WORD!
IT'S A SHAME TO SPOIL SUCH A GOOD FRIENDSHIP..
I SAY LET HIM FLOCK TOGETHER WITH BIRDS OF HIS OWN FEATHER!
SCHULZ

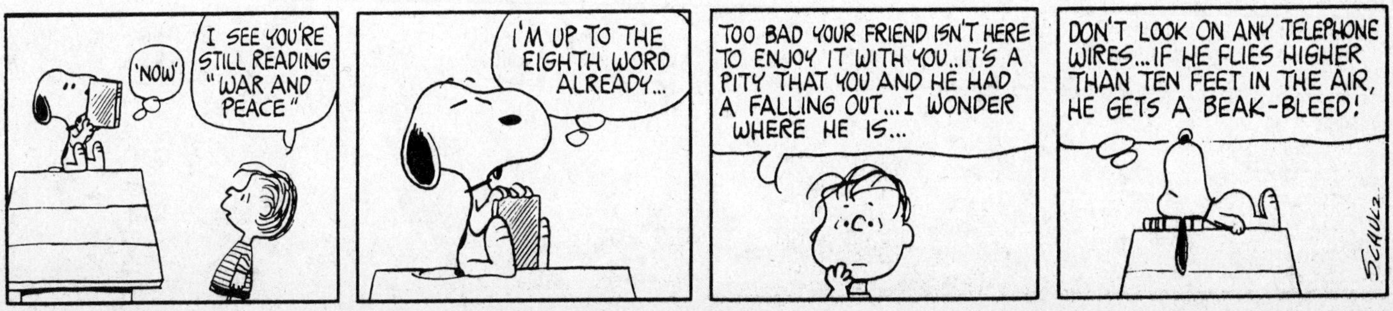
'NOW'
I SEE YOU'RE STILL READING "WAR AND PEACE"
I'M UP TO THE EIGHTH WORD ALREADY...
TOO BAD YOUR FRIEND ISN'T HERE TO ENJOY IT WITH YOU..IT'S A PITY THAT YOU AND HE HAD A FALLING OUT...I WONDER WHERE HE IS...
DON'T LOOK ON ANY TELEPHONE WIRES...IF HE FLIES HIGHER THAN TEN FEET IN THE AIR, HE GETS A BEAK-BLEED!
SCHULZ

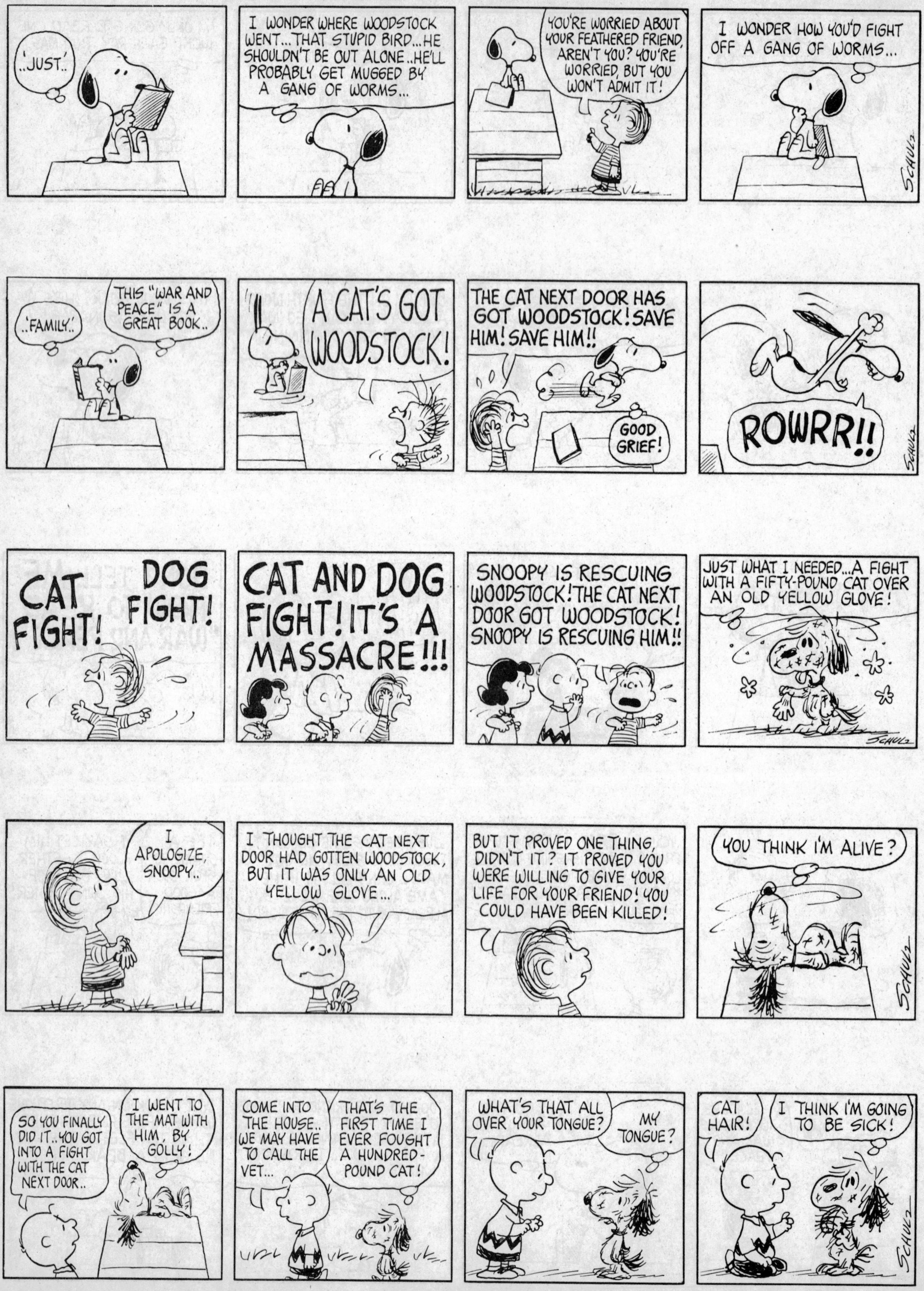

..JUST..
I WONDER WHERE WOODSTOCK WENT...THAT STUPID BIRD...HE SHOULDN'T BE OUT ALONE..HE'LL PROBABLY GET MUGGED BY A GANG OF WORMS...
YOU'RE WORRIED ABOUT YOUR FEATHERED FRIEND, AREN'T YOU? YOU'RE WORRIED, BUT YOU WON'T ADMIT IT!
I WONDER HOW YOU'D FIGHT OFF A GANG OF WORMS...
SCHULZ
..FAMILY..
THIS "WAR AND PEACE" IS A GREAT BOOK..
A CAT'S GOT WOODSTOCK!
THE CAT NEXT DOOR HAS GOT WOODSTOCK! SAVE HIM! SAVE HIM!!
GOOD GRIEF!
ROWRR!!
SCHULZ
CAT FIGHT!
DOG FIGHT!
CAT AND DOG FIGHT! IT'S A MASSACRE!!!
SNOOPY IS RESCUING WOODSTOCK! THE CAT NEXT DOOR GOT WOODSTOCK! SNOOPY IS RESCUING HIM!!
JUST WHAT I NEEDED...A FIGHT WITH A FIFTY-POUND CAT OVER AN OLD YELLOW GLOVE!
SCHULZ
I APOLOGIZE, SNOOPY..
I THOUGHT THE CAT NEXT DOOR HAD GOTTEN WOODSTOCK, BUT IT WAS ONLY AN OLD YELLOW GLOVE...
BUT IT PROVED ONE THING, DIDN'T IT? IT PROVED YOU WERE WILLING TO GIVE YOUR LIFE FOR YOUR FRIEND! YOU COULD HAVE BEEN KILLED!
YOU THINK I'M ALIVE?
SCHULZ
SO YOU FINALLY DID IT..YOU GOT INTO A FIGHT WITH THE CAT NEXT DOOR..
I WENT TO THE MAT WITH HIM, BY GOLLY!
COME INTO THE HOUSE.. WE MAY HAVE TO CALL THE VET...
THAT'S THE FIRST TIME I EVER FOUGHT A HUNDRED-POUND CAT!
WHAT'S THAT ALL OVER YOUR TONGUE?
MY TONGUE?
CAT HAIR!
I THINK I'M GOING TO BE SICK!
SCHULZ

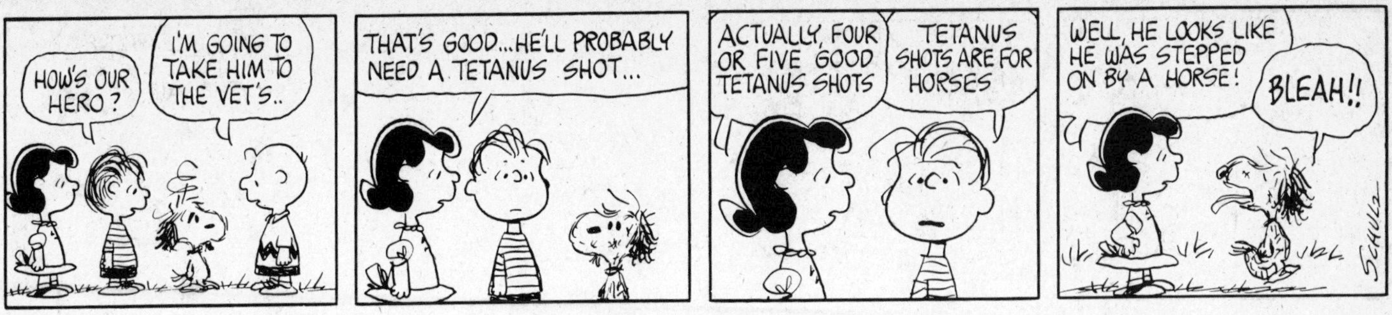
HOW'S OUR HERO?
I'M GOING TO TAKE HIM TO THE VET'S..
THAT'S GOOD...HE'LL PROBABLY NEED A TETANUS SHOT...
ACTUALLY, FOUR OR FIVE GOOD TETANUS SHOTS
TETANUS SHOTS ARE FOR HORSES
WELL, HE LOOKS LIKE HE WAS STEPPED ON BY A HORSE!
BLEAH!!
SCHULZ

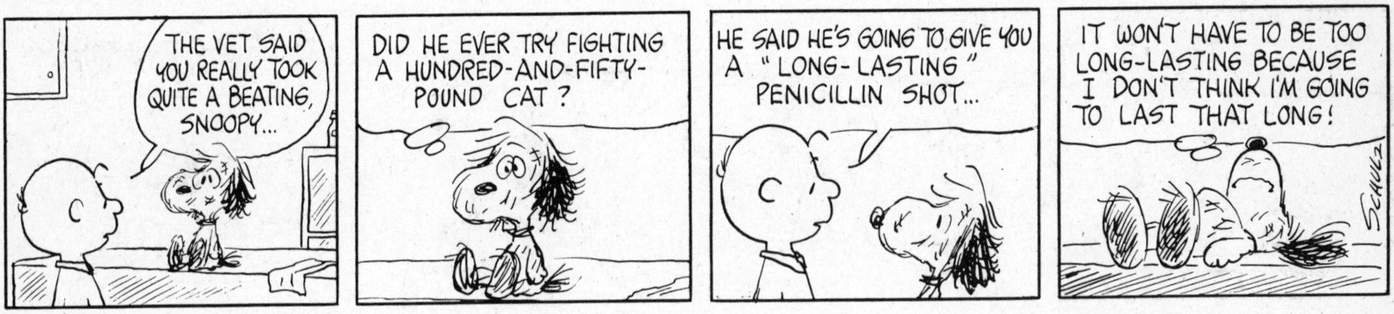
THE VET SAID YOU REALLY TOOK QUITE A BEATING, SNOOPY...
DID HE EVER TRY FIGHTING A HUNDRED-AND-FIFTY-POUND CAT?
HE SAID HE'S GOING TO GIVE YOU A "LONG-LASTING" PENICILLIN SHOT...
IT WON'T HAVE TO BE TOO LONG-LASTING BECAUSE I DON'T THINK I'M GOING TO LAST THAT LONG!
SCHULZ

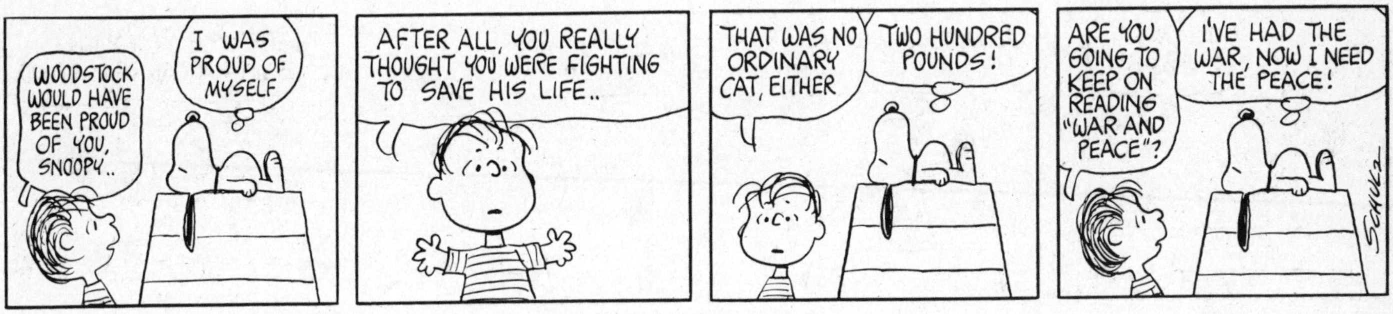
WOODSTOCK WOULD HAVE BEEN PROUD OF YOU, SNOOPY..
I WAS PROUD OF MYSELF
AFTER ALL, YOU REALLY THOUGHT YOU WERE FIGHTING TO SAVE HIS LIFE..
THAT WAS NO ORDINARY CAT, EITHER
TWO HUNDRED POUNDS!
ARE YOU GOING TO KEEP ON READING "WAR AND PEACE"?
I'VE HAD THE WAR, NOW I NEED THE PEACE!
SCHULZ

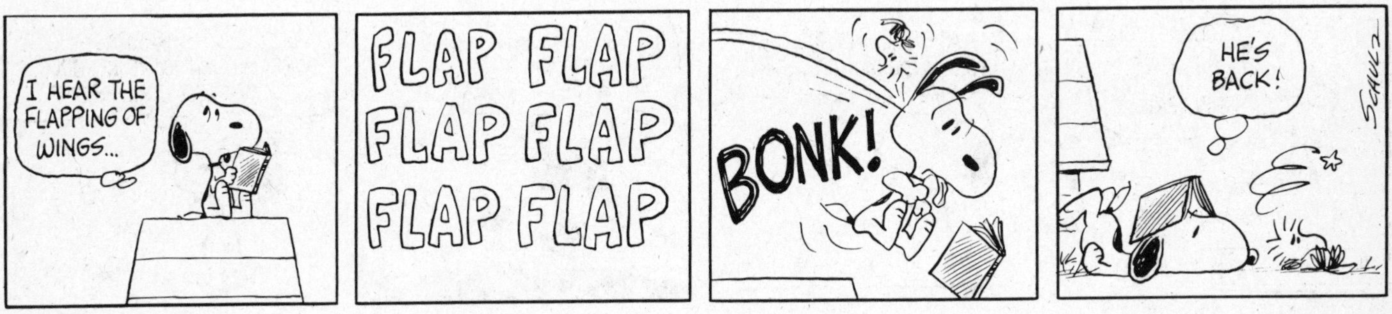
I HEAR THE FLAPPING OF WINGS...
FLAP FLAP FLAP FLAP FLAP FLAP
BONK!
HE'S BACK!
SCHULZ

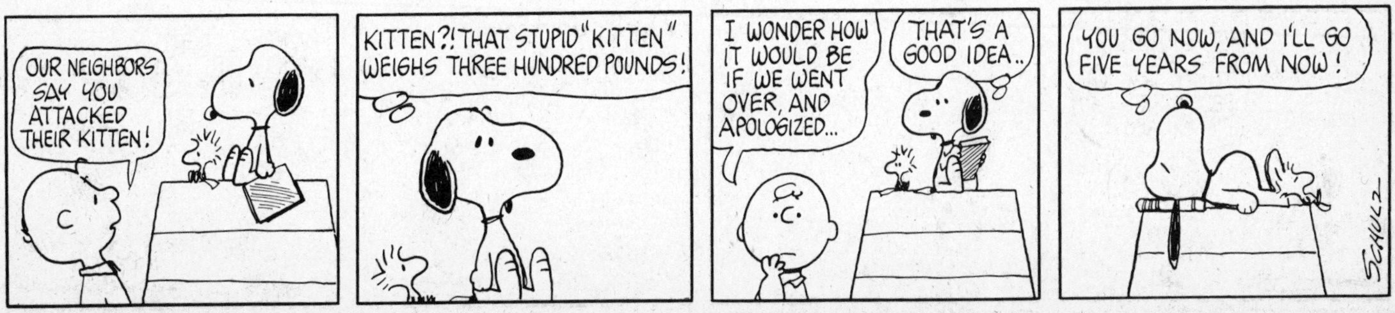
OUR NEIGHBORS SAY YOU ATTACKED THEIR KITTEN!
KITTEN?! THAT STUPID "KITTEN" WEIGHS THREE HUNDRED POUNDS!
I WONDER HOW IT WOULD BE IF WE WENT OVER, AND APOLOGIZED...
THAT'S A GOOD IDEA..
YOU GO NOW, AND I'LL GO FIVE YEARS FROM NOW!
SCHULZ

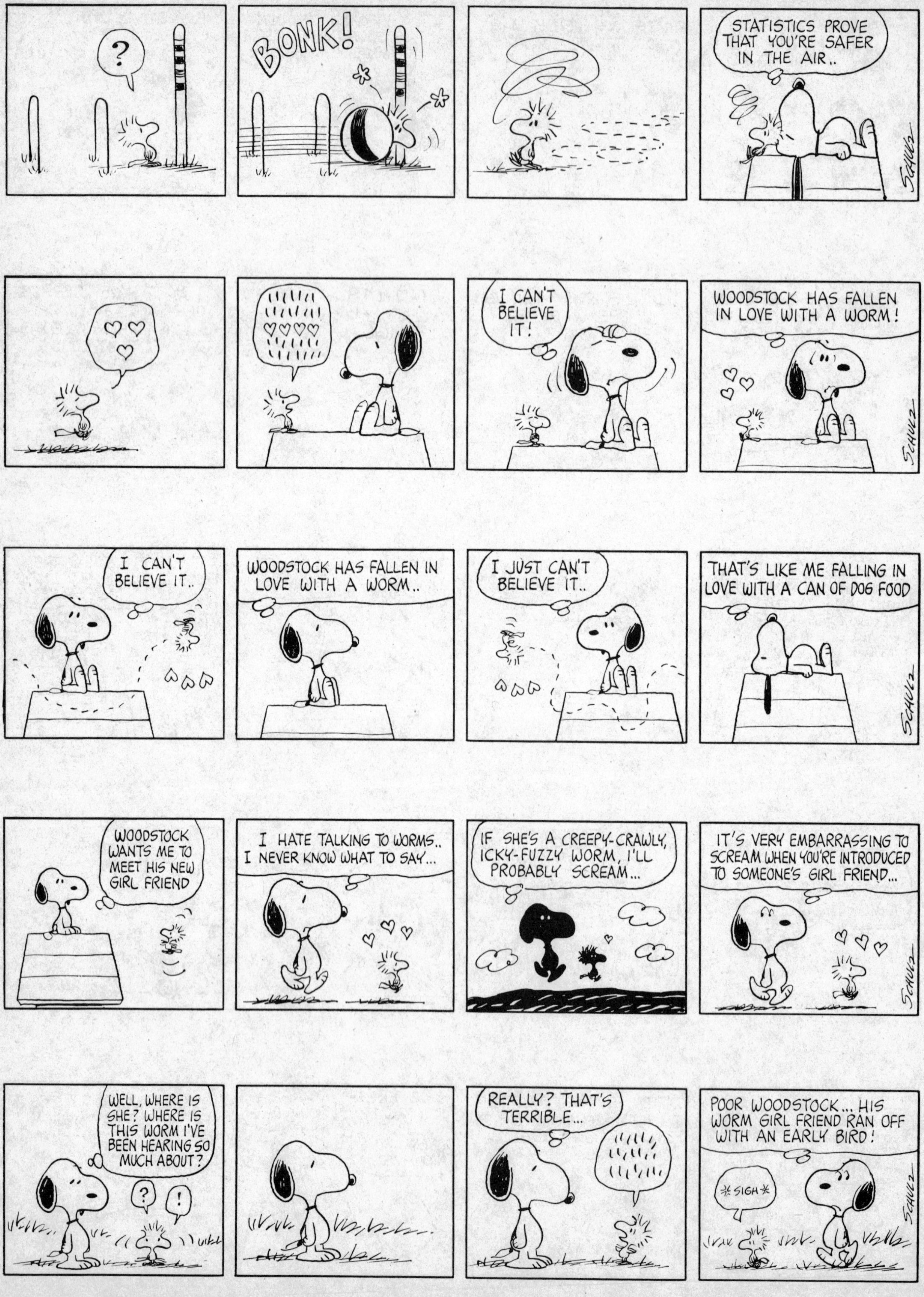
?
BONK!
STATISTICS PROVE THAT YOU'RE SAFER IN THE AIR..
SCHULZ
I CAN'T BELIEVE IT!
WOODSTOCK HAS FALLEN IN LOVE WITH A WORM!
SCHULZ
I CAN'T BELIEVE IT..
WOODSTOCK HAS FALLEN IN LOVE WITH A WORM..
I JUST CAN'T BELIEVE IT..
THAT'S LIKE ME FALLING IN LOVE WITH A CAN OF DOG FOOD
SCHULZ
WOODSTOCK WANTS ME TO MEET HIS NEW GIRL FRIEND
I HATE TALKING TO WORMS.. I NEVER KNOW WHAT TO SAY...
IF SHE'S A CREEPY-CRAWLY, ICKY-FUZZY WORM, I'LL PROBABLY SCREAM...
IT'S VERY EMBARRASSING TO SCREAM WHEN YOU'RE INTRODUCED TO SOMEONE'S GIRL FRIEND...
SCHULZ
WELL, WHERE IS SHE? WHERE IS THIS WORM I'VE BEEN HEARING SO MUCH ABOUT?
?
!
REALLY? THAT'S TERRIBLE...
POOR WOODSTOCK... HIS WORM GIRL FRIEND RAN OFF WITH AN EARLY BIRD!
SIGH
SCHULZ

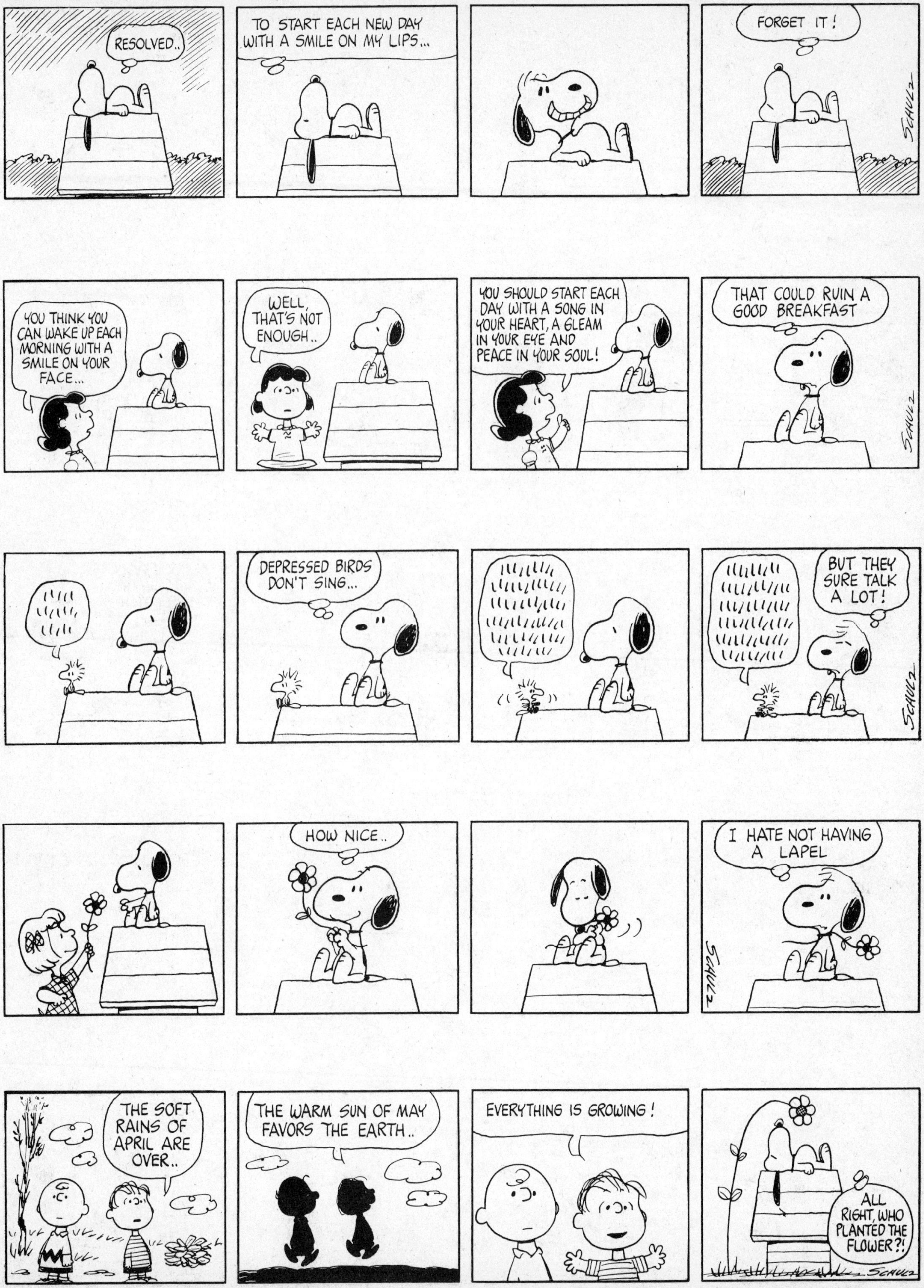
RESOLVED..
TO START EACH NEW DAY WITH A SMILE ON MY LIPS...
FORGET IT!
SCHULZ
YOU THINK YOU CAN WAKE UP EACH MORNING WITH A SMILE ON YOUR FACE...
WELL, THAT'S NOT ENOUGH..
YOU SHOULD START EACH DAY WITH A SONG IN YOUR HEART, A GLEAM IN YOUR EYE AND PEACE IN YOUR SOUL!
THAT COULD RUIN A GOOD BREAKFAST
SCHULZ
DEPRESSED BIRDS DON'T SING...
BUT THEY SURE TALK A LOT!
SCHULZ
HOW NICE..
I HATE NOT HAVING A LAPEL
SCHULZ
THE SOFT RAINS OF APRIL ARE OVER..
THE WARM SUN OF MAY FAVORS THE EARTH..
EVERYTHING IS GROWING!
ALL RIGHT, WHO PLANTED THE FLOWER?!
SCHULZ

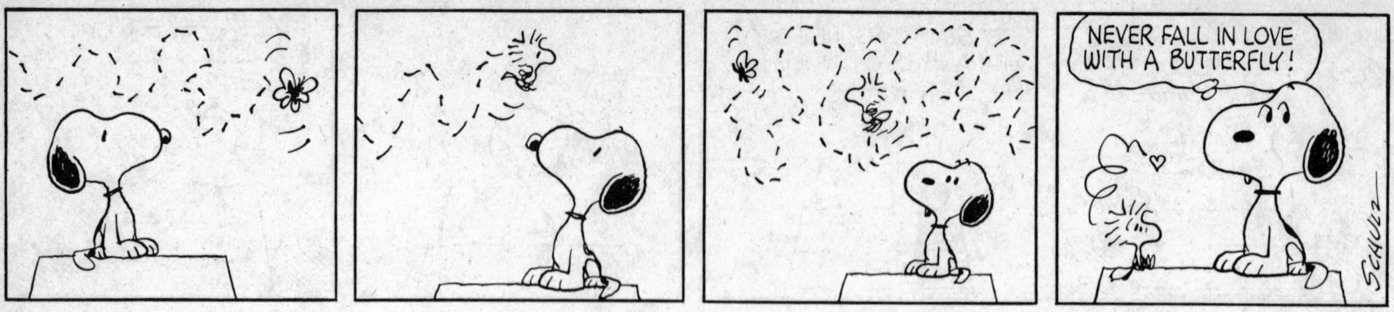
NEVER FALL IN LOVE WITH A BUTTERFLY!

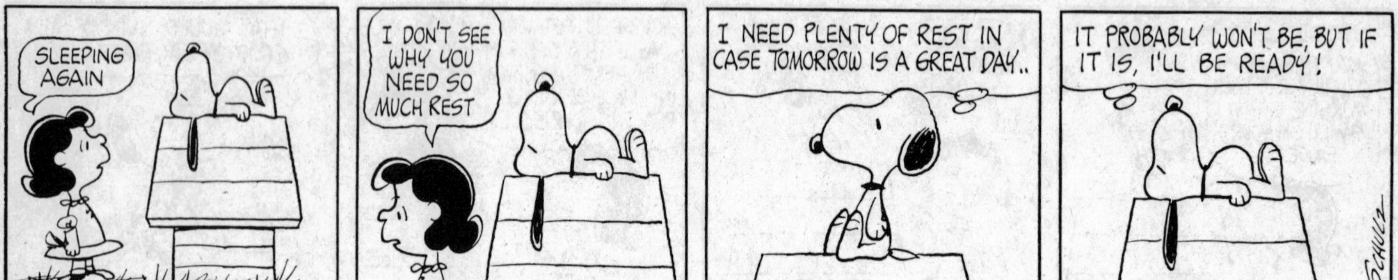
SLEEPING AGAIN
I DON'T SEE WHY YOU NEED SO MUCH REST
I NEED PLENTY OF REST IN CASE TOMORROW IS A GREAT DAY..
IT PROBABLY WON'T BE, BUT IF IT IS, I'LL BE READY!

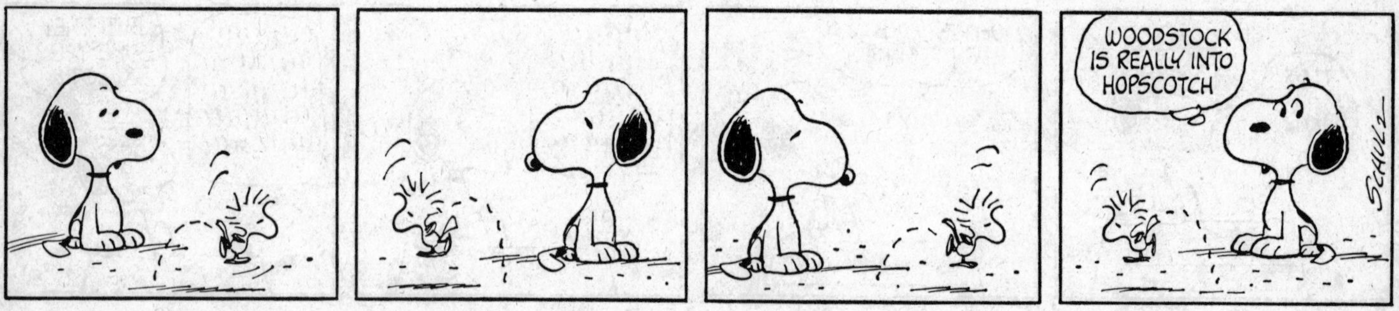
WOODSTOCK IS REALLY INTO HOPSCOTCH

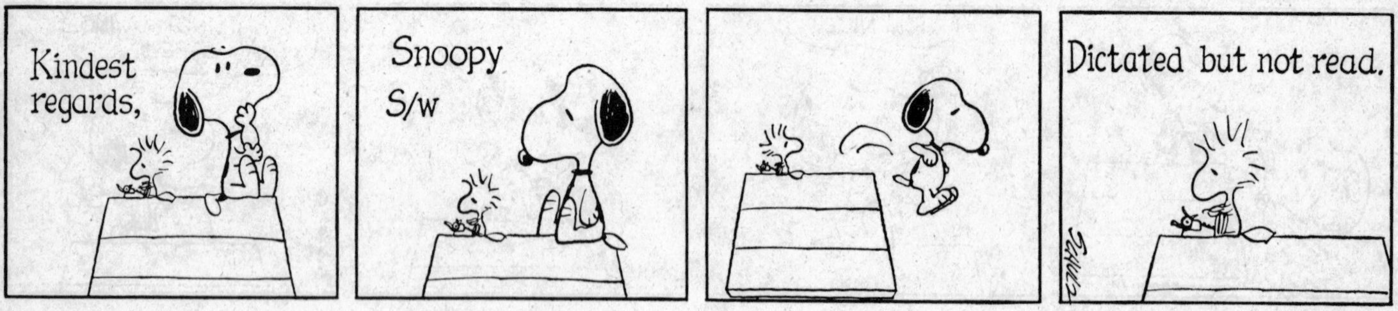
Kindest regards,
Snoopy
S/w
Dictated but not read.

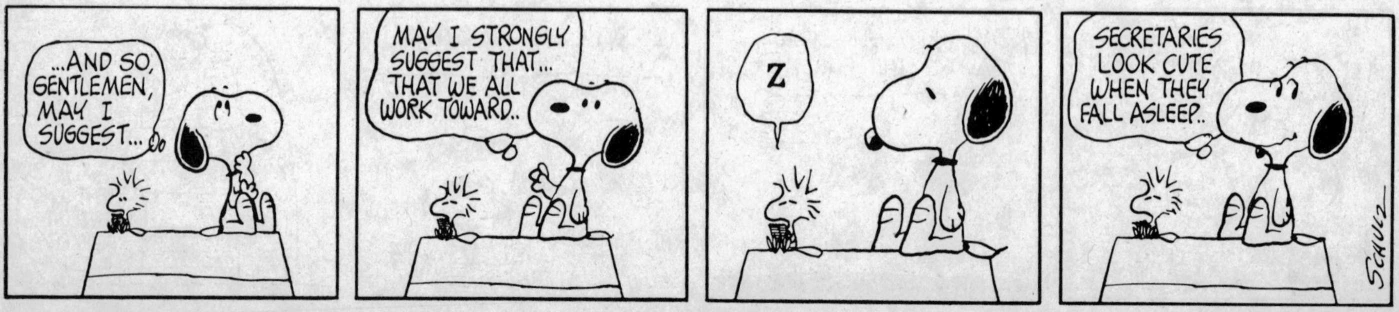
...AND SO, GENTLEMEN, MAY I SUGGEST...
MAY I STRONGLY SUGGEST THAT... THAT WE ALL WORK TOWARD..
Z
SECRETARIES LOOK CUTE WHEN THEY FALL ASLEEP..

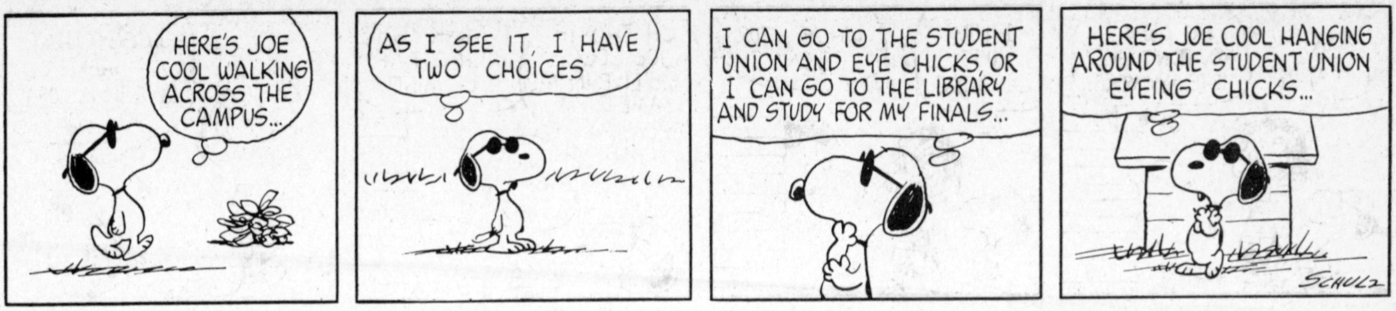
HERE'S JOE COOL WALKING ACROSS THE CAMPUS...
AS I SEE IT, I HAVE TWO CHOICES
I CAN GO TO THE STUDENT UNION AND EYE CHICKS, OR I CAN GO TO THE LIBRARY AND STUDY FOR MY FINALS...
HERE'S JOE COOL HANGING AROUND THE STUDENT UNION EYEING CHICKS...
SCHULZ

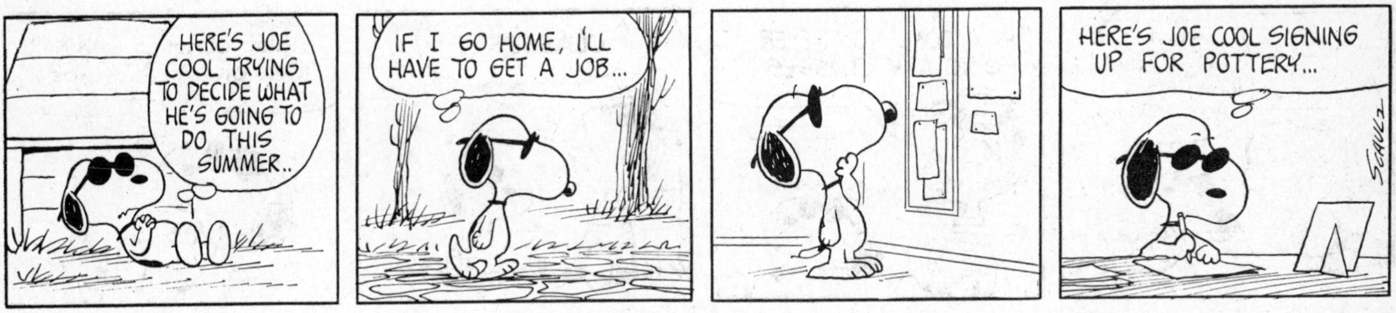
HERE'S JOE COOL TRYING TO DECIDE WHAT HE'S GOING TO DO THIS SUMMER..
IF I GO HOME, I'LL HAVE TO GET A JOB...
HERE'S JOE COOL SIGNING UP FOR POTTERY...
SCHULZ

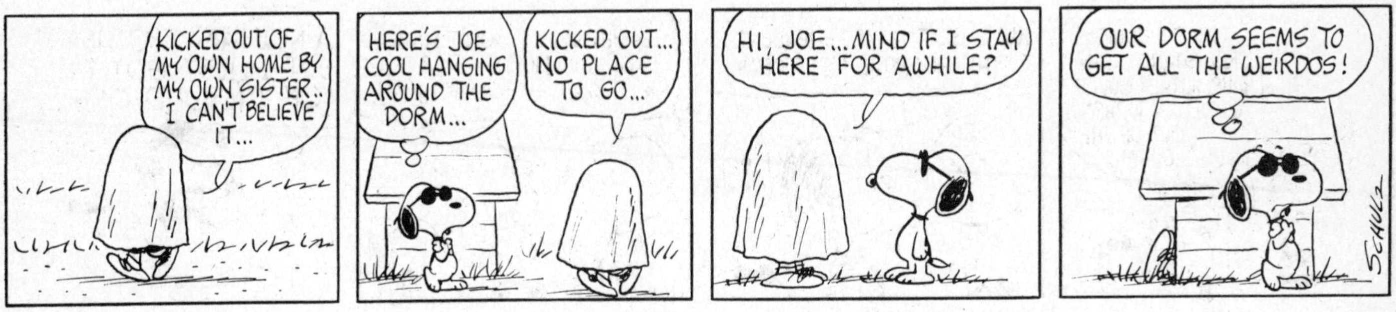
KICKED OUT OF MY OWN HOME BY MY OWN SISTER.. I CAN'T BELIEVE IT...
HERE'S JOE COOL HANGING AROUND THE DORM...
KICKED OUT... NO PLACE TO GO...
HI, JOE... MIND IF I STAY HERE FOR AWHILE?
OUR DORM SEEMS TO GET ALL THE WEIRDOS!
SCHULZ

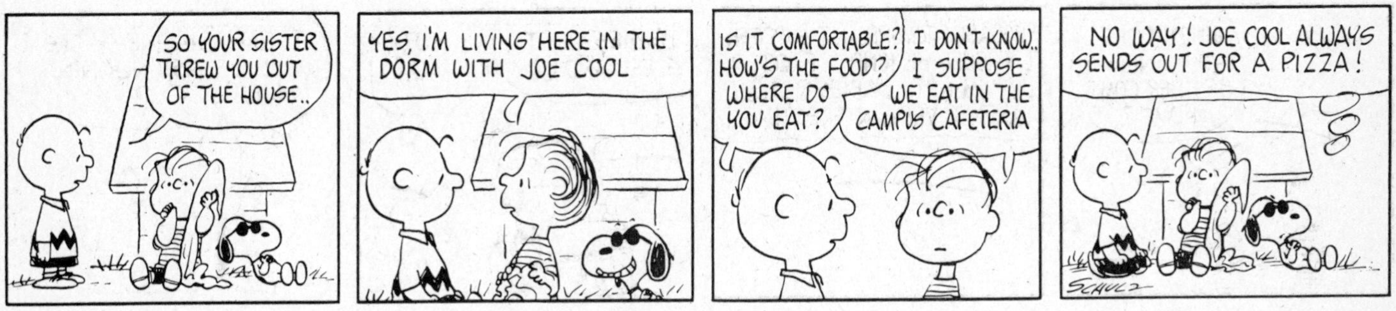
SO YOUR SISTER THREW YOU OUT OF THE HOUSE..
YES, I'M LIVING HERE IN THE DORM WITH JOE COOL
IS IT COMFORTABLE? HOW'S THE FOOD? WHERE DO YOU EAT?
I DON'T KNOW.. I SUPPOSE WE EAT IN THE CAMPUS CAFETERIA
NO WAY! JOE COOL ALWAYS SENDS OUT FOR A PIZZA!
SCHULZ

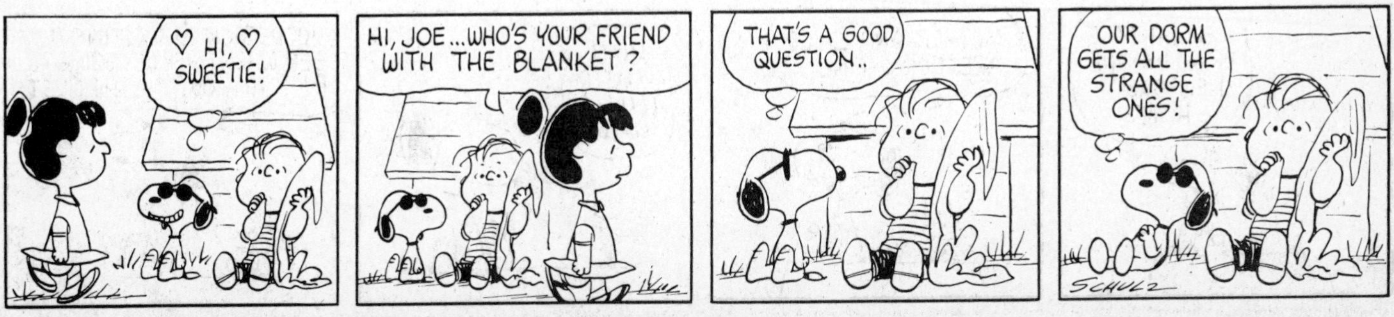
♡ HI, ♡ SWEETIE!
HI, JOE... WHO'S YOUR FRIEND WITH THE BLANKET?
THAT'S A GOOD QUESTION..
OUR DORM GETS ALL THE STRANGE ONES!
SCHULZ

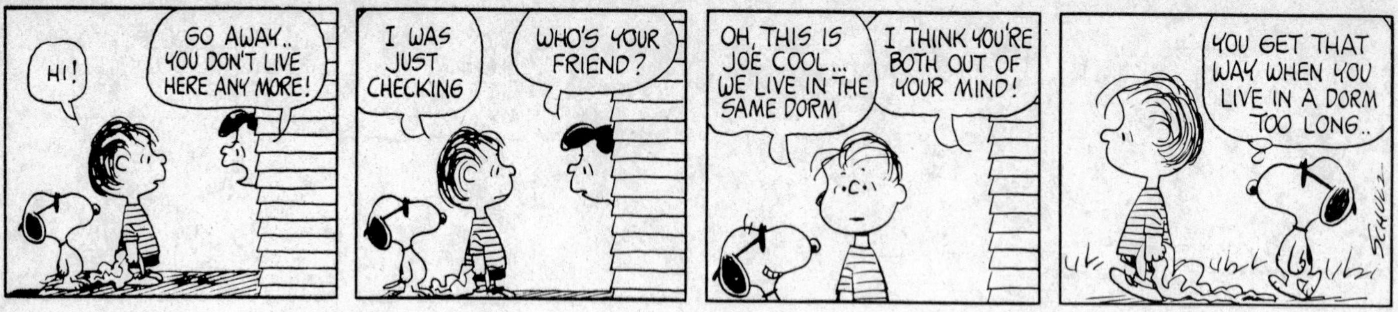
HI!
GO AWAY.. YOU DON'T LIVE HERE ANY MORE!
I WAS JUST CHECKING
WHO'S YOUR FRIEND?
OH, THIS IS JOE COOL... WE LIVE IN THE SAME DORM
I THINK YOU'RE BOTH OUT OF YOUR MIND!
YOU GET THAT WAY WHEN YOU LIVE IN A DORM TOO LONG..
SCHULZ

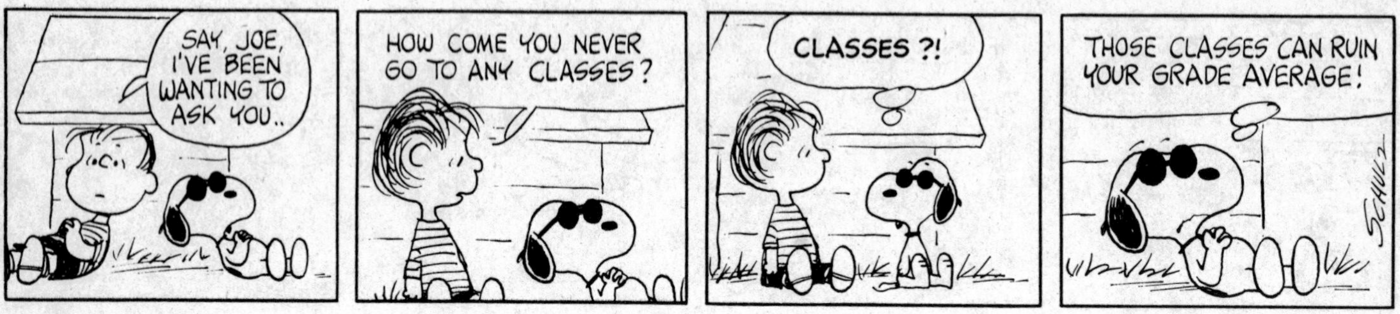
SAY, JOE, I'VE BEEN WANTING TO ASK YOU..
HOW COME YOU NEVER GO TO ANY CLASSES?
CLASSES ?!
THOSE CLASSES CAN RUIN YOUR GRADE AVERAGE!
SCHULZ

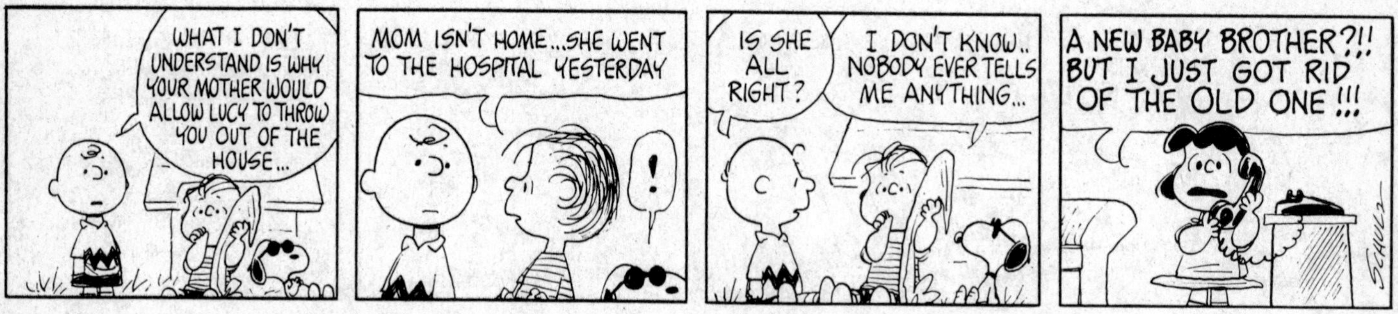
WHAT I DON'T UNDERSTAND IS WHY YOUR MOTHER WOULD ALLOW LUCY TO THROW YOU OUT OF THE HOUSE...
MOM ISN'T HOME...SHE WENT TO THE HOSPITAL YESTERDAY
!
IS SHE ALL RIGHT?
I DON'T KNOW.. NOBODY EVER TELLS ME ANYTHING...
A NEW BABY BROTHER?!! BUT I JUST GOT RID OF THE OLD ONE!!!
SCHULZ

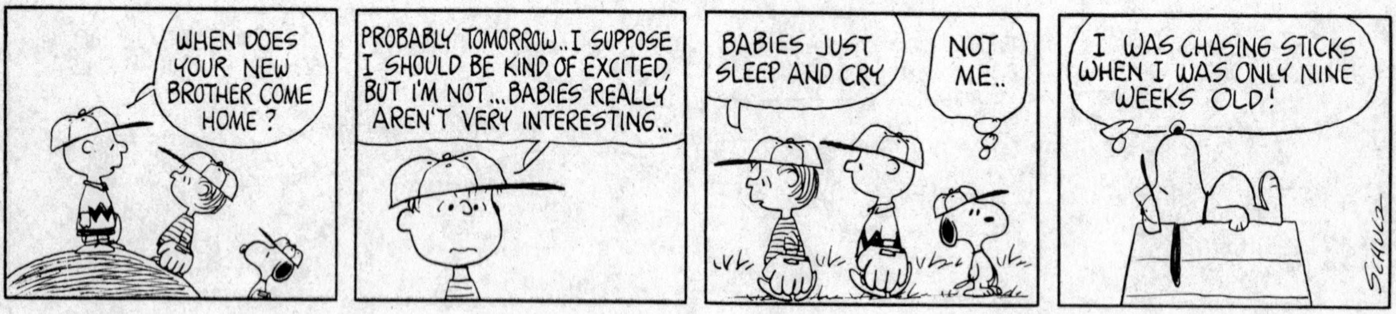
WHEN DOES YOUR NEW BROTHER COME HOME?
PROBABLY TOMORROW..I SUPPOSE I SHOULD BE KIND OF EXCITED, BUT I'M NOT...BABIES REALLY AREN'T VERY INTERESTING...
BABIES JUST SLEEP AND CRY
NOT ME..
I WAS CHASING STICKS WHEN I WAS ONLY NINE WEEKS OLD!
SCHULZ

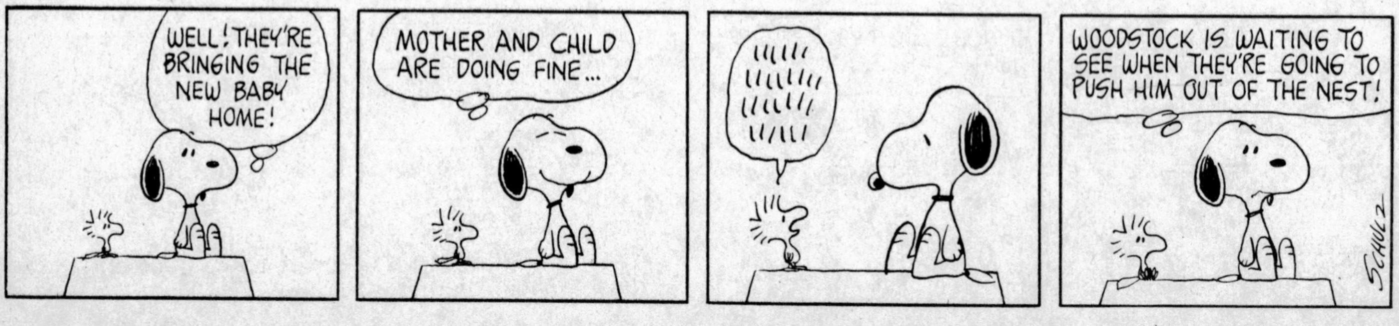
WELL! THEY'RE BRINGING THE NEW BABY HOME!
MOTHER AND CHILD ARE DOING FINE...
WOODSTOCK IS WAITING TO SEE WHEN THEY'RE GOING TO PUSH HIM OUT OF THE NEST!
SCHULZ

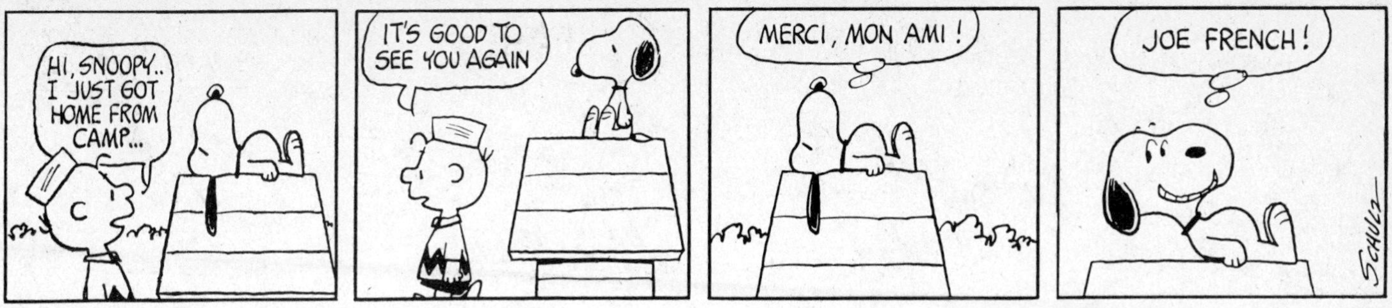
HI, SNOOPY.. I JUST GOT HOME FROM CAMP...
IT'S GOOD TO SEE YOU AGAIN
MERCI, MON AMI!
JOE FRENCH!
SCHULZ

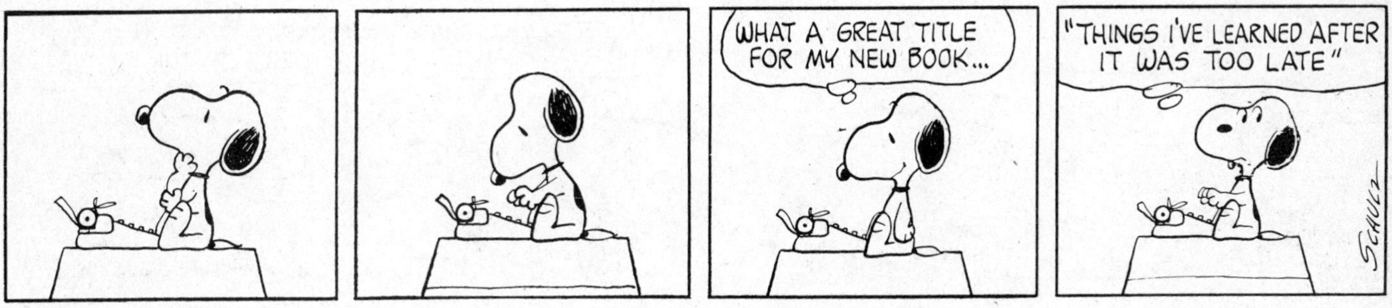
WHAT A GREAT TITLE FOR MY NEW BOOK...
"THINGS I'VE LEARNED AFTER IT WAS TOO LATE"
SCHULZ

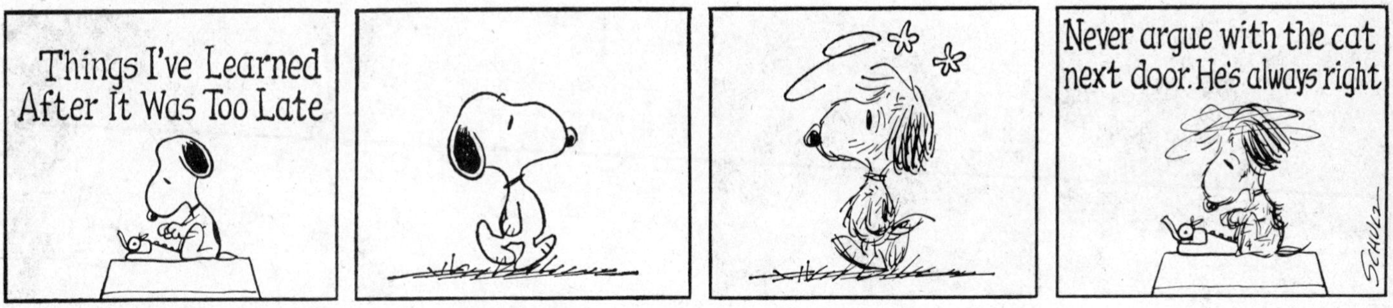
Things I've Learned After It Was Too Late
Never argue with the cat next door. He's always right
SCHULZ

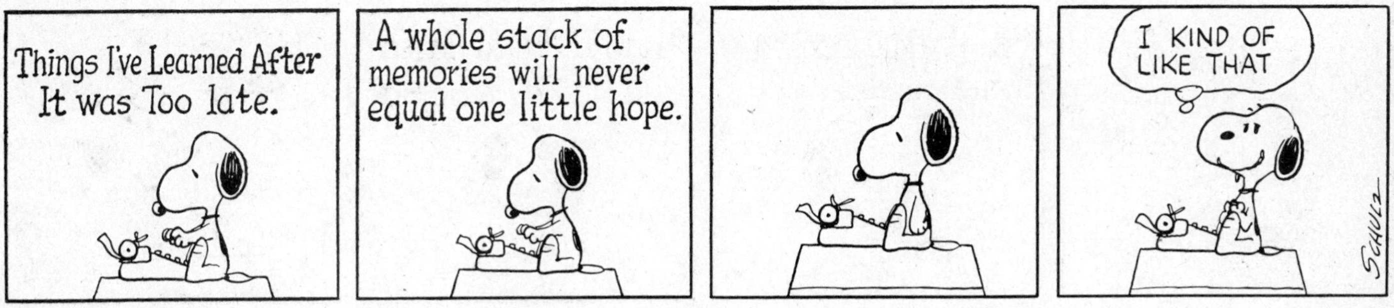
Things I've Learned After It was Too late.
A whole stack of memories will never equal one little hope.
I KIND OF LIKE THAT
SCHULZ

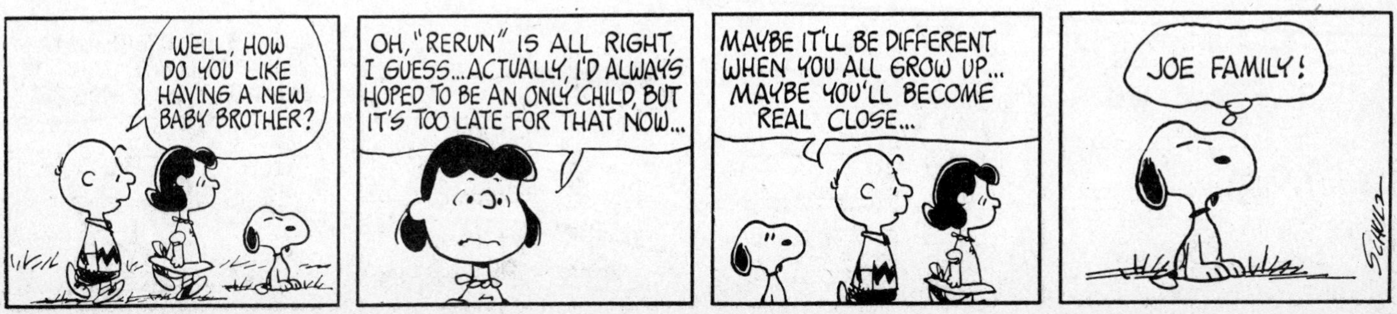
WELL, HOW DO YOU LIKE HAVING A NEW BABY BROTHER?
OH, "RERUN" IS ALL RIGHT, I GUESS...ACTUALLY, I'D ALWAYS HOPED TO BE AN ONLY CHILD, BUT IT'S TOO LATE FOR THAT NOW...
MAYBE IT'LL BE DIFFERENT WHEN YOU ALL GROW UP... MAYBE YOU'LL BECOME REAL CLOSE...
JOE FAMILY!
SCHULZ

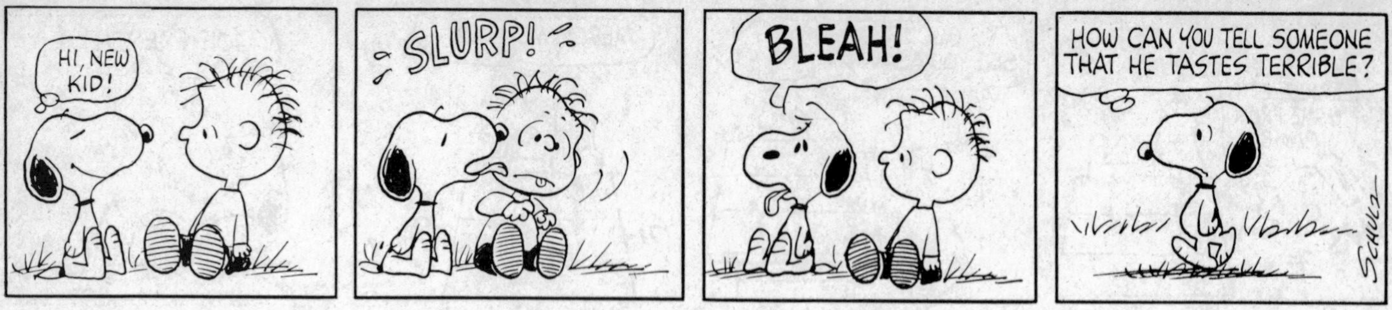
HI, NEW KID!
SLURP!
BLEAH!
HOW CAN YOU TELL SOMEONE THAT HE TASTES TERRIBLE?
SCHULZ

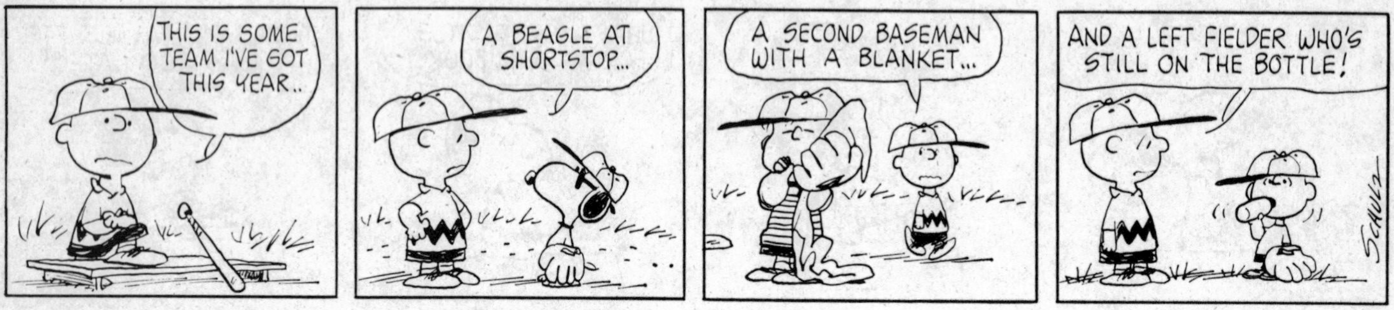
THIS IS SOME TEAM I'VE GOT THIS YEAR..
A BEAGLE AT SHORTSTOP...
A SECOND BASEMAN WITH A BLANKET...
AND A LEFT FIELDER WHO'S STILL ON THE BOTTLE!
SCHULZ

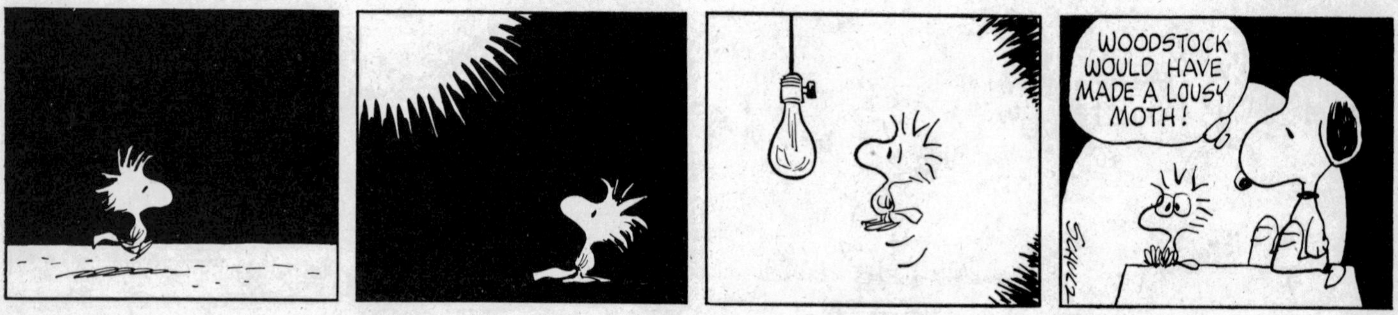
SCHULZ
WOODSTOCK WOULD HAVE MADE A LOUSY MOTH!

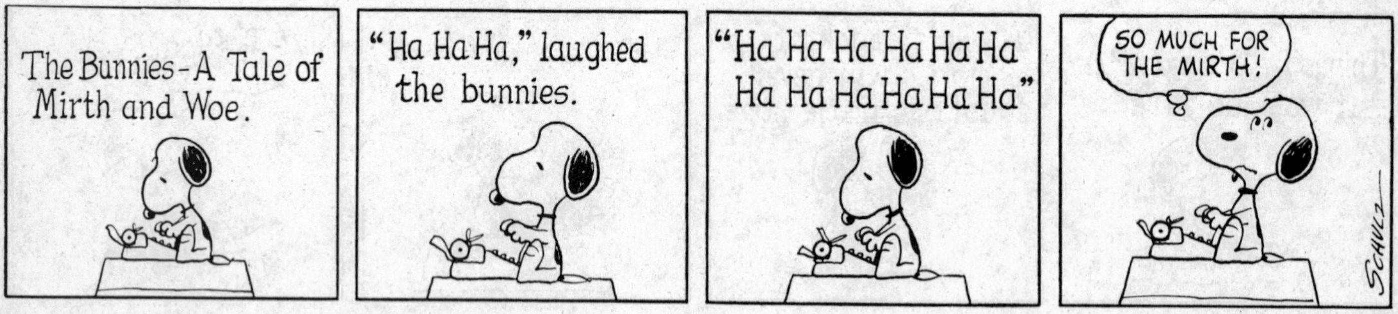
The Bunnies - A Tale of Mirth and Woe.
"Ha Ha Ha," laughed the bunnies.
"Ha Ha Ha Ha Ha Ha Ha Ha Ha Ha Ha Ha"
SO MUCH FOR THE MIRTH!
SCHULZ

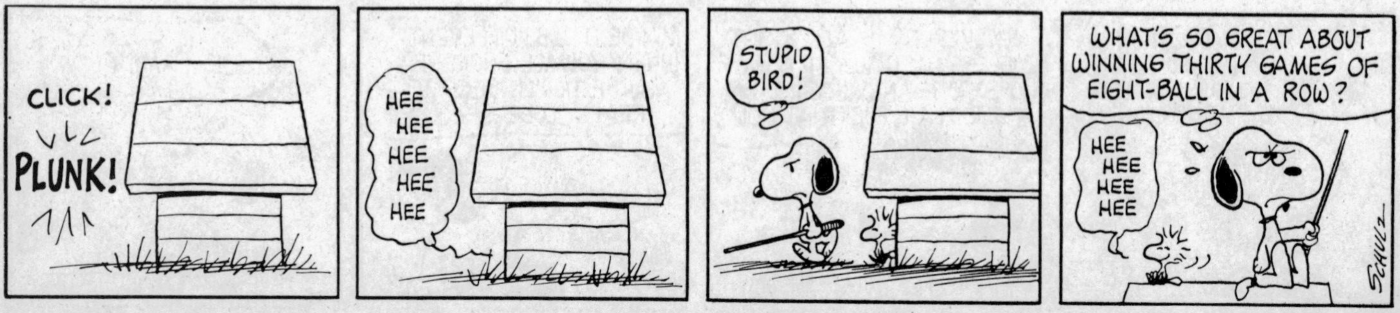
CLICK!
PLUNK!
HEE HEE HEE HEE HEE
STUPID BIRD!
WHAT'S SO GREAT ABOUT WINNING THIRTY GAMES OF EIGHT-BALL IN A ROW?
HEE HEE HEE HEE
SCHULZ

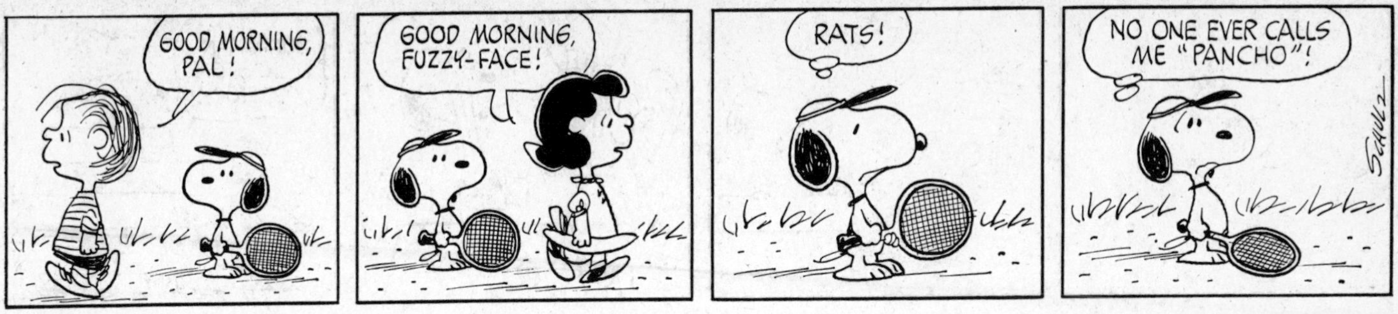
GOOD MORNING, PAL!
GOOD MORNING, FUZZY-FACE!
RATS!
NO ONE EVER CALLS ME "PANCHO"!
SCHULZ

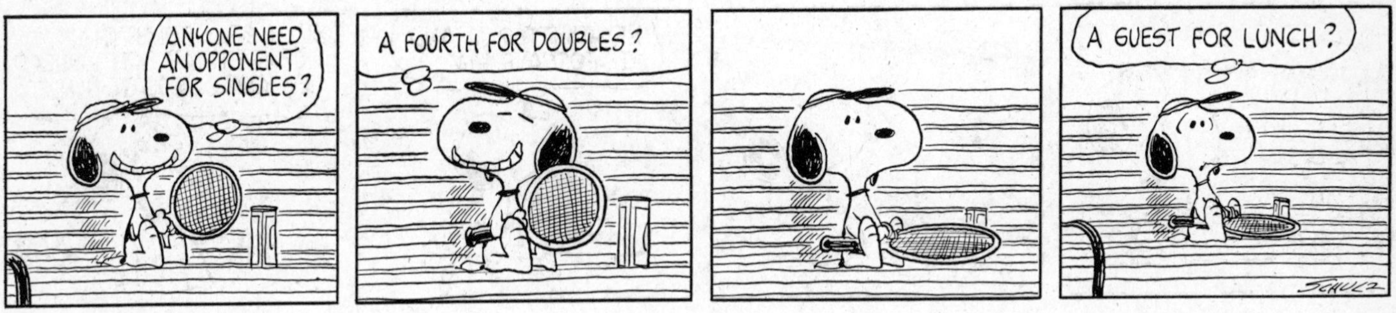
ANYONE NEED AN OPPONENT FOR SINGLES?
A FOURTH FOR DOUBLES?
A GUEST FOR LUNCH?
SCHULZ

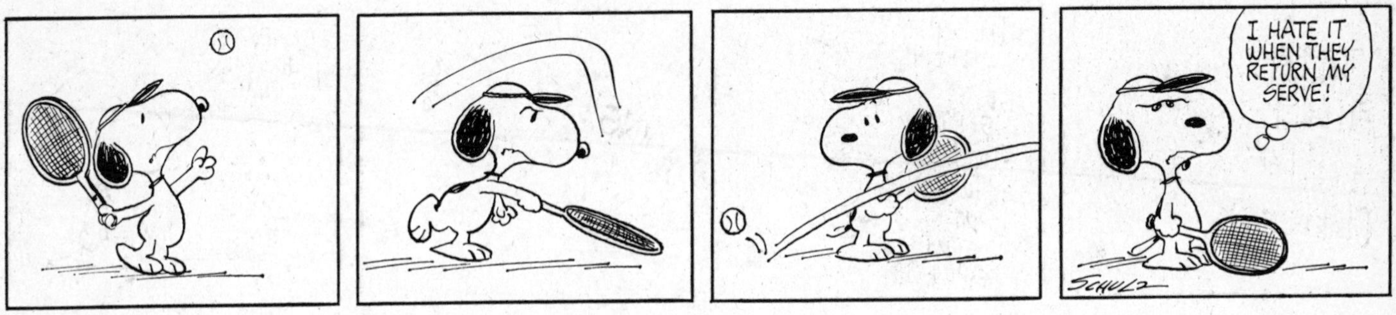
I HATE IT WHEN THEY RETURN MY SERVE!
SCHULZ

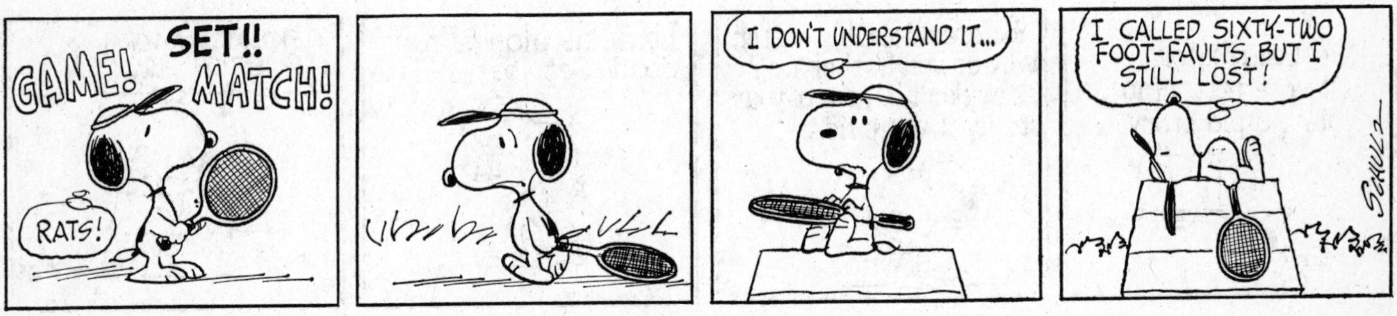
GAME! SET!! MATCH!
RATS!
I DON'T UNDERSTAND IT...
I CALLED SIXTY-TWO FOOT-FAULTS, BUT I STILL LOST!
SCHULZ

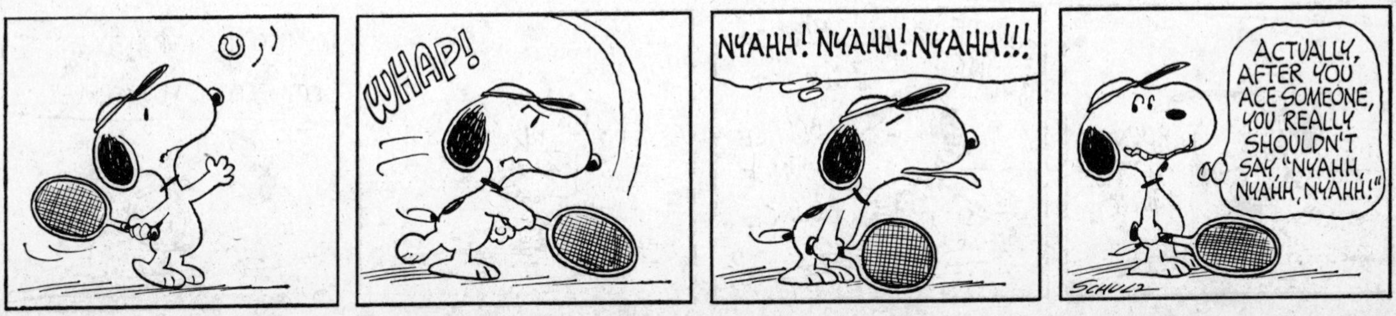
WHAP!
NYAHH! NYAHH! NYAHH!!!
ACTUALLY, AFTER YOU ACE SOMEONE, YOU REALLY SHOULDN'T SAY, "NYAHH, NYAHH, NYAHH!"
SCHULZ

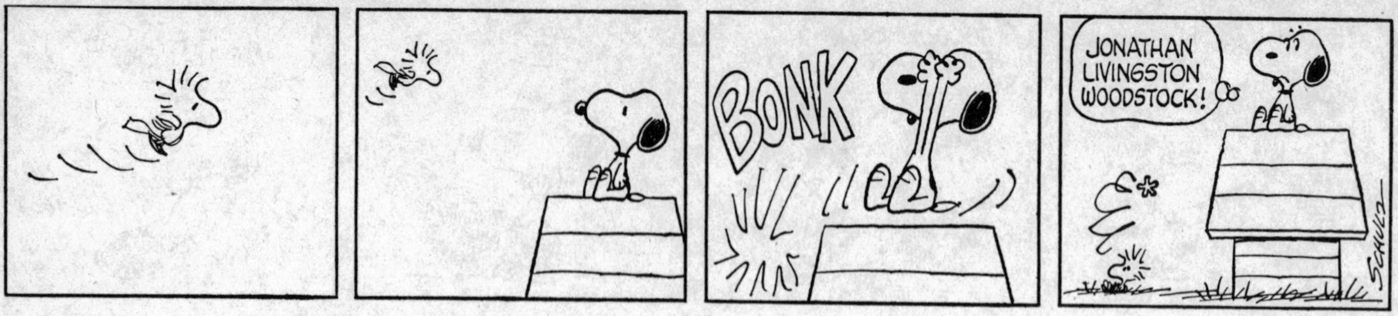
BONK
JONATHAN LIVINGSTON WOODSTOCK!
SCHULZ

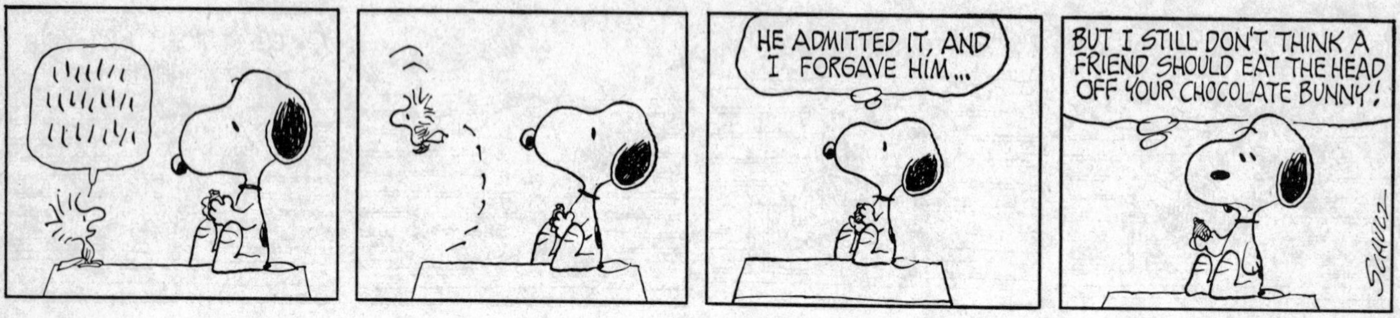
HE ADMITTED IT, AND I FORGAVE HIM...
BUT I STILL DON'T THINK A FRIEND SHOULD EAT THE HEAD OFF YOUR CHOCOLATE BUNNY!
SCHULZ

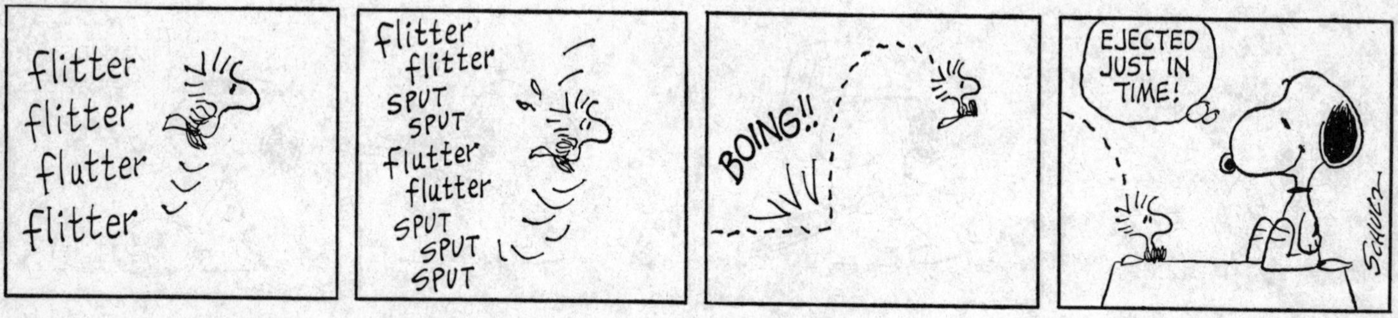
flitter flitter flutter flitter
flitter flitter SPUT SPUT flutter flutter SPUT SPUT SPUT
BOING!!
EJECTED JUST IN TIME!
SCHULZ

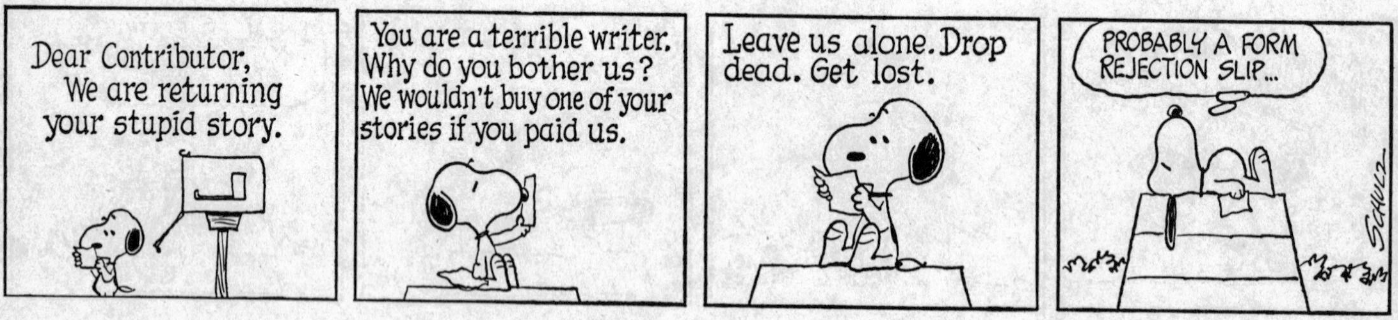
Dear Contributor, We are returning your stupid story.
You are a terrible writer. Why do you bother us? We wouldn't buy one of your stories if you paid us.
Leave us alone. Drop dead. Get lost.
PROBABLY A FORM REJECTION SLIP...
SCHULZ

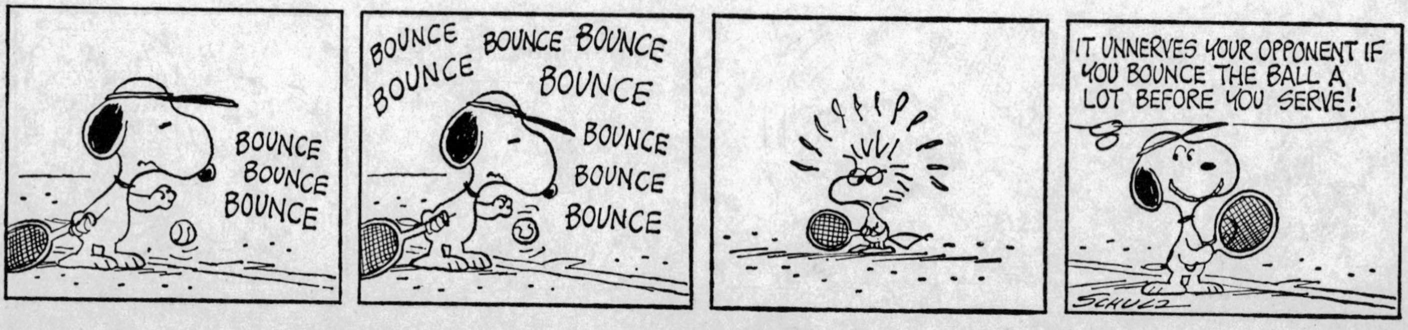
BOUNCE BOUNCE BOUNCE
BOUNCE BOUNCE BOUNCE BOUNCE BOUNCE BOUNCE BOUNCE BOUNCE
IT UNNERVES YOUR OPPONENT IF YOU BOUNCE THE BALL A LOT BEFORE YOU SERVE!
SCHULZ

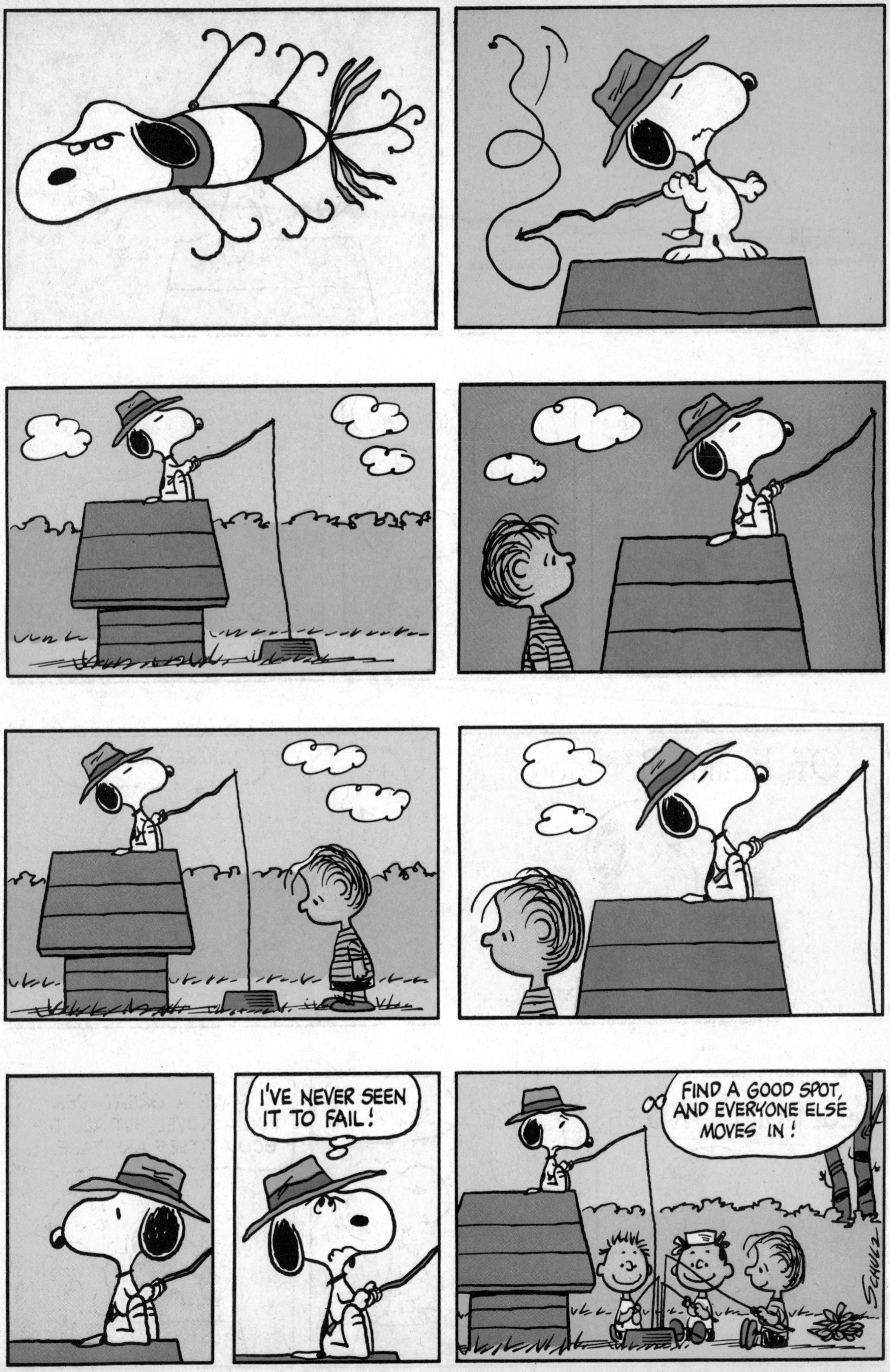
I'VE NEVER SEEN IT TO FAIL!
FIND A GOOD SPOT, AND EVERYONE ELSE MOVES IN!
SCHULZ

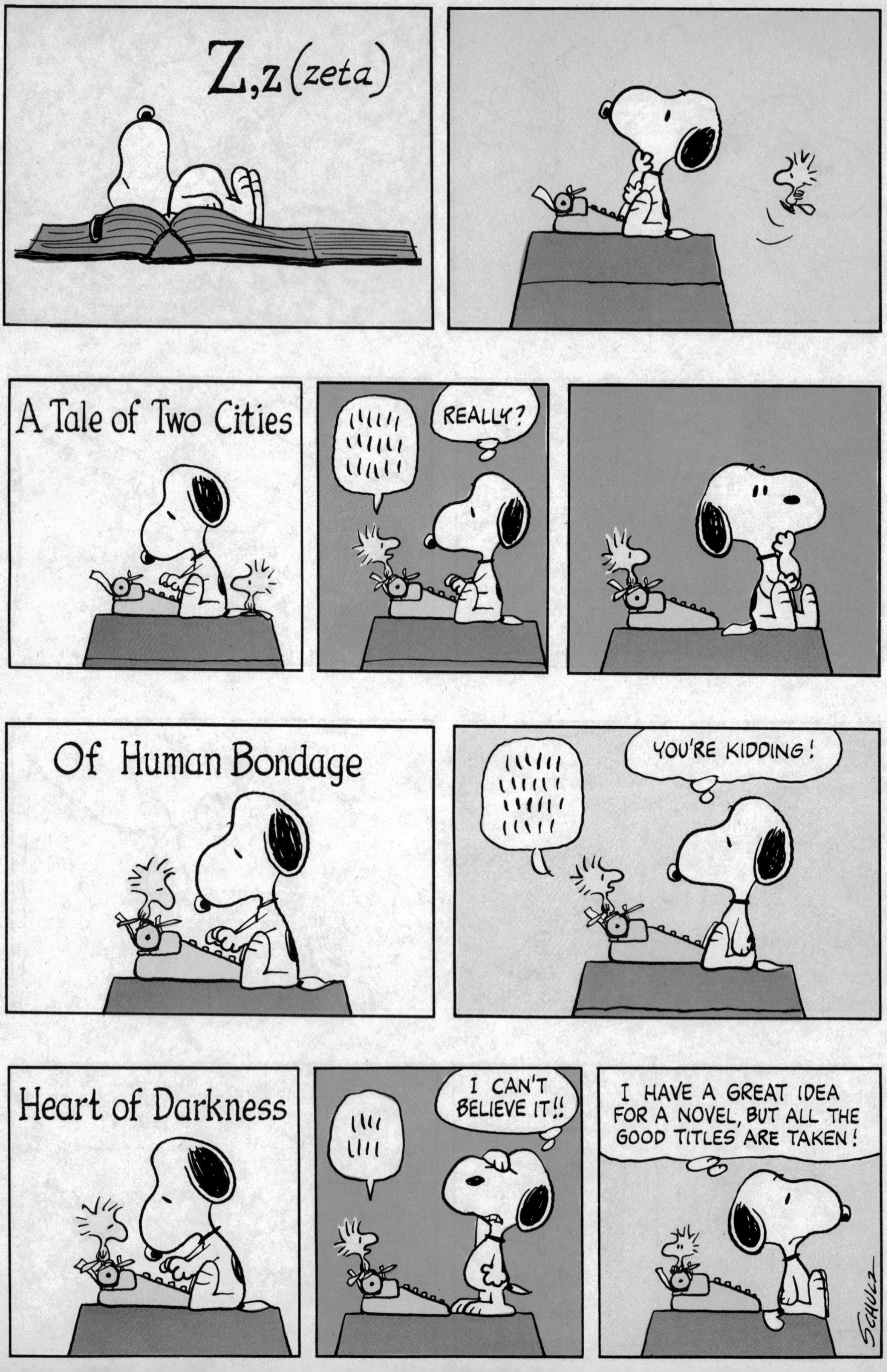

Z,z (zeta)
A Tale of Two Cities
REALLY?
Of Human Bondage
YOU'RE KIDDING!
Heart of Darkness
I CAN'T BELIEVE IT!!
I HAVE A GREAT IDEA FOR A NOVEL, BUT ALL THE GOOD TITLES ARE TAKEN!
SCHULZ

The last car drove away. It began to rain.

And so our hero's life ended as it had begun... a disaster.

"I never got any breaks," he had always complained.

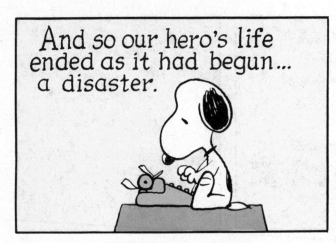

He had wanted to be rich. He died poor. He wanted friends. He died friendless.

He wanted to be loved. He died unloved. He wanted laughter. He found only tears.

He wanted applause. He received boos. He wanted fame. He found only obscurity. He wanted answers. He found only questions.

I'M HAVING A HARD TIME ENDING THIS..

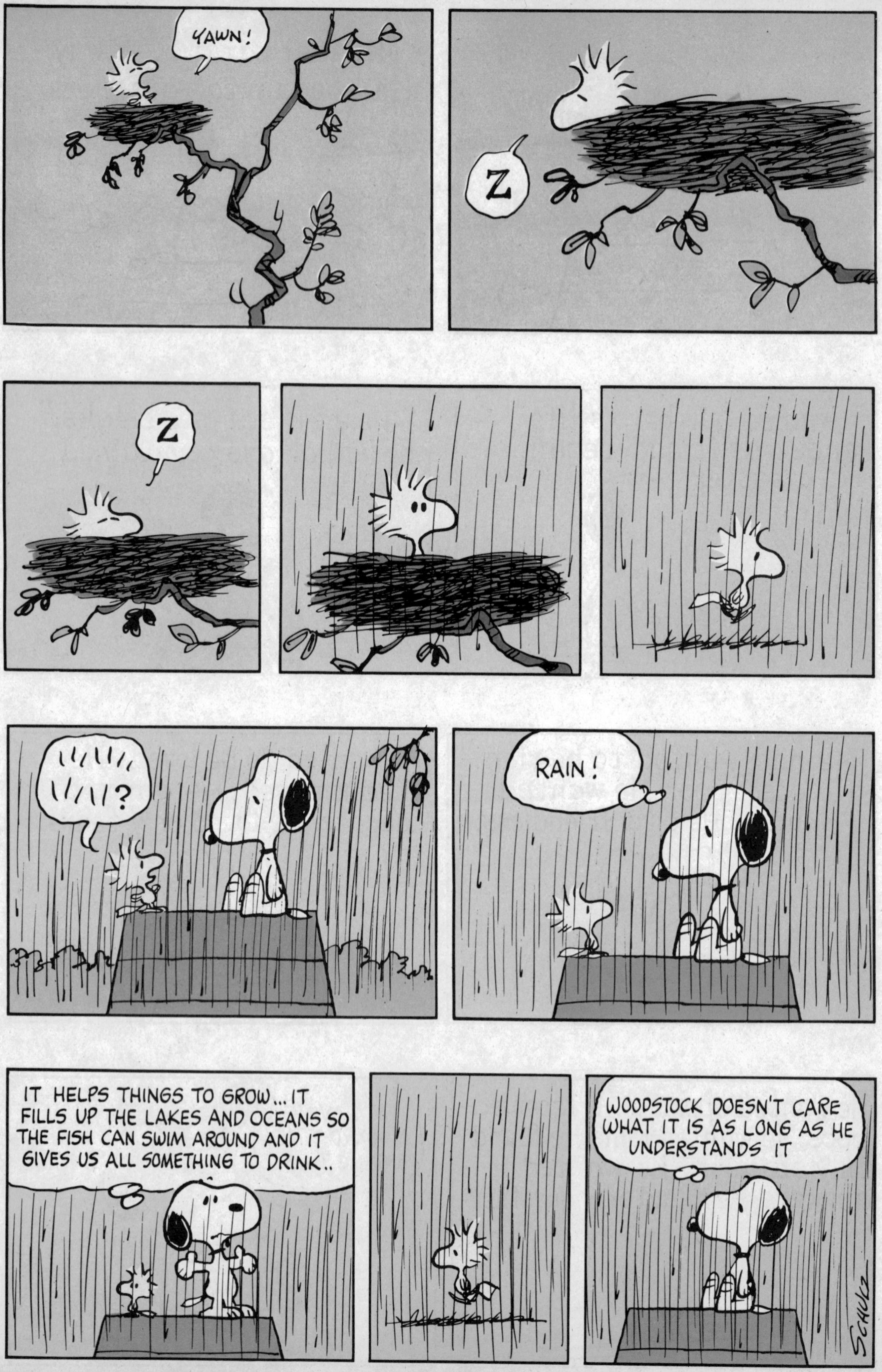
YAWN!
Z
Z
RAIN!
IT HELPS THINGS TO GROW... IT FILLS UP THE LAKES AND OCEANS SO THE FISH CAN SWIM AROUND AND IT GIVES US ALL SOMETHING TO DRINK..
WOODSTOCK DOESN'T CARE WHAT IT IS AS LONG AS HE UNDERSTANDS IT
SCHULZ

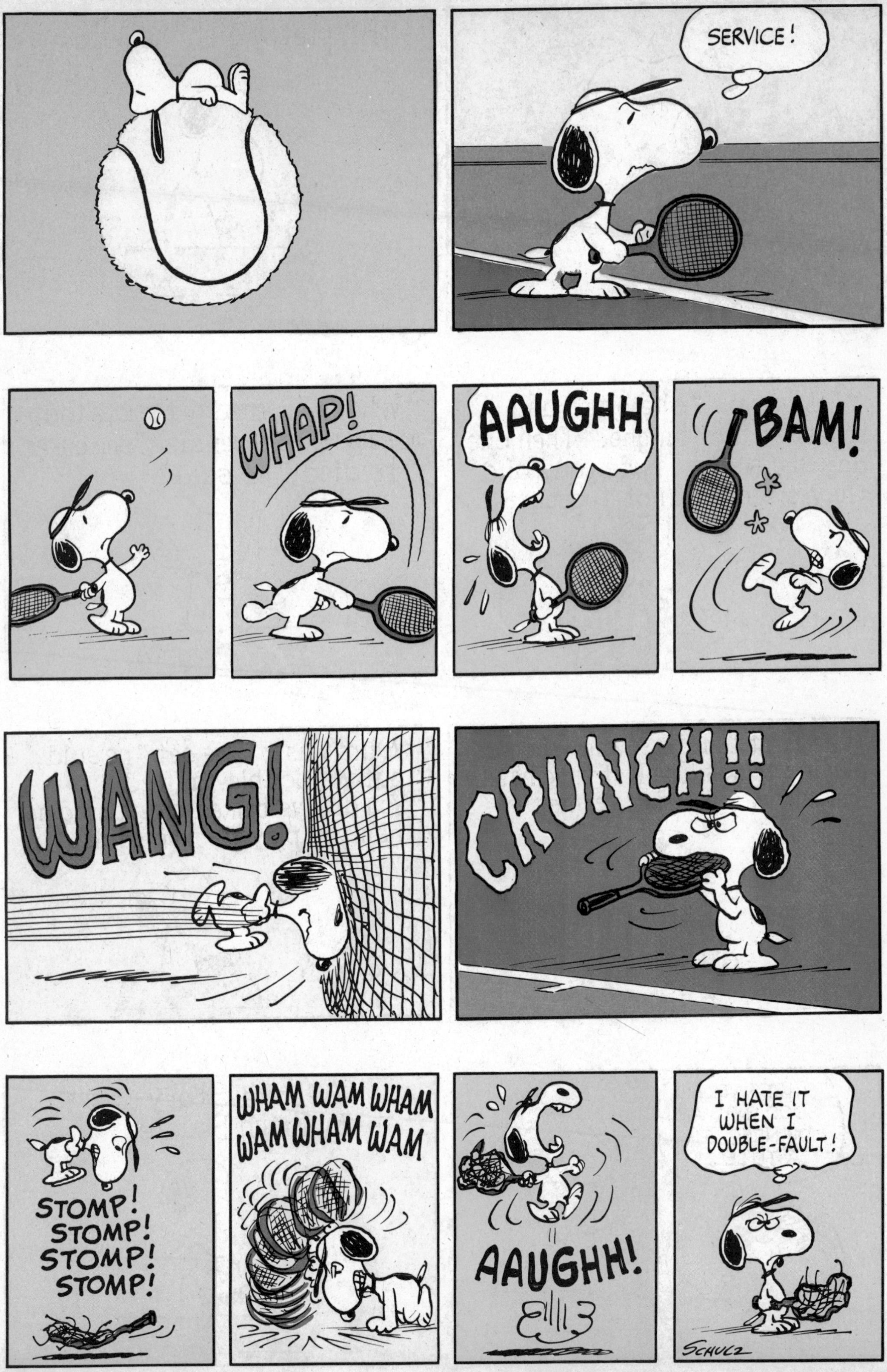
SERVICE!
WHAP!
AAUGHH
BAM!
WANG!
CRUNCH!!
STOMP! STOMP! STOMP! STOMP!
WHAM WAM WHAM WAM WHAM WAM
AAUGHH!
I HATE IT WHEN I DOUBLE-FAULT!
SCHULZ

"Hi, pretty girl," he said.

"I love you," she said, and together they laughed. Then one day she said, "I hate you," and they cried. But not together.

"What happened to the love that we said would never die?" she asked. "It died," he said.

The first time he saw her she was playing tennis. The last time he saw her she was playing tennis.

"Ours was a Love set," he said, "but we double-faulted." "You always talked a better game than you played," she said.

THAT'S VERY GOOD...NOW ALL YOU NEED IS A TITLE...

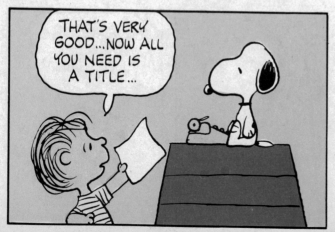

A Love Story by Erich Beagle

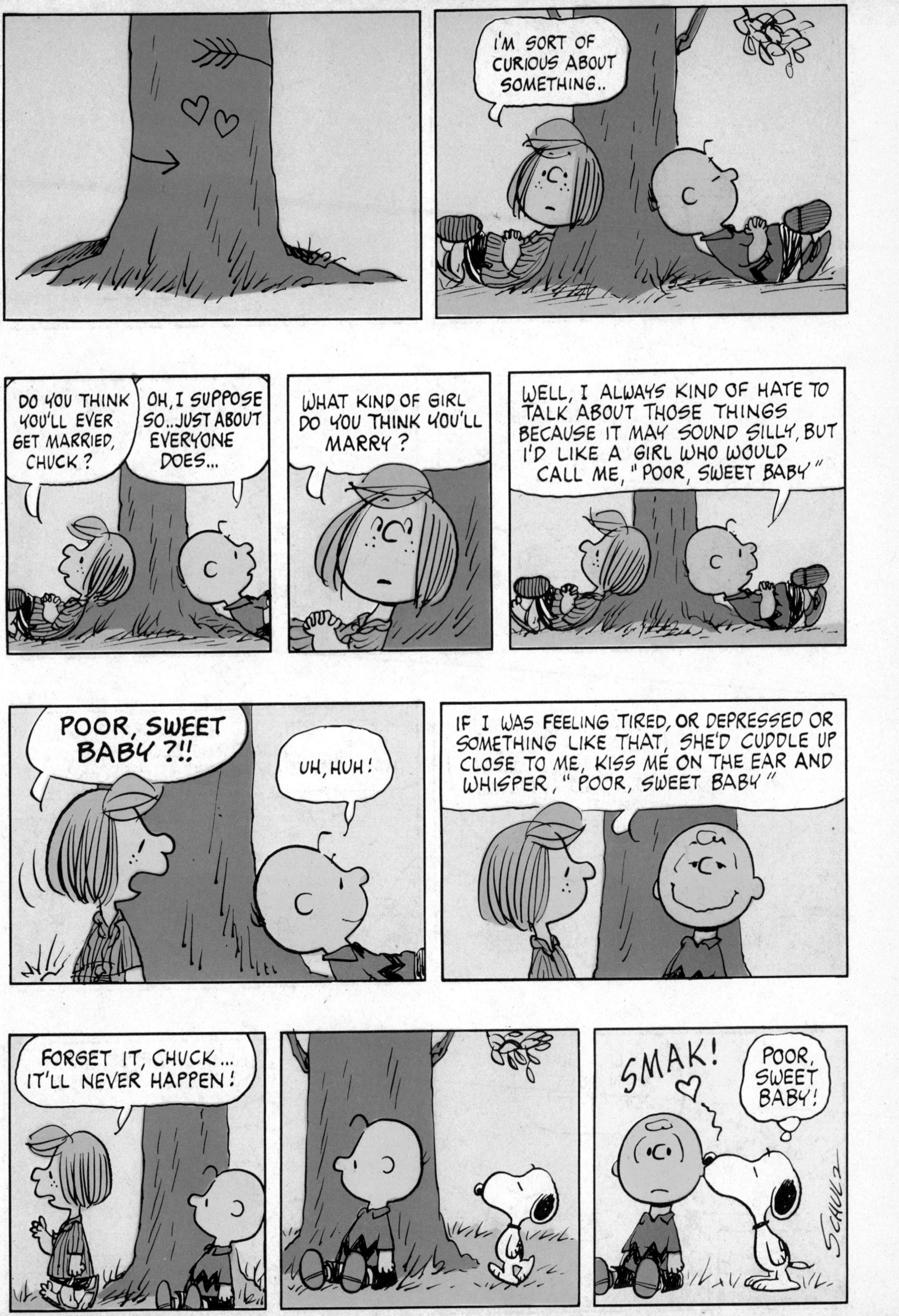
I'M SORT OF CURIOUS ABOUT SOMETHING..
DO YOU THINK YOU'LL EVER GET MARRIED, CHUCK?
OH, I SUPPOSE SO...JUST ABOUT EVERYONE DOES...
WHAT KIND OF GIRL DO YOU THINK YOU'LL MARRY?
WELL, I ALWAYS KIND OF HATE TO TALK ABOUT THOSE THINGS BECAUSE IT MAY SOUND SILLY, BUT I'D LIKE A GIRL WHO WOULD CALL ME, "POOR, SWEET BABY"
POOR, SWEET BABY?!!
UH, HUH!
IF I WAS FEELING TIRED, OR DEPRESSED OR SOMETHING LIKE THAT, SHE'D CUDDLE UP CLOSE TO ME, KISS ME ON THE EAR AND WHISPER, "POOR, SWEET BABY"
FORGET IT, CHUCK... IT'LL NEVER HAPPEN!
SMAK!
POOR, SWEET BABY!
SCHULZ

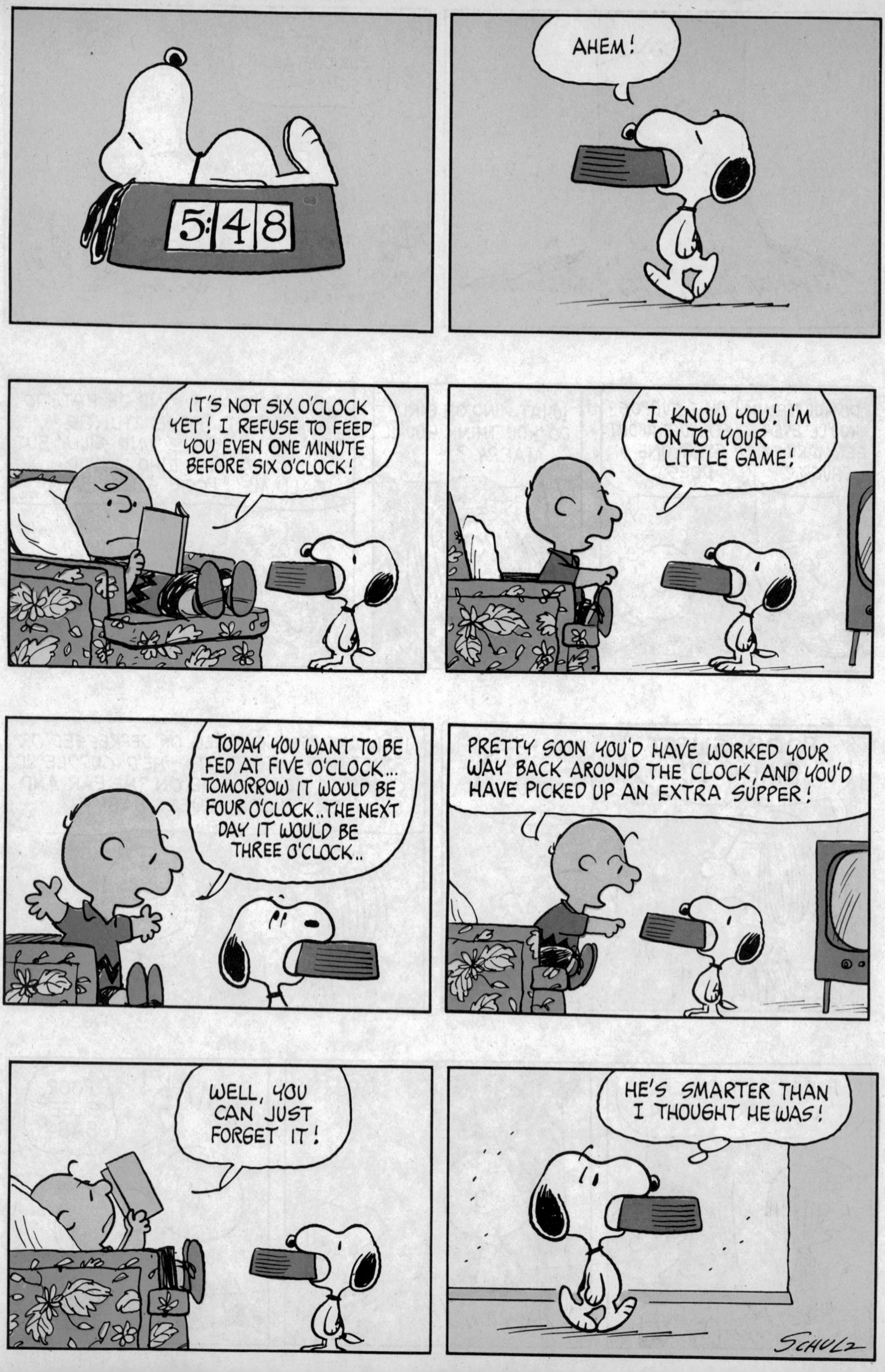
5:48
AHEM!
IT'S NOT SIX O'CLOCK YET! I REFUSE TO FEED YOU EVEN ONE MINUTE BEFORE SIX O'CLOCK!
I KNOW YOU! I'M ON TO YOUR LITTLE GAME!
TODAY YOU WANT TO BE FED AT FIVE O'CLOCK... TOMORROW IT WOULD BE FOUR O'CLOCK.. THE NEXT DAY IT WOULD BE THREE O'CLOCK..
PRETTY SOON YOU'D HAVE WORKED YOUR WAY BACK AROUND THE CLOCK, AND YOU'D HAVE PICKED UP AN EXTRA SUPPER!
WELL, YOU CAN JUST FORGET IT!
HE'S SMARTER THAN I THOUGHT HE WAS!
SCHULZ

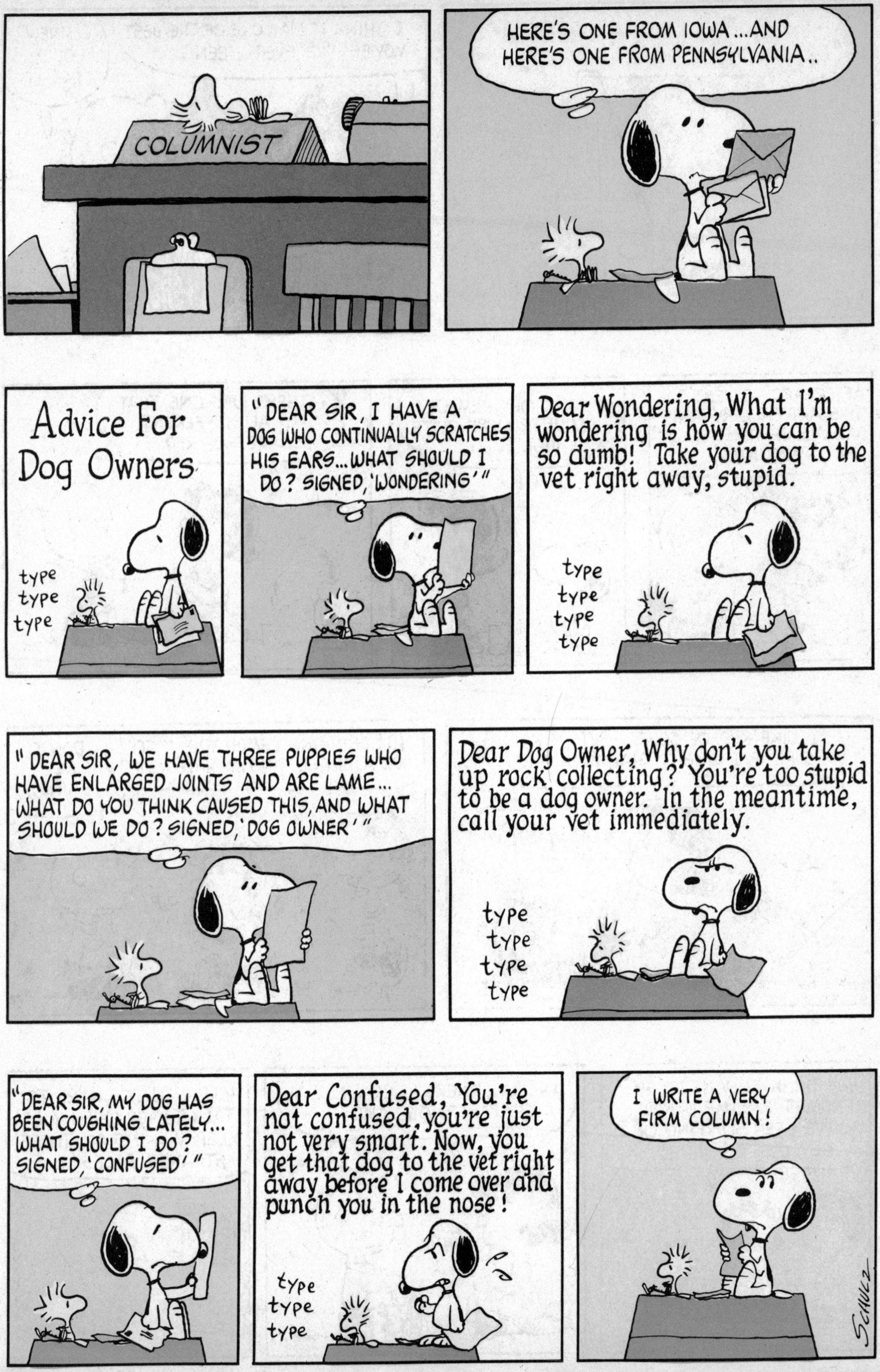
COLUMNIST
HERE'S ONE FROM IOWA ... AND HERE'S ONE FROM PENNSYLVANIA ..
Advice For Dog Owners
type type type
"DEAR SIR, I HAVE A DOG WHO CONTINUALLY SCRATCHES HIS EARS... WHAT SHOULD I DO? SIGNED, 'WONDERING'"
Dear Wondering, What I'm wondering is how you can be so dumb! Take your dog to the vet right away, stupid.
type type type type
"DEAR SIR, WE HAVE THREE PUPPIES WHO HAVE ENLARGED JOINTS AND ARE LAME... WHAT DO YOU THINK CAUSED THIS, AND WHAT SHOULD WE DO? SIGNED, 'DOG OWNER'"
Dear Dog Owner, Why don't you take up rock collecting? You're too stupid to be a dog owner. In the meantime, call your vet immediately.
type type type type
"DEAR SIR, MY DOG HAS BEEN COUGHING LATELY... WHAT SHOULD I DO? SIGNED, 'CONFUSED'"
Dear Confused, You're not confused, you're just not very smart. Now, you get that dog to the vet right away before I come over and punch you in the nose!
type type type
I WRITE A VERY FIRM COLUMN!
SCHULZ

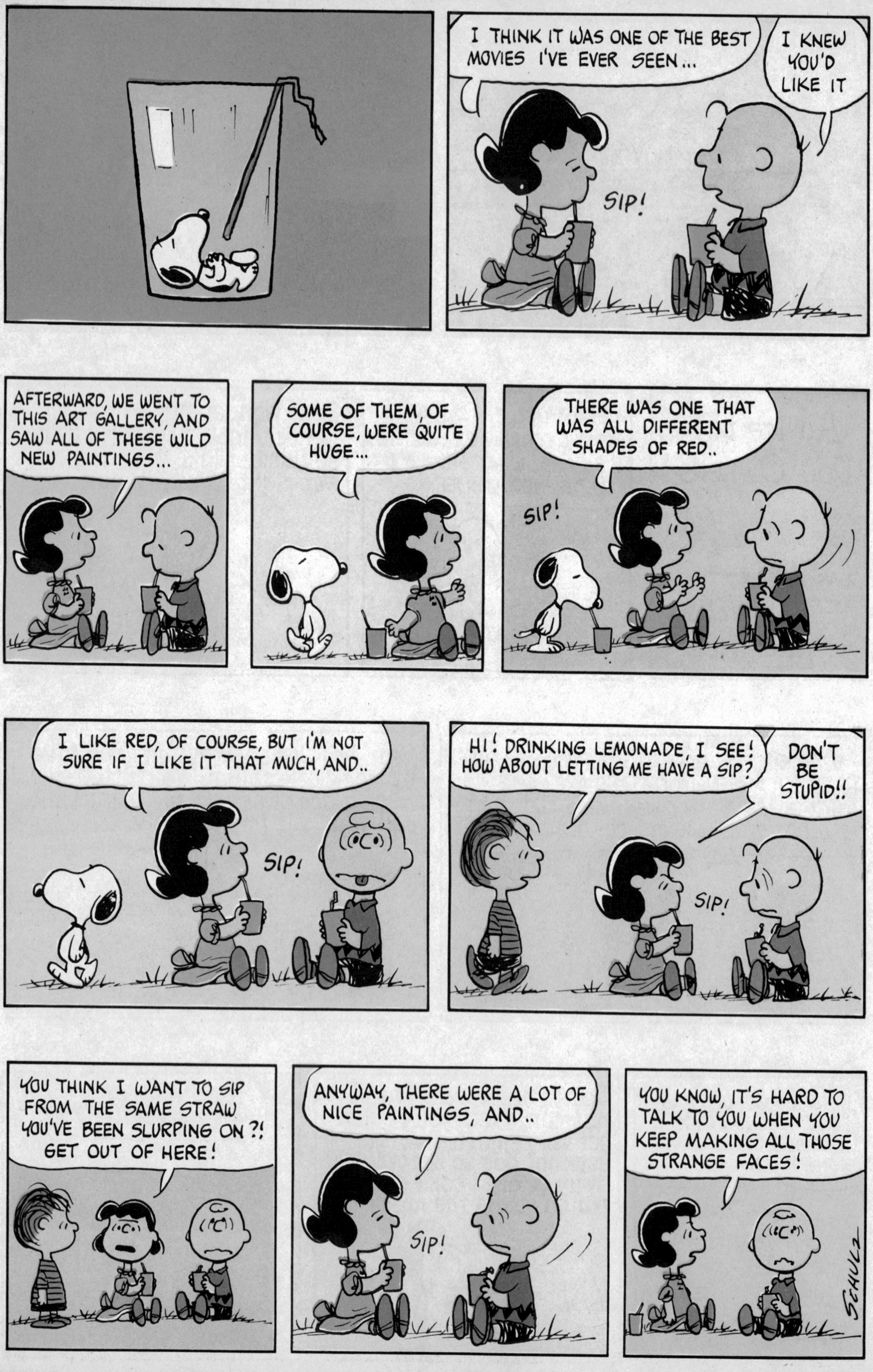

I THINK IT WAS ONE OF THE BEST MOVIES I'VE EVER SEEN...
I KNEW YOU'D LIKE IT
SIP!
AFTERWARD, WE WENT TO THIS ART GALLERY, AND SAW ALL OF THESE WILD NEW PAINTINGS...
SOME OF THEM, OF COURSE, WERE QUITE HUGE...
THERE WAS ONE THAT WAS ALL DIFFERENT SHADES OF RED..
SIP!
I LIKE RED, OF COURSE, BUT I'M NOT SURE IF I LIKE IT THAT MUCH, AND..
SIP!
HI! DRINKING LEMONADE, I SEE! HOW ABOUT LETTING ME HAVE A SIP?
DON'T BE STUPID!!
SIP!
YOU THINK I WANT TO SIP FROM THE SAME STRAW YOU'VE BEEN SLURPING ON ?! GET OUT OF HERE!
ANYWAY, THERE WERE A LOT OF NICE PAINTINGS, AND..
SIP!
YOU KNOW, IT'S HARD TO TALK TO YOU WHEN YOU KEEP MAKING ALL THOSE STRANGE FACES!
SCHULZ

I SAW A MOVIE RECENTLY ABOUT A BOY AND HIS DOG

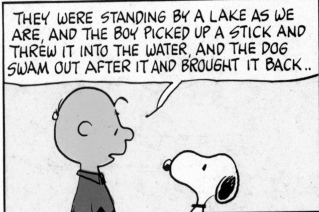

THEY WERE STANDING BY A LAKE AS WE ARE, AND THE BOY PICKED UP A STICK AND THREW IT INTO THE WATER, AND THE DOG SWAM OUT AFTER IT AND BROUGHT IT BACK..

I'M GOING TO HAVE TO STOP WATCHING THOSE MOVIES

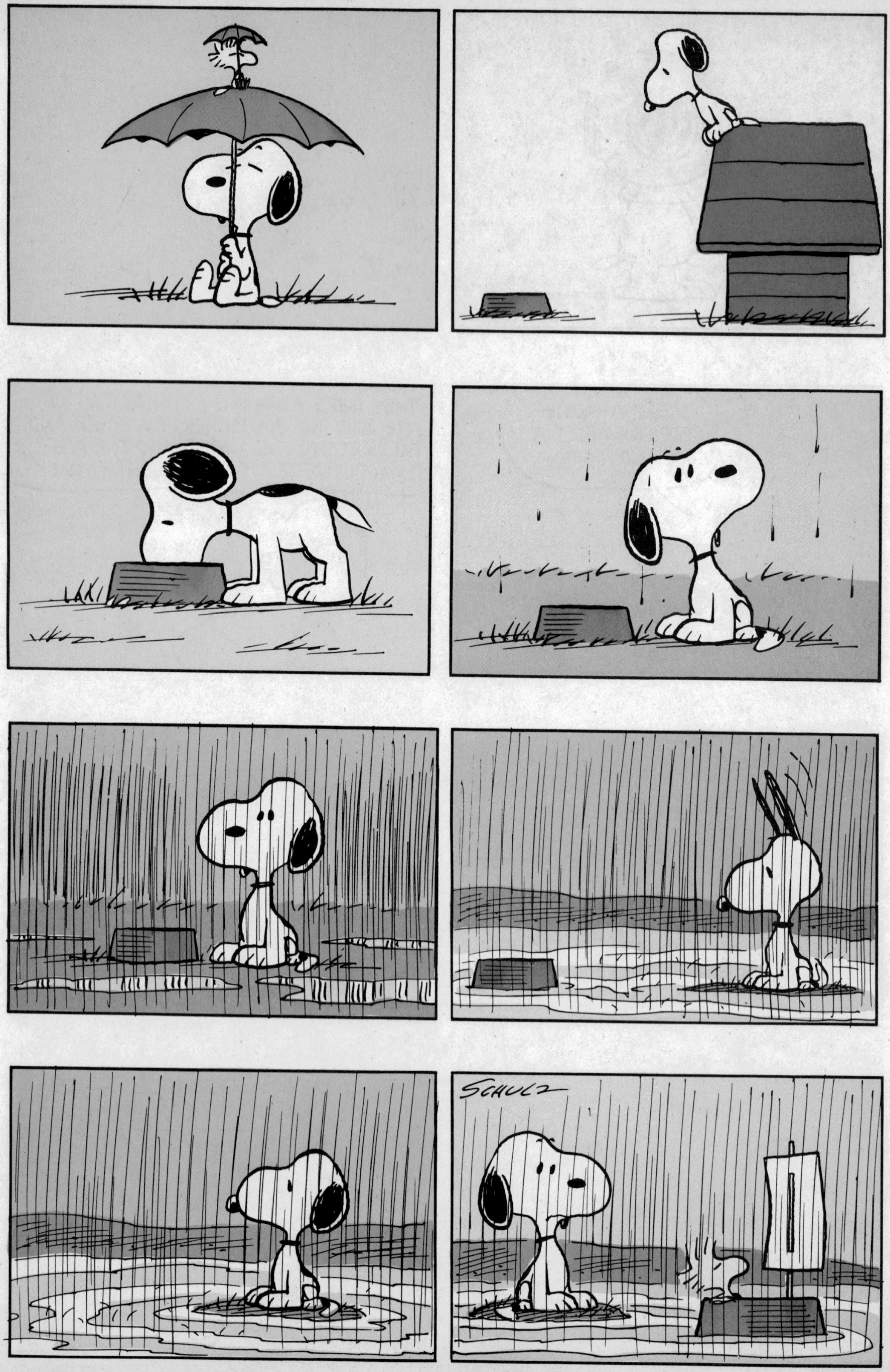
SCHULZ

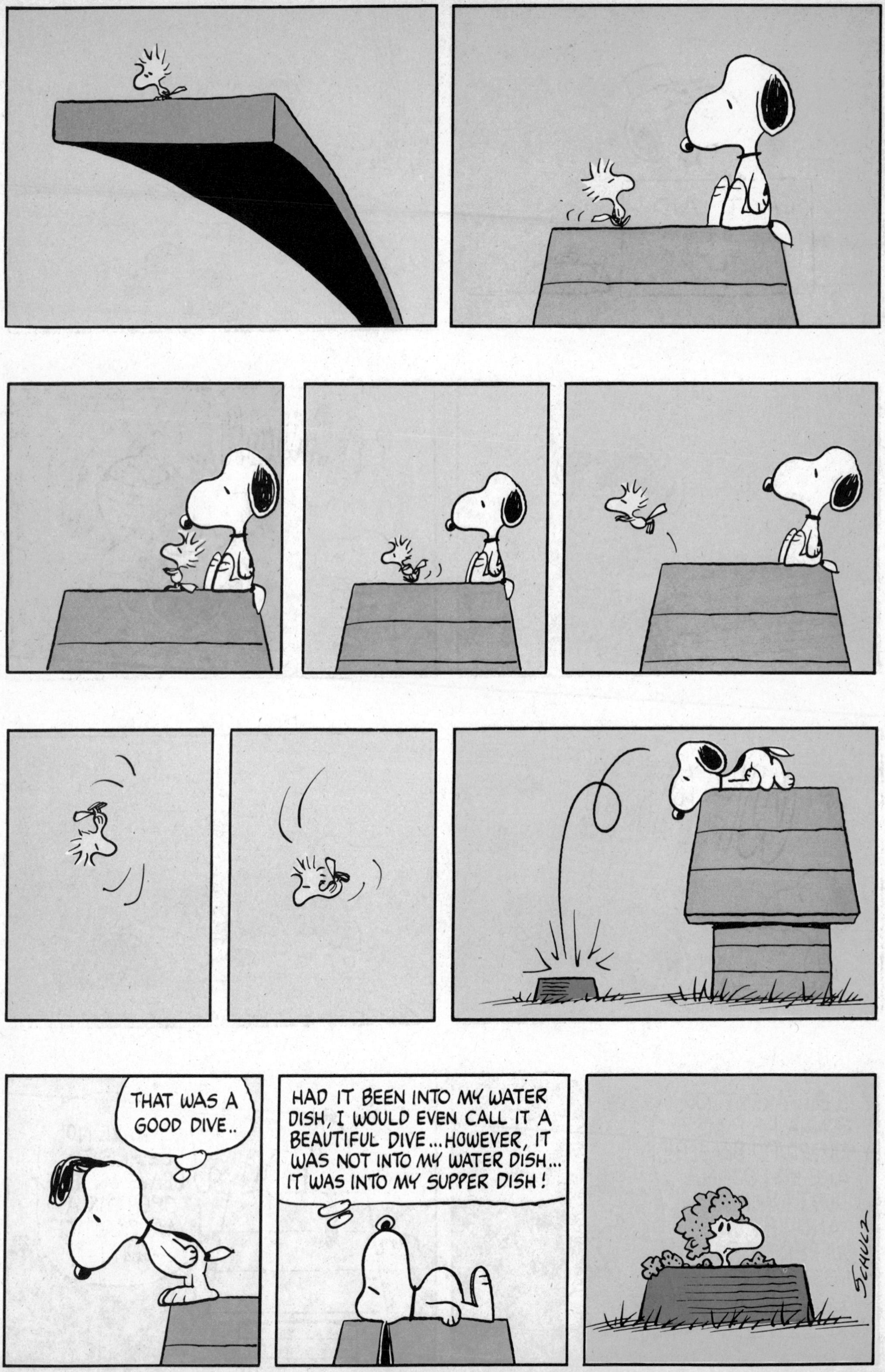
THAT WAS A GOOD DIVE..
HAD IT BEEN INTO MY WATER DISH, I WOULD EVEN CALL IT A BEAUTIFUL DIVE...HOWEVER, IT WAS NOT INTO MY WATER DISH... IT WAS INTO MY SUPPER DISH!
SCHULZ

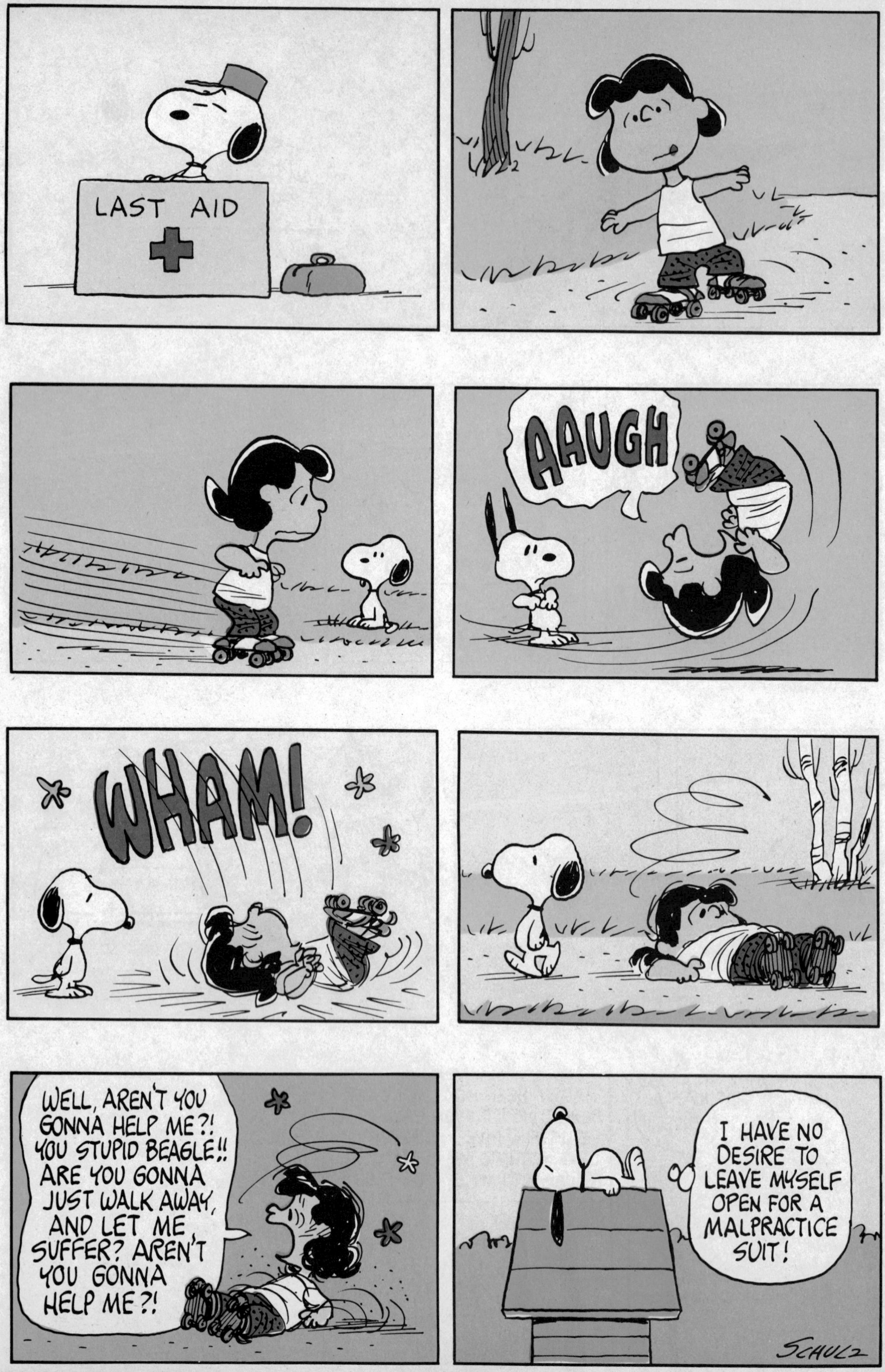

LAST AID
AAUGH
WHAM!
WELL, AREN'T YOU GONNA HELP ME?! YOU STUPID BEAGLE!! ARE YOU GONNA JUST WALK AWAY, AND LET ME SUFFER? AREN'T YOU GONNA HELP ME?!
I HAVE NO DESIRE TO LEAVE MYSELF OPEN FOR A MALPRACTICE SUIT!
SCHULZ

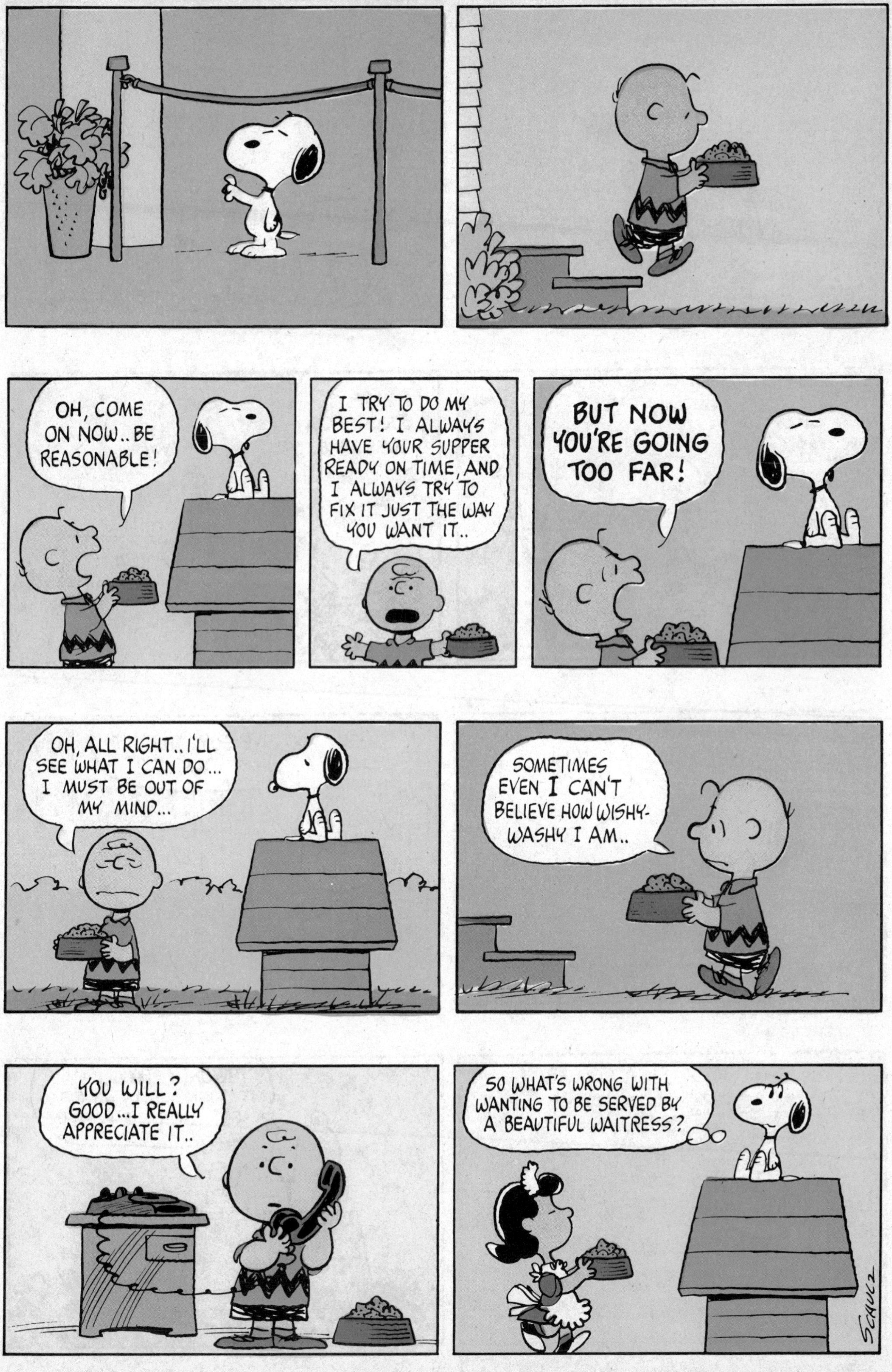
OH, COME ON NOW.. BE REASONABLE!
I TRY TO DO MY BEST! I ALWAYS HAVE YOUR SUPPER READY ON TIME, AND I ALWAYS TRY TO FIX IT JUST THE WAY YOU WANT IT..
BUT NOW YOU'RE GOING TOO FAR!
OH, ALL RIGHT.. I'LL SEE WHAT I CAN DO... I MUST BE OUT OF MY MIND...
SOMETIMES EVEN I CAN'T BELIEVE HOW WISHY-WASHY I AM..
YOU WILL? GOOD...I REALLY APPRECIATE IT..
SO WHAT'S WRONG WITH WANTING TO BE SERVED BY A BEAUTIFUL WAITRESS?
SCHULZ

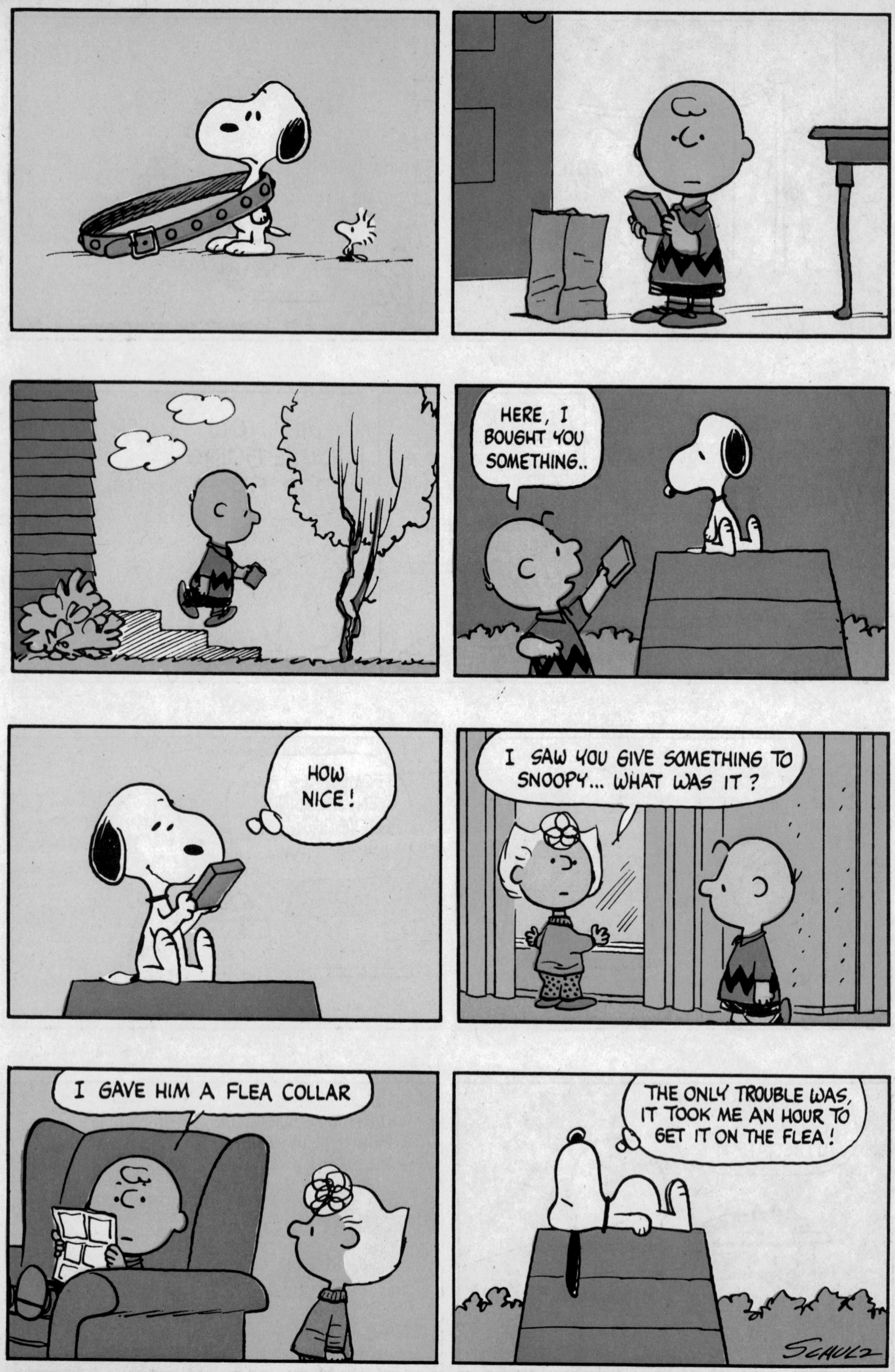
HERE, I BOUGHT YOU SOMETHING..
HOW NICE!
I SAW YOU GIVE SOMETHING TO SNOOPY... WHAT WAS IT ?
I GAVE HIM A FLEA COLLAR
THE ONLY TROUBLE WAS, IT TOOK ME AN HOUR TO GET IT ON THE FLEA!
SCHULZ

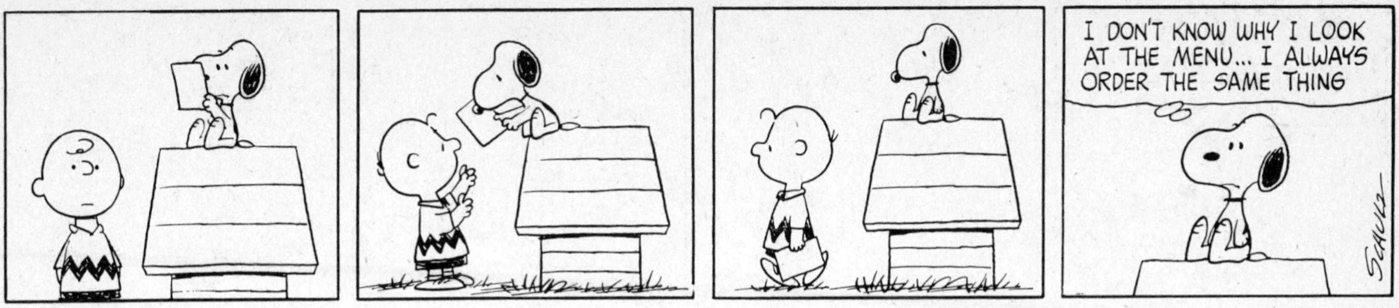
I DON'T KNOW WHY I LOOK AT THE MENU... I ALWAYS ORDER THE SAME THING
SCHULZ

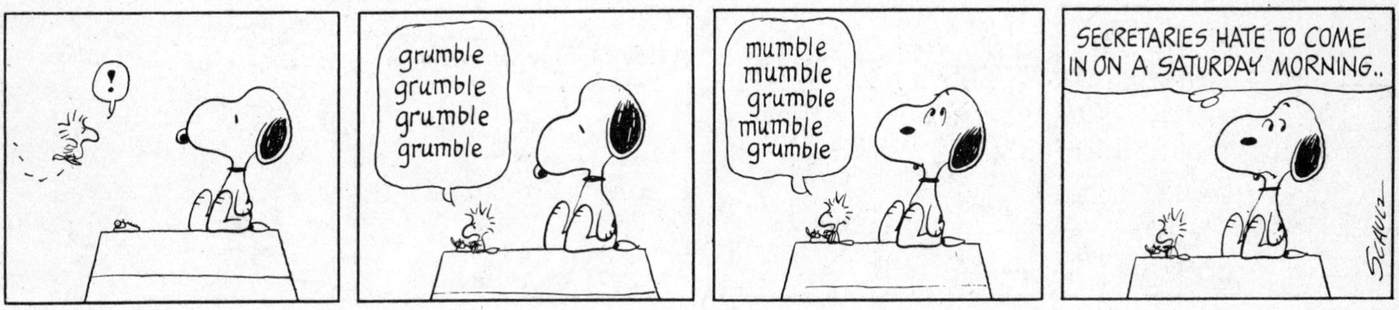
!
grumble grumble grumble grumble
mumble mumble grumble mumble grumble
SECRETARIES HATE TO COME IN ON A SATURDAY MORNING..
SCHULZ

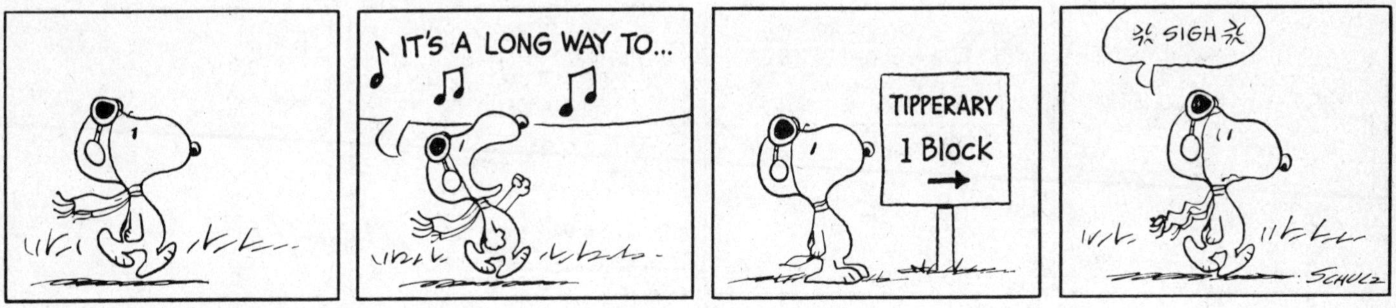
IT'S A LONG WAY TO...
TIPPERARY
1 Block
SIGH
SCHULZ

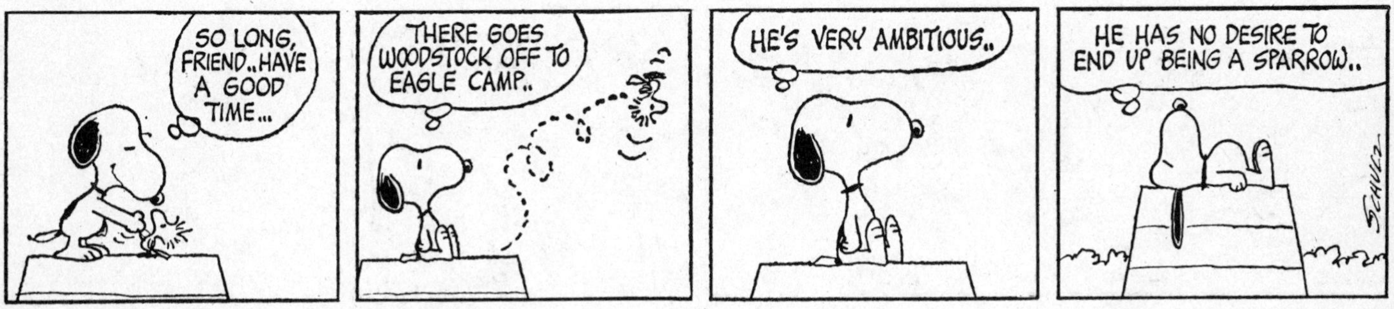
SO LONG, FRIEND..HAVE A GOOD TIME...
THERE GOES WOODSTOCK OFF TO EAGLE CAMP..
HE'S VERY AMBITIOUS..
HE HAS NO DESIRE TO END UP BEING A SPARROW..
SCHULZ

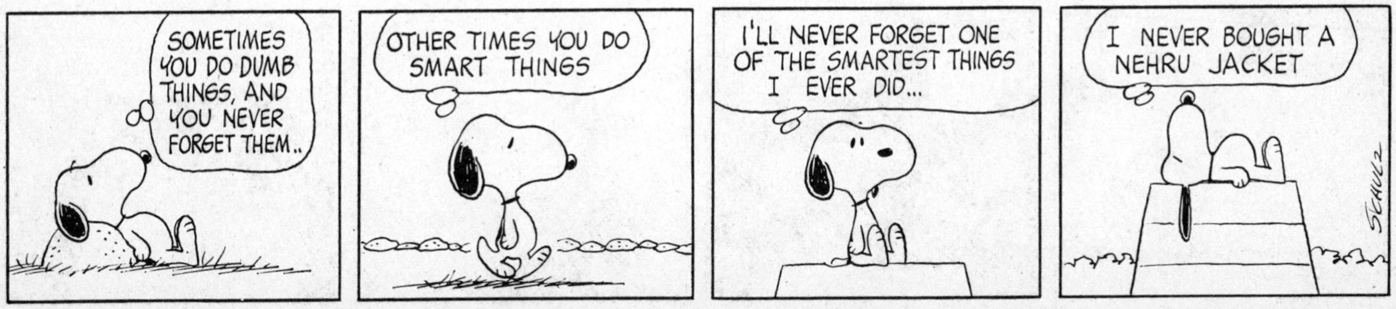
SOMETIMES YOU DO DUMB THINGS, AND YOU NEVER FORGET THEM..
OTHER TIMES YOU DO SMART THINGS
I'LL NEVER FORGET ONE OF THE SMARTEST THINGS I EVER DID...
I NEVER BOUGHT A NEHRU JACKET
SCHULZ

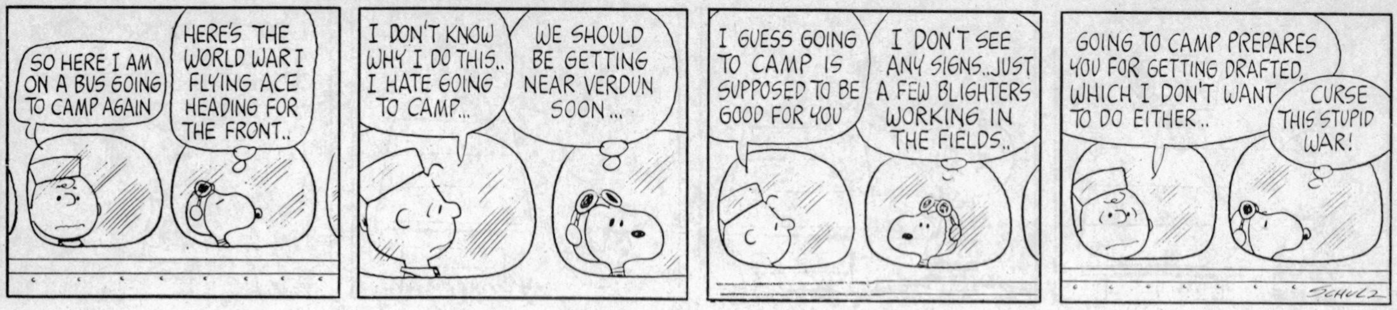
SO HERE I AM ON A BUS GOING TO CAMP AGAIN
HERE'S THE WORLD WAR I FLYING ACE HEADING FOR THE FRONT..
I DON'T KNOW WHY I DO THIS.. I HATE GOING TO CAMP...
WE SHOULD BE GETTING NEAR VERDUN SOON...
I GUESS GOING TO CAMP IS SUPPOSED TO BE GOOD FOR YOU
I DON'T SEE ANY SIGNS.. JUST A FEW BLIGHTERS WORKING IN THE FIELDS..
GOING TO CAMP PREPARES YOU FOR GETTING DRAFTED, WHICH I DON'T WANT TO DO EITHER..
CURSE THIS STUPID WAR!
SCHULZ

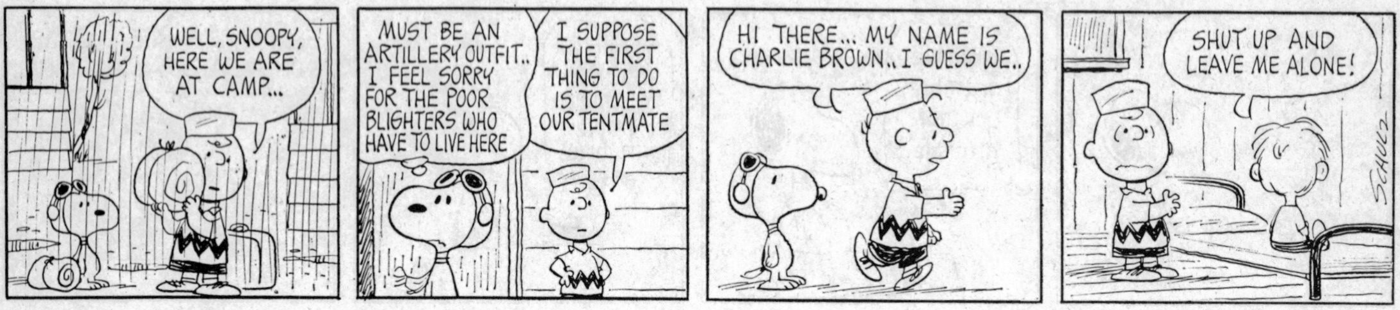
WELL, SNOOPY, HERE WE ARE AT CAMP...
MUST BE AN ARTILLERY OUTFIT.. I FEEL SORRY FOR THE POOR BLIGHTERS WHO HAVE TO LIVE HERE
I SUPPOSE THE FIRST THING TO DO IS TO MEET OUR TENTMATE
HI THERE... MY NAME IS CHARLIE BROWN.. I GUESS WE..
SHUT UP AND LEAVE ME ALONE!
SCHULZ

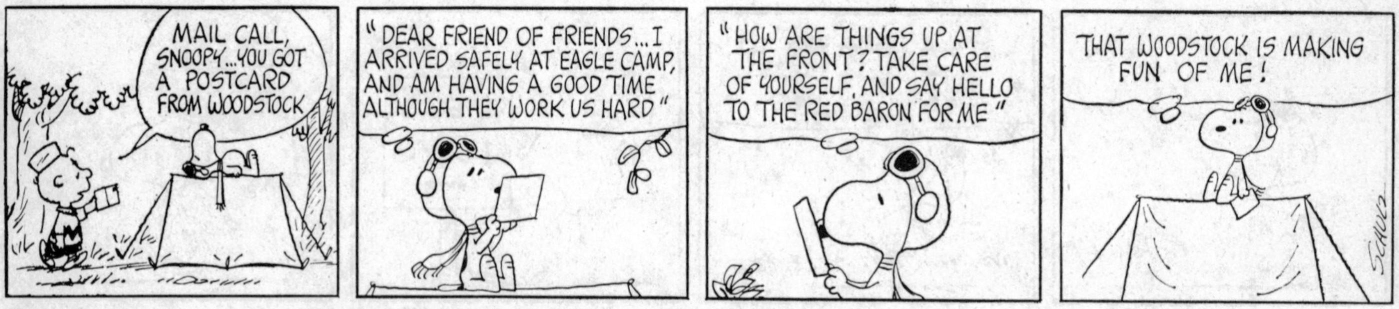
MAIL CALL, SNOOPY...YOU GOT A POSTCARD FROM WOODSTOCK
"DEAR FRIEND OF FRIENDS...I ARRIVED SAFELY AT EAGLE CAMP, AND AM HAVING A GOOD TIME ALTHOUGH THEY WORK US HARD"
"HOW ARE THINGS UP AT THE FRONT? TAKE CARE OF YOURSELF, AND SAY HELLO TO THE RED BARON FOR ME"
THAT WOODSTOCK IS MAKING FUN OF ME!
SCHULZ

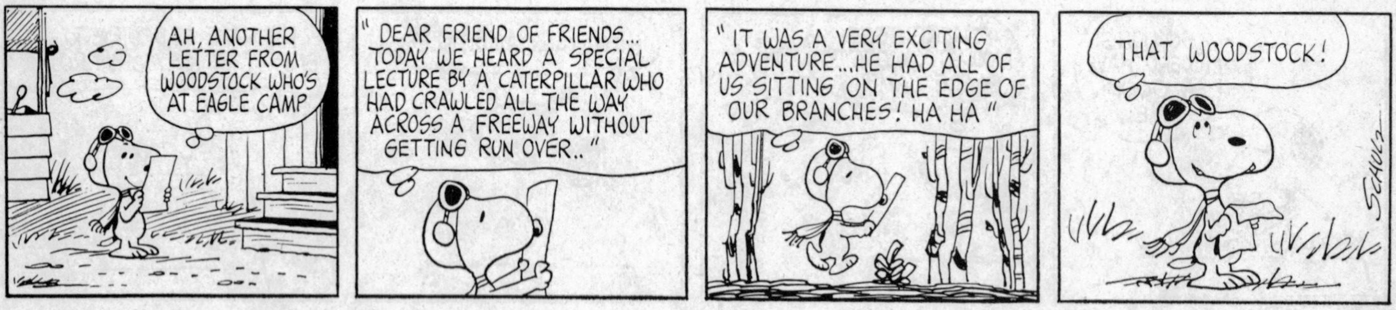
AH, ANOTHER LETTER FROM WOODSTOCK WHO'S AT EAGLE CAMP
"DEAR FRIEND OF FRIENDS... TODAY WE HEARD A SPECIAL LECTURE BY A CATERPILLAR WHO HAD CRAWLED ALL THE WAY ACROSS A FREEWAY WITHOUT GETTING RUN OVER.."
"IT WAS A VERY EXCITING ADVENTURE...HE HAD ALL OF US SITTING ON THE EDGE OF OUR BRANCHES! HA HA"
THAT WOODSTOCK!
SCHULZ

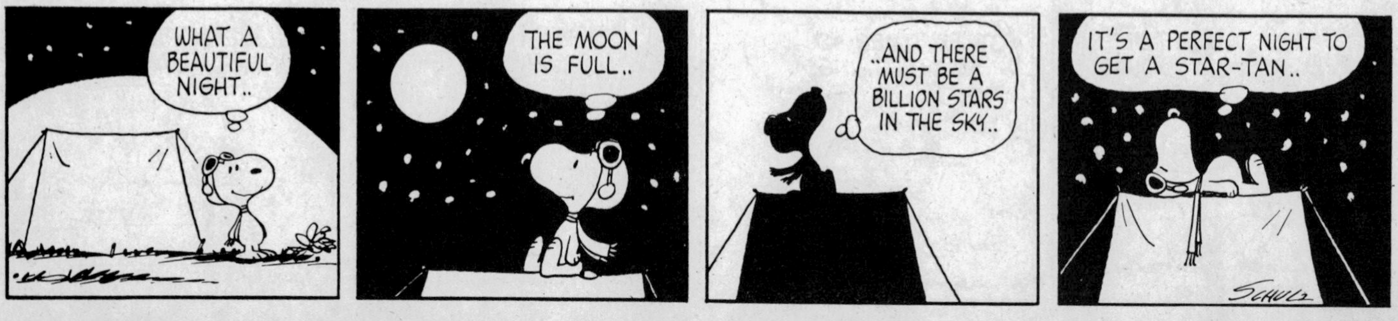
WHAT A BEAUTIFUL NIGHT..
THE MOON IS FULL..
..AND THERE MUST BE A BILLION STARS IN THE SKY..
IT'S A PERFECT NIGHT TO GET A STAR-TAN..
SCHULZ

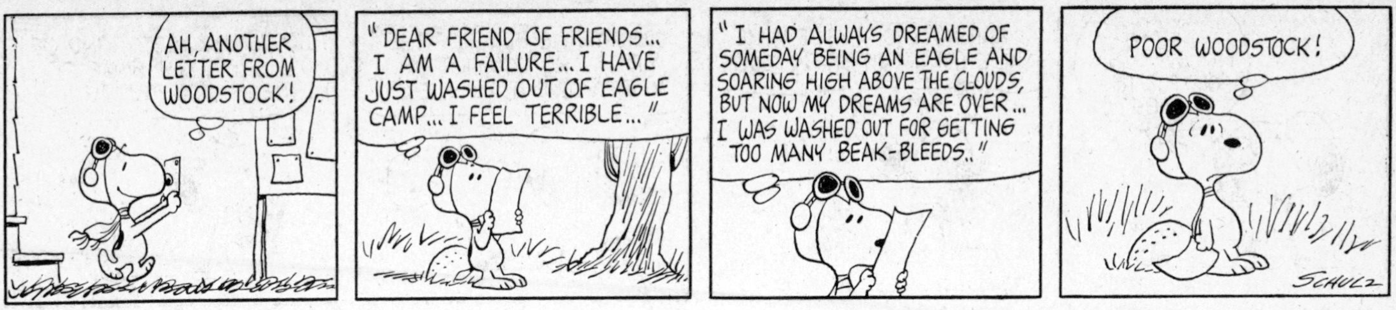
AH, ANOTHER LETTER FROM WOODSTOCK!
" DEAR FRIEND OF FRIENDS... I AM A FAILURE... I HAVE JUST WASHED OUT OF EAGLE CAMP... I FEEL TERRIBLE... "
" I HAD ALWAYS DREAMED OF SOMEDAY BEING AN EAGLE AND SOARING HIGH ABOVE THE CLOUDS, BUT NOW MY DREAMS ARE OVER... I WAS WASHED OUT FOR GETTING TOO MANY BEAK-BLEEDS.. "
POOR WOODSTOCK!
SCHULZ

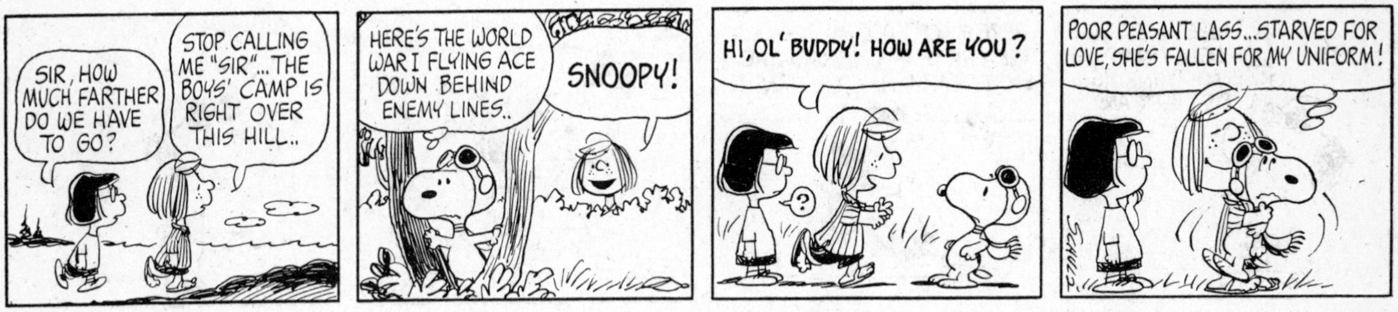
SIR, HOW MUCH FARTHER DO WE HAVE TO GO?
STOP CALLING ME "SIR"... THE BOYS' CAMP IS RIGHT OVER THIS HILL..
HERE'S THE WORLD WAR I FLYING ACE DOWN BEHIND ENEMY LINES..
SNOOPY!
HI, OL' BUDDY! HOW ARE YOU?
?
POOR PEASANT LASS...STARVED FOR LOVE, SHE'S FALLEN FOR MY UNIFORM!
SCHULZ

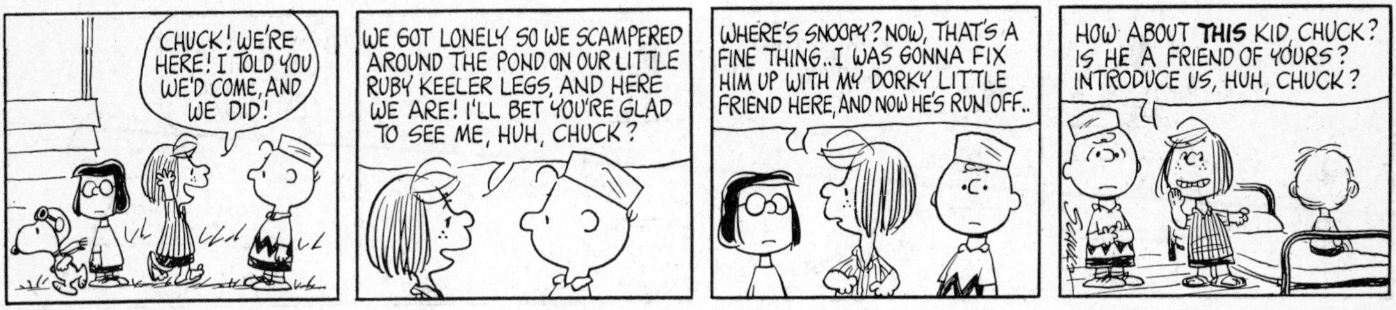
CHUCK! WE'RE HERE! I TOLD YOU WE'D COME, AND WE DID!
WE GOT LONELY SO WE SCAMPERED AROUND THE POND ON OUR LITTLE RUBY KEELER LEGS, AND HERE WE ARE! I'LL BET YOU'RE GLAD TO SEE ME, HUH, CHUCK?
WHERE'S SNOOPY? NOW, THAT'S A FINE THING..I WAS GONNA FIX HIM UP WITH MY DORKY LITTLE FRIEND HERE, AND NOW HE'S RUN OFF..
HOW ABOUT THIS KID, CHUCK? IS HE A FRIEND OF YOURS? INTRODUCE US, HUH, CHUCK?
SCHULZ

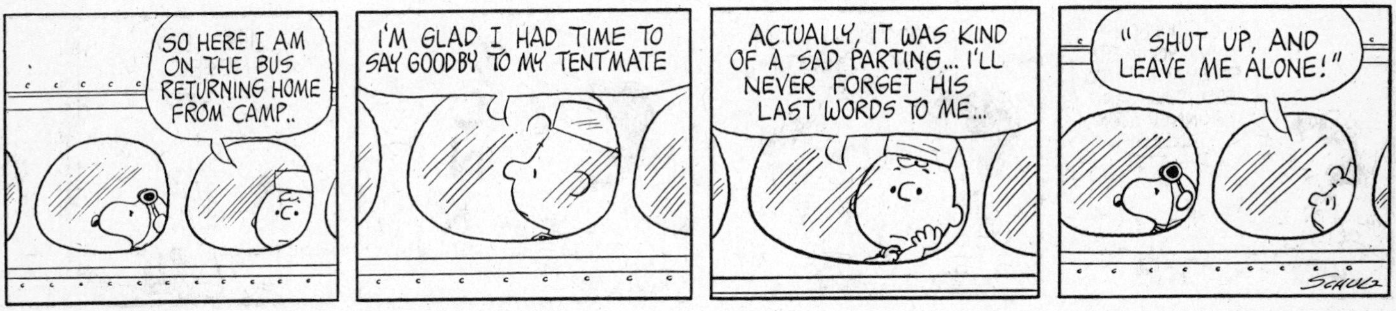
SO HERE I AM ON THE BUS RETURNING HOME FROM CAMP..
I'M GLAD I HAD TIME TO SAY GOODBY TO MY TENTMATE
ACTUALLY, IT WAS KIND OF A SAD PARTING... I'LL NEVER FORGET HIS LAST WORDS TO ME...
" SHUT UP, AND LEAVE ME ALONE! "
SCHULZ

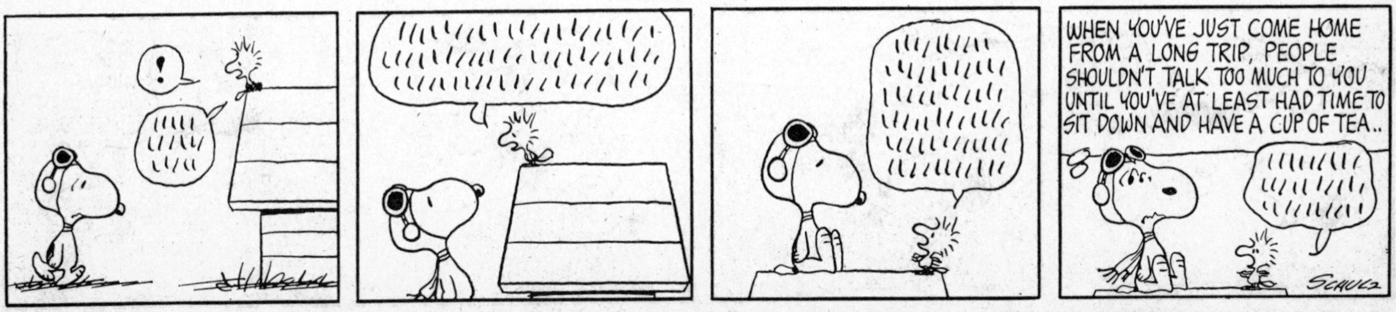
!
WHEN YOU'VE JUST COME HOME FROM A LONG TRIP, PEOPLE SHOULDN'T TALK TOO MUCH TO YOU UNTIL YOU'VE AT LEAST HAD TIME TO SIT DOWN AND HAVE A CUP OF TEA..
SCHULZ

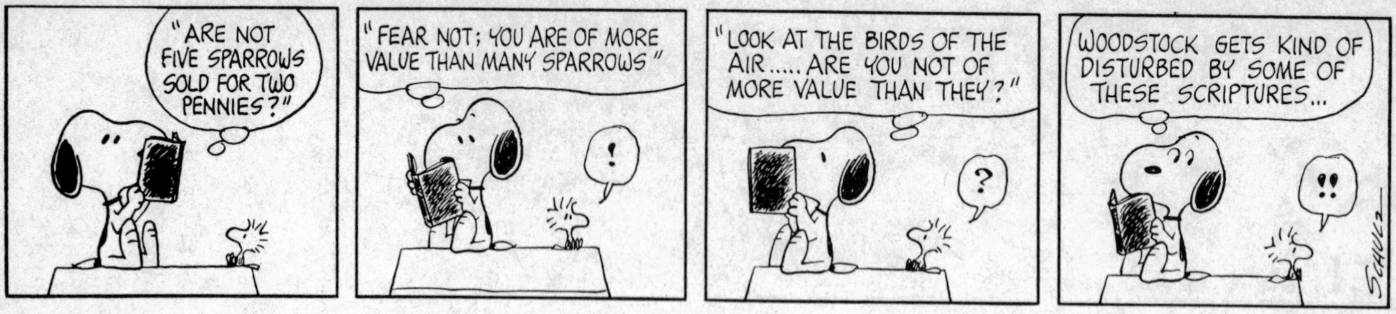
"ARE NOT FIVE SPARROWS SOLD FOR TWO PENNIES?"
"FEAR NOT; YOU ARE OF MORE VALUE THAN MANY SPARROWS"
!
"LOOK AT THE BIRDS OF THE AIR..... ARE YOU NOT OF MORE VALUE THAN THEY?"
?
WOODSTOCK GETS KIND OF DISTURBED BY SOME OF THESE SCRIPTURES...
!!
SCHULZ

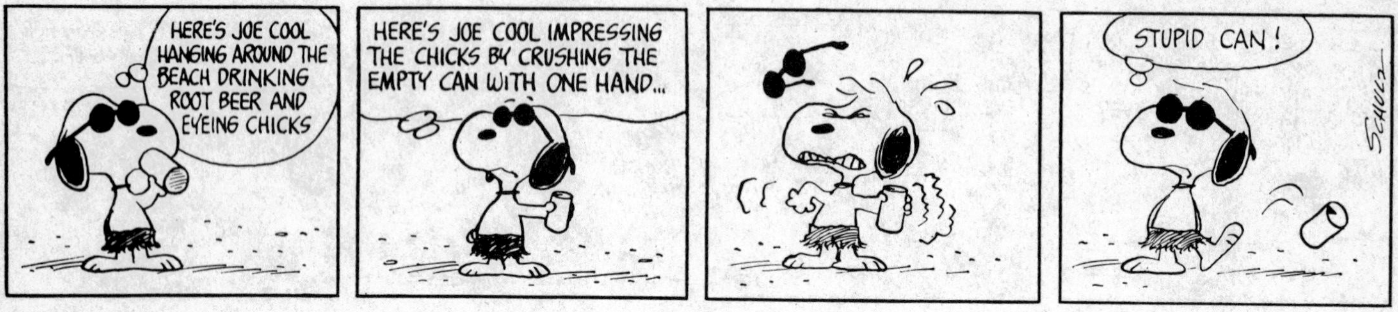
HERE'S JOE COOL HANGING AROUND THE BEACH DRINKING ROOT BEER AND EYEING CHICKS
HERE'S JOE COOL IMPRESSING THE CHICKS BY CRUSHING THE EMPTY CAN WITH ONE HAND...
STUPID CAN!
SCHULZ

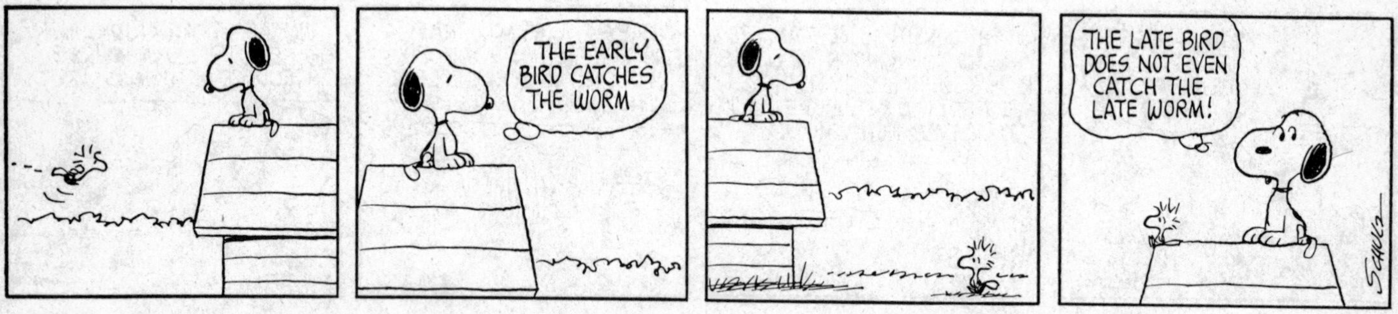
THE EARLY BIRD CATCHES THE WORM
THE LATE BIRD DOES NOT EVEN CATCH THE LATE WORM!
SCHULZ

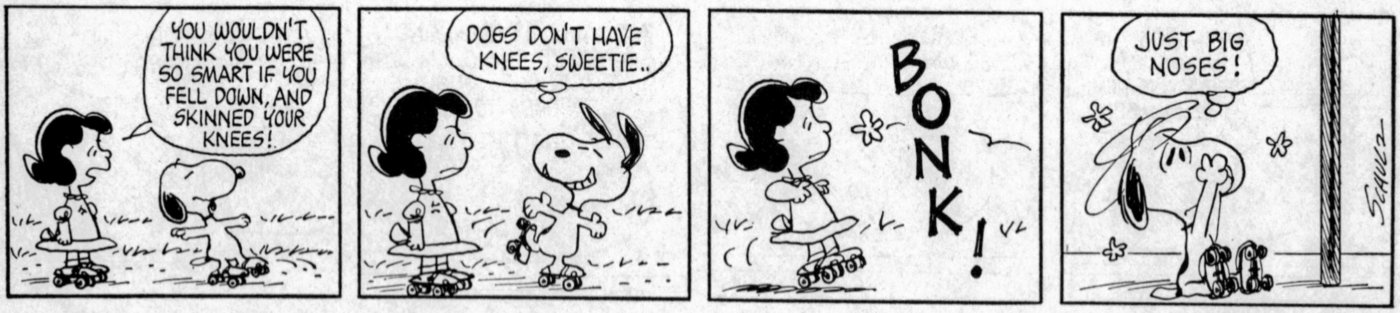
YOU WOULDN'T THINK YOU WERE SO SMART IF YOU FELL DOWN, AND SKINNED YOUR KNEES!
DOGS DON'T HAVE KNEES, SWEETIE..
BONK!
JUST BIG NOSES!
SCHULZ

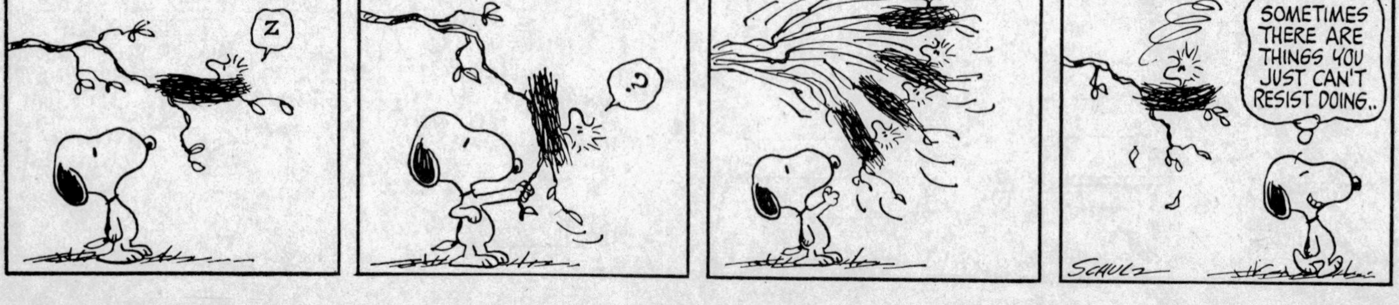
Z
?
SOMETIMES THERE ARE THINGS YOU JUST CAN'T RESIST DOING..
SCHULZ

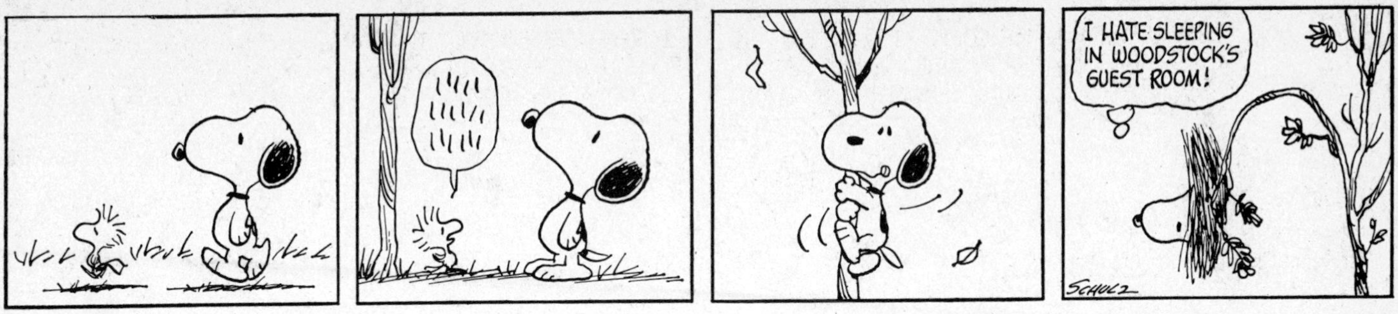
I HATE SLEEPING IN WOODSTOCK'S GUEST ROOM!

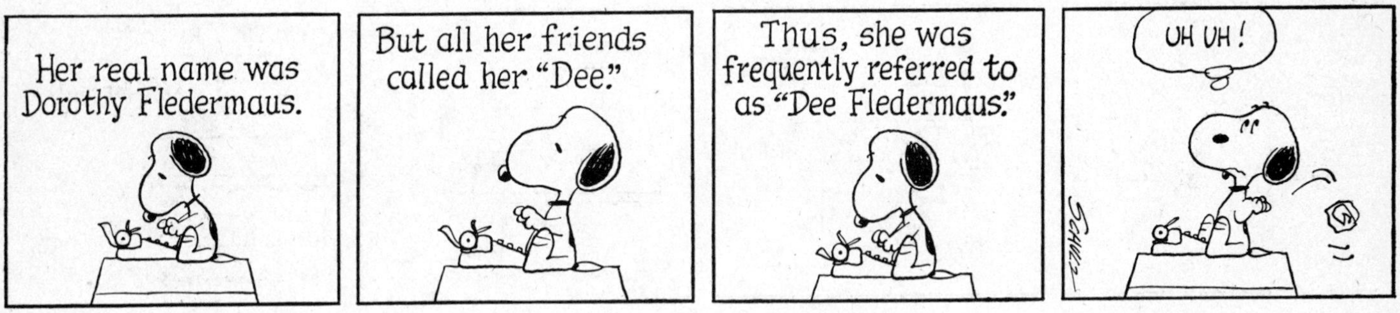
Her real name was Dorothy Fledermaus.
But all her friends called her "Dee."
Thus, she was frequently referred to as "Dee Fledermaus."
UH UH!

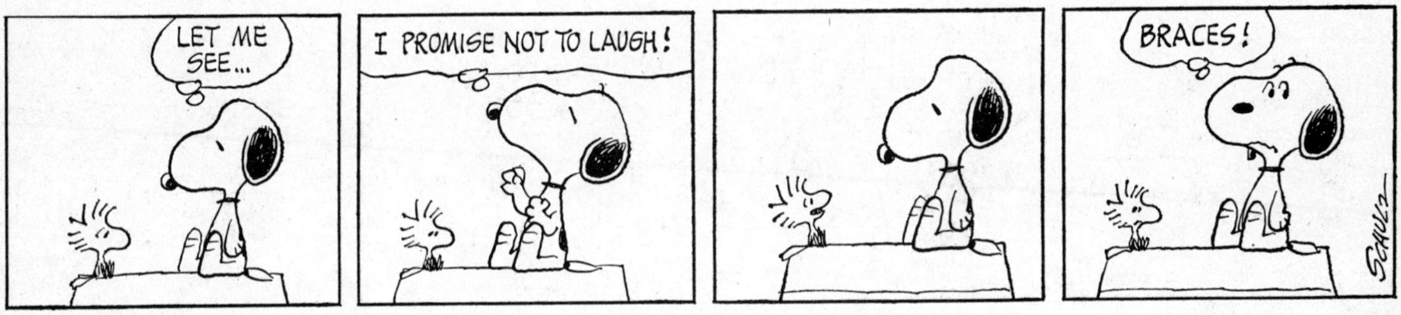
LET ME SEE...
I PROMISE NOT TO LAUGH!
BRACES!

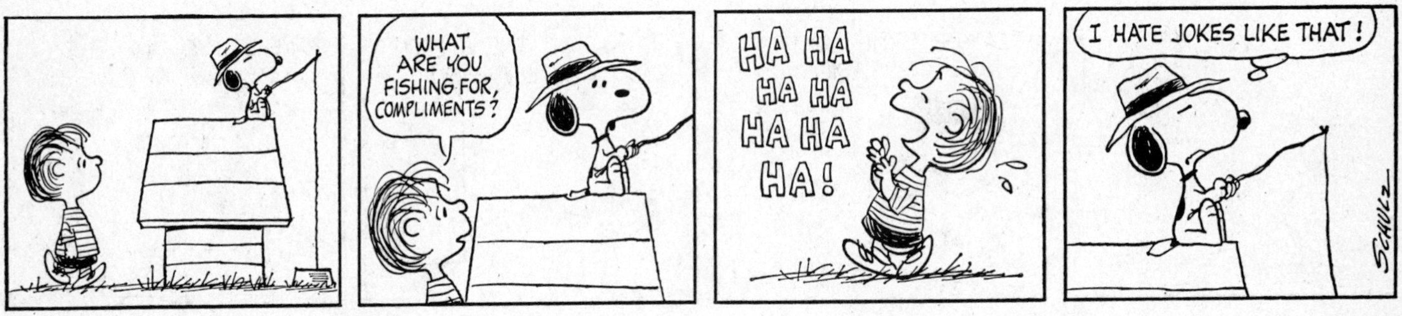
WHAT ARE YOU FISHING FOR, COMPLIMENTS?
HA HA HA HA HA HA HA!
I HATE JOKES LIKE THAT!

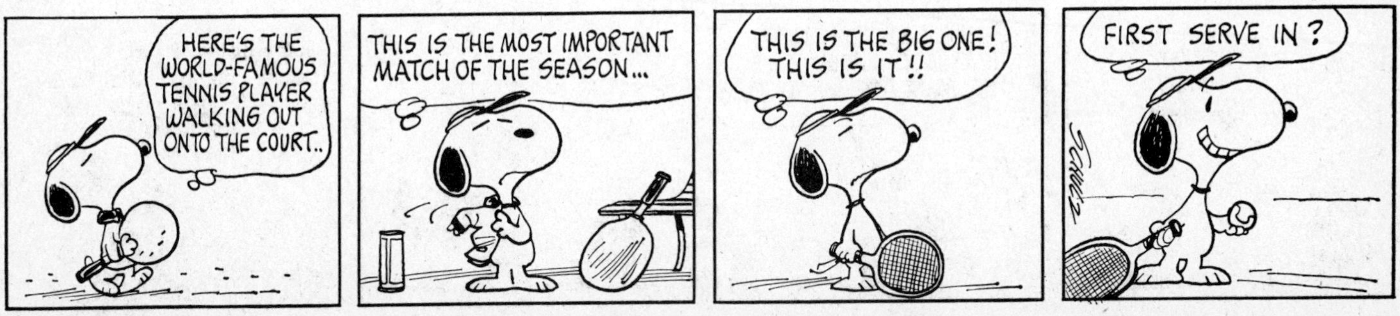
HERE'S THE WORLD-FAMOUS TENNIS PLAYER WALKING OUT ONTO THE COURT..
THIS IS THE MOST IMPORTANT MATCH OF THE SEASON...
THIS IS THE BIG ONE! THIS IS IT!!
FIRST SERVE IN?

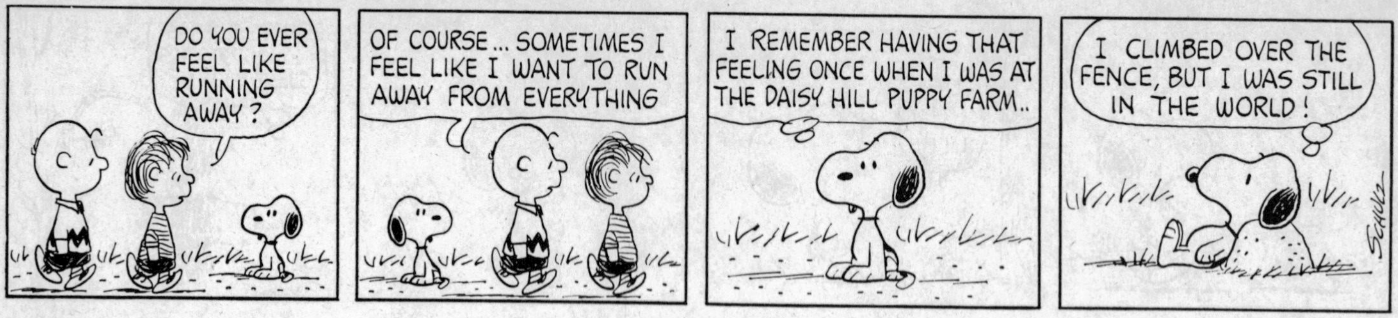
DO YOU EVER FEEL LIKE RUNNING AWAY?
OF COURSE... SOMETIMES I FEEL LIKE I WANT TO RUN AWAY FROM EVERYTHING
I REMEMBER HAVING THAT FEELING ONCE WHEN I WAS AT THE DAISY HILL PUPPY FARM..
I CLIMBED OVER THE FENCE, BUT I WAS STILL IN THE WORLD!
SCHULZ

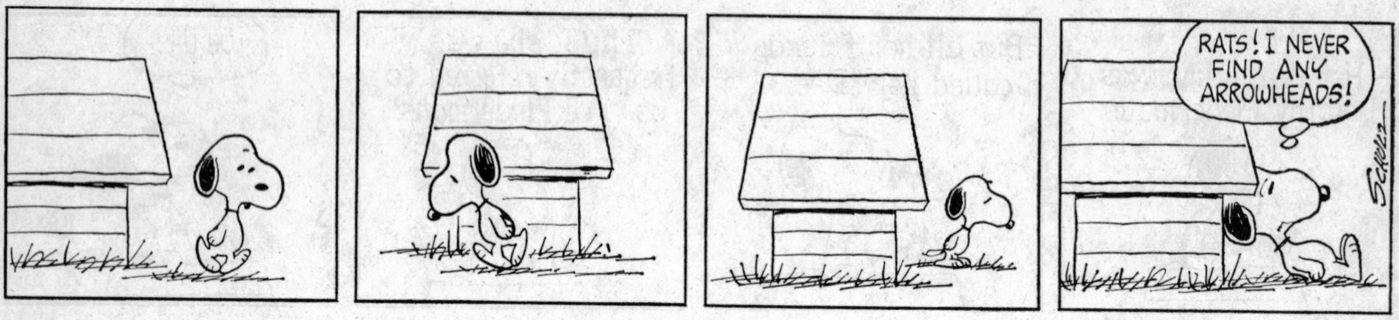
RATS! I NEVER FIND ANY ARROWHEADS!
SCHULZ

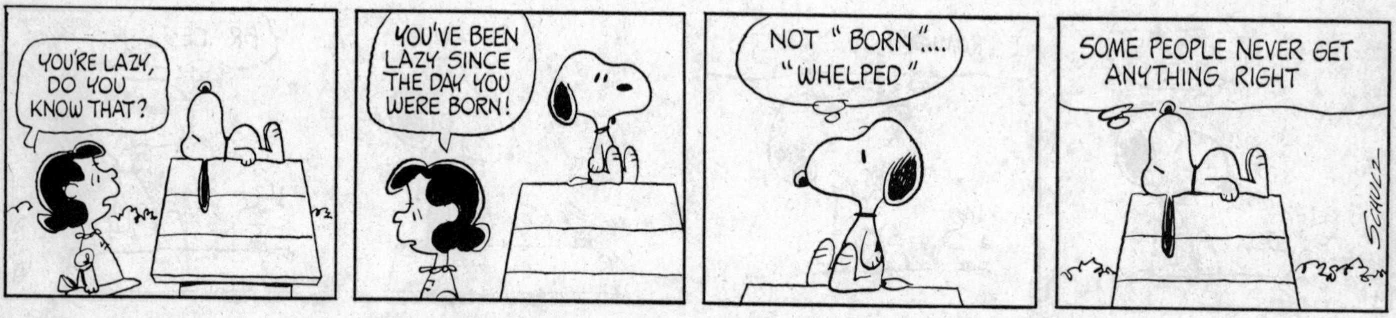
YOU'RE LAZY, DO YOU KNOW THAT?
YOU'VE BEEN LAZY SINCE THE DAY YOU WERE BORN!
NOT "BORN".... "WHELPED"
SOME PEOPLE NEVER GET ANYTHING RIGHT
SCHULZ

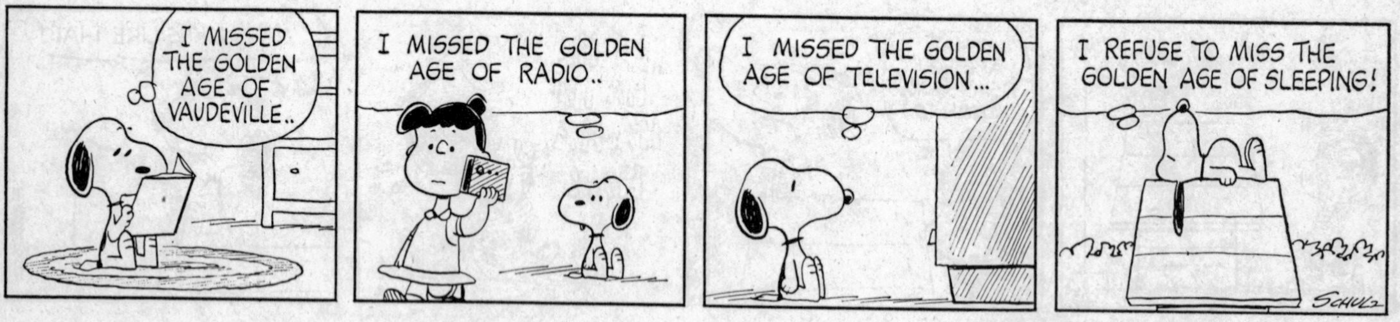
I MISSED THE GOLDEN AGE OF VAUDEVILLE..
I MISSED THE GOLDEN AGE OF RADIO..
I MISSED THE GOLDEN AGE OF TELEVISION...
I REFUSE TO MISS THE GOLDEN AGE OF SLEEPING!
SCHULZ

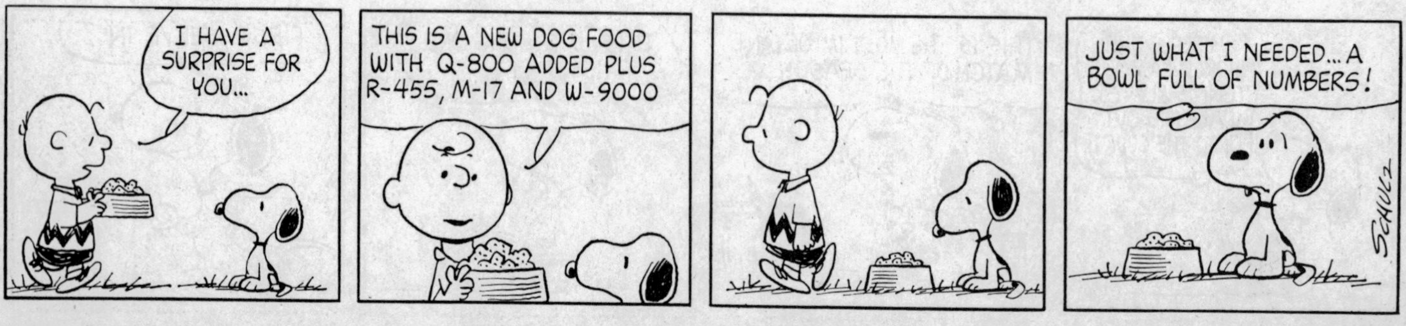
I HAVE A SURPRISE FOR YOU...
THIS IS A NEW DOG FOOD WITH Q-800 ADDED PLUS R-455, M-17 AND W-9000
JUST WHAT I NEEDED... A BOWL FULL OF NUMBERS!
SCHULZ

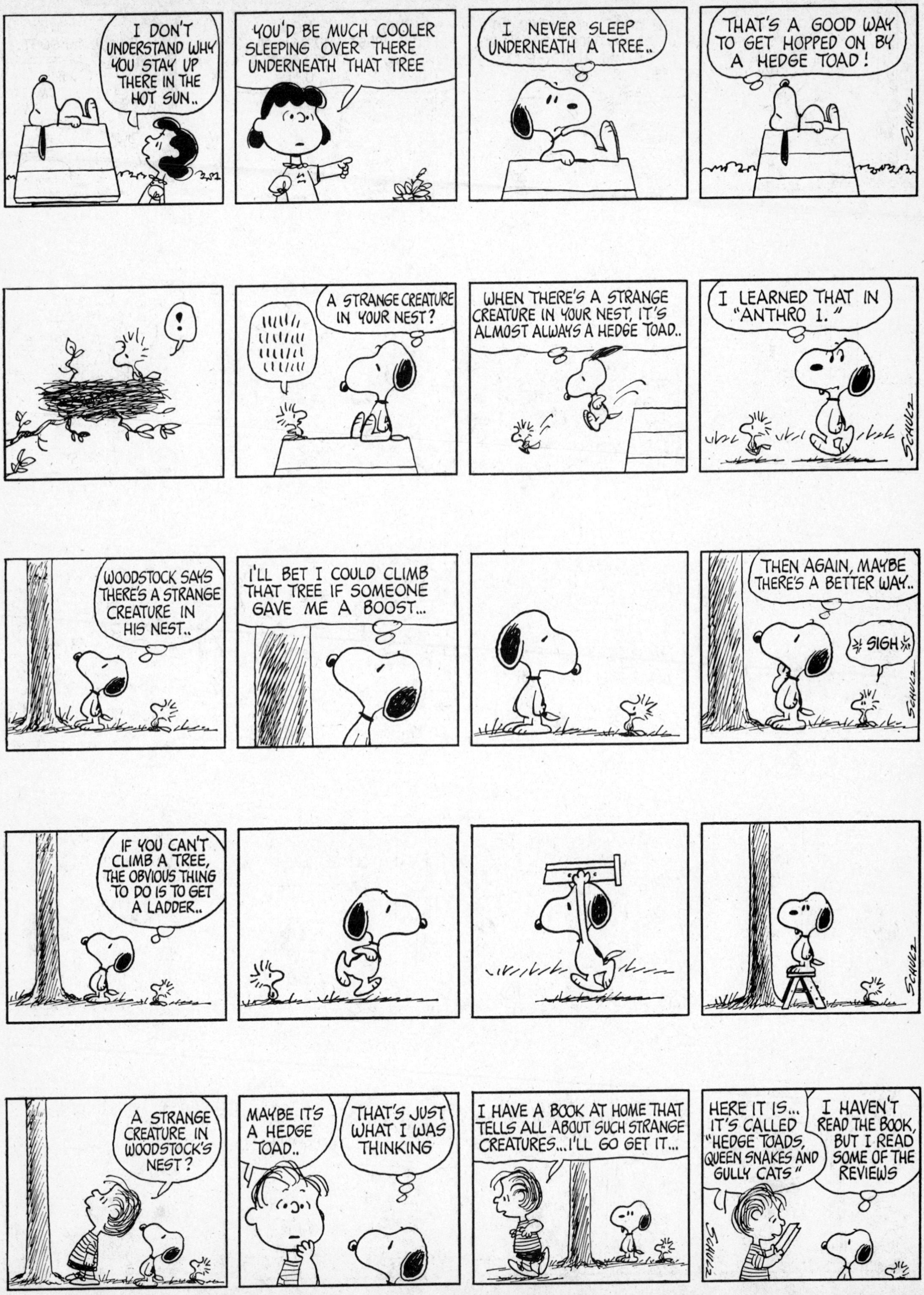
I DON'T UNDERSTAND WHY YOU STAY UP THERE IN THE HOT SUN..
YOU'D BE MUCH COOLER SLEEPING OVER THERE UNDERNEATH THAT TREE
I NEVER SLEEP UNDERNEATH A TREE..
THAT'S A GOOD WAY TO GET HOPPED ON BY A HEDGE TOAD!
SCHULZ
!
A STRANGE CREATURE IN YOUR NEST?
WHEN THERE'S A STRANGE CREATURE IN YOUR NEST, IT'S ALMOST ALWAYS A HEDGE TOAD..
I LEARNED THAT IN "ANTHRO 1."
SCHULZ
WOODSTOCK SAYS THERE'S A STRANGE CREATURE IN HIS NEST..
I'LL BET I COULD CLIMB THAT TREE IF SOMEONE GAVE ME A BOOST...
THEN AGAIN, MAYBE THERE'S A BETTER WAY..
SIGH
SCHULZ
IF YOU CAN'T CLIMB A TREE, THE OBVIOUS THING TO DO IS TO GET A LADDER..
SCHULZ
A STRANGE CREATURE IN WOODSTOCK'S NEST?
MAYBE IT'S A HEDGE TOAD..
THAT'S JUST WHAT I WAS THINKING
I HAVE A BOOK AT HOME THAT TELLS ALL ABOUT SUCH STRANGE CREATURES...I'LL GO GET IT...
HERE IT IS... IT'S CALLED "HEDGE TOADS, QUEEN SNAKES AND GULLY CATS"
I HAVEN'T READ THE BOOK, BUT I READ SOME OF THE REVIEWS
SCHULZ

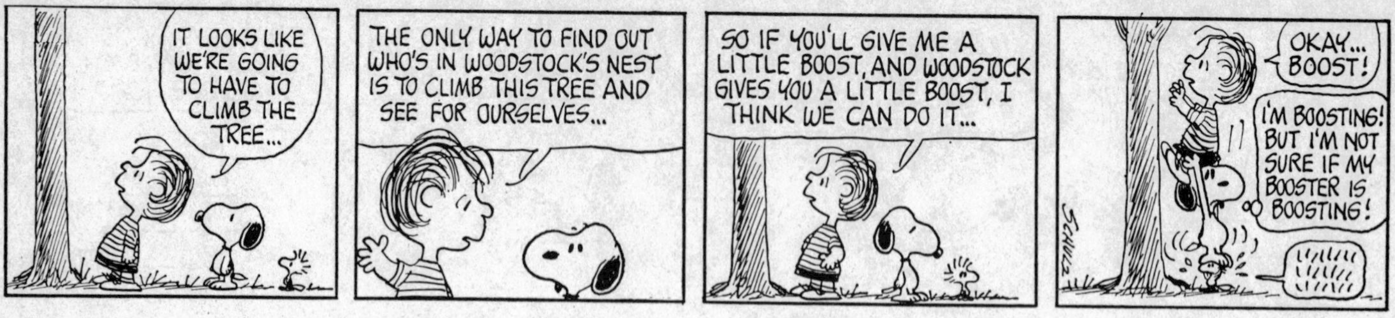
IT LOOKS LIKE WE'RE GOING TO HAVE TO CLIMB THE TREE...
THE ONLY WAY TO FIND OUT WHO'S IN WOODSTOCK'S NEST IS TO CLIMB THIS TREE AND SEE FOR OURSELVES...
SO IF YOU'LL GIVE ME A LITTLE BOOST, AND WOODSTOCK GIVES YOU A LITTLE BOOST, I THINK WE CAN DO IT...
OKAY... BOOST!
I'M BOOSTING! BUT I'M NOT SURE IF MY BOOSTER IS BOOSTING!

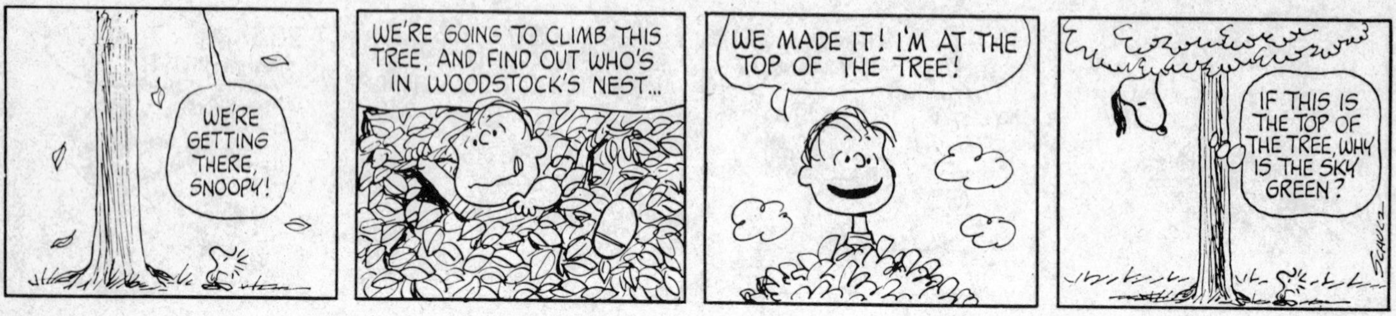
WE'RE GETTING THERE, SNOOPY!
WE'RE GOING TO CLIMB THIS TREE, AND FIND OUT WHO'S IN WOODSTOCK'S NEST...
WE MADE IT! I'M AT THE TOP OF THE TREE!
IF THIS IS THE TOP OF THE TREE, WHY IS THE SKY GREEN?

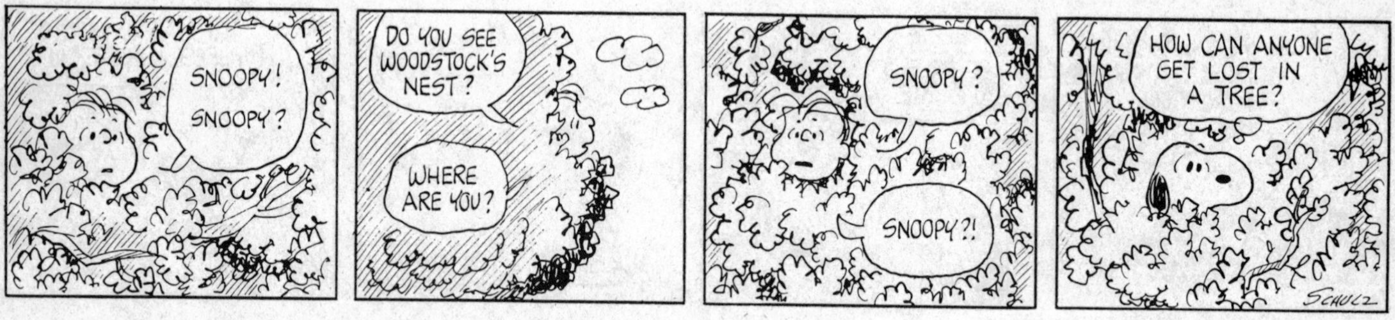
SNOOPY! SNOOPY?
DO YOU SEE WOODSTOCK'S NEST?
WHERE ARE YOU?
SNOOPY?
SNOOPY?!
HOW CAN ANYONE GET LOST IN A TREE?

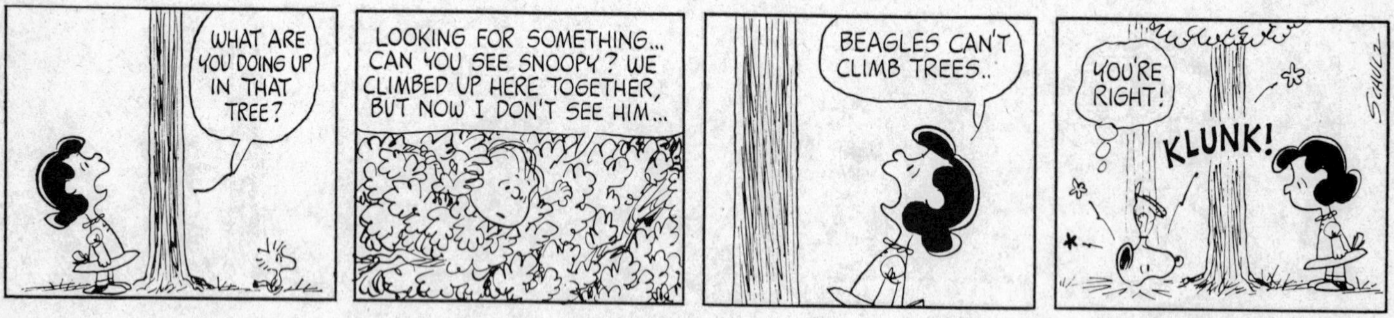
WHAT ARE YOU DOING UP IN THAT TREE?
LOOKING FOR SOMETHING... CAN YOU SEE SNOOPY? WE CLIMBED UP HERE TOGETHER, BUT NOW I DON'T SEE HIM...
BEAGLES CAN'T CLIMB TREES..
YOU'RE RIGHT!
KLUNK!

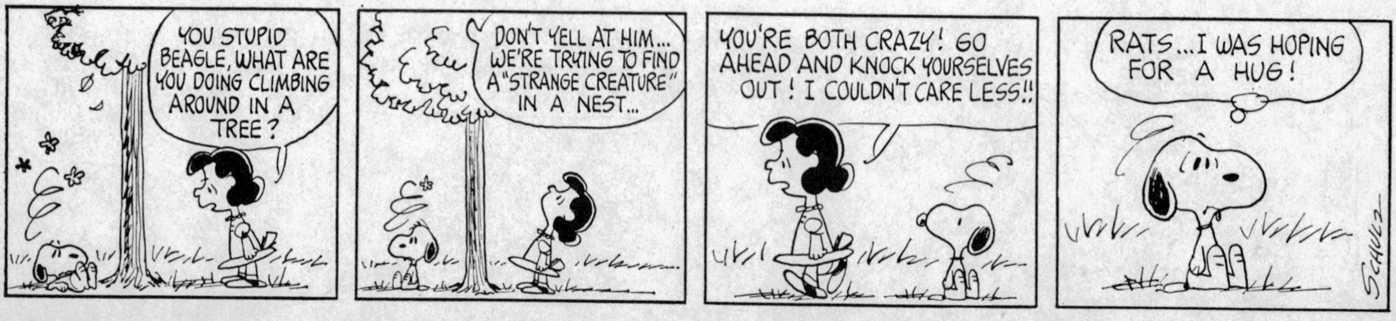
YOU STUPID BEAGLE, WHAT ARE YOU DOING CLIMBING AROUND IN A TREE?
DON'T YELL AT HIM... WE'RE TRYING TO FIND A "STRANGE CREATURE" IN A NEST...
YOU'RE BOTH CRAZY! GO AHEAD AND KNOCK YOURSELVES OUT! I COULDN'T CARE LESS!!
RATS... I WAS HOPING FOR A HUG!

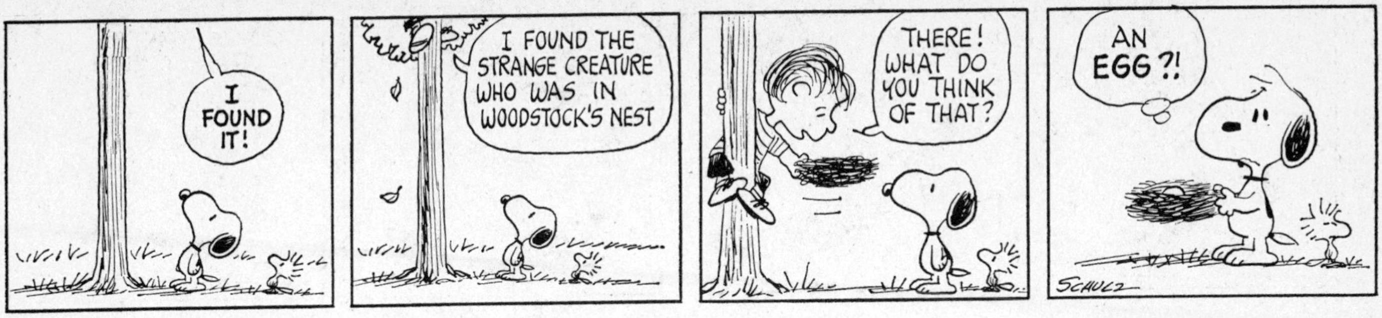
I FOUND IT!
I FOUND THE STRANGE CREATURE WHO WAS IN WOODSTOCK'S NEST
THERE! WHAT DO YOU THINK OF THAT?
AN EGG?!

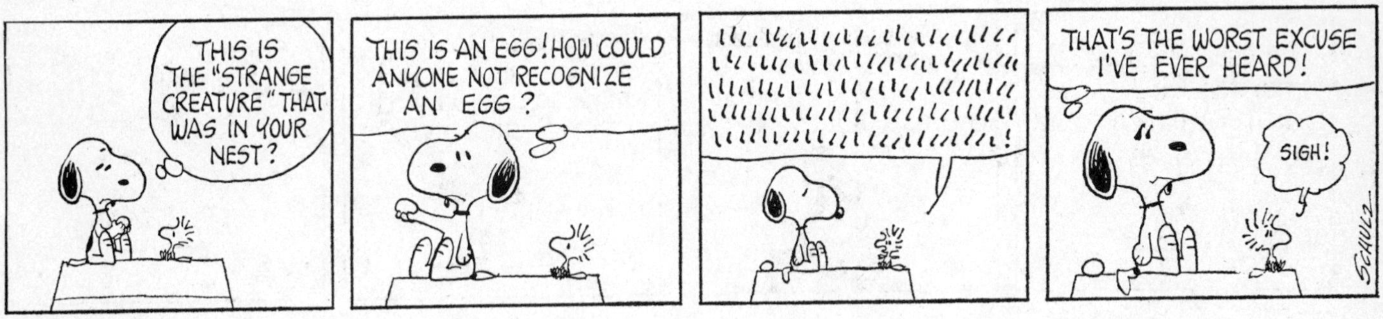
THIS IS THE "STRANGE CREATURE" THAT WAS IN YOUR NEST?
THIS IS AN EGG! HOW COULD ANYONE NOT RECOGNIZE AN EGG?
THAT'S THE WORST EXCUSE I'VE EVER HEARD!
SIGH!

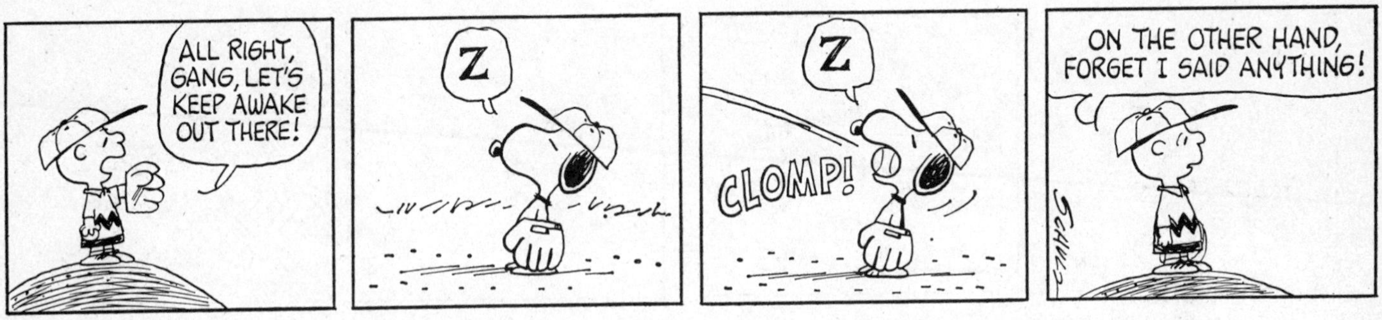
ALL RIGHT, GANG, LET'S KEEP AWAKE OUT THERE!
Z
Z
CLOMP!
ON THE OTHER HAND, FORGET I SAID ANYTHING!

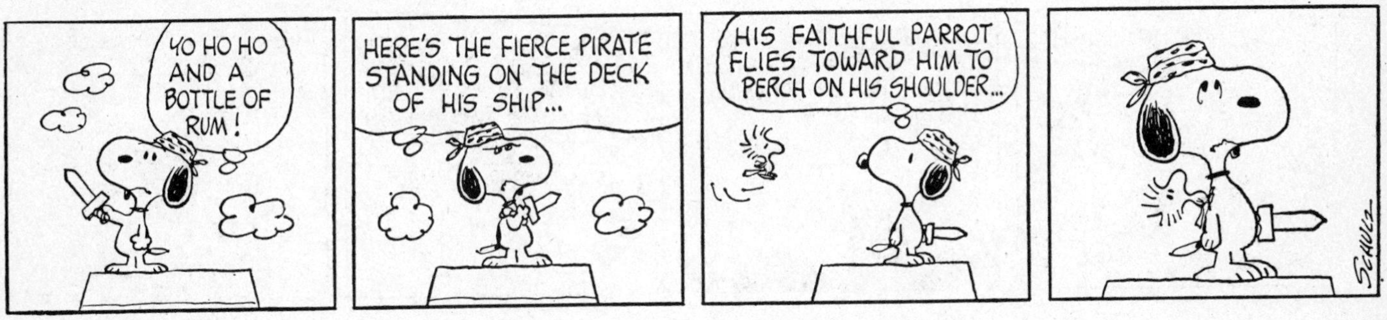
YO HO HO AND A BOTTLE OF RUM!
HERE'S THE FIERCE PIRATE STANDING ON THE DECK OF HIS SHIP...
HIS FAITHFUL PARROT FLIES TOWARD HIM TO PERCH ON HIS SHOULDER...

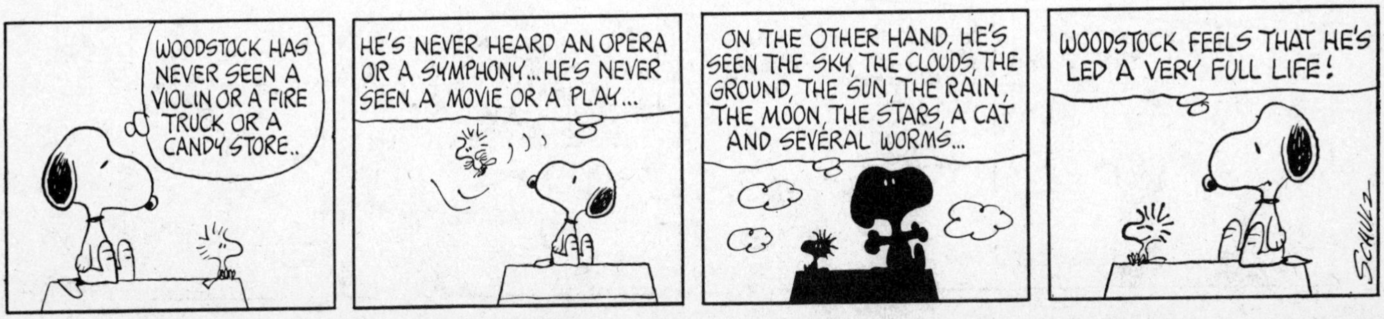
WOODSTOCK HAS NEVER SEEN A VIOLIN OR A FIRE TRUCK OR A CANDY STORE..
HE'S NEVER HEARD AN OPERA OR A SYMPHONY... HE'S NEVER SEEN A MOVIE OR A PLAY...
ON THE OTHER HAND, HE'S SEEN THE SKY, THE CLOUDS, THE GROUND, THE SUN, THE RAIN, THE MOON, THE STARS, A CAT AND SEVERAL WORMS...
WOODSTOCK FEELS THAT HE'S LED A VERY FULL LIFE!

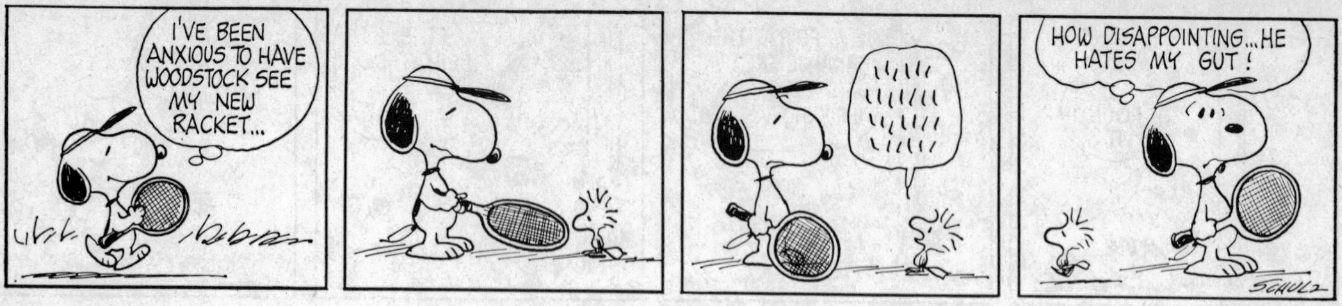
I'VE BEEN ANXIOUS TO HAVE WOODSTOCK SEE MY NEW RACKET...
HOW DISAPPOINTING...HE HATES MY GUT!
SCHULZ

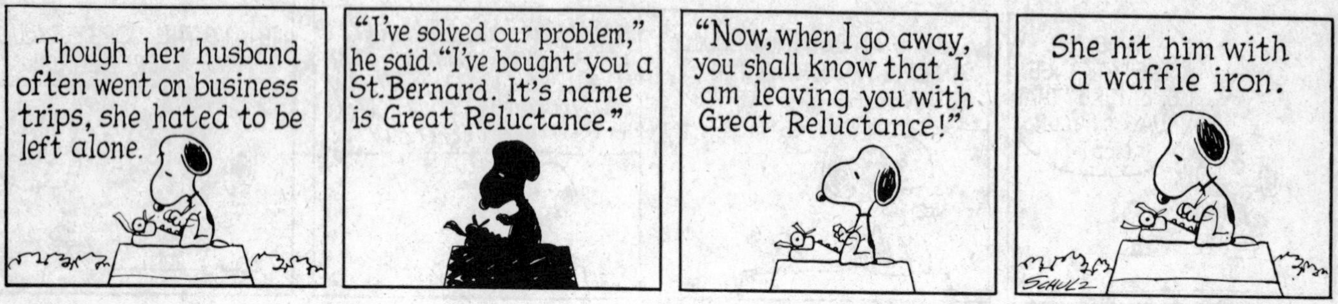
Though her husband often went on business trips, she hated to be left alone.
"I've solved our problem," he said. "I've bought you a St. Bernard. It's name is Great Reluctance."
"Now, when I go away, you shall know that I am leaving you with Great Reluctance!"
She hit him with a waffle iron.
SCHULZ

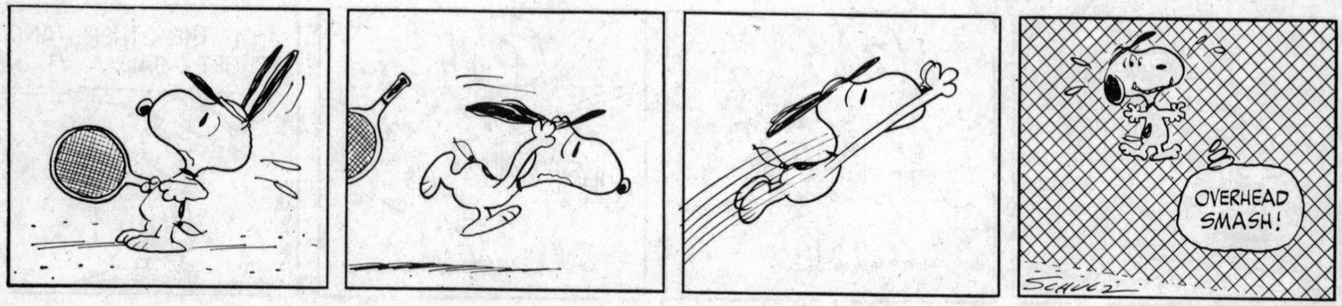
OVERHEAD SMASH!
SCHULZ

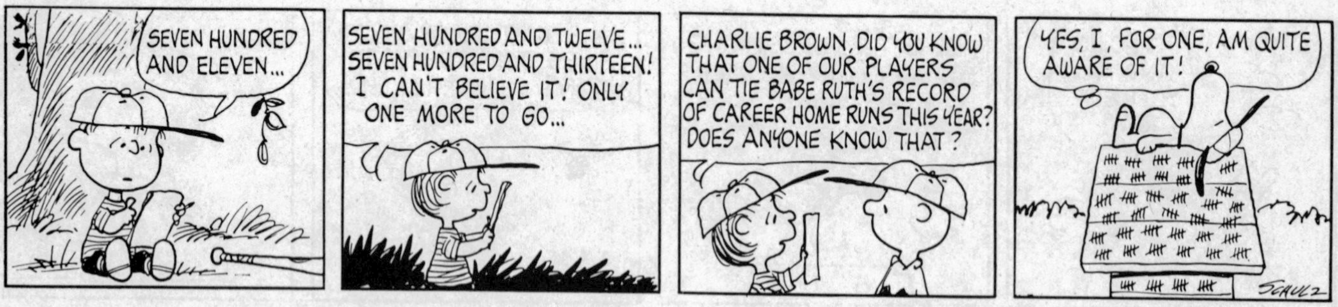
SEVEN HUNDRED AND ELEVEN...
SEVEN HUNDRED AND TWELVE... SEVEN HUNDRED AND THIRTEEN! I CAN'T BELIEVE IT! ONLY ONE MORE TO GO...
CHARLIE BROWN, DID YOU KNOW THAT ONE OF OUR PLAYERS CAN TIE BABE RUTH'S RECORD OF CAREER HOME RUNS THIS YEAR? DOES ANYONE KNOW THAT?
YES, I, FOR ONE, AM QUITE AWARE OF IT!
SCHULZ

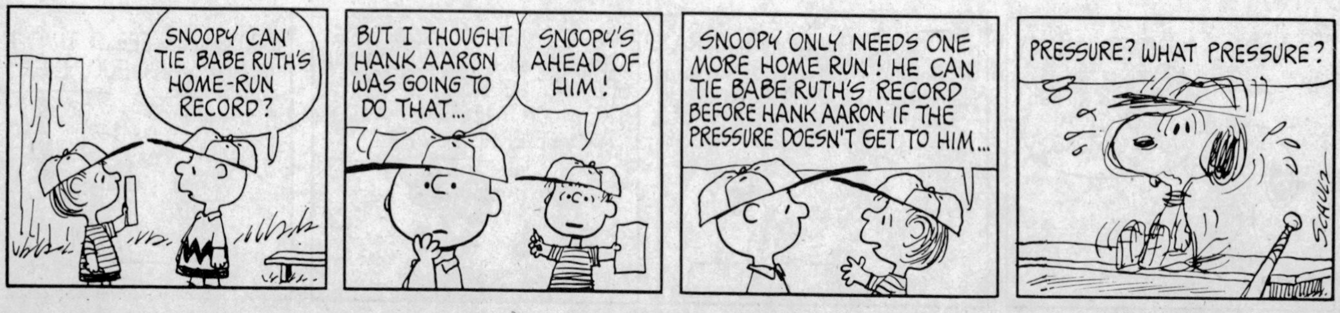
SNOOPY CAN TIE BABE RUTH'S HOME-RUN RECORD?
BUT I THOUGHT HANK AARON WAS GOING TO DO THAT...
SNOOPY'S AHEAD OF HIM!
SNOOPY ONLY NEEDS ONE MORE HOME RUN! HE CAN TIE BABE RUTH'S RECORD BEFORE HANK AARON IF THE PRESSURE DOESN'T GET TO HIM...
PRESSURE? WHAT PRESSURE?
SCHULZ

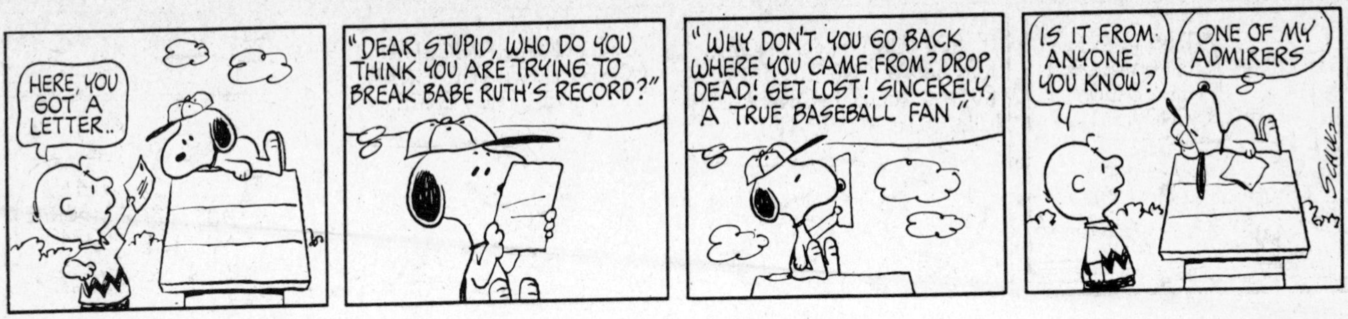
HERE, YOU GOT A LETTER..
"DEAR STUPID, WHO DO YOU THINK YOU ARE TRYING TO BREAK BABE RUTH'S RECORD?"
"WHY DON'T YOU GO BACK WHERE YOU CAME FROM? DROP DEAD! GET LOST! SINCERELY, A TRUE BASEBALL FAN"
IS IT FROM ANYONE YOU KNOW?
ONE OF MY ADMIRERS
SCHULZ

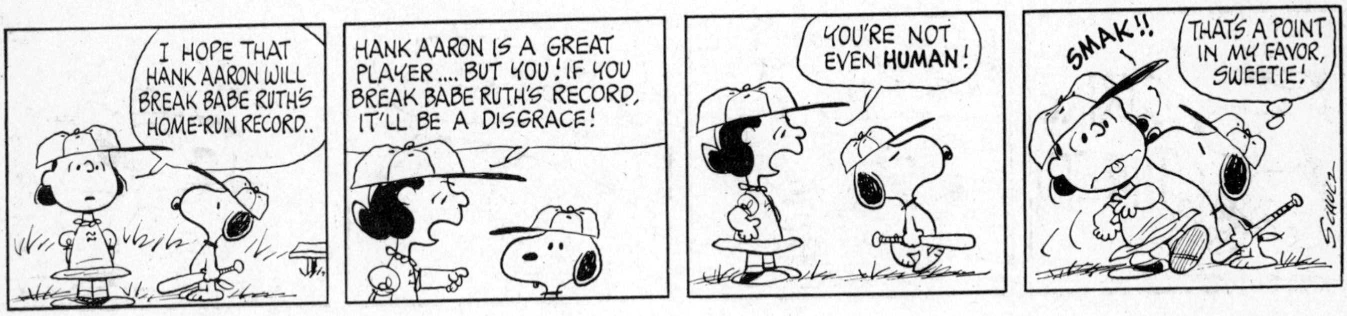
I HOPE THAT HANK AARON WILL BREAK BABE RUTH'S HOME-RUN RECORD..
HANK AARON IS A GREAT PLAYER.... BUT YOU! IF YOU BREAK BABE RUTH'S RECORD, IT'LL BE A DISGRACE!
YOU'RE NOT EVEN HUMAN!
SMAK!!
THAT'S A POINT IN MY FAVOR, SWEETIE!
SCHULZ

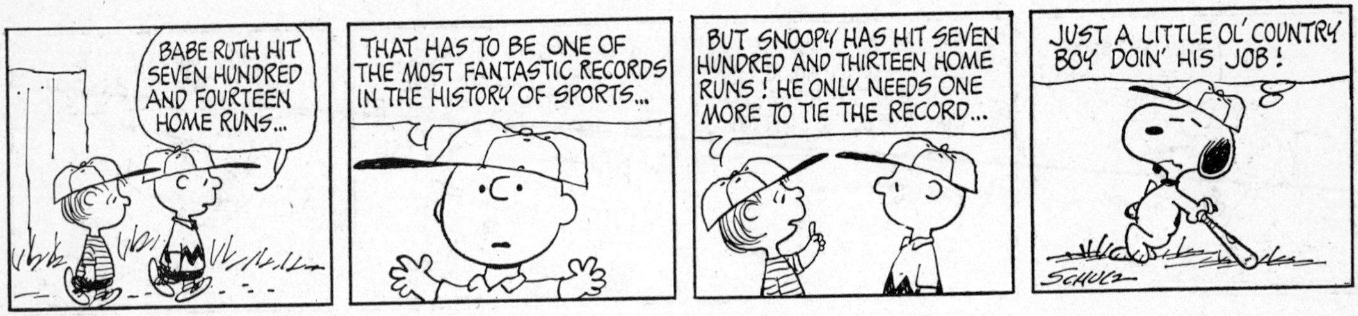
BABE RUTH HIT SEVEN HUNDRED AND FOURTEEN HOME RUNS...
THAT HAS TO BE ONE OF THE MOST FANTASTIC RECORDS IN THE HISTORY OF SPORTS...
BUT SNOOPY HAS HIT SEVEN HUNDRED AND THIRTEEN HOME RUNS! HE ONLY NEEDS ONE MORE TO TIE THE RECORD...
JUST A LITTLE OL' COUNTRY BOY DOIN' HIS JOB!
SCHULZ

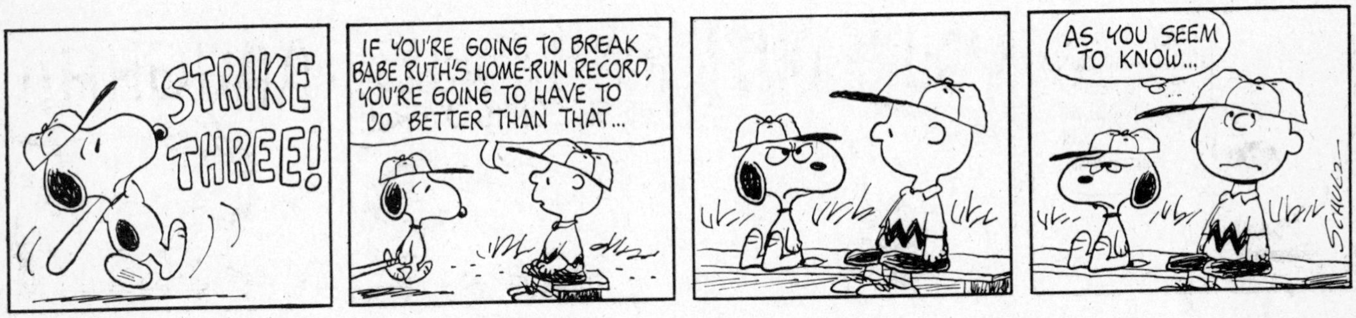
STRIKE THREE!
IF YOU'RE GOING TO BREAK BABE RUTH'S HOME-RUN RECORD, YOU'RE GOING TO HAVE TO DO BETTER THAN THAT...
AS YOU SEEM TO KNOW...
SCHULZ

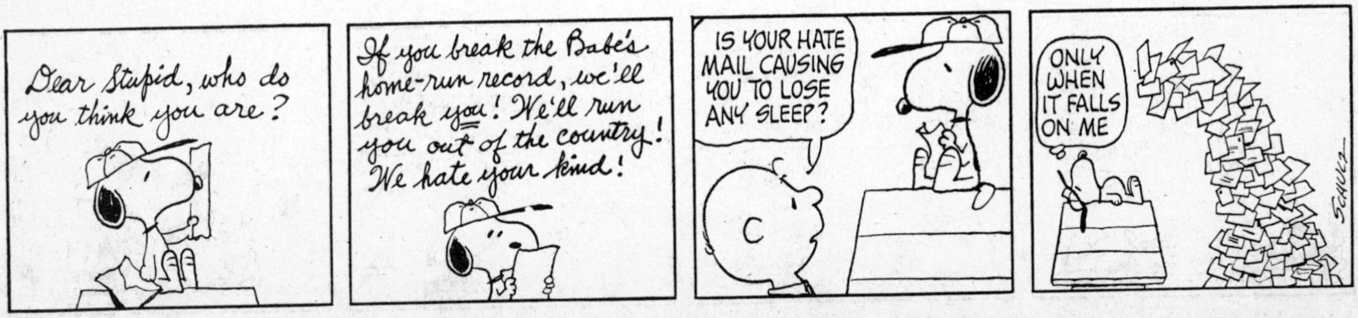
Dear Stupid, who do you think you are?
If you break the Babe's home-run record, we'll break you! We'll run you out of the country! We hate your kind!
IS YOUR HATE MAIL CAUSING YOU TO LOSE ANY SLEEP?
ONLY WHEN IT FALLS ON ME
SCHULZ

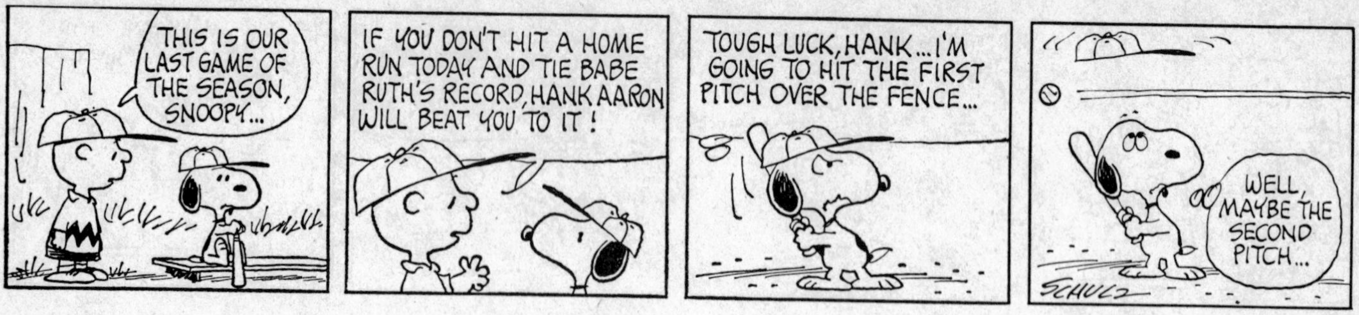
THIS IS OUR LAST GAME OF THE SEASON, SNOOPY...
IF YOU DON'T HIT A HOME RUN TODAY AND TIE BABE RUTH'S RECORD, HANK AARON WILL BEAT YOU TO IT!
TOUGH LUCK, HANK... I'M GOING TO HIT THE FIRST PITCH OVER THE FENCE...
WELL, MAYBE THE SECOND PITCH...
SCHULZ

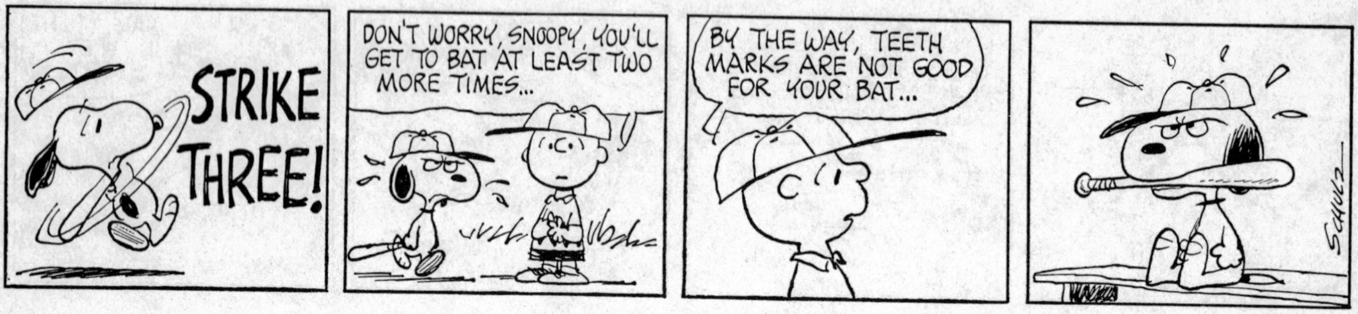
STRIKE THREE!
DON'T WORRY, SNOOPY, YOU'LL GET TO BAT AT LEAST TWO MORE TIMES...
BY THE WAY, TEETH MARKS ARE NOT GOOD FOR YOUR BAT...
SCHULZ

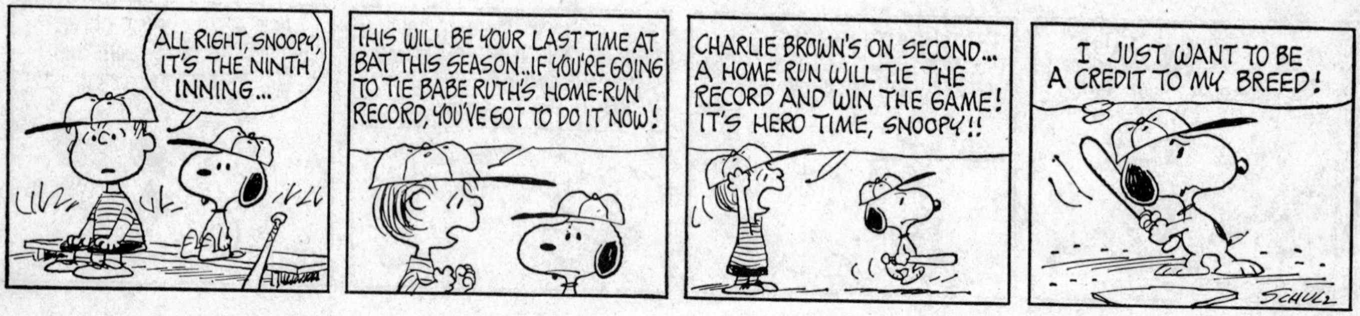
ALL RIGHT, SNOOPY, IT'S THE NINTH INNING...
THIS WILL BE YOUR LAST TIME AT BAT THIS SEASON.. IF YOU'RE GOING TO TIE BABE RUTH'S HOME-RUN RECORD, YOU'VE GOT TO DO IT NOW!
CHARLIE BROWN'S ON SECOND... A HOME RUN WILL TIE THE RECORD AND WIN THE GAME! IT'S HERO TIME, SNOOPY!!
I JUST WANT TO BE A CREDIT TO MY BREED!
SCHULZ

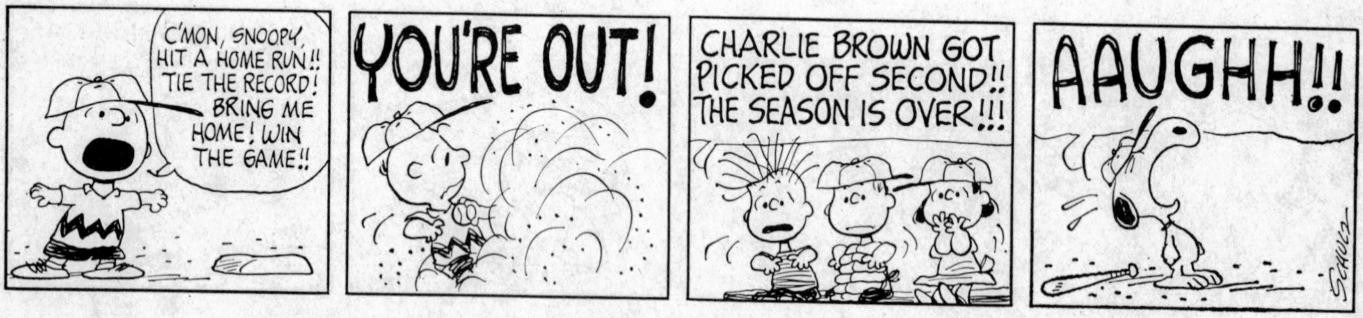
C'MON, SNOOPY, HIT A HOME RUN!! TIE THE RECORD! BRING ME HOME! WIN THE GAME!!
YOU'RE OUT!
CHARLIE BROWN GOT PICKED OFF SECOND!! THE SEASON IS OVER!!!
AAUGHH!!
SCHULZ

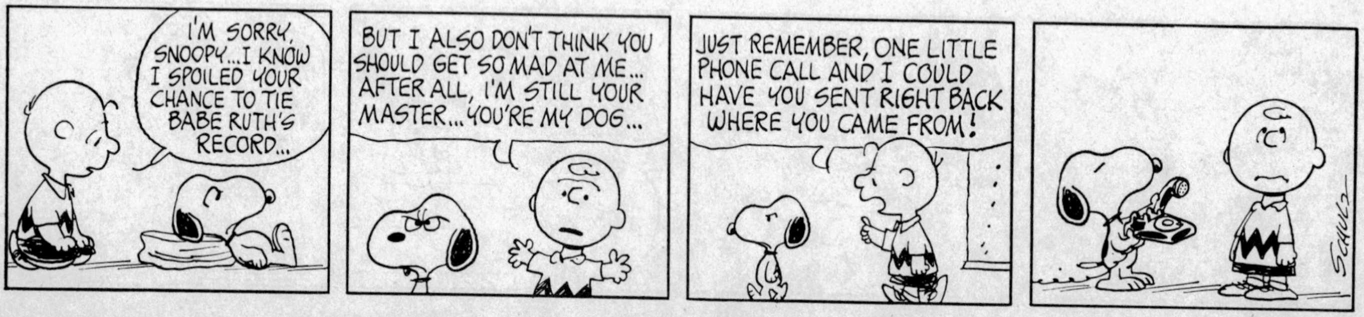
I'M SORRY, SNOOPY... I KNOW I SPOILED YOUR CHANCE TO TIE BABE RUTH'S RECORD...
BUT I ALSO DON'T THINK YOU SHOULD GET SO MAD AT ME... AFTER ALL, I'M STILL YOUR MASTER... YOU'RE MY DOG...
JUST REMEMBER, ONE LITTLE PHONE CALL AND I COULD HAVE YOU SENT RIGHT BACK WHERE YOU CAME FROM!
SCHULZ

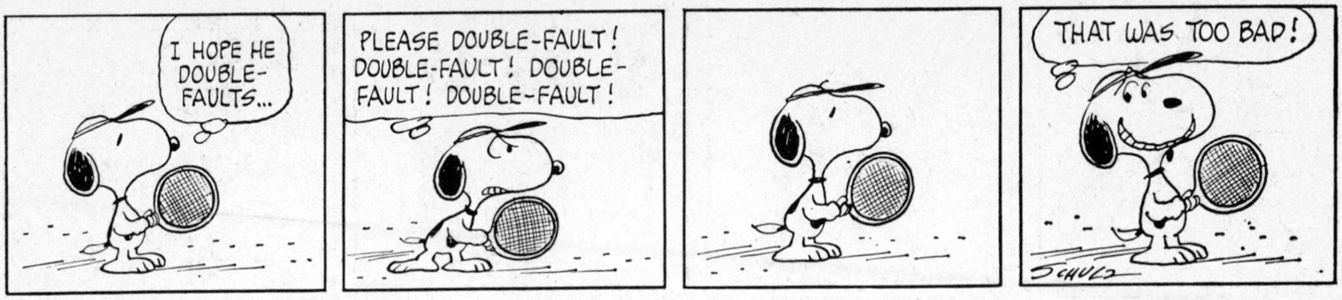
I HOPE HE DOUBLE-FAULTS...
PLEASE DOUBLE-FAULT! DOUBLE-FAULT! DOUBLE-FAULT! DOUBLE-FAULT!
THAT WAS TOO BAD!
SCHULZ

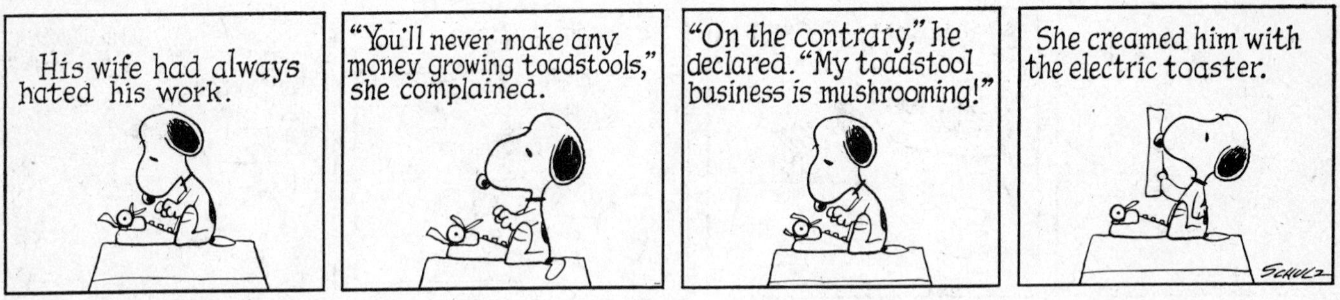
His wife had always hated his work.
"You'll never make any money growing toadstools," she complained.
"On the contrary," he declared. "My toadstool business is mushrooming!"
She creamed him with the electric toaster.
SCHULZ

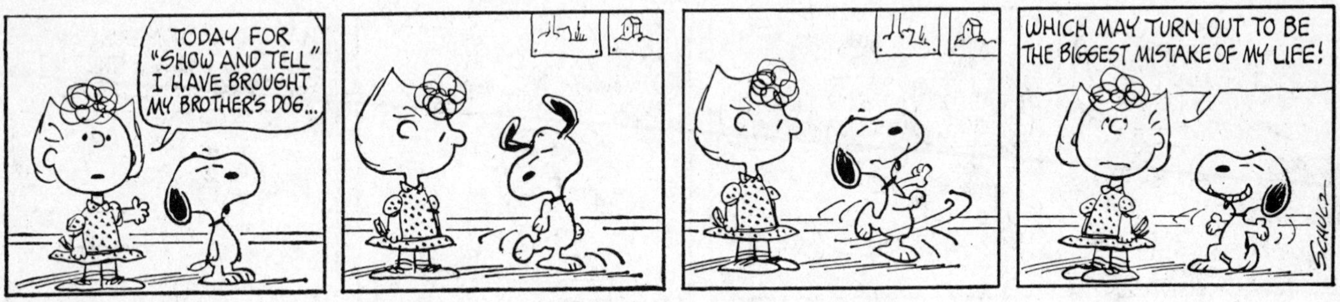
TODAY FOR "SHOW AND TELL" I HAVE BROUGHT MY BROTHER'S DOG...
WHICH MAY TURN OUT TO BE THE BIGGEST MISTAKE OF MY LIFE!
SCHULZ

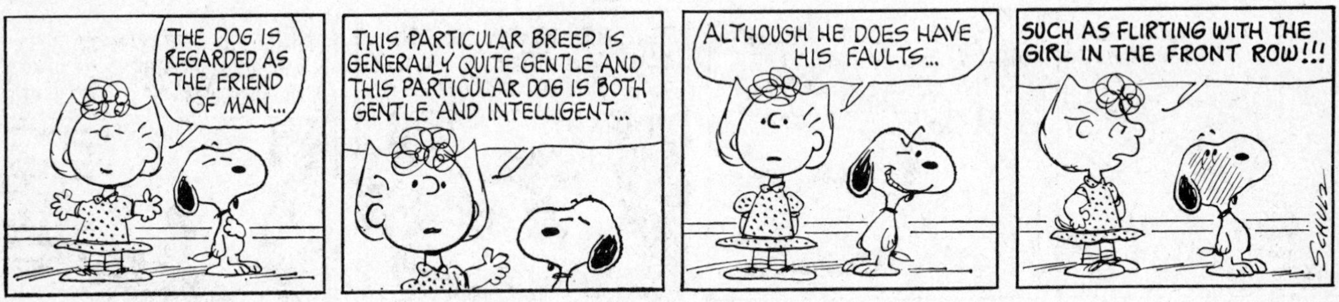
THE DOG IS REGARDED AS THE FRIEND OF MAN...
THIS PARTICULAR BREED IS GENERALLY QUITE GENTLE AND THIS PARTICULAR DOG IS BOTH GENTLE AND INTELLIGENT...
ALTHOUGH HE DOES HAVE HIS FAULTS...
SUCH AS FLIRTING WITH THE GIRL IN THE FRONT ROW!!!
SCHULZ

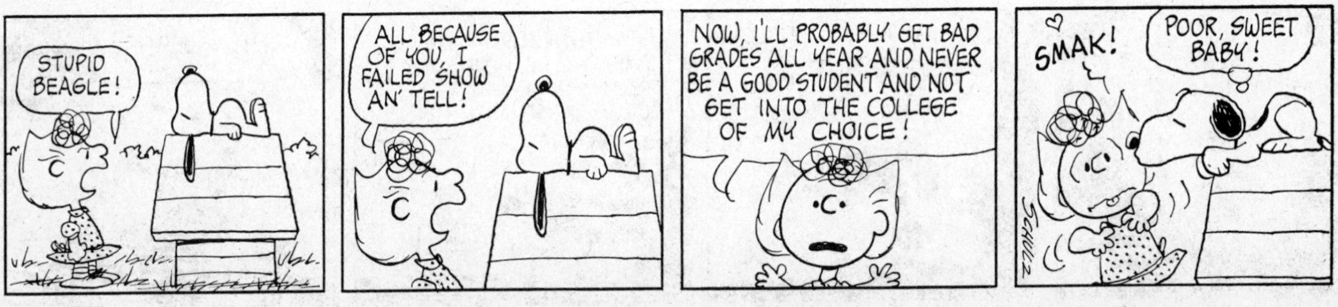
STUPID BEAGLE!
ALL BECAUSE OF YOU, I FAILED SHOW AN' TELL!
NOW, I'LL PROBABLY GET BAD GRADES ALL YEAR AND NEVER BE A GOOD STUDENT AND NOT GET INTO THE COLLEGE OF MY CHOICE!
SMAK!
POOR, SWEET BABY!
SCHULZ

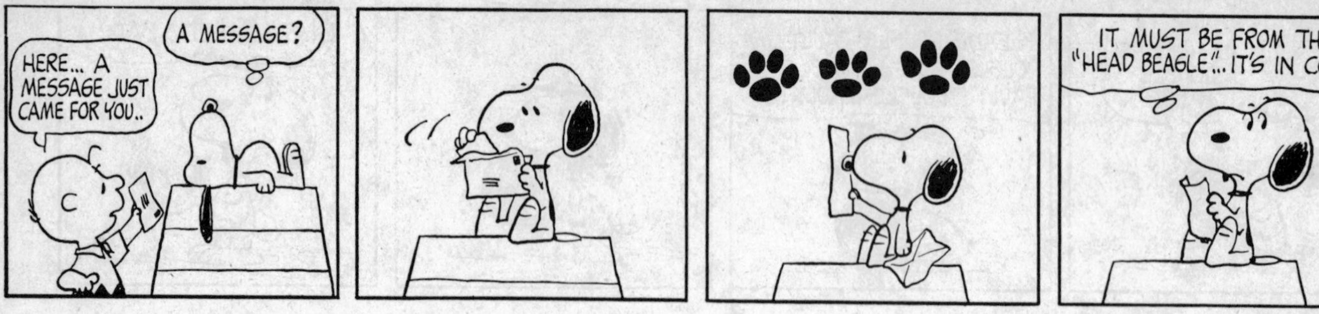
HERE... A MESSAGE JUST CAME FOR YOU..
A MESSAGE?
IT MUST BE FROM THE "HEAD BEAGLE"... IT'S IN CODE!
SCHULZ

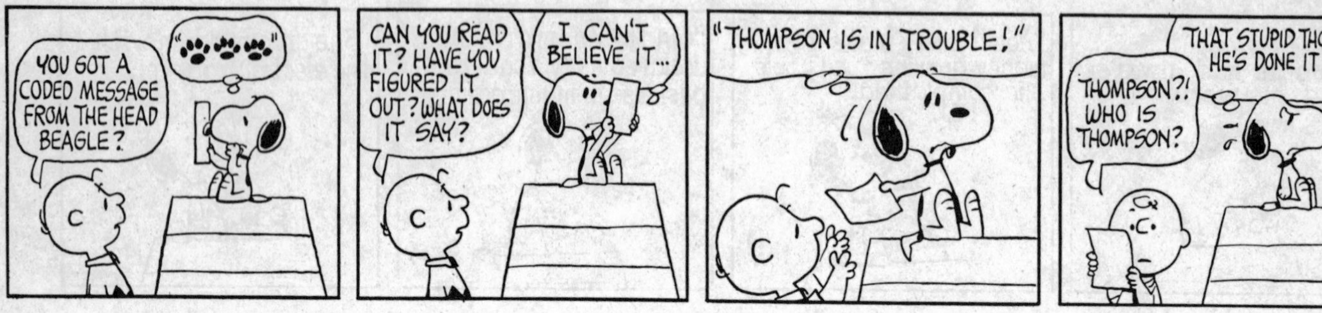
YOU GOT A CODED MESSAGE FROM THE HEAD BEAGLE?
CAN YOU READ IT? HAVE YOU FIGURED IT OUT? WHAT DOES IT SAY?
I CAN'T BELIEVE IT...
"THOMPSON IS IN TROUBLE!"
THOMPSON?! WHO IS THOMPSON?
THAT STUPID THOMPSON! HE'S DONE IT AGAIN!!
SCHULZ

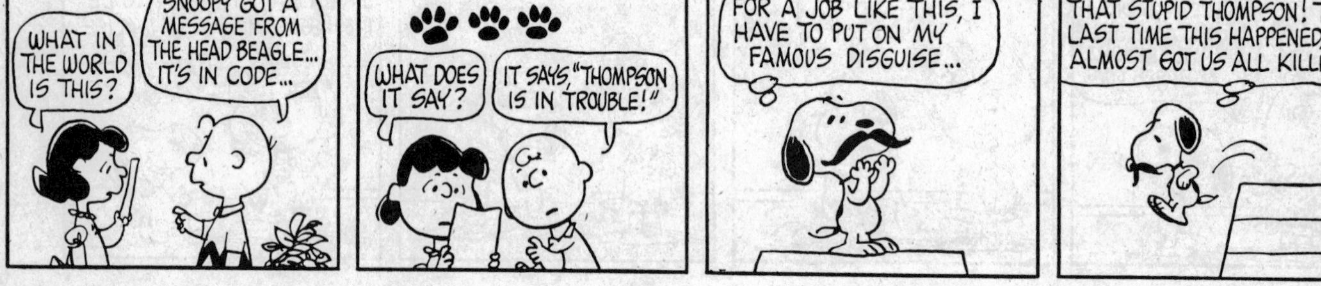
WHAT IN THE WORLD IS THIS?
SNOOPY GOT A MESSAGE FROM THE HEAD BEAGLE... IT'S IN CODE...
WHAT DOES IT SAY?
IT SAYS, "THOMPSON IS IN TROUBLE!"
FOR A JOB LIKE THIS, I HAVE TO PUT ON MY FAMOUS DISGUISE...
THAT STUPID THOMPSON! THE LAST TIME THIS HAPPENED, HE ALMOST GOT US ALL KILLED...
SCHULZ

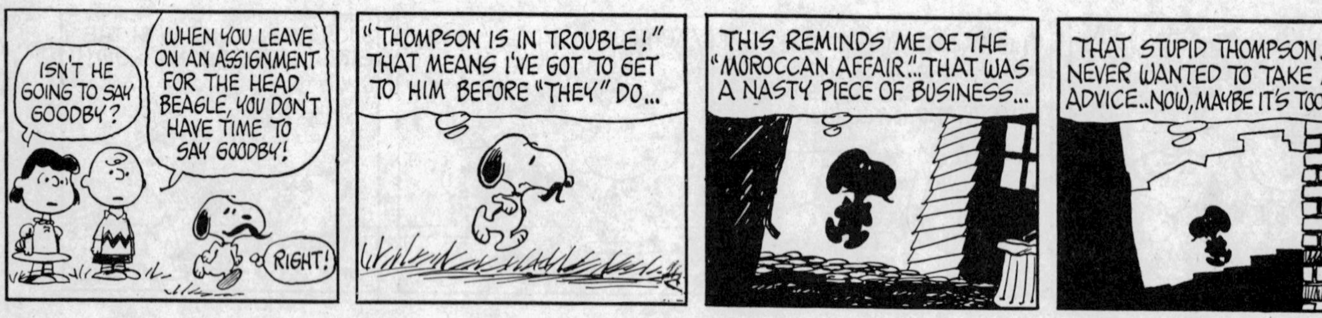
ISN'T HE GOING TO SAY GOODBY?
WHEN YOU LEAVE ON AN ASSIGNMENT FOR THE HEAD BEAGLE, YOU DON'T HAVE TIME TO SAY GOODBY!
RIGHT!
"THOMPSON IS IN TROUBLE!" THAT MEANS I'VE GOT TO GET TO HIM BEFORE "THEY" DO...
THIS REMINDS ME OF THE "MOROCCAN AFFAIR"... THAT WAS A NASTY PIECE OF BUSINESS...
THAT STUPID THOMPSON... HE NEVER WANTED TO TAKE ANY ADVICE.. NOW, MAYBE IT'S TOO LATE..
SCHULZ

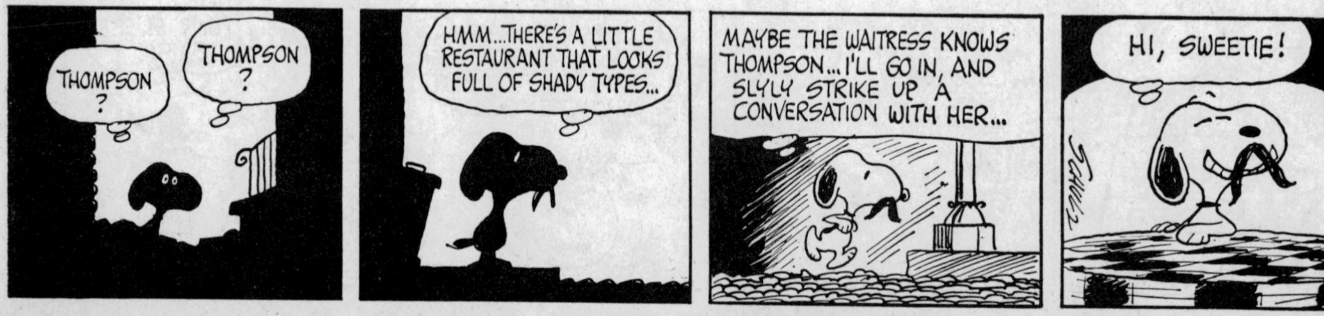
THOMPSON?
THOMPSON?
HMM... THERE'S A LITTLE RESTAURANT THAT LOOKS FULL OF SHADY TYPES...
MAYBE THE WAITRESS KNOWS THOMPSON... I'LL GO IN, AND SLYLY STRIKE UP A CONVERSATION WITH HER...
HI, SWEETIE!
SCHULZ

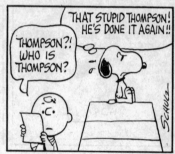

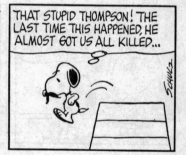

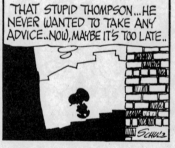

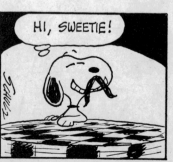

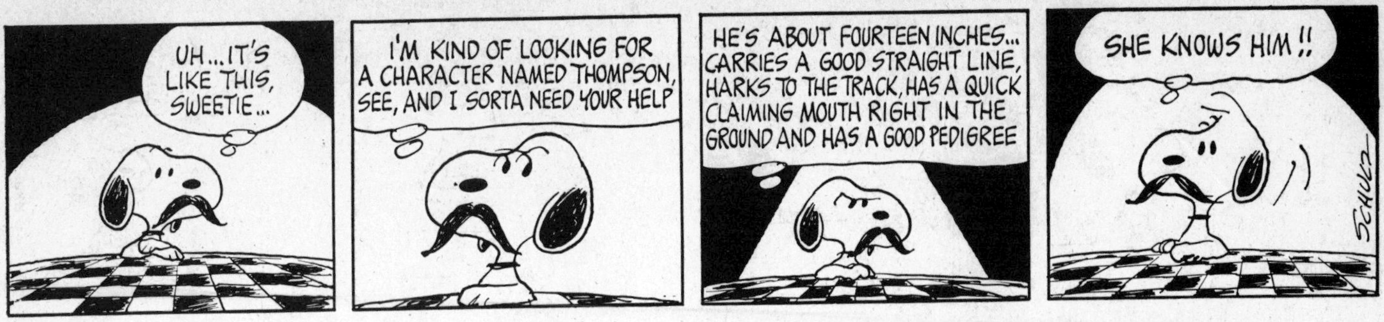
UH... IT'S LIKE THIS, SWEETIE...
I'M KIND OF LOOKING FOR A CHARACTER NAMED THOMPSON, SEE, AND I SORTA NEED YOUR HELP
HE'S ABOUT FOURTEEN INCHES... CARRIES A GOOD STRAIGHT LINE, HARKS TO THE TRACK, HAS A QUICK CLAIMING MOUTH RIGHT IN THE GROUND AND HAS A GOOD PEDIGREE
SHE KNOWS HIM!!

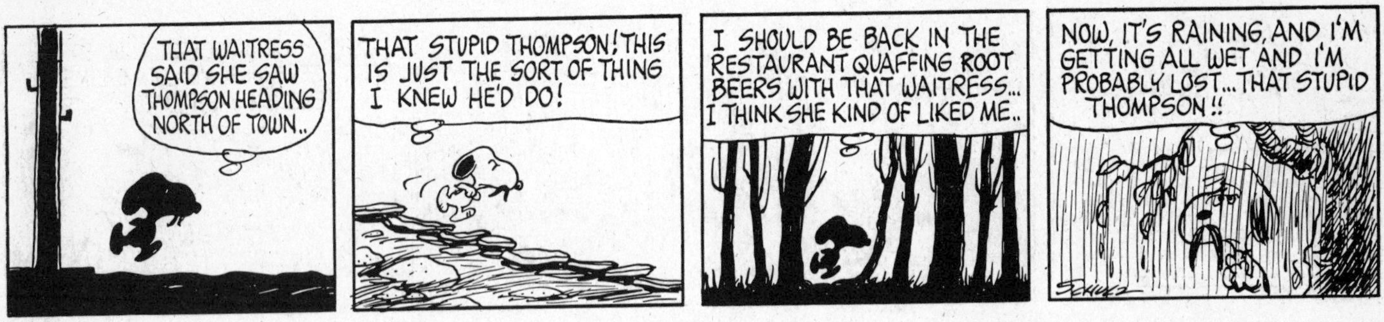
THAT WAITRESS SAID SHE SAW THOMPSON HEADING NORTH OF TOWN..
THAT STUPID THOMPSON! THIS IS JUST THE SORT OF THING I KNEW HE'D DO!
I SHOULD BE BACK IN THE RESTAURANT QUAFFING ROOT BEERS WITH THAT WAITRESS... I THINK SHE KIND OF LIKED ME..
NOW, IT'S RAINING, AND I'M GETTING ALL WET AND I'M PROBABLY LOST... THAT STUPID THOMPSON!!

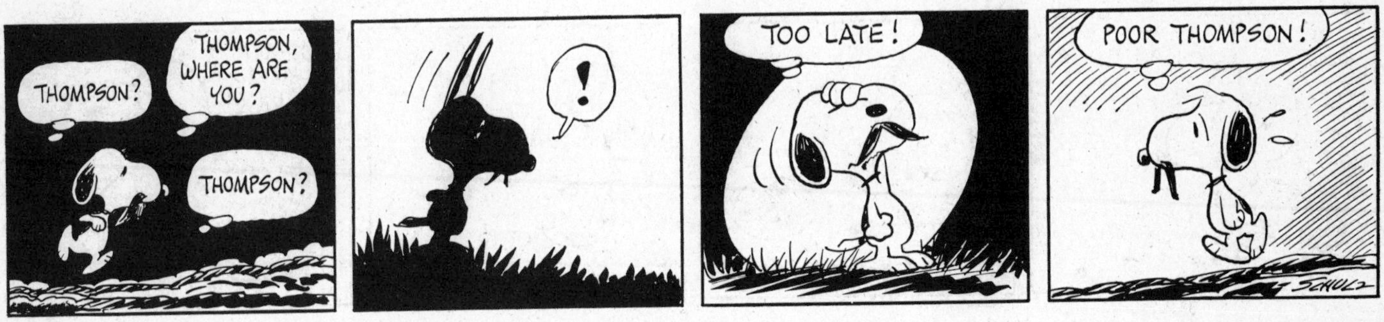
THOMPSON?
THOMPSON, WHERE ARE YOU?
THOMPSON?
!
TOO LATE!
POOR THOMPSON!

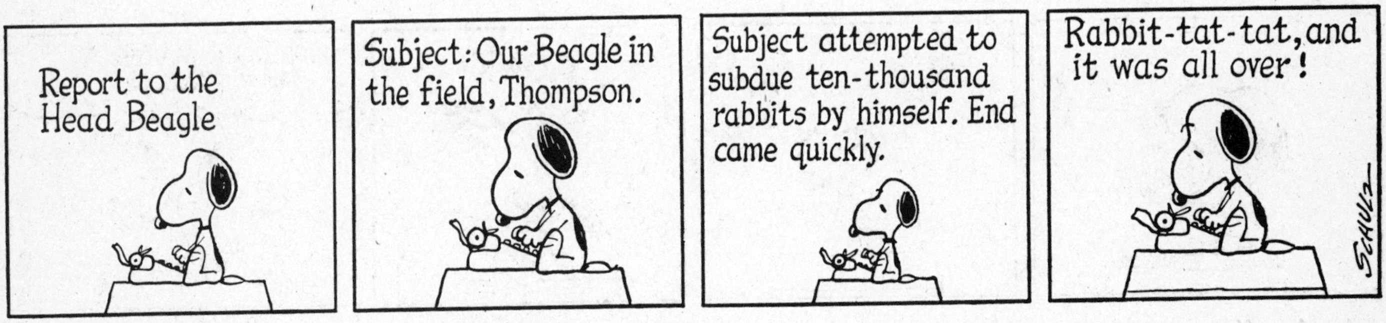
Report to the Head Beagle
Subject: Our Beagle in the field, Thompson.
Subject attempted to subdue ten-thousand rabbits by himself. End came quickly.
Rabbit-tat-tat, and it was all over!

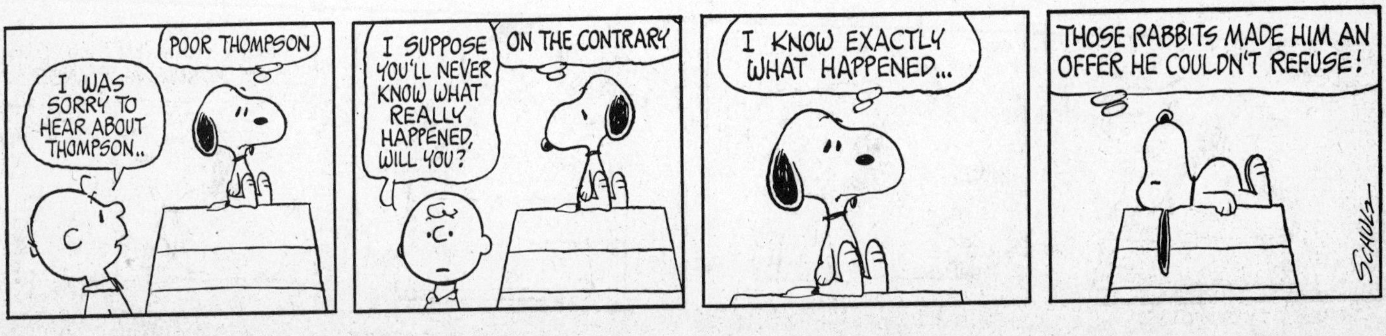
I WAS SORRY TO HEAR ABOUT THOMPSON..
POOR THOMPSON
I SUPPOSE YOU'LL NEVER KNOW WHAT REALLY HAPPENED, WILL YOU?
ON THE CONTRARY
I KNOW EXACTLY WHAT HAPPENED...
THOSE RABBITS MADE HIM AN OFFER HE COULDN'T REFUSE!

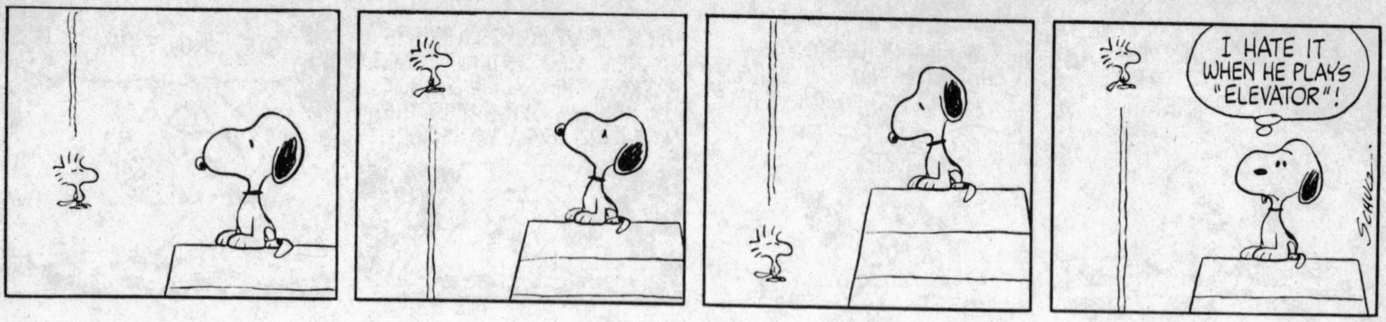
I HATE IT WHEN HE PLAYS "ELEVATOR"!
SCHULZ

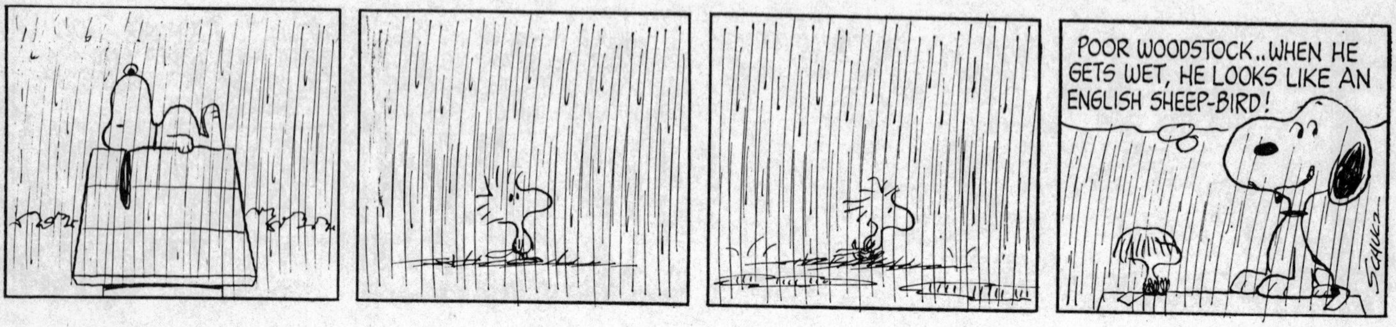
POOR WOODSTOCK..WHEN HE GETS WET, HE LOOKS LIKE AN ENGLISH SHEEP-BIRD!
SCHULZ

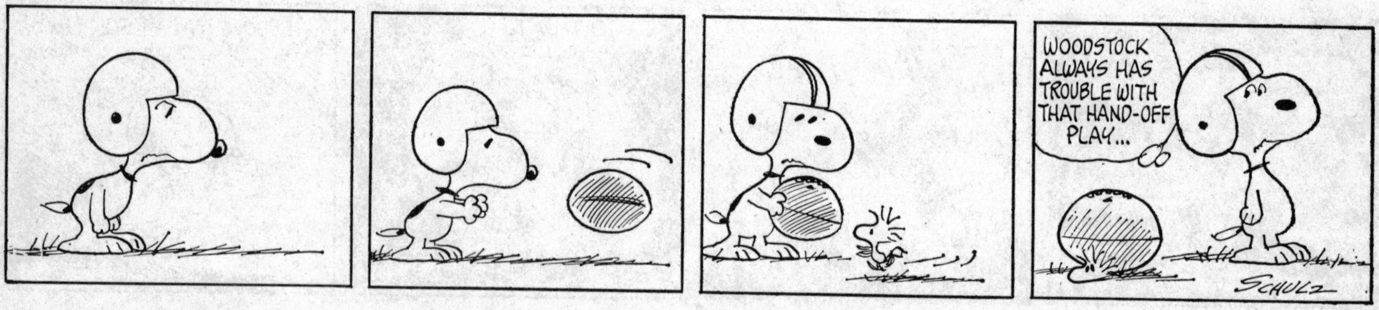
WOODSTOCK ALWAYS HAS TROUBLE WITH THAT HAND-OFF PLAY...
SCHULZ

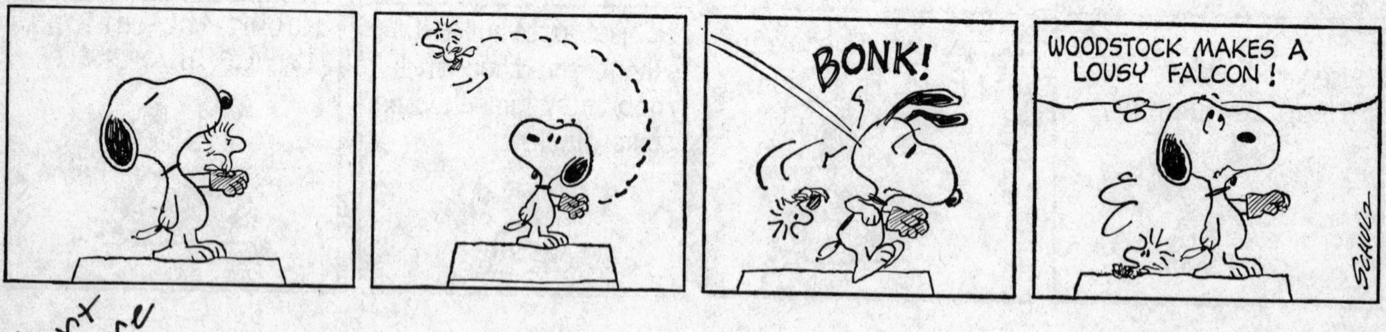
BONK!
WOODSTOCK MAKES A LOUSY FALCON!
SCHULZ

*Start here

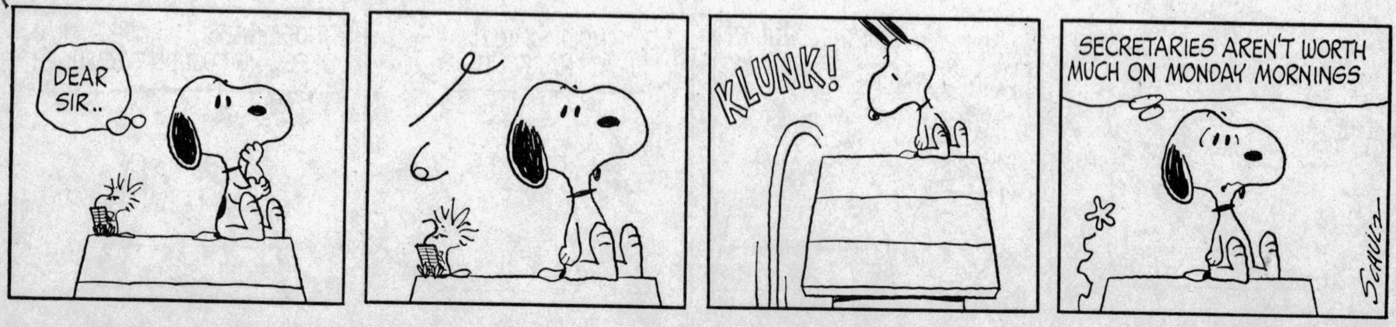
DEAR SIR..
KLUNK!
SECRETARIES AREN'T WORTH MUCH ON MONDAY MORNINGS
SCHULZ

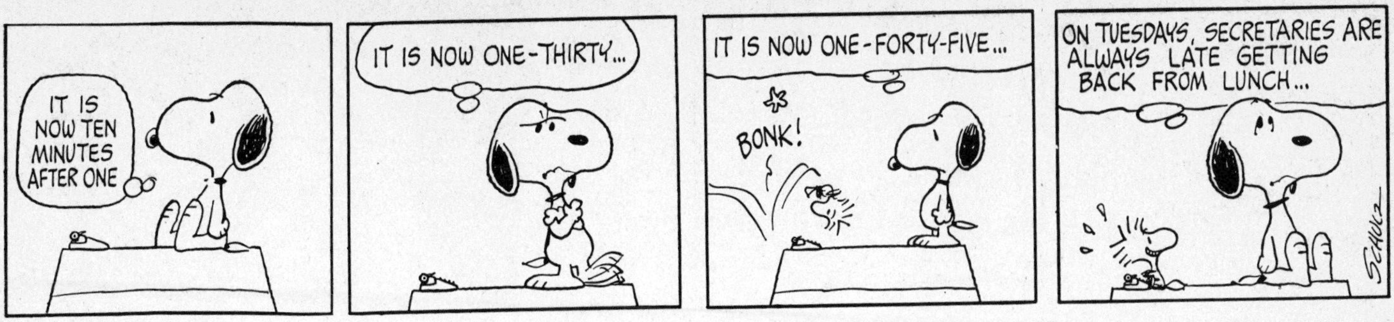
IT IS NOW TEN MINUTES AFTER ONE
IT IS NOW ONE-THIRTY...
IT IS NOW ONE-FORTY-FIVE...
BONK!
ON TUESDAYS, SECRETARIES ARE ALWAYS LATE GETTING BACK FROM LUNCH...
SCHULZ

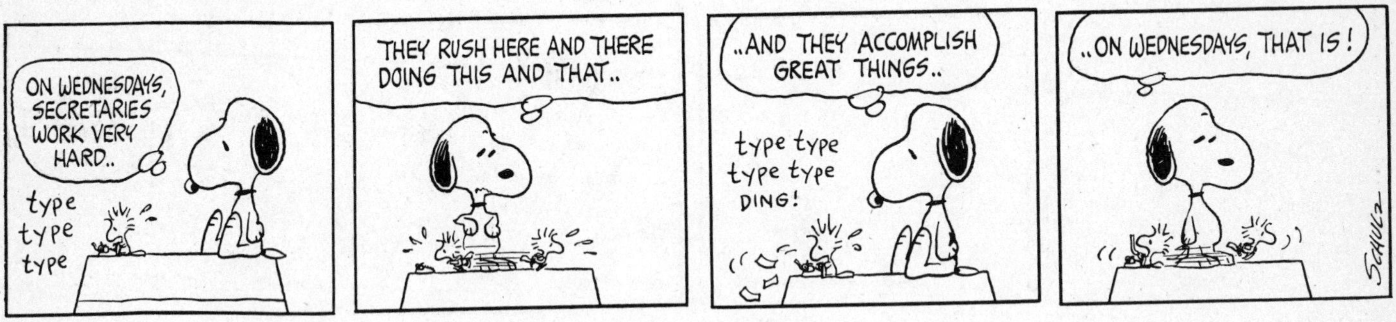
ON WEDNESDAYS, SECRETARIES WORK VERY HARD..
type type type
THEY RUSH HERE AND THERE DOING THIS AND THAT..
..AND THEY ACCOMPLISH GREAT THINGS..
type type type type DING!
..ON WEDNESDAYS, THAT IS!
SCHULZ

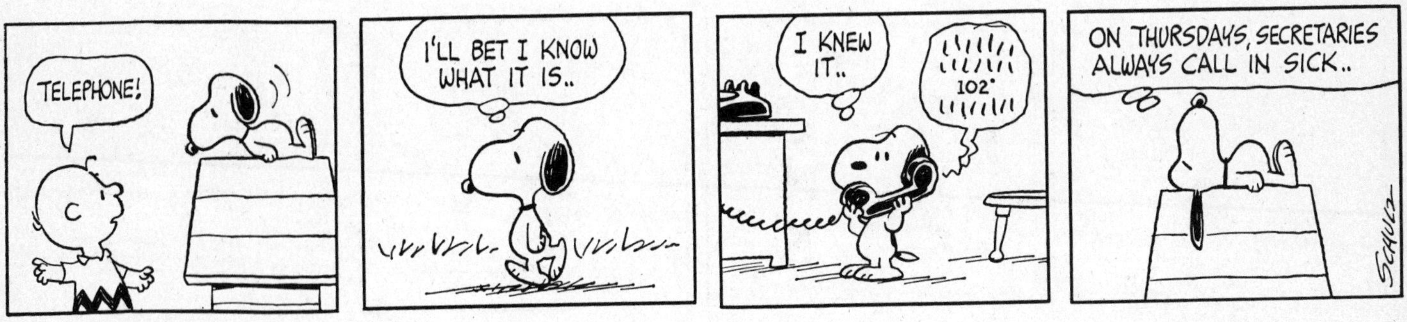
TELEPHONE!
I'LL BET I KNOW WHAT IT IS..
I KNEW IT..
102°
ON THURSDAYS, SECRETARIES ALWAYS CALL IN SICK..
SCHULZ

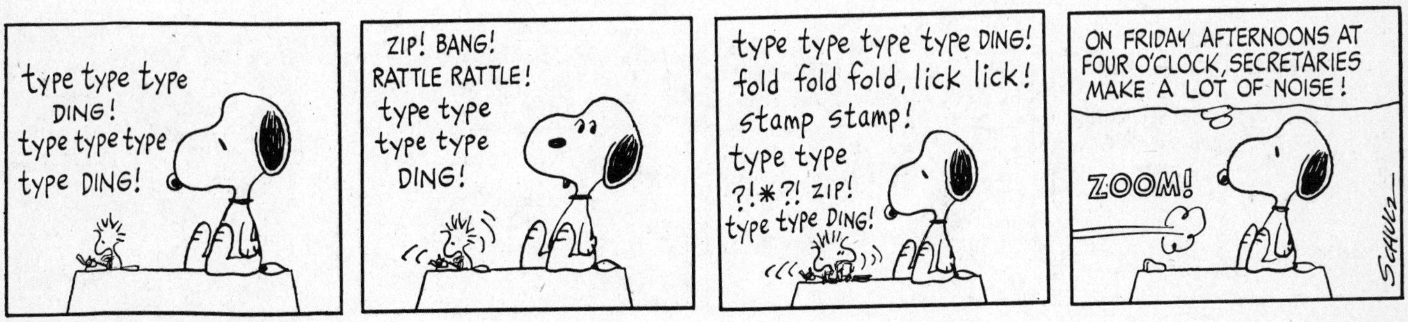
type type type DING! type type type type DING!
ZIP! BANG! RATTLE RATTLE! type type type type DING!
type type type type DING! fold fold fold, lick lick! stamp stamp! type type ?!*?! ZIP! type type DING!
ON FRIDAY AFTERNOONS AT FOUR O'CLOCK, SECRETARIES MAKE A LOT OF NOISE!
ZOOM!
SCHULZ

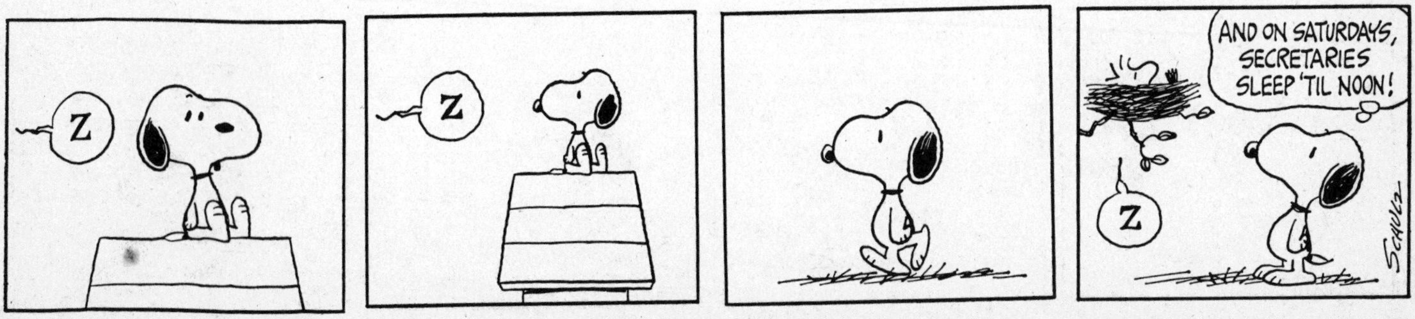
Z
Z
AND ON SATURDAYS, SECRETARIES SLEEP 'TIL NOON!
Z
SCHULZ

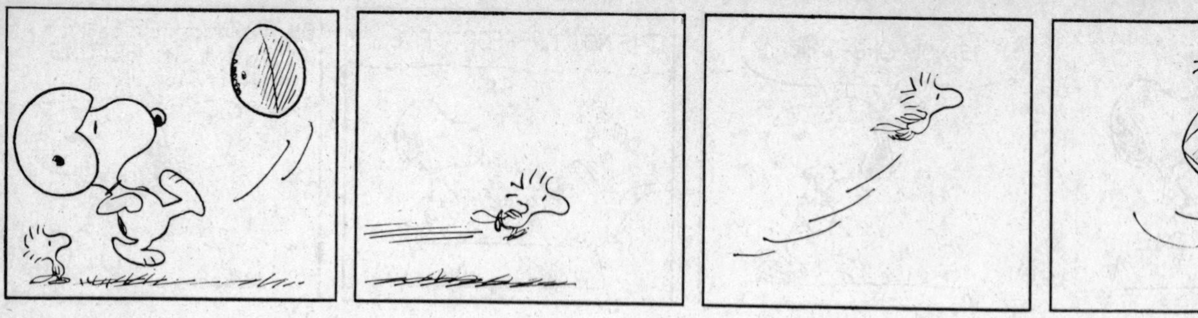
SCHULZ

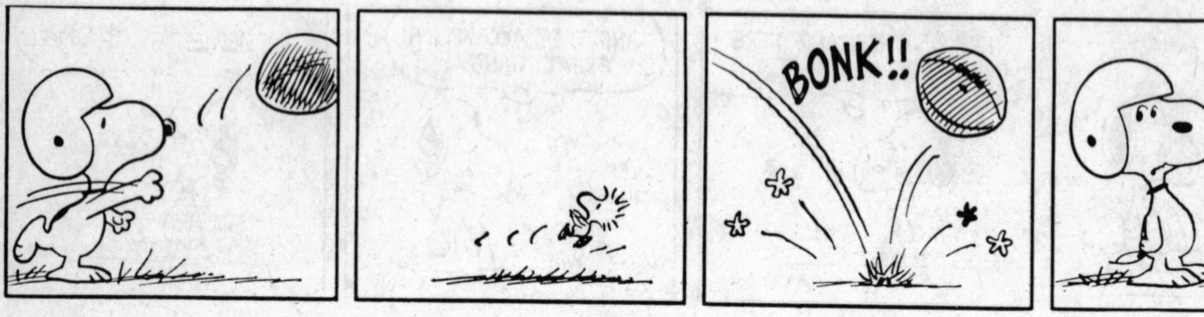
BONK!!
LAST ROUND DRAFT CHOICE!
SCHULZ

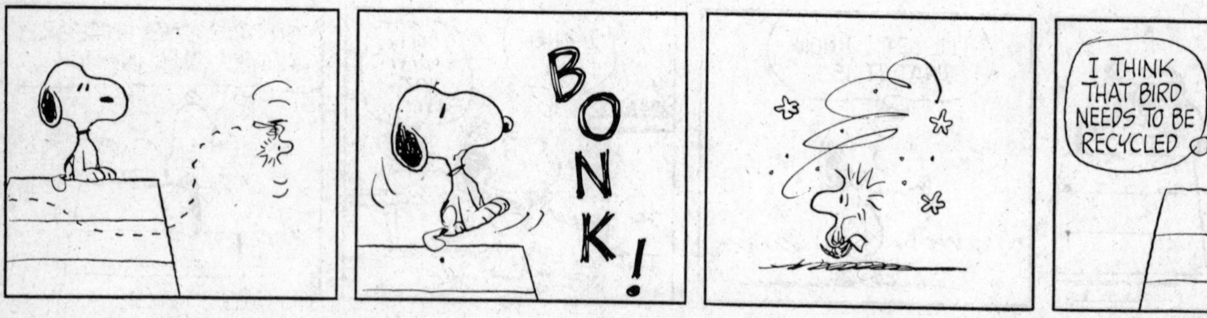
BONK!
I THINK THAT BIRD NEEDS TO BE RECYCLED
SCHULZ

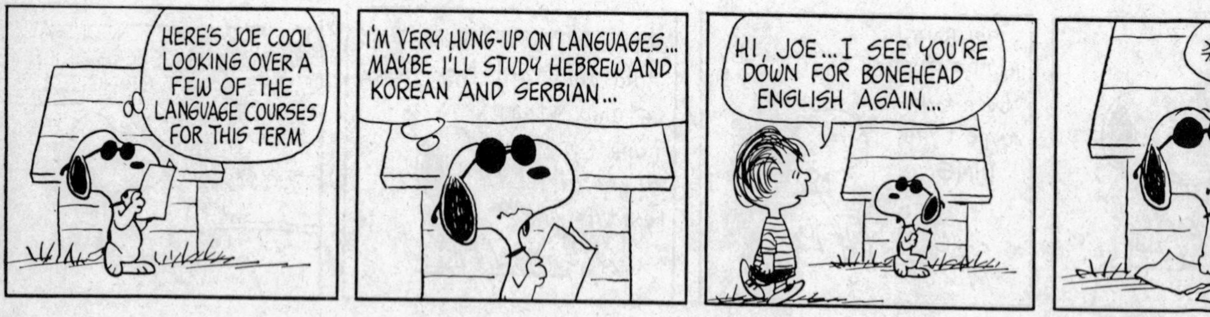
HERE'S JOE COOL LOOKING OVER A FEW OF THE LANGUAGE COURSES FOR THIS TERM
I'M VERY HUNG-UP ON LANGUAGES... MAYBE I'LL STUDY HEBREW AND KOREAN AND SERBIAN...
HI, JOE... I SEE YOU'RE DOWN FOR BONEHEAD ENGLISH AGAIN...
SIGH
SCHULZ

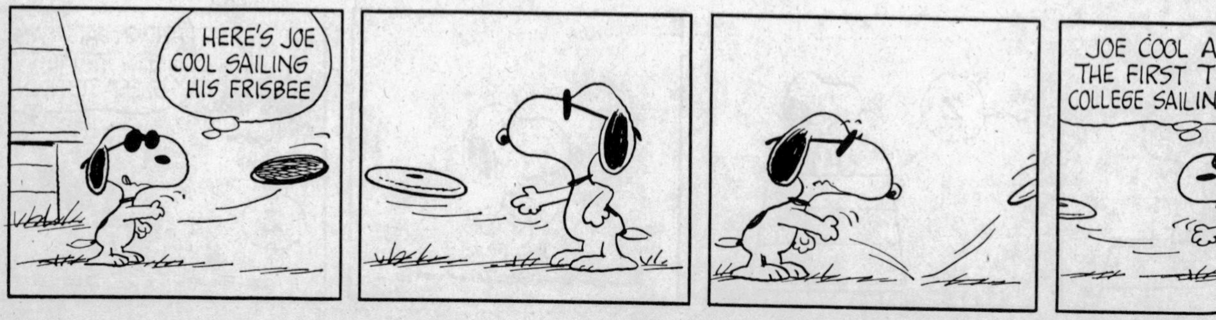
HERE'S JOE COOL SAILING HIS FRISBEE
JOE COOL ALWAYS SPENDS THE FIRST TWO WEEKS AT COLLEGE SAILING HIS FRISBEE
SCHULZ

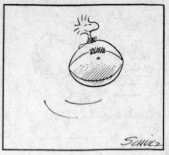

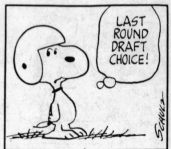

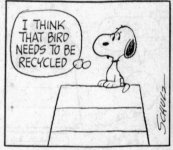

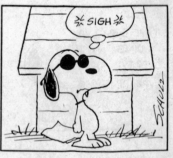

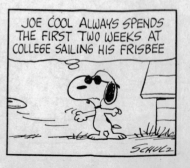

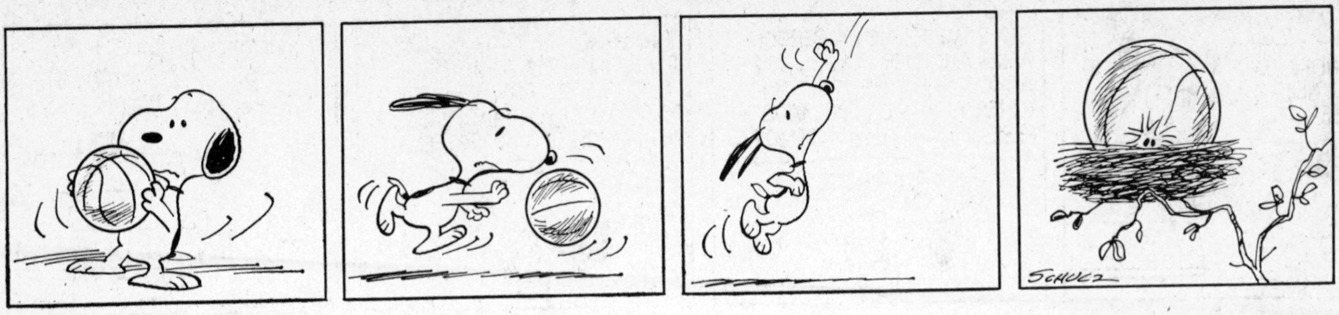

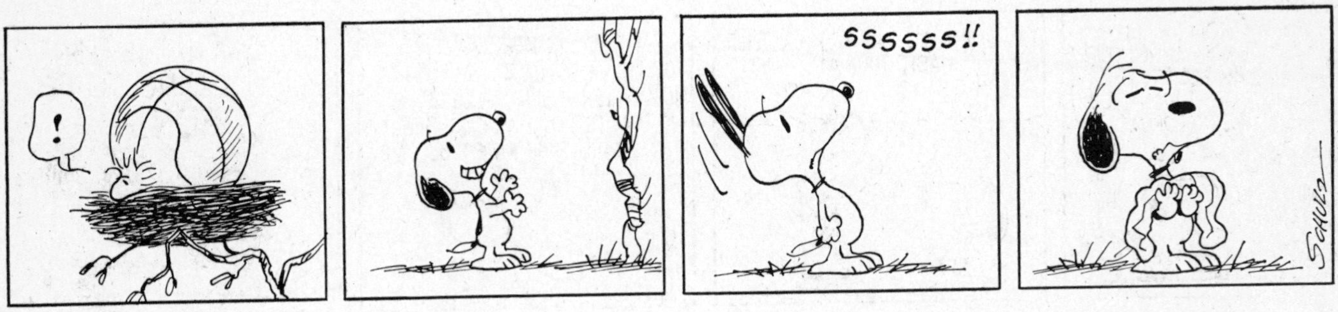
!
SSSSSS!!

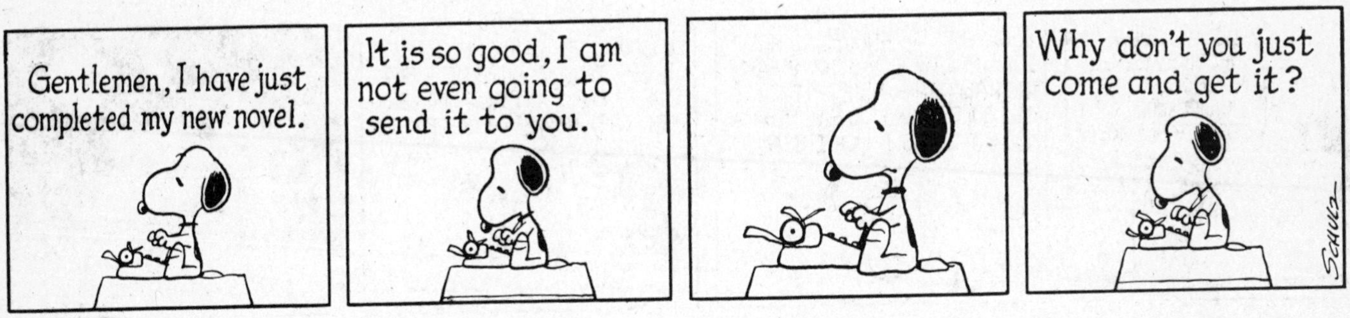
Gentlemen, I have just completed my new novel.
It is so good, I am not even going to send it to you.
Why don't you just come and get it?

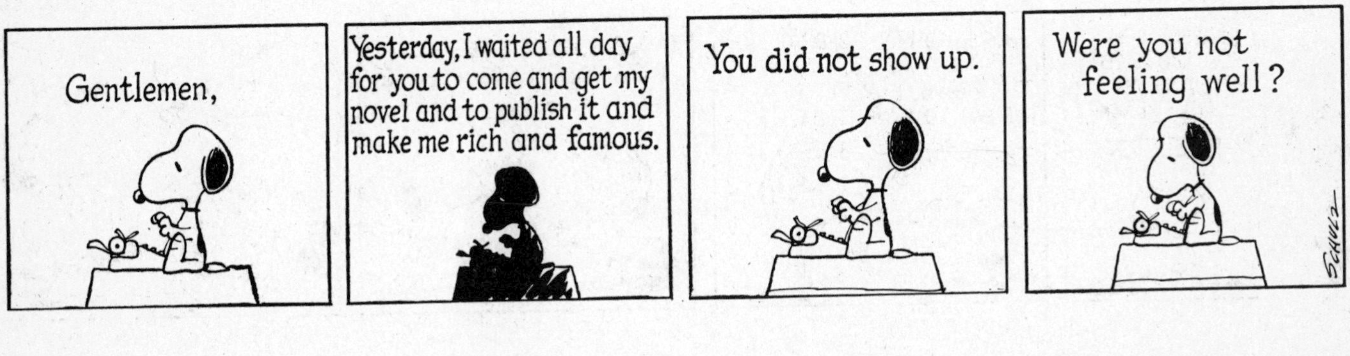
Gentlemen,
Yesterday, I waited all day for you to come and get my novel and to publish it and make me rich and famous.
You did not show up.
Were you not feeling well?

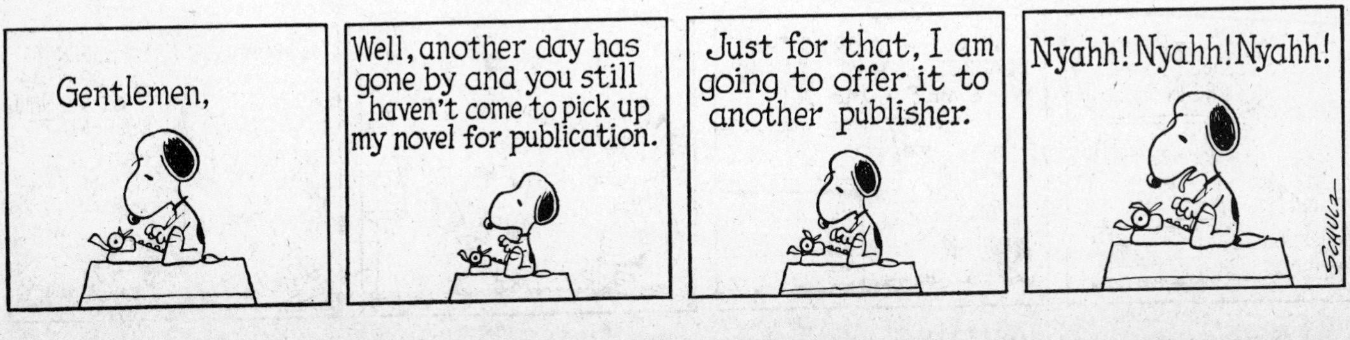
Gentlemen,
Well, another day has gone by and you still haven't come to pick up my novel for publication.
Just for that, I am going to offer it to another publisher.
Nyahh! Nyahh! Nyahh!

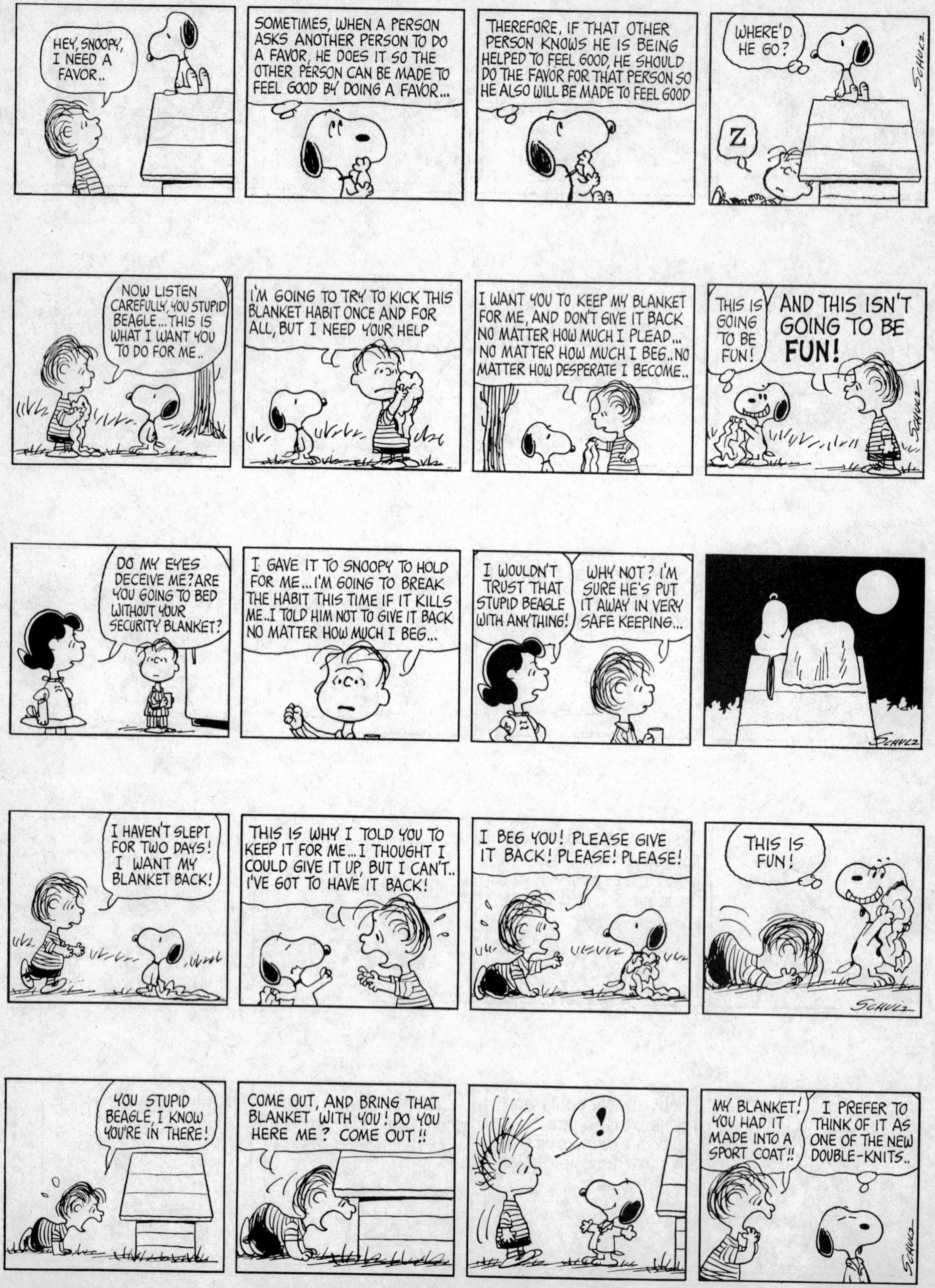
HEY, SNOOPY, I NEED A FAVOR..
SOMETIMES, WHEN A PERSON ASKS ANOTHER PERSON TO DO A FAVOR, HE DOES IT SO THE OTHER PERSON CAN BE MADE TO FEEL GOOD BY DOING A FAVOR...
THEREFORE, IF THAT OTHER PERSON KNOWS HE IS BEING HELPED TO FEEL GOOD, HE SHOULD DO THE FAVOR FOR THAT PERSON SO HE ALSO WILL BE MADE TO FEEL GOOD
WHERE'D HE GO?
Z
SCHULZ
NOW LISTEN CAREFULLY, YOU STUPID BEAGLE...THIS IS WHAT I WANT YOU TO DO FOR ME..
I'M GOING TO TRY TO KICK THIS BLANKET HABIT ONCE AND FOR ALL, BUT I NEED YOUR HELP
I WANT YOU TO KEEP MY BLANKET FOR ME, AND DON'T GIVE IT BACK NO MATTER HOW MUCH I PLEAD... NO MATTER HOW MUCH I BEG..NO MATTER HOW DESPERATE I BECOME..
THIS IS GOING TO BE FUN!
AND THIS ISN'T GOING TO BE FUN!
SCHULZ
DO MY EYES DECEIVE ME? ARE YOU GOING TO BED WITHOUT YOUR SECURITY BLANKET?
I GAVE IT TO SNOOPY TO HOLD FOR ME...I'M GOING TO BREAK THE HABIT THIS TIME IF IT KILLS ME..I TOLD HIM NOT TO GIVE IT BACK NO MATTER HOW MUCH I BEG...
I WOULDN'T TRUST THAT STUPID BEAGLE WITH ANYTHING!
WHY NOT? I'M SURE HE'S PUT IT AWAY IN VERY SAFE KEEPING...
SCHULZ
I HAVEN'T SLEPT FOR TWO DAYS! I WANT MY BLANKET BACK!
THIS IS WHY I TOLD YOU TO KEEP IT FOR ME...I THOUGHT I COULD GIVE IT UP, BUT I CAN'T.. I'VE GOT TO HAVE IT BACK!
I BEG YOU! PLEASE GIVE IT BACK! PLEASE! PLEASE!
THIS IS FUN!
SCHULZ
YOU STUPID BEAGLE, I KNOW YOU'RE IN THERE!
COME OUT, AND BRING THAT BLANKET WITH YOU! DO YOU HERE ME? COME OUT!!
!
MY BLANKET! YOU HAD IT MADE INTO A SPORT COAT!!
I PREFER TO THINK OF IT AS ONE OF THE NEW DOUBLE-KNITS..
SCHULZ

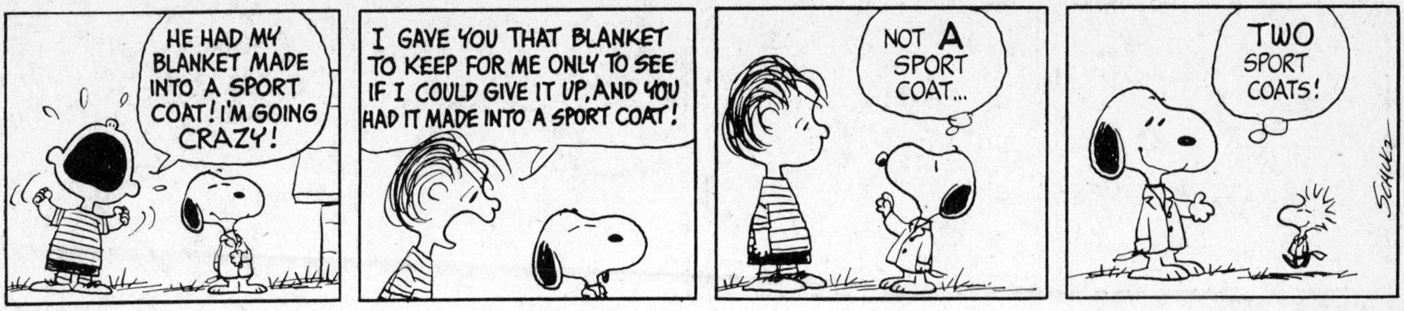
HE HAD MY BLANKET MADE INTO A SPORT COAT! I'M GOING CRAZY!
I GAVE YOU THAT BLANKET TO KEEP FOR ME ONLY TO SEE IF I COULD GIVE IT UP, AND YOU HAD IT MADE INTO A SPORT COAT!
NOT A SPORT COAT...
TWO SPORT COATS!
SCHULZ

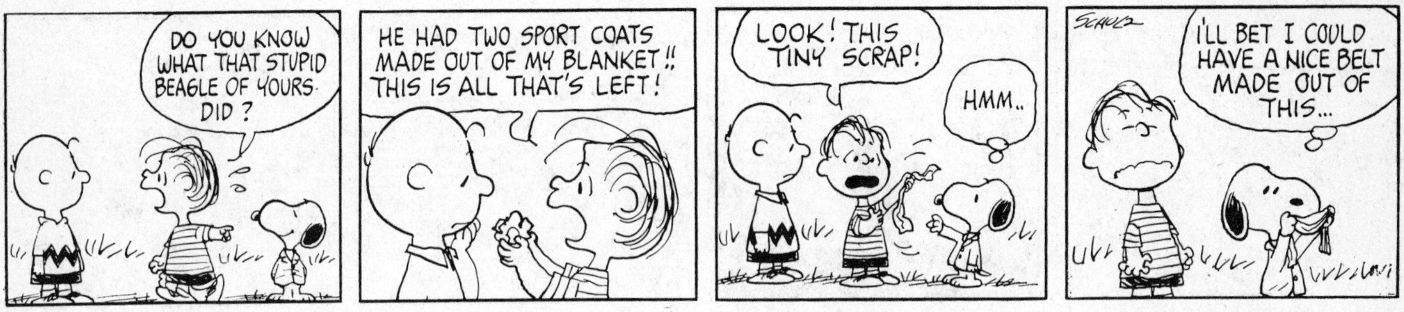
DO YOU KNOW WHAT THAT STUPID BEAGLE OF YOURS DID?
HE HAD TWO SPORT COATS MADE OUT OF MY BLANKET!! THIS IS ALL THAT'S LEFT!
LOOK! THIS TINY SCRAP!
HMM..
SCHULZ
I'LL BET I COULD HAVE A NICE BELT MADE OUT OF THIS...

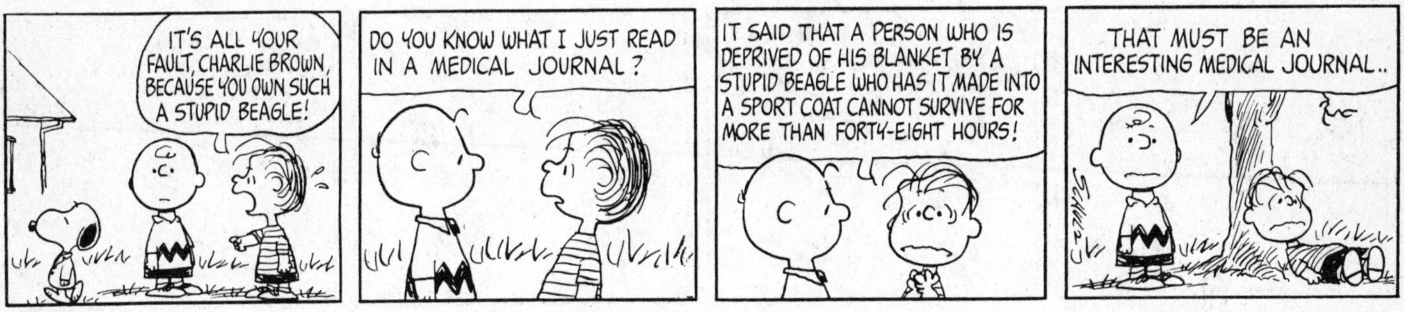
IT'S ALL YOUR FAULT, CHARLIE BROWN, BECAUSE YOU OWN SUCH A STUPID BEAGLE!
DO YOU KNOW WHAT I JUST READ IN A MEDICAL JOURNAL?
IT SAID THAT A PERSON WHO IS DEPRIVED OF HIS BLANKET BY A STUPID BEAGLE WHO HAS IT MADE INTO A SPORT COAT CANNOT SURVIVE FOR MORE THAN FORTY-EIGHT HOURS!
THAT MUST BE AN INTERESTING MEDICAL JOURNAL..
SCHULZ

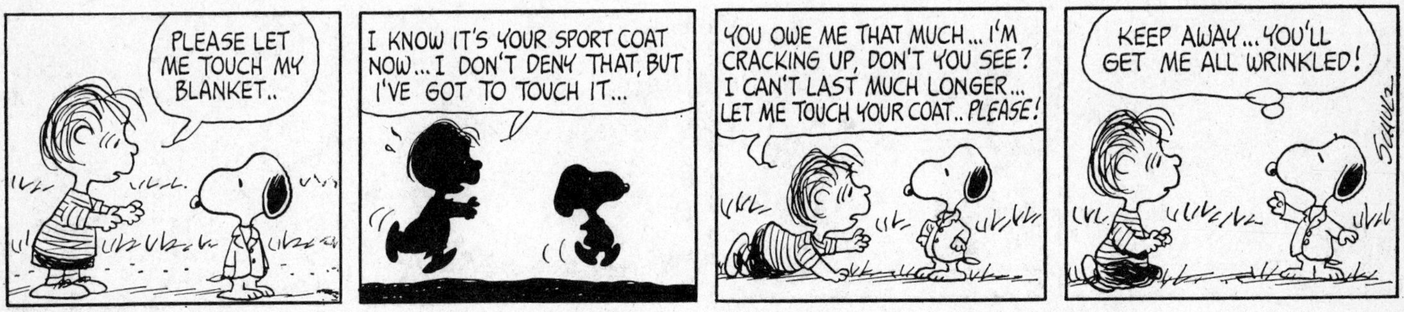
PLEASE LET ME TOUCH MY BLANKET..
I KNOW IT'S YOUR SPORT COAT NOW... I DON'T DENY THAT, BUT I'VE GOT TO TOUCH IT...
YOU OWE ME THAT MUCH... I'M CRACKING UP, DON'T YOU SEE? I CAN'T LAST MUCH LONGER... LET ME TOUCH YOUR COAT.. PLEASE!
KEEP AWAY... YOU'LL GET ME ALL WRINKLED!
SCHULZ

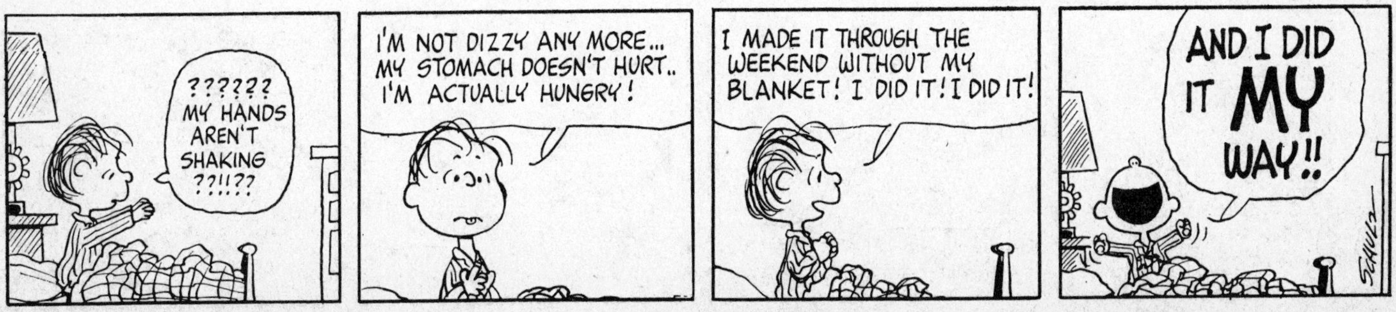
?????? MY HANDS AREN'T SHAKING ??!!??
I'M NOT DIZZY ANY MORE... MY STOMACH DOESN'T HURT.. I'M ACTUALLY HUNGRY!
I MADE IT THROUGH THE WEEKEND WITHOUT MY BLANKET! I DID IT! I DID IT!
AND I DID IT MY WAY!!
SCHULZ

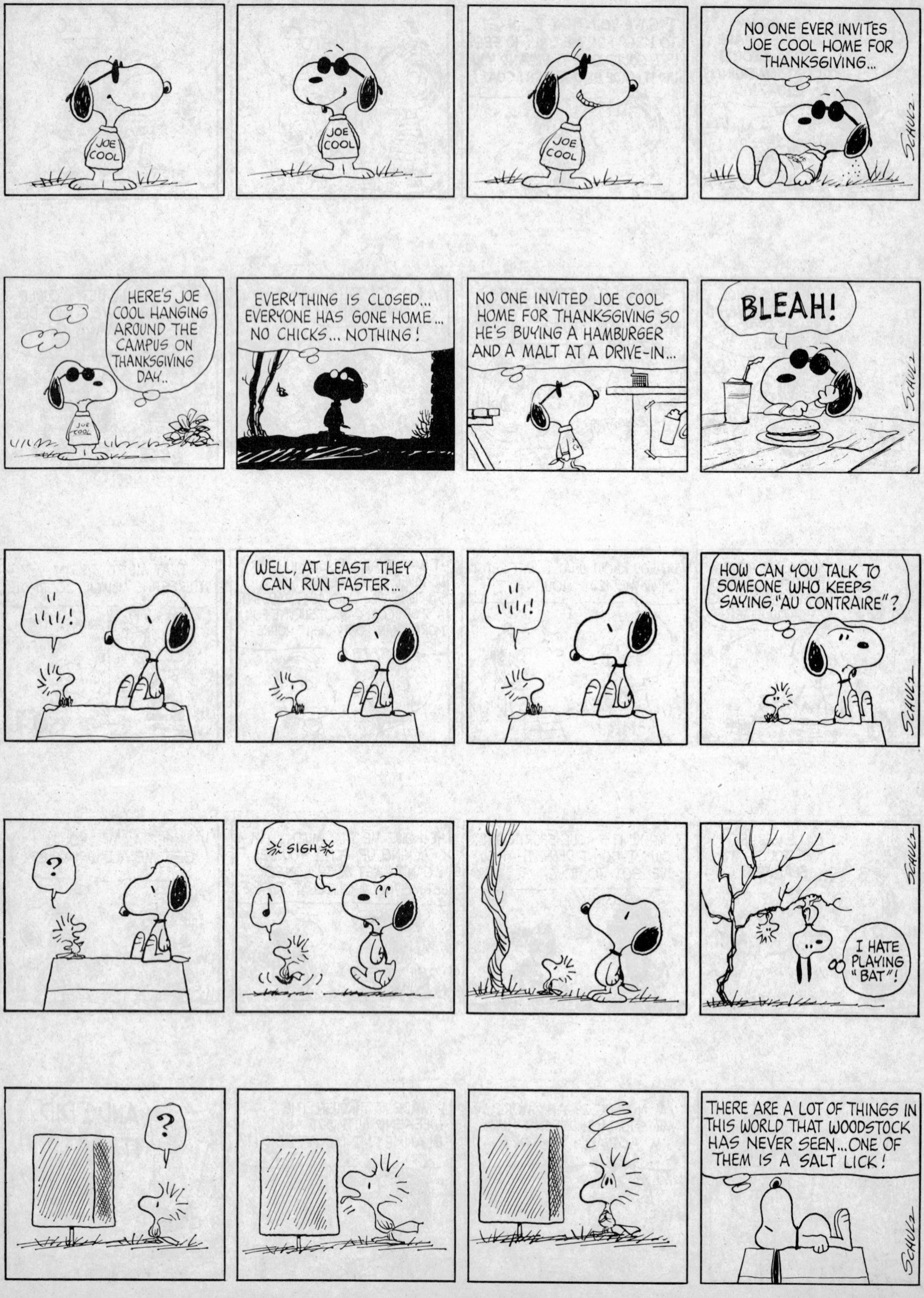

JOE COOL
JOE COOL
JOE COOL
NO ONE EVER INVITES JOE COOL HOME FOR THANKSGIVING...
JOE COOL
HERE'S JOE COOL HANGING AROUND THE CAMPUS ON THANKSGIVING DAY..
JOE COOL
EVERYTHING IS CLOSED... EVERYONE HAS GONE HOME... NO CHICKS... NOTHING!
NO ONE INVITED JOE COOL HOME FOR THANKSGIVING SO HE'S BUYING A HAMBURGER AND A MALT AT A DRIVE-IN...
BLEAH!
WELL, AT LEAST THEY CAN RUN FASTER...
HOW CAN YOU TALK TO SOMEONE WHO KEEPS SAYING, "AU CONTRAIRE"?
?
SIGH
I HATE PLAYING "BAT"!
?
THERE ARE A LOT OF THINGS IN THIS WORLD THAT WOODSTOCK HAS NEVER SEEN... ONE OF THEM IS A SALT LICK!

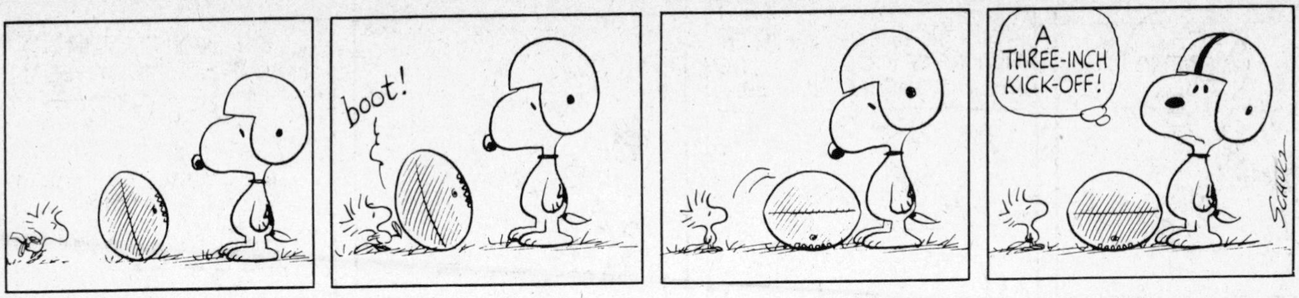
boot!
A THREE-INCH KICK-OFF!
SCHULZ

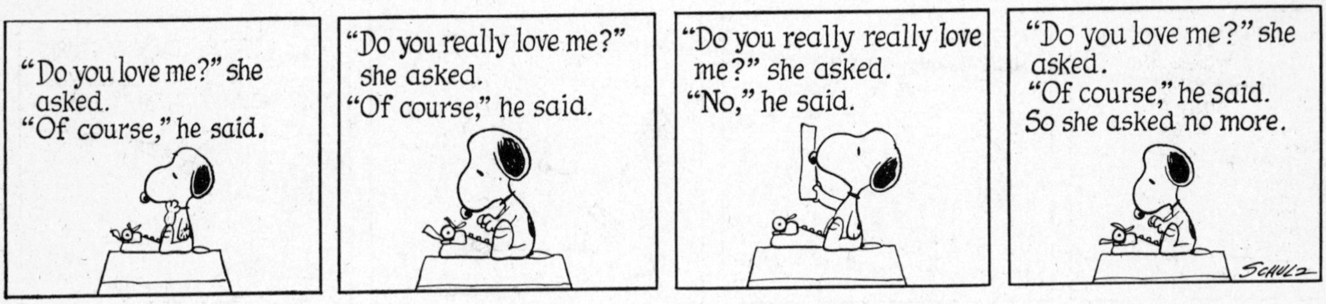
"Do you love me?" she asked. "Of course," he said.
"Do you really love me?" she asked. "Of course," he said.
"Do you really really love me?" she asked. "No," he said.
"Do you love me?" she asked. "Of course," he said. So she asked no more.
SCHULZ

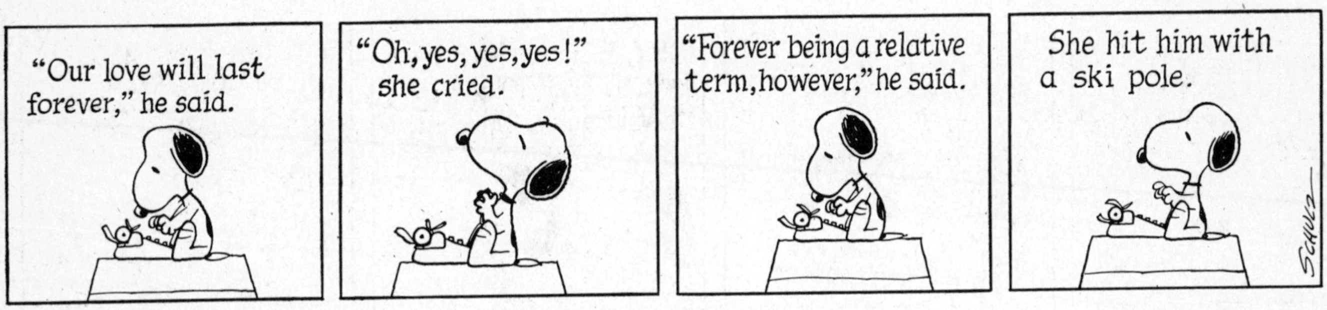
"Our love will last forever," he said.
"Oh, yes, yes, yes!" she cried.
"Forever being a relative term, however," he said.
She hit him with a ski pole.
SCHULZ

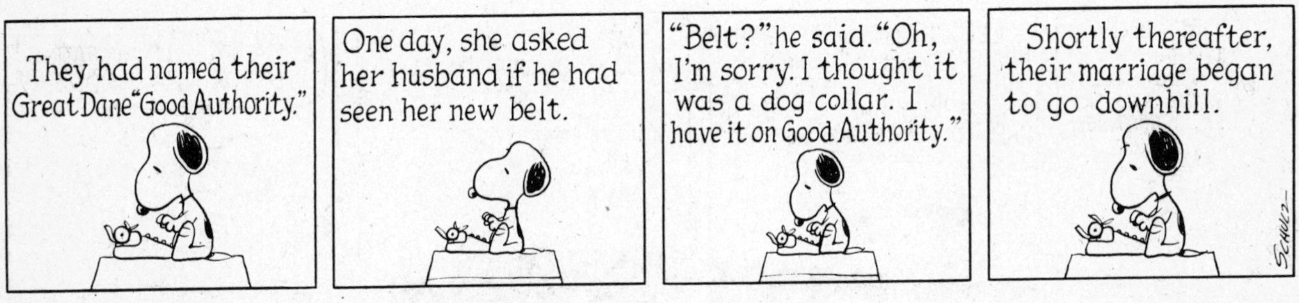
They had named their Great Dane "Good Authority."
One day, she asked her husband if he had seen her new belt.
"Belt?" he said. "Oh, I'm sorry. I thought it was a dog collar. I have it on Good Authority."
Shortly thereafter, their marriage began to go downhill.
SCHULZ

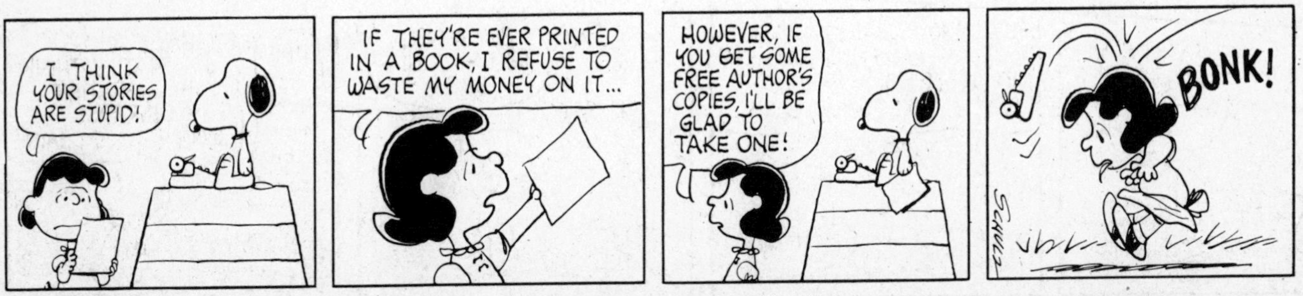
I THINK YOUR STORIES ARE STUPID!
IF THEY'RE EVER PRINTED IN A BOOK, I REFUSE TO WASTE MY MONEY ON IT...
HOWEVER, IF YOU GET SOME FREE AUTHOR'S COPIES, I'LL BE GLAD TO TAKE ONE!
BONK!
SCHULZ

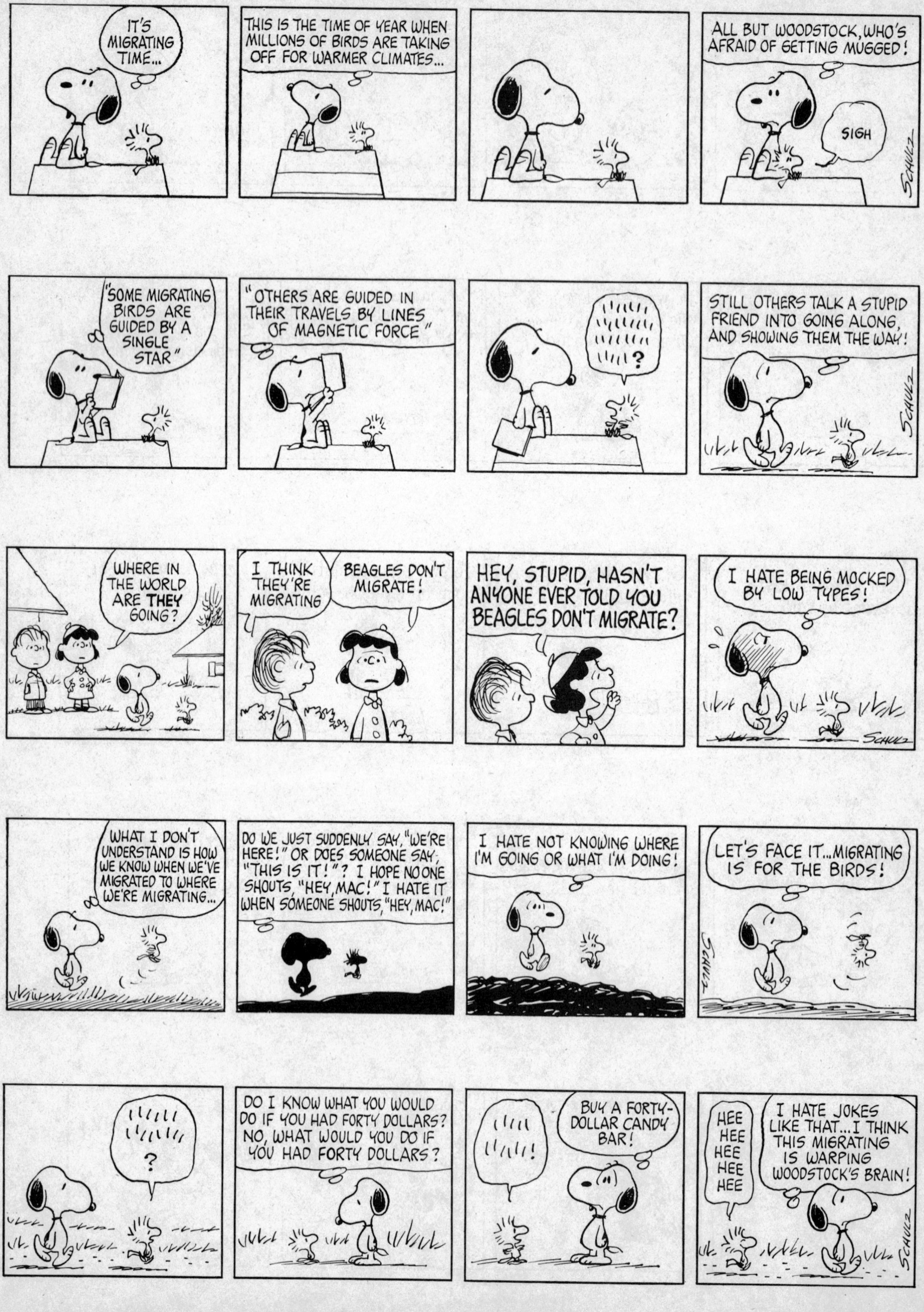
IT'S MIGRATING TIME...
THIS IS THE TIME OF YEAR WHEN MILLIONS OF BIRDS ARE TAKING OFF FOR WARMER CLIMATES...
ALL BUT WOODSTOCK, WHO'S AFRAID OF GETTING MUGGED!
SIGH
SCHULZ
"SOME MIGRATING BIRDS ARE GUIDED BY A SINGLE STAR"
"OTHERS ARE GUIDED IN THEIR TRAVELS BY LINES OF MAGNETIC FORCE"
?
STILL OTHERS TALK A STUPID FRIEND INTO GOING ALONG, AND SHOWING THEM THE WAY!
SCHULZ
WHERE IN THE WORLD ARE THEY GOING?
I THINK THEY'RE MIGRATING
BEAGLES DON'T MIGRATE!
HEY, STUPID, HASN'T ANYONE EVER TOLD YOU BEAGLES DON'T MIGRATE?
I HATE BEING MOCKED BY LOW TYPES!
SCHULZ
WHAT I DON'T UNDERSTAND IS HOW WE KNOW WHEN WE'VE MIGRATED TO WHERE WE'RE MIGRATING...
DO WE JUST SUDDENLY SAY, "WE'RE HERE!" OR DOES SOMEONE SAY, "THIS IS IT!"? I HOPE NO ONE SHOUTS, "HEY, MAC!" I HATE IT WHEN SOMEONE SHOUTS, "HEY, MAC!"
I HATE NOT KNOWING WHERE I'M GOING OR WHAT I'M DOING!
SCHULZ
LET'S FACE IT...MIGRATING IS FOR THE BIRDS!
?
DO I KNOW WHAT YOU WOULD DO IF YOU HAD FORTY DOLLARS? NO, WHAT WOULD YOU DO IF YOU HAD FORTY DOLLARS?
!
BUY A FORTY-DOLLAR CANDY BAR!
HEE HEE HEE HEE HEE
I HATE JOKES LIKE THAT...I THINK THIS MIGRATING IS WARPING WOODSTOCK'S BRAIN!
SCHULZ

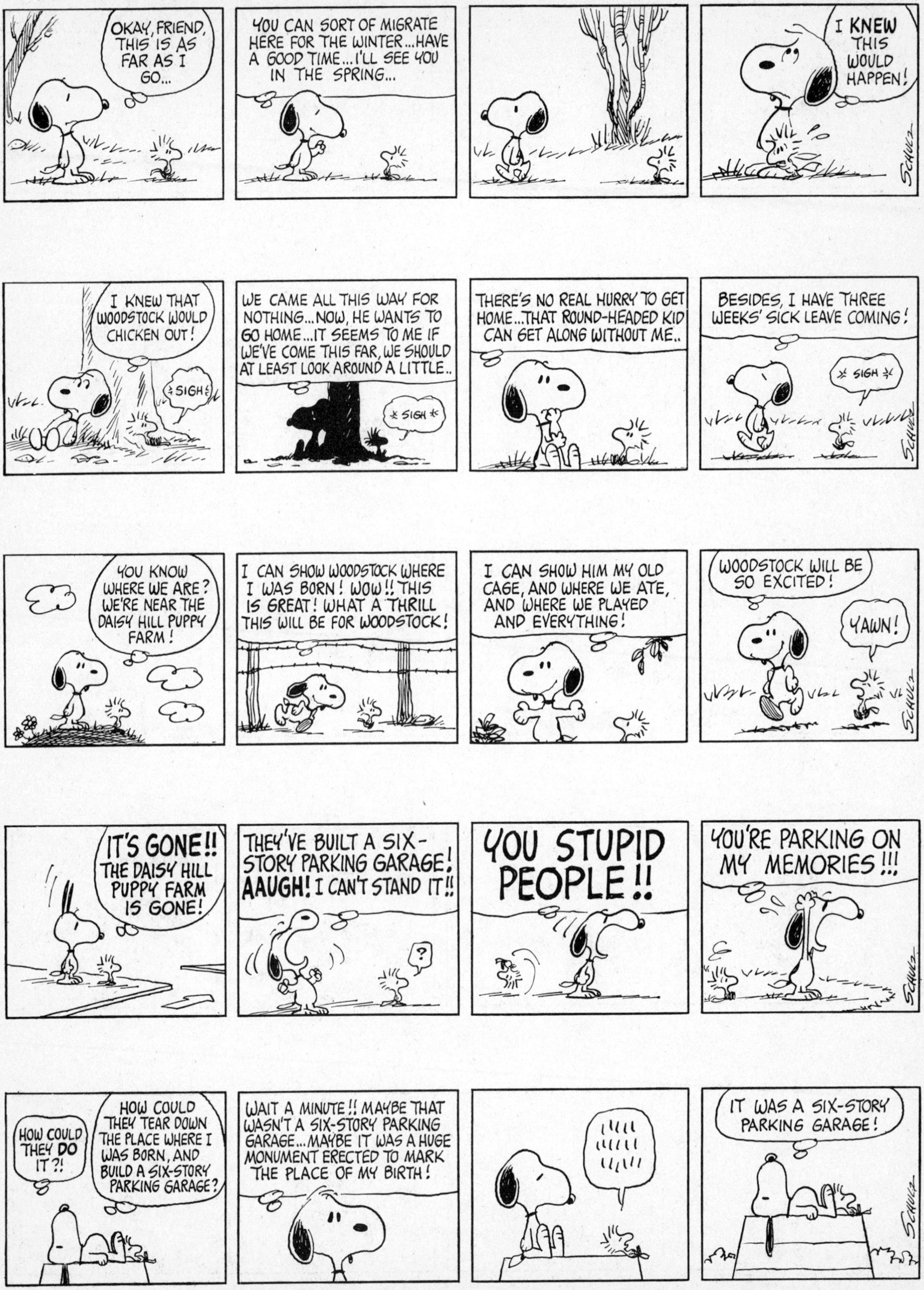
OKAY, FRIEND, THIS IS AS FAR AS I GO...
YOU CAN SORT OF MIGRATE HERE FOR THE WINTER... HAVE A GOOD TIME... I'LL SEE YOU IN THE SPRING...
I KNEW THIS WOULD HAPPEN!
SCHULZ
I KNEW THAT WOODSTOCK WOULD CHICKEN OUT!
SIGH
WE CAME ALL THIS WAY FOR NOTHING... NOW, HE WANTS TO GO HOME... IT SEEMS TO ME IF WE'VE COME THIS FAR, WE SHOULD AT LEAST LOOK AROUND A LITTLE..
SIGH
THERE'S NO REAL HURRY TO GET HOME... THAT ROUND-HEADED KID CAN GET ALONG WITHOUT ME..
BESIDES, I HAVE THREE WEEKS' SICK LEAVE COMING!
SIGH
SCHULZ
YOU KNOW WHERE WE ARE? WE'RE NEAR THE DAISY HILL PUPPY FARM!
I CAN SHOW WOODSTOCK WHERE I WAS BORN! WOW!! THIS IS GREAT! WHAT A THRILL THIS WILL BE FOR WOODSTOCK!
I CAN SHOW HIM MY OLD CAGE, AND WHERE WE ATE, AND WHERE WE PLAYED AND EVERYTHING!
WOODSTOCK WILL BE SO EXCITED!
YAWN!
SCHULZ
IT'S GONE!! THE DAISY HILL PUPPY FARM IS GONE!
THEY'VE BUILT A SIX-STORY PARKING GARAGE! AAUGH! I CAN'T STAND IT!!
?
YOU STUPID PEOPLE!!
YOU'RE PARKING ON MY MEMORIES!!!
SCHULZ
HOW COULD THEY DO IT?!
HOW COULD THEY TEAR DOWN THE PLACE WHERE I WAS BORN, AND BUILD A SIX-STORY PARKING GARAGE?
WAIT A MINUTE!! MAYBE THAT WASN'T A SIX-STORY PARKING GARAGE... MAYBE IT WAS A HUGE MONUMENT ERECTED TO MARK THE PLACE OF MY BIRTH!
IT WAS A SIX-STORY PARKING GARAGE!
SCHULZ

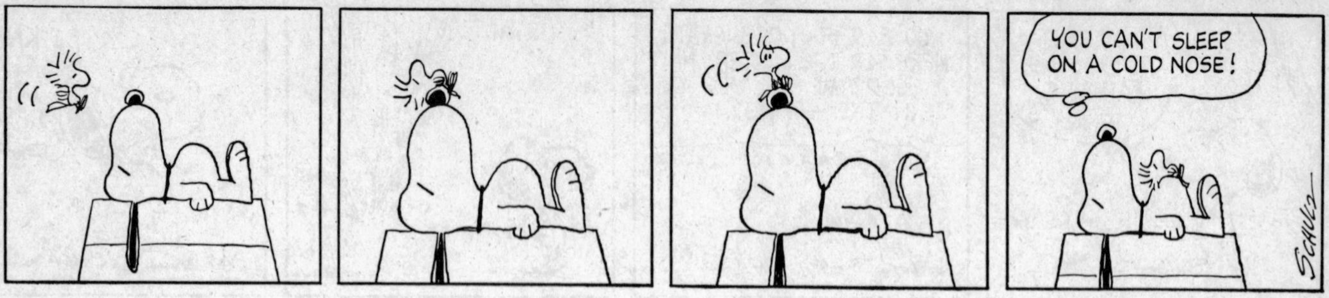
YOU CAN'T SLEEP ON A COLD NOSE!
SCHULZ

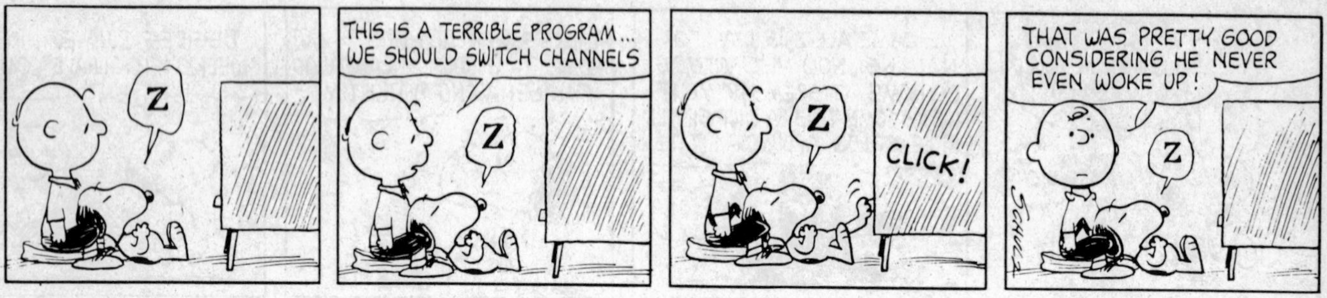
Z
THIS IS A TERRIBLE PROGRAM... WE SHOULD SWITCH CHANNELS
Z
Z
CLICK!
SCHULZ
THAT WAS PRETTY GOOD CONSIDERING HE NEVER EVEN WOKE UP!
Z

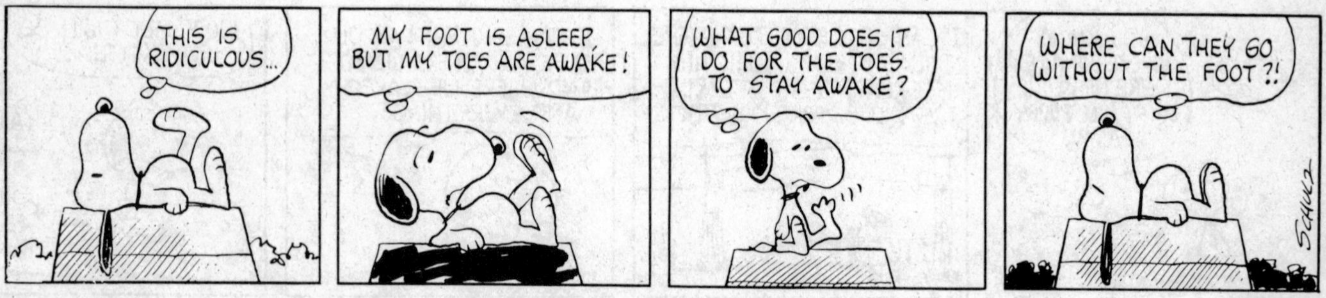
THIS IS RIDICULOUS...
MY FOOT IS ASLEEP, BUT MY TOES ARE AWAKE!
WHAT GOOD DOES IT DO FOR THE TOES TO STAY AWAKE?
WHERE CAN THEY GO WITHOUT THE FOOT?!
SCHULZ

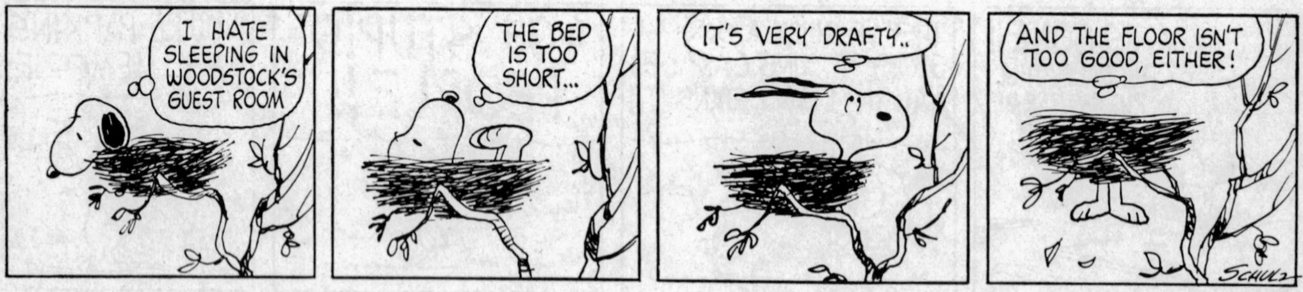
I HATE SLEEPING IN WOODSTOCK'S GUEST ROOM
THE BED IS TOO SHORT...
IT'S VERY DRAFTY..
AND THE FLOOR ISN'T TOO GOOD, EITHER!
SCHULZ

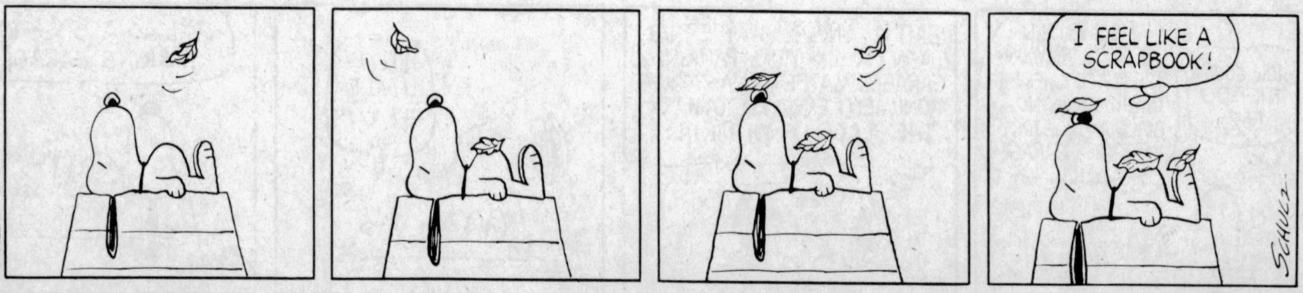
I FEEL LIKE A SCRAPBOOK!
SCHULZ

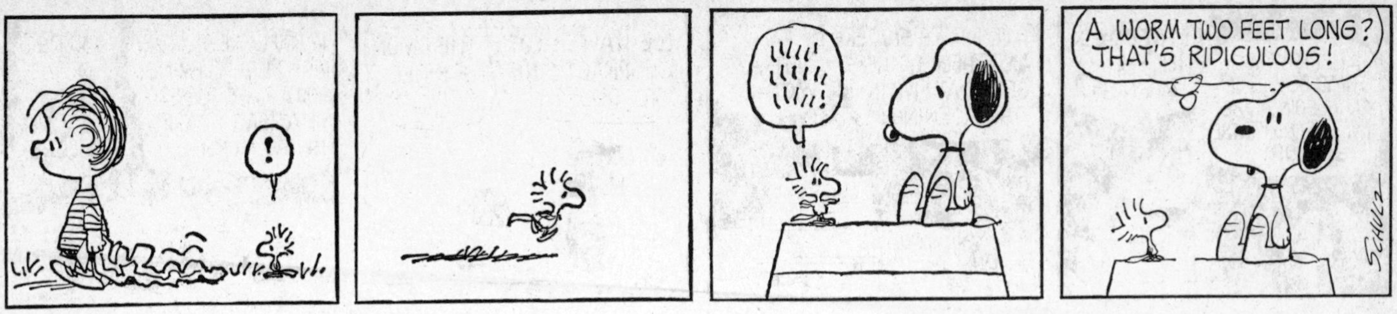
!
A WORM TWO FEET LONG? THAT'S RIDICULOUS!
SCHULZ

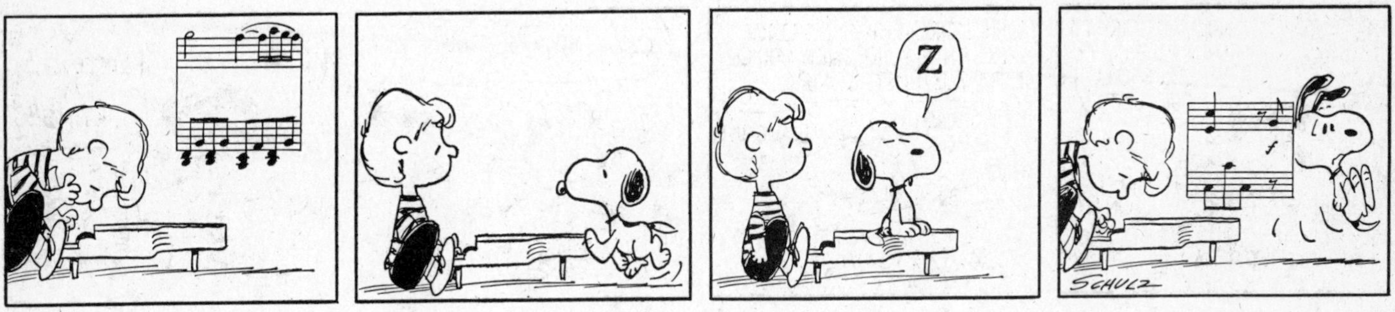
Z
SCHULZ

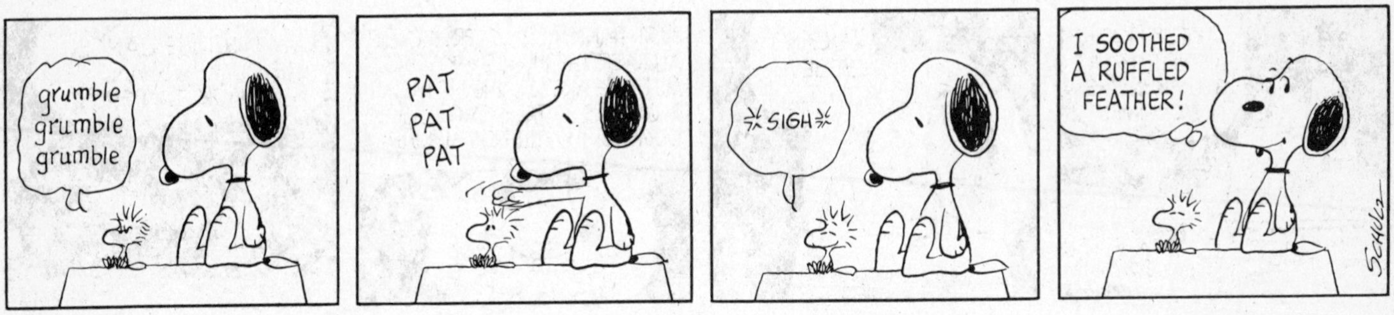
grumble grumble grumble
PAT PAT PAT
SIGH
I SOOTHED A RUFFLED FEATHER!
SCHULZ

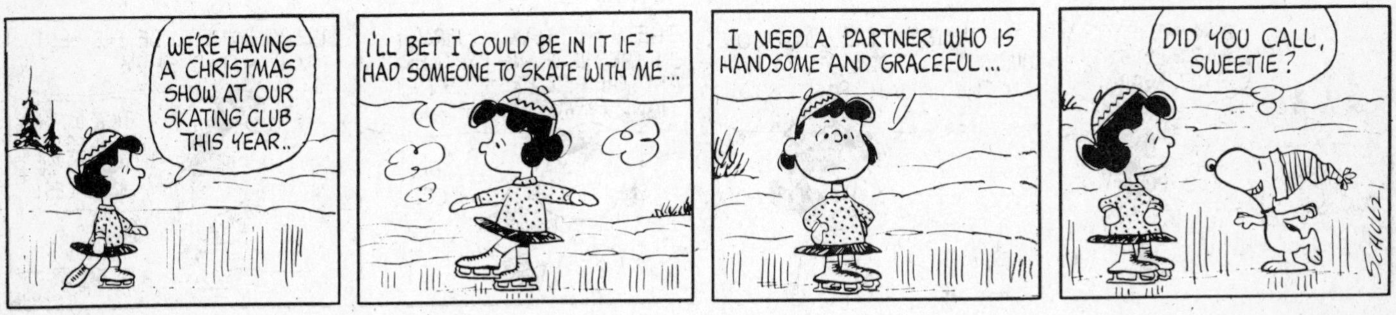
WE'RE HAVING A CHRISTMAS SHOW AT OUR SKATING CLUB THIS YEAR..
I'LL BET I COULD BE IN IT IF I HAD SOMEONE TO SKATE WITH ME...
I NEED A PARTNER WHO IS HANDSOME AND GRACEFUL...
DID YOU CALL, SWEETIE?
SCHULZ

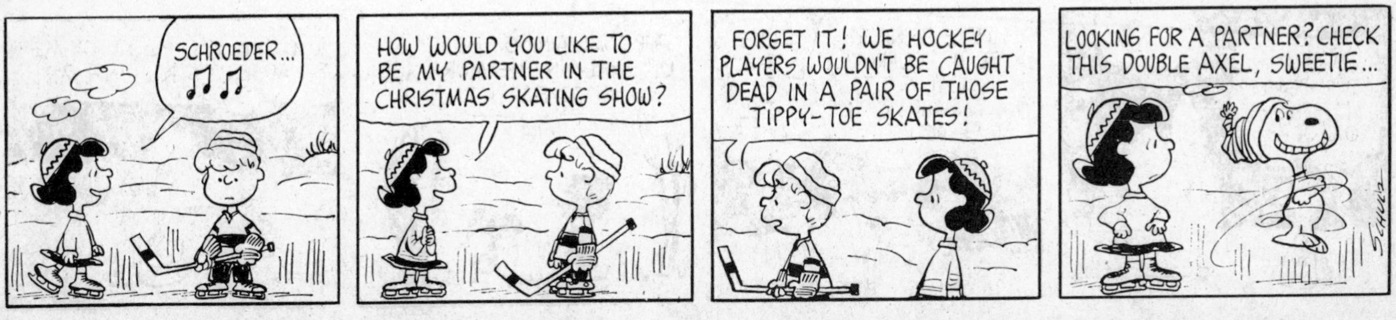
SCHROEDER...
HOW WOULD YOU LIKE TO BE MY PARTNER IN THE CHRISTMAS SKATING SHOW?
FORGET IT! WE HOCKEY PLAYERS WOULDN'T BE CAUGHT DEAD IN A PAIR OF THOSE TIPPY-TOE SKATES!
LOOKING FOR A PARTNER? CHECK THIS DOUBLE AXEL, SWEETIE...
SCHULZ

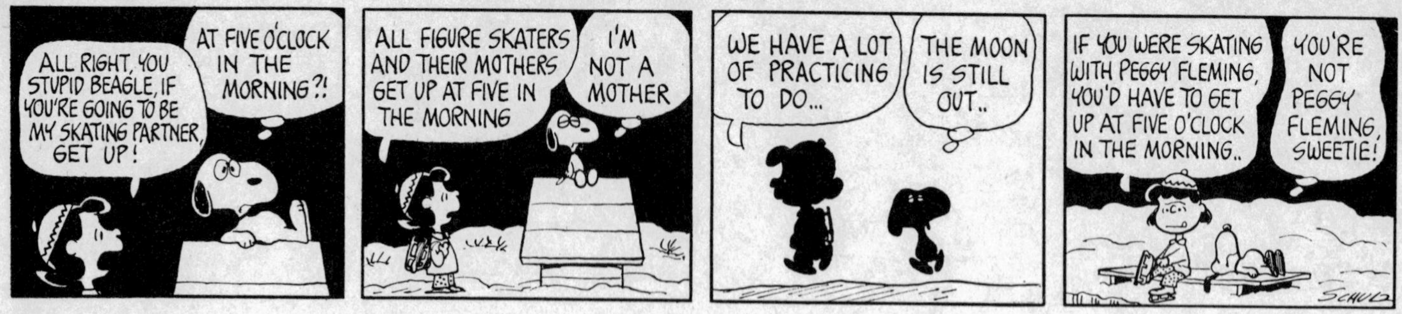
ALL RIGHT, YOU STUPID BEAGLE, IF YOU'RE GOING TO BE MY SKATING PARTNER, GET UP!
AT FIVE O'CLOCK IN THE MORNING?!
ALL FIGURE SKATERS AND THEIR MOTHERS GET UP AT FIVE IN THE MORNING
I'M NOT A MOTHER
WE HAVE A LOT OF PRACTICING TO DO...
THE MOON IS STILL OUT..
IF YOU WERE SKATING WITH PEGGY FLEMING, YOU'D HAVE TO GET UP AT FIVE O'CLOCK IN THE MORNING..
YOU'RE NOT PEGGY FLEMING, SWEETIE!
SCHULZ

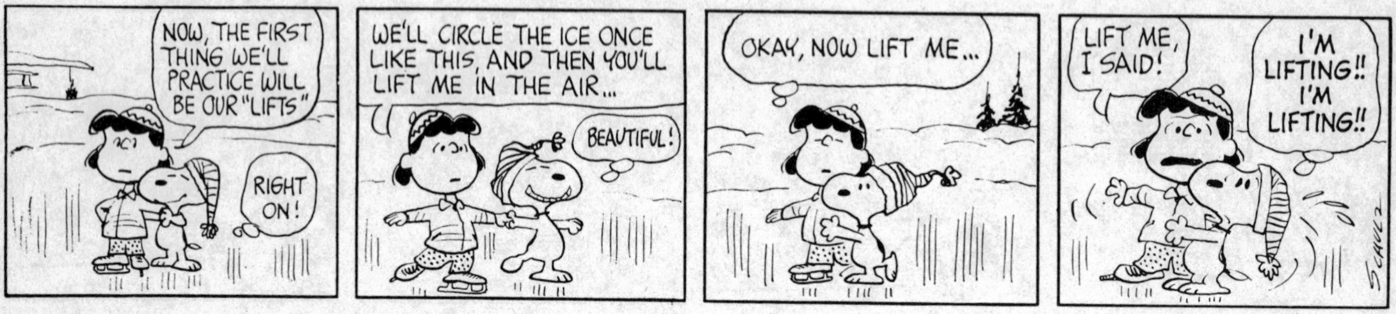
NOW, THE FIRST THING WE'LL PRACTICE WILL BE OUR "LIFTS"
RIGHT ON!
WE'LL CIRCLE THE ICE ONCE LIKE THIS, AND THEN YOU'LL LIFT ME IN THE AIR...
BEAUTIFUL!
OKAY, NOW LIFT ME...
LIFT ME, I SAID!
I'M LIFTING!! I'M LIFTING!!
SCHULZ

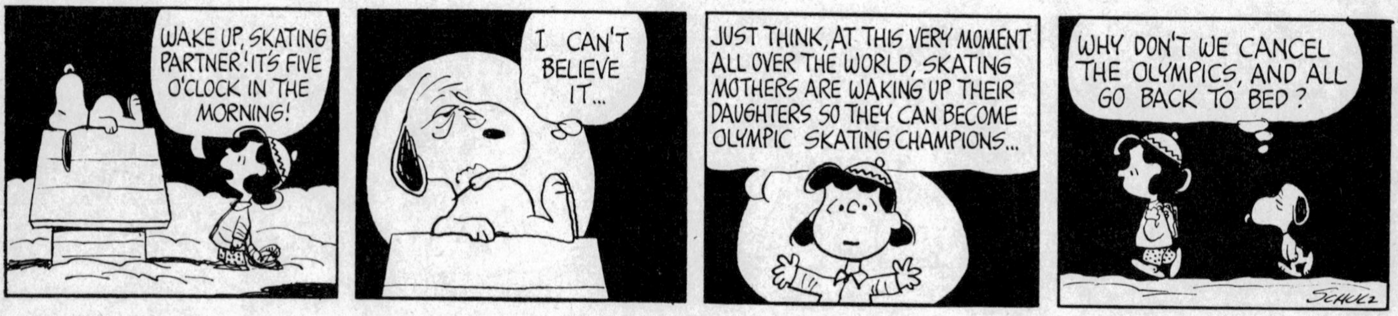
WAKE UP, SKATING PARTNER! IT'S FIVE O'CLOCK IN THE MORNING!
I CAN'T BELIEVE IT...
JUST THINK, AT THIS VERY MOMENT ALL OVER THE WORLD, SKATING MOTHERS ARE WAKING UP THEIR DAUGHTERS SO THEY CAN BECOME OLYMPIC SKATING CHAMPIONS...
WHY DON'T WE CANCEL THE OLYMPICS, AND ALL GO BACK TO BED?
SCHULZ

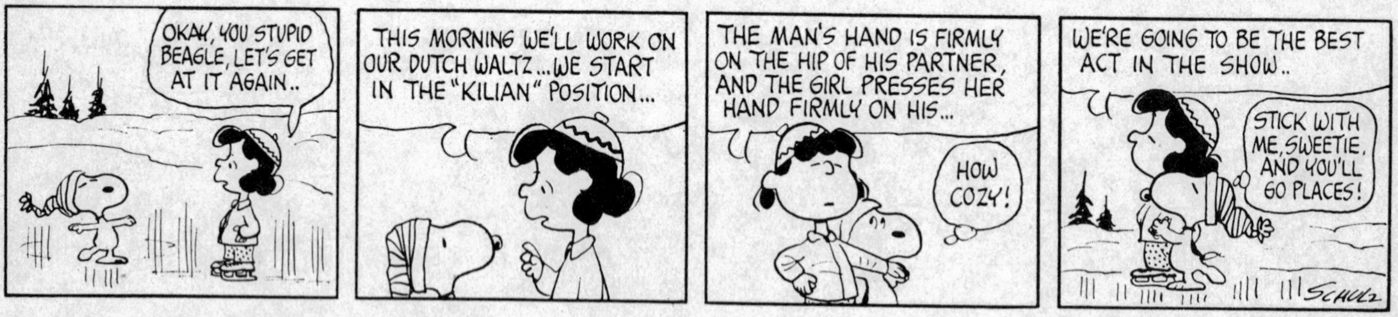
OKAY, YOU STUPID BEAGLE, LET'S GET AT IT AGAIN..
THIS MORNING WE'LL WORK ON OUR DUTCH WALTZ... WE START IN THE "KILIAN" POSITION...
THE MAN'S HAND IS FIRMLY ON THE HIP OF HIS PARTNER, AND THE GIRL PRESSES HER HAND FIRMLY ON HIS...
HOW COZY!
WE'RE GOING TO BE THE BEST ACT IN THE SHOW..
STICK WITH ME, SWEETIE, AND YOU'LL GO PLACES!
SCHULZ

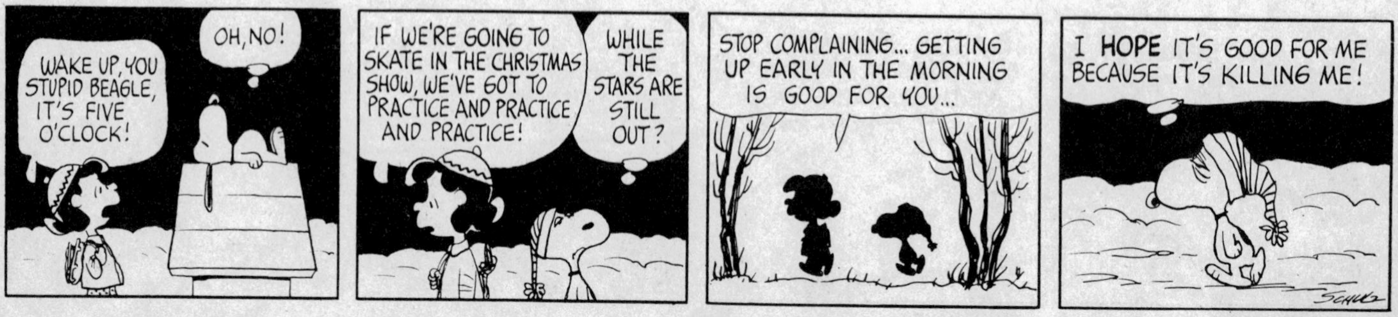
WAKE UP, YOU STUPID BEAGLE, IT'S FIVE O'CLOCK!
OH, NO!
IF WE'RE GOING TO SKATE IN THE CHRISTMAS SHOW, WE'VE GOT TO PRACTICE AND PRACTICE AND PRACTICE!
WHILE THE STARS ARE STILL OUT?
STOP COMPLAINING... GETTING UP EARLY IN THE MORNING IS GOOD FOR YOU...
I HOPE IT'S GOOD FOR ME BECAUSE IT'S KILLING ME!
SCHULZ

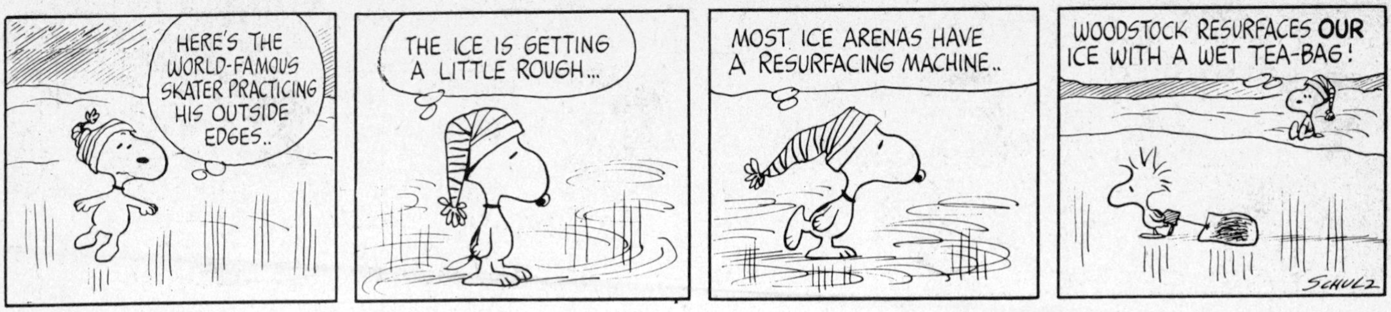
HERE'S THE WORLD-FAMOUS SKATER PRACTICING HIS OUTSIDE EDGES..
THE ICE IS GETTING A LITTLE ROUGH...
MOST ICE ARENAS HAVE A RESURFACING MACHINE..
WOODSTOCK RESURFACES OUR ICE WITH A WET TEA-BAG!
SCHULZ

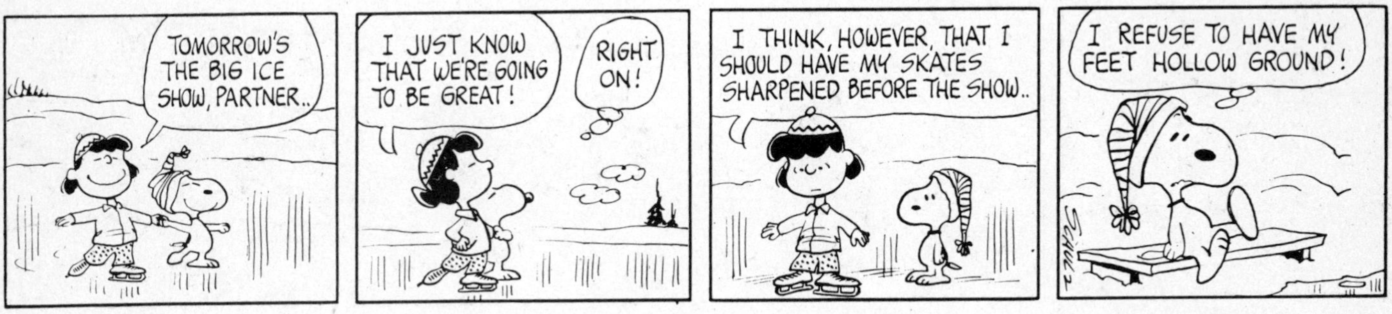
TOMORROW'S THE BIG ICE SHOW, PARTNER..
I JUST KNOW THAT WE'RE GOING TO BE GREAT!
RIGHT ON!
I THINK, HOWEVER, THAT I SHOULD HAVE MY SKATES SHARPENED BEFORE THE SHOW..
I REFUSE TO HAVE MY FEET HOLLOW GROUND!
SCHULZ

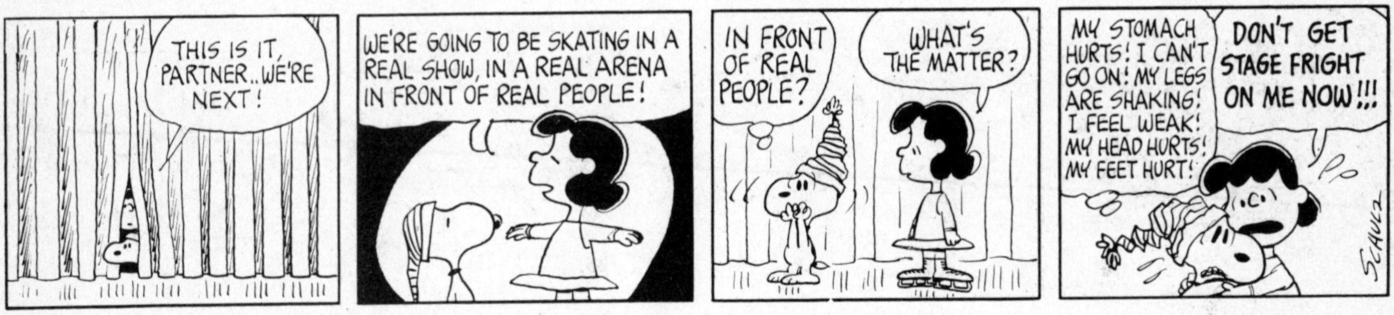
THIS IS IT, PARTNER..WE'RE NEXT!
WE'RE GOING TO BE SKATING IN A REAL SHOW, IN A REAL ARENA IN FRONT OF REAL PEOPLE!
IN FRONT OF REAL PEOPLE?
WHAT'S THE MATTER?
MY STOMACH HURTS! I CAN'T GO ON! MY LEGS ARE SHAKING! I FEEL WEAK! MY HEAD HURTS! MY FEET HURT!
DON'T GET STAGE FRIGHT ON ME NOW!!!
SCHULZ

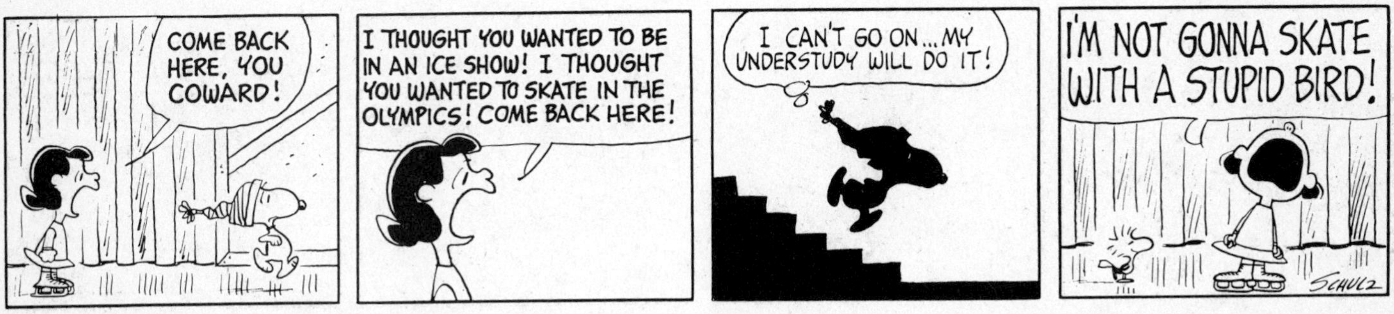
COME BACK HERE, YOU COWARD!
I THOUGHT YOU WANTED TO BE IN AN ICE SHOW! I THOUGHT YOU WANTED TO SKATE IN THE OLYMPICS! COME BACK HERE!
I CAN'T GO ON... MY UNDERSTUDY WILL DO IT!
I'M NOT GONNA SKATE WITH A STUPID BIRD!
SCHULZ

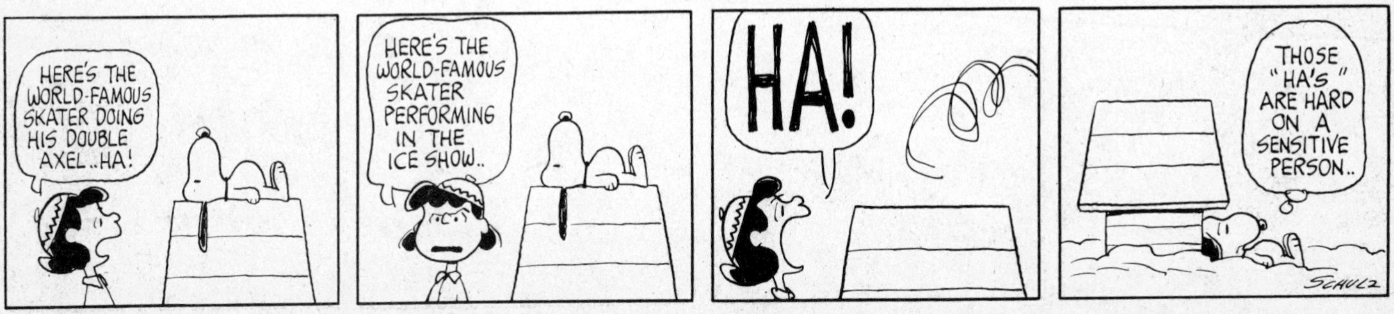
HERE'S THE WORLD-FAMOUS SKATER DOING HIS DOUBLE AXEL..HA!
HERE'S THE WORLD-FAMOUS SKATER PERFORMING IN THE ICE SHOW..
HA!
THOSE "HA'S" ARE HARD ON A SENSITIVE PERSON..
SCHULZ

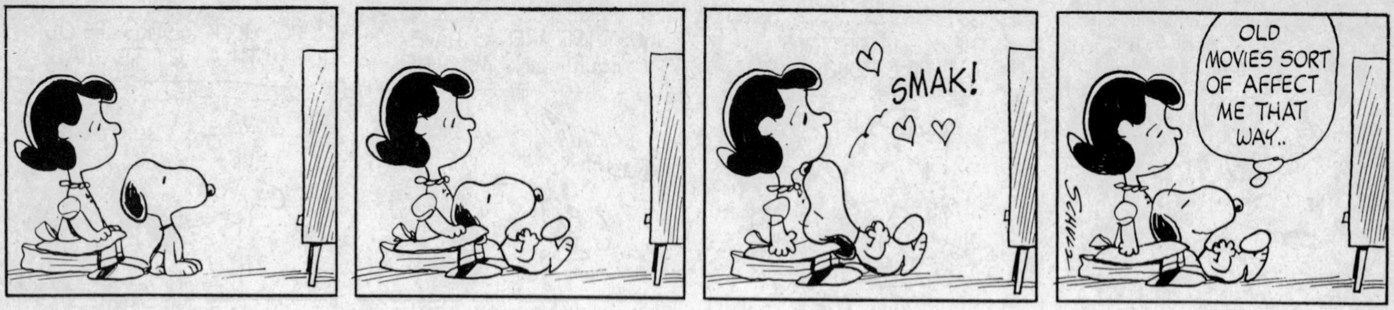
SMAK!
OLD MOVIES SORT OF AFFECT ME THAT WAY..
SCHULZ

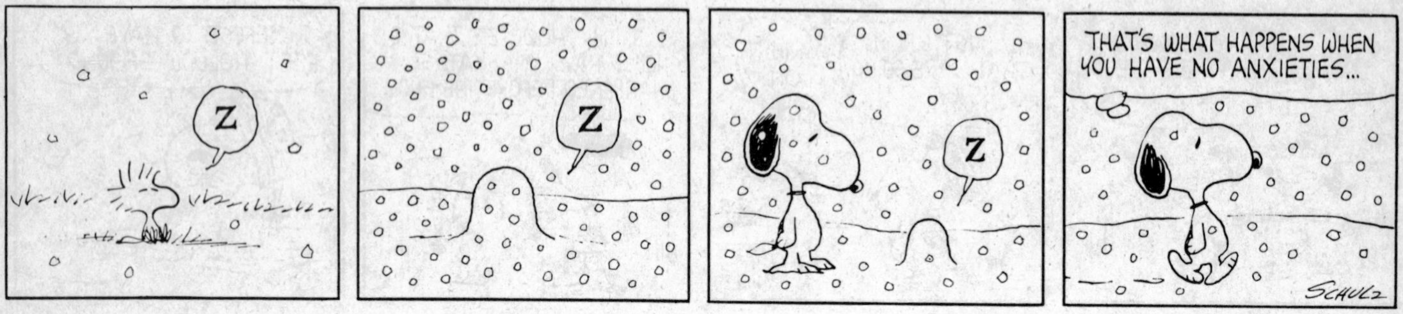
Z
Z
Z
THAT'S WHAT HAPPENS WHEN YOU HAVE NO ANXIETIES...
SCHULZ

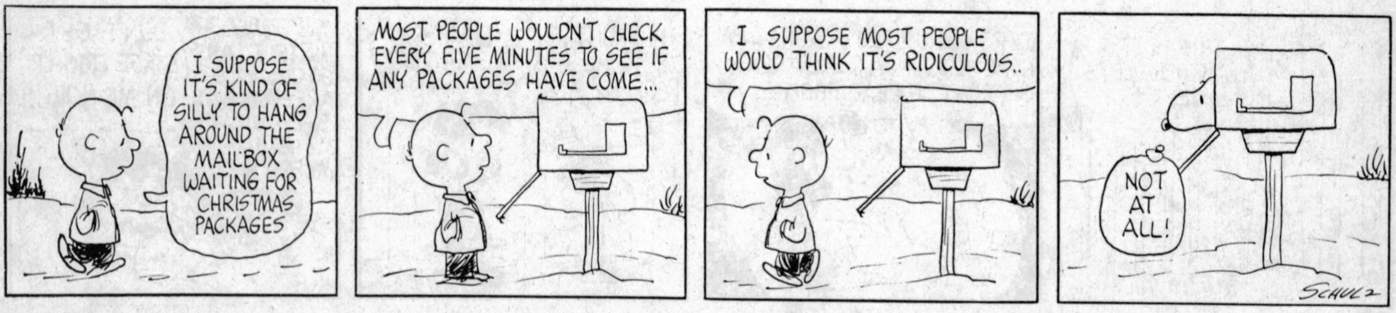
I SUPPOSE IT'S KIND OF SILLY TO HANG AROUND THE MAILBOX WAITING FOR CHRISTMAS PACKAGES
MOST PEOPLE WOULDN'T CHECK EVERY FIVE MINUTES TO SEE IF ANY PACKAGES HAVE COME...
I SUPPOSE MOST PEOPLE WOULD THINK IT'S RIDICULOUS..
NOT AT ALL!
SCHULZ

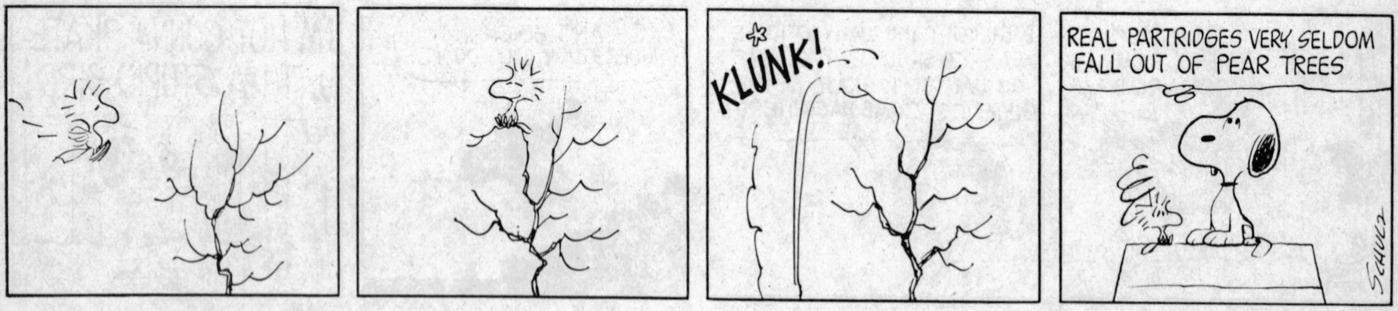
KLUNK!
REAL PARTRIDGES VERY SELDOM FALL OUT OF PEAR TREES
SCHULZ

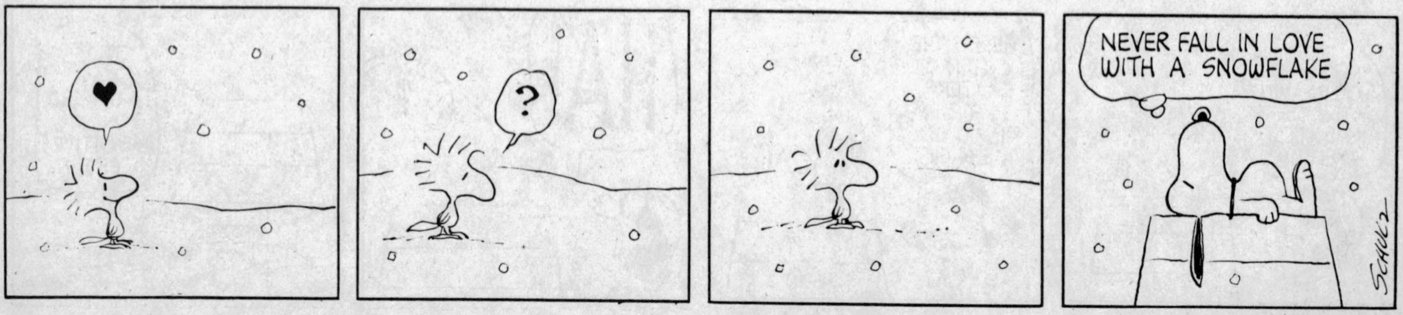
?
NEVER FALL IN LOVE WITH A SNOWFLAKE
SCHULZ

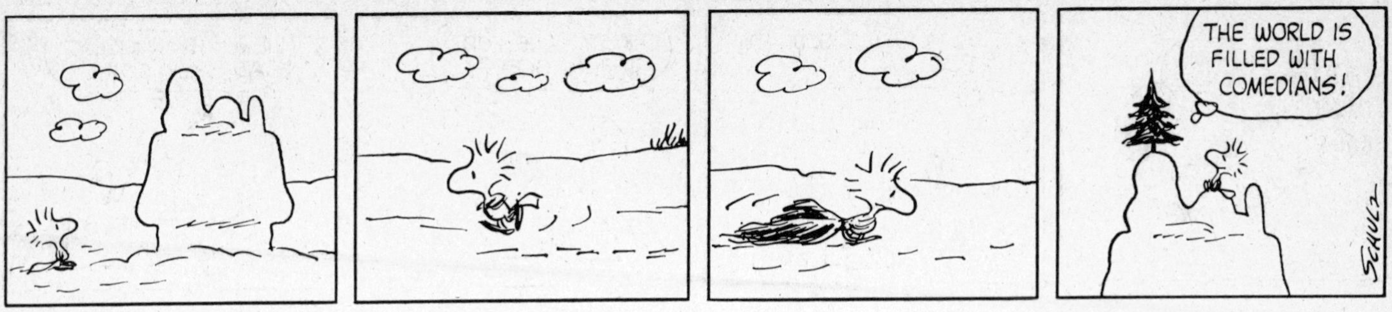
THE WORLD IS FILLED WITH COMEDIANS!
SCHULZ

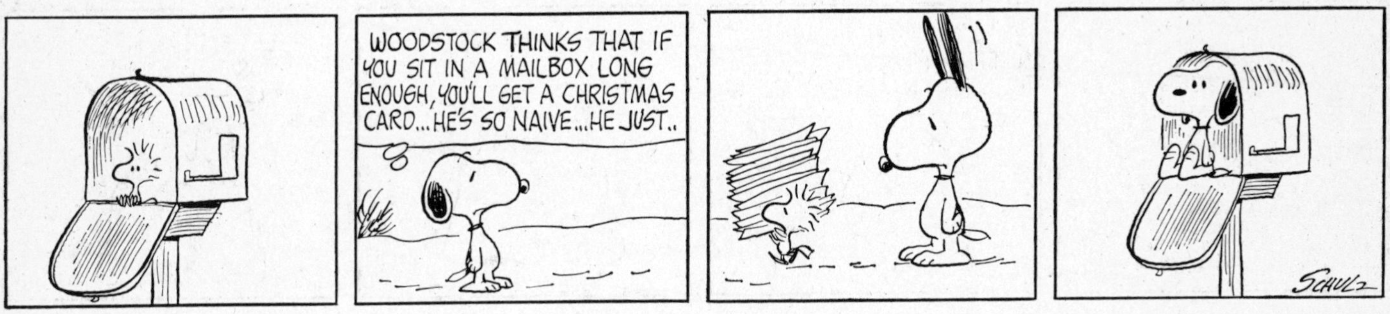
WOODSTOCK THINKS THAT IF YOU SIT IN A MAILBOX LONG ENOUGH, YOU'LL GET A CHRISTMAS CARD... HE'S SO NAIVE... HE JUST..
SCHULZ

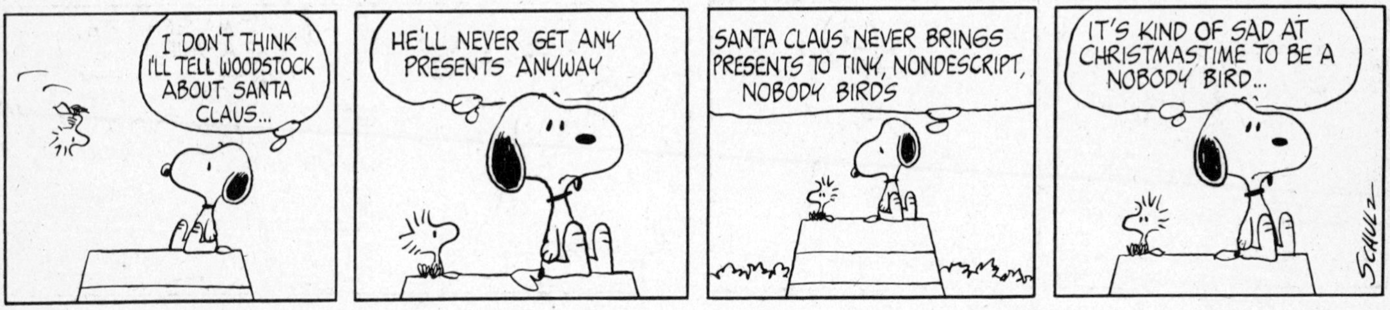
I DON'T THINK I'LL TELL WOODSTOCK ABOUT SANTA CLAUS...
HE'LL NEVER GET ANY PRESENTS ANYWAY
SANTA CLAUS NEVER BRINGS PRESENTS TO TINY, NONDESCRIPT, NOBODY BIRDS
IT'S KIND OF SAD AT CHRISTMASTIME TO BE A NOBODY BIRD...
SCHULZ

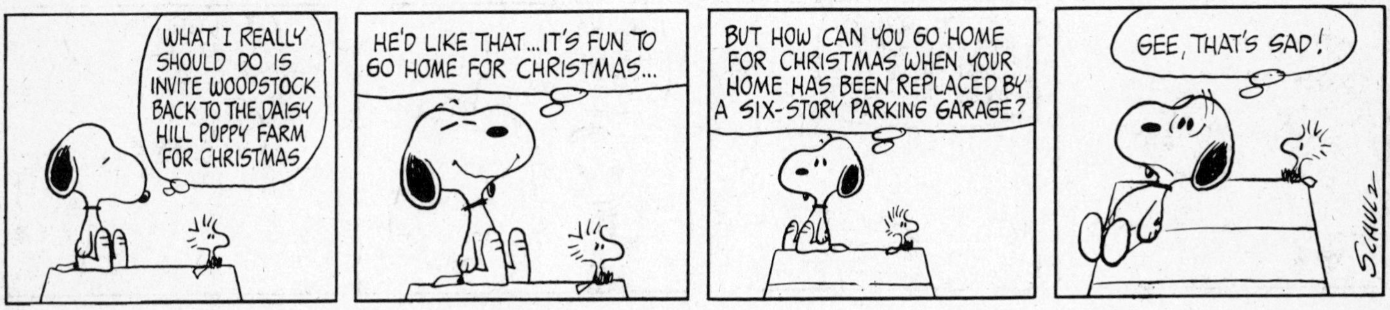
WHAT I REALLY SHOULD DO IS INVITE WOODSTOCK BACK TO THE DAISY HILL PUPPY FARM FOR CHRISTMAS
HE'D LIKE THAT... IT'S FUN TO GO HOME FOR CHRISTMAS...
BUT HOW CAN YOU GO HOME FOR CHRISTMAS WHEN YOUR HOME HAS BEEN REPLACED BY A SIX-STORY PARKING GARAGE?
GEE, THAT'S SAD!
SCHULZ

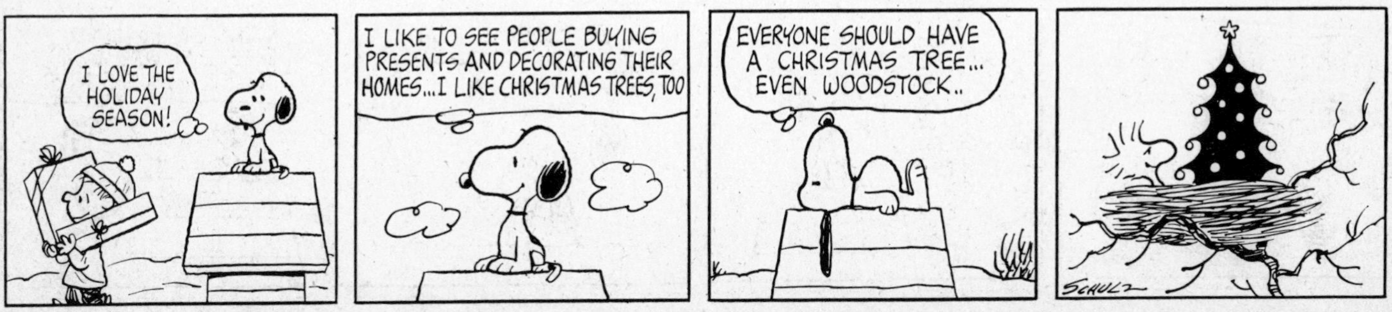
I LOVE THE HOLIDAY SEASON!
I LIKE TO SEE PEOPLE BUYING PRESENTS AND DECORATING THEIR HOMES... I LIKE CHRISTMAS TREES, TOO
EVERYONE SHOULD HAVE A CHRISTMAS TREE... EVEN WOODSTOCK..
SCHULZ

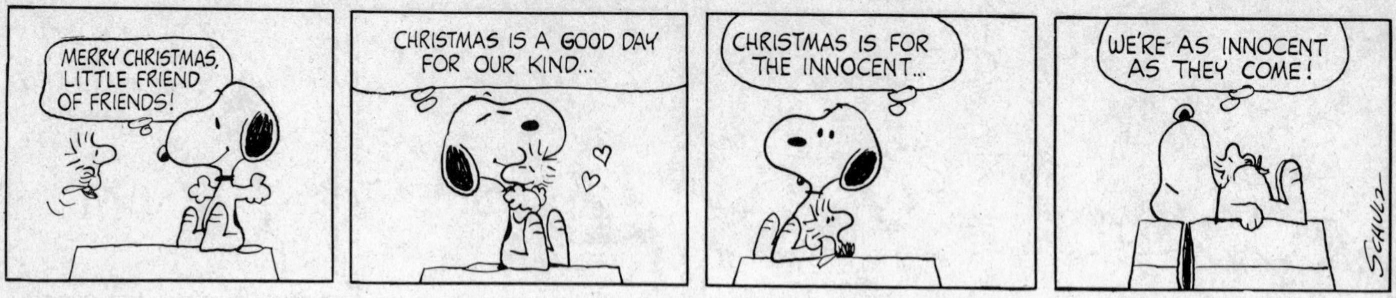
MERRY CHRISTMAS, LITTLE FRIEND OF FRIENDS!
CHRISTMAS IS A GOOD DAY FOR OUR KIND...
CHRISTMAS IS FOR THE INNOCENT...
WE'RE AS INNOCENT AS THEY COME!
SCHULZ

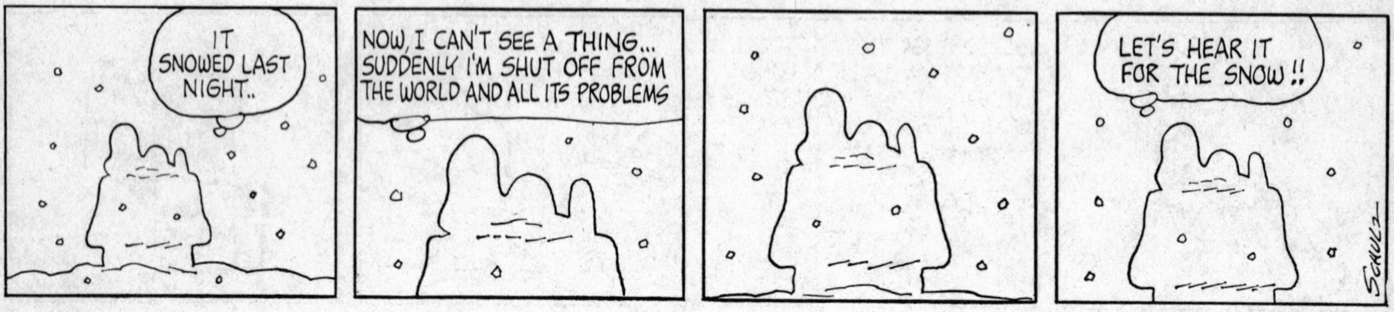
IT SNOWED LAST NIGHT..
NOW, I CAN'T SEE A THING... SUDDENLY I'M SHUT OFF FROM THE WORLD AND ALL ITS PROBLEMS
LET'S HEAR IT FOR THE SNOW!!
SCHULZ

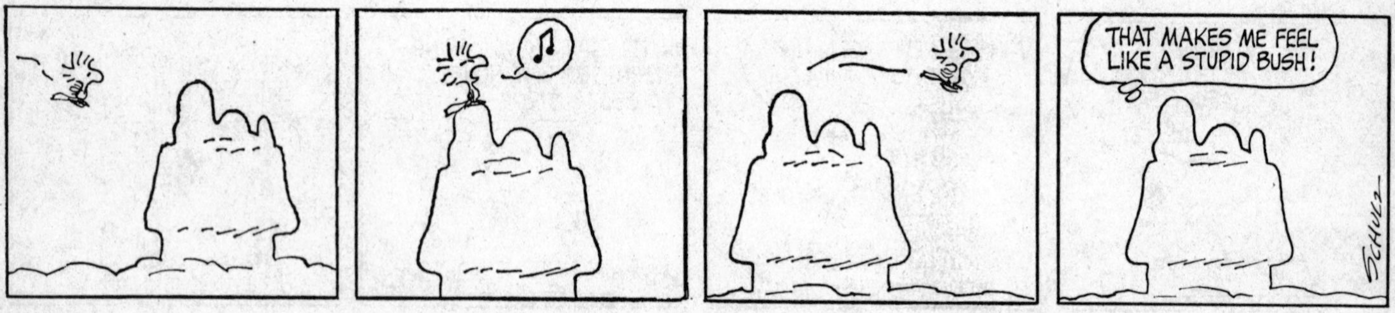
THAT MAKES ME FEEL LIKE A STUPID BUSH!
SCHULZ

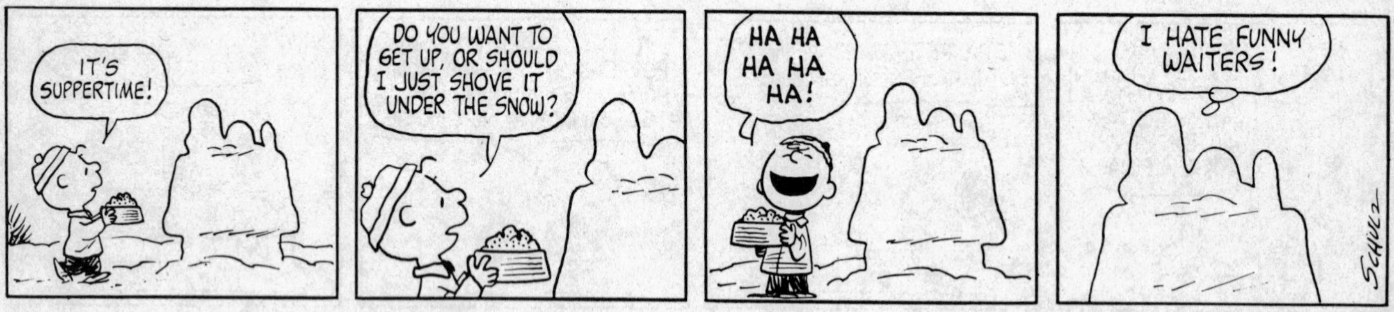
IT'S SUPPERTIME!
DO YOU WANT TO GET UP, OR SHOULD I JUST SHOVE IT UNDER THE SNOW?
HA HA HA HA HA!
I HATE FUNNY WAITERS!
SCHULZ

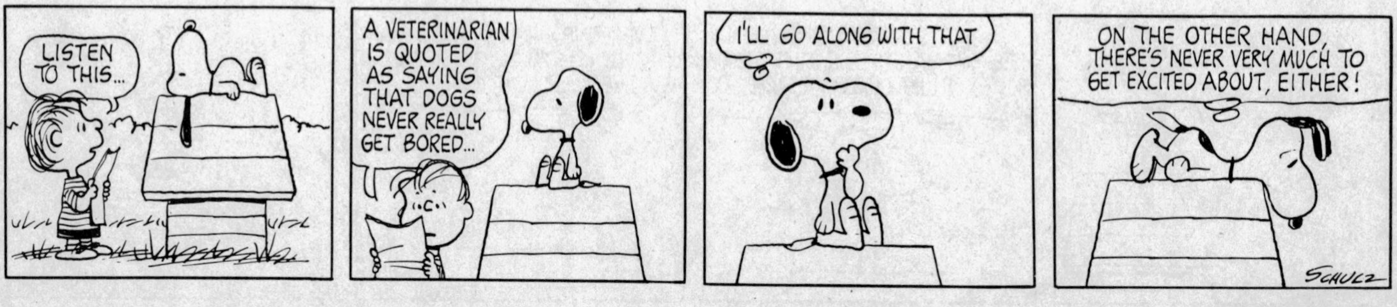
LISTEN TO THIS...
A VETERINARIAN IS QUOTED AS SAYING THAT DOGS NEVER REALLY GET BORED...
I'LL GO ALONG WITH THAT
ON THE OTHER HAND, THERE'S NEVER VERY MUCH TO GET EXCITED ABOUT, EITHER!
SCHULZ

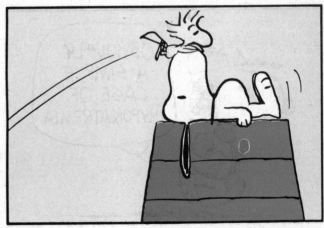

BLEAH!

SOMEBODY'S ALWAYS STIRRING UP THE ENEMY!

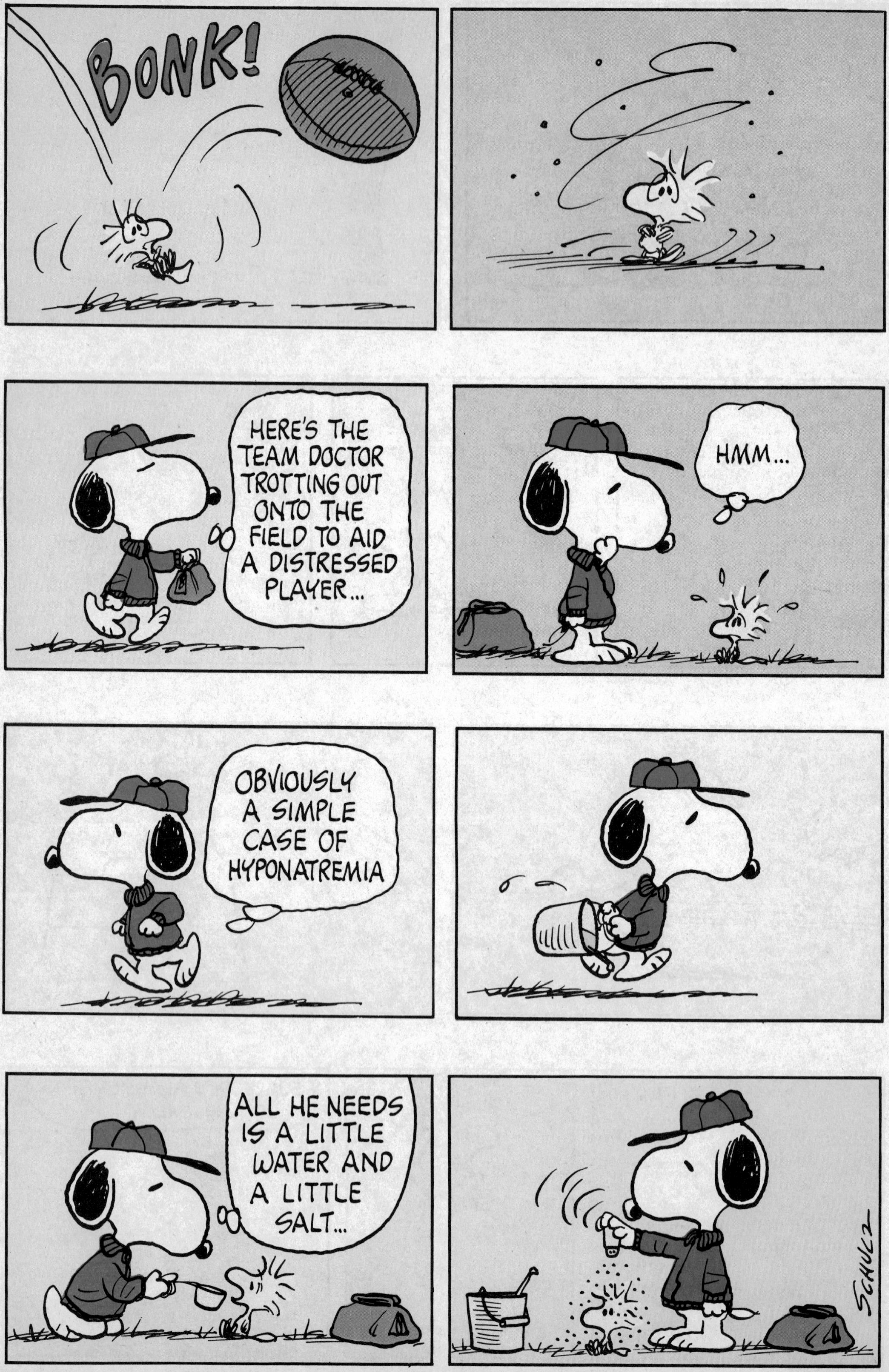
BONK!
HERE'S THE TEAM DOCTOR TROTTING OUT ONTO THE FIELD TO AID A DISTRESSED PLAYER...
HMM...
OBVIOUSLY A SIMPLE CASE OF HYPONATREMIA
ALL HE NEEDS IS A LITTLE WATER AND A LITTLE SALT...
SCHULZ

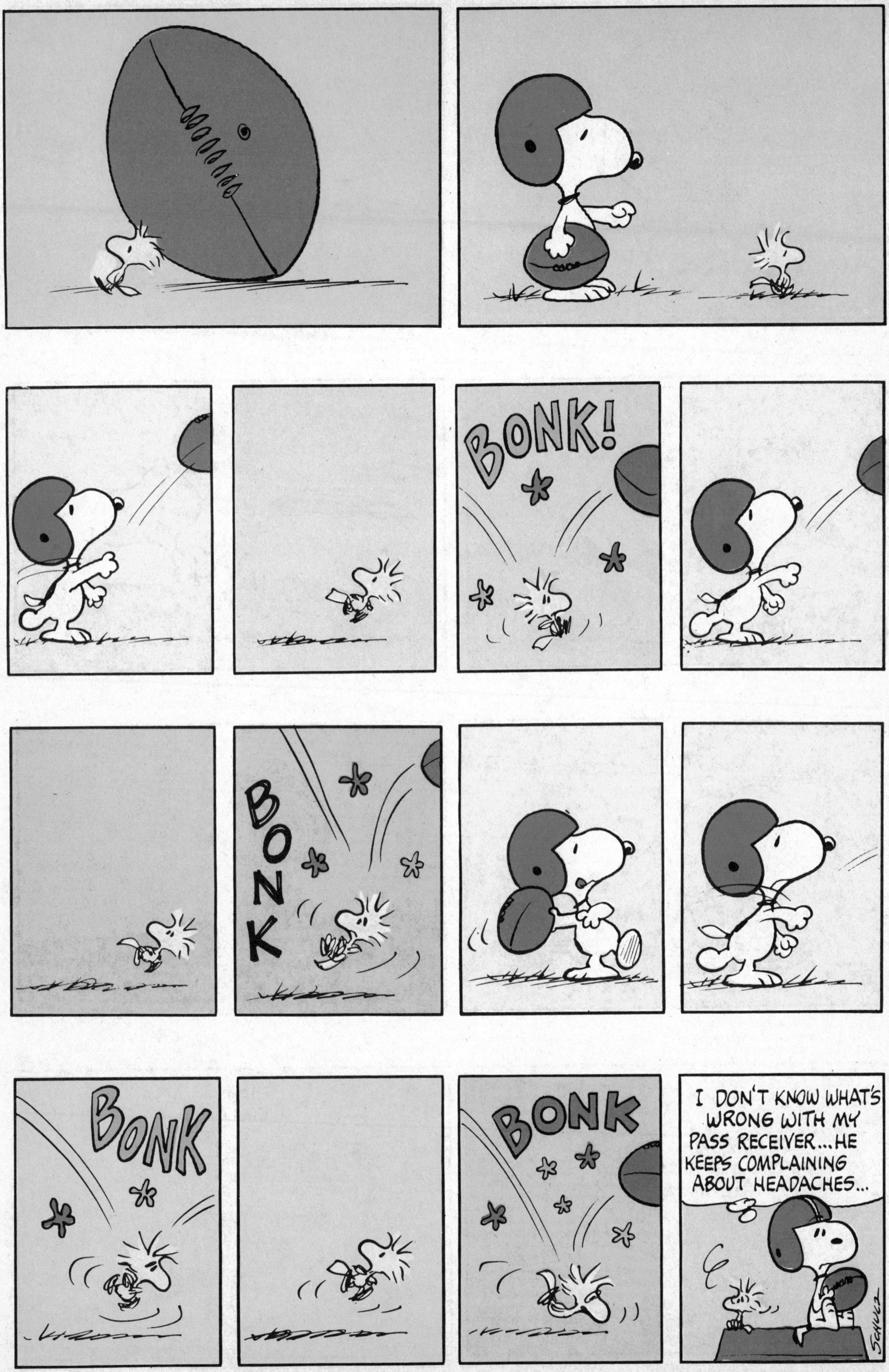
BONK!
BONK
BONK
BONK
I DON'T KNOW WHAT'S WRONG WITH MY PASS RECEIVER...HE KEEPS COMPLAINING ABOUT HEADACHES...
SCHULZ

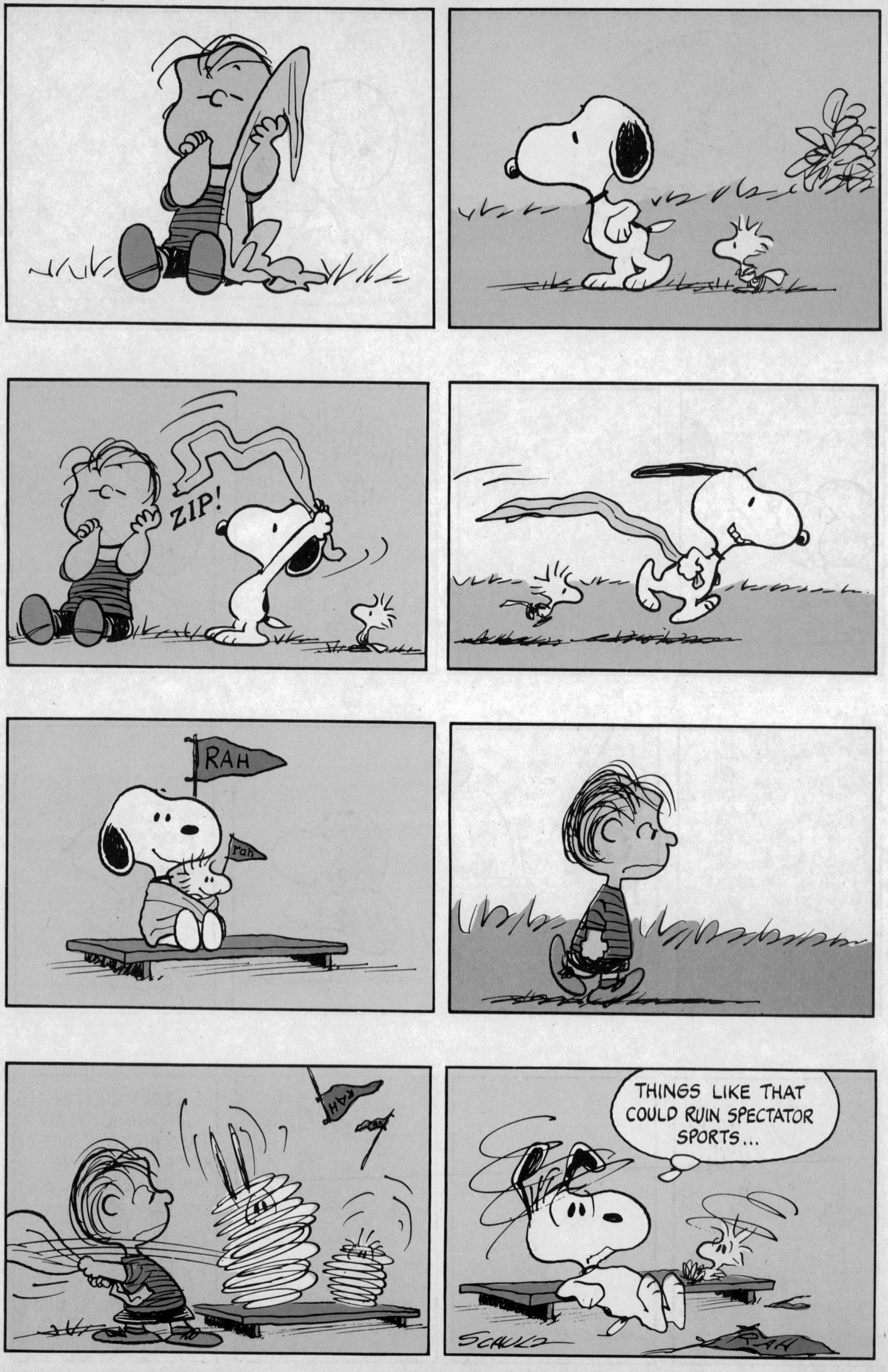
ZIP!
RAH
rah
RAH
THINGS LIKE THAT COULD RUIN SPECTATOR SPORTS...
SCHULZ
RAH

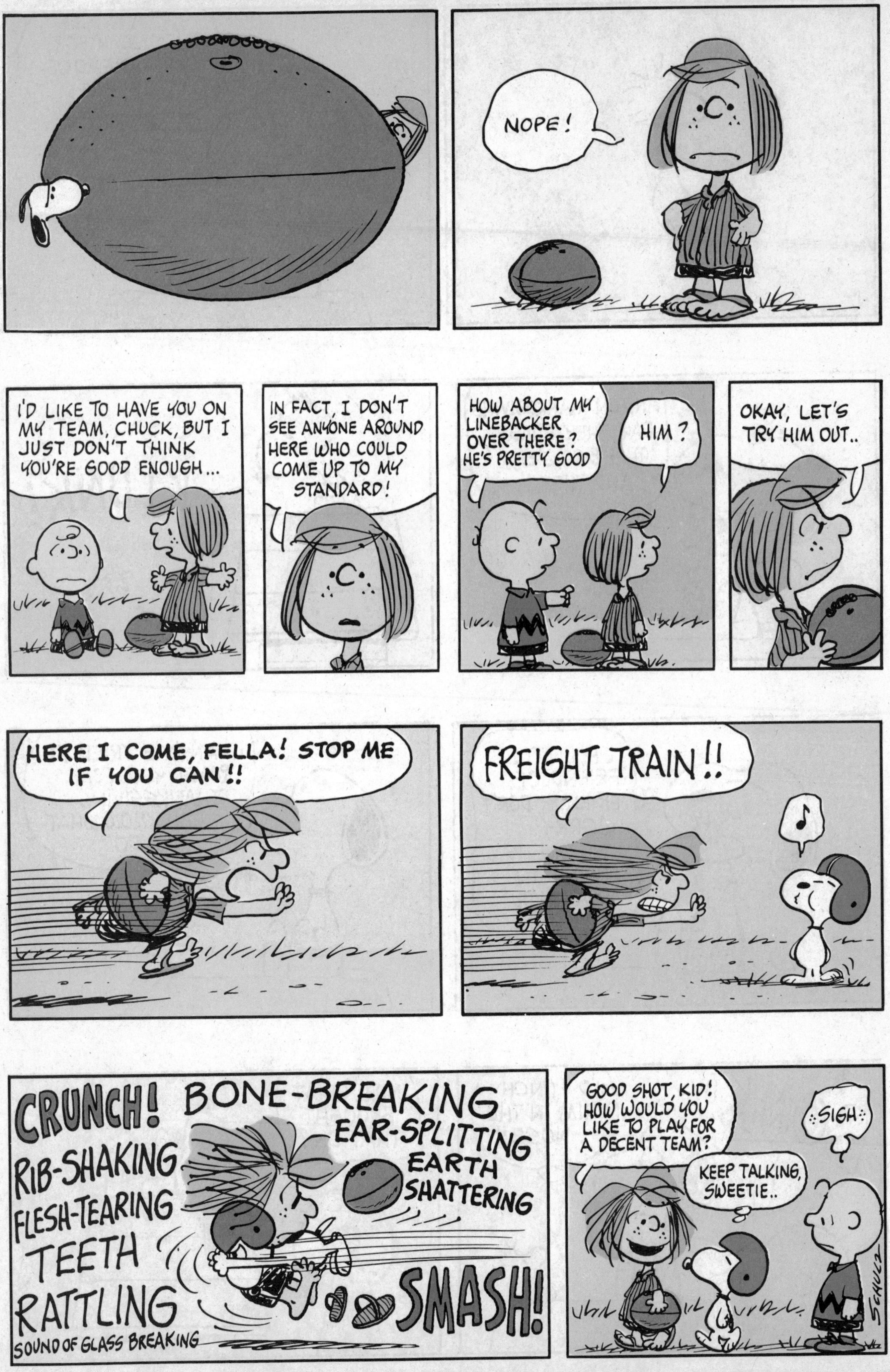
NOPE!
I'D LIKE TO HAVE YOU ON MY TEAM, CHUCK, BUT I JUST DON'T THINK YOU'RE GOOD ENOUGH...
IN FACT, I DON'T SEE ANYONE AROUND HERE WHO COULD COME UP TO MY STANDARD!
HOW ABOUT MY LINEBACKER OVER THERE? HE'S PRETTY GOOD
HIM?
OKAY, LET'S TRY HIM OUT..
HERE I COME, FELLA! STOP ME IF YOU CAN!!
FREIGHT TRAIN!!
♪
CRUNCH!
BONE-BREAKING
EAR-SPLITTING
EARTH SHATTERING
RIB-SHAKING
FLESH-TEARING
TEETH RATTLING
SMASH!
SOUND OF GLASS BREAKING
GOOD SHOT, KID! HOW WOULD YOU LIKE TO PLAY FOR A DECENT TEAM?
KEEP TALKING, SWEETIE..
SIGH
SCHULZ

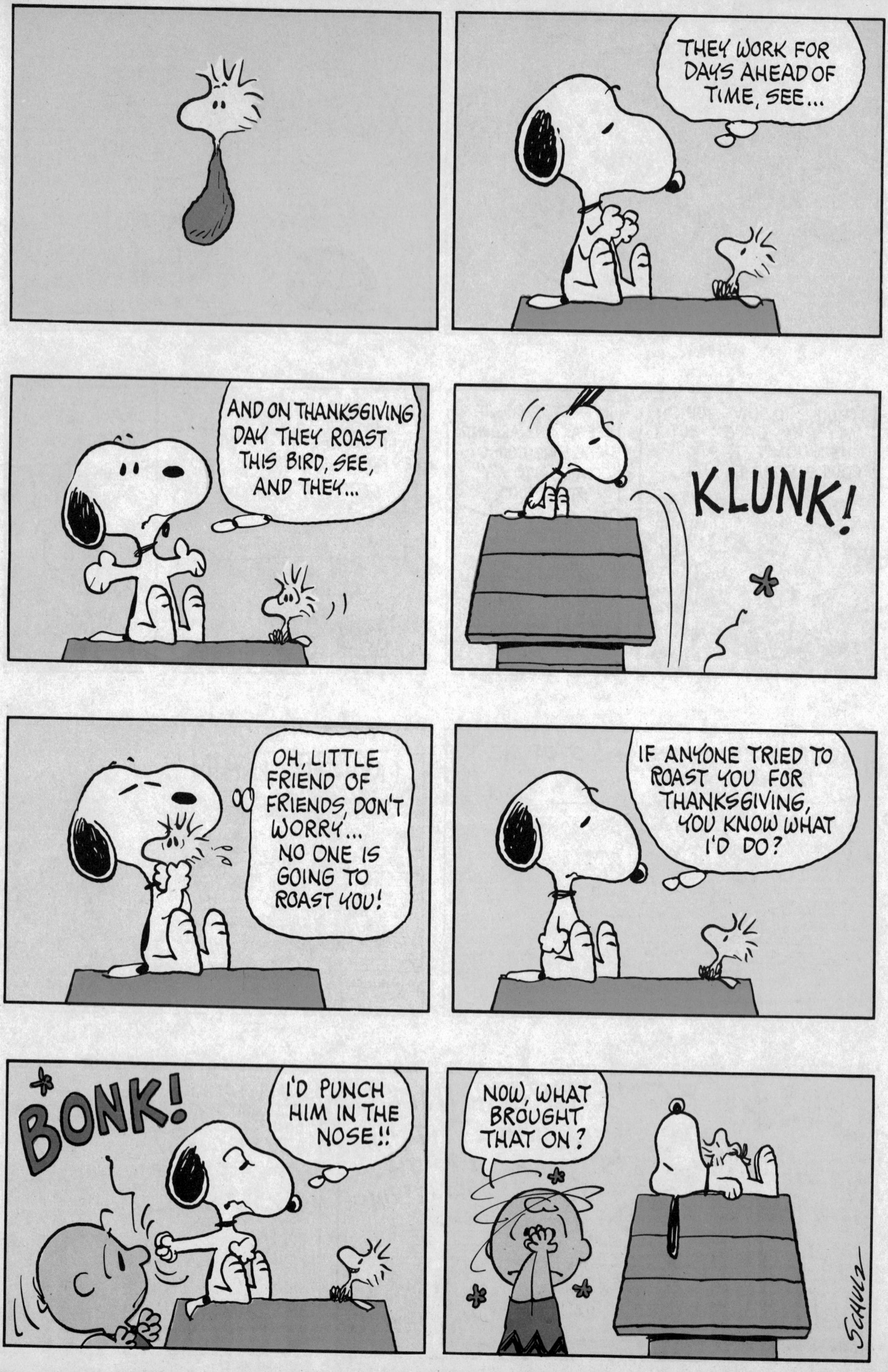
THEY WORK FOR DAYS AHEAD OF TIME, SEE...
AND ON THANKSGIVING DAY THEY ROAST THIS BIRD, SEE, AND THEY...
KLUNK!
OH, LITTLE FRIEND OF FRIENDS, DON'T WORRY... NO ONE IS GOING TO ROAST YOU!
IF ANYONE TRIED TO ROAST YOU FOR THANKSGIVING, YOU KNOW WHAT I'D DO?
BONK!
I'D PUNCH HIM IN THE NOSE!!
NOW, WHAT BROUGHT THAT ON?
SCHULZ

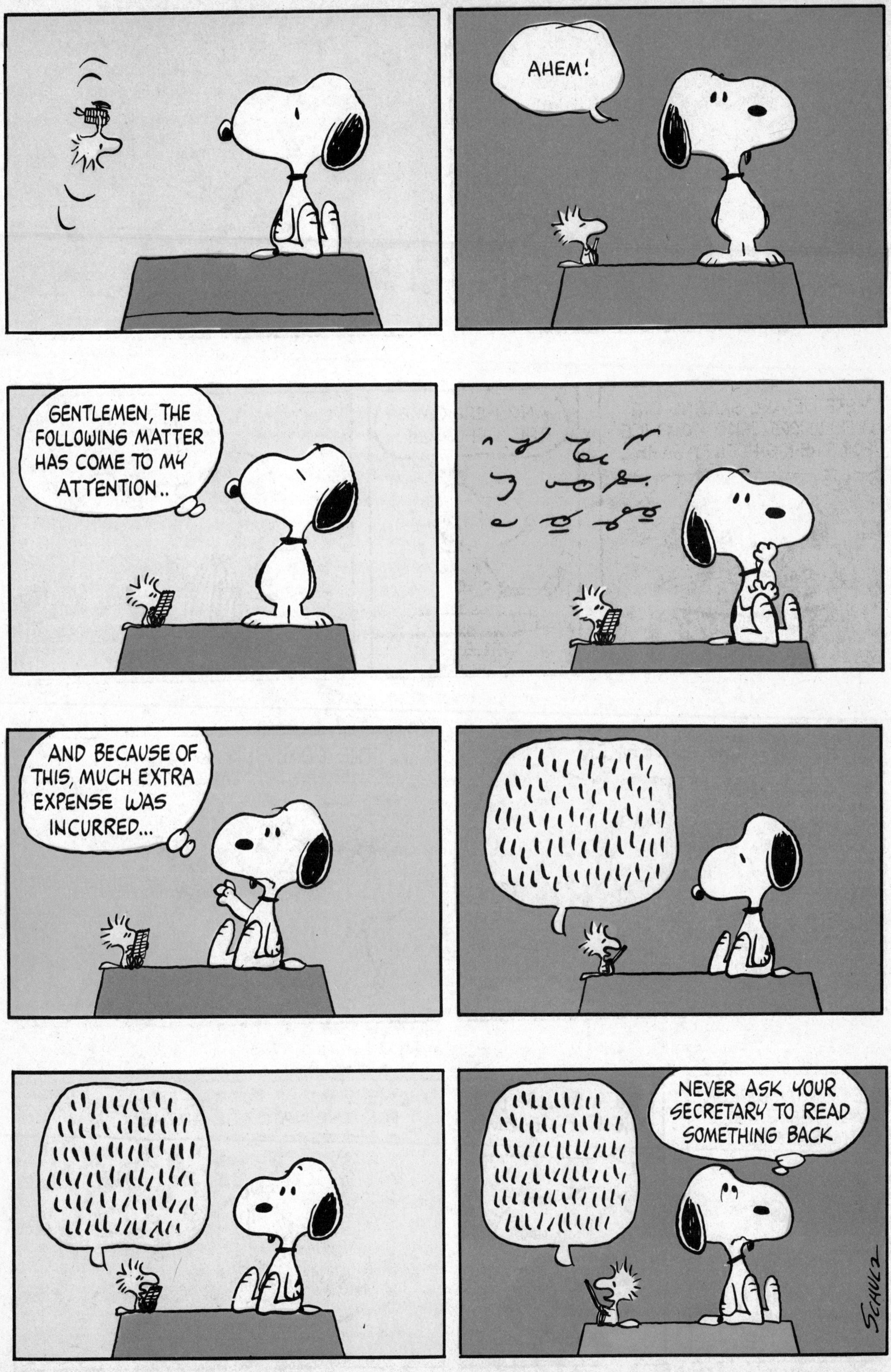
AHEM!
GENTLEMEN, THE FOLLOWING MATTER HAS COME TO MY ATTENTION..
AND BECAUSE OF THIS, MUCH EXTRA EXPENSE WAS INCURRED...
NEVER ASK YOUR SECRETARY TO READ SOMETHING BACK
SCHULZ

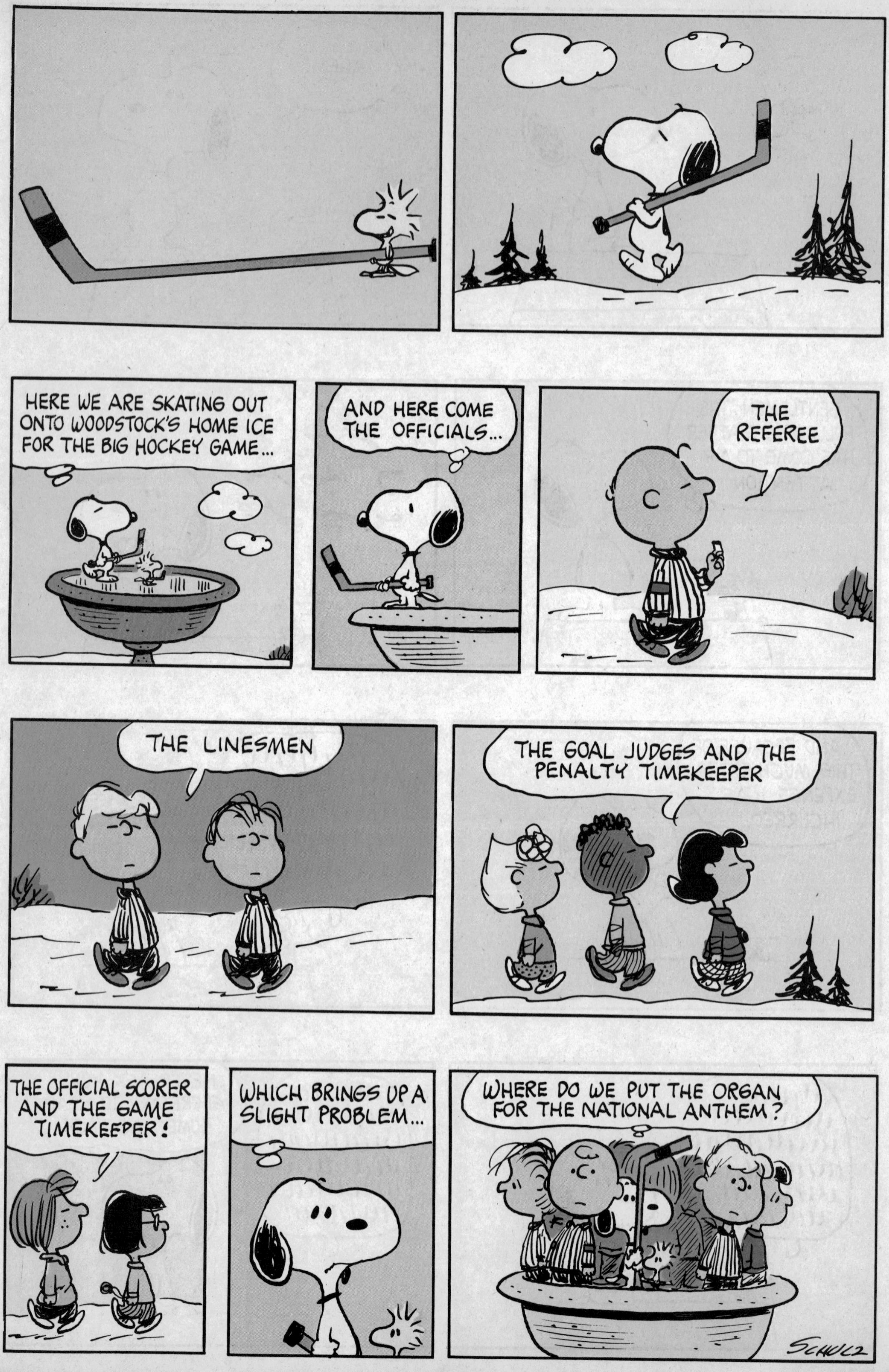
HERE WE ARE SKATING OUT ONTO WOODSTOCK'S HOME ICE FOR THE BIG HOCKEY GAME...
AND HERE COME THE OFFICIALS...
THE REFEREE
THE LINESMEN
THE GOAL JUDGES AND THE PENALTY TIMEKEEPER
THE OFFICIAL SCORER AND THE GAME TIMEKEEPER!
WHICH BRINGS UP A SLIGHT PROBLEM...
WHERE DO WE PUT THE ORGAN FOR THE NATIONAL ANTHEM?
SCHULZ

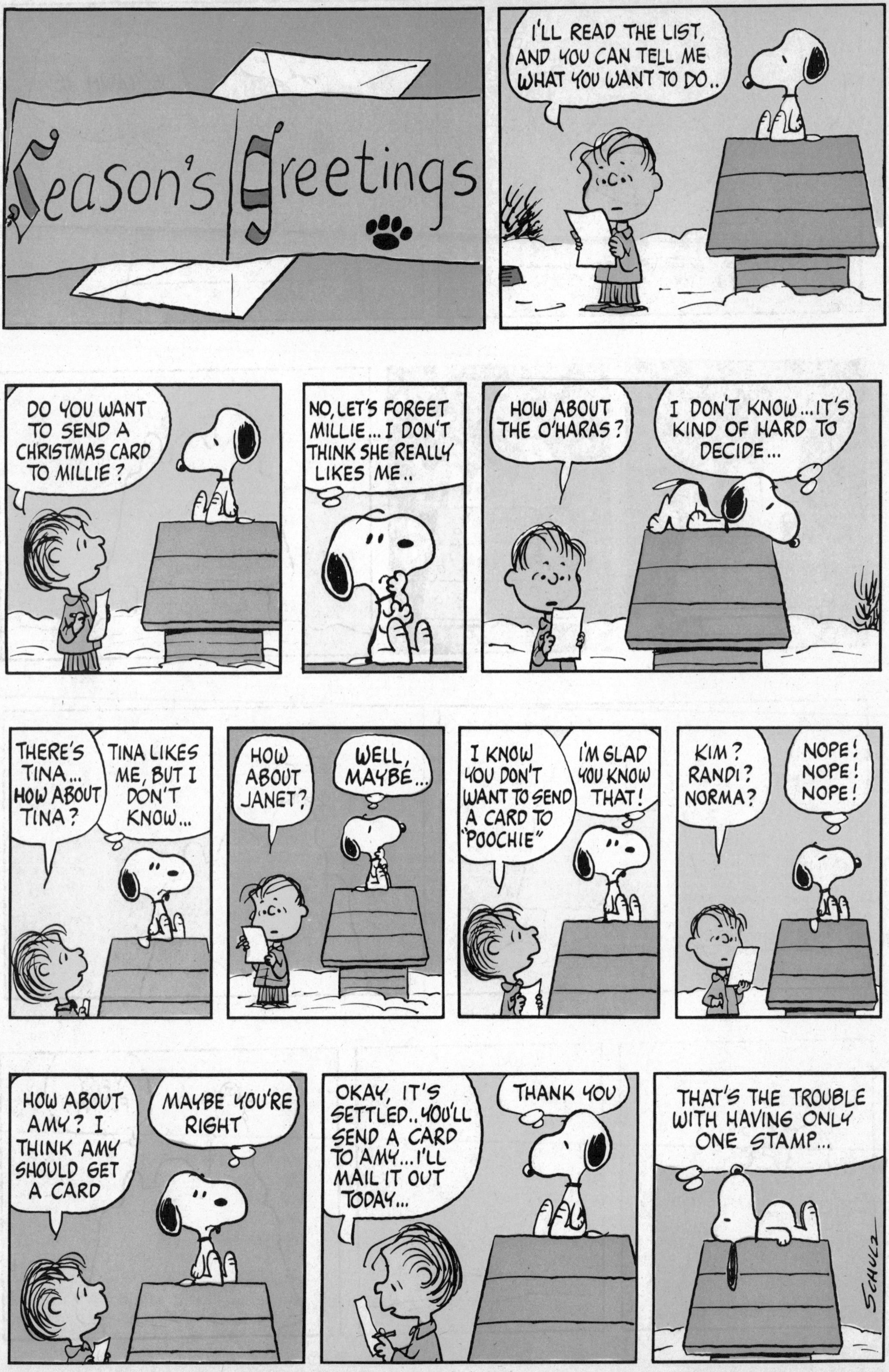
Season's Greetings
I'LL READ THE LIST, AND YOU CAN TELL ME WHAT YOU WANT TO DO..
DO YOU WANT TO SEND A CHRISTMAS CARD TO MILLIE?
NO, LET'S FORGET MILLIE... I DON'T THINK SHE REALLY LIKES ME..
HOW ABOUT THE O'HARAS?
I DON'T KNOW... IT'S KIND OF HARD TO DECIDE...
THERE'S TINA... HOW ABOUT TINA?
TINA LIKES ME, BUT I DON'T KNOW...
HOW ABOUT JANET?
WELL, MAYBE...
I KNOW YOU DON'T WANT TO SEND A CARD TO "POOCHIE"
I'M GLAD YOU KNOW THAT!
KIM? RANDI? NORMA?
NOPE! NOPE! NOPE!
HOW ABOUT AMY? I THINK AMY SHOULD GET A CARD
MAYBE YOU'RE RIGHT
OKAY, IT'S SETTLED.. YOU'LL SEND A CARD TO AMY... I'LL MAIL IT OUT TODAY...
THANK YOU
THAT'S THE TROUBLE WITH HAVING ONLY ONE STAMP...
SCHULZ

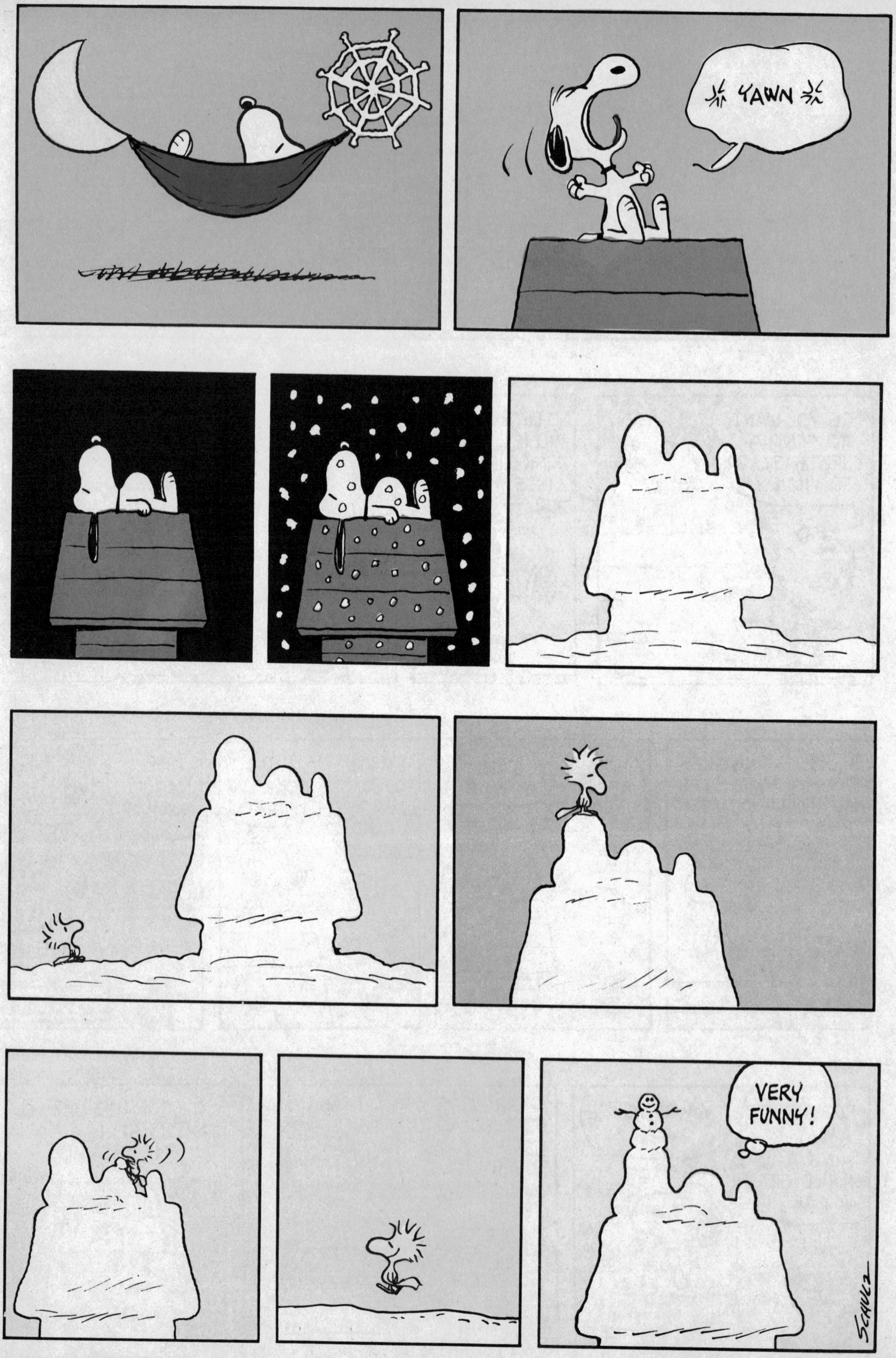
YAWN
VERY FUNNY!
SCHULZ

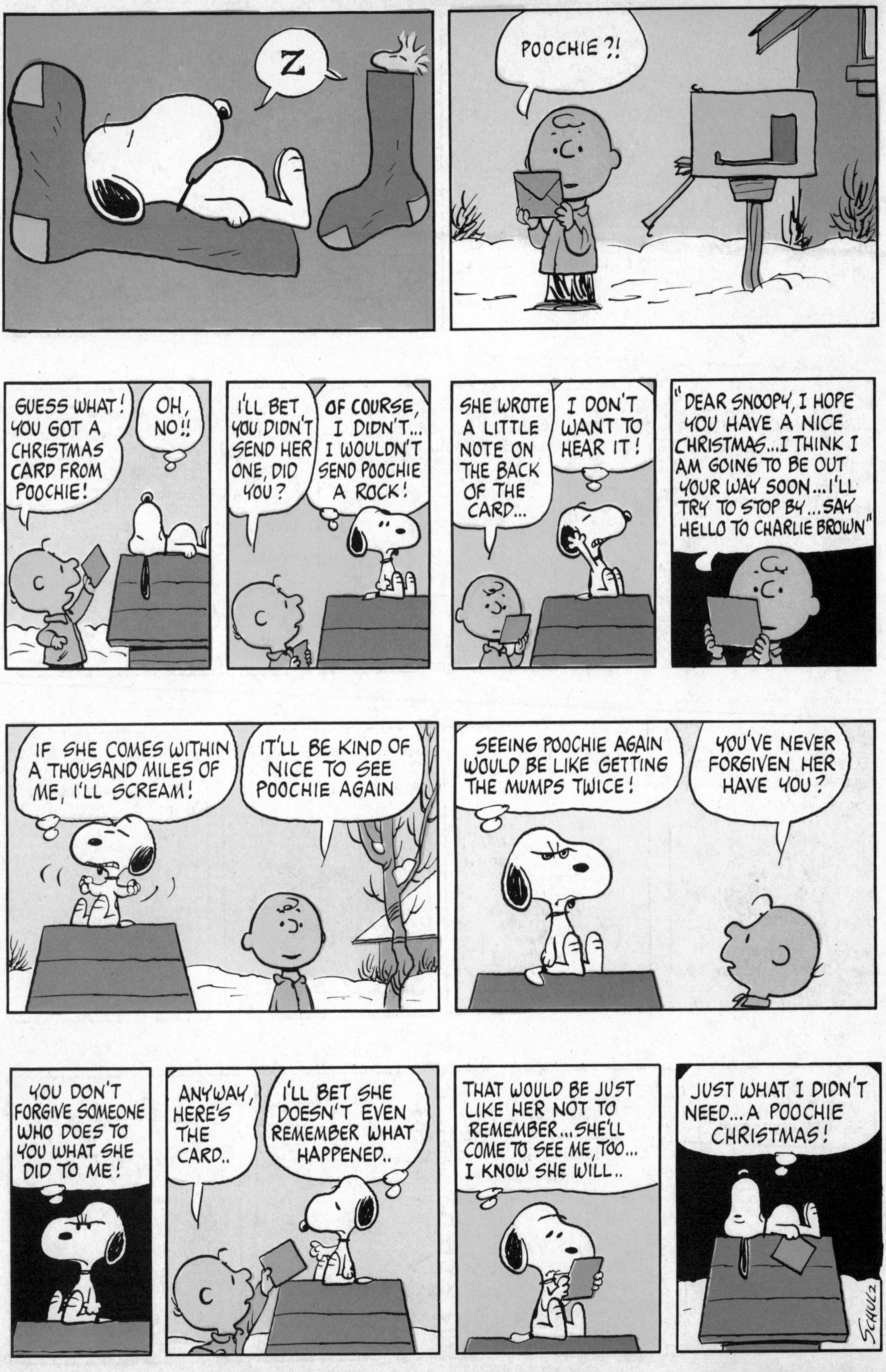
Z
POOCHIE ?!
GUESS WHAT! YOU GOT A CHRISTMAS CARD FROM POOCHIE!
OH, NO!!
I'LL BET YOU DIDN'T SEND HER ONE, DID YOU?
OF COURSE, I DIDN'T... I WOULDN'T SEND POOCHIE A ROCK!
SHE WROTE A LITTLE NOTE ON THE BACK OF THE CARD...
I DON'T WANT TO HEAR IT!
"DEAR SNOOPY, I HOPE YOU HAVE A NICE CHRISTMAS...I THINK I AM GOING TO BE OUT YOUR WAY SOON...I'LL TRY TO STOP BY...SAY HELLO TO CHARLIE BROWN"
IF SHE COMES WITHIN A THOUSAND MILES OF ME, I'LL SCREAM!
IT'LL BE KIND OF NICE TO SEE POOCHIE AGAIN
SEEING POOCHIE AGAIN WOULD BE LIKE GETTING THE MUMPS TWICE!
YOU'VE NEVER FORGIVEN HER HAVE YOU?
YOU DON'T FORGIVE SOMEONE WHO DOES TO YOU WHAT SHE DID TO ME!
ANYWAY, HERE'S THE CARD..
I'LL BET SHE DOESN'T EVEN REMEMBER WHAT HAPPENED..
THAT WOULD BE JUST LIKE HER NOT TO REMEMBER...SHE'LL COME TO SEE ME, TOO... I KNOW SHE WILL..
JUST WHAT I DIDN'T NEED...A POOCHIE CHRISTMAS!
SCHULZ

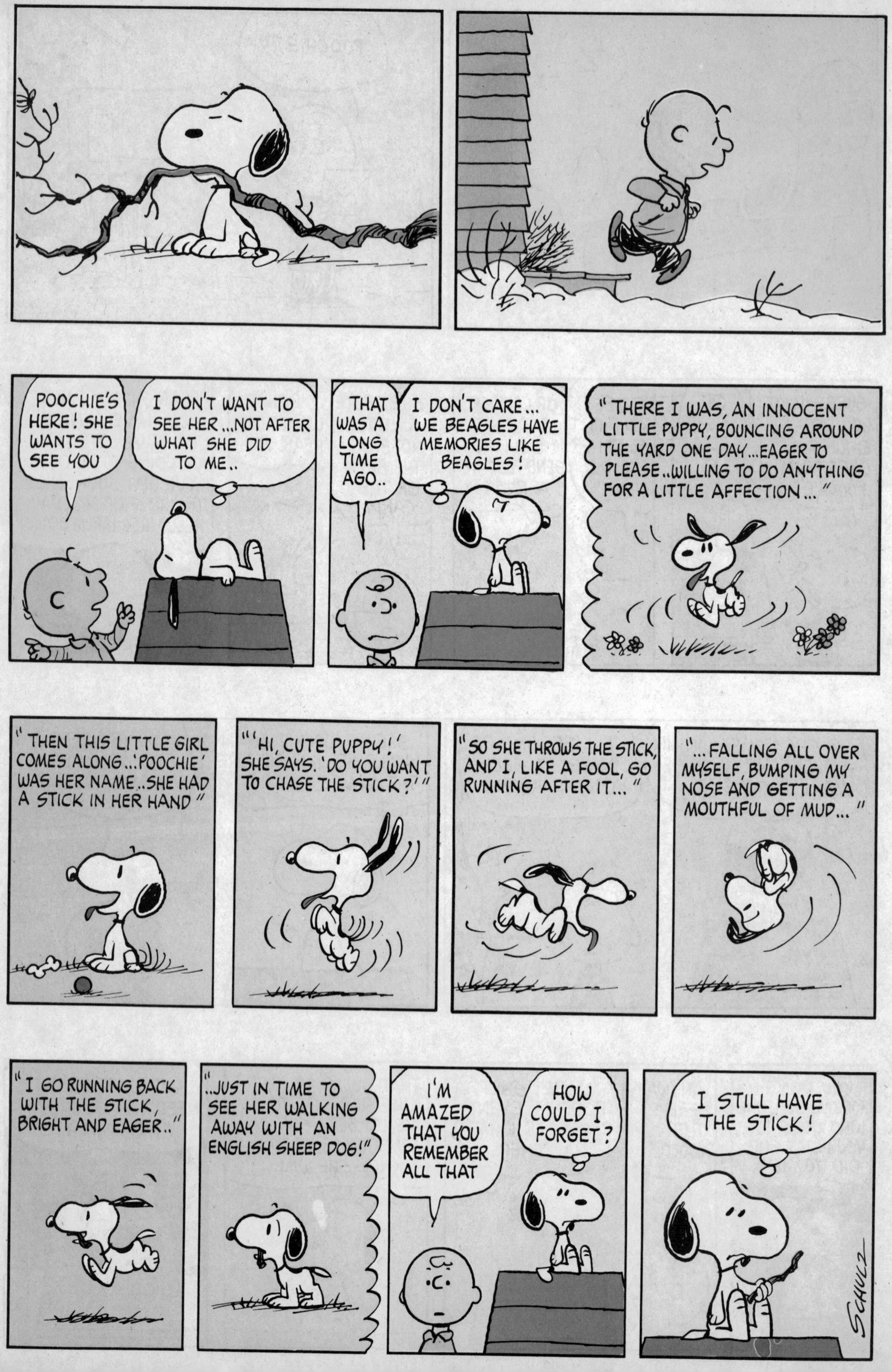
POOCHIE'S HERE! SHE WANTS TO SEE YOU
I DON'T WANT TO SEE HER ...NOT AFTER WHAT SHE DID TO ME..
THAT WAS A LONG TIME AGO..
I DON'T CARE... WE BEAGLES HAVE MEMORIES LIKE BEAGLES!
" THERE I WAS, AN INNOCENT LITTLE PUPPY, BOUNCING AROUND THE YARD ONE DAY...EAGER TO PLEASE..WILLING TO DO ANYTHING FOR A LITTLE AFFECTION... "
" THEN THIS LITTLE GIRL COMES ALONG...'POOCHIE' WAS HER NAME..SHE HAD A STICK IN HER HAND "
" 'HI, CUTE PUPPY!' SHE SAYS. 'DO YOU WANT TO CHASE THE STICK?' "
" SO SHE THROWS THE STICK, AND I, LIKE A FOOL, GO RUNNING AFTER IT... "
" ...FALLING ALL OVER MYSELF, BUMPING MY NOSE AND GETTING A MOUTHFUL OF MUD... "
" I GO RUNNING BACK WITH THE STICK, BRIGHT AND EAGER.. "
"..JUST IN TIME TO SEE HER WALKING AWAY WITH AN ENGLISH SHEEP DOG!"
I'M AMAZED THAT YOU REMEMBER ALL THAT
HOW COULD I FORGET?
I STILL HAVE THE STICK!
SCHULZ

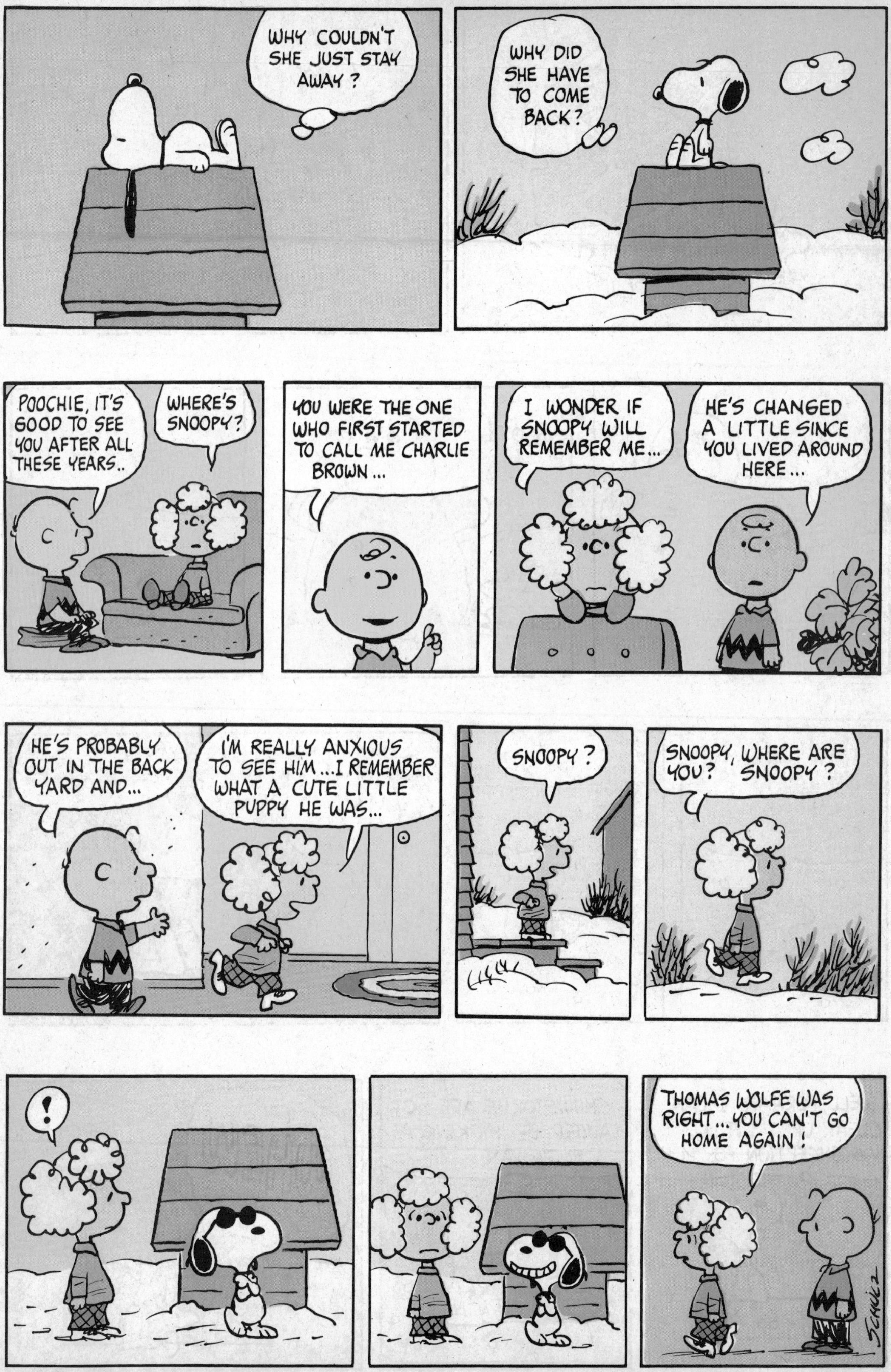
WHY COULDN'T SHE JUST STAY AWAY?
WHY DID SHE HAVE TO COME BACK?
POOCHIE, IT'S GOOD TO SEE YOU AFTER ALL THESE YEARS..
WHERE'S SNOOPY?
YOU WERE THE ONE WHO FIRST STARTED TO CALL ME CHARLIE BROWN...
I WONDER IF SNOOPY WILL REMEMBER ME...
HE'S CHANGED A LITTLE SINCE YOU LIVED AROUND HERE...
HE'S PROBABLY OUT IN THE BACK YARD AND...
I'M REALLY ANXIOUS TO SEE HIM...I REMEMBER WHAT A CUTE LITTLE PUPPY HE WAS...
SNOOPY?
SNOOPY, WHERE ARE YOU? SNOOPY?
!
THOMAS WOLFE WAS RIGHT... YOU CAN'T GO HOME AGAIN!
SCHULZ

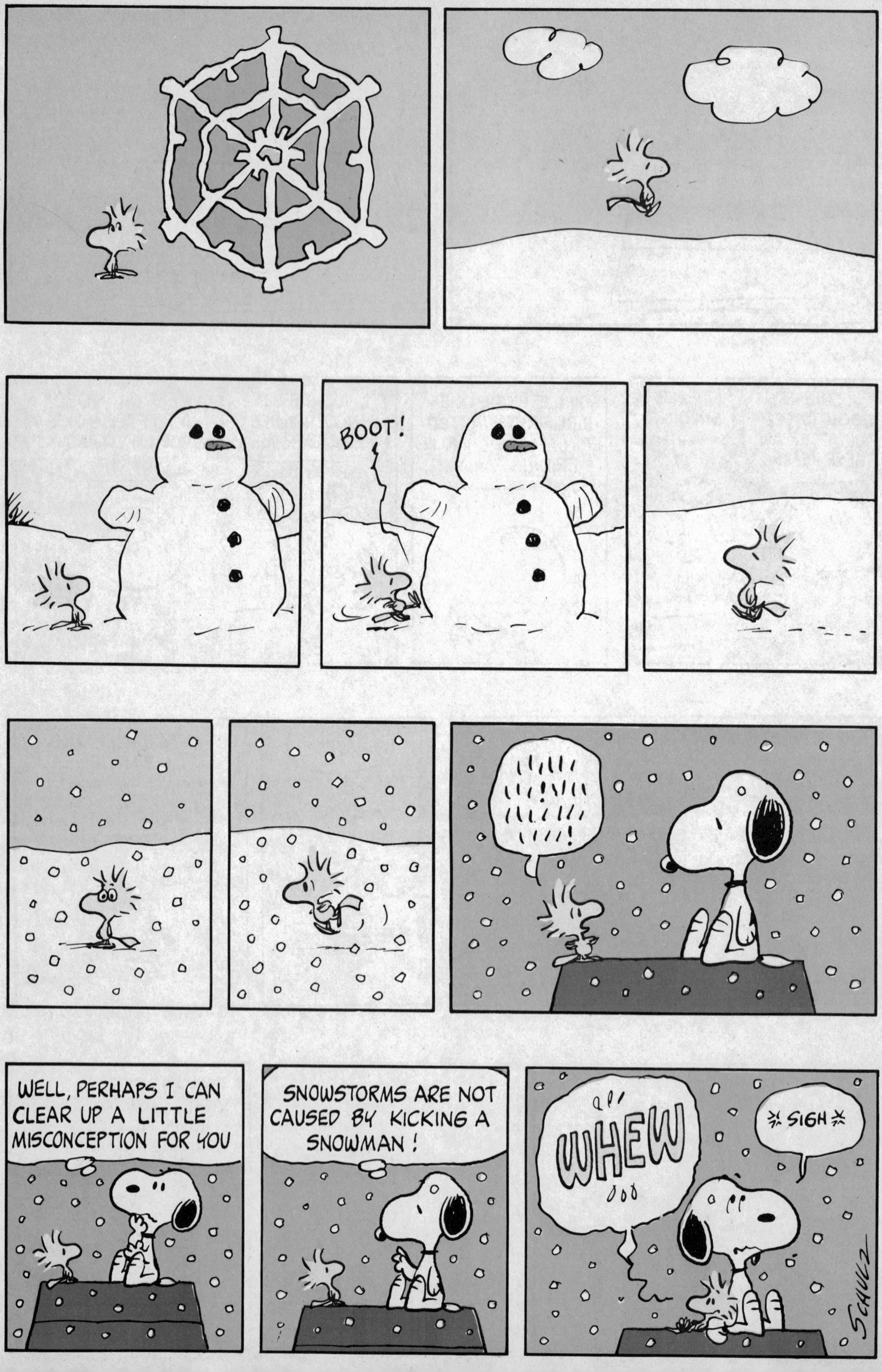
BOOT!
WELL, PERHAPS I CAN CLEAR UP A LITTLE MISCONCEPTION FOR YOU
SNOWSTORMS ARE NOT CAUSED BY KICKING A SNOWMAN!
WHEW
SIGH
SCHULZ

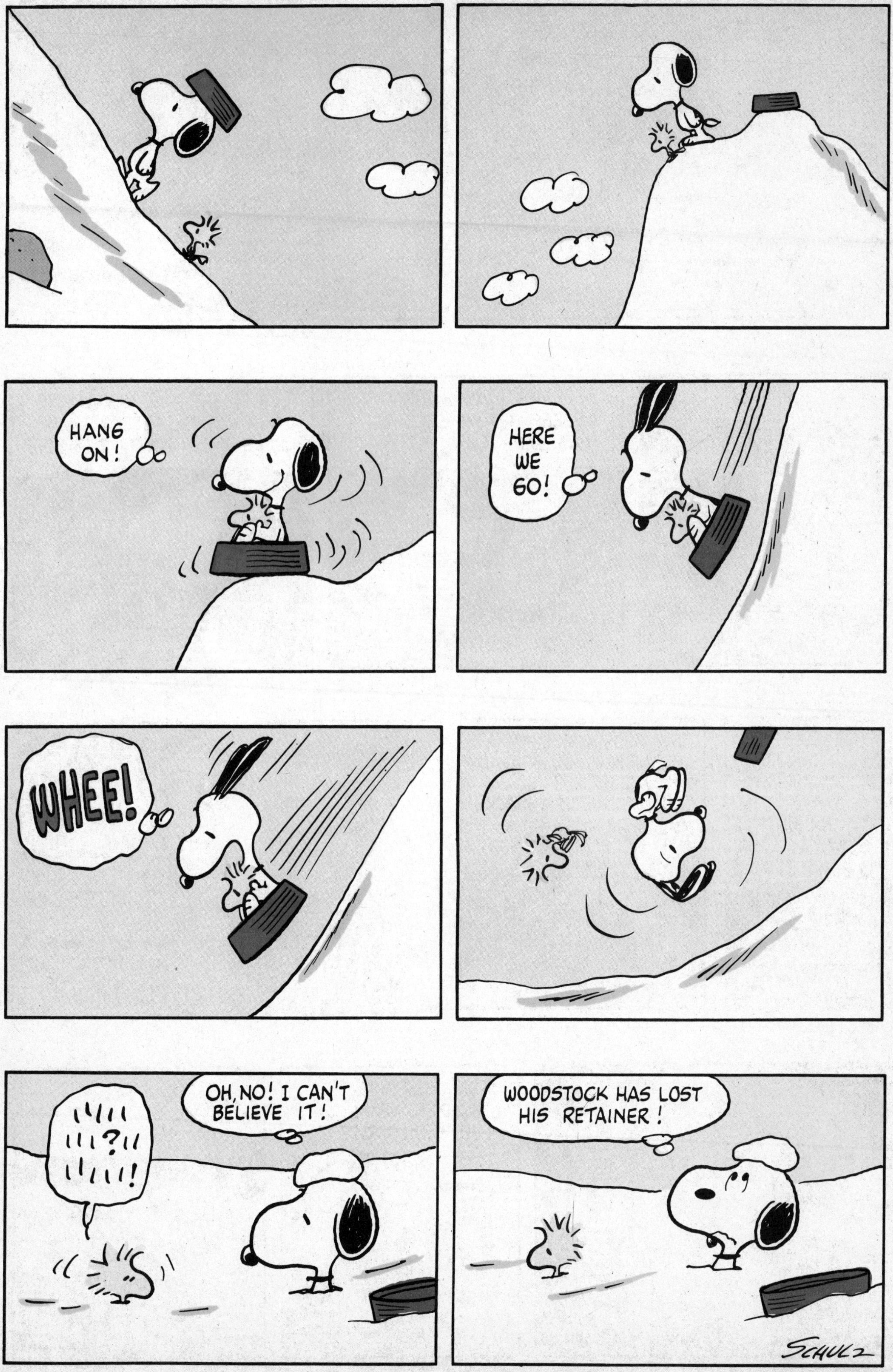
HANG ON!
HERE WE GO!
WHEE!
?!
OH, NO! I CAN'T BELIEVE IT!
WOODSTOCK HAS LOST HIS RETAINER!
SCHULZ

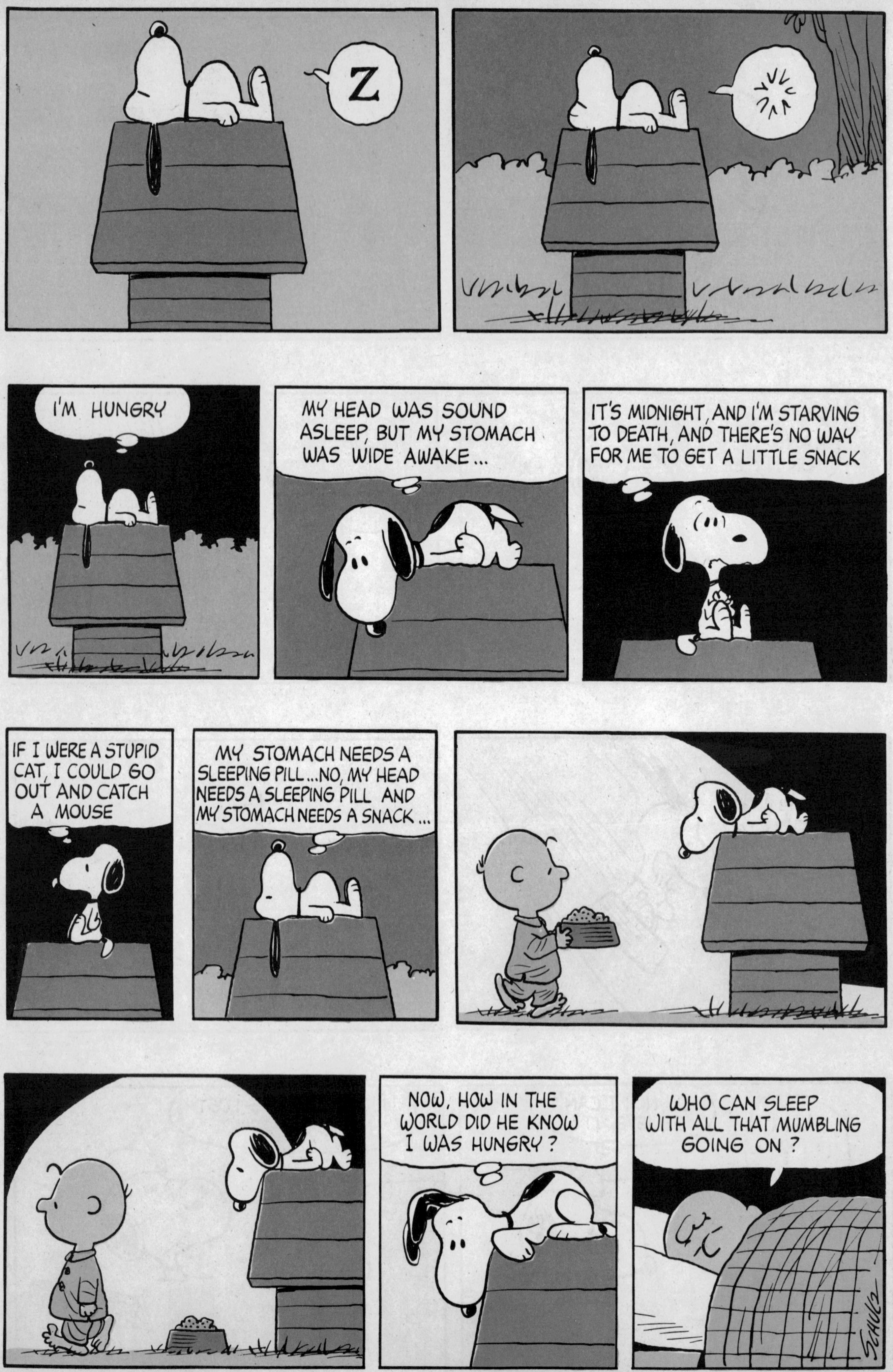
Z
I'M HUNGRY
MY HEAD WAS SOUND ASLEEP, BUT MY STOMACH WAS WIDE AWAKE...
IT'S MIDNIGHT, AND I'M STARVING TO DEATH, AND THERE'S NO WAY FOR ME TO GET A LITTLE SNACK
IF I WERE A STUPID CAT, I COULD GO OUT AND CATCH A MOUSE
MY STOMACH NEEDS A SLEEPING PILL...NO, MY HEAD NEEDS A SLEEPING PILL AND MY STOMACH NEEDS A SNACK...
NOW, HOW IN THE WORLD DID HE KNOW I WAS HUNGRY?
WHO CAN SLEEP WITH ALL THAT MUMBLING GOING ON?
SCHULZ